SPINNING JENNY

SPINNING JENNY

Ruth Hamilton

LONDON NEW YORK SYDNEY TORONTO

This edition published 1992
by BCA
by arrangement with Bantam Press Ltd.
Copyright © Ruth Hamilton 1993

The right of Ruth Hamilton to be identified
as the author of this work has been asserted in accordance
with sections 77 and 78 of the Copyright Designs and
Patents Act 1988.

CN 1032

Printed and bound in Germany
by Graphischer Großbetrieb Pößneck GmbH
A member of the Mohndruck printing group

For Dorothy Cann (née Hurst)

THANKS TO:

Sandra Heilberg of Sweetens Bookshops
Mike Lomas & Steve McMahon (School of Textiles),
and Such Datta (School of Art and Design),
all of the Bolton Institute of H.E.
Julia McMeans
David & Michael Thornber
Diane Pearson & Meg Cairns
The Rushtons of Bromley Cross and Harwood
Ruth and Graham Thomas

MUCH LOVE TO ALL MY ANIMALS:

Amber, Scooby, Benny, Soapy, Bodie, Ladybird, Basil, Mum One,
Cissie and Flicky

PART ONE
1920

Chapter One

SHE STEPPED OUT INTO WHAT WAS LEFT OF THE DAYLIGHT, her eyes narrowing against a sudden shaft of dying sun that pierced the air like a thin blade of steel.

It had been raining, and the brilliance was reflected on roofs, pavements and cobblestones, bouncing in violent flashes from a hundred windows in a mill shed across the way. A brewery horse ambled by, easy now, slower without his load of beer, nostrils flaring as he neared the stable. His ears pricked towards beckoning comfort, and the girl almost envied the animal his safe shelter. There would be oats and bran, sweet hay, perhaps a bucket of mash to take the edge off his enormous hunger. She smiled, approached the giant, running a hand along a quivering chestnut flank as he passed.

With another day of work over, and a night of chores ahead, she bowed her head against the skittish spring breeze, allowing its clean fingers to caress and cool a scalp made sweaty by a thousand movements between whirling cops of cotton. After the heat of the spinning room, even the smoky air of Bolton tasted good and fresh, simply because there was movement in it, a natural flow, not the screaming, deafening motion of machinery.

She wandered down Derby Street, pausing to stare in shop windows, her eyes resting on work shirts, books, sherbet dabs, shoes – anything and everything that was on display. In one window, there were three dummies, a father in dungarees, a mother in a wrap-over cover-all floral-patterned apron, the girl child dressed for school, gymslip and blouse, ribbons in the stringy false hair.

She gazed at this tableau for some time, seeming to soak it up, palms pressed flat against cool glass. That was what it looked like, then. That was family life, everybody smiling and ready for work, fingers stretched wide to express inner joy, feet spread apart to display stability, faces stained tan from walking free in a world that accepted just the normal.

She grinned ruefully, because she knew that the scene was a travesty. There were families in Claughton Street, dozens of them, and not one of them was perfect. Many a time she would sit in her enforced isolation, listening to their quarrels. Yet still she ached for ... for what? Something she'd never had, something she was too old to have now?

The Town Hall clock struck the hour, and she quickened her steps. It would be silly to invite trouble, so she forced reluctant feet to travel a path she could have followed blindfolded, a route she had walked too many times to count. They had lived at number seventeen since Jenny's fourth birthday, moving from the Chorley Old Road area with the sort of anxious swiftness that was so much a part of Auntie Mavis's nature. There had been many such moves, and most were outside the span of Jenny's memory, as they had taken place during her babyhood. Now, when she considered their last flitting, she wondered vaguely whether Auntie Mavis might be running from something. Or from somebody? How carefully the woman shut out her neighbours, how completely she dominated Jenny, controlling her movements, narrowing her life. Still, at least they had stopped running now, hadn't had a change of house for fourteen years. Perhaps Mavis had settled. Or perhaps she really was too ill to face another change of address.

She turned into Claughton Street, noticing immediately that the girls were at play again. It would begin now. Bracing herself, she approached the group, her heart lurching as she heard the familiar skipping song.

'Spinning jenny,
Spinning round,
Turning up,
And winding down,
Spinning cotton,
Spinning fast,
I am first,
And you are last.'

This home-made tribute to Hargreaves, inventor of the spinning jenny, was a common enough street-song, but there was another version, one specially created by the Claughton Street girls, a chorus they often used within Jenny's hearing, employing that cold, clear and judgemental cruelty that seems to be lent to the young until they achieve the age of true reason.

The children hopped in and out of curling ropes, a pair of washing lines expertly twisting in opposing directions. Although these street-urchins were ragged, they understood the concept of play, knew how to compensate for the lack of shop-bought toys. If they could steal no stump of chalk from school, they would scratch a hop-scotch pattern on flags with a chip of fallen roof-slate, or with a crumb of donkey-stone. The rim of a barrel provided a perfect hoop to bowl, while flattened bottle caps served as 'rollers' or 'casters', depending on the pre-decided nature of their gambling games.

Now, no doubt, two households at a safe distance from Claughton Street would be devoid of support for next Monday's wash. But the carefree ragamuffins gave no thought to their hapless victims. Play was the thing. Soon, they would be grown, and being grown meant the mill, so they crammed the hours of freedom with simple pleasures, pausing just for meals and, on occasions that were unavoidable, for distasteful pursuits like school and church.

They saw her coming, watched her from the corners of their quick eyes as she stepped carefully over rain-washed cobbles, the pale, blue-grey shawl slipping from a soft, feminine shoulder. She was not like the older mill women;

she never wore the shawl over her head, even when the weather performed its Bolton worst. Her neck, long, white and slender, was always on show, almost as if she were aware of its splendid beauty. The face was pretty, wide at the forehead, narrow yet not sharp at the chin. Her eyes, clear, large and bright, matched the freshened sky that showed now in patches between rain-clouds. Blonde hair was scraped back for work, piled into a huge, cotton-flecked bun on top of her head, but the children had caught glimpses of her hair in the mornings, and they knew that the flaxen mass was long enough to sit on.

She hesitated, a clogged foot lifted in mid-stride, dark eyebrows arched as if questioning the group, as if she hoped that they would accept her just this once. The ropes stilled themselves, while the chanting died away. They backed off from her as she resumed her walk, each child muttering, giggling, nudging a close companion. As though prompted by an unseen stage-hand, they began again, whispering at first, then unifying their voices until the song could be heard the length of the street.

> *'Spinning Jenny,*
> *Spinning Jenny,*
> *Hasn't got a mam,*
> *Crazy Mavie,*
> *Found a baby,*
> *In a pot of jam.*
>
> *Spinning Jenny,*
> *Spinning Jenny,*
> *Hasn't got a dad,*
> *He ran away,*
> *To save the day,*
> *'Cos Spinning Jenny's mad.'*

They fled, ropes trailing in their wake, arms waving in the air as they whooped in celebration of this small triumph. At the rear of the group, the smallest staggered, chubby legs still curved by infancy. But even she knew the words, the gestures. Just before turning left towards the safety of the back street, the three-year-old shook her fist, spat on the flags, then yelled 'Creepy Crawley' across the house fronts. The sounds echoed, as if they had been shouted into a cave. No door opened; once the children had left, the street was deserted.

Jennifer Crawley shook her head slowly, wondering why the young ones felt they had to run like that. She had never slapped them, never chided them for their misdeeds. But they had learned their pattern from older sisters, from girls of Jenny's age, and the females of her own generation had taunted her mercilessly all through her schooldays. The reason for such treatment sat behind one of these identical doors. Mavis. Auntie Mavis Crawley, who had imprisoned her young charge year after empty year. Jenny had never left the house except for school, shopping or work.

This was a clean street, a decent working-class area with varnished doors and steps that were always well scrubbed. The children in old play clothes had better dresses folded away somewhere; they were not real street tramps. Why then had they not been taught manners?

Her eyes travelled along house fronts, as if they sought the slightest kind response. She was so miserable here, so lonely. If only one of them would talk to her, treat her as normal. Because she was normal. And she mustn't – indeed she wouldn't – blame Auntie Mavis for this predicament. Not completely, anyway. Auntie Mavis might be strange, but she couldn't help it. And Auntie Mavis had always been there, was the only permanent and predictable factor in life. Even work was no escape, because Jenny's name had been passed around the sheds before she'd arrived to learn the job. So there was just number seventeen, Claughton Street. That was the only place she knew, the sole safety she had discovered in eighteen years. Yes, there was safety in containment. Yet she wanted . . . what? A husband, babies, her own house? All she knew was that she was changing. Soon, she must begin her life.

She closed the door with a soft click. Auntie Mavis might

be asleep, and Jenny had learned, during her lifetime in this house, never to disturb her aunt. She removed her shawl and hung it in its usual place, on a peg attached to the stair door, then she walked through to the scullery in search of food. It was difficult during the week, because she was full-time at Skipton's, and there wasn't much chance to shop. If she went for food in the evenings, there was not a lot of choice, particularly when it came to fresh meat and vegetables. But she'd picked up two extra meat and potato pies yesterday dinner time, and she would heat these, serve them with carrot and turnip and the dregs of gravy saved from a meagre week-end joint.

She busied herself peeling until the door opened. 'So, you're here, then?' The voice was scratchy, like a gramophone record that had been worn out with too much playing. Though under-use was more likely to be the excuse for Mavis Crawley's vocal rust. 'You know I'm stuck on me own all day, least you could do is give over dawdling, hurry up home and see if I'm all right.' There was hurt in the tone, a deep and self-righteous hurt that bordered on bitter resentment.

Jenny sighed, trying hard not to move her shoulders. The sigh must not show. None of her inner feelings must show, because Auntie Mavis was Jenny's one and only piece of security. Though wasn't it time to . . . ? Oh no, she should not think of abandoning this poor lady. 'Sorry, Auntie.' These words were delivered with the usual coating of gratitude and obedience. She was a good girl. She had always been a good girl, could not remember one single episode of naughtiness. For teachers, for her aunt, for the foreman at work, she had been swift to do as she had been bidden. Would it be like this forever?

Mavis climbed on her high horse again, resuming the lofty position she most enjoyed. 'Eighteen years I've devoted to you. I never had a life of me own since Dan left you with me as a foundling babe.'

Jenny turned her head slightly. 'I know,' she whispered. Every day the same thing was said; every day she forced herself to listen and to be thankful. Sometimes, forcing herself to be thankful was easy, but occasionally, a seed of doubt and rebellion would plant frail roots in Jenny's mind. As usual, she killed the growth by swamping it in the thousand items of trivia that occupied her everyday life. 'Do you want mashed or plain boiled, Auntie Mavis?' she asked now, the quickening of her own heart ignored once more.

'I don't care.' Mavis Crawley showed little real interest in her food, because she had no sense of smell. Food was something she took just to stay alive, though she did tend to indulge in liquids rather too frequently for Jenny's liking. A heavy throat-clearing was followed by, 'I might not live to eat it. Two turns I've had today, and nobody here to fend for me. I've had to fettle for meself, same as always.' Jewellery rattled as the head shook. 'One of these days, I'll just keel over. I'll go in a heap, crack me head on the flags, and then where will you be?' There was a clink as bottle touched glass. 'Eighteen years,' she breathed before taking a noisy sip of undiluted gin. 'What chance was there for me? I ask you, what sort of a life was that for an unmarried woman?'

Jenny turned fully and looked at her aunt. The skin was parchment white, bleached by lack of air and exercise. Three flat, brown inverted question marks lay in an evenly-spaced row on the forehead, while the rest of the hair was encased, as ever, in a gaudy turban. Large, fleshy ear-lobes depended even lower than nature had decreed, weighted by massive earrings that made a metallic noise each time they were disturbed. The rest of the body was completely covered by a long, emerald green robe with flowing sleeves and embroidered gold patterns. She was dressed for work, the only work she had known for many years.

'Oh,' said Jenny, her tone tired and resigned. 'You're busy tonight. How many?'

'Just the two, but they pay good money. What's up? Are you losing your nerve?' She cackled briefly, displaying a hideous array of black and yellow teeth. 'At least you get out of the house.' Her face had settled back into its habitual lines of misery. 'You're not stuck inside waiting for visitors. It's a good job I have my gifts, otherwise I'd see no face but yours. And sometimes, your mouth is in what I'd call a sulk, Jenny Crawley.'

Jenny pushed back her aching shoulders. 'I'm not sulking, Auntie. Anyway, you could go out. I could take you out. There's nothing to be afraid of, and I would stay with you all the time. You know I wouldn't leave you on your own in the street. You need fresh air, you need to get some exercise.'

'I can't!' The petulant stamp of a small foot was muffled by satin slipper meeting cold flag. 'You know I can't. It's me nerves, they won't let me go out. Next time I leave here, it'll be feet first in a box. And when I do, make sure I've got this best robe on.' A clawlike hand extended itself, the nails so long that they curled at the ends. 'I want a good coffin too, nothing shoddy, make sure the handles is solid brass. And put all my trappings in with me. I'm leaving nowt. My talent,' she picked up her glass and drained it in a single gulp, 'my special God-given gift goes to no bugger.'

'Yes, Auntie.' How could she mention God and then swear in the same breath? 'Shall I do a pudding? We've still some bottled fruit, and I can soon make custard.'

The robe swirled as Mavis Crawley swept out of the small room. 'No pudding,' she called over her shoulder. 'No time. They're on their way, I can feel it. This will be a good session. We shall get a visitation tonight.'

Jenny scraped and scrubbed, pausing occasionally to gaze out into the darkening yard. No wonder the children sang songs, no wonder they thought she was mad. There had to be a way out of this, but how could she just go, just leave without seeming downright nasty and unappreciative? She was grateful, she really was. Nobody had wanted her, nobody except this strange lady who had, at least, given Jenny a surname to use . . .

The parlour, an area of not much more than twelve square feet, was its usual sombre self when Jenny entered to do the preparations. There was a circular table in the centre, a dresser between front door and stairs, and several globed paraffin lamps on small tables that squatted around two over-stuffed armchairs. The curtains were brown, of thick, lined velvet, and the mantel cover matched the depressing colour, as did the floor-length tablecloth. Signs of the zodiac were scattered about the walls, framed drawings of a water-carrier and, further on, a strange insect with nasty claws, then twins, scales and all the other paraphernalia that demonstrated her aunt's weird calling. But it was the scorpion that Jenny hated most. As a child, she had suffered nightmares in which the poisonous beast had always played the chief role. Auntie Mavis used to say that Scorpio was a wicked sign, and that the good people born under it had to fight for their virtue. Of course, Jenny knew now that it was all a charade, though she still shivered whenever she dusted that particular picture.

She took the crystal from the dresser cupboard, dusted it on her apron, placed it on its mahogany plinth in the middle of the table. Folks' lives and fortunes were supposed to be visible in the glass orb, but all Jenny had ever seen was a distorted view of her own face. The tarots were in a drawer, while perfumed candles, their wicks already blackened from use, sat on the mantel next to a fat Buddha and a miniature totem. Auntie's guide was supposed to own this colourful pole, yet Jenny showed little respect for the object as she dumped it next to the cards in Auntie's place. She was getting just a little bit too old for this, she told herself. At eight or nine years of age, it had all been a game. Now, it was fraud, and she was a part of it. The whole thing was becoming too much for her, yet she could not find her way out of it.

She walked into the kitchen and took the pans from the grate, one filled with potatoes, a second containing carrot and turnip. With a sudden burst of energy for which she could not account, she attacked the vegetables, mashing them to smithereens within seconds. After adding salt and pepper, she distributed the meal on to plates, taking two heated pies from the range oven and pouring on a few spoonfuls of gravy. From the bottom of the stairs she called, 'Auntie? Your tea's out.'

'I am communicating.' This monotone floated listlessly down the stairs. Jenny shrugged, took up her aunt's plate, and placed it under a pan lid in the oven. Auntie would be sitting on her bed, legs curled beneath her, eyes staring into a different world, a world that existed only in the poor lady's twisted mind.

Jenny polished off her meal, filling her empty stomach with the only comfort she knew. The mill was hard, home life was difficult, food helped. With the end of a crusty cob, she mopped up the last vestige of gravy, then took the shovel from its place next to the black-leaded grate. It was such a stupid and dangerous exercise, but she would have to go through with it, or there would be no peace at all in the house.

She stepped carefully up the stairs, carrying in one hand a shovel filled with glowing coals taken from the kitchen, in the other fist trailing her shawl. She had to leave no evidence of herself downstairs, because Auntie must appear to be completely alone. Well, alone apart from the spirits, that was.

In the sparse back bedroom that was her own, Jenny tipped the coals into the tiny fireplace, adding some sticks of wood to produce the necessary smoke. It would be almost seven o'clock now. She needed to go down again, because she had forgotten to light the perfumed candles which were meant to mask the smell of singed kindling. That was for the benefit of the visitors, of course. Auntie wouldn't know if the house was on fire, not till she actually saw the flames, because even the most pungent of smells failed to register in the insensitive nostrils.

When she reached the bottom of the stairs, she saw that her aunt was already in the parlour, sitting straight as a ramrod at the table, thin hands stretched out on the cloth, the ghastly nails spread wide like ten sharp, yellowing weapons. Jenny closed the curtains, lit the candles, then slipped from the room. Auntie's meal would be ruined again. There would no doubt be a toast-making session later on, if there was any bread left . . .

'Jenny?' croaked the voice that was preparing to become ethereal. 'No noise. When you hear me scream "yes" very loud, I want ectoplasm in the fireplace corner. Then wait for "come to us". When I shout that, get to the front corner. And do it properly this time, they're paying five bob. For five bob, they want the heavenly bloody choir with harps thrown in.'

Jenny stood on the stairs, a small and very newborn bubble of rebellion forming in her chest. She did not want to take part in these horrible rituals any more. Apart from anything else, it was dangerous, skulking about in Auntie's bedroom with a bucket full of fire, directing smoke between gaps in floorboards, trying to waft it through the tiny cracks in the parlour ceiling. One of these days, the house would go up with everybody in it – herself, Auntie, and the foolish, misery-swamped people who came for messages from the other side.

She turned, paused, then crept back down the stairs. 'Auntie?'

'What?' The green eyes, stained now with dark shadow, flickered over the girl. 'What is it? Have you forgot summat?'

Jenny drew herself up to her full five feet and five inches. 'I . . . it's . . .'

'Well? Has the cat got thy bloody tongue?' Angry hands plucked at the tarot pack.

'It's wrong.' Jenny sank slightly, one of her shoulders drooping, while the arm stretched itself across her stomach, as if she were trying to hug and comfort her inner being. She should be stronger, should be able to speak up for herself. But she was afraid, afraid of hurting Auntie Mavis, scared of inviting her wrath. 'The smoke is wrong,' she added lamely.

Claws tapped quietly on the velour cloth. Jenny decided there and then that she would never have long nails. They were vile, ugly and threatening, and a person with long nails could never work properly, must always be idle, vain and up to no good. Whatever happened to her, she would definitely make sure her nails were cut neatly, though she wasn't criticizing Auntie Mavis, wouldn't dream of doing anything so nasty . . .

'Are you listening to me? The spirits do come, they do! Golden Arrow leads them to me – I see them, I breathe them. But these non-believers need convincing. So we give them a bit of smoke – what's bad about that? We're only helping them, giving them what they want, some hope, some peace.'

Jenny swallowed loudly, making a nasty, gulping noise. 'It's a lie. They told us at school about lies. The vicar came in and said you can act a lie, you don't have to say it. We are acting lies, Auntie, and you make me do it too.'

Mavis Crawley jumped up from her chair. 'You ungrateful little bitch. How many years have I clothed and fed you? Have I ever asked for thanks?'

Jenny blinked away the wet in her eyes. The word 'grateful' kept popping up all the time. It should be entered in the dictionary with an initial capital, just to remind everyone of its importance. 'Dan did it,' she said softly, wishing immediately that she had kept her mouth closed and her thoughts to herself.

'Eh?' The monosyllable was dragged out into a long, slow exhalation. 'What was that?'

'Uncle Dan. He brought money every month, saved up out of his wages.' And most of it, Jenny knew, had gone down Auntie Mavis's throat, swilled nightly from an outdoor-licence jug or from a gin bottle. She raised her eyes slowly. 'I know you gave me a home when my . . . mother didn't want me. But Uncle Dan paid for me, I know he did.' Emboldened for the first time ever, and not understanding why, the girl took another step into the parlour. 'Auntie, I don't want to do the smoke any more.' She was glad that she'd grown too old to make the noises, voices of dead children whose mothers used to sit in this very room hanging with hope on to every last hopeless word. It had been a cruel sham, was still cruel, even without the voices, and Jenny's heart felt like bleeding for the bereaved people who came to spend time and money here.

Mavis Crawley quickly covered the space between them, lifting her arm as if to strike. But there was something in the girl's face, an expression that stayed the raised hand before it could achieve its target. 'I shall put you out on the street,' she muttered, her decaying teeth clenched in anger. 'With your blinking stupid mother, where you belong.'

There followed a short, hollow silence. Never before had Auntie Mavis mentioned Jenny's mother, even though she had been closely questioned while the child was growing.

'Who is my mother?' asked Jenny at last. 'And where is she?'

'I don't know.' Mavis's knees were trembling. Dan had warned her often enough, 'You tell that child anything and I'll put her somewhere else, then see where you'll get your gin money.'

'My mother,' Jenny insisted. 'I know I've got one — everybody has a mother. Where can I find her?'

'She's dead,' snapped Mavis. 'Now, stop your stupid mitherings and get up them stairs. We've folk coming, so get yourself shaped before they—'

'Where did she die?' interrupted Jenny. 'And how? You've got to tell me, you've got to!'

Mavis grimaced, her mouth forming an inverted crescent. 'I don't know everything, do I? Even with my gifts, there's some doors closed. I just know she's dead. I looked at you one day, and I said to meself, "This child's an orphan." Her's been gone a good few years, so there's no use fretting yourself into stewed tripe.'

Jenny fixed her gaze on the crystal. 'Call her up,' she said. 'Do what you do for other people. If it works for them, it'll work for me and all.'

'It . . . doesn't work for family.'

Jenny inclined her head, knowing that it did not work at all. Ever. 'Am I your family?'

'Yes.'

Jenny nodded again, colour arriving along the fine, high bones of her cheeks. 'Then you were related to my mother. Does this mean you're my real auntie?'

'Eh? No. I mean, you're adopted. I can tell you nothing, nothing at all.'

'Except she was on the streets.'

Mavis was plainly floundering. Her eyes travelled frantically from clock to door, back to clock again. 'They'll be here any second. Be a good lass, go up and do the ectoplasm. Just this one last time, Jenny.' She was wheedling now. 'I'll not ask you again. From now on, you don't have to do anything. We can talk any time. Just do this one little thing for me, Jenny, you know I'm not a well woman.'

Jenny reached out and touched a thin, stiff shoulder. 'It'll soon be time for me to leave here, Auntie Mavis. I don't belong with you, don't belong with anybody.' She breathed deeply, seeking some confidence. 'I must start making my own road.' Perhaps this veiled threat would force Auntie to speak about Jenny's past.

Mavis allowed her chin to drop. 'Eh? Leave me on me own and me not able to put a foot across the doorstep? How shall I manage? Who'll get me errands? Who'll . . . ?'

A knocking at the door stilled her tongue. She stood, a look of pleading in her narrowed, greedy eyes, until the girl turned and began to ascend the stairs.

In her room, Jenny filled the bucket with fire, creeping softly across the small landing to the front of the house. Noiselessly, she rolled back the rugs in both corners, her mind empty even though her ears waited for the signal. When it came, she used the old bellows to puff smoke through the floor, moving across to the diagonally opposite corner as soon as the 'oohs' and 'aahs' had died down. Her second task completed, she righted the rugs, then tiptoed back to her own room, resting the dangerously hot bucket on the six tiles that fronted the fireplace. No wonder the kiddies called her names – the whole street knew about Mavis Crawley and her visitors from both worlds.

She straightened, sighed, then stretched out on her bed. In half an hour, she would be summoned downstairs, then, once the coast had been judged clear, she would be sent to the outdoor for brown ale. This was all because her mother had abandoned her. If her mother had loved her, she might have had brothers and sisters, someone to talk to, a life like everybody else's. Well, she intended to ask some very searching questions tonight. She would get the courage from somewhere, or she would pretend to have it, pretend to be braver than she really was.

She stared out of the upper half of the window, her ears

24

registering street-sounds. Someone shouted 'ta-ra', a door banged, children laughed, a dog barked. They were all so friendly, all so interested in the folk next door. Her eyes closed. No-one here wanted to know the Crawleys, mostly because of the spiritualist church Auntie used to attend before going funny with her nerves. And she'd dragged Jenny along to the services too, forcing her to listen while that queer, pale man delivered messages from the dead. It was daft, all of it. There was nothing holy about the pale pastor, because he used to put his hand up Jenny's skirt whenever he managed to get her alone, and proper vicars didn't do that sort of thing.

The front door slammed. Jenny rose and picked up the long-handled pincers, tipping the contents of the bucket back into the fire. That was the only good thing about one of Auntie's sessions – Jenny got a small fire in her room. Auntie's fireplace was boarded up because it had a bad draught, so Jenny always had the bonus of being slightly warmer after a seance.

'Jenny?'

She replaced the pincers, stood up and smoothed her skirt. 'Coming,' she called. Things were going to change tonight. Whatever she needed to do, she would find out about her mother.

In the parlour, Auntie was putting away the tarot cards and the crystal. She cast a sly, sideways glance in Jenny's direction. 'You did a good job there, love. Happen I should start splitting the money with you. Would half a crown suit?'

Jenny sniffed. She didn't want the coin, didn't want to touch the silver disc that had been left on the table for her. 'I've got my spends, ta,' she said.

'We'll go into partnership.' The drawer was closed, and Mavis stood fingering a seven-branch candelabra that sat in the centre of the dresser. 'Fifty-fifty?'

'No.'

'Nay, I can't say fairer than that, Jenny. I mean, I do most of the grafting, so you should be happy taking half the earnings. Come on, don't start sulking again.'

'But you take all of my wages Auntie. I only get a shilling

a week back. So I'd be happier just keeping a bit more of my wages.' She inhaled sharply. 'And anyway, I don't want any of their money.'

Mavis Crawley stood rigidly still, her hands resting for support on the rim of the mahogany dresser. She was angry, yet she struggled not to show it. The girl had grown up all of a sudden, had started to think for herself. There was no point in alienating her altogether. 'I don't want you to leave me, Jenny.' She bit hard on her tongue, forcing back the rage. After all, hadn't she sacrificed everything for this illegitimate brat? 'I don't think I could manage here on me own. You know how ill I am.'

'I'll have to go sooner or later.'

'Why?' The older woman spun round, her eyes gleaming in the shallow light cast by the twin candles across the room. 'Why will you have to go?'

Jenny shrugged. 'Happen I'll get wed.'

'Who?' snarled the slight, tense woman. 'Who's been looking at you?' Yes, she had dreaded this day, because the girl was beautiful, lovelier even than her wayward mother had been. 'Have you been carrying on with some daft lad? Is there goings-on in that bloody mill? Because if there is, you can sack yourself tonight, no need to give your notice.'

'No. There's no carrying on and I don't know any daft lads.'

'Then what do you mean about getting wed?'

Jenny was suddenly too tired for anything but the truth. Dressing things up took energy, the sort of strength that was not available, even to a healthy young woman, after a shift at a cotton mule. 'I shall meet nobody while I live here,' she said softly. 'Everybody reckons this is a queer house, and nobody will talk to me. They think I'm a spiritualist too, and I'm not. I don't believe in it.'

Mavis Crawley slapped a hand against her bosom, going through the motions of a near-faint as she folded herself neatly into a chair. 'You've seen,' she gasped. 'And you've heard . . .'

'I've seen Jimmy Sharples running up our stairs. I've heard him rattling chains for threepence. That's why the neighbours laugh, because Jimmy Sharples won't keep his mouth shut, not for a threepenny bit. Auntie, it's all a fake. I know you believe in some of it, but I don't.' She licked her drying lips. 'And it's sinful, making folk pay to get messages from their dead relatives. It's time I left here.'

The dresser clock chimed the quarter hour. Mavis Crawley sat, face in hands, earrings jangling as she waved her head from side to side. Jenny had always been placid, almost slow, and Mavis had believed that her own old age would be comfortable in such kindly and biddable company. 'You'll not go,' she said finally, poking her head upward in a gesture of defiance. 'Dan won't let you.'

'He will. He's always been nice to me, has Uncle Dan.'

'Has he? I've never known him say above two words to you, and one of them was "ta-ra".'

Jenny closed her mouth and kept her counsel. The meetings had been a secret, something they'd pledged under a tree in Queen's Park years ago. Dan had said that Mavis would likely be hurt by their trysts, so Jenny had never told about the quiet walks, moments stolen from Jenny's shopping time. It was true that he didn't talk much, but at least he had made time for a lonely girl, time that must have been precious to him, for he got few days off from his job as butler in the Skiptons' big house on the moors.

'Where will you go?' Mavis was asking now.

Jenny lifted a shoulder. 'I'll get a room. I might go away from Bolton altogether, find a living-in job down London way. I can cook and clean and sew.' Yes, a fresh start would be lovely, somewhere far from here, a new place where no-one would know about Auntie Mavis and her spirits.

'You'll have to make it right with Dan first.' She shifted in the chair, all ambition to look frail and ill seeming to disappear as the prospect of isolation filled her mind. 'And who'll look after me when you've buggered off to London?'

The girl's head dropped. 'I don't know.' There was a guilty edge to her tone.

'I can't go out. I shall have nowt to eat, nobody to fetch the doctor if I turn bad ways. What sort of thanks is this after eighteen years of bloody slavery?' She snorted and turned to address the Buddha. 'See?' she said shrilly. 'There's nobody as ungrateful as kiddies. You bring them up, you fettle and worry, then they go off chasing rainbows.'

Jenny studied her feet, her eyes fixed rigidly to the carpet slippers she was forced to wear while creeping about upstairs. 'You'll have to learn to go out again, Auntie Mavis. You're only about fifty, aren't you? Mrs Higginbottom still goes out, and she's well past seventy. I keep telling you there's no reason to be scared of the streets. And I can't . . . well . . . I just can't do it any more.'

'Do what?' In spite of firm resolve, the voice had grown shrill.

'I do everything, Auntie. I work in the mill, and I clean the house. Then there's the shopping and the washing.' She shook her head. How many times lately had she come close to falling asleep over a hot flat-iron at midnight? 'I do the meals when I come in, and then—'

'What do you think I did for years, eh? Who got up in the night to give you a bottle, change your nappy, fetch the doctor, boil steam kettles for your croup? Where was your real mam when the kids split your head open with stones?'

Jenny stood perfectly still, hands dangling loosely by her sides. If it hadn't been for Auntie Mavis's peculiarities, the street would not have turned, would not have thrown stones. She had been singled out from infancy, a freak, a monster, just another of Mavis Crawley's familiars. Yes, and they'd killed the cat, hadn't they? Poor little Blackie, strangled and suspended from a lamp because his mistress was an oddity. The notice under his body had read 'WICHES CAT'. They couldn't spell, but the meaning had been plain enough.

'I gave up any chance of marriage because of you.' Mavis was screaming now. 'I had men after me, men of substance, fellows who would have given an arm and a leg for a wife like me.' She puffed out her non-existent chest. 'But I took you in, girl. When Dan found you and brought you here, I opened my door. And how do you repay me? By threatening to leave me after you've worn me out.'

Jenny lifted her eyes and looked directly at the only

family she had ever known. 'Auntie,' she whispered. 'It's the gin that's worn you out, not me.' Never, for as long as she could sensibly remember, had this aunt of hers been fully sober. It was always 'a drop for my nerves' or 'a spoonful for this cough'. And on the worst days, there had been no speech at all, just a crumpled heap on a chair, a cold and empty grate, a hollow stomach, lessons at school floating over her head because she had been starved of food and warmth.

'You . . . you stupid little tart!' Mavis shot from her chair, propelled by temper and an indignation she felt to be righteous. 'How dare you say that to me? You're your mother all over again, just a jumped-up heap of slag with a pretty face and no bloody brain.' Thin lips curled back from the mouldering incisors. 'She earned her money on her back, you know. Finished up on the dock road in Liverpool, dropping her knickers every time a ship came in. She was a whore, your mam, a cheap, dirty . . .' Her words faded, while a look that was akin to terror invaded her pallid features. 'I didn't mean . . . I only . . . I can't be by myself.'

Jenny, shaken by the change in tone, stared incredulously at the trembling woman, noticing that the green eyes were fixed on the kitchen doorway. Slowly, Jenny turned her head. 'Oh,' she gulped. 'Uncle Dan.'

He stood stock still, a hand resting on the doorknob, his face twisting with emotions Jenny could not begin to define.

'Dan,' crowed Mavis. 'Come in. I didn't notice you standing there.'

He lifted the black bowler from his head, holding it close to his chest as if he were attending a funeral. Without taking his eyes off Mavis, he said, 'Pack your things, Jenny.'

Mavis shot forward. 'You can't. You can't take her. I'm still not right from the winter.'

He looked her up and down. 'You're not right from 1895,' he said scathingly. 'You weren't right when yon feller chucked you over, and thank Christ the poor bugger came to his senses in time. You were at it then with your potions, weren't you? Making dolls and sticking pins in. You're not a spiritualist, Mavis. They're decent folk, some of them. You're evil, that's what, and I should never have left this child with you. But beggars can't be choosers, and there was nowhere else to turn. Well, I can see to her now.'

'You can't!' She leapt across the room, talons flailing uselessly an inch away from the man's broad chest. 'You're me own flesh and blood, Dan, you're me brother, so you can't do this to me. She's all I've got. There's nobbut her to see to me, to—'

'To fetch and carry for you,' he said quietly. 'This has been my fault. I always knew you weren't right in the head, ever since we were children. But it's done now. All I can manage is to take her from this house and try to make up for what she's been through.'

Jenny sank on to the broad arm of an easy chair. 'Where am I to go?' she asked.

'With me.' His voice was gruff. 'I've got my own flat now, three rooms at the top of the house. I shall make it right with the master. You can stop with me from now on.'

Jenny tugged at a ringlet that had escaped capture, a slender lock that dangled from her left temple. 'I don't know,' she said cautiously. 'How would I get to my work from up there?'

Dan shrugged. 'The master owns yon mill, so happen he'll fetch you down.' He smiled encouragingly when he noticed her frantic expression. 'Nay, lass. There's a job for you, making beds, dusting and the like. You'll not live in my rooms, they'll give you one of your own over the new wing.'

'You'll be a servant,' screamed Mavis.

Dan fixed his sister with an iron stare. She had been pathetic and pleased when Dan had brought the baby Jenny to her. There had been no real chance of marriage for Mavis, and the foundling child had filled her empty days. 'And what's she been till now? A lady of bloody leisure? She'll get paid and she'll keep her wages. There'll be no drunks hanging on her pinny, nobody telling her lies about her mam.'

Mavis stepped back. 'They weren't lies.'

'Prove it,' he said.

'Then how did she get herself pregnant?' The earrings were on double time now, swinging back and forth as her head bobbed like a cork on a choppy sea. 'Her must have been a slut to get herself in that state. Then leaving the kiddy up at the hall, running off as if the devil was on her tail. What sort of a bloody housekeeper was she?'

'The sort I offered to marry.' These words arrived thin, forced between clenched teeth. 'But she was supposed to go home, back to Ireland. Her mam came down from Chorley, went mad at the idea of Oonagh taking up with a Protestant, so the girl was packed off in disgrace.'

Mavis fought a lewd giggle. 'Aye, as far as Liverpool. Then her mother was all over the place knocking on doors and looking for her. Your fancy Oonagh never left the docks, Dan. The sailors all knew her, the lads from round here. Oonagh Murphy was a by-word in her time, I can tell you.'

'Well, I never heard a word against her, so you're the bloody oracle, as per usual.' Dan's laboured breathing filled the room, then he moved his head, as if remembering the girl on the chair. 'Get your stuff together,' he said.

She sat frozen to the spot, her eyes round and glazed with shock. 'Oonagh,' she said at last. 'My mother's name was Oonagh.'

His expression softened. He was a handsome man, well over six feet tall, and every bit of him that showed was brown. Skin, hair and eyes gave off varying shades of the one colour, while his features were even and strong. He was a solid man, Jenny thought irrelevantly. 'I don't know what to do,' she managed in a voice unlike her own. 'Auntie needs me. There's work – what'll happen if I just don't turn up? And who's this woman that's supposed to be my mother?'

'I'll tell you later,' he said. 'Just trust me and come with me.'

Mavis grinned, her expression cold and mischievous. 'Happen you're looking for a wife?' she asked. 'Somebody as'll see to your old age? Aye, is that why Oonagh dumped her with you? So's she'd grow up and wed a chap old enough to be her grandad?'

He shrugged lightly. 'I'm nobbut forty-four, Mavis. And the rest is none of your flaming business.'

Jenny's fingers tightened until her fists were two tense balls of fear. Did she want to go and live at . . . what was the name of the place? Skipton Hall, that was it, named after the big mill family. Did she want to go up there among strangers? But wouldn't strangers be better, better than . . . ? She looked with pity on the shrivelled figure of her aunt. Alone, the woman would never cope.

Her eyes wandered to the tall, masculine figure that seemed to swamp the room, so huge he looked in this small space. She loved him, had always loved him, but she didn't want to marry him. Tears of confusion and frustration veiled the scene, casting a mist over her vision and her thinking. They were waiting. Both adults were waiting for her to make a move. 'I'm still not sure,' she said.

Mavis tried not to broaden her grim smile. 'There,' she said, a hint of satisfaction colouring the words. 'Her knows where her's best off.' She spoke to Jenny now. 'I'll try and fettle a bit better, lass. Happen you could take me out tomorrow, just as far as Noble Street. One step at a time, eh?'

Dan Crawley placed his bowler on the dresser. 'If you've a fancy for Noble Street, Mavis, you'd best get yourself gone. This lass is taking you nowhere.' He nodded slowly, as if he were suddenly endowed with great wisdom. 'I shall find her mother.' Before Mavis could comment, he continued, 'Aye, I've heard the tales, the ones you likely made up to suit yourself. I've even been to Liverpool to search for her, but there was never a sign.'

'Happen there was a ship in,' snapped Mavis. 'You'd have needed to go below decks to find the bunks.'

He planted his feet well apart, hands clasped behind his back where they could do no mischief to this hateful sister of his. 'Oonagh Murphy was a decent girl,' he said quietly. 'Tales have a habit of getting embroidered, like that daft frock you're wearing. There's no record of her at the bridewells, no knowledge of her in the dock road pubs.

She's not in Liverpool, and I don't know whether she ever was.' He sighed, the great chest expanding against the good cloth of his coat. 'If that lass had been up Lancashire way, I would have found her.'

'A name's easy changed,' barked the tiny woman. 'And it's best changed if you're going to make brass with a mattress strapped to your back.'

Jenny jumped up, hands clasped now over her ears. 'Stop it!' she screamed. 'It's wrong, it's all wrong, like the smoke was wrong. That's all this is, more smoke. Nobody ever tells the truth.' Frightened by her own outburst and uncertain of its cause, the girl stepped back towards the fireplace. 'Why are you fighting?' Her voice was young again, vulnerable and soft.

Mavis glanced at her brother, then averted her mean eyes. 'Your mam was a maid up at the hall,' she began. 'Got herself in the family way just after being promoted to temporary housekeeper, then disappeared. She came back one night and left you with our Dan. She said he was the only person she trusted. So soft lad here,' she jerked a thumb towards her brother, 'felt too sorry for you, wouldn't take you to the foundling home. And I brung you up.'

Jenny stared at the man she had always called Uncle. 'Is that the truth?'

He inclined his head.

'Then . . . then you must know my dad?'

Mavis mopped a glee-filled eye with the pointed end of a flowing sleeve. 'I think the names went in a hat, lass. It could have been any bugger.'

Dan strode forward, a large vein swelling and throbbing in his forehead. 'That's not true, Jenny. The lass made one mistake, and wherever she is, she'll have suffered for it ever since. And if she has changed her name, it'll be to keep away from her family, a load of Irish bigots, they were. She always said she'd come back for you, Jen, but happen she's been feared of her brothers. They'd kill her, you know. Just for having a baby out of wedlock, them drunken buggers would kill her if they caught her.'

'Even now?' Jenny's brow was creased. 'After all this while?'

'They never forget.' His tone was sombre. 'Drunks never forget injured pride, love. You've three uncles, every last one of them soaked in black beer and whiskey. They're in England too, likely road-making or some such thing, a job with ready ale money. As for your mam . . .' He lifted broad shoulders. 'I would have married her, but they wanted a papist. She'd have been flattened to pulp if she'd wed me.'

Jenny turned her back on a room that was filled by ill-feeling. She fingered the ugly Buddha, running a hand over its cold, rounded belly. 'I'm all mixed up,' she whispered. 'This morning, I had no mam and no dad. Now, I've got a mam who might be dead, or she might be alive and a bad woman, or she might be good.' She swallowed. 'And nobody knows who my father is.'

The ancient clock hiccupped before chiming the hour. 'Jenny,' he pleaded as the sound died. 'I'm a man of standing now. There's no need for you to stop here with all the daft carryings on. It's grand up yonder, fields and fresh air, a different life. I would have taken you up before, but I'd no position, no clout. And when I got promoted, Mavis wouldn't hear of you moving. Any road, you're coming with me now. The master won't sack me just for turning up with an orphaned relative that wants work.'

Mavis cackled. 'He might if the orphaned relative's left a mule untended.'

Jenny emitted a deep, shuddering sigh. Never before had she known Uncle Dan to talk so much. Yet never before had he said so little . . . She turned and faced them. 'Who is my father?' she asked simply.

'You've got none.' There was a nasty joy in Mavis's words. 'You're a bastard. He never even brung your birth certificate when you were fetched here. You haven't got a paper to say that you were born at all, just a bit of a certificate I got drawn up meself as your guardian.'

Dan gazed at the lovely, crestfallen child. 'You've a dad, all right,' he said. 'And documentation to prove it.' His large head nodded rhythmically. 'There was nowt denied at the time. There's a certificate up yonder, letters witnessed proper by lawyers and such like. You have a dad, love.'

Mavis gasped. 'Nay, you're not saying . . . is she? Is she a Skipton by-blow? Is there . . . cotton in her?' The broken sentences arrived shrill, punctuated by an excitement that was not containable. 'I've seen it in her cards, I have, I have.' She ran to the dresser. 'Every time, she gets money, good fortune and late love.' Her hand paused on the brass handle. 'A Skipton,' she breathed. 'All these years I've been housing the big boss's love child.' The crystal was cradled now in her claws. 'There's a house for her, a big house, servants, good clothes—'

'Shut up, Mavis.' He placed large, tanned hands on the table and leaned his upper body across the room. 'Come home with me, Jenny. I'll show you all the papers.'

Jenny, feeling stronger, shook her blonde head. 'No.' Her tone held certainty, even a borrowed maturity. 'I'll come when you tell me who I am. I don't need papers, Uncle Dan. Just tell me the truth, then I'll decide whether it's right for me to go up to Skipton Hall.' She stretched the slender neck. 'After all, I'm eighteen, so I should know what's good for me.'

He inclined his head towards Mavis. 'I'd sooner tell you when we're by ourselves.'

'No.' She needed to be sure of the man's motives. However kind he seemed, there might be something untoward going on. 'Now,' she insisted. 'Anyway, Auntie Mavis has a right to know who's been living with her all these years. Well?' She tapped her foot against the rug. 'Give me my father's name.'

Dan straightened, adjusting the dark tie at his throat. 'His name's Dan Crawley, lass. I'm your dad.' Mavis Crawley collapsed on to a chair, her features contorted by genuine shock, though her discomfort was ignored by her companions.

After a few seconds of total immobility, Jenny ran from the house. Life was suddenly too confusing to be faced, so she followed her animal instincts, running from a destiny whose course could not be denied or altered. The running was silly. But all the same, she ran.

Jenny was fleet of foot after school playtimes spent escaping the petty taunts of her peers. But Dan Crawley, a man endowed with long legs and not a little staying power, had the ability to catch up with her. Yet he seemed to be keeping his distance, as if he were giving her her head, allowing her literally to run out of anger or confusion or whatever negative emotions he imagined her to be feeling.

She flew like the wind past the opaque, blind eyes of closed mill windows, squeezing skilfully between the bars of the tall iron gates that separated Derby Street from the yard of McGinty's Brewers of Fine Ales. Breathless now, she leaned against a shed wall, her nose assaulted by the tang of stale spilled beer and the sweet smells of horse and hay. He would not get through the gates. The man she had always called Uncle Dan was too big to fit between the green painted bars.

A faint light showed in the far corner, announcing that the night watchman had arrived and was preparing for his dark vigil. His office was at the front of the brewery, allowing him to guard horses, stock and building without leaving his chair, and Jenny flattened herself against the stable wall in case a keen eye had caught her movements.

No-one came. After several choking seconds, Jenny edged her way round to the side where she would find her friends. She often came here, quite legitimately, on Saturday afternoons when the carthorses were being groomed. She even helped occasionally, when the old horseman was in better mood. He suffered from hangovers, did Billy Edge, and she had learned to search his face for signs of pain before entering the yard on Saturdays. Of course, he wasn't here now. Billy Edge would be in a pub collecting tomorrow's thumping headache.

She let herself into the nearest stall, pleased to recognize Amber's soft whinny of welcome. She was a fine mare, of a strange shade of chestnut that was lighter than usual, and with eyes that were, in daylight at least, reminiscent of a deep version of the precious stone for which she had been named. Jenny reached and grasped the wiry mane, pushing her nose against sleek, firm shoulder muscle, allowing her tears to pour into the animal's coat. There was something so comforting about a horse, she thought. So solid, so placid, so thoroughly dependable and clever. 'Amber,' she wept. 'Who am I?'

The horse turned, nostrils wafting warmth into Jenny's neck, large teeth grinding against a mouthful of fodder. This gentle mare who had, for fifteen years, carried barrels in weathers foul and fair, did not care about Jenny's identity. 'No, you don't mind, do you?' whispered the girl. 'It's what I am that matters, eh? What I'm like, how I act, things I do. But why didn't he tell me before, Amber? Even Auntie Mavis didn't know he was me dad – I could tell that from her face.' She patted the firm belly absently. 'I've got a mam, you know. She's not dead. I'd know if she was dead, I'd feel it in me bones. Amber, why is everything so cruel? Why do they make you pull that dray on the ice when they know your legs can break? And why don't they tell us who our mams and dads are?'

The teeth stopped grinding. Amber stood still and pensive, as if considering her companion's dilemma.

'Last summer,' said Jenny, 'I followed on the trams while you got taken up Tonge Moor for your fortnight off. There was you and Flora, it was your turn. I waited at the tram stop till you came up the road, and I watched your tails swishing when you got near. Billy Edge opened that gate, led you in and took your harness off.' She let out a deep, heartfelt sigh as the tears dried on her cheeks. 'Like two bullets from a pair of pistols, you were. No, more like spring lambs, I suppose. That's the only time I've ever seen Billy Edge smile, you know. That was the day I decided to like him. I watched you play, you and Flora. I didn't know a great big carthorse could lift all four feet off the ground at once. And you rolled about like a silly dog with your hooves waving in the air.'

Amber snorted, nodded, bent for more hay.

'I wish it could always be like that for you and me, old girl. Jumping and running in the buttercups. But you're stuck here with gallons of beer to shift, and I'm stuck . . . nowhere.'

'That's not true, lass.'

Jenny lifted her head and stared at the outlined figure in the doorway. 'How did you get in?' she asked, knowing that the answer did not matter.

'I climbed.'

'Over them sharp spikes?'

'Aye.' He moved to the other side of Amber, placing a large tanned hand on the horse's nose. 'Steady,' he said softly as the huge feet moved. The mare, having decided that the new presence was benign, continued to chew contentedly. 'Jenny.' There was tenderness in the tone. 'It were all done for the best.'

'Where is she?'

He dropped his head and thought for a moment. 'I don't know. I'd not be standing here in McGinty's yard if I had the answer to that question. I told her where I'd be putting you, then she went. I've not clapped eyes on her in eighteen years. Her brothers were on the rampage looking for her, and her mam too. But it seems they found nowt.'

'So I've uncles and a grandmother.'

He nodded, then raised his head to look directly at her, his sad eyes seeming to gleam like two points of soft light in the gloom of the stable. 'They'd not want you. She's Irish Catholic, your mam, and a baby out of wedlock is a disgrace. And they'd never have let her marry me, on account of me not being Catholic born. Even if I'd took lessons and turned, they wouldn't have given permission. And she was too young to be wed without consent. So she upped and went, said she'd be back when she got old enough to make her own decisions.'

Jenny edged along the wall, dropping on to a bale in the corner. 'What was she like?'

Dan drew a hand across his jaw, closing his eyes as he stared back into the past. 'Clever, she was. The old housekeeper dropped dead one day, and they gave the job to Oonagh on a temporary basis. But she was that good at it, they never bothered looking for another even though Oonagh was so young. I was just a valet at the time, so she was over me in a way, though I answered to the butler.' He looked hard at her, then turned away abruptly, as if the sight had caused pain. 'She looked like you,' he said. 'Happen a bit taller, but . . . like you.'

Jenny glanced down, surprised to see that she was still wearing slippers. The floor suddenly felt cold and hard through the thin, worn soles. 'Are you really my dad?'

'Yes.'

'Why didn't you tell me before?'

He stepped forward to close the lower half of the door, still keeping his back to Jenny. A great, tired sigh escaped his lips as he leaned against the jamb. 'I'd have lost me job if anybody had found out about me and Oonagh. We weren't supposed to . . . mix in them days. Even now, some of the masters don't like their servants pairing off. And I had to keep the job to pay Mavis and to stay in the same place, the place where your mam would come and look for me.'

'And she never came.'

'No.'

Jenny shivered. Her shawl was upstairs in the bedroom, and the work frock was thin, needed to be light because of the heat in the spinning room. 'What do we do now?'

At last, he swivelled in her direction. 'You come up yonder with me. You call me Uncle Dan, just like you've always done. When you get took on as maid, you call me Mr Crawley.' He lifted his hands in a gesture of despair. 'And we just carry on waiting.'

She wrapped her arms about her cold chest. 'Do they know anything about me up there?'

He nodded. 'They know you're Oonagh's and that I took you to my sister to wait for Oonagh coming back. I'm sorry. I couldn't tell them the truth. Happen the master could take it now, but there's others to consider, folk with closed minds.'

Jenny bit down on her lip to prevent the chattering of her teeth. 'Well,' she said after a moment's thought, 'it seems daft to carry on waiting after all this while. She'll not come now. Why don't you get a job somewhere else, have a fresh start, stop . . . hoping?'

He shook his head, walked over to Amber and began to

stroke the velvet nose. 'I'll stop where I am,' he said quietly.

Jenny gazed at him. 'You like horses, don't you?'

'I do.'

'So do I.'

'Yes, I know.' He reached out his arms and she hesitated fractionally before jumping up and running into the offered embrace. For a minute or two, she enjoyed being a daughter, holding close this strong, new parent, breathing in his scent, feeling the slight roughness of his chin. Then they separated and stared at one another, each knowing that such demonstrations of affection would be rationed, possibly totally forbidden, from now on.

When they left the stables, Jenny realized that she would always think of her father when she watched the drays. Yes, the big horses would remind her not of Uncle Dan, not of Mr Crawley, but of the father she had always known. The father she had never known.

Chapter Two

'YOU'VE SETTLED IN WELL ENOUGH, I'LL GIVE YOU THAT.'
Carla Sloane's blackcurrant eyes travelled over Jenny's
neatly clad figure. The housekeeper folded her arms,
pushing impossibly higher a huge bosom that looked as if
it had been encased in cement, so rigid and unyielding did
it appear. 'Mind, it's early days yet. As I said only this
morning to Mr Crawley, a month's hardly enough for a
trial. Still,' she exhaled, the breath whistling through gaps
in uneven teeth, 'you've been satisfactory up to now. Well,
as near satisfactory as we can get these days,' she
concluded grudgingly.

'Thank you, Mrs Sloane.' Jenny felt stupid, standing
here with a wisp of lace on her head and, round her
middle, a pinny that was no bigger than a pocket
handkerchief with a daft frill sewn on. She had been
'tweenying' for three and a half weeks now, a job that
meant fitting in anywhere and doing whatever was
necessary. She had, thus far, been answerable to Maria
Hesketh who was upstairs, to Briony Mulholland who was
down, and even to the small army of dailies and oc-
casionals who had shown her the tricks of the trade,
including how to cut corners while appearing to do a good
job, and how to keep on the right side of 'Stonehenge'.

Stonehenge was the formidable creature who was
currently circling Jenny, a hand to the square jaw as she
considered the new maid. She walked twice in a clockwise

41

direction, once the opposite way, subjecting the girl to the scrutiny for which she had become famous over the past decade and a half. One hair out of place, one scuff mark on a white shoe, and a servant might be sacked on the spot.

Jenny's glance moved from side to side until she felt dizzy from following the ritualistic moves of this over-whelming woman. She was, without a doubt, the ugliest person Jenny had ever met. The face was wide and craggy, like something that had been hewn by an apprentice mason out of solid rock. The forehead jutted over deep sockets that contained a pair of black, dead, tiny eyes, the sort of eyes one might have expected to find on a snake, or some similar cold-blooded animal. There was no spare flesh on the large-boned face, yet the body was ample, encased in the kind of corsetry that showed through clothing. Her lips were thin, as if they had been left unfinished, while large, tombstone teeth precluded the mouth from closing properly. It was the teeth that had labelled her Stonehenge, because they looked like some prehistoric arrangement of sacred tablets, a monument to mankind's stupid adherence to meaningless labour. It was important not to laugh, though, so the nervous girl tried to close her mind to Maria Hesketh's words, 'We use her on Midsummer's Day, let the sun shine through her teeth like they do down south with the real Stonehenge.'

Jenny shifted her weight to one leg, tired of standing, exhausted by the woman's stares. And Maria Hesketh was naughty, telling that tale just before this interview. Did they turn her upside down to get the best angle for the sun . . . ?

A hand reached out and prodded Jenny's spine, and the tense girl jumped against the hard touch. 'Are you strong? Capable of lifting properly?'

Jenny swallowed nervously, though there was no saliva in her mouth. 'I've run three mules, Mrs Sloane, my back's strong. I was a good piecer, never broke an end, no trouble bending for the cops.'

Stonehenge sniffed derisively. 'I'm not interested in your industrial experience, child. And I want you to know that there's no preferential treatment here, so we'll have that straight before we go any further. The fact that you are related by adoption to a senior member of staff does not entitle you to any favouritism.' She ceased her travels, standing in front of Jenny now, the dark, pebbly eyes seeming to burn with unfeeling energy. 'Have you been a carer?'

'Pardon?'

The housekeeper sighed again in the face of such stupidity. 'Your agoraphobic and alcoholic aunt. I understood that you have minded her for years and that you are discreet.'

'Yes.' She didn't know what else to say. There was a dictionary in the library – she would perhaps seek out the large word later. Discreet was all right, it just meant keeping your gob shut. And alcoholic meant the gin – but the other word . . . ?

'Are you listening to me, Jennifer Crawley?'

'Aye – I mean yes, Mrs Sloane.'

'So. Why did you leave her?'

'Oh.' Jenny wondered whether the nose had ever been broken, because it sat slightly off-centre, like an afterthought that had been stuck on in a hurry. 'Uncle Dan fetched me here. He said I had to come. So I came.' Her voice faded, swamped by the woman's bone-scalding glare.

'Yes, yes.' The perambulations resumed, and Jenny raised her gaze heavenward as the woman disappeared yet again. She must not giggle, she must not think about the summer solstice. Funny word, that. Solstice.

'It's loyalty I'm looking for, Jennifer.'

'Yes, ma'am.'

'There's a special and very responsible post available in this household. It is a rewarding job for a young woman of strength and sensibility.'

Jenny bit her lip. She knew what was coming, because the mad woman's nurse had fled just last week . . .

'Mrs Skipton is highly strung.'

'Yes, Mrs Sloane.'

'She needs someone she can trust, talk to, depend on. And there's a weakness in her bones, in her muscles, so she wants a strong, youngish person. I think you might be adequate in such a position.'

Jenny studied the copper-bottomed pans that hung from a beam, their bases glistening like a constellation of huge gold suns. She didn't want to nurse the lady of the house, didn't relish the thought of being trapped with yet another odd creature. After eighteen years with Auntie Mavis, she had done her fair share of good works. 'I'm not a nurse,' she ventured carefully. 'And I like housemaiding. I like the job I'm doing now.'

A firm hand closed itself round Jenny's upper arm, while a rasping voice whispered from behind, 'You should be grateful to this house, Jennifer Crawley, especially to Mr Crawley, who took you to his sister to be raised as family. You were abandoned on this very doorstep where you might easily have frozen to death had you been ignored.'

The word 'grateful' was cropping up again. 'My mother . . .' The words faded, choked by fear.

'Well? Finish what you started, miss.'

'She told my . . . Uncle Dan. She didn't mean me to freeze, Mrs Sloane.'

'But she left you.' There was amusement behind the cruel words. 'So you owe the Skiptons some loyalty. As for Mr Crawley, he agrees that you should be tried for this position of importance.'

'Oh.'

Dan Crawley entered the room, a huge silver dish tucked beneath an arm. 'The salmon platter, Mrs Sloane.'

'Ah yes. Leave it on the chopping block, Mr Crawley. Cook will be back directly.' There followed a pause, nobody moving. Jenny stared at the chopping block, a free-standing table with a top at least two feet thick except where it dipped towards its own centre from years of hacking knives and cleavers. The man who was her father, the man she sometimes called Uncle Dan, was a dark shape in the corner of her eye. Her nose began to itch, but she dared not scratch it. Stonehenge and nose-scratching did not go together. And it was awful having a dad when you couldn't call him Dad, when you couldn't ask for help from your own parent.

'Is something the matter?' asked Dan, his tone as mild and even as ever.

'Your niece does not wish to take over the care of Mrs Skipton. We have done our best, as you know, given her a delightful room in the east wing, the sort of room that is not usually allocated to a new girl. I remember when they started off over the stables, not much more than a candle to keep them warm.' Not without some difficulty, she extended her tongue and ran it over the edge of her jutting teeth. 'Yet she would pick and choose her work, Mr Crawley. I sometimes wonder what the world is coming to. In my day, we did not flinch at the idea of hard work.'

Dan crossed the room and stood directly in front of his daughter. 'It's a good job, Jenny. Just one room to clean, one fire to tend. And apart from that, you have to do as Mrs Sloane asks. She does know what she's doing, and she likely recognizes that you're right for looking after the missus.' He shook his head slowly. 'I told you, lass, you take your orders from this lady.'

Mrs Sloane came from behind, placing herself next to Uncle Dan so that they formed a wall of authority and adulthood, an obstacle Jenny could never hope to clear. It was useless to argue, so she might as well give in gracefully. 'I'll be happy to look after the lady,' she lied as prettily as she could. 'I just want to do it right, that's all. I mean, she is ... gentry, isn't she?' A look of near-amusement in Mrs Sloane's miniature eye passed unnoticed. 'I want to do it proper, Uncle ... Mr Crawley. I've only ever looked after Auntie Mavis, and that's not the same thing.'

'Your duties will be listed.' The granite chin turned towards Dan, and Jenny marvelled that it did not creak as it moved. 'She can read, I take it?'

He nodded.

'Then there should be no difficulty. Except,' she moved menacingly near to Jenny, so close that sour milk or bad cheese-flavoured breath fanned the girl's cheek. 'Except for discretion. Whatever occurs in the mistress's room, you will not discuss it except with myself and Mr Crawley. Even then, you will voice no opinion. Facts will suffice. Do I make myself plain?'

Jenny, working hard not to shake in her shoes, mouthed a quiet 'yes'. She was used to keeping her counsel, inured to having no-one to talk to. Though she had wished to make friends here, and Maria Hesketh had been ever so nice up to now. 'Will I lose my room?' she asked.

'You'll move into the bedroom adjoining Mrs Skipton's,' said the housekeeper. 'She needs constant surveillance, so your days off will be staggered.'

Jenny's shoulders slumped beneath the weight of further worry. 'My Auntie Mavis is used to seeing me on a Thursday. I do the shopping for her, 'cos she can't go out with her nerves. How will she manage if I stop going?'

'I'll go.' Dan's tone was resigned. 'She's my sister, so I'll see she's catered for. Happen I'll get somebody to go in a couple of times a week, a woman to do her errands and clean up a bit. There must be somebody round there that could do with a job.' He raised his chin and smiled down at Jenny. 'She's my problem. You just get on with your life.'

Mrs Sloane walked out to her office, a cupboard-sized room that butted on to the kitchen next to the laundry. Jenny watched the large figure as it squeezed itself behind the tiny desk which was occupied by accounts books, menus, duty rotas and, somewhat incongruously, a plaster statue of the Virgin and a rather ornate pince-nez. It was said among the servants that a person knew when he or she was in real trouble, because these strange glasses were always worn for dismissals and wage-dockings.

Dan placed the dish on the chopping block, then walked back to Jenny's side. 'You'll be all right,' he whispered. 'It's a bobby's job, is that, specially if you've got the right attitude. And if you haven't got the right attitude, then get it or pretend.'

'I don't want a bobby's job,' she whispered. 'I never wanted to be a policeman.'

'Bobby's job means easy, it's just a saying.' He forced these words from a corner of his mouth. 'Mrs Skipton's only another woman, just a bit strange, that's all.'

'I've had strange,' hissed Jenny. 'I've had enough strange already.'

He took her arm and led her out to the passage between kitchen and everyday dining room. 'Jenny,' he said pleadingly. 'Don't push your luck. If anybody realized that you were . . . that you are who you are, I might just be out on my ear as a bad influence. I've got to feel me way before I think of telling the master.' Aye, and Carla Sloane would make a meal of it, he thought. 'Don't be familiar with me. It's bad enough you being my adopted niece, but if they found out . . . well . . .'

'That you're my father.' Her voice was flat and emotionless. She had a dad now, and she couldn't even enjoy him.

'Don't say it aloud. I'd not have told you just yet, but for our Mavis turning sour. Mind you, she's always been the same, that one, all right as long as everything's going her own road.' He put his head on one side and studied her for a moment. 'You're better here, better fed, nicer dressed, warmer . . .'

'And still in charge of a sick woman. I saw that nurse running off, Uncle Dan. She looked as if the devil was on her tail, all staring eyes and her hair stuck up like a haystack.' She gulped back her misery. 'I'm scared, I'm frightened of folk who aren't right in the head.'

He glanced left and right, then lifted her chin with a strong forefinger. 'Trust me. Once she gets used to you – if she decides to get used – you'll be well on your road to promotion. Listen.' He dropped his hand. 'Wipe them baby-blue eyes and pay attention. Maria Hesketh upstairs, now she'll not reign long. No way will she ever make housekeeper, because she's too quick for her own good. She'll be back with her mother once the house empties a bit, she's only waiting for space at home. Briony'll get wed, that sticks out a mile, then there'll be nobody to train up.'

Jenny sniffed quietly. Briony Mulholland, downstairs maid and amateurish vamp, was after Dan, but he plainly lacked the wit to see it. Aye, he might be old enough to be Briony's dad – he was definitely old enough to be Jenny's – but he was still an attractive man.

'And Carla Sloane,' he said now, 'will be off to live with her sister in a couple of years, mark my words. This is your chance.'

'I don't want to live here,' she muttered, ashamed of her own petulance. 'Mrs Hardman doesn't live here, and she's the cook. Cooks always live in, so why—?'

'Jenny,' he interrupted softly but firmly. 'Mrs Hardman's the best cook this side of Preston. She . . . er . . . got special permission for a cottage.'

'Why?' Jenny's face was set in lines of stubbornness. 'Why can she live out while I've got to sleep next door to Mrs Skipton?'

Dan inhaled deeply. 'She's getting on, is Mrs Hardman, and cooks like her don't grow on trees.' He swallowed the real answer, the truth that had caused him to hesitate. If Mrs Hardman and Mrs Sloane had been forced to continue living together, then the services of a lion tamer might well have been required. The cook, a pleasant and motherly woman, had refused point-blank to breathe the same air as the housekeeper, so the master had granted Mrs Hardman a cottage. The two women followed some unwritten schedule, a tacit plan that usually allowed just one of them in the kitchen. 'Stop all the questions, Jenny,' he advised finally.

But Jenny wanted to have her say. 'I don't like mad people.' She stood her ground even though it was a bit uncertain, because her fear of lunacy was stronger than her respect for Dan. 'They should get somebody with a certificate.'

'Nurse Irene Morley had one, it was framed on the wall. It did her no good, she still ran away. A certificate doesn't give you backbone, love. Look. All Eloise Skipton needs is a firm hand and a bit of kindness. She's a thirty-odd-year-old woman with a wasting disease. There's nowt wrong with her brain, not as far as I know.'

'She's mad,' insisted Jenny stubbornly. 'Maria said she'd not take her on.'

He heaved a great sigh. 'The missus is a bit self-destructive at times. She has turns. But she's not bad, not an evil person.' He lifted his tone during this last sentence, as if he didn't really believe in what he was saying, as if he were trying to convince himself.

Jenny leaned against the wall. It was time to bow yet again to the inevitable. 'When do I start?'

'Tomorrow. The rest of today is yours, I'll make that right with Mrs Sloane. And you'll get new frocks, ordinary clothes, not a uniform. The missus doesn't like uniforms. You can read to her, help her with her sewing. It's a proper lady's job, is that, more like a companion.'

She watched him as he walked away, tall, broad, very sure of himself and of his position in this household. It was all right for him, she thought. He hadn't been pushed from one silly situation to another, from an aunt who looked for spirits to a mistress bent on suicide.

She picked a duster from the pocket in the side of her dress, holding it out like a flag of truce as she set forth to explore the house. Should she be questioned, she could flick it about, pretend that she was working.

There was no family around. The mistress kept to her room – in fact, Jenny had never set eyes on the woman. The master had been away since Jenny had arrived, reputedly holidaying in the Swiss Alps to clear his chest after a year in the Skipton mills. Though Jenny would have bet her life that Henry Skipton was never truly exposed to the heat and damp that were essential partners in the production of cotton. It was, she decided, an unfair world. Some sat beneath snow-capped mountains, others pieced ends. Some had mams and dads, brothers and sisters, others were landed with crazy aunts, bellows and a bucket of fire. Or with a yellow duster and a suicidal lady to care for. But this self-pity was doing her no good. Better to keep moving, better not to think at all.

It was an interesting house, oddly shaped, with bits added on in a haphazard patchwork that held no obvious pattern. The kitchen, with its office and laundry, faced out at the side on to a small yard from which the end of the family dining room was visible. A narrow passage led from the kitchen into the dining and morning rooms, while the drawing room was on the left, extending towards the hall. The latter large area stretched across the whole front of the building. It was a room in itself, with a huge brick fireplace, armchairs, couches, a grandfather clock and several small tables.

The ballroom, where large dinner-parties and dances were meant to be held, reached from the hall right through to the rear of the mansion, with a small conservatory tacked on to the back. This deprived the massive room of most natural light, so twelve chandeliers dangled from the ornate ceiling on heavy gold chains.

Off the ballroom were a study, a panelled library with thousands of books on its shelves, and a games room at the front. An east wing had been tacked on to the library, a special separate section built for guests. It contained two suites of rooms, with servants' quarters above. Jenny's current room was in this new block, though she would be losing it tomorrow.

With her mouth set in a defiant line, Jenny climbed the staircase next to the library. Although this access had been provided for servants, she was not supposed to use it unless she was actually tweenying. After meals, and during hours of rest, she was expected to use the outside stairway to attain the first floor. This was one of Stonehenge's stupid rules. In spite of her rebellion, she flicked the duster. Bravery was one thing, but tempting fate was another matter altogether.

The first floor was divided into two sections by a long landing area. To the rear of the house, there were the master's room and the mistress's room, with a bathroom placed between the two. Next to Mrs Skipton's bedroom was the nurse's room, the quarters that had been abandoned so hastily by the recent incumbent. Jenny paused, a hand resting on the knob. This was going to be her place in Skipton Hall, so she had better get her bearings, take a quick look.

She stood in the doorway, her jaw dropping to allow a quiet 'ooh' into the stillness. It was unbelievable. There was a beautiful bed with frilled canopy and brass frame, a full suite of white-and-gold furniture including wardrobe, chests of drawers and dressing table, and a plumbed-in washbasin with a cupboard beneath and blue tiles forming a splash-back.

She quickly shut off the sight of such splendour, blinking hard as if returning from a dream. There had been a couch too, one of those special things with a curly end – a chaise, she thought it was called. And lamps with pink shades, electricity, rugs . . .

The job must be terrible, then, if the certificated Nurse Irene Thingummy had fled from trappings as lovely as those! She moved along the landing, opening the last door into an airy bathroom. This too would be hers. Unless the four bedrooms at the front of the house were to be occupied, there would be no-one else to use this bath, because the master and mistress had their own facilities. Oh yes, the job had to be an awful one!

She sank on to a gilded and pink-cushioned chair on the landing, resting an arm on a nearby half-moon table. Absently, she drew the duster over its glossy surface, her eyes fixed now on the ceiling. Up there, in the six attic rooms at the front of the house, lived the butler and the housekeeper, each with a bathroom, a sitting room and a bedroom. Yes, her father lived up there. She would have been better off sleeping on Dan's sofa, and to hell with all the lovely furniture and scented soap shaped like roses!

There was a picture in her mind, though, an image of herself luxuriating in that lovely bath, soaking in perfumed salts and Eastern oils, hair piled up away from steam . . . But she would rather have peace of mind than a bathroom, yes she would.

There was movement in Mrs Skipton's room, and her spine stiffened against these muted sounds. She wondered obliquely where her mother was, where she had been all these long years. If she wasn't dead, then she should be here to protect Jenny from . . . from whatever lay behind that door.

That door flew open now, seeming to spit out the slender figure of Maria Hesketh. As usual, the ginger fringe stood to attention in spite of careful ministrations, while thousands of freckles were made bolder by drained skin. The girl's pale and bony hands had clenched themselves into tight balls of anger which beat rhythmically and repeatedly against a scrawny chest.

'Hello, Maria. What's going on?'

Maria Hesketh allowed the door to swing shut in her wake. 'Ever tried getting prune juice out of silk wallpaper? I could put up with this job for one day till it came to prunes. And no wonder Irene Morley hopped it – she got rice pudding, and not on the wall, either. I bet that wasn't part of her training at the hospital.'

'Oh.' Jenny rose from her seat, the duster dangling limply from a hand. She didn't know what to say, which questions to ask, didn't want any answers.

'She's bloody mad, bloody demented. She doesn't like anything ugly, she says, and prunes is ugly. Nasty and wrinkled, she says. Not fit for pigs, she says. Well, she needs the prunes to keep regular, but they're all over the wall now, so happen the wall will be healthier.' She looked Jenny up and down. 'When are you kicking off in this here job?'

'Tomorrow.'

Maria nodded vigorously, the pointed chin almost touching her chest. 'She'll take to you, I reckon, 'cos you're a long way off ugly. When old Stonehenge showed her face again a few months back, the missus went into a pink fit that went on for a fortnight. She said the last time she saw a face like that, it was fastened to a big church in Paris, something to do with rainwater drainage. But you're beautiful, you are.'

Jenny bit her lip sharply. 'Ooh Maria. I don't want to do it. I'd sooner clean grates and brasses, I would, honest. I'd rather do all the washing up till next Preston Guild.'

Maria leaned against the wall, feet planted well apart, arms folded beneath the slight swell of her bosom. 'Well, that won't be long, 'cos the Guild's on in a year or two. Listen, I've to go back in in a minute. I've got to go back and scrub the flaming wall. The best advice I can give is that you learn to be a good ducker. Watch her right arm, there's not much movement in the left one. And smile. Plaster a grin from east to west, don't look what she calls sullen. Sullen gets the right arm going. And mash the bloody prunes up, stick them in the bottom of a dark jelly or something, use your imagination.' She puffed out her thin cheeks and blew an exasperated breath. 'And to think she got all this from fish and chips. What's uglier than fried cod and soggy peas, eh?'

'You what?'

Maria grinned suddenly. 'Nay, you didn't think all this

52

glamorous stuff was from cotton, did you? Oh, the house is the Skiptons', right enough, but madam here brought a fair amount of cash in with her. The furniture's been made by some feller called Lewis Cans, she goes on about him, French, something to do with a king. But her mam and dad were dead common, kept a chain of shops, as far apart as Bermondsey and Edinburgh, so I believe. Aye, fish and bloody chips. But she's got all the blinking vinegar, I can tell you that for no money.'

'So she's not what you'd call a real lady?'

Maria stood up straight and posed with an arm angled behind her bright red hair. 'Ooh, she's had the elly-queue-shon lessons,' she said, emphasizing and splitting the syllables. 'And de-portment, how to walk about with a bloody library balanced on her head, but she's not gentry. Neither is he, but at least he's not airified. And he doesn't chuck prunes.'

Jenny shifted from foot to foot. She should be laughing at Maria, because Maria was very funny, a real mimic, but any laughter was swamped, pressed down behind a lead weight of anxiety and apprehension. 'She won't like me,' she said sadly. 'Nobody ever has liked me.'

'Don't talk so wet. Look at yourself next time you pass a mirror. Anyway, folk are bound to be jealous of some-body with a figure and a face like yours. And I like you.'

'You like everybody. That's how you are.'

'I don't like Stonehenge. She could stop the Town Hall clock with one of her looks, she could. In fact, they use her tongue when they want the paint stripping here.' She looked hard at Jenny, as if assessing her. 'Confidence, that's what you're short on. Now meself, I've always had plenty. I know I'm no Venus de Wotsit – her with no arms – but I've got it up here.' She tapped her skull with a forefinger. 'Anyway, I never could see the sense in being armless.' She giggled. 'Use what you've got, Jenny. Winning ways and a smile that makes the sun shine. Come on, love.'

'I'm dead scared, Maria.'

'We're all scared, pet. That's bloody life, being scared. When you stop being frightened, when you stop worrying, that's the time to start worrying, because you'll be dead. Every day's different, it's filled with new things, big ones, small ones, things that hurt or make you happy. We can't see the day till it's over, and if we keep waiting for it to be over, there'll be bugger all left. Me mam taught me that.'

'Live for the moment,' whispered Jenny.

'Aye, live and learn. Make a mistake today, make a different one tomorrow. Like me now. If I ever go back in there, I'll be pruneless. If they ask me to take a carthorse in, I'll do it, brasses, ribbons, bells – the lot. But from now on, no prunes. And I'd think twice about rice pudding too.'

Jenny nodded, her spirits lifting slightly. 'Don't ever leave this house, Maria. Not while I'm still here.'

'Well, I've not much choice at the moment. There's about five to a bed at home. When they wake up in a morning, they're putting their shoes on somebody else's feet, and our Sybil's not been seen for a month, 'cos she sleeps next to the wall and she can't get out. That's it, it's good to see you laughing, girl.'

At last, Jenny allowed herself to chuckle. She had a friend, her very first friend. If the days brought good things like Maria, then the edge would surely be taken off the bad. 'How many in your family, Maria?'

The slight girl shrugged. 'I don't know. I lost interest when I ran out of fingers to count them on. There was talk of me mam sending me dad down the vet's to get altered, but he kept slipping his lead. They call a register every morning, like school, but there's one called Anthony that gets somebody else to answer for him. We think he's took a crack-of-dawn job down the fruit market.'

Jenny was helpless with glee. 'Where . . . where do they all sit to eat?' she managed.

Maria said, 'On the stairs, of course. It's the usual place for big families down our end of the pool. They sit in rows going up, like the Romans did when them lions was eating the Christians.'

'The pool?' Jenny wiped a weeping eye.

'Liverpool. I only came here for a ride one day, sat on bales of cotton, I was. The horse slipped a shoe in

Skipton's yard, and Mr Skipton was talking to me and the driver. This driver's a mate of me dad's – me dad's a docker, see. Anyway, they took us in the office for a cuppa while the horse got seen to, and there was an advert on a board for an upstairs maid. Seems nobody wanted it 'cos of her in there.' She jerked a thumb towards the mistress's door. 'And I applied on the spot, got interviewed by himself. He says, "Have you done this sort of work before?" So I says, "Yes."'

'Had you?'

'No,' she replied without hesitation. 'So he says, "Have you got any references?", so I says, "Sorry, but this woman in this posh house up Crosby what I used to look after died", so he says, "Well, I hope you're not in the habit of losing your employers", then he took me on.' She raised her eyes heavenward. 'At least I don't sleep with our Sybil's big toe in me gob no more, but I could do without old Stonehenge. Anyway, I'd best get back before I'm missed.'

Liverpool. That was where Dan had searched for her mother, the city in which Oonagh Murphy was reputed, by Auntie Mavis at least, to have walked the streets. 'Will you take me to visit your family if we ever get time off together?'

'Course.'

'Won't they mind?'

'They won't notice.' She paused, a hand on the doorknob. 'Yes, they will. That's one thing about you, Jenny. You'll never get lost in a crowd, not with your looks.' She grinned, winked, then disappeared towards Eloise Skipton and her prunes.

Jenny wandered along the landing, no longer pretending to dust. At the top of the main staircase, she paused, sensing something different in the hall below. Uncle Dan, Briony Mulholland and Stonehenge were arranged in a silent line at a right angle to the front door. Opposite them, in a similar line, stood the four dailies, hair hurriedly pushed into the awful brown mob-caps they were forced to wear. The cook kept her distance, had placed herself in front of the grandfather clock. Jenny stared at the scene, sensing that Mrs Hardman was deliberately staying away from Stonehenge. So that was the real reason, then. Mrs Hardman didn't like Carla Sloane. Jenny grinned and decided that the cook was a good woman.

The front door opened fully, and in fell Howie Bennett, ostler and general dogsbody, a gawky youth who, at the moment, seemed to have more than the usual allocation of limbs. His face was bright red as he struggled with the unwieldy burden, a pair of skis and two sticks with circles at the ends. A man appeared behind him, a man of moderate height, slender, wearing a very good suit and the sort of tan that comes only from a holiday abroad. 'Drop them, Howie,' he said, his teeth flashing white in the sunbrowned face. 'I don't know why I took them anyway, the slopes were soft.' He greeted the servants, shaking each hand and grinning a lot. 'Sorry you got no warning,' he said. 'But we've a ship floating up the Mersey with a hole in her side, so my cotton's a bit damp. Insurance, you see. I'll have a look at the papers. Howie – drop the damn things.'

There followed a terrible clatter as metal hit parquet. Stonehenge did not budge, but Jenny could feel the housekeeper's eyes as they searched for scratches on the block floor. Howie bounced out to get the luggage while Briony Mulholland simpered and made eyes at the master. Jenny stepped back, suddenly anxious not to be included in the tableau below. She felt shy about meeting this man. Up to now, he had been a figure in a car next to the weaving sheds, a man who nipped in and out of the mill without ever really being seen.

But as she moved, he chose that moment to glance upward. 'Who have we here?' he asked, the voice even and pleasant.

The granite head swivelled on its axis. 'Come down, Jennifer. It's Crawley, sir. Jennifer Crawley. A . . . relative of Mr Crawley.'

'Come here.' He reached out a hand and beckoned. 'I don't bite, you know.' His smile broadened. So this was the little scrap who had been abandoned all those years ago. Dan Crawley was a good man, and this child was a credit to him and his sister.

Feeling extremely foolish, Jenny descended the main staircase, hoping that she would not trip and fall headlong at Henry Skipton's feet. Mrs Sloane was whispering in the master's ear, and Jenny hoped that she had cleaned her teeth, because the smell of cheese had been dreadful earlier.

'Jenny, is it?' he asked when she finally arrived without mishap.

'Yes, sir.'

'And you are to look after . . . my wife?' Was that pity in his eyes?

'Yes, sir.'

He nodded, the bright, clear irises twinkling beneath raised eyebrows. 'Welcome, Jenny. It's good to see a new face now and then.' He looked at her for what seemed a long time, then he turned to Howie who was dragging in a trunk. 'Dan will help you, son. We don't want you causing a mischief to yourself. Now, I shall eat in the study, Briony. Dan, when you've finished with this nonsense,' he waved a hand towards his luggage, 'come and give me a hand with the insurance stuff. If two of us read the small print, we might come up with a prize.' Again, he looked briefly at Jenny, his lips pursing slightly as he studied her. 'Good luck,' he said before striding away jauntily.

Briony Mulholland arrived at Jenny's side, managing to whisper beneath the commotion that followed, 'Notice he never asked how she was?'

'Eh?'

'His wife.'

'Oh.' It was none of her business, Jenny decided as she dragged in a suitcase. It was none of anybody's business, though it did seem strange, she had to admit that.

'Jennifer.'

She put down the bag and raised her eyes to Mrs Sloane. 'Yes?'

'"Yes, Mrs Sloane", if you please. Go and move your things to the room next to Mrs Skipton's. Make as little noise as possible. I understand that there have been . . . a few small difficulties today.'

'Yes, Mrs Sloane.'

'And wear something cheerful tomorrow. The mistress likes pleasant clothes.'

'Yes, Mrs Sloane.'

'The list of instructions, times for medicines, pills, various treatments and so on – this is all kept in my office. You will make a copy after your evening meal.'

Jenny gulped. 'Treatments? I can't do treatments, Mrs—'

'The therapists will come in. All you need to know is the times of their arrivals. Go along, now. I don't have all week to stand here and repeat orders that should be self-explanatory in the first place.'

Jenny fled outdoors, running round the end of the house until she reached the outside stairway. Where had Uncle Dan been when she'd needed him? Grimly, she hung on to the memory of Maria, Maria with her laughing eyes and silly hair, Maria with all the jokes about her enormous family. She would stick close to Maria, because the girl was a sane anchor in this odd house. This house in which she had a father she could not recognize openly, an immediate boss who was hateful and hideous, a mistress who was probably up the pole.

She packed her few clothes in the battered cardboard case and lifted a photograph of Auntie Mavis from the shelf over the bed. She was young in the picture, but it had faded with the years, leaving her face ill-defined and rather eerie. Like one of her spirits, Jenny thought as she pushed everything into the case. For a last few precious moments, she perched on the edge of the bed. It wasn't a particularly comfortable room, just a table, a chair, a small cupboard and this bed, but it had been her home for the best part of a month, and she'd always known that Maria was just next door.

On leaden legs, she made her way along the passage that connected the servants' quarters to the main house, glancing over her shoulder one last time before taking that final step on to the deep red carpet that covered the long landing. It was deathly silent up here, like a morgue, she mused. There was no sign of Maria, no sign of anyone. She was alone. Except for the woman behind that dreaded door. Her heart pounded so loudly that she felt sure it could be heard all over the house.

In the room that was to be hers, she stealthily put away her sparse belongings, anxious to make no sound that might prompt an early summons from next door. She still couldn't believe that she would be sleeping here among all this opulence. The carpet was blue, and felt very thick underfoot, even through work shoes. Bed drapes and curtains echoed this colour, relieved by sprigs of cream flowers. Lampshades, cushions and chaise were of a deep rose pink, while the rest of the furniture was white with gild-edged panels and golden handles. The main luxury was the washbasin. She longed to turn the tap just to make sure that she really had running hot water all to herself, but she could not trust the plumbing to be silent. Tomorrow, she would wash here; tomorrow night she would take a bath, a real bath that didn't have to be carried in from the back yard.

When she had put away her things, she perched nervously on the edge of the bed, unsure about what to do next. It was too early to go down for the evening meal, too late to go for a walk. She took off her shoes and lay flat, staring up into the fancy folds that decorated the bed. For want of something better to do, she started to count the bunches of flowers. When she reached forty-seven, her eyelids began to droop, so she shook herself to wakefulness and began again. In spite of firm resolve, her eyelids drooped. The bed was so comfortable, the room was so cosy . . .

'Jenny!'

'Eh?' She jumped up, wondering where she was.

'Your dinner's out. And Stonehenge's nose is out too, out of joint. She says she can't spare the time to be sending messages to servants what don't turn up for their dinners. Come on, hurry up before she comes herself.'

'Oh, Maria. I must have dozed off.'

Maria glanced round the room. 'It's posh, eh? Her mother used to sleep in here when she came to stay. Yes, this was Lois's mam's room.'

'Lois?' Jenny jumped from the bed and smoothed her wrinkled dress.

'She changed it to Eloise when she got herself educated, stuck an E at the beginning and another at the end. Lois is all right if you're serving cod and chips, but it's no good when you're Lady Muck. Come on, get the cap straight. And your hair's coming down, but we've not time to mess with it.'

Jenny fumbled with her hair, the weight of which was a permanent problem. She must get some of it cut off now that she had left Auntie Mavis. Auntie Mavis would never allow her to get her hair trimmed.

She ran along the landing in Maria's wake, stumbling as they reached the east wing.

'Steady, now.' The voice came from behind.

She turned and looked at Mr Skipton, straightened the stupid cap, performed an odd curtsey, then threw herself through the doorway.

They fled down the outside stairs, round the corner and into the kitchen. Carla Sloane, a look of patient martyr-dom cutting deep into her features, stood just inside the kitchen door. 'Is this too early for madam?' she asked sarcastically. 'Perhaps I should have sent a tray to your room?'

'I was . . . sorting my things out, Mrs Sloane. And . . . er . . . listening for the mistress in case she wanted anything.'

'Yes, she was,' said Maria, her face as straight and serious as she could possibly make it. 'Sat with her ear 'ole to the door, she was, Mrs Sloane. In fact, I had a job to shift her.'

Stonehenge sniffed. This made an awful sound, because the teeth forced her to sniff open-mouthed, and Jenny dreaded the day when the woman might catch a cold. 'Sit down,' she ordered now. 'And eat the good food provided for you.'

Jenny placed herself opposite Dan, who was just finishing his pudding of prunes and custard. It was then that Jenny made her first real mistake. She started to laugh. It all flooded back, Maria and the prunes, Maria and her family . . . The cause of this unwarranted merriment stood to one side, the red hair flattened now by copious applications of water. 'Hysterics,' she declared helpfully. 'It's that room, Mrs Sloane. She hasn't never seen nothing like it in all her life before. I think she's very . . . grateful. Everything's got on top of her, you see.'

Maria's 'grateful' stuck fast in Jenny's mind, causing a renewed fit of giggles.

Dan frowned and put down his spoon. 'Pull yourself together, lass,' he said, not unkindly.

Carla Sloane crossed the room quickly. 'We do not encourage this sort of unseemly behaviour at table, Jennifer Crawley. It is not good for the digestion of others, and it is certainly bad for your own system.' She looked at Dan. 'Is she often like this?'

'No, but she's nobbut a lass, Mrs Sloane. They get in a state, young girls, have to let the steam off.'

'There'll be no steam in this kitchen, Mr Crawley, unless it comes from the cooker. Stop this!' she screamed at Jenny, who was doubled over with the pain of laughter. 'Or get out and leave the rest of us in peace.'

'I'm . . . I'm sorry. I can't . . . seem to . . .'

Carla Sloane picked up Jenny's plate, carried it across the room and tipped the contents into the pig-swill bin. 'There,' she said, a look of triumph in the mean eyes. 'Let's see how amused you are with an empty stomach.'

Dan stood up, pushing back the chair with one hand, making a fist with the other. His face had turned pale beneath its perennial tan, and Jenny stopped laughing when she saw anger pulsing in a vein just above his temple. 'The girl will eat, Mrs Sloane,' he said. 'She will eat if I have to prepare the food myself.'

Briony Mulholland entered with a wooden, squeaky-wheeled trolley, pausing in the doorway as if she could feel the tension in the large room.

'Mr Crawley.' Stonehenge's face was an interesting shade, something between mauve and magenta. 'There will be no favouritism.'

'And there'll be no starvation,' he answered quietly. 'If it was Briony or Maria, I'd say the same. This child is not going without food until breakfast. I'll get her some bread and cheese from the pantry.'

Housekeeper and butler stared at one another for

several seconds, the atmosphere so heavy that the room suddenly seemed to lose illumination, as if a cloud had descended from the beamed ceiling. But the large, brown man was too big in more ways than one for Stonehenge. After a last meaningful sniff, she marched out, slamming the office door so loudly that it trembled in its frame for some moments.

Dan looked at the three girls. 'Briony,' he said. 'Leave that and come back later.' He turned to Maria. 'Go on, lass. I need to talk to my . . . to Jenny.'

Jenny studied the table, unsure of where to look. 'I'm sorry,' she whispered.

He glanced over his shoulder to ensure that the other two maids had left. 'We choose our friends,' he said quietly. 'And sometimes, we choose our enemies too. I know you don't like her, Jenny. None of us likes her, but she's efficient, good at the job. We've all learned to stop on the right side of her. Except you – you haven't learned. You've picked a bad enemy, lass. Her's like a bulldog with a bone once the teeth go in. And I thought you had more sense than to carry on like that.'

'I was only laughing.'

'Aye, and she thought you were laughing at her. Have you never thought how it must be to walk about all your life looking like the result of a bad accident? She's ugly, she's mean and now she's angry on top. She can make your life hell, Jenny.' He turned his head slightly, muttering something that sounded like 'ask the master, he knows', but Jenny barely heard these words.

She raised her eyes. 'Then I shall leave. I'll go back in the mill and do the job I trained for.'

'No.' He shook his head slowly. 'You'll stop here where I can keep an eye on you. Too long I've left you floating in the breeze, pretending to myself that you'd be all right, that you didn't need me. But you do need me, don't you?'

'I don't know.'

'Well, I do. You're not going back to our Mavis, and you're not living on your own.' He turned away, his eyes blinking rapidly. 'Spitting image,' he said to himself. 'Except for the mark.'

'What mark?' She was fully alert now. 'What mark, Uncle Dan?'

He touched his face with a forefinger, placing it next to his right eyebrow. 'Your mam had a beauty spot here. It was in the shape of a small heart. A bit uneven, but still a heart.'

'Oh.' Some instinct ordered her to ask no more questions.

He brought bread, cheese and butter, slicing two rough shives from the end of the new loaf. 'Eat,' he commanded.

She ate, though the food stuck in her throat, and she had to force it down with water. 'I have to have a list,' she said when the silent meal was finished. 'A list about Mrs Skipton's medicines and people coming to do treatments.'

'I'll get it.'

She copied out the instructions, glancing from time to time at the closed office door. Although Dan stood between her and Stonehenge, the awful woman was still her boss. 'You'll be fine,' Dan said more than once as she copied out columns filled with blue pills and yellow pills and exercises for wasted limbs. 'Get the mistress on your side. She might not move about much, but she does carry a little bit of clout round here.'

Jenny climbed the stairs at nine o'clock, heart and feet still heavy with dread. She would have to sort out the 'something cheerful' to wear, then she would be forced to sleep right next door to another nightmare, one she hadn't met yet.

But the nightmare she had already encountered loomed large in her fitful sleep that night, the rock-hard face smirking and twisting its way through many dreams. She had made a bad beginning.

When dawn came, she prepared herself for another start that held little promise. But at least her father had given her bread and cheese. At least her father loved her . . . Didn't he?

Chapter Three

AT EXACTLY SEVEN O'CLOCK, JENNY OPENED THE DOOR THAT joined the two rooms. She stood, legs turning to jelly, hands wet with fear, an awful mass of foreboding swelling in her chest. But she was not like Auntie Mavis, oh no, she could not see into the future through a glass ball or by selecting sets from a pack of evil-looking cards. Perhaps it would be easier if she could see at all, because the whole area was shrouded in the leftover gloom of night time.

Across in the opposite corner, she could only just make out the shape of the other door, the one that led to the landing. At eight o'clock, she would have to go through the second door to pick up the mistress's breakfast from the half-moon table where Maria would leave it. But before that, she had to face this first grey and lonely hour.

The instructions were plain. Everything was to be done quietly. Any noisy task must be left until the mistress had stirred from her rest. Jenny was to make or mend the fire, whichever was appropriate, and this essential chore was to be performed in near-silence so as not to disturb the sleeping Mrs Skipton. Once the fire had been tended, there would be the carpet to sweep, the furniture to dust and polish, several ornaments to wash. The washing of ornaments would accord to a rota made by the mistress, and such ablutions would take place in the bathroom at the end of the landing. Every single piece of Spode, Wedgwood and Sèvres was to be washed weekly in soap and water.

Naturally, anything that became chipped or damaged by Jenny's attentions would reflect in the calculation of her wages. She frowned deeply. Breaking a few ends of cotton was one thing; smashing an irreplaceable piece of china would be a different kettle of fish altogether. She pursed her lips. It would be better not to think about fish or chips. There'd been enough damage done by her nervous giggling last night.

As her eyes adjusted to the twilight provided by heavy, lined curtains, Jenny began to take in the details of the huge and confusing room. Hardly an inch of wallpaper was visible. There were at least twenty paintings and, between paintings, shelves were loaded with figurines, crystal bells, plates, vases, rosebowls. With only one good arm, Eloise Skipton must have an incredibly accurate aim if the hurled prunes were to miss her treasures. The floor was crammed with furniture – tables, delicate chairs, armoires, display cabinets, a desk, dressing table, wardrobes, a wide, shrouded bed.

She stepped inside and closed the door. The bed drapes were diaphanous, but they were fully closed, so she could not see the woman behind them. This was not going to be easy, because she was plainly expected to work in near-darkness until breakfast time, and she was terrified that something of great value might get lost as she moved about the light-starved area.

Trembling at every slight sound, she cleared ashes into the bucket, then fed the fire with new coals, placing each piece by hand in an attempt to cause less disturbance. At the end of this first task, her hands were filthy, so she scuttled out to the landing and along to the large bathroom on the end. After washing her hands, she mopped her fevered brow with cold water. It was getting late; there was still the carpet and the dusting . . . Anxious not to fall foul of the mistress so early in her new career, she barged out of the bathroom, colliding heavily with Mr Skipton. 'Ooh,' she gasped, a hand to her mouth. 'I'm sorry, sir.' This was just typical, she thought. She did tend to become all fingers, thumbs and left feet when agitated.

He steadied her with his strong arms, then took a step

backwards. 'First day?' The eyebrows were raised again. He seemed to have a very mobile face, yet she guessed that the man seldom showed his real feelings to the full. Happen he couldn't, being a big boss and suchlike.

'Y . . . es, sir,' she stammered. 'I've done the fire, so I had to wash my hands. I didn't want to dirty the nice ornaments, see, and I must get back because—'

'Take things slowly,' he said, folding a newspaper and placing it under his arm. 'There's no need to rush about. My wife is like clockwork. She will wake in exactly . . .' He glanced at his watch. 'Forty-five minutes. Just do your best. If you don't finish the cleaning, then you will have to do it later on. A routine takes time to develop, and you have hardly had time, Jenny.'

'Yes, sir.'

He stepped back even further, a hand straying along the banister rail. 'Don't be bullied.' He said these last words in a hurry, as if he were slightly angry, though his expression betrayed next to nothing.

This was a man of average height, yet his bearing was good, and this straightness of neck and spine gave the illusion of greater stature. His most riveting feature was a pair of dark-lashed hazel eyes whose irises were clearly marked by flecks of green and brown, shafts of varying colour that seemed to flow into the pupils like the spokes of a wheel. Hair and whiskers were light brown, and of a smoothness that owed some debt to careful grooming. The shoulders were broad for a man of his height, and were currently clad in a jacket of dark grey wool. Matching trousers displayed straight, knife-sharp creases. His shirt was brilliant white, with a stiff collar and one gold cufflink showing just above the hand that gripped the newspaper. He looked – even smelled – like the physical embodiment of power. Confidence seemed to ooze from his pores, as if he would never need extra clothing to keep him warm.

Jenny lingered, unsure of what to do. Should she go back to work, or must she wait to be dismissed? Henry Skipton was, Jenny thought, a man of quick and certain decision, a person who would seek no help from outside himself. Yet there was a gentleness about him, a kindness that appeared not to differentiate between servant and peer. He said now, 'Go easy, child,' and his voice was almost tender. He was probably the same with everyone, and yet she wished with all her might that he would go away before she stumbled again. But he stood, surveying her carefully, as if he were assessing her worth, putting a price on her appearance.

Jenny backed away from him, tightening the belt of her blue and white print frock before turning. The dress was her best, yet she knew that the fabric was poor and that he, a cotton king, would recognize its shabbiness. She could feel him standing there, knew he was watching her progress along the landing. It was with something akin to relief that she let herself back into the mistress's bedroom, because the man had strangely penetrating eyes, the sort that seemed to see inside and beyond a face. Again she had to wait for her own vision to accept the darkness before carrying on with her exhaustive list of duties.

At five minutes to eight, she replaced the shepherdess, the six white Spode ladies and the Sèvres plates that had been on today's washing list. She stood, a hand on the doorknob, her heart beating wildly as she waited for Mrs Skipton's alleged mechanism to come into force. Seconds ticked by, their progress marked by an ornate clock on the mantelshelf.

At one minute to eight, a clatter from the landing announced the arrival of a breakfast tray. Jenny's own breakfast would be waiting in the kitchen when she took down Mrs Skipton's used dishes. Her mouth was like sandpaper. A cup of tea would have been welcome, though she doubted whether she would have been able to swallow anything.

There came a groan from the bed. 'Can't reach it,' said a snappy voice. 'Don't know why they put it so high. Girl? Are you there? Do something about this, for goodness sake.'

Jenny walked across on unsteady legs, opened the curtains at one of the two tall windows, then parted the bed drapes. Eloise Skipton, her face contorted by effort, fell back on to her pillows. Above her head there dangled a bar suspended from the ceiling by chains, obviously a means provided to help her into a sitting position.

'I've slipped down in the night.' Cool eyes swept over Jenny's body. 'And who are you?'

'Jenny, ma'am.'

For several further seconds, Eloise stared at the new girl. So this was the one. This was the one who had been born here when Henry had been a single man. They had joked about the baby, she and Henry. The laughter echoed now in her mind. 'Is it yours?' she had asked jokingly. 'Have you been exercising your droit de seigneur?' And his reply had been, 'Of course. All pregnancies within a five-mile radius of the hall are my fault.'

This was not Henry's daughter. If she had been Henry's daughter, he would have told his wife. They had kept no secrets in those days. The love had been strong enough, big enough . . . No, she refused to grieve. He did not deserve any tears, because he cried no longer for his poor crippled partner.

'Well, Jenny-ma'am,' she said quite sharply. 'Don't just stand there, get me up. Do something with these pillows. I've been sleeping all night on a bag of bricks, I think.'

Jenny lifted the slim woman, padding bolster and pillows into a more comfortable shape. 'Is . . . is that all right for you now, Mrs Skipton?'

A pair of clear, slate-grey irises stared steadily into Jenny's face. The woman was exceptionally beautiful, yet pathetic because the illness had obviously taken something away. There was a frailty about the porcelain complexion, and a pain line had etched itself here and there, drawing the face slightly inward, as if it had shrunk without completely losing its original shape. 'I shall manage, thank you. Do you have the pills ready?'

'Yes, ma'am.'

'Breakfast?'

'I'll get it now, ma'am.'

Eloise Skipton's pretty mouth pouted. 'Don't call me ma'am. I am still a relatively young woman, you know. Don't call me anything.' No, this was no kin of Henry's. If she had been, he would have taken her in by now, would have adopted her in spite of wagging tongues. This Jenny would have replaced . . . Again, she cut off her thoughts. Some areas of the past were best severed, though she had remembered the little one frequently of late.

'Right.' Jenny walked out to get the tray. This was daft, this was. How the heck could she just talk to the mistress like an equal? There had to be some sort of title. Mrs Skipton. Yes, she would call her Mrs Skipton. 'There you are, Mrs Skipton.' She angled the hinged legs on the tray so that it sat astride the woman's long, silk-covered lower limbs.

'Don't call me that, either.'

'Oh.'

Eloise pushed a forkful of scrambled egg into her mouth while Jenny poured tea. In accordance with her instructions, she added a splash of milk and no sugar.

'Get your cup.'

'Pardon?' Jenny knew that her chin had dropped and that she must be looking very foolish and senseless at this moment.

'Blue mug at the end of that shelf.' The fork waved in the air. 'Have a drink.' The girl was beautiful too. There had been another blonde beauty in this house, someone who might have looked like Jenny eventually. But the maid had none of Henry's features. And anyway, Eloise repeated to herself, he had always been honest with her. She knew all about his pre-marital activities, and this was not on the list.

'Er . . . thank you. Yes, I would like a cup of tea.'

She perched on the edge of a bedside chair sharing tea with a very calm, well-behaved lady whose manners seemed perfect except for the fact that she spoke with her mouth full.

'Irene ran off, I believe. Couldn't manage my tantrums. Have you heard about my performances?' These short sentences arrived muffled, because the words had to fight their way past a large amount of food.

'No,' lied Jenny. 'All I've got is a list of medicines and so on. I wasn't supposed to come here for this job. I'm just a housemaid, what they call a tweeny.'

Through a sizeable bite of toast, Eloise Skipton grinned impishly. 'They're looking for a fool, of course. Somebody who will let me have all my own way so that I will cause the least trouble. Though how a person can have all her own way when she can't even walk . . .' She shrugged meaningfully. 'Will you let me get away with things, Jenny?'

'I . . . I don't know. I don't know how I'll stop you. After all, you're paying my wages. I'm not used to being in charge.' No, that wasn't true, was it? She'd run a small household for long enough . . .

'It's temper. I get angry because I'm going to die.'

'Oh.' It was so difficult to form a sensible answer.

'It's a slow death too. And there's little to occupy me while I lie here dying. Can you occupy me, Jenny? Can you amuse a dying woman whose humour is unpredictable?'

She swallowed the dregs of her tea. 'I can try. Do you ever get downstairs?'

'Only when they take me to the funny farm for my annual holiday. I go into a rest home so that the staff here get a break from me. But apart from that, I stay in here.'

Jenny piled up the dishes on the tray. 'Get a lift put in. There's plenty of room for one.'

The woman in the bed laughed. 'He wouldn't like that. He wouldn't like it if I went up and down spreading gloom and despondency. I am supposed to be tidied away, you see, left like unsightly rubbish waiting to be collected.' She nodded pensively. 'So perhaps we shall have a lift. What else is there for me to do? I seem to be here just to annoy, so I may as well do it properly.'

Jenny hesitated. 'Have you not talked about a lift?'

'We never talk.'

'Oh.'

'You say "oh" a lot, Jenny.'

'Yes.' She lifted the tray and placed it on the floor. 'Shall I see to you now? Get you washed and dressed?'

Eloise Skipton's eyes narrowed. 'I think you'd better get the other one to help you this first time – that plain girl with the awful hair. Giving me a bath can be quite an interesting experience, you know. I can swing into the wheelchair, but I do tend to get wet in the bath, so it's a slippery job.' The eyes moved now over Jenny's face, as if exploring it in great detail. 'You are beautiful.' This was said in an ordinary tone, as if to underline itself as a plain statement of well-considered fact.

'Thank you.'

'I never saw such hair. My own,' she placed a finger at her temple, touching an auburn strand, 'was lovely before I became ill. It has lost some of its sheen, I'm afraid.'

This was a strange conversation, not at all the sort of talk Jenny would have expected from a mistress, from a mistress who was supposed to be next to raving mad. 'You are still a pretty woman, Mrs Skipton. But fresh air would do you good.'

Blue-veined lids came down now to veil the expression. 'I am a wife in name only, Jenny, and the name means nothing to me. If you must call me something, use the word "miss". You and I will have to learn patience with each other.' She turned her head. 'They don't usually let me have a pretty one,' she said, almost to herself, the tone bordering on wistfulness.

Jenny picked up the tray and walked to the door. 'I'll be back in about half an hour, miss.'

'Take your time.' Was there a hint of sadness in the resigned tone? 'I'll still be here when you get back. I'm going nowhere, there's plenty of space in my diary.'

Jenny stood on the landing for a few moments. The woman was not crackers, not at all. She smiled, grateful for Eloise Skipton's attitude thus far. But a picture flashed briefly into her mind, the image of Maria yesterday, the poor girl angry and confused because the mistress had turned on her. Would this happen again? And if it did, what would be the best way of coping?

In the kitchen, Carla Sloane presided like an evil crow over the breakfast table. Jenny placed the dishes next to the sink where a daily stood, great ham-like arms up to the elbows in suds. After taking her plate from a rack above the stove, Jenny sat at the table, as far away as possible from Stonehenge. She took eggs from a dish and began to eat, eyes lowered so that she did not have to look at anyone. Maria, the only other servant present, was munching toast.

'In favour then, are we?' The voice was strangled by something akin to rage. 'I see the blue mug's come down. Gave you a cup of tea, did she?'

Jenny continued to eat, though it was not easy.

'I'm talking to you, Jennifer Crawley. It starts off like that if she takes a fancy to you. But she'll soon lose patience once she realizes how stupid you are.'

She swallowed with difficulty. 'Yes, Mrs Sloane.'

'I give you four weeks at the most. The last pretty one hung on for two months, but after that, things started to happen to her.' The chair was scraped back, then heavy feet stamped through to the office. At last, Jenny raised her eyes and looked at Maria, waited for the door to slam, noticing that the cook entered the room as soon as Stonehenge had left. 'What did she mean?'

Maria shrugged. 'I wasn't here when the missus had her last pretty one. She plays games, I think. She likes nice things round her – ornaments and stuff – and a pretty nursemaid is just another nice thing, something to be enjoyed.' She nodded thoughtfully, then took a noisy draught of tea. 'Black hair, the last one had, the last good-looking one. That's what they say, anyway. She just disappeared one night, left all her things and buggered off, never heard of since. I wonder if she got murdered?' She grinned. 'I'm having you on, girl. She's alive and well by all accounts.'

Jenny placed the fork on the edge of the plate. 'Mrs Skipton seems all right to me. She gave me a cup of tea and told me to call her "miss". She doesn't like her name—' She glanced fearfully at the cook, that large, solid and seemingly dependable woman who went home every evening to a little cottage in a nearby lane. The cook continued to roll her pastry, while the mob-capped daily at the sink hummed quietly and tunelessly into the bowl of suds.

'Don't worry about them,' said Maria cheerfully. 'One's deaf and the other pretends to be, so nothing will get repeated. She doesn't like her husband.'

Momentarily confused, Jenny frowned until she realized that Maria's quick mind had reverted to the mistress. 'Oh? Why not?' she asked carefully, though she knew that she didn't really want an answer.

Maria sucked the toast crumbs from her teeth. 'Well, I couldn't say. I mean, there's loads of folk married to one another that can't stand the sight of one another. Mind you, I've a feeling that this goes deep, as if there's . . . well . . . like real hatred at the bottom of it, you know what I mean?'

'He seems a nice bloke.'

'Yes, I think he is. He's dead fair when it comes to his workers, straight as a die, no messing. But what goes on between a man and wife is different, Jenny. Me mam always says that you don't know a feller till you've seen him with his clothes off and his belly full of black beer.'

Jenny stifled a giggle. 'That's a funny thing to say.'

'Well, it's likely true, and not just about men. I mean, here I am in the maid's frock, done up to act a certain way. The bit that's me is hidden underneath. We see Mr Skipton all decked out in a suit, hair combed, beard trimmed and shaved – he's acting a part. We all do it, from dockers to dukes. Clothes make you what you are. Till you take them off.'

Jenny decided to end this conversation by finishing her breakfast in silence. It was nothing to do with her, any of it. All that mattered was getting through this day of initiation. 'You've to help me get her ready,' she said when she had eaten the eggs.

'I know. Old Po-Face told me. Christ, I wish I could take a chisel to that physog of hers and carve a smile on it. She's gutted over last night, you know. You laughing like that's done her no good. She'll get her own back on you, just mark my words.'

'What'll she do?'

'She'll think of something.'

'But the missus seems to like me. She gave me the blue mug, didn't she? If Mrs Skipton takes to me proper, then nobody can hurt me.'

Maria pushed her empty plate to the centre of the table.

'Listen. The mistress has hardly any say here. She can't walk about much, so she knows nothing about what goes on from day to day. As long as Stonehenge has it in for you, there's no protection. I'd keep me gob shut if I were you. Just do the job and come down for your meals. If Mr Skipton has one fault, it's that he's under his housekeeper's thumb. I can't work out whether he really likes her, or whether she's got some sort of hold on him. It's a queer place, this. The boss carries on as if he thinks the sun shines out of his housekeeper. Give her her due, the house runs like Big Ben, and Stonehenge is good at keeping everything in order. Mr Skipton has enough to worry about with the business, so he wants no trouble here. When push comes to shove, it'll be you that goes.'

Jenny raised her hands. 'Happen that's what I want. I never asked to come here, Maria. It was Uncle Dan that fetched me. I can soon get a job back in the mill.'

Maria rose to her feet, casting a wary eye in the direction of Mrs Sloane's office. 'You'll get no job in no mill if she blackens you. I don't know how or why, but Carla Sloane carries a lot of weight with Mr Skipton. She's bloody powerful, take my word for it. If you get a bad name in his mills, then no bugger in any other factory will take you on. So get that tea swallowed and we'll get up the dancers and sort the missus out.'

As they walked up what Maria called the dancers, Jenny found herself wondering about Henry Skipton's words. 'Don't let yourself be bullied,' he had said – something of that sort. Who was he expecting to act the part of bully, then? There was only one real bully in this house, and that was the ugly housekeeper, and the boss apparently placed a lot of faith in her. Was he meaning his wife, then? Surely a crippled woman who never even left her own room could not do any damage? What about the dark-haired pretty one, though . . . ? In this confused state of mind, Jenny entered the mistress's room with Maria.

Eloise Skipton remained silent while the two girls ministered to her needs. Jenny found herself almost overwhelmed by pity, because it was plain that the lady's illness had removed all chances for privacy and normal, everyday dignity. They lifted her on to and off the lavatory, sat her at the washbasin while she cleaned her teeth, then they bathed her. Her body was a series of hollows, sunken grooves at the base of her neck and above her hipbones, a concave belly, slack and shrivelled leg-muscles, tired, veined breasts the size of small apples, their skin wrinkled by rapid weight loss. Several purplish weals on the wrists advertised earlier suicide attempts. Jenny's heart fluttered. If Mrs Skipton tried again, she wouldn't know what to do, how to manage.

Once she was back in her bed, she lay flat and still for at least ten minutes while Jenny tidied the bathroom. The woman was plainly exhausted, even though most things had been done for her.

Jenny, her task completed, returned to the bedside. Icy grey eyes stared up at her. 'In a few minutes, you may sit me up. Then you will do my hair and put on my make-up. Today, I shall wear the pearls.' She watched Jenny's face, clearly seeking some reaction. 'I have pearl days, diamond days – whichever takes my fancy.'

'Yes, miss.'

'Aren't you surprised?'

'No.'

'Why aren't you surprised? Don't you think it strange that a cripple should wear jewellery? It's not as if I get many visitors, unless you count doctors and nurses. So why do I dress up?'

Jenny, unsure of her ground, simply smiled.

'Well? Has speech deserted you altogether?'

'No.'

'Then why do I take so much care with my appearance?'

'Because . . . because it's in your nature. You like pretty things around you, and jewels are pretty things.'

Eloise sniffed. 'I was a pretty thing once. That's why I took his fancy, you see. Though I sometimes wish I'd never set eyes on him.'

Jenny picked up a vanity case from the bedside cabinet, taking from it a pot of expensive French cold cream. This was stuff she shouldn't be hearing, it was none of her concern. It didn't seem right that the mistress should talk so openly about her marriage. She smoothed a small amount of cream on to Eloise Skipton's dry cheeks.

'I had a child once, a live one. All the others I lost, then I finally gave birth to this one little girl.' It was in her mind again and, like a sack of air in water, it bubbled upward to the surface from time to time.

'Oh?' Jenny's hand paused fractionally, then busied itself once more with the powder puff. 'Where is she now?' she asked, knowing that this question was expected. Yes, the coral lipstick was the best . . .

'Dead. Died when she was three months old.'

'I'm sorry.' Jenny was indeed sorry, and the pity must have shown in her face and in the temporary stillness of her hands.

Eloise shrugged carelessly. 'She'd never have had a proper mother anyway. I couldn't enjoy her now, couldn't do the things that mothers normally do with a daughter. Of course, he's never forgiven me.'

'Oh.'

'Back to "oh" again, are we?'

Jenny stepped back to study her handiwork. 'I'll do your hair now. Do you want it up?'

'Yes. But not severe, leave a few wisps on my forehead and in front of my ears. That way, I feel more like a woman and less like a pathetic patient.' She lowered her head so that Jenny could brush the back of her hair. 'The young things in London are all talking about bobs, short hair cut straight as if a basin has been used. Do you think it will ever catch on?'

'I don't know.'

'You won't do it, will you?'

Jenny thought for a second. 'I might. This lot gets in my road, it's so heavy.'

Eloise studied herself in a hand mirror once her toilet was completed. 'You have an eye, Jenny. I haven't looked as good as this in ages. And don't cut your hair. Your hair will get you noticed. That's the secret, you see. Get noticed, get a man, get out.'

Jenny paused, the silver-backed hairbrush still in her hand. 'Get out of what, miss?' she asked eventually.

'Out of service.' The woman tutted her impatience. 'You're not considering a life of drudgery, are you? Can you see yourself in twenty years cleaning someone else's house, bathing cripples, fetching and carrying plates? Well?'

'I've not thought.'

'Then think.' The voice was shrill now. 'Life's a staircase, something you have to climb. In fact, it's more like a slippery mountain with very few footholds. The grey people make camp in the valley. They never look up to the summit, never notice how bright the sky is at the top. They're too scared of the journey, frightened of slipping back.' She settled into the mound of feather pillows, her tone quieter now. 'Find the path, Jenny. Look to the sky, or remain grey.' She was exhausted, yet fire seemed to smoulder behind the smoky eyes.

This was likely what Auntie Mavis would have called a soap-box job. Mrs Skipton was on her hobby horse, so it would be best to humour her. 'I've no head for heights.'

The small attempt at humour was completely ignored by the mistress. She fixed her gaze on Jenny, eyes narrowing as she spoke. 'And remember, you don't need to have a lift put in to get yourself moving. You've got youth, beauty and strength. All you need is to take the first step upward. Look at me, now. Can't walk, can't dance, can't breathe some of the time. But when I had my legs, I climbed. If I'd kept my legs, there would have been no holding me. Anyway . . .' Her glance wandered over Jenny's face. 'I don't know you well enough yet. But when I do, I shall find you a path, Jenny. And I'll throw in a few climbing lessons.'

Jenny coughed self-consciously. 'What if . . . if I don't want to go that way?'

Eloise shrugged carelessly. 'The first step is to make you want it. Fetch the cards and I shall teach you whist.'

While they played, Jenny mused over her mistress's words. What was this strange woman planning? And did these plans have anything to do with the last 'pretty one' leaving so suddenly? She felt uncomfortable, almost wary, every time she caught Eloise's eye. There was more than just whist being taught here, because the frail lady kept pausing to comment on Jenny's posture or to correct her speech. It was becoming quite a lesson in what Maria would have called 'elly-queue-shon', all weird vowels and clipped, clear endings to words.

'Do you know who your father is?' asked Eloise without warning.

Jenny picked up the trick of cards that she had just won. 'Yes,' she said, wondering immediately whether she should have lied. 'But I can't tell anybody.'

'Is he . . . a businessman?'

'No. He works, but he's not in business.'

Eloise knew that the girl was telling the truth. It was all the confirmation she had needed. No, she told herself sharply. She had not required any answer from this chit of a girl. The love between herself and Henry, the love that had existed, the lost, dead love . . . Yet even now, while convinced, she wondered . . . No, no, no! Henry had had just one daughter, just Sophie. 'She was in your room,' she said suddenly.

'Eh?'

A thin hand raised itself in a gesture of near despair. 'Don't say "eh". It betrays your origins. She stopped breathing, died in your room.'

Jenny swallowed. 'Who did?'

'My daughter. I went in, because I could still walk at that time. And there she lay in her cradle, all still and cold. He blames me, of course. I never did manage to do anything right for him. Every other pregnancy had ended in disaster, then I carelessly lost Sophie. When I became a cripple, I was of no further use. He hates me.'

The ensuing short silence was uncomfortable. 'Shall I get your coffee from the kitchen?' Jenny found herself sitting rigidly on the edge of the chair.

'And I hate him for hating me.'

Jenny collected the cards from the tray. 'Do you take sugar in coffee?'

Long bony fingers grasped Jenny's wrist. 'It's about paying me back, all this. He never comes near me. Since my parents died, I see no-one except the doctor, the masseuse, the physiotherapist.' She released her hold, picked up the remaining cards, then tossed them across the room. 'For wasting to death, I am punished,' she screamed.

Jenny inhaled deeply. 'Stop it,' she said softly.

The face on the pillow darkened ominously. 'Who the hell are you to tell me what to stop? A mill girl, a child of the gutter? Oh, I know your history, Jenny. A foundling left on this very doorstep, some streetwoman's illegitimate brat, a product of the slums. Your mother probably laid herself down next to every handsome man in the village.'

Something odd and powerful stirred in Jenny's breast, forcing the breath from her lungs in a quick gasp. And yet the feeling wasn't new, not completely, because she remembered the sickening sensation. From when, though? Ah yes. She had felt like this on the stairs in Claughton Street, just before she'd told Auntie Mavis that the seances were wrong. 'Shut up,' she surprised herself by saying now. 'I don't want this rotten job anyway.' She had a father, a good, gentle man with more sense in his head than this woman could ever have. 'You are a very rude person,' she said, her heart racing with fear of her new-found anger. 'First you want me to stand me ground – better meself and all that. Then you tell me off for being cheeky.' She paused, considering. 'And there's not much difference between fillings cops and frying chips.'

'How dare you?'

Jenny lifted her head high above the helpless form in the bed. 'Because I don't care whether I go or stay. Because you're throwing no prunes or playing cards at me, Mrs Skipton.' She bit briefly on her lower lip. 'I'm not a rude girl usually. I never answered back at school, and I always did what Auntie Mavis wanted. 'But . . .' She remembered a voice on the landing outside this very room. 'I will not be bullied,' she finished, her face arranged into a shape she imagined to be determined.

Eloise Skipton's lips were set in a thin, mean line, so that the words were forced out of a mouth that was almost immobile. 'I never fried a chip in my life. My parents and grandparents made the money, and I was educated. Yes, I climbed my mountain. And it was very hard, getting "finished" in a school filled by upper-class cabbage-heads. I never did a day's work in my life. And why I should bother explaining all this to a skivvy—'

'Then don't! Don't bother. Save your breath and your energy, because you've little enough.' Jenny stopped in her tracks, arms akimbo, feet wide apart as she studied the poor creature on the bed. Oh, what was she doing? Why was she carrying on like this when Eloise Skipton couldn't even sit up properly to defend herself? The woman's last remaining weapon was speech . . . 'I'm sorry,' she said lamely.

'What for?'

'Answering back, being nasty.'

Eloise smiled, though the eyes remained untouched. 'You have spirit, girl. I think I can make something of you.'

'What do you mean?'

A thin shoulder raised itself in an attempted shrug. 'I don't know what I mean yet. It's early days, isn't it? But there's character hidden beneath that shell of niceness. And you are . . . superbly equipped.'

Jenny shivered involuntarily. There was a look on the mistress's face, an expression she'd noticed Auntie Mavis wearing from time to time. Like when the 'visitors' had left a good tip, a shilling or two over the odds because Auntie Mavis had 'brought back' a long-lost loved one. Yes, this was another greedy and selfish woman, though perhaps the illness had some bearing on her temperament. Jenny turned and gathered up the scattered cards.

'Are you going to give up the position, then?'

Jenny pushed the pack into a mother-of-pearl box. 'I'll stay for a while with Uncle Dan.'

'The butler. The man who found you on the doorstep.'

'Yes.'

'And his sister brought you up?'

'Yes.'

'Tell me about your life.'

Jenny straightened the ornaments on a circular, lace-covered table, placing the card box in the centre. 'I am your nursemaid, miss. There is no need for you to know about my business, and there is no call for you to tell me about yours, either. I look after you, I get paid for it.' She faced the bed. 'And that's the top and bottom.'

'What if I dismiss you?'

'Then I pack my bag and go.'

Eloise forced her face to soften. 'I want you to stay. If we get along satisfactorily, then I shall take you under my wing, teach you to speak properly, show you how to dress, how to act like a lady.'

'Why?' Jenny folded her arms and put her head on one side. 'Happen we don't all want the same things. Some of us might be happier staying the same road as we already are.'

Eloise nodded wisely. 'At the foot of the mountain? In a grey cave with water running down the walls? Wouldn't you like something better?'

'I don't know,' said Jenny truthfully. 'But I'd like the chance to find out for meself what I want.' She turned and left the room without waiting for dismissal.

Maria was on her way upstairs with the morning coffee. 'You're supposed to come down for this, you know,' she grumbled gently.

'Yes. She's been throwing things.'

'Oh. Did you duck like I told you?'

'It was just a pack of cards. I . . . er . . . sorted her out.'

Maria thrust the silver tray into Jenny's hands. 'You what?'

'I think I shouted at her.'

Maria's narrow jaw dropped. 'I don't believe it.'

'I told her to behave.'

'And you're still stood up with all your skin on? Christ, you're lucky. She can walk a bit, you know. Get her mad, and she'll be out of that bed like sh— . . . like muck out of a goose's bum.' The ginger head nodded rapidly. 'I reckon she must like you. Nobody tells her off, never. Even the bloody doctor comes out of there looking as if he's seen the inside of hell.'

As Maria scurried away to continue her tasks, Jenny stood, tray in hands, head bent in deep thought. The confrontations were no good, she decided. Mrs Skipton was a sick, weak woman with nothing but death in front of her. The invalid's remaining life was mapped out for her, its scope and breadth dictated, predetermined by her illness. A brief picture of Amber flashed into Jenny's mind, that good, brave and gentle horse whose lifestyle was restricted by the confines of labour. Like Amber, Mrs Skipton had no choices, few chances to improve her lot.

Jenny turned to carry the coffee in to her mistress. From now on, she would humour this dying soul, give her some pleasure. If such meagre compensation had to include the 'improvement' of a nursemaid, then that too would be endured. Jenny's newborn anger and resentment must remain out of sight for now. There would be time enough to search for Oonagh, time enough to run her own life later. The one thing Eloise Skipton had little of was time, so Jenny would lend some of her own.

It had been long, this first unforgettable day. Except for two hours in the afternoon, during which brief free time Jenny had slept in her own sumptuous room, she had been on duty for fifteen hours. Yet when midnight arrived, marked by the muted chime of the grandfather in the hall below, Jenny still lay wakeful.

She reached across to the bedside cabinet and switched on a pink-shaded lamp. As the resulting pool of light flooded over and around her, she followed its course with her eyes, taking in the details of her surroundings yet again. This was a strange place to be. She was, she felt, a weed or a cabbage in a rather fine rose garden. It wasn't that she was ugly, it was just that she didn't fit in somehow. Some weeds were very pretty, and even cabbages held a certain neat charm in the scheme of things. But they didn't belong in a landscaped flower garden.

Anyway, lying here having daft thoughts wasn't going to improve matters. The best idea would be to go downstairs and warm up some milk, because a cup of hot, sweetened milk had proved, in the past, to be the best weapon against insomnia.

She crept downstairs like a thief in the night, her coat

gathered close to her body as if it were protection against the unknown. She was doing nothing wrong, she told herself repeatedly. It was quite acceptable, quite normal for a sleepless person to seek comfort and sustenance. But this was not her house. She glanced fearfully around the dim landing and staircase, trying hard not to disturb anyone by missing her way in the gloomy light provided by the odd electric lamp. If Mr Skipton were suddenly to appear, she would have to flee back to her room, because she was clad only in night attire and her one good, grey coat. Also, the thought of Stonehenge made her shiver. No, that was not the sort of face one would wish to meet in near-darkness. Even in daylight, the woman's ugliness and sour disposition were terrifying.

Light showed under the kitchen door, so she hesitated before entering. What if Stonehenge should still be here? Could she face that special nastiness at this hour of night? She opened the door a fraction, surprised to see Maria bent over the table. 'What are you doing?' she stage-whispered. Maria ought to have been in bed hours ago, because her working day always began at six in the morning, seven at weekends.

Maria clapped a gloved hand against her own open mouth. 'By all the saints in heaven – why don't you just poison me? It'd be kinder than frightening me to bloody death. Come in and shut that door.' The hand moved to her breast, pressing hard against a heart that was apparently bent on escaping from its cage of ribs. 'You could have made me spill all the blue,' she complained. 'And I'm running out, 'cos I used most of it last night to make purple with me spare red.'

Jenny entered the kitchen stealthily. 'You're whipping up a right mess there,' she commented, her glance sweeping over the paraphernalia on the newspaper-covered table top.

'I'll clean it all away, just like I always do.' Maria waved half a potato, dipped it in a saucer of royal blue dye, then stamped it against a square of white cotton cloth. 'What do you think?' she asked, her eyes gleaming with a mixture of pride and self-criticism. 'It's a bit Greekish, isn't it?' With her head tilting to one side, she considered her latest design. 'It'll do,' she said. 'Till I can get something better than spuds to cut. They deteriorate, see. I want something more permanent, and the wood I've found round here's no good, it soaks too much up.'

Jenny studied the blue-patterned cloth. 'That's pretty,' she said. 'But what's it for?' It was odd, watching a grown girl playing at potato prints in the middle of the night. This was something that happened at school on the rare occasions when there was powder paint to spare.

Maria shrugged. 'It's for our Anthony, the one that's never there when the register gets called. He flogs them as headscarves on the street corners in Liverpool, round the markets and that.' She picked up two lengths of metal which had been welded together just at the ends, using the gap between these parallels as a stencil to form a blue border at the edge of the cotton square. While she worked, her tongue protruded from her mouth, and her forehead was furrowed by lines of deep concentration. 'That'll have to do,' she pronounced before carrying the finished item to the oven.

Jenny inhaled gingerly and glanced round the room. 'What's that smell?' There was something cooking, and it definitely wasn't anything edible.

'Me headscarves. I'm using the oven to set the dyes.'

'Oh.' Jenny was flabbergasted to find this small hive of industry operating during the hours of darkness. 'What if Stonehenge finds out?' She didn't know what else to say or ask, because the situation was beyond her, somehow . . .

Maria giggled. 'She won't. She's got half a bottle of vintage port for company tonight – I saw her sneaking it out under her pinny. She'll not move a muscle till six in the morning. I'm not saying she's a soak, but she likes the odd drop of good stuff at the end of the day, something to help her sleep.'

The intention to make a warm drink was completely forgotten by this time. Jenny sat at the table, maintaining a careful distance from dishes of dangerously colourful dyes. 'How long have you been doing this?'

Maria was wrapping her potatoes in copious amounts of

newspaper. 'Only a few weeks. The master gave me some cotton, said me mam could have it to make sheets from. But I kept it.' She placed the parcel in the fire, using the poker to push it well into the dying embers until it caught alight. 'See, I've always been good at patterns, so I thought I'd give this a go. Our Anthony's got some ideas for making a screen, like a frame for printing with. When we get going – if we ever do get going, like – we'll be able to sell to the shops, do it proper.'

She walked across to the oven and pulled out some finished items. 'You have to do them coolish, else they burn. I've lost a few, but I'm learning.' The squares were stretched out on strange and obviously home-made contraptions, unwieldy objects manufactured from thick wire and pieces of what appeared to be broken housebrick or red stone.

Jenny watched, fascinated by her friend's quick, deft movements. There was determination in the set of Maria's mouth. Ambition too. Yes, a person who would work hard all day, then deliberately miss out on sleep, must surely have a clear goal in life. 'You want to set up in business, then, you and Anthony?'

Maria paused, a bright crimson and white square stretched between her hands. 'I'm not sure, Jenny. I'd like to be me own boss some day. But it takes money. All I've spent this far is a few coppers on dye and sewing cotton for the hemming. But to make it work proper, we'd need something called an injection of capital, that's what our Anthony says. And who's going to lend money to a couple of kids from the Liverpool slums?'

Jenny considered this problem before asking, 'What about Mr Skipton?'

Maria smiled broadly at her friend's foolishness. 'Don't talk so soft. Our Anthony never went to school for a full week, always wagging off, he was. They'd never give him a decent reference, 'cos he's not done a proper job since he left school official, like. Been doing odd bits since he was about eight, always mucking out stables and selling fruit. Then there's me.' She shrugged lightly. 'An upstairs maid what's good at patterns. Oh, and I'm not bad at telling lies, which is handy when it comes to business, I suppose. But I've no way of proving my worth, Jenny. Why should Mr Skipton start giving me money?'

'But if you're good . . . ?'

'It's not what you know, Jenny. It's not what you can do. The ones that have will only lend money to others that have already got it. They'll only invest in what's safe, and things what's safe already have a fortune behind them.'

'Sounds stupid to me. How does anybody ever get going, then?'

'They don't. Not in this day and age, specially if you're a woman. Best you can hope for is a job in a works owned by some big bugger.' She dropped her prints on to the clear end of the table. 'I'll make some cocoa. It's me bedtime in a minute, I can't manage on less than five hours. And I've still got to hide me stuff round the back of the stables.' She waved her hand towards the makeshift frames. 'Our Anthony made them for me.' There was pride in her tone. 'He can do anything, that lad.'

Jenny insisted on making the cocoa while Maria tidied up her mess and stacked her implements behind the stables. When all the evidence had been removed, the red-haired girl stripped two pairs of cotton gloves from her hands, scrutinizing the fingers for tell-tale spots of dye. 'I do this two or three nights a week,' she explained. 'I'm stealing nothing, 'cos I just use the oven when it's cooling down anyway. But if she found out . . .'

Jenny inclined her head. There was no need to identify the 'she'. 'I look at it this road, Maria. Mr Skipton spins and weaves cotton. Now, as far as I can see, this here cotton gets took away to places where they put patterns on it. Am I right?'

Maria jerked her head in agreement, almost spilling her cocoa. 'It's a different thing altogether, is printing. He couldn't take it on, girl. And anyway, I don't want nothing to do with these places where they churn it out by the cartload. I'd like to do it in a small way, like exclusive designs. It may sound daft, only I need to do something special with me life, something people will remember me for.' She blushed a deep and unbecoming red that clashed fiercely with her bright hair. 'Our Anthony's the same. No education, but plenty of ideas. Do you think I'm trying to get past meself, love? After all, I am only a girl. Is it all daft and too much to hope for?'

'No.' It was then that Jenny remembered Mrs Skipton's words about mountains and valleys, about those who climbed and reached, about the grey masses who stayed at the bottom without ever looking up. Mrs Skipton obviously believed that the only way for a woman to ascend was on a man's back, but here was a female who was trying to find her own mountaineering equipment, and good luck to her. 'If I had the money, I'd lend it,' she said softly.

Maria reached out and touched Jenny's hand. 'I know you would.' Her colour remained high. 'You're a good pal, Jen. Soon as I clapped eyes on you, I knew you'd had your share of bother. Different from me, like, 'cos my trouble was overcrowding. Your cross has been loneliness, hasn't it, queen?'

Jenny smiled sadly and made no reply.

'Well, you don't need to be lonely no more. You and me, we'll be friends till the day one of us pops her clogs. I'll tell our Anthony about you. If we ever get a shop, we'll put you in it, because folk like buying from a pretty girl.'

'What'll I sell?'

Maria spread her arms wide, as if seeking to embrace a world that held few boundaries for her. 'Cloth things. Scarves for a kick-off. And cups of tea in a corner, scones with jam and honey. Like a little café with my things on show as well.' She laughed at herself. 'It's a dream, Jenny. A big, beautiful dream full of rainbow patterns. But where would we be without our dreams?'

Jenny stared down into her empty mug.

'Have you got a dream?' enquired Maria.

'Yes. Yes, I have.'

'What is it?'

Jenny bit her lip. 'Do dreams spoil with telling? Are they like wishes?'

'No.' Maria shook her carroty head. 'A wish is something out of sight. A dream is a thing you might just make into truth one day.'

A long, slow breath escaped from Jenny's parted lips. 'I want to find me mam,' she said. 'She's called Oonagh and she might be in Liverpool.' The face opposite her own was so trusting, so trustworthy . . . 'Some say she was a streetwoman. My . . .' No, she didn't dare to speak about her father, not quite. Not yet. 'My Uncle Dan says she wasn't. No-one can find her.'

'Have you got a picture of her?'

'No. She looks like me, only taller, and she's got a sort of heart-shaped beauty spot here.' Jenny placed a finger at her temple.

'Right.' Maria rose and lifted the cups. 'Our Anthony's your man. Once he's had a look at you, he'll get searching. There's nothing happens in the pool what he can't find out about. He knows everybody, does our Anthony, from road sweepers to the Archbishop himself. So find a photo of yourself and I'll get it posted.' She paused and looked at Jenny. 'Why did she leave you in the first place? No need to hang your head in shame, it doesn't matter to me if you came out wrong side of the blanket. But how could she go off and leave a baby as pretty as you must have been?'

Jenny gripped the edge of the table. 'Her brothers and her mother. They got angry about her being a mother without a husband. They were Catholics, see—'

'Huh!' Maria tossed her head angrily. 'We're Catholics. Nearly all our street's Catholic, and most of the weddings are done in a hurry. There's many a priest down our way keeps the holy water handy and the lid off the font in case the baby pops out before the couple's blessed. We've even had some right arse over tip, with the baptism before the bloody wedding.'

'They were Irish.' Jenny knew that she was doing her best to defend a mother she had never seen, and she could not understand her own motives. 'She got an offer of marriage, but the man was a Protestant and they wouldn't allow it. So she ran away, had me, then brought me back and left me with Uncle Dan because she trusted him.'

'Then she ran away again.' There was a caustic edge to Maria's words.

'Frightened,' insisted Jenny.

Maria pursed her lips. 'Was it Mr Crawley who offered to marry her?'

'Yes. She was housekeeper here, so she knew him well. He loved her. And he offered to marry her too.'

'But Oonagh's family wouldn't allow it.'

'That's right.'

Maria perched on the table, feet swinging from the bottom of her long white nightdress. 'Briony's set her cap at him, you know.'

'Yes.'

'Only she'll not get him, will she?'

Jenny shrugged, trying hard to look unconcerned.

''Cos he's your dad, isn't he?' Maria left a small space for a reply, but none was forthcoming. 'It's a way he has of looking at you, Jenny. When he thinks there's nobody watching, like. I'm right, I know I am. And don't worry, your secret's safe enough with me. And if your mam's anywhere in Liverpool, my brother will find her.'

'Thank you.' Jenny hesitated. 'He'd lose his job, Uncle Dan, I mean. If—'

'If they found out he's your dad. Yes, he might, though I doubt it. Anyway, this is nobody's business. Let them carry on thinking he's just a kind man who took you to his sister when you were dumped here. Now.' She jumped down from her perch. 'I'll hide the rest of the evidence under me loose floorboards. We made three bob each last week, me and our Anthony. Just one thing bothers me, Jenny.'

'What's that?'

Maria giggled. 'How fast are these bloody dyes? What if it rains? Can you see all that lot in Liverpool running round with purple hair and green faces? Ooh God, our Anthony'll have to stow away on a ship if these colours don't hold.'

Jenny joined in the laughter. 'Doesn't the baking make the dyes stick?' she asked.

'I don't bloody know, do I? I'm working off the top of me head, just using common sense. Tell you what. Next time it rains, we'll go out with these scarves on. If we come back in looking striped, we'll tell me brother to emigrate to

89

Australia. Mind, they'd still find him. There's nothing worse than an angry Liverpool woman.'

They gathered up the cloth, turned out the lights and went out into the corridor. After a whispered good night, they separated, Maria making for the library staircase, Jenny entering the morning room on her way to the main hall.

Mr Skipton stepped out of the drawing room just as Jenny passed the door. 'Ah,' he said, delivering this syllable in several tones that displayed his surprise. 'And what are you doing out of bed at this hour, young lady?'

She clutched at the neck of her age-thinned coat. It was too short, too tight, and she must have looked terrible to him, really poor and scruffy. 'I went for some cocoa, sir.' Those hazel eyes were piercing the semi-darkness, making her feel vulnerable and almost naked. It was probably guilt, she thought. Yes, she was hiding Maria's secret now, as well as her own . . .

'Was the day . . . difficult?' he asked.

'No.' He hadn't asked had his wife been hard work, hadn't even asked whether she was comfortable. 'Mrs Skipton played cards, then I read to her,' she volunteered timidly.

'I see.' He stretched out an arm, indicating that she should continue her journey towards the stairs. 'Don't be taken in,' he whispered so quietly that no-one heard. No-one except himself.

Angrily, he walked back into the drawing room, leaning against the door as soon as it was closed. She would be at it again, no doubt, trying to mould the girl, trying to get her to do things, say things, make things happen. He picked a decanter from the desk, pouring a large measure of brandy into a globe which had already been used twice. That woman. That damned spiteful, evil woman.

She had no legs now, no ability to move about among decent people. So she borrowed children, little girls like this one, little girls not much older than Sophie would have been . . . With a muted cry of rage, he hurled the glass into the marble fireplace. Sophie. She would have been nine now, nearly ten.

He sank into a Queen Anne chair by the grate, his hands gripping tightly on to finely carved wooden arms. He could feel Eloise's presence even now, even though he hadn't set eyes on her for months. She was like a gas, a silent, deadly and invisible element that permeated the house, curling and twisting its ghostly fingers around everything and everyone, soaking in, seeping through, filling cracks and crevices with its undiluted malice. What did she say to these young maids? What did she do to make them run off into the night, no messages, no apology?

Only Carla Sloane knew the full extent of Eloise's abilities. Only Carla Sloane was in possession of the unabridged facts. He stared into the dead grey ashes in the fireplace. No. There was one other person who carried the pictures, the memories, the grief. And that person was himself.

His head sank to his chest. A few splinters of crystal lay at his feet, the shattered remains of a lovely piece of Waterford. How many fragments? How much glue would it take to make it whole again? What sort of magic could ever make the glass look good after such terrible treatment?

No, there was no mending it. Best to pretend that the brandy globe had never existed. Best to imagine that Henry Skipton had never been born, because he, the mill owner, the boss, the man of property, was just a shadow. An illusion now, no more than that. Because she had thrown him at the wall, and there was no glue, no magic. Not for him.

Chapter Four

THE PINCE-NEZ SAT ASTRIDE THAT PART OF CARLA SLOANE'S face which was reputed to be a nose, though the shape of this feature left its ultimate denomination open to a degree of question. 'Under a mattress in this house, certain things have been discovered,' she announced to a bemused and dumbstruck Jenny. 'What have you got to say for yourself, Crawley?' The hideous proboscis made a sniffing sound, and the silly spectacles shifted and swung until one lens sat considerably lower than the other, thereby lending a rather comical atmosphere to the nasty scene.

'Er . . .' What could she say? Maria had been hiding her scarves, but why should Jenny be questioned about them? The main thing was not to laugh, not to start giggling at the sight of those skew-whiffy glasses. She concentrated hard on a crack in the wall just above the open door.

'Well? Is this dumb insolence on top of everything else?' A hand came up and righted the pince-nez, removing completely any danger of merriment.

Jenny shifted her weight from foot to foot, realizing that no matter what she said, this awful woman had already made up her twisted mind about something or other. And the less said, the better, because she didn't want to be the one to betray Maria and bring the clandestine printing venture to a premature end.

The hideous face darkened even further. 'Two knives

and three serving spoons,' she announced, a note of triumph trimming her words. 'Antiques too, solid right through. The Skiptons don't go in for this plated rubbish.' She was wagging a finger now, waving it about in time with her words.

'Eh?' At last Jenny found her tongue. 'I don't know anything about knives and spoons. Cutlery's nothing to do with me, not since I took over looking after Mrs Skipton.' But the seeds of fear were flourishing by this time, their small shoots taking nourishment from a few remembered words whose roots lay beneath the shallow topsoil of recent memory. What had Maria said? Something about Stonehenge finding a way of paying Jenny back for that imagined slight, for laughing at the table . . . ?

Thin lips curled in a mean sneer. 'I know that. I knew that when I got you to clean the fish knives, because you had to do them twice before they were half-decent. You'd never set eyes on a good piece of silver till you came here. And now you've set more than eyes, haven't you? Oh yes, you've started a nice little collection for yourself. Well.' The arms folded themselves beneath iron breasts that seemed to form a potentially useful storage shelf between chin and waist. 'Your bags are packed out in the yard. You will leave immediately and, of course, without a reference. Thieves do not get a character statement from me.'

Jenny's jaw fell, then snapped shut with a click that echoed through her heated brain. What was happening here? What was all this about knives and spoons? 'Where were these things found, Mrs Sloane?' she managed at last.

'As if you don't already know! Under your bed, of course. They'd have fetched a penny or two in a pawnshop, wouldn't they? You're a thief, and those who steal are dismissed on the spot with no warning, no opportunity for a second chance.'

Jenny's head moved slowly from side to side. 'I am not a thief,' she said, her voice low and careful. 'I have never stolen anything in my life. Where's my un— . . . where's Mr Crawley? He'll tell you I'm honest.'

The slit that was punctuated by wide-spread and crooked incisors now curled itself into a smirk. 'Day off.

He's gone to town, then on to visit his sister, the woman you call your aunt. He's not here to protect his precious adopted niece this time. You'd best follow him, because you've nowhere else to go.'

Jenny stood her ground, determined to make some small effort to fight such an unfair attack on her moral reputation. Although she held few chances to clear herself, she thought before forming her next words. 'I want to see Mrs Skipton,' she insisted quietly.

Stonehenge nodded just once. 'I bet you do. I bet you want to have a go at wheedling your way out of this disgusting crime. No. The mistress does not associate with common offenders. So get yourself gone.'

Before the ensuing pregnant pause had an opportunity to bear fruit, Maria stepped into the kitchen, her usually pale face aflame with temper. 'If she goes, I go.' She turned to look at Jenny. 'I've been stood outside listening, girl. This one's tame monkey will have stashed the stuff under your mattress.' Thin arms gestured wildly in the air. 'Briony bloody Mulholland's at the back of the missing silver, because she'll do exactly what the ugly old cow asks. And that just goes to show how soft and daft you need to be to work in this rotten house.'

She rounded now on Carla Sloane, hands stilled but clenched into fists so tight that her knuckles formed white peaks at the base of each finger. 'Broke any mirrors lately with that mush of yours? This is all because Jenny laughed the other night, eh? Well, she wasn't laughing at you, 'cos your gob would make a grown man cry, it would.' The red head tossed itself bravely, as if freeing its owner of all inner restraint. This was not a lost temper; this was a temper deliberately mislaid.

She tore the apron from her waist and threw it towards the housekeeper. 'Take your rotten job and stick it up your backside. God knows the job's a whopper, and there's only your bum big enough to stow it. And I'll tell you this as well.' She stalked up to the furious woman, standing just inches away from the dangerously frozen mask of anger. 'You are a mess outside and in. You're deformed, you are, deformed and horrible, specially in your mind. Briony wants rid of Jenny, 'cos she don't like anybody standing between her and the butler. She wants the master to let them get wed, doesn't she? And Jenny, being Mr Crawley's niece, might have stopped that, so Briony put the silver in Jenny's room when you asked her to. Just you listen to me, you nasty bugger. I'll get the truth beaten out of Briony Mulholland. I'll fetch me family over from Liverpool, and we'll knock her about till she admits what she's done. Then me and Jenny will get the pair of you put in prison.'

Jenny ran forward and gripped Maria's slender arm. 'Stop it. Please don't get in trouble for me.'

But Maria remained in full flood, her fury living up to the reputation bestowed on people with her colouring. 'Don't interrupt me, Jen.' She didn't even move her head when she spoke to Jenny, but continued right away her verbal assault on Carla Sloane. 'I'll get you for this, Stoneface. I don't know what kind of a hold you've got over this family, but it must be something big for them to keep such an ugly animal in the house. It's not that Mr Skipton respects you for being good at the job. You've got him in your clutches, so he has to carry on as if the sun shines out of your rear end.'

Carla Sloane took a series of stumbling backward steps, gasping as if she were in pain.

'I wasn't born yesterday,' snapped Maria. 'We soon get old where I come from, and we learn a lot about people. You're a bad one. I was saying to Jenny only the other day that Mr Skipton's only blind spot was his faith in you. But it's not faith, is it? It's bloody fear. Which bloody barrel have you got that man over, eh? Another of your cock-and-bull stories? Did you stick something under his bed?'

'Get . . . out of this . . . kitchen.' These words, heavily contaminated with venom, were pushed slowly from between teeth that refused to clench completely because of their strange placement. 'You'll not work again in this area, either of you.'

Maria raised her sharp chin. 'Don't threaten me, missus. I come from what you'd call a bad lot, a big family what doesn't take kindly to insults. I can set half a dozen dockers on you before this week's out, and they'll chuck you right into the middle of next Christmas Eve before you can sing one line of bloody "Jingle Bells".' Her head bobbed about like a cork on choppy waters. 'I'll get to the bottom of you, mark my words. I'll find out what makes you tick and why this family keeps you on. As for Mulholland, she'll get what's coming to her as well.' Without waiting for a reply, Maria stamped out of the room to pack her bag.

Jenny stood very still with her gaze fixed on Stonehenge, who also appeared to be rooted to the spot. The roughly chiselled face was motionless, yet there was expression in the usually dead eyes, as if a fire were burning behind the mask of composure. After several seconds had elapsed, Jenny moved to leave the kitchen.

'We all have our secrets, don't we, Jennifer Crawley? Like why did a grown man take pity on a newborn child? Why did he take it to his sister instead of shoving it into the orphanage?'

Without looking at the woman, Jenny said, 'Some people are naturally kind, and Uncle Dan's one of them. Happen you'd better talk to him about why he took me to live with Auntie Mavis, because I don't know the answers, I was just a baby at the time.'

'A slut's bastard.' These words were delivered slowly, separately, as if to underline the intended cruelty.

Jenny swivelled round. 'I don't understand what you're on about, Mrs Sloane, but if you're looking to push my uncle into trouble, you'll not get far. He's an asset to the master, helps him with all kinds of things.'

The big woman inched forward, dragging her body so slowly that she now truly looked as if she had been fashioned from some heavy and almost inert material. 'Just keep that Maria Hesketh and her family away from me, or I'll dig up the past until this place is littered with corpses. Do you get my drift, girl?' She looked even more monstrous now, because the small black eyes were beginning to bulge beneath the overhanging brow. 'There's plenty of skeletons in these parts, believe me.'

Jenny had read a story once about the undead, folk who got up out of their coffins and walked about doing murderous things. It was silly, but this person might have been one of those zombies, cold, stiff, malevolent and completely devoid of any positive human emotion. She suppressed a shiver, wishing that her own imagination would go to sleep for a while, just until she had managed to get away from this unusual and terrifying creature.

'I want an answer from you, Jennifer Crawley.'

Jenny shrugged, hoping to seem not to care about any of it. 'Whatever Maria does is her own business, so I can't speak for her. I'd just forget it all if I were you,' she said with transparently false sweetness. 'You've enough on with a housemaid and a nursemaid to find. Mrs Skipton will be difficult when she gets told I've been sacked, and she won't allow you in her room, will she?' An exaggerated sigh was followed by, 'Poor Briony will have a lot on her plate. Including one or two solid silver knives and forks, I shouldn't wonder.' While this final small comment still hung in the air, Jenny ran outside to collect her belongings.

Mid-morning found the two girls trudging wearily along a country lane in the direction of Bolton. Maria was worst off, because she carried not only her small bag of clothes, but also some of the wire contraptions on which she had 'baked' her printing. Although Jenny offered to help, Maria muttered momentous statements about this being her burden and her blessing, a thing she would carry through life until it got big enough to take its turn at supporting her instead. After a while, Jenny stopped volunteering assistance, because her head was filled by pictures of Auntie Mavis and her seances, while her heart sat in her chest like a heavy lump, weighted by anger and frustration because she had done nothing wrong. She had committed no sin, yet she was out of a job. Just because she'd laughed at a plate of prunes and custard.

If Uncle Dan had been there, today's sacking wouldn't have happened. But she had no intention of asking for his help now. Nothing would persuade her to go back into Stonehenge's lair, not even the kindness of her new-found father.

They sat at the edge of the road, burdens scattered around them in the weeds. 'I don't know what to do,' said

Maria at last. 'Because I can't go home, me mam's got enough without me turning up again like a tin penny.' She pushed the ginger fringe from her eyes, causing it to stand to attention above the furrowed forehead. 'Me mam's not a coper. She'd be sad if she knew I'd got the boot from me job.'

Jenny stared up the lane, hoping that some transport would arrive soon. 'You'll have to come with me to Claughton Street. There's no spare bed, but you're welcome—'

'How many in a bed?'

'Just the two of us. Auntie Mavis has her own room.'

Maria smiled. She needed very little encouragement to revert to her usual cheerful self. 'That's all right, then. Only I wouldn't like to start playing sardines again. At our house, when one of us turns over, everybody has to shift. It's like dancing in slow motion, all keeping time even when we're asleep.' She paused, a blade of grass clenched between her teeth. 'Will she mind if I just land on her doorstep with no invite?'

Jenny lifted a shoulder. 'She'll not have to mind. If she won't take you in, then we'll both leave. And she hates being on her own.' She hugged her knees tightly. 'Maria?'

'What?'

'She's . . . a bit queer, a bit on the strange side.'

Interest flickered in the pale eyes. 'I heard something about that. Takes all sorts, you know.'

'She drinks and talks to ghosts.'

Maria smiled. 'I don't care. Me dad drinks, and he talks to lamp posts and stray dogs, so I'm used to it. One night, he even had a long conversation with an angel in the cemetery, one of them marble things with posh wings all spread out. I know it's not the same as a ghost, but it's on the right lines. It wouldn't talk back to him, so he took it personal and punched it right in the hymn book. Broke three fingers on his left hand, he did, then had six months off work because he'd been "struck from above". I think he stopped drinking for at least two days that time.'

Jenny folded the dress round her knees, drawing her feet inward so that she could hug herself. If only she could laugh, if only she could be like Maria. She sat, rocking gently to and fro, creating the sort of movement a baby in a cradle might enjoy. She didn't want to go back, hated the thought of returning to Auntie's constant whining, to the drudgery of running that poky house, to the tarot, the crystal, the buckets of so-called ectoplasm. 'I don't want to go to Auntie's,' she said plainly. 'I hate it there, Maria.'

'We've got to go somewhere, queen.' This advice was delivered in Maria's habitual no-nonsense Liverpool tone. 'It's either Mavis and her spirits – both kinds – or it's some shop doorway. We'll think while we're at your auntie's, take a day or two to sort out a plan.'

Jenny blew out her cheeks. 'She'll not let go a second time. I'm all she's got, all she's had for eighteen years.' She thought for a minute. 'Mind, Joe Soap might give me a house of me own, 'cos I always made sure Auntie didn't drink the rent money, and he was grateful for that.'

'Joe Soap? What was his mother thinking the day she christened him?'

Jenny smiled tightly. 'His real name's Joseph Wright but everybody calls him after the coal tar soap. If we could get wages coming in, he might find us somewhere to live, even if it's only a couple of rooms. Mind, he's just the agent. I've no idea who really owns the houses. And I'd still have to escape from Auntie for the second time.'

Carrying these half-formed plans along with their chattels, they climbed gratefully on to the flat back of an empty coal dray that had just finished some country deliveries. The driver, a taciturn man whose cap was pulled down so far that it almost met his downturned mouth, asked no questions about their plight, so they completed the bulk of their journey ensconced in relative comfort and coal dust.

After being deposited in the centre of town, the grimy girls set off to walk the last mile to Claughton Street, Jenny's feet beginning to drag as they neared their goal.

'Come on,' chided Maria. 'I could do with a cup of tea and a good rub down with a damp cloth. Any slower and you'll be going backwards.'

'The street hates me.' Jenny knew that she sounded

infantile and petulant, but the thought of facing the children's taunts was the last straw on the bale. 'They call me names, Spinning Jenny, Creepy Crawley and—' She stopped when Maria tossed her belongings down to the pavement. 'Why are you throwing . . . ?'

'Listen, you've got me for company now, and I wasn't called Big Gob for nothing, you know. Just let them start. A Scouser's a good match for a Woollyback any day of the week. Hold your head up, will you? Christ came home on a donkey, and He didn't care. We've done better than Him, 'cos we got a coal cart.' She reached out a hand and touched Jenny's shoulder. 'Grow up, love,' she said gently. 'Stop worrying about who thinks what about you.'

Jenny gulped back the pain. 'They say I'm queer like Auntie. They call me a sorcerer's apprentice, as if I'm learning to be another weird one. And I never even took the knives at Skipton Hall, did I? Wherever I go, there's no fairness . . .'

Maria clicked her tongue. 'You can stop this feeling sorry for yourself for a start. If you walk about looking like a wet rag, then you will get used to clean the floors, yes, they'll all wipe their doorsteps with you. Life's hard. Know that, accept it, and the hardness gets easier.'

'And another thing.' Jenny was in no mood for Maria's pearls of wisdom.

'What now?' Maria was struggling with her bits and pieces of metal. 'God, wouldn't you know I'd take an interest in something like this, something that won't fold up and be tidy. Well? Come on, tell me. No use standing there with a gob on you.'

Jenny sighed. 'She's after Uncle Dan as well.'

'Briony? She's after anybody in trousers as long as he's stood up and not drooling from the mouth.'

'No, I don't mean her. It's Stonehenge. She suspects something about me and Uncle Dan, says she'll get to the bottom of everything, if you try to sort her out over me being sacked. He could lose his job, Maria. He can't afford for anybody to find out that he's me . . . me father. It's bad enough Auntie Mavis knowing, but he can shut her up with money.'

'So you want me to let things lie?'

'Yes.'

Maria tucked the small suitcase under an arm, the dyeing frames clanging as she moved. 'That's all right. Like I said before, you and me are pals. We work as a team now, try to suit each other, like a matched pair of dray horses.'

Smiling sadly at her memories of Amber and Flora enjoying their holidays, Jenny followed her friend homeward. Though this was hardly home, hardly where she wanted to be. Yes, like Amber, she had few choices. And most of all, she would miss that nice big bathroom . . .

Claughton Street stank. Not only did it smell, but it was full of people, folk standing in the middle of the cobbles, others leaning against house walls, a few hovering singly in doorways.

Maria and Jenny paused at the corner, their eyes moving from side to side as they took in the scene of chaos. Blue-clad policemen were stalking about looking official, and a horse-drawn fire cart was parked halfway up the street. At the edge of the pavement, a figure crouched low, doubled over by the power of a loud and racking cough. A plain wood coffin lay in the gutter, its lid propped against a window sill. Next to the lid stood a large axe with a bright red handle. Jenny felt sick. Only this morning she'd been thinking about coffins and the like, and here was a real one stuck in the street in broad daylight . . .

'Jenny?'

'What?'

Maria pointed with her suitcase. 'That man who's coughing – isn't it Mr Crawley?'

'Eh?' Jenny stared, her breathing suddenly quick and shallow. Yes, it was Uncle Dan. Somebody was shouting orders, telling everybody to pour water on their fires and not to strike any matches. The word 'evacuation' reached her ears, though it arrived muffled by a roaring in her head. Something had happened, something terrible, and it was likely her fault. The smell. It was all connected to this awful smell, and that fireman's axe had been used to break down a door. She knew which door. It was number seventeen . . .

The street began to shiver, as if she were looking at it through a haze of heat, then her legs turned to rubber just before a blessed darkness arrived, and she threw herself gratefully into the silence, relieved to absent herself for a while. Her last thought was that she should have been here, that she should have stayed with Auntie Mavis. Though she would have been at her mule anyway at this time of day, so what difference . . . ?

She woke in a strange house. The fireless grate was shiny with new leading, and firebrasses gleamed in the hearth. A woman bent over her, someone she knew, a fat neighbour with a jolly face that was serious for once. 'Drink of water, love?' asked the owner of the ruddy, plump cheeks.

'Where's Maria?'

'I'm here.' The pointed face appeared at the end of the sofa on which Jenny lay. 'Are you all right, Jen?'

'I feel funny.'

'We all feel funny, it's the gas,' said the lady of the house.

'Uncle Dan?' There was a hysterical note in the two words.

'Gone to hospital,' replied the woman, pushing a cup under Jenny's nose. 'They couldn't keep him out of the house, the firemen. As soon as they broke the lock, he was in there trying to save her, so he breathed a lot in, you see.'

Jenny sipped, moaned, then gripped a warm, fleshy hand. 'Is she dead?'

A small moment of hesitation was followed by, 'I'm sorry, lass. There were nowt anybody could do for her. See, she wouldn't notice, would she? She wouldn't know about the room filling with gas, because she couldn't smell nothing.'

It would have been easy to slip away again into darkness and quiet, but some part of Jenny hung on, though the room was misty. 'My fault. I shouldn't have left her. She'd only me to live for. Now she's gone and done that, killed herself because there was nobody to talk to. I . . . never . . . loved her, never loved . . . anybody . . .'

She began to scream, pouring out words that made no

sense, words that were not complete words at all. Auntie Mavis had committed suicide. Agoraphobia meant the fear of going out, it was in a dictionary in the library. Jenny had been Auntie Mavis's sole contact with the outside world. Mrs Skipton liked pearls and diamonds, there was something wrong with the knives and forks and the door had been broken down with a long-handled axe . . .

A substantial hand made sharp contact with Jenny's left cheek, its action cutting short the bout of hysteria. 'It were an accident,' said the neighbour. 'I've been going in cleaning for her, 'cos your uncle took me on. This morning, she'd no pennies for the meter, so I got her some when I did her shopping. If it's anybody's fault, it's mine. I knew she was forever leaving the gas tap turned on after it had run out. She's put her money in the meter, then gone into one of them trances of hers, forgot to light the ring under the pan. She could have done that when you were living here, love. This might just as easily have happened while you were at the mill. And she'd no intention of doing away with herself, 'cos she'd took to me a treat and she was happy, new customers, she had, so there were plenty of folk popping in for . . . for what she did.'

Jenny giggled unexpectedly, shocked to hear the sound of her own apparent heartlessness. 'That was her last trance, then. I bet she thought it was real this time. It was real, wasn't it? Because she's reached the other side, just like she always hoped. I wonder if they're there, the folk she used to talk to? Why am I laughing, Mrs . . . ?'

'Burke. Me name's Ena Burke, and you're giddy because of the shock. People often laugh and cry all at once when they get bad news like this. I laughed when me husband died in the pit ten years ago, and that weren't particularly funny either. You'll settle down once you get the funeral over.'

Jenny was suddenly sober. 'If she'd been deaf or blind, I would have stayed, wouldn't I? But I never thought she'd die because of having no sense of smell.' Another thought struck her. 'Did they put her in that awful coffin?'

Maria, who had remained unusually quiet thus far, leapt to Jenny's side. 'Don't think about it.'

'But she's got to have brass handles. I promised her she'd have her best robe on too, and she wants her crystal ball and her cards and all sorts buried with her.'

Ena Burke nodded wisely. 'They've only took her temporary, while they have a good look at her. Sudden death, you see. When they've done, you can fetch her home and do things proper.'

Maria glanced at the door as somebody pushed it open. A fireman's helmet poked itself into the room. 'I've fixed the door,' announced a voice from within the headgear. 'You can go home now, if you like. The boss has decided not to evacuate the street after all.'

Maria stared hard at Jenny. 'Do you feel up to it?'

Jenny hesitated for several seconds. 'Where else can we go? Mind, it's going to be horrible, walking in there, knowing what's happened to Auntie Mavis.' She felt calmer now. Her thoughts were emerging in the right order, and her tongue seemed able to follow her brain's instruction at last.

'It'll get worse if you wait,' advised Maria. 'You'd be best facing up to it right away, as soon as you feel strong enough.' She glanced at the fireman. 'Has the gas gone altogether?'

He took off his hat, revealing a pleasant face topped by jet-black hair that was beginning to recede, probably a victim of erosion due to the weight of the helmet. 'Still smells a bit, but it's safe. Is there anything I can do for you?'

Maria pointed to the pile of luggage. 'Stick that in the house,' she said. 'And thank you.'

Jenny lifted her head. 'Will you go to the hospital and find out about Uncle Dan? He's the man who went in and tried to . . . get her out. He's breathed some gas, and I want to know how he is.'

'I'll do that.' He backed out, clattering Maria's frames in the doorway.

After several cups of tea and many words of encouragement from Mrs Burke, the two girls stood in the doorway of number twenty-nine. 'You know where I am,' said Ena Burke. 'Just run down and get me if you need anything.'

Jenny found herself wondering vaguely where Mrs Burke had been for the past eighteen years, but she kept her counsel. This was no time to indulge in another bout of stupid self-pity. Yet the woman volunteered an answer without ever hearing the question. 'I've only lived here a few months. You'll have seen me in passing, but I spend a lot of time round at me daughter's. Well, I did till I started looking after your auntie. Anyway.' She smoothed her flowered wrap-over apron. 'Happen they'll treat you better after this tragedy. I know what they say, lass. I know they didn't like Miss Crawley's ongoings. But they should sweep their own back yards before mouthing off about other folks' bits of bother.'

With this small piece of comfort, the neighbour pushed the two girls into the street, steering them gently in the direction of number seventeen. 'You'll be fine in an hour or two,' she advised Maria quietly. 'Just keep her out of her auntie's room, 'cos it might upset her seeing the lady's things.'

Curtains twitched as Jenny and Maria walked past the part of the terrace that stretched between numbers twenty-nine and seventeen. It was as if a thousand eyes were watching them, while a similar number of voices seemed to be passing muted judgement on their newly returned neighbour.

The house was cold inside, because every window had been left open to allow gas to escape into the street. A stale odour hung in the air, and it was plain that the very fabric of the building had been soaked in fumes. Everything was the same. Buddha sat on the mantelpiece next to the totem, the candelabra rested on the dresser, Auntie Mavis's seance chair was pulled out from the table, as if expecting to be occupied at any second.

'I can't.' Jenny stood in the doorway, a hand against patched wood where the axe had bitten. 'I don't want to go in, Maria.'

'Then I'll do it.' The slender girl pulled her companion back into the street, then strode past the dresser, her arms stretched out at each side of her thin body. 'See? It's just a house. And there's nowhere else we can go, Jenny.'

Jenny crossed her arms, each hand gripping the opposite shoulder and kneading nervously, trying to pull the tension to the surface where, like the carbon gas, it might evaporate into the atmosphere. But calm continued to be elusive. 'It's easy for you, she wasn't your auntie.'

'Well, you'll have to sleep in the street, then. Look, I know this has been a terrible shock, but we have to carry on, get some food, light a fire. It's cold for early summer, isn't it? And it'll be colder still if you sleep outside all night.'

Jenny could not argue with such obvious logic. She stepped gingerly into the room, a hand sliding along the dresser as if looking for courage and support. 'I ought to get down to the infirmary and see about Uncle Dan meself. But I'm tired, so tired.' She sank into Auntie's chair. 'What if he dies and all? Won't it be awful if . . . ?'

'Yes,' said Maria firmly. 'It would be awful. And you can't do anything to make anything different. It's not your fault. He shouldn't have come in the house – they told him not to. But he's like that, Mr Crawley. He's brave and he always makes his own mind up about things. Come on, we'll have you out of that chair and in your bed, lady. I'll sort things out and take messages.' Without ceremony, she dragged Jenny from her seat and pulled her towards the stairs.

Once she had settled her friend into bed, Maria Hesketh stood on the landing, a hand to her brow as she considered her next move. Jenny was in a state, still hovering on the brink of hysteria. If she did settle to sleep – and that would be a miracle in itself – then the poor girl would probably wake up screaming.

Halfway down the narrow staircase, Maria made her decision. There wasn't time to consider the rightness of her judgement, so she simply followed her instincts into the sombre front room. With those quick, deft movements of the practised housemaid, she cleared the small area of all objects that might offend Jenny, everything that seemed to pertain to Mavis Crawley's odd vocation. Within ten minutes, the zodiac signs had been relegated to the back yard, while Buddha and the totem had found a new place of rest in the dresser cupboard.

But the room looked bare and sad, as if it were mourning the recent departure of its mistress. Maria stood, hands on hips, eyes following the shape of the walls and taking in every clean patch left by the twelve discarded pictures.

She found a box of tin tacks in a drawer and hauled some printed scarves from her suitcase, pinning them over the tell-tale gaps. The result was unusual but colourful. Four further squares were laid on the table, each representing a place mat. Beneath the hinged lid of a footstool, she discovered sewing materials, and she used these to quickly tack together three cushion covers. They were rough and ready and would require finishing at some stage, but the effect was pleasing. After more printed cotton had been placed on the backs of armchairs, Maria walked into the kitchen and stood for a few minutes before stepping back towards the parlour. She wanted to pretend that she hadn't already seen it, to imagine how Jenny would feel when she noticed the changes.

Maria had never spread her work out before, had never had the chance to view the printing as a whole collection. It was beautiful. She wondered briefly whether she might be biased or proud or too hopeful, but the stirrings in her breast owed nothing to such sins. In that moment, she knew that she was good, that her gift was true and strong, almost something separate from herself. Her eyes pricked with unshed tears born of emotions that were very mixed. She was clever, she could do it, she could make patterns. Jenny's aunt had died, and this death had given Maria the chance to know her own destiny. Jenny had lost a job, Maria had thrown one away. Mr Crawley was in hospital with a chestful of gas, while an ugly little Scouse urchin stood here in a dead woman's house with a chestful of pride. Fiercely, she rubbed at her eyes with the heel of a hand. She would not cry. However shocking this day had been, she would be strong for her friend, for poor Jenny.

The door opened a crack. 'Is that you?' asked a deepish male voice, one Maria had heard before.

'No,' she said, her customary Liverpool-Irish wit returning instantly. This was her defence, a ploy she often used in strange company or in difficult situations. 'It's not me,' she added. 'It's somebody else altogether.'

He poked his head into the room. 'I said I'd come back,' he explained almost sheepishly.

'Did you?' She studied the apparently disembodied head. 'Where's your daft hat?'

'At the station.'

Maria sniffed meaningfully, aware that the meaningfulness of her sniffs was legendary in some parts. 'I'd leave it there if I were you, it's wearing your head out, your brains are showing through in patches. Have you tried castor oil?'

The tall man stepped into the room. 'No. Does it work?'

She shrugged. 'Depends what you do with it. You can rub it into your head or swallow it. Rubbing it into your head will give you something to do between fires.' A smile tugged at the corners of her lips. 'So will the result of swallowing it,' she said. 'How's Mr Crawley?'

'Oh, he'll be all right in a day or two. The bobbies went up yonder and told the Skiptons what's happened. Me mother's a beggar for castor oil,' he continued without pause, determined to keep up with this cheeky madam. 'She used to give it us for everything from a headache to athlete's foot.'

'Did it work?' She bit her lip immediately, realizing that she had fallen into his trap.

He nodded slowly. 'It kept us occupied, took our minds off the other kinds of pain. Where's the blonde girl?'

'Upstairs. I'm trying to get her to take things easy. She's lost a lot today. Her job, her auntie and her . . . her uncle's in hospital. I'll look after her.'

His eyes wandered round the room, taking in the dramatic alterations. 'Last time I was in here, it was like a blinking mausoleum. A lot brighter now, isn't it? Are these yours?'

'Yes.'

'They're different, aren't they? Nice and colourful. Most houses are all brown and green, pictures of grandmas and stuff. I see a lot of houses in my job, but I've never clapped eyes on owt like this lot. Where did you buy them?'

'I made them.'

He took a few more steps into the room, picking up a cushion for closer inspection. 'That's grand, is that. Aye, it's time we got away from all this Victorian misery.'

She tried hard not to look pleased. 'Our Anthony – he's me brother – says I'm years ahead of meself. So I'm going to do some in quieter colours. Mind, these are really headscarves, and they're just for practice. But one day . . . oh, never mind all that. You'd better get back to your job or your tea. And we've a funeral to see to.'

Made awkward by this reminder of the earlier tragedy, he backed towards the door. 'Eeh, I'm sorry. I didn't mean to be disrespectful, honest.'

'It's not disrespect.' Maria's voice was almost heated. 'It's keeping sane in an awful job, and I know what that's like. Anyway, I never knew Mavis. It's Jenny upstairs who's grieving, 'cos this woman brought her up. She's had a terrible time today, one way and another.'

He fingered the doorknob. 'Will I come back and see you again?'

'What for?'

He shrugged shoulders that were broad and capable beneath the thick, black uniform jacket. 'Well, I could help you. I'm handy when it comes to odd jobs.' A large finger tugged at the collar of his shirt. 'And we could happen go out some time.'

'Where?'

'Park, penny rush, Grand Theatre—'

'I don't sit in penny seats, thank you. I'm a tuppenny girl and I like a bag of toffees too.' This was stupid. He couldn't like her – she'd seen herself in a mirror often enough, knew what to expect in the glass. She was a scrawny, red-haired runt with eyes of such a pale blue that they were next to colourless. She had no chest, no bum and she'd seen better legs on an underfed sparrow in the middle of a cold spell. And her arms were like twigs, except that they were too pale and freckly to belong to any self-respecting tree. The biggest parts of her limbs were the elbows and the knees, great knobbly lumps stuck halfway up or halfway down, depending on your vantage point. 'I'll be busy,' she almost snapped.

'Oh. Well.' He twisted the knob. 'No harm in asking, I suppose.'

Something like panic rose in Maria's gorge. He was going. He was going and she might never see him again. 'Hang on a bit.' God, she was blushing like a child on its first day at a new school. 'There might be a few things . . .'

'Right.' He turned and leaned against the door. 'I'm all ears.'

Maria swallowed and took a deep breath. The house still stank of coal gas. 'It's . . . her auntie's bedroom. We might have to shift things if Joe Soap lets us take over the rent book. See, Jenny could want everything of her auntie's moving out. Then again, she could want it all saving for . . . sentimental reasons.' She was doing well, so she inhaled another load of confidence and stale fumes. 'We might need a strong man.'

'I'm strong.'

'I can see that.' He was nice-looking too, in spite of the receding hairline. In fact, the tall forehead made him look alert and very intelligent. He had soft brown eyes and thick eyebrows, as if the hair from his head had simply done a midnight flit downward to the next street. The lips were thin but not hard. Maria had never liked men with fleshy lips. There was something unseemly about a lad with a generous mouth, something feminine and untrustworthy. 'Come back in a few days,' she finished somewhat lamely. He was staring at her, and the staring was making her feel uglier than usual.

'One condition. You let me walk you out some time.'

Maria crossed her ankles and leaned against the wall in an attitude that was supposed to express nonchalance. 'Oh.' This monosyllable came out squeaky, so she said 'oh,' again, giving herself time to think and her voice a chance to drop an octave. 'I'm no oil-painting,' she said flippantly. 'Why ever should you want to be seen out with me?'

'I like you.'

'Why?'

'I don't know. I just like you, that's all. Do you want me

110

to write a bloody book about it?' His skin reddened right up into the bald patch. 'Or is there a form to fill in? I'm sick of flaming forms, report books, sign for this, sign for the air you breathe. So don't you start, I get enough paperwork with this rotten job.'

Maria pursed her mouth while she thought. 'I'll have to see her through her mourning before I can go gallivanting. She's me best friend, like.'

'Aye, I know all that. I'm not as daft as I look.'

'You couldn't be,' she parried neatly. 'Come round in a few days, then.'

'I will.' He opened the door.

'Hey,' she shouted. 'Hang on a minute. What's your name?'

He hesitated. 'What's yours?'

'I asked first,' she declared indignantly. 'Well?'

'Don't laugh.'

'I won't.'

'You will.'

'Listen.' She abandoned the casual stance and stood with her arms akimbo. 'I'm not walking out with no stranger. What do you think I am?'

He grinned broadly, displaying very white and even teeth. 'You're a Scouser called Maria. I've no idea of your second name, but I listened out for the "Maria" this afternoon. Now, straighten your face.'

She sucked in her cheeks, praying that she would not fail him by giggling.

'I'm Denis,' he said finally.

'What's wrong with that?'

'Not a lot. Unless your second name's Dandy.'

'Denis Dandy?'

He nodded. 'Bloody terrible, isn't it?'

Bravely, she maintained an air of seriousness. 'Better than Willy Wyre,' she said carefully. 'I was at school with a lad called Willy Wyre. The day he got baptized, his mam was bad with childbed fever, so his dad took him up to church on his own. When he got there, he couldn't remember what he was supposed to call the lad, 'cos he'd stopped on the way at the Pig and Whistle for a drop of the hard stuff. In fact, he had more than a drop, and he left the poor baby in a shopping bag under the hatstand, the landlord had to run after him with the left luggage. Anyway, he got very confused, did Mr Wyre, and when he got to St Gregory's with his bagful of baby, he had to pull round by leaning on a gravestone. Now, the fellow in this here grave had had his name chipped into the marble, and this name was William. So Mr Wyre went into church with "William" sort of engraved into his head. It was supposed to be Christopher, but that's life, isn't it? Your dad gets drunk and you finish up being called Willy Wyre.'

The grin on Denis's face was huge now. 'That's why I like you,' he said happily.

'Eh? 'Cos of Willy Wyre?'

'No,' he said. 'Because you're daft. Maria.' He rolled the name round his tongue, as if savouring it. 'But I'll call you Tuppence.'

'Why?' The light blue eyes were round with surprise.

He waved a finger at her. 'Nay, it was you who put a price on your own head. You said you were a tuppenny girl. Some of us,' he twinkled, 'get our names by accident. And some of us choose what we get called. It's your own fault, Tuppence.' He tipped an invisible hat and walked out of the house.

Maria 'Tuppence' Hesketh sank into a chair as soon as his ringing, iron-tipped footfalls had died away. This was unbelievable! She had an admirer, a real, actual man who was interested in her, in plain Maria Hesketh with red hair and no chest and a horrible Liverpool accent! And he was nice, handsome too in his way. She couldn't take this in. Even the pretty and simpering Briony Mulholland would never get a chap as special as Denis Dandy. And Jenny was the beautiful one, Jenny was the girl who should be getting all the chances. Was Denis using Maria to get to Jenny? She shook her head in answer to this silent question. No. That had all been real, it had happened. He liked Maria, he liked the tuppenny girl.

Jenny stepped into the room. 'Who was that?'

Maria cleared her throat. 'Oh, it was just the fireman. He's been down to the infirmary, and Mr Crawley's going to be all right soon, once his chest has cleared.'

'That's good.' Jenny lowered herself into the chair opposite Maria's, her movements as slow as those of a very old woman. 'Maria?'

'What?'

'I didn't love her. That's why I feel so awful, because I didn't care about her. She was a lonely, sick old lady, she couldn't smell the gas, and I left her. Even if she could have smelled the gas, she was frightened of going out. I should have loved her.'

'Some people aren't lovable,' said Maria, her voice steady and sensible. 'You can't make yourself love somebody.'

'She used to say I wasn't grateful.'

'And were you grateful?'

'No.' Jenny's hands tightened on the chair. 'I think I was scared of her. She had this power – nowt to do with ghosts and all that – just a kind of strength that made you do exactly what she wanted.' She paused, staring into the empty grate. 'My Auntie Mavis was a cruel and selfish woman. I think she was lazy. All that stuff about not being able to go out was likely put on, just so I'd do everything for her. I'm speaking ill of the dead, aren't I?'

Maria looked hard at the sweet, gentle face of her troubled friend. 'You're growing up, that's what you're doing, Jen. She kept you a baby when it suited her, then turned you into a working grown-up overnight, just so that you'd see to her and earn a wage. You've been used, love.'

'Yes.' Large bright eyes scanned the walls. 'That's lovely, Maria. Just what we need to make the place our own. We can stay here, you and me. If we can get some work and pay the rent.'

Maria tapped the chair arm with her nails. 'Can you cook?'

Jenny nodded.

'Pies and hotpots?'

'Yes.'

'Then you make saucer pies and pans of stew and I'll take in sewing and washing.' The sharp chin jerked itself upward in a movement that spoke of inner determination. 'We'll not need references from Stonehenge, Jen. You feed them and I'll dress them. Between us, we'll run this bloody town in the end.'

The craziest thing was that she actually believed the words she spoke at that moment. And this new faith in the future had nothing to do with bushy black eyebrows and calm brown eyes, she told herself firmly. She, Maria Hesketh, needed no man. And she would knit him a nice warm scarf for next winter . . .

It was Maria who found the policy, tucked away under a pile of old letters and bills in an ancient butterscotch tin at the bottom of the dresser. Jenny, who was as near to next of kin as could be found while Dan Crawley was in hospital, signed for the money at the door. The Wesleyan and General chap knew Jenny well, so if he had any qualms about passing over the cash to a female minor, they did not show. He folded the documents into his pocket, making a mental note about visiting Mr Crawley for a second signature in case the boss kicked up again. This poor lass had an auntie to bury, so the money was going to the right place as far as he was concerned.

The life insurance policy bought Mavis Crawley her special funeral, though few attended the ceremony. Her brother Dan was still a patient in the infirmary, having developed a slight pneumonia in a lobe of his right lung, so the hearse was followed by just three people. There was a beautiful blonde girl, her thin, red-haired friend, and an off-duty fireman with a black arm-band sewn round the sleeve of his good brown suit. But Jenny was satisfied, because she had kept her promise. Inside the coffin, Mavis was all decked out in robe and turban, while crystal ball, tarot cards, Buddha and totem accompanied her on this last journey. Perhaps there had been no love, but there had, in the end, been obedience and attention to detail, right down to the gleaming brass handles and a bunch of hideous lilies.

The service took place at the nearest Church of England church, simply because Jenny refused to face that groping pastor again. In the last few years of her life, Mavis had allied herself to no religion, so her final blessing was administered by someone Jenny considered to be neutral. The Church of England was everybody's church, and it was there just to christen, marry and bury folk, because only the rich and idle spent time with such a watery and meaningless faith.

After the burial in a civic cemetery, and when Denis Dandy had gone to do his shift at the fire station, the two girls had the usual funeral meal of ham sandwiches followed by trifle and several cups of tea. They sat in the late Mavis's front room, having opened the curtains just enough to let in sufficient light to illuminate the table and its contents. Jenny tugged at the waistband of her best skirt, which happened, fortunately, to be black. 'I'll never eat again,' she pronounced, pushing away the remaining trifle.

'You like your food. Tomorrow, you'll be at it again with the egg and bacon. Anyway, how much money have we got and what did Mr Crawley say about it?'

'Thirteen pounds, sixteen shillings and elevenpence. Uncle Dan says I can have it, do what I want with it, only it's spoke for.'

Maria took an enormous bite of ham and bread. 'You what?' she asked, almost choking on the food. 'What are you going to live on? Fresh bloody air?' These words, struggling for life past half an ounce of thin-cut best boiled and no fat, arrived strangled, but Jenny was good at interpreting foreign languages. 'She's got to have a stone,' she said stubbornly. 'The least I can do is get her a stone. Italian marble, she liked.'

Maria swallowed loudly. 'Can you eat Italian marble? Can you? Just because you feel stuffed at the moment doesn't mean you'll not starve the rest of the week. You could use that money to start a business, buy some sewing stuff and some meat for the stewpot. God help us, you've not the sense you were born with. You could save up for her memorial, or get it on the knock.'

'The knock?'

'Yes, that's when they knock at your door every week for a shilling in the pound. So if you buy something for five

115

pounds, you pay five bob a week for twenty-one weeks.'

'Don't you mean twenty?'

'No, the extra's interest.'

'Then I'm not interested in their interest.'

Maria jumped up and began to pace the floor. 'Don't go clever on me, Jen. There's enough with my acid, no need for you to come over all carbolic. We've no jobs, queen. In case you hadn't noticed, we're both out of work. And it was a grand idea, to run our own little business, you going round with your basket of pies and me making skirts and—'

'Jenkins wouldn't be best pleased if I started selling pies.'

'Who's he? What's flaming Jenkins got to do with it?'

Jenny shook her head patiently. 'He's the bread and pie man.'

'Well, bugger him and all.' Colour arrived in the pale, freckled cheeks, allowing Maria a brief spell of what almost amounted to beauty. 'It's a free country, isn't it? And we'd not be selling enough to wipe out his shop, 'cos we've not got a big oven. As for a few bits of frocks, I can't see the court dressmakers getting worked up about my share of the trade.' She fell to her knees beside Jenny's chair. 'Aw, come on, love. She'll not know whether she's got a headstone or not, will she? It won't do any harm to hang on a month or two, and we can shop round, find her a really nice one.'

'But I'll know she hasn't got one.'

'So?'

'So it's not right, not comfortable.'

Maria swivelled on her knees, then dropped into a sitting position, holding the dark blue skirt round her thighs as she gazed into the fire. 'Well, you'll be broke in a fortnight, and I've only got three bob left. I'll take these scarves off the walls tomorrow, go down the market and flog them.'

Jenny sighed and dropped her head. It was happening again. Somebody was telling her what to do, and she would likely do it just for peace and quiet. 'All right,' she said quietly. 'We'll do the pies and sewing.'

Quick as a flash, Maria was on her feet again. 'You'll not regret it, I promise. Where are you going?' Pale reddish-brown eyebrows were arched with surprise as she watched Jenny taking the shawl from its peg.

'I'm going to the hospital.' Shoulders drooped in resignation, while the blonde head seemed to be struggling to hold itself up.

'You look battered, girl. Can't it wait?'

Jenny stared past Maria and at the mantelpiece where Buddha had used to squat. 'No, it can't.' With a supreme effort, she forced the exhaustion out of her bones and into the back of her mind. If absolutely necessary, she would find time to be tired later on. 'He's me dad, remember. Not that anybody's supposed to get told that he's me father, but he is and that's an end of it. He's a nice man and I'm going to visit him.'

Maria's eyes seemed to cloud over as she looked with pity at her forlorn friend. 'You've had it hard up to now, love. We've both had it bloody hard, and it's up to us to change it. Yes, it's been a long life, even though we're only eighteen. Stop being frightened, Jenny.'

'I'm not frightened.' Due to sheer weariness, the tone stopped well short of indignation. 'Fed up, is what I am. It's all about pleasing folk, and if you please one, you let another down. One day,' she walked to the door and opened it, turning just before she stepped outside. 'One day, I shall please meself.'

The door slammed. Maria picked up the poker and prodded idly at the feeble fire. Jenny had looked so cowed, so downright miserable. Mind, that was probably how most people took funerals, on their shoulders rather than on the chin. She'd been kept down, had Jenny, so now she had no sense of her own value. It was a shame. And Maria intended to change Jenny's life as well as her own. They were young, they were healthy and they were at a crossroads. Well, for a start, as from tonight, Maria would sleep in Mavis Crawley's room, to hell with the ghosts. It was a squash with the two of them in Jenny's little bed, so it was time to get on with the big job.

The front bedroom had been closed off since the day of

the death, and it was with some trepidation that Maria set foot across the threshold. It was like Aladdin's cave, all draped shawls and necklaces and rugs with funny patterns. She would keep the rugs, they were covered in the sort of geometry that appealed to Maria's own unorthodox tastes. The bed cover was interesting too, with its large golden pentagon embossed in the centre of a purple circle. How could she achieve things like this in print? Not with an ordinary oven and a few bits of wire, that was for certain.

There was a wooden chest beneath the window, and Maria quickly emptied this of linen, replacing spare sheets and towels with Mavis's bizarre clothes. This left an obvious problem, and Maria solved it by simply stuffing the linen on to the top shelf of the wardrobe. She picked up all the beads and chains, which had hung – for some considerable time judging by the dust – on the edges of mirrors and pictures. These, together with the dead woman's footwear, were placed in the chest. Denis could shift this lot eventually, sell it or take it to the corporation tip.

After sitting on the lid of the chest for some moments, Maria decided that this was as closed as it was going to get. Right. It was her room now. She sniffed, breathing in the mixed odours of mothball, dust and something like incense, a smell only too familiar to a good Catholic girl who had kicked herself out to benediction once a month. Almost choking against the cloying air, she threw up the sash window, expecting an immediate improvement. Nothing happened. Summer had arrived at last, and the air hung outside in the street like a theatre fire curtain, solid, thick and impenetrable.

A through draught, that was what she needed. Her eyes settled on the boarded-up fireplace. If she could clear the blockage without breaking the wood, then it could be put back in place for the winter. It took a nail file, some large scissors and about a pint of sweat, but at last she lifted the wood away from the gap to reveal the usual metal basket and a small ceramic fire-kerb.

The basket was full, but not with ashes. There were two

parcels, each wrapped in brown paper and tied with ribbon that had once been red. On both sides of the parcels, a large blob of sealing wax had been applied where the lengths of ribbon crossed, and someone had obviously pressed a ring or coin into the wax, leaving a shallow but definite mark.

Carefully, Maria lifted the packages. The wrappings were old and partially decayed, threatening to crumble at a touch like dried leaves in autumn. She blew away the grime of years, noticing that there were cracks here and there, tears along ageworn folds. But the contents were still not visible, because layers of newsprint lay beneath the brown paper.

The writing was faded, but she managed to read it. 'FOR MY NIECE, JENNIFER CRAWLEY. TO BE OPENED AFTER MY DEATH, BUT NOT BEFORE JENNIFER CRAWLEY'S 21ST BIRTHDAY. Signed Mavis Crawley.' This legend was inscribed on both packets.

Maria dropped on to the bed, testing the springs absently by bouncing gently on the edge of the mattress. Three years. Jenny would have to wait three years before opening these things. Why, they might be full of money! Her fingers itched to rip away the frail coverings, but she forced herself to be calm. What should she do with them? If she gave them to Jenny, it would be just another worry for the poor girl, something else to feel guilty about. Because opening them would be betraying the dead auntie, and not opening them might cause even more discomfort and uncertainty. Who with human blood in her veins would be able to resist getting hands on a legacy?

She lifted a package to her ear and shook it gently, and no sound came forth. But paper money wouldn't make a noise, would it? A vision flashed into her brain, a clear picture of a nice little shop with a printing room in the back, some sort of continuous feed machinery pushing cloth through rollers or across screens. 'Maria Hesketh,' she said gravely. 'Put Satan behind you.'

There were no two ways about it, she would have to hide the damn things and say nothing. For the time being, at least. Jenny had enough on her plate without facing any more life-altering decisions. Yes, it would be best to forget these parcels, stick them in the bottom of the wardrobe.

And at least there was a through draught now. Even if it was a bit sluggish.

Chapter Five

His long, slim fingers drummed rhythmically and relentlessly against a leather-edged blotter that sat squarely in the centre of the desk. This was a massive piece of furniture, with knee-spaces and chairs at both sides, so that partners could do business properly, sensibly, without a lot of bending and stretching of the left hand just to see what the right limb was doing. Dan Crawley often occupied the second seat, but he was in hospital with pneumonia, while Henry was here in the small study of Skipton Hall with a headache and servant problems.

He flicked idly through a price list from some conglomerate in America. They seemed to be offering him a free bale with every dozen purchased, but he didn't like the prices, so the tantalizing offer, having failed completely to tantalize, sailed in the shape of a paper aeroplane right past the bin and under the bookcase where it joined its older brothers. Henry had taken to aeronautics recently, and copies of minutes were currently parked with balance sheets and rough notes in the dark hangar beneath a bit of Shakespeare, the translated plays of Molière and a gigantic book entitled *A Brief History of Cotton*. He was glad he'd had the foresight to buy the brief history. A larger tome might have shot through the bottom of the case and into the aerodrome. Which would not have been fair play on his air corps.

The place was like a morgue, and the sound of his nails,

tap-tapping again on the desk top, thrummed gently across the study and into the library. The connecting door hung wide, and Henry Skipton fixed his eyes on the vast store of knowledge that was stacked in the next room. Knowledge. Learning. Skills. The intellectual wealth of ages occupied those shelves. Yes, they were there, all the things he ought to have passed on to his children, all the things he might have bequeathed to Sophie if *she* hadn't . . .

She. The 'she' in question lay upstairs, doubtless still cursing like the fishwife she really was. The cursing had arisen out of the fact that Jenny Crawley had been sacked, probably unfairly, probably by the orang-utan in the kitchen, the one that called itself a housekeeper. Briony Mulholland, who had been forced to take Jenny's place as nursemaid, was not exactly flavour of the month, so the wife who was far from dearly beloved was also far from pleased at this moment. On top of all which, Briony Mulholland had been threatening all day to leave. Matters were not improved by the fact that Mrs Sloane could not go upstairs because Eloise hated the sight of her. Everyone disliked Carla Sloane, but he had to admit that the creature was currently having a bad few days and was therefore entitled, temporarily, to a degree of pity.

He clapped a hand to his aching head. Oh God, life was so complicated. Dan Crawley was a patient in the infirmary, the man's niece had been sacked for stealing, and the little red-haired girl had walked out without notice. Mrs Sloane was not acceptable in the sickroom because she was ugly and Eloise could not abide ugly things. And yes, there was a deeper and more sinister reason than that, wasn't there? The reason why the dreadful housekeeper had continued to reign for all these years. Oh no, it wasn't just her looks that kept Carla Sloane out of her mistress's room. It was knowledge, the sort of knowledge that could put a rope round someone's neck . . . He threw the thought out of his mind and concentrated on the one remaining servant. Briony, according to the lady of the house, was a damn fool of a girl . . .

As if conjured up by his thoughts, Briony Mulholland's nut-brown face appeared before him. She was a pretty girl, though the strain was beginning to show in her features, a frown line, a downturned lip, small but frantic movements in the eyes. She inhaled deeply, then approached the desk, hands clasped as if in prayer against the bib of the white, lace-trimmed apron. 'I'm sorry, but I'm off,' she said abruptly, a thick curl of hair tumbling forward to conceal confusion in the yellowish-brown irises.

He leaned back in the chair, pushing his palms against the desk's edge until he had projected himself backwards by several inches. 'This will leave us in something of a mess,' he said carefully.

'I know, but it's nowt to do with me.' The voice carried a familiar ring, the sort of tone a tackler might produce when the weaving failed to come up to scratch. Self-righteous and self-pitying, those were the adjectives. 'I mean . . .' One hand pushed back the hair, while the other limb waved wildly in space above the desk. 'I mean, she wants Jenny. She keeps going on about Jenny this and Jenny that, then she went and threw a pot of cold cream at me. It missed, but she cracked one of them fancy French plates, so now she's screaming fit to bust. Honest, I can't stick it no more, it's terrible.'

He studied her closely. Yes, there was panic here. The young woman probably did fear for her sanity at this point, just as so many had worried about their state of mind after a closer than absolutely necessary encounter with Mrs Eloise Skipton. 'I'll get a nurse tomorrow.' He managed, barely, to keep his voice from shaking. Pleading with a maid was not a good idea. He liked his servants, but it was important that they should not be given an opportunity to steal the upper hand.

Briony's head shook itself in a movement that seemed slow and thoughtful. 'No. I've had enough. What I'm getting at is it's not just today, is it? When you work here, you're all the time wondering when it's going to be your turn to go in with the mistress. Jenny didn't seem to mind, but Maria hated it, so it's not just me being awkward. Last time Maria got the job, it was prunes everywhere.

Plastered them all over the place, did Mrs Skipton. There's only Jenny can do owt with her.'

Henry Skipton rose and stretched his legs, pressing flattened palms into the small of his back as he straightened. 'She'll be on her own if you go, Briony. Wouldn't it be rather unfair of you to walk out without any notice?'

The chin jutted forward. 'I don't care. She could have killed me with that big pot of cream. I'm telling you now, Mr Skipton, they'll be needing pit boots, special clothing and danger money if they're going in yon room. And a proper insurance policy wouldn't be a bad idea either.' The wayward locks tumbled once again, but this time she simply blew them away, allowing her frantic eyes a series of brief glances at a world that had ceased to be sane.

Something uncomfortably akin to hysteria lurked at the edge of Henry's mind. 'I thought you were . . . interested in . . . er . . . continuing to work for Mr Crawley?' The girl's intentions towards Dan had been plain for some time, plain to everyone except, apparently, Dan himself. 'Don't you want to wait until he comes out of hospital before making any final decisions about a change of career?'

'No.' She sniffed away her recent disappointment. She'd gone out on a limb to get rid of Jenny, shoving stuff under the girl's bedding when ordered by Stonehenge. Getting rid of Jenny had seemed important, because Briony had wanted Dan to herself. Now Stonehenge, up to her eyebrows in brandy last night, had said that Dan would probably never marry anyone, that he'd likely been 'crossed' early in life and that no-one should hold out any hope where Dan Crawley was concerned. Briony suddenly felt more than angry. She planted her feet wide apart and folded her arms tightly. 'It was her in the kitchen,' she said breathily, as if trying to push out the words in a rush. 'She told me to do it.' Well, there was nothing to lose now, was there?

Henry pondered, his head on one side. 'Who told you to do what?'

Briony faltered, guilt rising to the surface where it sat brightly on rounded, creamy-bronze cheeks. But she squashed the negative feelings quickly and deliberately, informing herself mutely that Stonehenge had been her boss and that she, Briony, had been forced to obey just to keep her job. Well, she didn't need the rotten job any more. There was a post for her at the Red Cat, live in, all found, just tidy the guest rooms and change a few towels. Emboldened by thoughts of such a promising future, Briony threw caution to the winds. 'Best if I get it all off me chest,' she announced. 'She told me to put knives and things under Jenny's bed. She wanted rid of Jenny, 'cos Jenny laughed at the table.'

'I beg your pardon?'

She felt sorry for him. He looked like someone who had just gone ten rounds with Mrs Skipton – lost, mystified and somewhat depleted in spirit. 'Listen, sir, you have to do as Stonehenge tells you, whether it's right or wrong. The upshot was that she managed to sack Jenny for stealing stuff what Jenny had never stole in the first place, if you get my meaning.'

'Oh.' He walked round the desk and perched on its edge, giving himself time to interpret Briony's message. They were no more than eighteen inches apart when he asked, through a mist of near-comprehension, 'Why did you do that, Briony?'

She stared steadily at him. 'Why do any of us do anything she asks? We're feared to death of her, that's why. If she tells you to stash silver under Jenny Crawley's bed, you do it, no questions. Because she's the boss, because she's there. Why is she there? It's up to you to answer that one, Mr Skipton. And don't bother sacking me for cheek. I've got a job what doesn't need references because me mam knows the family in the pub.'

He let out a long, slow breath, not deigning to answer the maid's impertinent question. 'You shall have a reference, Briony. I shall write one for you. Now, tell me.' He walked to the window and gazed outside. 'Where is Maria Hesketh?'

'I don't know, do I?' came the swift response. 'She was with Jenny when the auntie got found dead in the house, so happen she's still there. She might even have got herself another job, I shouldn't wonder.'

He blinked against a sharp stab of migraine. So, it looked as if the red-haired girl had come out in sympathy. Yes, that would be the case. Workers were uniting at all levels. There was a distinct possibility that labour might be universally withdrawn at some stage, but he had not the time to dwell on such notions at present. The withdrawal of labour in his own household was causing enough grief without him worrying about the social and economic state of a whole nation.

'I shall double your wages,' he said quietly, marvelling anew at the power of being a boss, a master. All it took was nerve, organization and terminal tomfoolery. Oh yes, this was real power, wasn't it? Having to pay double wages so that the servants wouldn't make a mass exit? 'Everybody's wages,' he said quietly, caution thrown with gay abandon into the mouth of a passing force nine gale. Then, to himself, he added, 'Assuming that I can bloody well find everybody, that is.'

Briony hesitated, her eyes aglow at the thought of so much spending money. But it wasn't enough. With a certainty that showed no inclination to waver, she placed her faith in the knowledge that Henry Skipton would have to go even further in his quest for assistance. 'They'll not work for Mrs Sloane,' she announced, completely sure of her ground at this juncture. She was telling no lies. Mrs Hardman would back her up, if necessary, because the cook detested the housekeeper, couldn't bear to be in the same room for more than a minute or two. 'Everybody hates her. Mr Crawley's very polite to her – you know – pretends to respect her and all that. But it's just to keep things running smoothly. All the same, we can tell he doesn't like her. Even Howie can't stand Stonehenge, and Howie's about as sensitive as the fire back. As for the girls, they'll not come near her again, and she'll not have them in the house neither.' Wonderfully satisfied with her oratory, Briony placed her weight on one foot and rested an arm on the opposite hip. She had him where she wanted him. Like a hunter, she contemplated her quarry with near-indifference to its eventual fate.

He inclined his head deep into thoughts that were

obviously too sobering to be viewed straight on. 'Then Mrs Sloane will have to go,' he muttered beneath his breath. After all, the blasted woman had cost him enough good staff over the years. There was only Howie Bennett who seemed suited at the moment, but Howie worked and ate outside the house for most of the time and was, anyway, as daft as a row of cabbages gone to seed . . .

After a moment's pause, Briony asked, 'Pardon, sir?'

He pulled himself together, dragging up his head until it stood in line with the rest of him. 'Nothing. Briony, see to your mistress, please. I'll get someone else tomorrow. And I shall go out myself to find Jenny and Maria.'

Briony studied her white-shod feet. 'Double?' she asked. 'Did you say I'd get twice the wages?'

'Yes.'

'And . . . did I hear right just then? Did you say you were getting rid of Stonehenge?'

He nodded once.

The details were immediately unimportant. Briony crammed the cap low over her brow as if to express solid determination, then swung round and left the room. If he wanted to chuck his money about, it was fine with her. As for Stonehenge – well – he could do what he liked about her and all. It might even be fun to be around when the granite woman got her marching orders. For double the wages, Briony Mulholland would take cold cream, insults, plus the peculiar cruelties of Skipton Hall's resident freaks.

Henry's temper was not improving. He already paid his servants well, because he had known for some time that workers at the Hall had a lot to tolerate. There was Eloise's wickedness, and Carla Sloane's undoubted malice, as well as the usual grind of daily household tasks. He watched Briony as she walked away towards the stairs. For twice the pay, she would no doubt manage the screaming and the missiles without Wellington boots, pit helmet and a policy covering acts of God and female devils.

He set his mouth in a thin, determined line, pushed back his depressed shoulders and made for the kitchen, hesitating just fractionally with his hand on the latch that would open the door of the witch's lair. This was an awful, evil woman, and he approached her not without a degree of fear. Still, it was time to clear the decks, time to get things sorted. There'd been enough threats and blackmail in this house, so perhaps he should grab this chance to call someone's bluff and simply let the worst happen. After all, the worst might even suit him once the scandal had died down.

She squatted in her office, looking for all the world like a malevolent toad waiting for prey to fly past. A small snuff-box lay open on the desk between account books and a statue of the Virgin. She looked up, simultaneously snapping shut the snuff-box, so that the movement of her head seemed to be responsible for the accompanying sharp click. The edges of her nostrils were stained yellow by the fine powder she had recently inhaled. 'Sir?' There was a mocking, almost patronizing ring in her voice.

He stood in the doorway, hands in pockets, elbows angled out towards the jambs. 'Pack your bags,' he said softly. 'I want you out of here within the hour, Mrs Sloane.'

Her face had never shown much colour, but now it seemed to drain itself completely of the parchment sepia that was usually etched deep into the chiselled cracks of her extraordinarily unpleasant features. 'What did you say?'

He noticed that no 'sir' was appended to this question, there was no attempt to mimic respect. 'You heard me. I want you off the premises today. For good, this time. I'm paying for no more of your holidays. It's all over, Mrs Sloane, and you are free to leave.'

She stood up abruptly, the chair falling back against a wall in the cramped space of her study. 'You can't do this,' she snarled, her voice dropping to the level of a whisper. 'As much as you might want to, you can't afford to let me go.'

'Can't I?' The room was so tiny that he could almost feel the sickening breath fanning his cheek. 'This is my house. You are just a servant in it, no more than that. I will not be dictated to by a housekeeper. Do your worst, it is no longer of any consequence to me.' He turned on his heel.

'Hang on.' She was behind him, panting heavily, frantically. 'If I spill the beans, your name will be mud round here.'

'Will it?' He stopped in his tracks so abruptly that she almost shunted into the back of him. 'Not if I act the ignorant fool,' he said. 'Perhaps I knew nothing until today. Perhaps . . .'

'What do you mean?' She stamped past him and stood, hands on ample hips, eyes fixed to his face. 'I told you the night it happened.'

'Yes.' His voice was barely audible. 'You spoke of the accident the night it happened, Mrs Sloane. You described the events to me, then to the police, in great detail. The fact that you gave out two different versions is not my concern. Of course, you told me later that this was all done in an attempt to save my name. But no. You have used your so-called loyalty to blackmail me for years. If you were lying to officers of the law, then you have been accessory after the fact for all these years.'

'So have you!'

'No. I knew nothing until today.'

Her voice rose in panic. 'But I told you, showed you,' she screamed, sounding childishly hysterical. 'The minute I saw, the minute I realized . . .'

'No.' His features remained calm except for a slight flicker in a lower eyelid. 'I have been unaware, completely in the dark until today. Prove something different if you can. I shall not be a character witness at your trial, believe me. You will go down alone for shielding a criminal, for withholding evidence.' He slowed his heart by taking deep draughts of oxygen into lungs that suddenly seemed starved. 'You told me nothing, Sloane. Nothing at all until today. And now, when I dismiss you for being deceitful, you invent this dreadful pack of lies and threaten to make it public.' He nodded. 'A few years ago, I would have heeded your demands, but I have now ceased to care. You cannot blackmail a man who refuses to be afraid. You have no hold over someone who does not value life.'

The upper lip curled above protruding fangs. 'She's a murderer. I watched her with my own eyes, saw her suffocating her own baby. How will it look in the papers when I tell them that Eloise Skipton took a pillow, held it over the face of her struggling daughter, pressed hard, threw her own body across the couch to stop the limbs from flailing—'

'Shut up,' he screamed, a hand coming up to his face as if to defend himself from the verbal onslaught. 'There is no need for you to be so graphic.' He bit his lip, giving himself time to grow calmer. 'But then you always were a cruel bitch. Inflicting suffering is your hobby, your pastime. Well, you can't hurt me. Bring in the police, the press, the king himself, and I shall stick to my story. This will all be new to me, Mrs Sloane. I shall say that I know nothing, that I knew nothing at the time, and that the death is recorded as . . . accidental suffocation.' He seemed ready to choke on the lie, as if he too were running out of air to breathe. 'As for the lady upstairs . . .' He shrugged expressively. 'Will anyone listen to the ramblings of a dying woman? Will anybody prosecute her when she may not even live to the end of a trial? Get your horse saddled, Sloane. I want you off my land inside the hour. If you are still here this afternoon, I shall perhaps arrange another accident. After all, some of my guns could benefit from a wipe with an oily rag.'

Her hanging jaw shut with an audible click. He was right. The bloody man was right – there was nothing she could do. Unless she told the police that she had been threatened for all these years, that Mr Skipton had promised her the sack if she were to speak of that fateful night. Would that work, though? No. The threat of dismissal should not, in the eyes of the law, constitute a good enough reason for shielding a murderer. Almost bursting with frustration, Carla Sloane swept past Mr Skipton and out of the kitchen.

He leaned against the chopping block, a hand pressed into his side, as if he were suffering from a stitch after a long run. Yes, it had been quite a distance, hadn't it? The years with Eloise had dragged, especially since . . . since she had killed their daughter.

His eyes screwed themselves tight against several kinds

of pain. There was the actual headache, a recurring discomfort that had plagued him for some months. Then there were the images, the memories of his beautiful baby daughter, blue eyes, buttercup hair, a smile as sweet as sunrise. She was dead. She would never come back. She was in his head. And above it all, like a heavy raincloud, hung the biggest hurt of all. This final aching agony had auburn hair, grey eyes, multiple sclerosis and a sick dislike of crying babies.

His head was in his hands again. This was happening more and more, this inability to cope, this giving in to raw emotion whenever he was alone. Surely he should be over it by now? Surely it should not be hurting still, so long after he'd supposedly accepted his wife's insanity?

He peeped through his fingers, staring at the quarry-tiled floor. She was not insane. In that fact, in his understanding of that certainty, lay the source of all his grief. His wife, while sound in mind, had taken a pillow and had deliberately snuffed out the light of his life. Now he was biting his knuckles again. Sometimes, when he woke in the mornings, his fingers were bleeding. In the night, during what passed for sleep, he had no control. Sophie died over and over in his dreams. Eloise Skipton had killed his child, had murdered her own daughter because she could not stand the noise and because she could not bear the child's beauty. Eloise had been jealous of the attention lavished on Sophie. So she had killed her.

The kitchen clock croaked and creaked, seeming to match the uneven rhythm of his heart. He tried to dwell on matters mundane. There was just one resident servant now, just Briony. Perhaps he should let her go; perhaps he should finally face the nightmare. Just himself and Eloise, a cleaver, a gun, a spoonful of rat poison. The method was not important, but he wished she were dead. And she would not go into the Skipton crypt, oh no, she would not join Sophie. Eloise would be burnt and scattered to the winds, the evil dispersed, spread out, diluted. He heaved a great sigh of hopelessness. If only she would die. If only she would hurry up, because he had not the courage to do away with her. His attempt to concentrate on practicalities had failed . . .

He was a failure. As a failure, he sank into a chair by the range, his head drooping so far that his chin almost rested on his chest. He should have told the police. He should have said, 'She did it. Mrs Sloane tried to stop her, but the child was already dead . . .' The truth was that he hadn't wanted to believe in his own wife's evil, hadn't been able to encompass her wickedness. By the time he had realized the depth of Eloise's depravity, the lie had gained the credence of folklore, had grown too mature to change. The Skipton babe had perished in its sleep, poor little soul. Heads had shaken, tongues had stumbled over sad words about money not being everything, and Sophie had been relegated to history, one of the shorter strands that occupied the canvas of the cotton barons.

He looked at the fire, watched the thin, yellow flames licking at the bars. What had he felt then, when Sophie had just died? Shock? Grief? Why hadn't he sought to avenge his child? The answer was there, just beneath the surface of his tired mind. He had loved Eloise. It had been a blinding, all-consuming passion, too hot to last. Again, he considered the fire in the grate. It was pale and struggling, but it would endure because it was balanced – just the right amount of fuel, just the right amount of air. His love for Eloise had been unhealthy, red-hot, bound to burn itself out sooner or later. The Skiptons had objected to the match, and this had added spice to the situation. She had been a forbidden fruit, so he had grabbed at her and she had withered after producing just one sweet blossom . . .

His fingers curled into tight knots of fury. He hated her. With every fibre of his being, he loathed the woman he had married. She was sly, selfish, manipulative, envious, destructive. The outer demonstration of abnormality was appropriate, because it illustrated quite graphically the crippled state of the woman's mind. As her limbs twisted, as muscle slackened and grew weak, Eloise Skipton's mind shrivelled into a dry and merciless ganglion of contempt for the world and all its inhabitants. She was, he thought, the very embodiment of bitterness.

Oh Sophie! He gritted his teeth, forcing the scream inward where it echoed in the corridors of consciousness, a silence that was too loud to bear. With a grunt of exasperation, Henry leapt across the room and into the yard, crossing the space between kitchen and dining room until he reached the stables. In the first stall, he stroked a weary hand the length of Barney's flank. Barney the chestnut was not much of a horse to look at, rather low in the belly, a bit thin round the mane, stringy and slack in the neck. But Barney was a character, a horse of wisdom, fortitude and great understanding. His ears pricked themselves to attention as he became aware of the master's mood. There was sadness here. With his warm muzzle, he touched Henry's shoulder.

'I could kill her, I suppose, if I could find courage and energy. She wants to be off anyway – I've heard her screaming the words along the landing. She's always saying that she wants to be dead. Barney?'

The large red-brown head nodded.

'She killed my baby. And I did nothing about it. I suppose I was worried about the scandal, but I don't remember thinking about that sort of thing. She didn't come to the funeral. She stayed in bed, weighed down by what she called grief. By the time I'd taken in what she'd done, by the time I accepted fully the fact that I was living with a murderess, she'd started with this multiple sclerosis. It was too late, Barney, too late to get her paid back.'

The horse whinnied softly. There was no comfort to be offered, so he simply carried on just being a horse, just being something warm and substantial to lean on.

'You know, lad? I couldn't care less what happens now, to any of us. Carla Sloane can get a handbell and a three-cornered hat and she can cry our business all over the Town Hall Square, if she likes. No-one can hurt me any more. I'm numb, numb and cold all over.' He shivered, leaning heavily now against his equine companion. 'So I don't feel strongly enough to actually finish off that so-called wife of mine. Except when I let myself think properly about Sophie, and that's a thing I try to avoid.'

Barney nodded and snuffled against Henry's hair.

There might be a sugar lump in a minute, but sometimes, when Henry was upset, there were no treats. Then Howie came in with a carrot, so Barney got his bonus after all.

'All right, sir?' asked the stable lad. He knew that the master came down to the stables when life was getting on his nerves. 'They're good creatures, aren't they? I always wanted to spend me life with horses, Mr Skipton. Very . . . comfortable, they are. Now, that Jenny girl – her who just got the sack – she used to come down a lot during her time off. I'd watch her when she didn't know I was watching. Not spying, sir, just keeping an eye on me horses. She were particular fond of Barney here. She used to just stand and lean her head against him. It were a lovely sight, that. All that yellow hair laid on Barney's back. She sang to him.'

'Did she?' Henry tugged gently at the horse's mane. People were strange, he thought. It was amazing to hear that a little servant girl had such a fondness for horses. Yet why should it be surprising? Did a person need to be born into money before an affection for expensive animals might be conceived? Ah, what did it matter . . . ?

'It were summat to do with two horses, carters I think they'd be. I heard her telling Barney about them. One of them was called Amber. Jenny's life's ambition is to set Amber and this other one free to run in a field. That's what she told old Barney, any road. Shame she had to get the sack, sir. She brightened the place up a bit.'

With a click of his tongue, Henry Skipton pulled himself together. He had several things to do. For a start, he must get down to the infirmary to check on Dan's progress. And he would have to find Jenny and Maria, persuade them to come back, restore the household to some sort of order. There would be no housekeeper, of course. The maids would have to run the place between them, and Dan could take over the purse strings as soon as he was well enough.

He left the stables and walked round to the front of the house, leaning against a window sill as he watched Carla Sloane staggering down the wide pathway with her possessions in two suitcases and a pair of canvas bags. At that rate, she might reach Bolton by Christmas, but he didn't care. It was difficult to care about anything, difficult to summon up the energy to go to the hospital and speak to Dan.

So, she talked to horses, did she? Was this a smile on his face, was he actually amused by the vagaries of a servant? She wasn't like a servant, was she? No, the head was proud. It was as if she had stepped out of one of those illustrated Victorian books in the library, a gentlewoman fallen on hard times, or a daughter who had ceased to be the apple of her father's eye. She was lovely. And he was going to try to bring her back to that travesty of a woman who festered upstairs like a fast-wrinkling windfall in an autumn orchard. He remembered a certain dark-haired servant, one who had seemed eminently suitable for several weeks. What had happened there? he wondered. Here one minute, gone the next.

But the question was indeed rhetorical. Eloise was capable of what almost amounted to mesmerism, so thoroughly did she take in her intended victims. She wasn't like Carla Sloane, didn't sit there as ugly as sin and twice as hungry, tongue all but flicking in anticipation of the kill. Oh no, Eloise Skipton was too clever for that. She picked up her specimens, stroked them, fondled them into a sense of security, then sent them out to perform whichever tasks might provide some amusement at a given time. Eloise used pretty girls to live, vicariously, the life that had been denied her.

He straightened and strode towards the car. No more of that. He might be tired, he might be feeling slightly self-destructive at the moment. But he had finally found the courage to get rid of the hideous housekeeper, so he might as well go the whole hog and put Eloise in her place at last. For a reason he did not completely understand, a reason he would not even begin to think about, young Jenny Crawley, if she returned to the hall, must be made aware of her mistress's evil web. So why, he asked himself as he steered the Riley through the front gate, why was he going to fetch Jenny? Surely another nursemaid would have been adequate . . . ? He shrugged, his mind too over-worked to deal with any more self-analysis. Like a wild animal, he was simply following where nature led.

Carla Sloane was out on the lane, her huge flat feet surrounded by cases, umbrella and bags. Driving past her felt terrible – it was almost worse than sacking her all over again – but he dared not stop. Out here in the Lancashire countryside, it was almost a law that people with transport would pick up and carry those on foot. But the whole day had, thus far, been outside the general run, so laws no longer applied here. He was a man with several missions, the chief of which was to find himself a reason for continuing alive in a very lonely world.

He turned and she was staring at him, the tiny, wicked eyes seeming to bore through the very fabric of the car, shredding metal, melting glass, making him tremble in the chill, unnatural heat. She was, he thought in that brief moment, a monster, something from a fairy tale, a creature thought up by parents who would will their children to be good by threatening the arrival of the bad fairy.

He steered round the bend, glad that he could no longer see the hideous features. But no, he thought as he gripped the wheel. Eloise was the bad fairy. Carla Sloane was more of a troll, something that was at least honest enough to express its own nastiness. But the lady of Skipton Hall hid her wickedness behind a mask of beauty into which real pain had etched itself, giving the whole visage a pitiable and creditable air. Her persuasive ways had caused the black-haired girl to escape some months ago.

What did she get these girls to do? he wondered as he sat waiting for a flock of sheep to make its silly way across the lane. A man with a stick waved ineffectually, while a small black-and-white dog made some small attempt to control the baa-ing and panicking beasts. Henry knew how they felt. Not the sheep, the man and the dog. Sometimes, no matter how hard you brandished your fist, no matter how loudly you barked a protest, the world continued on its way without even noticing that you were there.

After a long, slow drive, Henry left the car on Derby Street, choosing to walk the last few hundred yards to the house where Mavis Crawley had recently breathed her last taste of poisoned air. Better, he thought, to leave the car away from his destination, since cars always brought out children and comments to be aired in more or less equal proportion at this end of town.

It was so different here, such a marked change from his usual environment. The place was grey, yet unpleasantly colourful at the same time. Faded women stood in doorways, arms folded against chests of various sizes, some scrawny from near-starvation, others plump from over-indulgence in cheap, filling foods. The cheeks of these females were often raspberry-to-beetroot red, scalded into great dry patches whose size was no doubt dictated by the number of years spent so far in a wash house. He could imagine them crowded into the steam-wreathed room, each woman bent double over her tub, every pair of lungs seared by the stenches of carbolic, bleach and starch. But it was their hands that saddened him most, because they looked as if the skin had actually been scraped away. Perhaps the dermis had been eroded, worn out by the rhythmic movement of fabric against ridged washboards, by the constant use of noxious cleaning chemicals.

Not all the women were old. In some eyes there lingered a left-behind trace of hope, a hope that bordered on pain because it was diminishing so fast that only unattainable dreams remained. He hated it here, hated even the colours, because the colours themselves accused him, screamed aloud of want. Red noses, purple hands, hair bleached a premature white by anxiety and poverty.

He strode round the corner into Claughton Street, almost colliding with a gang of children who had collected round Pol O'Gorman's cart. He could have done without this, he thought grimly. A reception committee of such size was not exactly what he had needed. Boys and girls stood in a jagged line, each child clutching a bundle of rags, a pair of very worn boots, a length of piping or some other object that might prove acceptable to Pol.

Pol herself was resplendent as ever in her red-and-white dirndl skirt, nearly white blouse and red ear rings that dangled to her shoulders. About Pol's person there hung a thick air of not-quite-cleanness, the smell of discarded clothing, rotting leather and cheap perfume. An Irish woman of indeterminate age, she plied her trades in the streets of Daubhill during the hours of daylight, then on Bradshawgate after sunset. Her evening job paid best, as some of her regular gentlemen were quite free with their wallets, but she liked kiddies, so she carried on with the rag-and-bone just to be neighbourly and because it paid the bills. She also had an affection for her pony, a love she kept well hidden beneath screams of 'Is that the best you can do or did you think we were at a funeral?' and 'With the cost of hay going up I'll be rid of you unless you shape.' Pol's pony lived in the lap of luxury, stabled in a meadow at the back of Blackburn Road in the company of some very superior horseflesh. She believed in the best of everything did Pol, and her faith showed in the cream of her nearly clean skin, in the gloss of her tangled hair. 'Would ye be wanting a donkey stone, sir?' she asked coquettishly, stepping without thought into her evening role.

'No, thank you. I'm looking for Jenny Crawley.' In spite of depression, Henry had to fight a smile. Pol was someone he had glimpsed only from a distance in the past, but his workforce thought she was a 'scream' because she clung so tenaciously to her accent. Pol had not seen Ireland since she was a small child, and the resulting mix of Irish and Lancashire speech caused much glee.

A brown-haired child with a runny nose giggled and dragged a filthy sleeve across the mucus-covered upper lip. 'Her's potty,' he declared to no-one in particular. 'And her Auntie Mave were mad and all. Done herself in with the gas, she did.'

Henry addressed Pol, who was the only other adult at the scene. 'Do you know which is the Crawley house?'

Pol pointed a jangling, braceleted arm. 'But they'll not be in there, I'm thinking. The two girls would be down now at the hospital looking to see did Mr Crawley get any better.' Actually, she said 'bether' rather than 'better', tossing the rich, black mane as she spoke.

'Spinning Jenny's bloody mental,' insisted the brown-haired urchin. 'It's a daft house, is that, belongs to Creepy Crawley.'

Henry grabbed the unsavoury boy by a greasy shoulder. 'What do you mean?' he asked evenly.

The lad shrugged and struggled against restraint, but the grip on his upper arm was akin to iron. 'Auntie Mavis did ghosts. She used to pay me to rattle chains up in the loft, and that Jenny girl made smoke come through the ceilings. She were mad. They were both mad. Me dad says Mavis Crawley had a few spots missing off her dice, and their Jenny's stupid too.'

Henry released the filthy child, his eyes resting on the almost-Irish whore who faced him with her head thrown back and a hand resting on each wide, round hip. She was like an extension of her cart – gaudy, exciting and rather smelly. The well-fed pony sulked between the shafts, seeming to bear no relationship to the rest of the picture, which was vibrant with balloons, spinning tops, and even the odd flash of gold where small carp swam in buckets waiting to be swapped for old clothing or ironmongery. She smiled seductively, revealing teeth that were strong, white and even. 'The child's right in his own way, sure enough. Mavis Crawley told the future and communicated with the past, the dead past and—'

'I know that. Her brother is my . . . friend. No matter. I shall go to the hospital and find the girls myself.'

'Girls, is it?' Lustrous eyes swept the length of his body.

He swallowed, suddenly nervous, but not knowing why. 'Servants of mine,' he said slowly.

'Ah.' The children backed off as she walked round Henry in a large circle, her movements ritualistic, as if she were part of some pagan festival of dance. 'Now I can place you. Yes, I thought I recognized your clock,' she said, her tone becoming harsh. 'You'll be Skipton, then, the mill boss.'

'Yes.'

She stopped in her tracks, neck arching like the throat of a snake just before it strikes its prey. With her nose tilted skyward, she coughed, then straightened before sending a large glob of saliva across the space between them. The missile caught the edge of Henry's left boot, but he did not flinch. Some instinct told him not to move, and he felt sure that this same instinct had kept many a man alive while in the presence of an offended wild animal.

'Ye're the scum of the earth,' she hissed, her mouth contorted by emotion. 'She was a good woman, my mammy, never a cross word for anyone, always a smile on her lips. But the smile wasn't the only thing on her gob, was it? Naw, there was her lifeblood too. Years she stood in yonder sheds, cleaning up after the carders had broke the bales. And what did she get for it? Lungs filled by dust, that was her reward. Didn't she finish up with the consumption and breathing so painful that the whole street heard it and wondered how did she carry on?' She laughed, but the sound held no humour. 'And for that we left the old country? Did we turn our backs on Mayo just to die in the graveyard you call England?'

'I . . .' He raised his arms, looked at the woman's bitter frown, then at the sea of young faces that formed the audience. His arms dropped uselessly to his sides. What could he say? Should he tell her to go back across the water if she didn't like it here? No, that would simply stoke her anger to further excess. And she spoke a kind of truth, didn't she? Cotton killed them, killed them by the dozen every year. But then starvation would have been just as cruel, slow and effective.

He was sorry, but he could not say so. He was sorry for the mill workers, the dirty children, the women with their dry, work-battered faces and twisted hands. He was sorry for Sophie who had not lived, who had never been given the chance to complain or weep about the unfairness of existence. He was sorry for himself, for his own unbearable and hopeless loneliness. Yet he would not let this almost-Irish creature see any of it, would not let her penetrate an armour whose chinks he fought daily to disguise. He turned on his heel, but she pursued him.

'Skipton!' She ran round him, stopping in front of him with her arms held wide to bar his progress. 'Was the love-child yours? Did you do that too? Did you ruin poor Oonagh before tossing her out into the cold—?'

'No,' he snapped as soon as he had made his way through the woman's train of thought. 'Jenny is not my daughter.' Did people really believe that she was? he wondered for a moment or two. 'She was adopted by my butler and his sister – the lady who recently died here. But Jenny Crawley is no relation of mine, Mrs . . . er . . . ?'

'Well now, isn't this all very lah-de-dah?' She wagged her head from side to side, her voice making a poor stab at imitating proper English. 'We never talk of Oonagh,' she said now, her tone dropping to a whisper. 'Us in the Irish community – we keep our business out of the Murphys' doings. A bad lot, Oonagh's brothers. If they'd thought for one minute that you were the father, they'd have had you separated from your inner tubes. She disappeared. Just went like that.' Long fingers snapped then waved in the air. 'They looked for her, the three boys. Even the mother got down off her broomstick to search for Oonagh. But no trace was ever found. Of course, they cared nought for Oonagh's child. A fatherless brat is not a favoured being in our part of the world.' She fell silent, nodding to herself as if nursing many distant memories.

He cleared his throat. 'What has all this to do with me, Mrs . . . ?' The damned woman had still not said her full name.

'O'Gorman,' she snapped, pulling herself out of the reverie. 'And I'm Miss O'Gorman, for I didn't yet find a man good enough. All I'm saying is that ill-luck plagues all who pass your doors, whether it's up at your house or down at the mills. Me own mammy passed away with the consumption, then Oonagh disappeared. Now there's Dan Crawley in hospital with the pneumonia, and poor Jenny is penniless by all accounts. Did it never occur to you that you might carry some kind of curse?'

He gasped, almost biting on his tongue. Perhaps there was a curse and perhaps little Sophie's death had been a part of it. No, this was fanciful rubbish, brought on, no doubt, by the ramblings of the Irish tinker. 'You talk a lot of nonsense,' he said mildly. 'Your head is like your cart – laden with scrap and junk.'

She pushed out her not inconsiderable chest, causing the buttons to strain on the front of her cheap, greyish-white blouse. 'I am worth a fortune, Mr Skipton,' she pronounced, laying great emphasis on the 'misther'. 'There's money in muck, and you should know that, for you murder folk every day with your filth, then stick the money in the bank. But I'm a wealthy enough woman, sir.' Again, a heavy layer of sarcastic mock-respect was laid on the title. 'One day, I'll get you back for what you did to my mammy.'

The children were becoming restless. Cries of 'I want a goldfish' and 'Me mam's waiting for a donkey stone' reached the ears of the two adults. 'Threats mean nothing to me,' he said softly. 'Because, you see, I have very little to lose.' He cursed himself inwardly, knowing full well that he should bare no part of his soul to this woman.

She drew a hand across her upper lip. ''Tis a sad man ye are, Henry Skipton.' Her voice, mellowing now, bore no obvious resemblance to the earlier nerve-jangling scream she had used. 'And you with the world at your feet now. Would it be presumptuous of me to ask why you are so miserable?' The word 'presumptuous' carried great weight, as if she could not help allowing mockery to encroach each time she spoke. 'For I'm sure that the tale of me mammy's death would not bring you so low in spirit.'

He shrugged and gave her a look that was meant to be withering. 'If I'm sad, that's my concern. I'm not here to chat to you. I came to reinstate two young girls who were dismissed unfairly from my household. As you cannot properly locate them for me, I can think of no reason why I should continue this discussion.' He marched across the street, knocked on Jenny's door and waited. When no reply came, he strode off towards Derby Street, casting not one single glance in Pol's direction.

But her voice followed him. 'The grief will only go when you pass those mills on, Henry Skipton. You lost a child, your only child, and many of us have lost people because of you. We know loss. You know loss. Get rid of the cotton . . .'

Out of reach and sight at last, he leaned against a wall. Rage bubbled just beneath the surface of his mind, a blind anger caused by the fact that she had accused him of being Jenny's father. While mill bosses were accustomed to being denounced for having 'bits on the side', he wanted no-one to think that he had fathered this particular child.

Why he felt so strongly he did not know, but the idea of people believing that he was Jenny Crawley's father seemed to disturb him unnecessarily. Yes, he remembered Oonagh, yes, he had known her, though never in the biblical sense. The sweet, beautiful Jenny was somebody else's daughter, and he was glad about that.

He lurched forward, a hand to his chest. Why was he glad? Oh no, it couldn't be that he was interested in her! Surely not! But she stood before him, as if her image had been indelibly printed on the insides of his eyelids. There was a cheap work frock of blue-and-white cotton, then this changed to a black dress, a garland of lace crowning thick coils of bright, blonde hair, a silly apron round a slender waist. Something moved in a hand; he thought it might be a duster. This was stupid. He was old enough to be her father, he was a married man, she was a servant.

He marched towards the main road, head down as if to squash the disobedient thoughts that chased each other through his crazy brain. If he were infatuated, if he were drawn to a woman's physical charms, then he would not be so unhappy, so beset by hopelessness. Wouldn't he be positive, at least imaginative about the possibilities? No, he was not, could not be drawn to the little servant girl. Perhaps she might be something of a daughter figure, someone who needed guidance or protection. That was the most she could ever be, a poor substitute for the child he had lost.

But she was extremely beautiful, lovelier than any of the others who had caught his eye and, occasionally, his attention through recent wifeless years. He cursed himself inwardly and tried to thrust the whole matter to the back of his mind. But the back of his mind was full, tenanted by unpleasant memories, and the vision of Jenny, as if refusing to take up residence in unsavoury company, continued to pop in and out of immediate consciousness.

He steered towards the town. It was impossible, he told himself severely, to have any meaningful affection for a girl he had spoken to just two or three times. He knew nothing of her except that she was called Jenny Crawley and that she was extremely pleasing to the eye. Eloise had been beautiful, hadn't she? How idiotic it was for a man of forty to allow his head to be turned once more by prettiness. After all, he had no idea of Jenny's character. She might be another whited sepulchre, magnificent on the outside, yet inhabited by deep piles of rot and filth.

But a smile played on the corners of his downturned mouth as he pulled into the infirmary grounds. She loved horses, she talked to horses. Right from childhood, he had recognized that these great beasts had potential for almost limitless friendship and loyalty. Eloise had disliked them, had found them noisy, smelly and hairy. But Dan Crawley's adopted niece clearly shared Henry's faith in the equine world. Horses needed no comprehension of English, no lessons in psychology. They simply understood the human condition, were born knowing man's frailties and needs. There was nothing like a horse for leaning on, complaining to, arguing with.

He got out of the car. She knew all that, the girl with the corn-coloured hair and the eyes like dew-washed forget-me-nots. She had found it in the dray horses and in Barney, who was a singularly unimpressive animal except for his listening skills.

Henry was wasting his time and, as if to underline this fact, he glanced at the clock tower. Even if and when Eloise died, a girl as pretty as Jenny Crawley would never look at a middle-aged man. And a middle-aged man with three mills and no intention of making a second marriage should not pursue a serving girl. He tut-tutted under his breath. What had Eloise been? A lady, a daughter of the nobility? No. She had been a moneyed wench from parents who had made their fortune in fish and chips. What was the difference, then, between Eloise (really Lois) Robinson and Jenny Crawley? A few pounds in the bloody bank?

Angrily, he pushed open the front door of the infirmary. What would people think if he were to have a liaison with Jenny? What the hell did he care what people thought? What had they thought when Sophie had died, when he had been consumed by a grief too large to express? Had they believed him to be hard and uncaring? And did it matter?

He straightened his shoulders. The murdering bitch could not last forever. This time, Henry Skipton, soon to be widower of this parish, might even start pleasing himself for a change. Should he aim to deflower a servant girl, a beautiful woman who, if she could not love him, might at least be sufficiently grateful to allow him a child? In spite of firm resolution, his shoulders drooped again, almost of their own accord. She would not have him. With a clarity that was blindingly sudden, he stared steadily down a seemingly endless hospital corridor and into a future that was empty and totally without point.

And in that moment, he knew that he was desperately infatuated with Jennifer Crawley, foundling, cotton spinner, housemaid, nursemaid, maid of great gentleness and beauty. There was, he thought as he made his way towards Men's Medical, no intelligence in feelings, certainly little sense in looking for love from someone like Jenny. She was not suitable, while he was just a miserable, confused and rather stupid man who had matured in body, but not in mind. Was he looking for a reason in life, a raft to cling to, a daughter who would make the years to come bearable?

No, he told himself firmly. He was not seeking a daughter. Perhaps he merely sought diversion, an affair to fill his time, a joyous coupling with a beautiful young woman. The girl was not suitable for marriage to him, and he had been foolish to consider it, however briefly. Nor was she the right candidate for a brief fling. Deflowering virgins was not, had never been, his pastime. He would have to forget her.

He turned as if to leave the hospital, but his feet were disobedient. Feeling more than foolish, he swivelled on the spot like base metal responding to magnetism. He was, he thought, out of control. With his mind a blank, he walked up the corridor to visit a sick butler.

Excitement seemed to bubble in the air above the two girls' heads; they were obviously discussing something of great interest and import. He watched the crowning glories merge as secrets were shared, a blonde head leaning

145

against a carrotty crop of amazingly fierce colour, while hands raised themselves to lips as guards against laughter that would have been unseemly in a hospital.

Henry strode with determination towards the pair of girls who sat in wooden chairs under a poster about consumption and the importance of sputum disposal. He cleared his own ominously clogged throat, considering irrelevantly and very briefly Pol's mother who had died of consumption, and remembering Pol herself, who disposed of her own saliva on other folks' boots. Lately, his thinking had displayed a tendency to flutter about rather aimlessly, and it settled now like a disturbed and ready-to-jump butterfly halfway between the word 'consumption' and a crude drawing of a sputum mug. 'May I . . . er . . . ?' he began ineptly.

Maria bounced to her feet. 'Ooh, Mr Skipton. Do you want to sit down?'

She offered him her chair, and he shook his head miserably. At home, it would have been Maria's place to find him a chair. Here, on the outside, he was the gentleman, so she must keep the seat. He was sick of everything, especially of the laws of what was generally called 'polite society'. 'How's Dan?' he asked, trying to keep the situation on a normal and even keel. Though he could not look at the pretty one . . .

'They're messing about with him now,' sighed Maria, dropping back into the hard seat. 'Can't have visitors, 'cos they're thumping him on the chest and chucking him round like a bag of spuds. That means he's ready for home. You can tell when you're getting better, 'cos they do their best to make you ill. Bloody doctors,' she finished somewhat breathlessly.

He tried again to look at Jenny, but his eyes seemed to stick somewhere round her neckline. She was wearing a navy scarf with a little gilt pin fastened to one side. The pin was in the shape of an alligator and it displayed a single eye of gleaming red glass. 'Is he coming back to Skipton Hall?' he asked. Her throat was creamy-white, young, healthy.

'Yes, I think so.' The voice emerged low and quite well

146

modulated, though the accent was broad. 'Mind, he'll need to rest a while before doing a full day.'

'Yes.' He pretended to take an even closer interest in the depressing poster. 'Are you coming back to work, Jenny? And you, Maria?'

Maria's jaw stuck at half-mast for a moment, then she seemed to snap herself to life with a shake of her vivid head. 'I wouldn't come back and work for that woman for all the pans of scouse in Liverpool, sir. I'm sorry, but she's rotten all through. And it's that Briony's fault as well—'

'I know,' he said, thereby damming just temporarily Maria's powerful flood.

'You know?' The Liverpool girl's hackles were clearly rising. 'You know what old Stonehenge did to Jenny?'

'Yes.' He leaned against the wall, his back turned against the list of instructions on what to burn and what to fumigate. 'It wasn't Briony's fault. She's just a girl, not much older than the two of you.'

Jenny rose to her feet and came to stand in front of him, her clear eyes searching his face. 'Did you believe that I was a thief?'

He inhaled slowly, allowing the breath to escape gradually from between slightly parted lips before answering. 'I didn't even know why you had been fired. Then Briony confessed her part.'

Jenny nodded. 'Short-staffed, are you?'

At last, he looked at her. There was no mockery, no malice in her expression. 'Yes, we're short,' he answered. 'Especially since I fired Mrs Sloane this morning.'

Maria dashed to Jenny's side. 'But that means . . . that means there's only Briony and the dailies.' Her quick, pale eyes flitted from Jenny to the master. 'You got rid of Stonehenge? And there was me thinking she was rooted. You actually sacked the dragon?'

'Yes.'

Maria grinned impishly. 'Ooh, I wish I'd seen that. I'd pay balcony prices to look at her face now. But hey – Briony won't like being stuck with the missus. And the missus won't let a daily into her room. What the hell are you going to do?' Somewhat tardily, she added a quiet 'sir' to the impertinent question.

His arms lifted themselves, then dropped limply to his sides. 'I'm asking the two of you to come back to work at the Hall for double wages.' There followed a small silence that was interrupted by a distant clatter of metal from the ward where some poor nurse was probably doing a bedpan round.

Maria, unladylike as ever, whistled under her breath. 'We've plans,' she said. 'I've a brother coming over from Liverpool to see if we can start our own business, me and him and Jenny.'

'I see.' He pulled at his heavily starched shirt collar. 'What sort of business?'

'Pies and stuff,' said Jenny quickly. She didn't understand why, but she still needed Maria's printing to be a secret. 'We're keeping Auntie Mavis's house on, and we'll live there.'

He met her gentle gaze. 'The brother too?'

'I suppose so.'

'Won't you be somewhat . . . crowded?'

'We'll manage,' interspersed Maria. 'We're used to managing, Mr Skipton.'

Yes, they were used to managing, weren't they? So young, yet so capable. It was almost as if they were senior to him, because they certainly held the upper hand in this particular situation. He coughed behind a tan-coloured hand. Servants were easy to come by – he could perhaps get Briony to do some poaching. The girl could probably tempt some help away from one of the other large houses. But he didn't want . . . or rather he wanted . . .

Heat coursed into his face, and he prayed that it did not show. 'Jenny,' he began, carefully forcing a false steadiness into his voice. 'Won't you come back and look after my . . . Mrs Skipton?' His flesh crawled at the thought of Eloise getting her claws into this lovely child, yet he could think of no other possible tack to take. 'You're needed,' he said lamely, then added, 'As I said earlier the wages will be doubled.'

Maria pulled at Jenny's sleeve. 'Remember our plans,' she mumbled indistinctly.

Jenny studied Henry Skipton. He looked a bit worn out, as if he'd missed a few nights' sleep. Money wasn't everything, then. He was likely in a pickle, what with Uncle Dan being ill and just one maid left to do the lot. A sensation akin to pity invaded her breast, and she tried to squash it, because it wasn't her place to feel pity for someone as rich and important as Henry Skipton. 'We'll have to think about it,' she said quietly. 'We need to talk a few things over, me and Maria, what with Auntie Mavis's house and everything to sort out.' She dragged her arm away from Maria's indelicate nudging. 'I shall come up tomorrow, Mr Skipton, after I've made me mind up. Whatever gets decided, you'll be the first to know.'

'The third,' said Maria acidly. 'Might even be the fourth if our Anthony turns up.' She had no intention of being anyone's servant ever again, and the idea of her friend even considering the possibility of returning to Skipton Hall was appalling.

He shook Jenny's cool hand. 'Until tomorrow, then. And please give my regards to Dan.'

'Yes.' She watched him as he walked away, his shoulders not quite so firm as usual. 'I feel sorry for him, Maria.'

'You what?' Maria took a swipe at her own face, batting the fringe from her eyes until it stood to attention like a very hot private on parade. 'There's no need to feel sorry for him, Jen. He's got the sort of money you and I can only dream about.'

Jenny nodded. 'Aye, and happen money's not everything, Maria. I was just thinking that, when he was stood here talking to us. The man's miserable. And he's sacked Stonehenge, so things can't be as bad as what they were up yonder. Happen I'll go back just for a while, see him through this bad spell. You can keep the rentbook in my name for when I want to come back. With double wages, I can pay the rent, give you a bit extra towards the business, help you get started. Be practical. You're always telling me to be practical. A few bob a week will be more use than a couple of dozen potato pies that might not sell.' She paused, fidgeted with her scarf. 'And to be honest . . .' Shyness overtook her and stole the rest of this sentence.

Maria tightened her thin lips before asking, 'Well? Can't you finish what you started if you're being honest?'

Jenny swallowed. 'There'll be Anthony living at number seventeen, and there's only two bedrooms.'

'We'll share, you and me.' The mouth remained stubborn.

'Aye and what will the neighbours think if I'm there? It's all right for you, you're his sister, but—'

'Shut up,' spat Maria furiously. 'Who cares what who thinks? He's nothing like me except for his hair, we don't even look as if we come from the same tribe, let alone the same family. So your neighbours might think I'm living over the brush, but I don't care.'

'Well I do. I've had enough of being talked about, everybody whispering about Auntie Mavis's seances, everybody blaming me just for living with her.' She pushed back her shoulders and faced Maria squarely. 'It's nice that you're so brave and strong and cheerful, Maria. I'm glad you haven't had a life like mine. But stop pushing me, stop expecting me to change in the twinkling of an eye. I'm used to doing what folk tell me to do, teachers, bosses, Auntie, Stonehenge. If I listen to you, you'll be another one I've obeyed, won't you?'

Maria breathed deeply, as if seeking patience. 'I want you to be your own self, Jen.'

'But I don't know who I am yet. Eighteen years I've spent waiting for somebody to say "jump", then jumping like a circus dog just to keep the peace. Stonehenge has gone, so I reckon I can do me bit of growing up at Skipton Hall. Then, when I've done it, I can come back down and help with the business.'

'That,' said Maria slowly through tightening lips, 'is a load of tripe and onion. Daft bloody Lois'll have you dancing through hoops, mark my words.'

'I can manage her.'

'Then you'll be the first. There's been queer goings on with her and nursemaids. They all run away in the end. Some of them don't even bother to pack their clothes, they just hop it in the nightie with a coat on top. There was the one with the—'

'Black hair,' interrupted Jenny, quite sharply. She rubbed a hand across her mouth, nodding for several seconds as she considered the pros and cons. 'I'm going back. I'm needed.'

'You've always been blinking well needed. Your auntie, the boss at the mill, now Mr Skipton—'

'And you,' said Jenny quickly.

Maria's jaw fell, but formed no words.

'You need my house, and you're welcome to it. You think you need me to help with the business, and that's why you don't want me to go back into service—'

'Rubbish,' snapped Maria. 'I just thought—'

'You thought you'd be the one telling me what to do for a change. Stop it. I'm going to see if Uncle Dan's ready for us now.' She turned on her heel and made for the ward door.

Maria followed slowly. This was one of the few times she'd found Jenny to be firm, even argumentative. Ah well, perhaps Jenny should have some rope for a while – as long as she didn't wind it round her neck. She'd be back and the business would happen, Maria felt sure of that.

Through a window, Henry Skipton watched the two girls until they disappeared into the ward. He was stupid, he told himself firmly. He was not in love with anybody. His feelings for Jenny were no more than a reminder of the onset of old age and possible dementia. All the same, he looked forward to tomorrow. She would come. It was easy to see that she was a woman of her word. He would trim his whiskers tonight . . .

Chapter Six

POL O'GORMAN NURSED AN ALMOST INEXPLICABLE TENDER spot for anybody who seemed 'different'. She was known far and wide for her generosity to street urchins whom she would feed and clothe somewhat haphazardly, taking them into her heart and into her pleasant, if rather untidy house where hollow bellies would be filled with Irish stew, jam butties, or whatever turned up in the depths of her meatsafe.

Clothes and footwear were distributed in the same careless fashion, and some strange sights could be glimpsed emerging from her back gate, little girls in old frocks that almost swept the floor behind them, boys with odd boots and trousers whose waistbands rested just below armpits. But she loved children, so she lavished on these wandering souls all the generosity in her lonely and childless breast.

Her affection for the unusual was not confined solely to the young. Although she had never taken the trouble to analyse her own attitude, Pol probably empathized strongly with all folk who were outside the so-called normal mould. Somewhere, in the recesses of her cluttered mentality, she no doubt kept a faded memory of a mother entering England well before the turn of the century, ill clad, ill shod and with a thin female bastard clinging fiercely to her skirts.

It was Pol's warm if somewhat volatile nature that caused her to trot the cart twice past the tramsheds on that balmy evening in June 1920. She was late, and Franklyn Finnegan's weighing-in yard would be closing its gates soon, but the strange figure seated on the wall outside the tramshed acted like a magnet, drawing the laden cart twice round the block.

With her second tour completed, the gaudy tinker stopped her pony, jumping down to separate boots from rags and to push a few treasures into a special box labelled 'KEEP FOR CHILDREN'. The person sitting on the low wall did not move, even when Pol cast a meaningful stare in its direction. Never in all her life had the rag-and-bone woman seen anything quite like this. It was female – that was obvious from the clothes, which were plain and grey, but good. Cases and bags were stored against a gatepost, giving Pol the distinct impression that the well-fed and possibly well-bred woman was accompanied by most, if not all of her worldly possessions. The word 'ugly' did not serve in this instance, because it did not adequately describe the monstrous face. There was a terrible stillness about the woman's frame, and such immobility caused Pol to shiver as she wondered whether a human heart could bear to beat in such an ill-conceived container.

Drawing about her shoulders a shawl made from colourful squares of crocheted wool, Pol tossed back the free-flowing mane of black hair before approaching the wall. She was neither nervous nor shy by nature, yet her stomach lurched against her ribs, as if it were trying to digest the powerful cocktail of fascination and sympathy that was so heavily laced with revulsion.

'Were ye looking for a tram?' Pol's voice emerged high from a throat constricted by pity and something akin to fear. She coughed. 'These vehicles are all put away now and they'll not run again till morning. There's some still about, but fewer at this hour with not so many workers on the move.' She shivered slightly, pulling the shawl close to her throat. 'A chill in the air,' she muttered vaguely while her skin crawled. Pol's mammy had used to say that a sudden shiver meant that someone was walking over a grave, usually the grave of the one who quaked.

The head turned with a slowness that looked painful. 'I

am just getting my breath, thank you. When I'm rested, I'll find a hotel room for the night.' Tiny, cold eyes swept up over the tall, work-stained female. 'There is no need for you to concern yourself on my behalf. I shall be ready to move on shortly.'

Pol studied the pile of cases. 'They look heavy, sure enough. Would you like me to throw them on the cart, save you carrying them?' Making herself bold, she stared full into the colourless face, taking in the craggy forehead that almost concealed the eyes, then allowing her gaze to follow the wandering path of gristle that formed a nose, finally glancing at a row of jutting and splayed teeth. A bubble of anger rose in Pol's throat, but she squashed it quickly. Sinner though she was, she still refused to be angry with God, who was this creature's Maker. She smiled grimly, hoping to conceal the shock brought on by close proximity to such total and unrelieved misfortune.

'You're Irish.' For once, the words were spoken in a tone that fell short of the accusatory.

Pol tried to broaden her grin, though it remained stiff on her face, as if it had been glued there. 'As a matter of fact, I've not seen the old country since I was knee-high to a leprechaun. But me mammy talked this way and I've kept it on. Mind, you'll hear a trace of Lancashire in me from time to time, even though I do try to sound like a real Mayo girl. I suppose it's a form of pride, as if I'm saying to people, "I'm proud of me beginnings."' As her courage returned, she sidled closer. 'Did ye lose your place?'

'I beg your pardon?'

'Your house – has the landlord turned you out? Could ye not manage the rent?'

Carla Sloane's tongue snaked out from behind the ill-formed teeth, running its thirsty edge across the dry lower lip. She felt no grief, but a dull anger thudded like a drum in her temple. Not only had she been cast from the Skiptons' door, but her last living relative had refused to take her in. Maude Unsworth, who had for years provided bed and board for her sister during brief holidays, was unwilling to offer shelter on a more permanent basis. Being unloved and unlovable had become the norm, but homelessness was another matter altogether. 'I resigned my post,' she finally replied. 'It . . . it ceased to be suitable.'

'And where was that?'

The stiff shoulders moved in a shrug that almost failed to happen. What did the pseudo-Irish tinker matter? There was nothing to be lost, in this instance, by telling the almost-truth. And the thirst was becoming unbearable, so any offer of help would be welcome at such a juncture. 'Skipton Hall,' she snapped, her tongue tripping over the 'Skipton'. She could scarcely say the name now without the hatred rising like thick bile in her gullet.

'Bastard,' whispered Pol beneath her breath, then she lifted her head before asking, 'What position did you hold?'

'Housekeeper.'

Pol settled herself on the wall next to the unfortunate woman. It was a shame, it really was. To be born with a face that would frighten the devil himself was one thing, but to finish up at the mercy of this particular cotton baron was something else altogether. 'I saw him just the other day.' Her tone was confidential and quiet. 'And I told him there and then in front of the whole street what I thought of him and his spinning machinery.'

Pol breathed a deep and mournful sigh. 'For he killed me mammy. Well, to be truthful, 'twas his father before him that did for her, but I'm a great believer in the sins of the fathers being the responsibility of those who follow. The consumption,' she muttered, her voice suitably grave. 'The poor woman died strangulated and smothercated by her own blood.' With due reverence to her mother's memory, Pol O'Gorman made the sign of the cross. 'May she rest with all the saints in peace.'

Carla Sloane quickly squashed the feeling that she had found not a friend, but someone with whom she might share a common interest. Too often in her youth she had sought affection, even tolerance, but now she knew better. People might, on occasion, be useful, but they would never like her. She sat and stared across the road, wondering how she might use this common collector of rubbish. 'You don't have much time for Mr Skipton, then?' she asked, her voice as lightweight and uncaring as she could manage.

'Thinks only of himself,' came the swift response. 'When I look back, it was your resignation that caused our meeting, for he was searching for Jenny Crawley, looking to get her back into service at the hall. It was in her street I met him, but I filled his ears with fleas before I'd done.'

'He's taking her back, then?' No emotion showed in the flat, evenly spaced words.

'I believe so. He said something about they'd been unfairly dismissed. Who's the other one? I'm sure he said there were two of them.'

'Maria Hesketh, a cheeky young imp from Liverpool, the sort who's ready with the quick answers. So they're to be reinstated? I always said that Henry Skipton had lost the sense he was born with.' She tutted loudly, deciding that a degree of sympathy could perhaps be dragged from the rag-and-bone woman. After all, it was rather late in the day to try to save face, and any port would be appreciated in a storm of this severity.

Deliberately cooling her anger now, the housekeeper said, 'I don't know what to do.' Simplicity would be best at present, for this brightly garbed and rather unclean female was probably not overendowed with brains. 'I've no reference from him,' she stated baldly. 'Because, like yourself, I've little time for him and I said so. Plain speaking does not encourage the writing of good character references.'

Pol clapped a grimy hand on her companion's rigid shoulder. 'Look, you come along with me, walk beside the cart.' The miserable and spoilt pony had enough to pull without this solid female climbing aboard. 'It would not do for a lady of your position to ride alongside me,' she gushed. 'But I'll carry your luggage. We can go to my house and have a nice bite to eat, then we'll decide what are we to do about your trouble.'

'I have no wish to inconvenience you.' This was said stiffly in order to disguise the fact that Carla Sloane would have gladly inconvenienced anybody for a sandwich, a cup of tea and a soft cushion to sit on.

'It's no bother at all. I can weigh this in tomorrow.' She waved a hand towards the pile of debris on the cart. 'And

Amos can spend the night in the back yard shed, no need to take him to his stable.' Without waiting for a response, Pol began to gather the cases together. When they were placed on the cart, she turned to find the woman standing behind her. 'I'm Pol O'Gorman,' she said almost defiantly. 'Me reputation is not good, but I've a heart of gold when it comes to misfortune and injustice.'

'Carla Sloane. I'm criticized for doing a good job, for making sure his house ran smoothly. Of course, like a lot of men, he prefers his women young.' With these formal introductions completed, she stepped back to the middle of the pavement.

Pol climbed on to her seat at the front of the cart, urging the pony onward with a click of her tongue and the gentle stroke of a leather rein. Carla Sloane walked along the flags, wondering vaguely what people might think if they saw her in the company of a tinker. But her feet were sore, her back ached, and the complaints of her empty stomach were becoming audible. For a chair, a drink and some bread and cheese, she might well have considered making this journey in fancy dress and to the accompaniment of a full brass band with morris dancers.

'Do you reckon she might be his?' asked Pol.

'I beg your pardon?'

Pol flicked a rein and shouted loudly, 'I'll be getting a handcart and you'll be for the glueworks, Amos. Can ye not pick up the feet a little?' She turned to glance at her companion. 'Jenny Crawley. I never did go much on that tale, meself. Don't you think Dan Crawley might have been doing his young master a favour when he took the child to his sister's house? She was a pretty lass, was Oonagh Murphy.'

'Well, I—'

'And now Henry Skipton is walking the streets looking to find his butler's adopted niece. Can you see the sense in all of that, now? Wouldn't it seem strange that Henry Skipton should be wasting his time on the likes of her? Unless she's very special, if you take my meaning. Did ye need to stop for a while?' she asked as the woman's pace slowed.

'I don't think so.'

Pol pulled gently on the rein until the pony shambled to a halt. 'Are ye meaning that ye don't need a rest, or that Henry Skipton isn't father to Oonagh Murphy's daughter?'

Carla Sloane tried to purse her lips, though the resulting grimace, caused by the crowded incisors, did nothing to improve her gargoyle face. 'He's desperate for a child, someone to inherit his wealth,' she said. Her large head turned its unblinking stare on Pol. 'Perhaps we can find him one,' she muttered. 'If the town got to hear about a bastard daughter . . .'

Pol giggled. 'And who better than meself to pass on such a rumour? Sure, I'm out and about every day and some evenings too.' She pushed out her bosom and patted it as if it were a pet dog or cat. 'The men listen to old Pol, Carla. I get many a drink bought for me, and I listen to endless lists of troubles once folk climb feet first into their cups.'

The cold eyes blinked just once. Yes, this woman was a whore, and who was more satisfactorily placed than a streetwoman when it came to the passing on of opinion? Opinion which could become rumour, rumour which might gather sufficient weight to become doctrine? That would damage Skipton, certainly. She swallowed, causing pain to her rusty throat. Some instinct told her that Jenny Crawley was not Skipton's daughter, yet she refused to enlighten Pol O'Gorman. It was better to say nothing and to convey, by the quality of her silence, a level of tacit agreement.

After travelling a distance that seemed endless to the pedestrian, they reached Pol's house. It was an end-of-terrace with rounded bays overlooking the road and a tiny patch of grass at the front. This midget garden was beautifully kept with its precise and verdant square surrounded by marigolds, white alyssum and royal blue lobelia. Pol handed a doorkey to her companion. 'Bring yourself into the house now, get the kettle on and your whistle wetted. There's brandy and whisky in the decanters and some sweet sherry near the stove in the kitchen if you've a mind for something stronger than tea. I'll just take this young feller into the yard.'

Carla Sloane opened Pol's front door and stepped into a wide hall. The stairs were to the left, on the outside wall of the house, and their banisters gleamed with varnish and polish. A good hallstand of carved wood was on the right, while the three interior doors shone, as if bragging about recent attention.

Still feeling very much the housekeeper, she peered into the three rooms. The furthest door led to a green-painted kitchen with a central table, four gas rings and an assortment of cupboards with ill-fitting doors and broken handles. The room was cluttered but not filthy. In the rear living room, she found a lovely mahogany table with a central pedestal and six matching chairs, two with carvers' arms. A sideboard in similar wood was covered by an assortment of boxes out of which spilled clothes and discarded household linen. The huge blackleaded grate occupied the chimney wall, the oven hanging open to reveal a dozing blue-grey Persian curled on a tea towel. Disapproval sniffed its way up Carla Sloane's off-centre nose. Cats were not her cup of tea. The thought galvanized her to move, because a cup of tea with a splash of brandy would be just the thing. Out of the corner of her eye, she caught a movement in the back yard, so she scurried from the room, remembering that Pol was settling the pony. She had no wish to be caught snooping.

When the kettle was on, the grey-clad visitor slid like a ghost into the hall, opening the last door. The front room was something of a treasure cave, filled by things which Pol had obviously 'come by' on her travels. The tinker plainly knew what she was about, because there was not one single piece of junk to be seen. Four chairs pushed into a corner looked distinctly Chippendale, as did a couple of desks and occasional tables. A piano in near-black shiny timber lined a wall, its top covered in leather-bound books, some of which were probably first editions from the previous century. Fire-irons and brass fenders cluttered the carpet, while framed prints were stacked in cardboard boxes all over the room.

'I've an eye for the good stuff.'

Carla Sloane stiffened, though her pride forbade her to feel guilty. 'This is a remarkable collection,' she said grudgingly, willing the envy not to be obvious. This tramp had money, real money and good furniture to show for her labours. And what did Skipton's ex-housekeeper have? Nothing. No pension, no cottage, not even a reference.

'It's me insurance for me old age.' Pol stepped past the visitor and stood near the centre of the room. 'I deal, you see. To the world I'm good old Pol, the rag-and-bone woman who likes a pint of black and a glass of Irish in good company. But I've a talent for the antiques, though the good Lord alone knows how I came by it. Those vases are Ming, worth a few bob. And the grandmother clock's a one-off, commissioned by the original owner for some beloved daughter's wedding over a hundred years since. There's a box of real Regency miniatures somewhere. Never mind, sure it's all written down in me catalogue, no need to check the stock.'

'Don't you worry about burglars?'

The dark head shook above a creamy neck that was firm and youthful in spite of more than thirty-five summers and winters. 'No-one in his right mind would touch Pol's belongings,' she replied somewhat smugly. 'I've followers galore who would rip out the throat of any thief who tried to steal from me. Come on, now, sit yourself in the dining room till I fetch our suppers, for we're both weary-worn and faint for lack of nourishment.'

As if by magic, she appeared almost immediately in the doorway with a tray that held two ham salads and a huge pot of thick, dark tea. After another swift foray to the kitchen, she brought soda bread, Lancashire cheese and wedges of golden-brown potato cake liberally spread with butter the colour of cream. 'Irish,' she explained. 'Just a touch of salt and churned with a delicate hand. The English are a heavy-fisted lot when it comes to dairy farming.'

Carla Sloane, who had a mouthful of ham and no particular opinion on the subject of agriculture, nodded wisely, chewed, then slaked her thirst with the contents of a fine china cup. 'That's the best ham I ever tasted,' she said by way of thanks. 'Irish?'

Pol's eyes twinkled as she threw back her head. 'Ah, no,' she said, suppressing a giggle. 'The English make fine pigs, I'll say that for them. Some of the larger pigs strut about in three-piece suits, collar and tie, then eighteen-carat gold watch-chains stretched across their bulging bellies. Didn't ye work for one of them until just lately?'

'His belly didn't bulge.'

'Not yet,' replied Pol smartly. 'But the fat of the land will show on him in the end. He'll finish up with the gout, a red nose and so many chins you'll wonder where did his Adam's apple go. 'Tis the way with them. His father was the size of a whale when he went off into the nursing home. Mad as a bull too, for the drink had addled his brain to pulp.'

The visitor finished her third potato cake and decided to revise her opinion of the tinker. There was intelligence here. Intelligence, wit and strong instinct. 'That was splendid. I am too full to move. Thank you.'

A crystal decanter and a pair of matching globes were placed on the table. 'Here. Take a good swig while I fetch in your bags. You'll stop here the night, for I can see you're too tired for more travel.'

'But—'

'Away with your bothersome buts. Let down your hair for once, loosen your stays and take the iron out of your backbone. I've little time for English niceties. Back home, a traveller is always taken in, or so me mammy used to say. No questions, no charge, just a bellyful of good food and a cheery word for the road.'

'Have you ever been back?'

Pol sighed so deeply that she seemed to be dragging air from the soles of her shoes. 'No, not yet. I was nine when we came here and I haven't dared to go back. Because if I had gone back, I would have stayed before I'd made me fortune out of your fellers. That was why I was fetched here, so that I could make a grand pile of English money. When I return to Ireland, it will be for good.' She grinned widely, turned on her heel and went out to the large yard.

Carla Sloane could not help feeling a degree of reluctant admiration for this odd female specimen. Alone in the room, she pondered about the lot of womankind as she helped herself to several mouthfuls of French brandy. The cognac was not quite up to Skipton's fine Napoleonic standards, but it hit the spot with unerring accuracy. She listened while Pol bounced upstairs carrying cases, wondering at the woman's undoubted strength of body and of character. Some would look down their noses at the whore, the collector of rags, though they would need to be fairly tall to top Pol's unusual height. Carla felt, at this moment, that Pol had done her best with the gifts she had been born with. Every woman had to do the same, must capitalize on her abilities, sell what was saleable, prepare herself for the downslide into unavoidable old age.

With her tongue loosened, with inhibition floundering in mature brandy, the guest spoke to her returned hostess as soon as the second brandy globe was charged and cupped in Pol's none too clean hand. 'You've done right,' muttered the slurred tongue. 'It's up to us lone women to get the best we can, whatever we have to do to stay in one piece. Take me, now. I've been in service since I was thirteen, so I was saving up the years, just as you save up your collection. At the end of my time, I should have been given a lump sum, a pension and a cottage to live in. It hasn't worked out for me. I don't know what I shall do with the rest of my life.'

Pol twisted her glass, swilling the amber liquid beneath her fingers so that it would warm. 'Imelda Finnegan,' she announced with wisdom in her tone.

'I beg your—'

'They've a house on Chorley New Road, and Imelda without the common sense of a rabid dog – or should I say bitch? They keep a big yard over to Folds Road, doing well out of rags and scrap metal. Howandever, didn't Imelda take it into her head that she and Franklyn were on the brink of notoriety? So they bought themselves a great big house, and them so used to living in a couple of rooms above the rag shed. They could be doing with a house-keeper, somebody to show them how to live the good life.'

'Residential?' The desperation was plain, even though she tried to pull it out of her voice.

'You couldn't live with them two, no matter what the size of their palace. They spend half the time touching and kissing one another, then for the rest of the week, it's knife and pot throwing. They have what's called an up-and-down relationship, so nobody will straighten the house. She can fry a kipper and boil a ham, but she's not what you'd call a home maker. You can stop here till you're settled in work, then I shall sort out a place to stay.'

'I don't know what to do, you see. It's difficult for me, harder than it is for most people, because of . . . well . . .'

'Because of how you look? Come on, you can lay your cards on the table in this house. You do have an unusual appearance. That's a fact of life, just as it's another truth to say I'm a rag collector and a woman of loose morals. At the Finnegans', your appearance would be a godsend, for Imelda is certain sure that every female in the land is waiting to pounce on Franklyn and have her wicked way with him.' She drank, patted her hair, then gazed into the near-distance, a twinkle in her eye. 'He must have something very special, must Franklyn Finnegan, only he keeps it well hidden, for a plainer looking man I have yet to meet. Perhaps he keeps his treasure in his trousers, and for my money it can stay where it is till Pancake Tuesday falls on a Friday.'

As ever, Carla became expansive in drink. 'Most of them keep their brains in their trousers. There are many decisions made by a man's private bits and pieces. Take Skipton. He wanted Eloise Robinson and he got her. That was nothing to do with sense and reasoning. The choice was made by a part of him that was as far away from his head as it could be. And much good it did him, following his baser nature in that way. They're like chalk and cheese, those two, should never have married.'

Pol drank deeply, running a healthy red tongue over her lips once the glass was drained. 'You know, Carla.' She leaned her elbows on the table in an attitude of comradeship. 'If it were all to be run proper, in a sensible and organized fashion, more of these high-flying gentlemen should avail themselves of my services. Wouldn't it be a sight easier if they kept their passion for a paid mistress? Sure, the wife should have money and brains, and I suppose she ought to be easy enough on the eye for big parties and the like. But lust is unseemly in a lady of standing. Most of them have no passion at all, thank the Lord, so an occasional husband comes to me till I send him home grateful, calm, and not likely to make awkward advances where they might not be welcome. It's normal enough and should be made more official.'

'Yes, I see what you mean. You'd be taking a burden from the wife, just as I do with the housekeeping.' The drink was loosening her brain as well as her tongue, she thought fleetingly.

Pol's head bobbed quickly. 'That's it! Staff provide the services that are deemed too lowly for the wife. So I should be a member of staff.' The bobbing stopped, and an enormous gale of laughter was followed by, 'Can you see it? "Come in, Lord Wotsyername. This is my cook, my housekeeper, my maid" – all along the line they'd go. And at the end there'd be me in a scarlet gown with purple feathers on me shoulders. "Oh yes, Lord Wotsyername. This is Pol O'Gorman, my partner in fleshly lust." That would be great, wouldn't it? Oh, that's desperate funny.'

The bulky woman across the table, who was not amused at the turn taken in the conversation she had unwittingly started, tried to sober up, breathing deeply through lips that were permanently parted. She ought not to be discussing the base nature of mankind, certainly not with a woman of such recent acquaintance. 'He's got nothing now,' she said, unable to comply with a near-drowned determination to keep her counsel. The brandy was sharper, rougher than her usual spirit, and it seemed to continue oiling her tongue when she would have preferred it to remain fastened. 'The wife's a cripple in her bed, the child's long dead, and he can't keep his servants because his wife's considered to be a crim— . . . she's not fit to go near. Let him struggle on and find a housekeeper of my calibre in this town. Hmmph.' The 'hmmph' ended with a huge hiccup followed by a larger-than-average belch of wind. 'I beg your pardon.'

'No matter. Why, King Henry the Eighth might have cut off your head had you not burped your appreciation.' A criminal? Was that the gist of the severed word? Ah well, best left at this stage.

'I think I need my bed.' Carla rose and stood swaying like a large, crudely made statue about to tumble from its plinth. 'It's been a long day, and the journey from Bury was dreadful.'

Pol tapped her fingers on the table. 'Bury? What in the name of all that's sacred were you seeking in Bury? Was there a place, a job you were after getting?'

'No.' The tongue flicked nervously before leaping back behind the craggy teeth. 'I went to my sister's, to Maude's. I've always spent my holidays there, and I assumed that she would welcome me as a more permanent resident.' She paused momentarily, folding protective arms across the inflexible bosom. 'I was wrong. It seems that a few days is the extent of her patience with me. Her husband left her well catered for, so she spends her time with other widows, in sewing circles and having pretty tea-parties.' The grandmother clock in the next room chimed, its tune slightly off-key for want of some qualified attention. 'She never had a party while I was there, never invited anyone to the house during my stays. She was . . . ashamed of me. I was not acceptable, you see. I did not belong in her world of small talk and recipes, tatting and embroidery. So she showed me the door.'

Pol rose to her feet. 'So, you've nobody who gives a damn?'

Carla shrugged. 'I'm used to it. As a child, I was treated as the school hobgoblin. If a fairy story was read in class, the others would turn and stare at me. I was the bad dwarf, the troll under the bridge, the wicked demon that spoiled a princess's plans. In the yard, they would set about me. Until I learned to pick them off one at a time and give them the thrashing they deserved.'

'And as a young woman?' Pol's voice displayed no pity,

though her heart felt as if it had been twice through the wooden mangle on washday.

'I was put to service. The first two years were spent in a scullery with endless dishes and pans to wash. Gradually, people got used to my appearance, and I made my way up the ranks. The interview for Skipton's was uncomfortable, but there was just Henry Skipton present and he seemed not to care. The staff were under my command – except for the butler – so they were forced to accept me.' She paused for a moment. 'There was just one who laughed. Just one who stepped out of line.'

'Laughed at you?'

'I think so.' She pulled at the hem of her tailored jacket, a nervous movement that did not escape Pol's watchful eye. 'It's of no importance now. I'm away from the place.'

Pol stood in the doorway watching as the unfortunate grey woman stumbled up the flight. 'The door to your room is just to the right at the top of the stairs,' she called before going back for an extra dose of brandy. Carla Sloane had something on the Skiptons, Pol sensed that. It would no doubt be useful in time, as would Pol's suspicion that he had fathered a bastard. Though it would be a shame to damage poor Oonagh's daughter, so perhaps that idea needed storing out of the light for a while.

She drained the glass swiftly, pondering yet again the reason why she hated the man so much. He was quiet enough, fair to his workers by all accounts, the sort of chap who seemed to give little offence. She turned and picked up a silver-framed picture, a brownish photograph that was always displayed on the range mantel. A slight, dark-haired and definitely beautiful woman sat on a studio chair. Behind her, the backdrop depicted some dejected and very limp trees, possibly willows that had practised their weeping rather well. Pol's head nodded, because they were right to mourn, those trees.

She replaced the portrait, sniffing the tears from an elegant, well-formed nose. 'They killed you, Mammy,' she whispered hoarsely. 'They put you in a prison, in a scalding hot jail full of noise and smell and dirty cotton.'

She'd been a healthy young woman, had Kathleen

O'Gorman, a free spirit from the wild side of Ireland where wind pushed wave against rugged rock, where animal and child shared shelter and food, where a travelling Englishman had broken her heart. He had sold no farm equipment to the O'Gorman family, but he had increased their number by one.

Pol walked to the window and stared out at the large wooden shed that served as Amos's quarters when he stayed at home. The cart, under a thick tarpaulin, filled the rest of the yard, but Pol did not see it, because her mind's eye was straying backwards in time, fixing itself on memories that would never be erased.

Her father had left a false address on a scrap of paper. None of Kathleen's family had mastered reading at the time, but letters written on their behalf had been returned marked 'not at this address'. Kathleen's mother had visited all the neighbours, which task was not a small one with the nearest houses miles away. No-one could remember the name of the company represented by the handsome young Englishman.

The pony poked his head out of the half-door and fixed a sullen stare on his mistress. For once, she did not heed him. Her lips moved as if in silent prayer as she stared up into the evening sky, but prayer was the last thing on her mind tonight.

She cleared the dishes and set two pans to boil on the rings. While waiting for hot water, she sat among her treasures in the front room, running her fingers along precious wooden surfaces, breathing in the scent of good beeswax polish.

The hatred was because of who he was and what he was. The hatred was because of a few words spilling with blood from a mother's dying lips. Pol closed her weary eyes, picturing yet again that awful scene, hearing once more the cough-splintered syllables as they fought for life in a room that reeked of death.

'Your father was killed, Polly. He was killed by one of his silly machines, dead before you were ever born.'

'Who was he, Mammy?'

'No proof.'

'Never mind about proof. Just tell me.'

Pol opened her eyes to the present, but her mouth framed a message from history as she repeated the last words ever spoken by Kathleen O'Gorman. 'Mr Skipton's brother,' whispered Pol to the grandmother clock, her voice mingling with its ticking and with an echo from twenty years ago.

Pol slammed the door and walked into her cluttered kitchen. It wasn't his fault, she was sufficiently rational to know that. But the urge for revenge, the need for a pound of flesh, was too elemental to be ignored. She was of a proud people, a people who had suffered much over the years, a breed that tended to look after its own.

With hands that trembled, Henry Skipton's cousin poured water into the enamel bowl. She would not beg from him, could never try to claim whatever might – or might not – be hers by rights. Her fingers tightened on a soap-slicked china saucer, the strength of her anger almost forcing it to leap back into the bowl. 'Cousin Henry,' she muttered softly, 'I shall dance on your grave.'

He was staring at her scarf, causing her to tug at the colourful square that adorned her neck. Maria had made it. She had made it out of cotton intended for bedsheets, a gift from this man. Jenny felt that his eyes saw and understood everything, and she feared that he might, at any moment now, accuse her of being an accessory to petty theft. Were sheets petty? she pondered obliquely.

'That's a fine piece of work,' he said. 'The printing, I mean. Very artistic and unusual. Cheerful too.'

'Thank you.'

'Cotton,' he continued. 'A good, fine weave, probably from a Lancashire mill. Who designed the pattern?'

She shrugged, hoping to give the impression of knowing nothing and caring even less. 'It was a present,' she mumbled.

'I see.' He walked round the desk, waving a hand at a chair until she realized that he was inviting her to sit. When she was settled, he placed himself in a similar chair and rested his hands on the blotter. 'Will you come back, then?' he asked. 'There's a nurse here at the moment, but you are the person . . . Mrs Skipton prefers. The cook has taken on the job of housekeeper, though she won't be living in. Mrs Hardman has grown used to her independence, and I have no wish to curtail her freedom. Of course, Briony is still with us.'

Jenny tried not to notice the telling pause that had occurred before he had managed to speak his wife's name. 'Briony was the one who put . . .' Her voice faded immediately, as did a little of her righteous anger, because a shamefaced Briony stood in the doorway with a tray. 'Coffee, Mr Skipton,' said the girl brightly. 'And I've brought a spare cup for the visitor.' She put down the tray, then turned to Jenny. 'I'm sorry. Mr Skipton knows what I did, about the silver under the mattress. She made me. It was Stone . . .' She glanced quickly at the head of the house. 'It was Mrs Sloane,' she amended carefully. 'Because you laughed.'

'I wasn't laughing at her,' said Jenny, suddenly forgetting the master. 'It was the prunes. Maria told me about prunes flying about upstairs, then when I saw Uncle Dan eating some, I went a bit silly. I wasn't making fun of Mrs Sloane. She can't help how she looks. Any road, I was terrified of her.' A small ripple of temper stirred again in Jenny's breast. It was all very puzzling, because she had never been a particularly ill-tempered person. 'And you wanted rid of me, Briony Mulholland. You had your reasons, I suppose.' As if reminding herself where she was, Jenny ended the conversation by standing up to pour coffee while the maid fled from the room, tanned cheeks further stained by embarrassment.

Henry Skipton hid a grin behind his hand. So the girl did have some spirit, then. Perhaps she might, after all, survive his wife's strange whims. If she came back, that was. 'Will you come back?' he asked again.

'It's a bit awkward, but I'll look after Mrs Skipton for a while, say a couple of months.'

'I see. Do you have other plans for the long term?'

'Maria has.' She hoped that the heat in her face did not show. If he asked too many questions, what would she say? It was daft, a girl like Maria wanting to become a famous printer, and Jenny was too fond of her friend to risk exposing the girl's tremendous faith in herself. If Maria succeeded, then everyone would sit up and take notice. But Jenny, determined to be a true and loyal supporter, was hedging Maria's bets. If the venture was destined to fail, then it ought to be allowed to peter out without folk standing by in floodlit and contemptuous judgement.

'Maria would have a head filled with ideas,' he said, his tone heavy with something neither of them understood. Jenny might have called it sarcasm, but all he felt was an emotion that bordered on disappointment. He sipped his coffee before continuing, 'You'll be secure here. Maria is a fanciful girl, probably tormented by ambitions that are not realistic, especially for a young woman. And she'll no doubt return to Liverpool once there's a slightly emptier bed in her parents' house.'

Jenny studied her Sunday best shoes. They were shiny and black, with shallow uppers and three narrow straps buckled over feet that were elegant and high-arched. 'Liverpool's coming here,' she said finally. 'Well, one of them's coming, a brother – I think we told you about him at the hospital. We've took over the rent on Auntie Mavis's house, so Maria and their Anthony will be living there for the time being.' She raised her head. 'Until they get settled, till he finds somewhere else to stop, it would be . . .' She struggled for an end to the sentence.

'Unseemly for you to live there with a single young man?' he interspersed helpfully. 'He is single, I take it?'

She nodded. 'They're looking to start some kind of a business, see. Selling odds and ends, probably on the market.' That should be enough for him to know, she decided. With any luck, he wouldn't be getting a microscope out to study the details.

'Such as?'

Her shrug fell rather short of careless; it was plain to him that Maria had plans and that Jenny knew more than she was prepared to put into words. 'All sorts of trankle-ments,' she muttered somewhat lamely. If he wanted further magnification, she thought, he could blinking well go elsewhere for it.

He replaced the cup in its saucer and leaned forward. 'I beg your pardon, Jenny?'

'Tranklements. Bits and pieces. Anthony will have some ideas from Liverpool – he's worked on markets and in shops – and Maria will . . . get some other things,' she finished, completely lame at this juncture.

His eyes twinkled merrily, seeming to send out light and warmth. It occurred to Jenny that he was probably capable of being really amusing if he wanted to. 'Me Auntie Mavis always said tranklements, sir. It's like when you've got a box with a few different things in. It saves time and long lists if you just say, "Oh, these is all me tranklements." Is it not a proper word?'

He grinned hugely. 'It's a splendid word. I can almost hear the tranklements banging and clanking together in the bottom of a box.'

'They're not always noisy. They can be anything, even dusters and mops, the kinds of things that don't clatter. But I know what you mean, it is a loud word.'

A shaft of sunlight illuminated the crown of her head, giving her a decidedly hallowed appearance, as if she were posing as one of those Catholic saints whose pictures were used on small cards to punctuate a worshipper's prayer book. There was a stillness about her, a calm that was not usually noticeable in a girl of her age, especially in one supposedly destined for service. She was elegant, yet simple. Her looks were her riches, he reckoned, because he had seldom seen hair so completely blonde, eyes so large and definite about their blueness, skin so downy and perfect. He cleared his throat. The girl was a stunner, yet it would seem that she did not notice, did not care about her appearance. No powder, no rouge, no overwhelming smell of cheap perfume.

She was looking at him now, so he coughed once more against a sudden dryness at the back of his mouth. 'I suppose you'd better go upstairs and see her. She's been asking for you often enough, or so I've been given to understand.'

Jenny stared at him levelly. She would not ask him why he never visited his crippled wife, why he seldom spoke her name. It was not her place to ask. And anyway, there was a current in this house, something that a poor swimmer ought to avoid at all costs. The woman in the bed had already tried to pull Jenny into the flood; it was no use jumping in willingly and letting the pair of them use her as a lifebelt. That was what it was all about, she thought as she studied the muted pain in his face. He was unhappy with Mrs Skipton and Mrs Skipton was unhappy with him. They both needed to talk, but it would be better if they each talked to different people. And she hoped fervently that neither of them would choose her, because she had no desire to become the rope in their tug-of-war. 'I'll see the mistress tomorrow when I start work,' she said crisply. 'There's no point in exciting her now. If she sees me, she'll want me to stop, and I've things to do.'

He glanced quickly out of the window, needing to rest his eyes after the dazzling sight of such heart-stopping beauty. If he had a painting of her, he would have to turn it to the wall sometimes, would need to rest and gaze for a while at things less stimulating, more ordinary. Perfection was tiring . . . wasn't it? Hadn't he had perfection once before . . . ?

'Mr Skipton?'

'I'm sorry, yes. Where were we?' He looked at her hands. They did not accuse, were not yet work-reddened.

'I said I'd see Mrs Skipton tomorrow. She'd likely want me to stop if she saw me now.'

Perhaps she did have an idea of her own value, then? 'I shan't be here tomorrow,' he said. 'I'll be at the mill.'

'Yes.' She rose and picked up a cheap bag. The gilding was flaking off a clumsy clasp and some stitches had broken on the handle, leaving it frayed and shabby. He wanted to give her a bag, buy one, take one from the dozens stacked upstairs along with all the other bounty that had been culled by a wealthy and spoiled wife. The wish to buy a bag for Jenny Crawley was unreasonable, and he sat on it firmly. His head would never again be turned by a pretty woman. Would it?

She walked to the door, turned and bade him farewell. He nodded, muttered a curt 'goodbye', then inhaled deeply as her footfalls, muted by carpet and rug, marked her progress towards the outside world. Half wishing that he had never asked the wretched girl to return, he poured two fingers of fine single malt into a glass, shuddering when the liquor scalded his throat. What was it about her? he wondered. Was it that she was blonde, just as Sophie had been blonde? Did he really seek a replacement for his dead daughter, was he searching for comfort in his old age? And how many more times was he going to ask himself that stupid question? No, he was not old, not old enough yet to be coddled into true dotage by a compliant daughter or by a pretty nurse.

Eloise might alter her, that was another possibility, and he had failed to warn her, had been unable to frame his sentiments. After all, he had little to go on – the evidence was too flimsy. But every pretty maid had left, some without notice, others picking lame excuses from a hat. There had been sick mothers, sudden marriages, several funerals of grandparents who had mysteriously resurrected themselves in time for work at the mills. Whatever Eloise said or did to upset young nursemaids remained a mystery to him.

The young woman was plainly inexperienced, so her head might easily be turned by gifts and sweet words. She could be sweet when it suited her, that damned wife of his. And there was a distinct danger of Jenny being turned against him, of Eloise weaving her pattern of lies so cleverly that the girl would be taken in. No matter.

He slammed the glass on to his desk. Jenny was a mere servant, a working-class girl who needed his money to survive. She would be paid, very well paid. And he had had enough of such people. A fish and chip heiress had proved that the class system was there for a good reason. He was a working man himself, but his position placed him far above and beyond thoughts of cotton cops and fish batter. His parents had been right, he should have married someone similar, a girl separated by several generations from the trade that paid the bills.

He grinned unexpectedly. 'Henry Skipton,' he asked out loud, 'are you a bloody snob after all?'

'I've never been so shown up in all me life. Your mouth was hung that far open – we could have took your tonsils out with nail scissors. I bet Jenny could see what you had for your dinner yesterday.'

'But I—'

'Don't start. Don't start till I've finished.'

'When will you finish?'

'When I stop. You'll know when I've done, 'cos I'll stop talking.'

'Oh, has somebody fitted a washer to your gob to stop it dripping, then?'

Maria crossed the room and belted her older brother across the back of his head with yesterday's copy of the *Bolton Evening News*. Anthony did not flinch. The Hesketh household was populated by red-heads, so flying fists and boots were the norm for him. A newspaper was of little consequence and of negligible weight; it was, therefore, an item to be ignored. 'I only looked at her,' he grumbled gently. 'Do I have to get me bloody passport stamped before I look at her? Or shall I get blindfolded?'

'You'll have no need to get blindfolded, lad, 'cos I'll poke your eyes out. Have you gone soft or what?'

'What,' he answered sullenly.

'What do you mean, "what"?'

He grinned. 'You asked me had I gone soft or what, and I know I'm not soft, so I said—'

She clouted him again across the back of his skull, this time with the flat of her hand. 'I've been trying to get her to come in with us, to stay here, live here and help us till we get going. I mean, this is her house.'

'So? And will you stop rattling my brains?'

'Huh, you'd need one more brain cell to qualify as a plant, you would. Even then you'd be a weed or poison ivy. Listen, daft lad – do you think she'll hang about here with you slavering after her? I told her you were all right. I said there'd be no bother, she could come in with me and you could have the little room. But oh no, you've got to carry on all Rudolph Vaselino, eyes crawling on her like ants at a picnic.'

174

He leaned back in the chair. 'Have you finished now?'

'No. What's in that case in the back yard?'

He craned his head round as if expecting to find a third person in the room.

'Anthony!'

'Oh, were you talking to me? Only you said I had to wait for me turn, like, so I—'

'All right, all right.' She let out a long sigh of despair. 'What have you brought?'

He shrugged broad shoulders. 'Stuff,' he said.

'What stuff?'

'Odds and sods that me dad didn't want.'

Maria's arms folded themselves across her slender waist, fingers digging into the fabric of her one good skirt. 'We're going legit, Anthony,' she said quietly. 'No more of that, no more things what's fell off a cart on the dock road. Me dad's too far gone, he'll never alter since he qualified as 70 per cent proof. They'll be slapping tax on him soon, he's that pickled. But we've got a chance to start a proper business. See, we've got to save. The money we get for sewing and washing—'

'Hang about,' he said, suddenly coming to life. 'That's woman's work. I'm not standing in no kitchen with no flowered pinny on washing knickers in the dolly.'

'Will you shut up?' screamed Maria. 'You'll be out every morning selling what I can print in the back kitchen at night. There'll be no sleep for me, Anthony Hesketh, so there'll not be much for you, I've no faith in the idea of suffering single-handed. I've sorted things out with the landlord at the Prince William. I told him you were strong, used to humping crates since you were about eight years old. You'll be working the cellar if he takes to you. Evening shift, serve in the bar when he's short.'

'What? Bloody what? I've left Liverpool for this?'

'You've left Liverpool for your own bed and three square meals. You can go back if you want, squeeze in with the rest of the lads and eat when me mother remembers to put her book down.'

'Don't start on me mam when she's not here to hold her corner,' he said sharply.

175

Maria sighed and pushed at her fringe until it stood like stiff bristle on the top of her head. 'I love me mam. I speak me mind, that's all. She's done her best, but she's got her faults like everybody else. The truth is that she should have been a lady and—'

'You what?' He guffawed loudly, displaying good teeth and a tongue that had remained healthy in spite of poor diet. But Anthony had always known how and where to supplement the meagre meals provided at odd intervals by a dreamy mother. 'Me mam a lady? Christ, she batters the life out of the awld feller at least twice a month.'

'That's because she should have been a lady reading and painting pictures. She gets mad at him for drinking.'

'And she doesn't talk like a lady—'

'She would have talked like a lady if she'd been a lady.'

'True. And chalk would be cheese if it had been cheese.'

'Anthony!'

'All right, keep your hair on. It's stuck up again like a yardbrush, you could be an extra out of a Charlie Chaplin film.'

Maria dashed to the mirror, licked her palms, then flattened the carrotty spikes into something that resembled order. 'Jenny'll not stop,' she said glumly to her reflection. 'She'll go working at Skipton Hall again when she should be here, should be backing us up with her potato pies.' She turned to face him, her thin face bright with fury. 'You shouldn't have looked at her like that. And you shouldn't have waded straight in with your boots on, telling her you couldn't find her mam. You've got no . . . no dignity, no idea of what's proper.'

'Oh hey, I'm sorry, queen. This is me face, you see, me one and only mush.' He jabbed a thumb against his cheek. 'It's what God gave me and I can't swap it, same as you can't do anything about your hair. It's not my fault if I look at people funny. And she is a bit of all right, you know. I thought that when I saw her picture, but she's even better in the flesh.'

'You haven't seen her flesh,' roared Maria. But her mouth twitched in reply to his cheeky grin, and she sighed, visibly letting go some of her tension. Anthony was her favourite brother, and she couldn't stay mad at him for long. He was handsome, their Anthony. His hair was what Maria called 'a quieter red' and he had clear green eyes, well-shaped eyebrows, a straight nose (how he'd kept that through all the fighting she would never know) and a good Irish skin that was dotted with very few freckles. 'I feel as if we're chucking Jenny out,' she said. 'She might have stopped here if you'd never come.'

'Right, I'll bugger off home, then.'

'I'm going to need you.'

'What as? A bloody doorstop? I can't talk, can't look at people, can't tell people I haven't found their mother. What flaming use am I?'

She lifted her sharp little chin. 'You're a man,' she said, her tone trimmed with something that sounded like disapproval. 'If we put you in a suit, you might even look normal. I'm not sticking in here with gaslight and candles, lad. I shall want a shed with some sort of power, like electric, and—'

'What's it got to do with me?' His eyebrows shot up till they almost disappeared beneath his hairline.

'They'll lend you money. You're good at lies.'

'Eh? What sort of mad scheme are you working on? We've had enough of your capers. It was you who took Sybil treasure hunting in that condemned house. It was you sent her along a beam in the loft—'

'I never pushed her, did I? I never knew she was going to fall through the bloody ceiling and get knocked soft. Mind you, she finished up no softer than she'd set out in the first place. No, this is different, I'm grown up now.' She paused for a moment to grab some breath. 'You'll have to pretend to be me,' she finished.

By this time, Anthony was completely lost. 'I don't mind wearing a suit if I'm pressed, and if the bloody suit's pressed, but I'm not putting one of your frocks on, girl.'

Maria's back straightened as if it were supported by a steel rod. There was an expression in her features too, one he recognized as don't-stand-in-my-way-or-else. Her eyes flashed with intelligence, while two small spots of colour in her cheeks lent the face something that was strangely reminiscent of beauty. 'Listen, you great big nelly. The firm will be called Maria Hesketh. Not Mar-ee-a, Mar-eye-a, 'cos that sounds posher. You can build the machines, get down the library for a couple of books.'

'Machines? Books? What the hell are you on about now? You just said yourself, this is the grown-up world now. You can't organize the family like you used to, a bucket of water and a step stone each, knock on the doors, penny a step.'

'I'm talking about real business,' she said. 'Printing. This town's full of cloth, we can get it cheap, especially the fents.'

Exasperated, he blew out his cheeks. 'What's a fent?'

'An end,' she said, plainly straining to reach some patience. 'Or a roll with a couple of flaws. We print it, cut it up, sew it into whatever, then sell it.'

'In here?'

'Wherever we can get. In here first, later on in a proper shed. You'll be a director of Maria Hesketh, so you can handle all the negotiations and the engineering. They'd not listen to me, the bank people.'

He clapped a hand to his head. 'Have you gone doo-lally all the way? Folk like us, we don't own sheds and print machines. You're mad.'

She tapped a small foot on the rug. 'I am mad, Anthony, you've got that right. I'm hopping mad, mad 'cos all I can be is a servant or a factory worker. Best I can hope for is a shop job. I'm mad because I'm just a girl and girls can't have anything, can't be bosses. The only way a girl gets stuff is if her dad pops his clogs and leaves her a few bob. And I'm mad at you, you've no ambition. I believe in my dream, lad. I know what I can do.'

He stared at her. The power of this gawky young woman surrounded her like some invisible force, almost as if she were producing enough electricity to run a machine by herself. 'Right,' he said. 'I'll be in it, we'll give it a go.'

'You won't be sorry. And Denis'll help.'

'Who's Denis?'

She studied him for a moment. 'He's me young man, works for the Bolton Fire Brigade. I might marry him if he's lucky. Anyway, I'll go and make our tea.'

Anthony Hesketh nodded to himself as soon as his sister had left the room. She was a bloody pest, their Maria. She'd started many a riot back home, had been the cause of endless trouble between the Heskeths and their neighbours. Perhaps this was why she'd always been a nuisance, he thought as he lit a cigarette. Their Maria was going places, so he might as well keep her company. He liked making and mending, had a marked instinct for understanding things mechanical.

So she had a follower, did she? That was nice, she could do with settling. He leaned back in the chair, a slight smile playing on his lips. This could all turn out for the best if he played his cards right. And that one called Jenny might just be his queen of hearts.

Chapter Seven

ELOISE RESTED AGAINST HALF A DOZEN PILLOWS, TRYING YET
again to become accustomed to sleeping in an upright
position. It was for her chest, the physiotherapist had said.
If she carried on lying down all the time, she might
develop congestion of the lungs, bronchitis, even pneumonia. The woman was right, of course. As time went on,
her chest occasionally felt anaesthetized, turning simple
breathing into an act of will, a boring exercise that took a
great deal of stamina. Inch by inch, Eloise was dying.

She didn't want pneumonia, not at the moment. There
was much to do, a great deal to accomplish before she
shuffled off the planet into what she hoped would be
silence, just a great big nothing. Because if there really was
some kind of retribution on the other side, Eloise Skipton
might not fare so well in the eternal pecking order. In fact,
she would probably finish up somewhere rather warm and
smelly, a place not unlike the fish and chip shops she had
visited with Daddy and Grandpa to check on staff and the
quality of merchandise. Hell, for Eloise, could well turn
out to be full of fish batter, sliced potatoes and boiling fat.
Except that it didn't exist at all, and such wanderings of
her mind were a waste of time, time that hung heavily on
hands that were growing increasingly useless.

The physiotherapist had become more than helpful
during recent weeks. After Jenny's sudden departure,
Eloise had felt betrayed, abandoned and completely

lonely. In desperation, she had turned to her daily therapist and, as time passed, the white-garbed female had become a valuable ally. Resident nurses came and went, none of them suitable, none of them as promising as Jenny had been. The constant factor during the time without Jenny had been Sara Browne. She was pleasant, dutiful, respectful and obedient. Though, as Eloise frequently reminded herself, many women of Sara Browne's calibre would have chosen to be useful when bribed. Especially when the nosebag held a pale blue Ceylon sapphire and two adequately flaw-free white diamonds set in eighteen-carat yellow gold. Sara Browne's calibre was easily defined – she was of the newly emerging lower middle or upper working classes – used to little, grabbing much and offering expensive services to those with older money. Still, such ambitious types had their uses.

Eloise was, at last, almost equipped. According to Briony Mulholland, Henry had been preoccupied of late and had spent long hours at the mills. Now that the dragon-lady had been removed from the kitchen, there was no-one to question the presence of workmen. And anyway, the hefty Mrs Browne had marched the fellow upstairs and he had taken his instructions from Eloise. The result of weeks of clandestine planning sat now inside the bedside cupboard. A shiny new black telephone, an extension that would enable the mistress to know what the master was doing.

She grinned to herself. No longer would she call Mrs Browne her torturer. The therapist had understood, had agreed that poor Mrs Skipton should have a telephone, had thrown up her muscle-roped arms in dismay on hearing of Mr Skipton's frugality. And she had expressed no overt surprise on being asked to obtain certain telephone numbers for her patient. By that time, the dainty sapphire ring had hung on a chain round the large woman's neck, safe from massage oils, resting against the sexless chest until it could be altered to fit fingers that resembled a pound and a half of pork sausages. The adornment, thought Eloise smugly, would not sit well amidst so much blubber.

It was wonderfully comforting too, just knowing that an

operator sat at the other end of the wire, a disembodied and neutral voice that would summon help should the need arise. Yes, he would have got her a telephone if he had cared at all for her. No cripple should be left alone in the night with just a bell that might – or might not – summon a dozing servant.

Everything seemed to be working out well. Jenny would be back tomorrow, and she seemed malleable enough. Whatever – the girl was the last resort, would have to be persuaded, cajoled, even bribed if necessary, because this was probably Eloise's final opportunity, the sole remaining chance.

The dark-haired girl – what had her name been – ah yes, Lucy. Lucy had been rather worldly-wise, had not bent readily to Eloise's will. She would need to be clever this time. It was vital to instil in the guinea-pig a desire to better herself, yet it was also important to retain, even to nurture a degree of *naïveté*. A strange mixture was required then, a blend of aspiration and gentleness. A girl imbued with such qualities would be very special and extremely dangerous. Jenny was, Eloise hoped, the ideal candidate. Like an author, Eloise would write what she chose on the blank page, would turn Jenny into her own creation.

A slight feeling of unease invaded the thin breast. Jenny had fought back. Jenny had stood her corner when things came to a head. But there needed to be some character there, some instinct for self-preservation, a degree of imagination too. Eloise nodded. She would produce the thread, then Jenny would spin and weave, unaware that the pattern was being dictated by her mistress. A slight chuckle escaped from her throat, the result of a sudden realization that she was thinking in terms of cotton. Perhaps he might have liked that.

Her head turned itself towards a darkening window. The bed drapes were parted tonight because it was hot. There had been good days, she thought self-pityingly. Days when he had loved her, almost worshipped her. Months and years when he had marked each special occasion with a gift. Birthdays, anniversaries, Christmases.

Sometimes, he had invented a special day, like 'two years since we met' and 'fourteen days since you last burnt the toast'.

They had always made toast in the winter evenings, stretching that long brass fork towards the log fire, holding each other close while butter melted and bread scorched to cinders. They had needed no food for their bodies then, because each fed the other's soul, each filled the other's thoughts. The toast had been a game, an excuse to sit before a fire that raged too hot, a reason to be naked and to hold each other.

Holding each other. Her throat held no sign of a chuckle now. The parts of her body that were still adequately supplied with intact nerve stiffened with rage, and she could feel her face setting in tight lines. The loving. That had been their hottest flame, hotter by far than any mere kindling of coal or logs. Even now, she could not forget the loving, which was why the bitterness had become so strong, so completely overwhelming.

There had never been anyone else, so she could not assess their intimacies by comparison. She only knew that everything had been good, that there had been joy and abandonment, that the idea of shame had never entered her head while they had explored each others' bodies. It had been important – no – it had been more than important. Essential might provide a nearer explanation. And he had taken it away, had taken himself away after . . . after Sophie's death.

Tears began, and she sniffed angrily, but her defiant eyes continued to produce salt water. He had taken away her happiness, then the disease had arrived to remove the crushed remains of her will to live. Uncaring, she blew her nose on a silk sheet. Her body once felt like this wonderful rich fabric, smooth and perfect. Now it was a wrinkled mess, skin sagging and drying to crêpe, or reminding fingers of the outer covering of one of those seedless tangerines that always appeared at Christmas.

The will to live had returned slowly, had nurtured itself on the terrible loathing that grew daily inside her heart. Hatred was, she found, just as hot as love. It was the same emotion, but in reverse. She was still obsessed by him, but now she was destructive, had spent years working on a scheme that would hurt him, perhaps destroy him altogether. He was lonely, therefore he was vulnerable. She would cut open his Achillean zone, and she would pour in the poison. Just a little drop at first, just enough to cause some festering. But finally, she would make of it an ulcer, a running sore that would never heal. As soon as the new skin showed signs of forming, she would drip in a little more venom.

And in the end, she would have his money. His money, his house, his land, perhaps even his bloody mills! She didn't need them and would probably bequeath them to the building of an institution for people with multiple sclerosis, but that didn't matter. Getting them, whipping them away from beneath his nose, that was the thing. Yes, that would be her triumph.

The tears dried stiff on her cheeks. She didn't care about others with this disease. No-one had suffered as she had, no-one had lost what she had lost. His love had been everything, all she could ever possibly want. Like a flower, she had bloomed in his radiating warmth. Like a flower, she had been cut down by him, a buttonhole that did not quite please the eye, a decaying bloom cast out of his sight to be emptied away with the rest of the refuse. But yes, she would get what she could and she would bequeath it to other cripples, just to remind him of his wife's importance. He would outlive her, that fact was certain. And people would weep at her funeral, would bemoan her husband's ill-treatment of a helpless wife, would bless her name for leaving so much to the unfortunate victims of such a harrowing disease. Happily, the urge to commit suicide was itself long dead, buried beneath her need for revenge. Whatever happened to him, he deserved it.

With difficulty, she shifted on to her side. A faint glimmer in the corner of the room was caused by the spokes in her wheelchair, the latest acquisition from Sara Browne. This was sturdier than the previous model, which had been used just to get Eloise from bed to bath. The new one was a roadworthy item, and Jenny could push it around the grounds. Crawley should be out of the convalescent home shortly and he could carry her downstairs. It would soon become necessary for her to leave this room, to be out and about as often as the illness would allow. But yes, the hatred would burn, would give her the necessary staying power. And, once the whole thing had got started, she would be able to sit, like a theatre director, to watch the play that was her own brainchild. She was writer, producer, director, choreographer. And she had chosen the cast rather well too.

The rubber ring had slipped again, and she made some small attempt to replace it beneath buttocks that had wasted. She was so thin now that the bedsores felt as if they were welded to bone. In future, she would do as she was told, would sit in a padded chair sometimes, lie on her stomach occasionally, go out in her new chariot. She needed all her wits and what was left of her strength in order to follow the grand plan.

And above all of that, she needed Jenny Crawley.

'You came back to me, then.' Eloise was practising her new look, an expression that spoke of godliness and inner suffering, bravery and sympathy for others. No, not just for some others, for everyone. Temper must abate now. No screaming, no throwing of dinners, few selfish demands.

'How are you, miss?' Jenny placed the coffee tray on the bedside cabinet.

'I'm fine, thank you. Get the blue mug and we shall share the coffee. Mrs Hardman is an excessively kind woman – she always sends me plenty of coffee.'

Jenny fetched the mug, poured the coffee, sat down.

'My poor, dear girl,' effused the mistress. 'You look so pale and sad, and you seem a great deal thinner. I am sorry, Jenny. Losing your aunt like that must have been a terrible shock. Was she your only living relative?'

Jenny choked on a mouthful of coffee while groping for a reply. 'There's Uncle Dan,' she said quietly as soon as the ticklish cough had righted itself.

A skeletal hand reached out and placed its transparent

digits on Jenny's arm. 'Ah yes, I was forgetting your uncle. My unhappy, beautiful little friend,' she continued. 'How you must have suffered.'

Jenny, who was shocked at the show of affection, sat rigidly still. Had the illness got to Mrs Skipton's brain? Was she going to become properly doo-lally any minute, shouldn't they be getting the doctor in?

'I am nearing my time,' said the frail woman mournfully. 'And I must improve my soul, because there is no hope at all for my body. Yes, I have been ill-tempered in the past, but prayer is so healing, so relaxing. I have no wish to meet my Maker while I'm in one of my screaming fits.' She patted Jenny's hand. 'There is so little time for me now, you see.'

Jenny decided to stick to more practical areas. 'Have you had your bath?'

'Yes,' came the smiling reply. 'Little Briony helped me earlier, before you arrived. It's amazing that a small girl like that can have so much strength.' The sigh that followed was filled with gentle sadness. It was a sigh that spoke of reconciliation, a sigh that said, 'Yes, I have accepted my lot, however short its span.'

'Is Maria not with you? I used to laugh at her hair, you know, and that was extremely unkind of me. We must show her how to make the best of herself.'

'She's not here.' Jenny was still clinging desperately to the notion of everyday duties, but here was the mistress carrying on in a way that went straight past the mundane. After a mouthful of coffee, the bemused girl continued, 'She's living with her brother.'

'In Bolton.'

'Yes, miss.'

A smile erupted over the coffee cup. 'Then you must bring her to visit me. Bring the brother too, if you like. I cannot get out into the world very often, and I'm not able to venture too far. You, Jenny, must bring the world to me.'

'Oh. Right. Yes.' Jenny backed towards the landing door, the tray balanced precariously on hands that were trembling. Once escaped, she took a few deep breaths.

What the heck was going on here at all? At least Auntie Mavis had been predictable. At least Jenny had known that she would be either drunk or in a state of trance. This was like . . . like two completely separate people. Should she tell Mr Skipton that his wife was going odd? No, he wouldn't care. And Briony was too daft to talk to, and Uncle Dan wouldn't be here till tomorrow.

She carried the tray into a kitchen where, although nothing had changed, the atmosphere seemed lighter, brighter and fuller of air to breathe. 'Mrs Hardman,' she began.

'What, love? Oh aye, she's finished her coffee. Leave it yonder near the big sink, Iris'll see to it after. Get yourself a drop of tea out of yon pot if you want some.'

'She's gone all funny, Mrs Hardman.'

'Iris? She's never been right since the Zeppelin, that's why she moved out to the country. Still keeps all the lights out at night in case the bother starts again. Can't do nowt with her, love, least said soonest mended. To top it all, she's deafer than ever.'

'No, it's Mrs Skipton.'

The cook-housekeeper stopped pummelling the bread dough, wiping her large hands on a capacious white wrap-over apron. Her forearms, huge and smooth, were like two hams ready for hanging. The round face was set in lines of something that almost became seriousness, though her nature was not normally grim. 'Watch yourself, lass. Her's even started being nice to Briony, and she can't stand nobody excepting you most of the time. I reckon she's play-acting.'

'But why?'

The enormous shoulders raised themselves and dropped immediately. 'Who can say? The road she's treated my good food over the years, nothing would surprise me.'

'She's trying to make her peace with God, I think. She's not got much longer and she knows she hasn't always been . . . nice.'

'Nice?' shouted the cook. 'Don't have me laughing, Jenny. I'm no use at bread if I crack off laughing. Listen to me. There's more goes on in that little head of hers than you'd find between the pages of Mr Skipton's library. Her'll not change her spots at this stage, love. Even if she could, they'd likely go to stripes, 'cos she's all cat, believe me. She can jump from purring to scratching and spitting quicker than you can say cheese.'

'Oh.'

'Never mind "oh"! Just watch your back at all times. Keep her fed and warm, mind the sores on her bottom, look out for dark skin, 'cos it could mean gangrene, read to her when her eyes get tired. Yes, I know she's a sick woman, Jenny. Sickness brings out the worst or the best, and she never had no best. Happen she can't help it, happen she's been badly treated, but that's no reason for the rest of us to suffer. Go on, now.'

As Jenny left the kitchen, Minnie Hardman eased her bulk into a chair. She'd heard the stories – everybody had heard the tale about Jenny being abandoned here as a baby. Did the evil bitch believe that Jenny was Mr Skipton's? Was she looking to get revenge, would she try to get rid of the girl? Permanently rid?

The bread dough was starting to rise before its time, so Minnie jumped up and tackled the job in hand. No use crying over milk that had been spilt long before Minnie's own time in this house. But her eyes were moist all the same, and she had to wipe her face before dividing the dough. She fought the sweat and tears brought on by anger, reminding herself sharply that her baking was no good when she came over all emotional. Bread, she thought, was a living thing, an agile barometer that spoke clearly about the temper of whoever had made it.

Still. It was a blinking shame, it was a pity the woman upstairs hadn't lost her power of speech as well. Because she had a funny effect on young girls, did Eloise Skipton. A very funny effect.

'Jenny, do you have a birth certificate?'

Jenny, perched on the top step of the ladder, just managed to save herself from tumbling to the ground. 'Yes,' she answered feebly before giving herself time to think. Taking care not to stumble, she climbed down to floor level, grateful for stability once she stood on the thick carpet. It was almost as if the mistress had tried to catch her unprepared and off-balance.

'Might I see it?' Henry had laughed at the time, had giddily whispered that he was the father of many such babies, so Jenny had been swept beneath the rug as a joke, something to smile about occasionally. 'I am about to make a will,' she said through a smile that was suitably pathetic and weak. Perhaps she had never really known her husband. She certainly did not know him now. Had he been lying? If so, and if this Jenny should turn out to be his daughter, then the plan would need to change . . .

'Uncle Dan's got it,' muttered Jenny, her face burning with nervousness.

There would be a different ending to Jenny's story if . . . if . . . no! It didn't bear consideration. 'Where does he keep it?'

'In his rooms.' The washleather, twisting and turning in her fingers, was almost in knots. 'Anyway, miss, why ever would you need that just to make a will?'

Eloise sniffed, trying and failing to produce a few tears. 'I intend to give you just a token, my dear. I would not embarrass you by leaving a lot of money to your name. But I do need to know who exactly you are. It's a legal matter.' She sensed that Jenny would not know too much about the law in such areas.

'I can't have me birth papers unless he says. Uncle Dan, I mean.'

'Nonsense.' The old coating of steel was entering the voice, so she moderated it immediately. 'Your birth certificate is your own property. My solicitor will need to see it—'

'No. I don't want you to leave me anything.'

'Again, I say nonsense. Surely you do not wish to forget me?'

Jenny stared at the totally unforgettable. 'I'll remember you, miss.'

'Jenny?' Once more, the words held a faint echo of command and demand. 'I want to know who you are, who your parents were. Of course, I've heard about Oonagh, but we don't have an inkling about your father.' She paused momentarily. 'Do you really know who he is or was?'

Jenny cursed her blazing cheeks. If she told the truth, Uncle Dan would suffer. It was still hard to think of him as Dad, but he was her father and he might lose his job. No, Mr Skipton would never sack him. Would he? But even if he didn't get the sack, folk would likely look at him different, as if he were a bad man. 'I can't tell nobody,' she said eventually.

'You can tell me, Jenny. You can tell me anything, because I am going nowhere, except to the grave. Your secret will lie with me in my coffin. I shall tell no-one. No-one at all.' She spoke softly, smoothly now, her voice almost hypnotic. 'Say the name, Jenny, say the name.' She was sure, almost sure that this was no Skipton off-cut, yet in spite of that, she needed the confirmation to be absolute.

Jenny blinked rapidly, like one returning from an absorbing daydream. 'I'll have to talk to Uncle Dan first.'

'No! No, you mustn't. Think how hurt he will be if he discovers that I am naming you in my will. You and not him. I have no desire to cause pain to a man who has been so long in our employ. Just listen to me . . . Where are you—?' The voice cut itself off when its owner found herself speaking to an empty room.

Jenny flew up the attic stairs two at a time, sitting breathless on the landing as soon as she reached the top. Uncle Dan was resting, had only got back from the convalescent home this morning. What should she do, what must she do? It seemed unfair to bother a man who had been so ill, yet she couldn't go back to the mistress, not now. There'd be all that mithering again, and Jenny was past coping with it, had taken just about enough. The right thing needed to be done. The right thing was probably to tell the mistress to mind her own flaming business, but she was ill too, iller than Uncle Dan . . .

'What's up, lass?'

The tears streamed as she jumped up, turned and threw herself into large brown arms that looked so comfortable beneath the rolled-up shirt sleeves. 'She wants me certificate, Uncle Dan. She wants to know who I am for her will, so she can leave me summat or other.' The message arrived fractured by noisy, ugly sobs.

She felt a hand patting her back, heard a whisper that sounded like, 'She wants to know who you're not, more like,' then she was guided through to Uncle Dan's sitting room and placed in a chair with a flowered cover and a loose spring that dug into her behind. 'Whatever am I to do, Uncle Dan?' she moaned.

He pushed a glass into her hand. The base of the container was covered in a yellowish liquid. 'Get yourself on the outside of that for a start. I'm going down yonder to talk to her highness.'

'You can't!'

'Swallow it. Do as you're told, I'm your father. From now on, come what may, you shall call me "Dad". It's none of your doing, this mess, and we'll manage some road. Just you wait here while I put yon missus in her place.' He was still breathless after his brush with pneumonia, but anger overcame frailty. 'I'll burst her bloody balloon for her,' he muttered.

The whisky stung, so she gasped a few times before replying, 'But you might get the sack. If you go, it'll be my doing.'

'Why, what have you been up to?' shouted the man who had never raised his voice before. He inhaled to steady the beating of a heart that had been sorely tested of late. 'Did you get bloody born, was it your idea?' Seeing the fear in her eyes, he dropped to his knees in front of the chair. 'I loved your mam, lass,' he said, the words arriving soft and gentle as ever. 'And you are a piece of that love, the only part of it that's left to me.' The strong, handsome face worked, seeming to blur at its edges as the large man fought his emotions. 'In bed all that while, I started thinking on, you know, meditating over things. I'd already decided to tell Henry,' he said. 'I call him Henry on the quiet, when there's just us two. Before, with Sloane here, I couldn't bring meself to say I was your dad, 'cos she would have made a picnic out of it once it had got out.'

Jenny bent her head to the empty glass. 'She was an unhappy woman, Uncle Dan.' She glanced upward and grinned weakly in spite of fraught nerves.

The thick eyebrows had raised themselves, while a mischievous smile did battle with the grief in his eyes.

'I mean Dad,' she whispered shyly.

'Say it again, love.'

'Dad. Dad, Dad, Dad.'

He swallowed quickly, 'We can go to Mavis's house if we're not wanted here.'

'Maria and Anthony are there.'

'That's all right, we can double up all round. I've slept in worse places when I've been on the road looking for . . . for Oonagh.'

'Will we ever find her?'

He shrugged, trying to throw off the pain. 'I don't know. She might be dead. If she is, I can accept that. If she's not, and she's stopped away all this time, then we'd be best not mithering anyway. I've give over waiting, Jenny.' He stood up. 'And that woman had better stop mithering my daughter and all.'

He touched her hands, threw on his jacket, then smoothed down the thick brown hair. Without another word, he left the room.

Jenny placed her glass on the floor and went to stand at the window. It was set on the roof at the front of the Hall, and the view over rolling countryside was magnificent. He would miss being here, would Uncle Dan. She corrected herself firmly. Views from windows didn't count anyway. Her dad, not her uncle, would be looked after no matter where they went. He was her dad. At last, she had a proper family.

'I didn't send for you, Crawley.' She tried to smile, tried to adhere to the decision to be nice, gentle, a harmless woman who was dying.

'It's Jenny,' he said without preamble. 'She's fretting herself over this birth certificate.' He did not address her as 'miss' or as 'ma'am', but simply stood and stared right into her eyes as if he were an equal.

192

The reply tripped smoothly from her lips. 'Oh, I am sorry if I have upset her.'

'Are you?'

'Of course I am.' Temper threatened, but she still retained her tenuous dignity. 'Jenny is a good friend to me, someone I value.'

He strolled to the window, hands pushed casually into trouser pockets. 'But you still want to see her pedigree, eh? Were you thinking of having her registered with some kennel club?'

'Not at all. I simply wondered . . . well . . .'

'Whether she was your husband's love child? Whether she might be his daughter, someone who could claim from him?'

'No.' She was plainly floundering in a whirlpool of her own making, and she realized that this servant would see her confusion the moment he turned his head. 'I am doing some work on my will,' she muttered. 'And I needed to know Jenny's . . . position. I don't want to make bequests to someone who might squander them. If her father were an inebriate, or a gambler—'

He swivelled, said sharply, 'He is neither,' then watched as her face worked in an effort to appear calm. Slowly, he approached the bed, aware of the quick eyes that seemed sufficiently alert to survive the death of the body which contained them. 'You don't need to know who he is,' he said softly, so softly that she strained to hear. 'Jenny's a good girl. I've known her since she was born, since she was left here eighteen years since. Whoever her dad is, she's still a trustworthy servant.'

'Yes, I understand that.'

He leaned over her, frowning so deeply that the eyebrows seemed bent on meeting. 'Then understand this, if you can. Jenny is my daughter – mine. That's why I've paid for her to be kept all these years. Did you think your husband was paying, slipping me a few bob now and then so that my sister would rear his shame? I'll tell you this for nowt, if Jenny had been his, he'd have brought her here and adopted her.' He bit back some words concerning the dead Sophie. This woman had lost a child, and he didn't want her to think that Henry hadn't shared the pain, that he could have replaced the baby with another infant.

She was looking at him steadily, no emotion showing in the slate-grey eyes. 'I will tell no-one,' she said evenly.

He straightened and pulled at the sleeves of his jacket. 'Well, I will,' he said. 'It's time the record was put right. I was going to do it anyway, tell the master. Tonight's as good a time as any.'

Behind the mask, Eloise's mind had jumped into a faster gear. How would she manage to follow her plan while Jenny had a father in the house, someone who might interfere, someone with a paternal right to guide, advise, protect?

'I'll get back to my rooms,' he said coldly.

'Very well. I hope your health will be back to its usual robust self soon.' She pondered. Yes, she would put the idea to Jenny. Jenny would be pleased to think of her father recuperating in Bispham at the Skiptons' expense. It had happened before, servants getting a holiday by the sea after illness, so no precedent would be set. Of course, she would have to send one of her notes to Henry. One of her billets-doux, as she bitterly named them these days. How many women were forced to write to their husbands, men who lived in the same house, shared the same bathroom? 'You may go now, Crawley.' She had not been able to resist this last small attempt to underline her superiority.

He half-smiled, swung round, then ambled from the room with a slowness that spoke of contempt, but she was too busy to notice the slight.

The situation was promising now. She had the final confirmation that Jenny was not Henry's child, so the original plan was going to suffice. None of it promised to be easy, but at least she didn't have to work out a different plot, one at which she had enjoyed no practice. Her previous stumbling attempts had taught her to be more subtle, more devious in her approach.

Once Dan had gone away for a month's recuperation, Jenny would fall ripe from the tree. And the fruit of

Eden's garden would be recreated, the serpent would writhe again.

Claughton Street had been invaded. There were no bombs, no huge silver balloons hanging in the sky, no soldiers parading up and down to show off their uniforms before embarkation. This particular breach of the peace did not come dressed in khaki; the whole platoon had arrived on foot from the station, umpteen children, a weary-looking woman with a torn coat and a vague expression, then finally, bringing up the bedraggled rear, a man who would have been tall except for a stoop that only just failed to render him hunch-backed. Both adults disappeared into number seventeen, leaving the younger trespassers to indulge in a variety of outdoor pursuits, all of which were far from seemly.

Curtains twitched, infants were dragged screaming into houses, doors slammed. A woman who was doing a tardy step-stoning tipped up her bucket and spoiled her pattern; even the butcher's lad seemed amazed, standing rigidly at the end of the street, a short string of three sausages dangling unnoticed from his basket.

The residents of Claughton Street were not visible, but every front door had at least one ear fastened to its panelling. In some cases, a mother listened near the top of the door, while youngsters applied their attention lower down, one hand gripping Mam's skirts just to be on the safe side.

It was the noise of the aliens that caused the sudden silence among the permanent inhabitants of the terraces. Nothing like this had ever happened in Claughton Street before. Where had they come from? And were they going to stay? The looks of them had been enough, every one of them with red hair and clothes that looked as if they'd been slept in, jumpers inside out, hems jagged, socks and stockings full of holes and of a universal ill-washed grey. But the din was something else, because whoever they were, they didn't speak English.

'Cum on out, I seen yer, gizza go of yer skippin' rope,' yelled a voice that sounded female.

''Ey Missus, open yer door, let's see de size o' your lad's marbles.' This arrived plainer, was presumed delivered by a boy child.

It was a form of English, then, a strange form with rather posh *o*'s and some *t*'s that were distinctly *s*. *Th* seemed to have disappeared altogether from the ex tremely odd vocabulary, had been replaced by *d*, so the street echoed with 'dis' and 'dese'.

No-one ventured out, even though the strangers had been identified as probable residents of mainland Britain. Everyone who didn't live at numbers fifteen and nineteen was suitably grateful to be in relative peace, and sorry for those condemned to flank such chaos. Those across the way claimed ringside seats on wooden chairs, each sitter shielded by a thick cotton-lace curtain.

They were everywhere, swinging from the gas lamps, doing handstands against walls, sitting on folks' steps and spoiling the donkey-stoning. Many of the furtive onlookers tried to do a head count, but the red-haired vandals were quicker than cockroaches, more agile than fleas. They seemed to range in age from three-ish to fourteen-ish, and the older ones should doubtless have been at work, as should the man with the stoop. It was plain that they could do with the money, if only to pay for a bar of soap, preferably Lifebuoy because of its antiseptic qualities.

The bent man appeared in the doorway of seventeen. 'Gerrin 'ere,' he yelled in a voice that brooked no argument and hardly matched the weariness in his back. 'All of yerz,' he added after taking a hefty swig from a blue-and-white striped pint mug of tea.

They crowded into the house, pushing and shoving, several smaller ones seeming to get so stuck that a 'pop' was expected when they finally shot inside. It was like something out of a film; the Keystone Cops might have made a fortune out of copying this lot. Mavis Crawley's door remained open, probably beause there was no room to swing it shut. The watchers remembered Mavis with a degree of regret; she might have been a bit on the peculiar side, but she'd never brought a circus this size into a decent neighbourhood with nice clean windows and stoned steps.

Ena Burke sallied forth from number twenty-nine, her gait determinedly nonchalant, a large covered tray in her hands. She had made two dozen scones for Maria's visiting family, but after what she'd just seen, she reckoned five dozen might have been just about enough. There were nine children, or so she'd managed to count during all the acrobatics. Now, if they ate two each, that would be eighteen gone, leaving just six for Mr Hesketh, his wife, Maria, Anthony and that fireman, if he turned up. That meant one apiece for the grown-ups and one left over. She should have made a sponge to top things up, a quick one would have done, one of those Crestona mixes.

The door was still open, and she had no spare hand to knock with, so she stepped into a din the likes of which she had not encountered since the war had ended. Within ten seconds, she had been relieved of her tray and was squashed against the dresser by three or four children with enormous smiles, two of which were enhanced by missing teeth. There was something very touching, Ena thought, about a kiddy with gaps.

She heard Maria shouting, 'It's all right, Mrs Burke, I've got your cakes,' then the man swept the little ones away, brushing them aside as if they were no bigger than insects and just as troublesome. 'Ta, queen,' he said. 'You seen to our Maria an' her mate when de gas killed de auntie.' This was spoken so quickly that Ena had to think before replying in a voice loud enough to be heard above the bedlam, 'Oh aye. That were nowt, Mr Hesketh.'

A sudden quiet arrived in the stifling room. The nearest child looked round at her from behind her father, large green eyes staring solidly at the visiting neighbour. 'You don't talk proper,' she said almost distinctly. 'Dey never talked proper at de station too.' She turned and looked at the quiet woman who sat fingering a copy of the *Daily Sketch*. 'Mam?' she asked.

Mrs Hesketh didn't look up from the paper. 'What's that, Josie?' Her voice was softer, gentler than the others.

'Are we still in Liverpool, Mam?'

'No, love.'

'Is dis a different part of England, Mam?'

'Yes, love.'

The girl smiled at Ena. 'Dat's all right, den. Dat's why you don't talk proper. 'S not your fault.'

Ena burst out laughing and reached for the little girl who had judged her to be a poor communicator. 'Eeh lass,' she giggled. 'It takes all sorts to make a world, and you'll do for me, sunshine.'

Josie lifted her thin arms and found herself hoisted up against a huge maternal breast. 'We're noisy, aren't we, missus?' she asked solemnly. 'Dey don't like us in our street neider. Me mam's de only one what's quiet. An' she gets loud when me dad's drunk. Next door gets de police in to us on Sat'day nights.'

The general hubbub had started again, so Ena and Josie's conversation was reasonably private. Ena looked over the child's head to where the quiet mother sat with her face bent to the newspaper. That poor, thin, weary woman had given birth to this lot. Though she seemed not to notice them, apparently had the ability to block them out, even to forget about them. Did Josie get the attention she needed? Did any of them receive love?

'I like you,' whispered Josie.

'And I like you too. How old are you?'

'Seven. I've gorra noder loose tooth. See, it wiggles about. Do you want to 'ave a pull on it?'

'No, I'll not bother, you might get hurt.'

'Oh.' Josie glanced shyly at her new friend, then batted the thick, dark gold eyelashes almost seductively. 'Can we go in your 'ouse?' she whispered.

'What for?'

The narrow shoulders lifted and fell. 'To look at it.'

'It's nobbut a house, lass.'

'Nobbut?'

Ena grinned, creasing her fat face until her eyes almost disappeared. 'Nobbut's short for nothing but. It means only. It's only a house.'

Josie sighed deeply. 'Is it nice?'

'It's . . . well, it's all right.'

'Is dere mill-yuns of people in it? Me dad says our 'ouse 'as a popperlation exp-erlosion. Means we've got mill-yuns at ours. I've got me own spoon now, 'cos I'm seven. It 'asn't got no 'andle, 'cos it fell off, like, bur it's me own spoon.'

Ena blinked. Her own spoon? What the hell did she use before she got a spoon? Had she eaten with her fingers, had she shared, waited for another to finish? She coughed. 'Mr Hesketh?'

'Call me Ernie.'

There was a sudden rush for the kitchen and food, and Ena found herself breathing more easily once the other children had left. It was as if they had been using up the oxygen, as if their hot bodies had drained all the energy from such a small, confining space.

'Josie wants to see my house,' said Ena. Mr Hesketh made no reply. He simply shrugged, then followed the crowd into the back kitchen.

At last, the mother looked up, a slight frown creasing the strangely smooth forehead. 'Josie likes houses,' she said. 'She's always going in somebody's. And she sometimes comes out with more than what she went in with. Take her, but watch your stuff.' This was said in a matter-of-fact tone. A thief in the family was plainly no novelty, no cause for shame.

Ena led Josie out, relieved to get away from such a crush.

Maria watched her family swooping on the food, saw eyes light up at the sight, the taste of good, home-cooked scones. Her mother only served up shop-bought, and even then it was a case of first come, first served, last in gets an empty plate, no sign of a crumb. Frances Hesketh had never been organized. Their home was dirty, had always been dirty. As more children arrived, the mess increased, piling up in corners, collecting in the back yard and in the loft. Dad had floored the roofspace somewhat half-heartedly after some of his booty from the docks had crashed through a bedroom ceiling, but there was scarcely room up there now for his ill-gotten gains.

She carried a cup of tea and a scone to her mother. The kids had spilled out into the yard and were making a racket, but the front room was quiet enough. 'Here you are, Mam.'

'Ta, love.' The hand was thin, bony, almost transparent, but it was as steady as a rock. This was why her mother had survived, thought Maria. Nerves of iron and a mind that could fix itself on the unattainable, daydreams found in books and newspapers, periodicals, even comic papers. 'That's a lovely scone, Maria. You'll have to thank that woman.'

Maria knelt by her mother's chair. 'They're cheaper if you make your own, Mam. You'd never get that many from a shop for the price of flour and stuff.'

Frances Hesketh placed her cup in the fireplace. 'I've no time for all that.'

'Make time.'

The older woman smiled and nodded knowingly. 'I could stand at the sink all day, Maria. I could cook and wash and sew my life away. The only thing that keeps me going is my bit of imagination.'

Maria dropped her chin and inhaled deeply. Taking a mother to task was a somewhat daunting thing. 'So the best way you can manage is to ignore your children? Mam, it's first up, best dressed. And I mean that, it's not a joke. We used to fight over one skirt and the decent blouse. There's so many of us. You should make some kind of a rota, get one to shop, one to help with the washing, do some proper cooking. You'd enjoy things more if you got the house sorted out.'

'I'm past caring, love.'

'But the kids care. They hate it. I know that, because I hated it.'

Frances licked the scone-crumbs from her lower lip. 'I never asked to have so many babies.'

'Then you should have done something about it.'

'I'm a Catholic and he's my husband.' The tone was neutral, devoid of sentiment. 'I love you all.' Even now, while speaking these words of affection, there was little warmth in the voice.

'They'll go wild, you know. The lads'll end up like me father, pinching, working when they can't get money any other way. I was lucky, being one of the older lot. But these little ones are getting away with murder because you're always reading and dreaming and—'

'Maria!' At last, some vigour. 'Do you want me to die? Do you want me to finish up like Mary Clarke's mam, worn out at thirty-eight, down a hole at forty? The way I cope is by standing back, away from it all. At least I'm here. How would they go on without me to watch his drinking? And how would you manage in my shoes, just one pair in three years? Would you be any better than me with all these mouths to feed?'

Maria sniffed back her tears. In a way, she had always understood this strange mother of hers. It was a weary life, a tedious existence. In the books, Frances Hesketh saw how things might have been, how they could have been. 'Mam?'

'What?'

'Can I save just one of them? Can I have our Josie?'

The grey-green eyes were suddenly old. Old, wise and almost unbearably sad. 'I'd give all of them away if I thought they'd be looked after,' she said. 'I'd give all of them a chance away from Ernie. He's my man and I love him, but there's neither of us cut out to mind this tribe. You have her, see to her, give her a good time.'

'Oh, Mam.'

'What?'

'Isn't life sad?'

Frances Hesketh stared down into her cup, as if she were looking for answers in the coarse leaves that floated muddily in its base. 'I told you that years ago,' she said. 'It's a vale of tears, girl. And it's better if you cry on your own, because no man's shoulder is strong enough to bear the tears of woman.' She looked up. 'Remember that, my queen. Smile. And when your smile fades, turn to another woman. Don't ever let a man see you weep, or he'll just take advantage of the weakness.'

'I wouldn't swap you, Mam.'

Frances ran a slow finger down her daughter's serious face. 'And I wouldn't swap you for all the angels in heaven. I don't know how you did it, but you've turned out great.' She glanced at the clock. 'We'll have to be getting that train. We've to change all over the place, then get trams. I don't know where he got the money for all the fares, but I think it's something to do with a new pile of boxes in the loft. God knows what he's got his hands on this time.'

Maria stood, leaned against the fireguard. 'I wish you could stop near, where I could keep an eye on you.'

'Hey,' smiled Frances. 'Who's the mother here?' She was improving herself, was their Maria. There was a bit of flesh on her face at last, a twinkle in the eyes, one or two curves beginning to fill out the skirt and blouse. And only their Maria would have thought of putting that big jug of orange flowers in the empty grate. She carried her own sunlight, this one, made colour wherever it was lacking. Maria would go far, certainly a lot further than the streets that butted on to the dock road.

'Mam?'

'What is it, love?'

Maria faltered, a finger to her lower lip. She breathed deeply, dropped her hands and stood with them folded in front of her. 'Mam, if you had something of somebody's, and somebody else had told you that the first somebody couldn't have it yet, and you didn't know whether to give it to the first somebody in case the second somebody turned in her grave . . . ?'

'I'm with you, girl.'

Maria smiled. Only her mother could have kept track of such a rambling and unfinished question. 'Well, what do I do?'

Frances tapped her teeth with a frayed fingernail. 'I'd use me judgement. See, the second somebody isn't here – right?'

'Right, Mam.'

'And the first somebody doesn't know about the second somebody's wishes, am I on the ball?'

'Liverpool one, Bolton nil,' chuckled Maria.

Frances straightened in her chair. 'There'll come a time in the first somebody's life when it's right to give them whatever it is. Like if there's a change happening, going away or getting married or having a baby. You'll just know, love.'

'Thanks, Mam.' Frances might be a bit of a scatterbrain

when it came to scones, but she was excellent at dealing with the less tangible aspects of life.

Anthony tumbled in at the front door, the rumpled hair giving him a startled appearance. He stopped in his tracks, grinning lovingly at the woman who had given him life, the mother whom nobody slandered in his presence, not if they valued their teeth. 'Hiya, Mam,' he said breathlessly. 'I've run all the way from the pub.'

'Oh God,' sighed Frances. 'Another drinker?' She was confident that there was little danger of Anthony staggering in his father's footsteps.

Anthony's face seemed ready to split, so pleased was he to see his mam, so happy to have her almost to himself for a moment or two. 'No, I've been humping boxes. The boss was testing me, I think. So I showed him what I could do.'

'And you, Maria?' asked Frances. 'Have you got work?'

Maria grimaced comically. 'I'm the seamstress for a few posh folk on the other side of town. I'll have to do some jobs on the spot, and bring the others home. Then I'm making frocks and things from people's odds and ends, material they can get cheap at the mill shops.'

'Your patterns?' There was a trace of anxiety on Frances's face, as if she cared deeply, probably so deeply that it seldom showed, about her daughter's dream coming true.

'I'll carry on in me spare time.'

A man's face poked itself round the open door. 'Have you got room for a little one?' He was a long way from little, thought the other occupants of the room. Maria voiced the joint opinion. 'If you're the little one, don't go bringing your big brother round here. Mam,' she went on almost shyly, 'this is Denis. Denis, this is me mother.'

The tall man stooped to shake a cool hand that felt like glass in his too-strong grip. 'Sorry,' he muttered. 'Did I hurt you?'

'No,' answered Frances. He wouldn't hurt their Maria either . . .

'Frank?' yelled a loud voice from the kitchen. 'Dey've ate the bloody scones and now dere's two of them stuck on top of de lavvy roof, dey can't get down.'

'Who's Frank?' asked Denis.

'Me mam,' replied Maria. 'He'll not tire himself, me dad. He cuts all the names down short, so he'll save wear on his vocals.'

Frances simply smiled. Maria had got herself a nice man with a brave, romantic job, a fellow who wouldn't go drinking and pinching all over the dock road. He saved lives for a living, did Denis. And she'd have to have some new shoes before long. For the wedding.

Chapter Eight

CARLA SLOANE ENJOYED HER WORK AT THE FINNEGANS'. SHE was finally in receipt of the appreciation that was her due, so she threw herself into the job if not happily, then with a degree of contentment she had never encountered before.

Imelda was a woman with few useful abilities. She had borne no children, therefore her maternal depths had never been plumbed, but she adored her husband and spent most of her days preparing for his homecoming. Domesticity found no place in such preparations. The whole of Imelda's energy went into 'improving herself', to which end she washed and set her hair repeatedly, pressed her clothes, painted her face and, when the Angelus bell sounded, prayed to a God who, in Carla's books, should take a dim view of time wasted on such personal and egocentric embellishments.

Imelda's friendly and affectionate concern for 'poor Carla' was immediate and enduring. She provided the unfortunate woman with Ven-Yusa Oxygen face cream, Harlene Hair Food and even New-Pin washing soap to protect Carla's hands during chores. Lotions and potions frequently found their way into Carla's bag, turning up at odd and sometimes unfortunate moments, during searches for fares, or when she groped in the capacious compartments for a refreshing mint. At such times, she felt a stab of unbidden, certainly unwanted, self-pity, and she would eat another sweet to send the pain away. She was ugly, had accepted her deformities, and she tried to hope that Mrs Finnegan too would learn to accept them. Even as she hoped, she knew that she hoped in vain. Imelda was like a terrier with a bone, a miniature and supposedly docile animal who was quite capable of proving strength of character should anyone try to take away her prize. Yes, Imelda was on a mission, and Carla knew only too well the reputations of Catholic missionaries. They never knew when to give up.

But Carla thought that things had gone a little too far when denture advertisements, culled from various national and local presses, began cutting themselves away, as if by magic, from surrounding newsprint. They turned up all over the place – on the wooden drainer, under the pillow of the Finnegans' unmade bed, on the living room mantelpiece. The housekeeper never mentioned them, though she was aware of some searching glances from her employer after the cuttings had been screwed up and relegated to fireplace or bin. Getting the teeth done would no doubt be an expensive business, so Imelda's so-called home assistant and cook studiously ignored the printed messages.

A full frontal approach was certain to come, and Carla did her best to be girded against such a confrontation. She had opened up to Pol, who had become the nearest ever to a friend, and Pol had laughed heartily about the whole matter. 'Ah, she's a great girl, is Imelda. Straight from the potato fields and into marriage with himself, she went. There's not a bad thought in her, nor a bad bone in that idle little body. She's only trying to improve you, Carla, for she'll want you to get a man.'

'I don't want a man,' Carla had answered. It was the truth. A further piece of veracity lay in the fact that Imelda could not embrace the concept of life without a husband. Every last Eve should have her Adam, according to the tiny, self-appointed sage. A woman without a man was no woman at all. Except, of course, for the wonderful and truly exceptional brides of Christ who had given themselves up into poverty, chastity and obedience. Imelda, like the nuns, adored her master. It was always

'Franklyn says' and 'Franklyn thinks', as if Imelda had been born simply to magnify and glorify the funny little man. Though she did display the odd slip in the obedience vows, and Carla was sometimes left to clear up after such heinous indiscretions.

Carla was thinking about all this as she cleaned the brasses in a kitchen that positively shone at last. She sat at a large, scrubbed, white-wood table, rubbing hard at some greenish crevices in a heavy wall plaque. Her life had worked out quite well apart from all the creams and tonics. Pol had invited her to stay indefinitely, because the two blatantly ill-matched characters got on together extremely well. The job was fine and would undoubtedly improve once Mrs Finnegan forgot about Carla's appearance . . .

A shadow cast itself across newspapers that were spread out to save the table. Carla, still working furiously with a polishing cloth, raised her head. 'Did you want something, Mrs Finnegan?'

The minuscule dark-haired woman shook her daring bob. She had had the hair savagely cropped the day before, and was coaxing some kiss-curls into place with the aid of sticking plaster and hair grips. Carla cleared her throat. It wasn't her place, but someone ought to tell the silly creature that the plasters would probably pull her hair out. And it was such a stupid style, the hair all straight, then suddenly bursting into such obviously false curls on forehead and along cheekbones.

'I just needed a word,' pouted the scarlet cupid's bow mouth. 'And I wish you'd call me Imelda.' The voice was harsher than Pol's, genuinely Irish, but lacking in the softness that usually lilted through the speech of a daughter of Eire.

'It's not what I'm used to.'

Imelda shrugged. 'And the house isn't what you're used to either. This is no stately manor out in the wilds.' She waved a hand towards another detached house at the bottom of the garden. 'This is a normal place to live. Can't you get it into your head that Franklyn and I are your friends, just ordinary people who have made money? And what's money for, Carla?'

The big woman assaulted the brass, sniffed, lifted a shoulder. 'It's to do as you like with. To save, to spend—'

'Exactly. And sure Franklyn says to me the other day, he says, "Meldy" – he calls me Meldy when we're alone – "Meldy, can you not do something for Carla? It would do her a lot of good to be rid of them teeth," he says. You see, they're not good teeth, Carla. You've black holes in quite a few, for I've seen them with me own two eyes. Franklyn says they'll have what he calls an adverse effect on your stomach.'

'Indeed?' Carla gave her attention to a brass bell, a crinoline lady with a clapper of dirty base metal enshrouded beneath the silly wide skirt. Imelda was a woman of poor taste. And, no doubt, she was putting her own words into Franklyn's mouth again. Yes, this would be one of Imelda's ideas, another item with which to plague the long-suffering man.

'And you can't close your mouth, can you?' continued the shrill, somewhat birdlike voice. Though it would have to be a very noisy and persistent bird, perhaps an irate budgerigar . . . ?

'I've managed so far,' answered Carla, applying a firm rein to her rising temper. 'I'm how I was made, no excuses for it. The teeth don't bother me,' she lied, remembering last week's pain in a molar. 'If I can live with them, so can everyone else.'

Imelda stamped a foot. 'Put that stuff down till I talk to you.' A stamped foot meant serious business, business that would not wait its turn.

Carla dropped the rag and placed the bell on the *Daily Sketch*. The reckoning was coming, so she might as well just let it arrive without struggle, have the thing over and done with.

The lady of the house placed herself in a chair opposite Carla's. 'Now, listen. When I got me grown-up teeth, the two at the front were crossed, because I've just a small mouth, not enough room for such big teeth. So Daddy paid for me to go into Dublin for a plate. They took out the two teeth and gave me some nice pot ones. Ah, they were beautiful. But they sent me others loose and bad, so now I have all false at the top. And aren't they lovely? Would you know if I hadn't just now told you?'

'No,' said Carla lamely but truthfully. This argument was not going to be easy. So far, nothing but sense had been spoken. Not that it seemed sensible to get good teeth pulled just because they were crossed at the front. But the fact that Carla's own incisors would be better in the dustbin could not be refuted.

A childlike hand crept across the table and touched Carla's elbow. 'You wouldn't know yourself. It would make a mile of difference to your appearance.'

'Yes, I suppose it would.' She didn't want to be a painted beauty, normal would be enough.

'And they'd fit properly, which is more than can be said for those God gave you, may He have infinite mercy on me for the criticism. If your teeth lined up right, you'd do better with your food. Won't you let me bring you into town to get them ordered? Franklyn will pay. He is concerned for you. So am I. It is only right that I should take care of my own domestic assistant.'

Carla stared at the adult infant who was her employer. She had the body and mind of a child, the face of a woman past forty. But Imelda Finnegan was astute, strong in instinct. She worried about things like teeth and hair, skin and nails. She had probably forgotten more about self-improvement than Carla had ever known. But this would be such a drastic step. Pol had been no help, had simply said, 'Do as you like, do what feels right.' Carla decided to ask a sensible question. 'Doesn't food get stuck under the teeth?'

'Sometimes. Sure, you just manage, you just learn how to eat with them. See, I've cut out an advert for you.'

She spread it on the table, pushing aside brass, cleaning fluid and cloths. 'There you are, fifteen shillings for a full set, seven years' written guarantee. There'll be another two bob for the gas, I think. And if they break ever, sure they'll mend them the same day while you wait.'

Carla swallowed. She didn't much relish the idea of gas, but the toothache had plagued her more frequently of late. 'I don't want to walk about all gummy while they heal,' she said, knowing full well that, even without teeth, she could not possibly look any worse than she did now. A complete lack of mouth furniture might even be an improvement, though eating would be difficult.

'No need to be without,' insisted Imelda firmly. 'There, it's written down, fitted in four hours. You come home, then when the bleeding slows down, you go back for the teeth. It's all done in a flash these days. No running about with a great gap like I had.'

'Won't it hurt?'

Imelda pushed non-existent hair from her shoulder, forgetting that her locks had been fiercely shorn. 'I miss me long hair,' she sighed. 'Anything that's worth doing hurts. They'll give you tablets for the pain, then you just eat soft stuff for a few days.'

'I'll think about it.'

'Remember, Carla, your face will be lovely afterwards. When Pol came to ask could you have the job, she said you were taunted about your appearance when you were young. This will make a whole world of difference.'

'Will it?'

Imelda looked up at the ceiling. 'Haven't I prayed to all the saints up there about this? And didn't I get the strongest feeling that this is the right thing for you?'

There could be no answer to this. The housekeeper folded the newspaper and continued to clean brasses. Mrs Finnegan was probably right. Without these teeth sticking out all the time, she might even look human. And they were sore, so sore that the oil of cloves didn't have much effect any more.

'Will ye do it, Carla?' A 'you' often turned to 'ye' when she was pleading, usually when she was begging clothes money from Franklyn.

'I think,' said Carla slowly, 'I think I well might. But I don't like dentists.'

'Nobody does. They're a necessary evil, like the woman who sawed off all my lovely hair. Does it suit me?'

'Yes,' lied Carla heavily. 'It looks very nice. Shall I make a pot of tea?'

'Now that would be marvellous,' purred Imelda, effusive,

just as she always was after a victory. 'And I'll make an appointment for you with Mr Williams. He's a good dentist. He stopped all Franklyn's holes for six bob.'

Carla rose from her seat, knowing that she would gladly pay at least that sum if someone would stop the hole in Imelda's face, just dam the chatter for a while.

But Imelda was by no means finished. 'Pol tells me you've a statue of Our Lady on your bedroom window sill. But she also says that you're not a Catholic.'

The sound of cold water gushing into the kettle drowned Carla's loud thoughts. She was so irritated that even her mental functions seemed angry enough to be heard. The statue had been a gift from Maude, one of the few presents she had received from her sister. Maude had converted to Catholicism in order to marry her husband. After his untimely death, she had passed the figure on to Carla as a memento of a wonderful man. And he had been a wonderful man, the sole male person who had ever come close to making his wife's sister feel normal. He had discussed with Carla matters arising from newspaper articles, problems at his work, the inadequacies of Bury's civic dignitaries. So she had kept the statue to remind her that one person had considered her to be ordinary.

'Carla?' The water had stopped running and the kettle sat on the hob. 'Are you a lapsed Catholic?'

'No. I'm not anything.'

Imelda's tongue clicked to illustrate her impatience with such an attitude. 'Everybody's something. Even Protestants are something.'

'There was no praying in our house.' She placed a plate of crackers and cheese on the counter, then swept all the brasses off the table with one movement of her strong arms. With the ornaments cradled in the skirt of her large white apron, she attempted a smile. 'There's a nice bit of Lancashire,' she said, seeking to recover the comradely atmosphere. If she was going to be forced to listen to Imelda's witterings, she could at least discourage her from carrying on 'something mortallious', as Franklyn usually described such moods. 'And some Irish butter.' She must not lose her temper here. Few houses would take her on without recent references, and while the Finnegans were not strictly up to standard, she owed them some civility for employing her. And Pol would not be too pleased either if the job came to an end.

'Would ye go to mass with me, Carla?'

How much further was this pushing going? Spine and neck stiffened as the large woman left the room with her apron filled with brasses. 'I'll be back in a moment,' she said quietly. Panic rose in her throat as she replaced the ornaments. In what Imelda called the drawing room, Carla was alone, but she would have to get back into that kitchen, or Madam would surely pursue her quarry. Imelda Finnegan wasn't one for letting go. She worried away at her husband like a small and angry rat tackling an even smaller rodent. And when the nibbling didn't work, words and plates flew thicker than autumn leaves in an orchard, splinters of porcelain littering the floor. The words would hang in the air; they were almost tangible on the day after a row. Words could not be shifted, but Carla was often left with the job of sweeping up the truly visible evidence of discontent. There wasn't one complete set of china; even some of the nicer vases and ashtrays had disappeared of late, and Carla had no intention of joining her master as a recipient of such missiles. Better, then, to simply agree. Imelda might well enter one of her monumental sulks if faced by resistance.

'Did you hear my question?' asked Imelda as soon as her housekeeper got through the door.

'Yes.'

'And you've no answer? Surely there's no earthly reason why you should not come with me to mass? If you were a member of some other faith, then I wouldn't ask.'

'I'll come.'

The small, prematurely wrinkled face split into a grin. 'Well, isn't that just great? You've had me worried desperate, for it's no life if you haven't religion. Even Protestants – and the good Lord knows how mistaken they are – have something to hold on to. I sensed your need, Carla. If you can take to the one true faith, you will be greatly comforted.'

Carla poured the tea and sighed inwardly. This was going to be a lovely weekend, then. She had weekends off, and looked forward to a bit of peace and quiet. On Saturday and Sunday evenings, Pol went out to ply the trade that was never discussed between the two women. Where she took her 'gentleman friends' was a mystery, a riddle that Carla chose not to solve. Alone in the house, Carla would read, take a bath in front of the dining room fire, wash her hair. On Sunday mornings, she had a lie-in, seldom rising before ten o'clock. Pol emerged even later; she never went to church, preferred to say her prayers alone in front of a statue with a red light burning at its feet.

Oh well, there was no use arguing. Carla would go, this Sunday, to be greatly comforted. There was no alternative.

He ran into the house, his breathing shallow and fast, head jerking quickly from side to side as he searched for some sign of life. 'Damn and blast that bloody motor,' he swore softly. When he had bought the wretched thing, he had done it with hatred in his heart, even though the purchase had been inevitable. Everybody owned one now. Everybody with a business, at least. Some had two of the things, one for work, one for Sunday best or for the wife and children to play around with.

Well, there was a lot to be said for the horse-drawn cart. A horse would never have done this. The brake on a cart was visible, understandable, needed no oil and little coaxing. These flaming engines wanted mothering every five minutes, water for the radiator, soft chamois for the frail skin of paint, a persuasive and even rhythm on a starter handle that could break a man's hand whenever it decided to sulk. Like twice a day. But a cart obeyed every time, just a flick or a slight pull on a leather rein. And anyway, horses were imbued with sense and discretion. No, a good horse would have stopped well short of this kind of accident.

He ran from the hall, a bloody bundle clutched to his chest. Heedless of good clothes, he nursed the animal, kept it close to the heat of his own body, as if he could will

213

it to live. The kitchen was empty. Mrs Hardman would be at home now with her cats, a pot of cocoa and a penny dreadful.

Jenny. He would find Jenny, because she was not the sort to flinch. Briony would never cope, and Dan was away at the seaside for at least two months. *She* had insisted, in her note, that the good man should have the whole summer as paid leave. What was she up to now? No, no time for that.

He flew up the stairs two at a time just as the hall clock celebrated midnight in soft, musical chime. Even Mrs Hardman would be asleep by this time, cats in cardboard boxes, love stories stacked away for tomorrow, princesses abandoned to their passionate and breathless expectations of white knights.

He did not pause to knock, simply throwing open the door and touching a switch that caused the room to flood with light. Her hair was spread all over the pillow like pale yellow silk. Another princess waiting for her . . . ? He must really try to stop these mental wanderings. 'Jenny?'

She sat up slowly, eyes narrowing against unwelcome and intrusive brightness. 'What?' she asked. Almost immediately, she realized who this was, first pulling a sheet against her body to acknowledge that a man was present, then adding an 'oh sir' as she quickly completed her identification of the intruder.

'I've hit a pup,' he whispered. 'Can you help me?'

'Dear God,' she exclaimed softly, taking in the stains on his coat. 'I'm coming.' She leapt from the bed and grabbed at a newly-purchased cheap dressing gown, swiftly covering the white cotton nightdress. From a drawer she pulled an old wool cardigan. 'Give him to me.'

He hesitated just fractionally. 'It's a mess.'

'I don't mind. You run down and make sure there's hot water. Take some clean towels from my bathroom.' My bathroom? she thought as she received the limp body. But the slip of tongue was forgotten as she looked at the pretty pup. 'Hurry up,' she said, her tone stronger. 'Did your wheels go over him?'

'No. He bounced off the side, then rolled into a ditch. I

214

had a devil of a time finding him in the dark.' He fled away to search for more help and towels.

With the young animal wrapped in her cardigan, Jenny crept through the house and into the kitchen. There was a strange mixture of smells in the room, soap and bread and beef gravy. A small black head lifted itself to sniff the air, and Jenny decided that this was a good omen, a sign of interest and hunger. But there seemed to be little strength in the creature's neck, and soon the eyes closed again as the puppy re-entered his sleep of shock.

'Has he moved?'

Jenny did not look at the master. 'He shifted a bit, could smell food, I think.'

'He's had quite a bump. The vet's on his way, that's why I took so long. I wanted someone to watch the dog while I telephoned – that was my reason for waking you. I've brought the towels, but we'd better do nothing until we've had some advice.'

She lifted her head and glanced at him. Her hair was a cloak now, a beautiful satin garment that covered her from head to waist. A few knots and tangles made her less ethereal, as did a streak of blood across the perfect chin.

Henry moved forward and wiped her face with his handkerchief. 'Spit,' he ordered when his ministrations failed to remove the dried mark. She licked at the white square and he cleaned her skin with the spittle. 'He won't be long,' he said.

'Will the dog die?' Her voice trembled slightly. 'The bleeding's stopped.' Her brand new dressing gown was a mess. She would have to accept the gifts offered by her strange mistress, all that silky lingerie, otherwise she'd have nothing to wear in bed, nothing to put on over a nightie when going to the bathroom. 'Will he die?' she asked again.

'We've to keep him warm and still. It all depends on internal bleeding according to Stuart Cross. He's a good horse doctor, so let's see what he can do for the canine variety.'

They sat opposite one another in a pair of wooden chairs that flanked the grate. Her chair was a rocker, but she remained rigidly motionless in an effort to accord with the vet's telephoned instructions. A tiny heartbeat thrummed against her fingers; even through the thick wool, she felt the dog's pulse as it struggled to maintain this almost exhausted little life. 'Don't die,' she muttered from time to time. 'Keep going, he'll be here any minute.'

Henry could not take his eyes off her. She was a giver, a lover of all creatures, a born nurse. Too bad that she had to nurse such a cold and vicious mistress, then.

'Are you all right, Mr Skipton?'

'Yes.'

'You're shaking. I can see from here that you're shivering. Are you cold?'

'No.' As if to verify and illustrate the reply, a few beads of sweat ran down his forehead. With determination, he gripped the arms of his chair. Somehow, he would keep these silly hands still. There was no reason on earth why he should be in this dreadful state. Other men would have left the dog, wouldn't have cast a second thought in its direction. But he had to be different, of course. He had to care what happened to the little beast.

'It wasn't your fault.' Her voice was clearer now. 'You didn't do this on purpose. You'd never hurt a dog, not deliberate. I know that.'

'How do you know?' His tongue felt thick and the words seemed to rattle against his teeth before coming out into the open.

'I just do. Some people hurt animals and others don't.' He was suffering from shock. In near-disbelief, Jenny stared at her employer. This was the man with all the mills, all the money. This was the man who didn't give a tuppence-ha'-penny care for his sick wife. Henry Skipton, owner of a big house, a car and lots of other lovely trappings was shaking because he had hurt an animal. 'You need sugar and something warm,' she said. Happen he had his reasons for not talking to Mrs Skipton. He didn't seem the sort of man to be cruel and nasty on purpose, just for the fun of it. 'Make some tea. Do you know how to make tea?'

'Yes, I do, strange as that might seem.' He stumbled

across the large room and lit a gas hob, rattling the kettle to assess its contents. 'I often get up in the night for a cup of tea,' he said.

'Well, put plenty sugar in it. And don't have it too hot. Hot's good for shock, but too hot'll make you worse.'

'Who told you that?' This was a banal conversation, yet he clung to its ordinariness. He didn't want to worry about the dog, didn't want to look at the beautiful servant who was hugging the result of man's careless need for speed.

'Auntie Mavis.'

'Ah yes.' At last he gave her a quick glance. 'The lady who died, the lady for whose gravestone you are saving.' He wanted to bite out his tongue. Once more, the talk had wandered off to uncomfortable ground, and he was the leading sheep.

'Oh. Who told you?' Her mouth had dried slightly, and the words came out thin and weak.

He moved his head and stared at the kettle, willing it to boil more quickly so that he could use his hands to do something sensible and constructive. 'Your father told me.'

'Right.' She searched for words, staring hard into the puppy's matted coat, as if the syllables might be hidden in its density. 'I gave the change to Maria, you see. The change from the insurance policy. It should have been used for the stone, but there wasn't enough to do both. Maria needed it for . . . for the house. Bits and pieces.'

'Tranklements.' No humour coloured the borrowed term.

'Yes.' The young animal stirred. 'Keep still,' she chided softly. 'The doggy doctor's coming.' She addressed the master again. 'He offered to pay. My . . . father said he'd buy the stone. But it's . . . like it's my duty. She brought me up, you see, looked after me when I was a baby.'

He tried to clear a throat that was too tight even for coughing. 'Dan did what he thought was best for you. He's a good man. The best father you could have.' Again, he attempted to clear his mouth of a taste that had arrived with the accident. Perhaps it was the taste of distaste . . . ? 'He couldn't have kept you here. My parents didn't approve of marriages between servants. And once . . . your mother disappeared, Dan found it impossible to claim parentage. We thought he was just being kind, and that your mother would come back for you eventually.'

She watched the last dying embers of the fire. 'Even Auntie Mavis didn't know he was me dad. She thought he'd just taken to me, that he felt sorry for me after . . .' Her shoulders straightened. 'After Oonagh went away. Oonagh is my mother. She was housekeeper here for a while.'

'Yes, I remember her.'

Her eyes strayed to his face, but she could see only the profile. 'What was she like?' Yes, it would be good to hear somebody else's opinion. Her father's memories of Oonagh were embedded in stained glass, making the missing mother into something of a saint, a saint whose life had been difficult.

'She was pretty.' He stirred the tea, his back completely turned towards Jenny. 'There was a mark on her face, a beauty spot. French courtiers – and probably some English too – used to stick false ones on their skin. But your mother had a real mark, very dark brown, almost black.'

She clicked her tongue quietly as the pup jerked his limbs. He was probably dreaming, poor little soul, probably reliving the accident in his sleep. 'Was she a good person?' she asked.

'Oh yes. Very efficient, very kind and soft-spoken. A pleasant girl with a sweet singing voice. We used to listen to her when she couldn't see us. Oonagh was too shy for a visible audience. Yes, she would have made a good wife and mother, but her family . . .' His words faded to nothing.

'I know about her mother and her brothers. She had to run.'

He swivelled on his heel. 'Shall I make a cup for you?'

She smiled and answered, 'No hands.'

He almost offered to be her hands, but immediately thought better of it. She was lovely, and lovely women ought not to intrude into the lives of lonely men. Lonely and lovely were separated by just one consonant; they should really have miles between them, those two adjectives.

'Mr Skipton?'

'Yes?'

She inhaled deeply before speaking again. 'I hope you won't get mad, only Auntie Mavis thought she knew who my dad was.'

His head moved in a very slight, almost imperceptible nod. 'She thought I was your father. Oh, don't worry about it – I've heard it all before. Oonagh was beautiful, but I was . . . otherwise engaged. Engaged, in fact, to be married.'

'To Mrs Skipton.' She was blushing, and could not account for the sudden heat in her face. Yes, she could. It was this awkwardness between master and mistress, the awful tension in the house. She should not have mentioned Mrs Skipton, must learn to do the job, just the job and no more. Never mind, she told herself firmly. He would think she was blushing about Auntie Mavis's mistake.

'That's right,' he said eventually. 'I was engaged to Eloise when I was just nineteen, and I assure you that I indulged in no dalliance with Oonagh Murphy.' He returned to the chair, using his cup to hide the expression on his face. 'First love is always intense,' he said gruffly. 'And often misleading. Many young people are confused, led astray by strong feelings. But to endure, a marriage needs more than simple attraction.'

'Yes.' Was he speaking of himself, Jenny wondered, or of Dan's intense passion for Oonagh, for a woman he had sought for so many years? Whatever, she decided to be brave. This was an unusual situation, an opportunity to be candid for once. Somehow, in the middle of the night, status did not matter. It was as if they had entered a different dimension, a place where there was no division among people. 'Where do you think she went, Mr Skipton? My mother, I mean.'

He placed his empty cup on the floor. 'To Liverpool for the boat. But she never reached Ireland. There's quite a family over there, lots of cousins and so forth. No-one has seen her since the night she left you here. Her brothers came by, a noisy lot they were, too. We told them nothing of your whereabouts and they seemed not to be interested anyway. Oonagh's mother also visited. Your grandmother was quite a harridan, I'm sad to report. After that – nothing.'

She dropped her gaze to the bundle in her lap. 'She must have gone somewhere, Mr Skipton. People don't just disappear like that. And Unc— my dad would have married her. She could have come back when she was a bit older, could have seen us both again, lived with us like a proper family.'

'Complicated things, humans,' he said soothingly. 'Never try to work them out, Jenny. Philosophers have been going insane for hundreds of years in an effort to find the meaning of life. We are the oddest animals, because we don't often rejoice about life. Every morning, birds sing simply because they are alive. Dogs, cats, horses – they all have a sense of fun, an in-built *joie de vivre*. But we humans – what do we do in the morning?'

'Light fires and wash ornaments,' she answered.

'Shave, wash, eat, then curse the petrol engine.' He was smiling.

She answered his grin with one of her own. He was lovely to talk to, a really nice man. She could not understand what the missus had against him, because he was excellent company. It would be part of her illness, of course. Lying in bed like that must have made her bitter and unpredictable. 'He's taking his time,' she complained. 'Poor dog'll be dead if he doesn't shape and hurry up.'

'I'll go to the front,' he said. 'We don't want him ringing that damned great bell. No point in disturbing . . . anyone else.' In the doorway, he paused, a hand to his face. Without looking round, he said, 'Don't let yourself get sucked in, Jenny. When I asked you to come back here, I told myself that you must be protected. And now that I know your parentage . . . remember that Dan is my friend.' His shoulders heaved themselves upward, as if he were preparing himself for something of import. 'Friends are rare. Colleagues, acquaintances – they are ten a penny.

As my friend's daughter, you must take care of yourself.'
He walked out before she could frame a reply.

Jenny, her mind torn into two tired and jagged parts, simply sat and waited for the pup to either live or die. The worry about the little dog took up half of her thinking, while the portion that was left seemed to concentrate on Mr Skipton's words. 'Don't get sucked in.' 'You must be protected.' These statements clattered around in her head, ominous, unexplained, confusing. Could she ask him to make his warning clearer? Could she use this after-midnight island as a true leveller, an area in which she might question closely a man who had always been her boss? Right from leaving school, she had been answerable, ultimately, to Henry Skipton. Even in these grey hours before dawn, he continued her master. Was he advising her not to work too hard? Was he telling her to beware of his wife? Mrs Skipton had changed of late, she was all kindness and sympathy and gentleness. Should Jenny tell him that, then? Tell him that Eloise seemed to be nearing her time, that the woman was reaching out for God as her life ended?

The puppy opened his eyes. They were warm and brown, they were good eyes. 'Hello,' she whispered as the limbs began to move against the sure but soft restraint of her arms. 'Don't start getting frisky. You'll hurt yourself if you're not careful.' The animal, seeming to absorb her meaning, stopped moving. She was sticky with his blood, could smell the metallic tang of spilled life. Yet she smiled, because movement in the limbs meant a possible wholeness of bone, while open eyes were always a good sign, a message that the brain might be intact and undamaged.

Mr Skipton returned with the vet in tow. This was a short man with no hair on his head, plenty on his chin. A fluffy, light grey beard decorated the jaw, while twinkling eyes made of him a Santa Claus, a small benevolent man filled with happiness and good intentions. He took the pup and laid him on the table. 'Sit over there, you two,' he said in a deep, booming voice that contradicted his physical stature. 'There's a bit of stitching to do, and I know you can't stand blood, Henry. Blood and illness always make you run a marathon.'

Jenny stared at Mr Skipton. Perhaps that was the answer, then. He hated illness, so he stayed away from it. His fear of blood had been overcome tonight because of his desperate need not to be a killer of animals. She had heard of people who were scared of hospitals, terrified of being ill, of seeing others ill. Auntie Mavis had suffered from that phobia thing, the fear of going out, of standing in a place that was not enclosed. Mr Skipton was the same, but about other things. He was scared of sickness, and that explained, at least in part, the odd situation at Skipton Hall. Because he was a kind man, he likely didn't want Jenny 'sucked into' a sickroom. It was a shame, because he was a lovely person, the sort that was easy to talk to. You could tell your troubles to this man, she thought. Even the most secret thoughts would be safe with him.

'His head's been bashed about a bit,' announced Mr Cross. 'Nothing broken, but a bit concussed, I'd say. This gash on his rump is mendable. No broken bones. Lucky chap.' His tongue stuck out at a corner of his mouth as he began to shave the fur from unconscious flesh.

'I'll stop down here with him, ' ventured Jenny. 'You've your work tomorrow, Mr Skipton.'

'I see.' He stretched out his legs and folded his arms. 'And you haven't your work, I take it?'

'Yes, but I can get time off.'

'Can you?' His eyebrows had shot upward again. They were always doing that.

'When I say about the dog, Mrs Skipton—'

'She doesn't like dogs,' he interrupted, almost snappily. 'Dogs, cats, horses. Especially young ones. No patience with anything of the infant variety. Even dislikes foals.'

'She's . . .' Jenny collected her courage. 'She's different now.'

'Really?' He looked at the vet. 'Nearly finished, Stuart?'

'In a moment.'

Jenny looked down at her bloodstained clothing. There was no point in explaining things to Mr Skipton. If he was afraid of seeing ill people, then nothing could alter the grim situation here, the terrible division between man and wife. It was a bit like that canyon in America, the deepest place on earth. Nothing would knit up the canyon at Skipton Hall, either.

'I'll take the dog to my room,' he said. 'We shall keep him.'

'Keep him?' she asked. 'In the house?'

'Yes. Mrs Hardman loves animals, and there's plenty for him to eat, lots of grass to run on. Whoever owns him must have let him wander, so they don't deserve to have him back.'

'He's a mongrel,' said the vet. 'God knows how he'll finish up, because these feet are enormous.'

'Then he needs space,' answered Henry. 'A big dog needs a big house with grounds. And I have never admired these overbred, neurotic, pedigree affairs, all brushed hair and ribbons. There's a certain mentality to the owners of those creatures too. Snappy little terriers with bows in their hair are usually owned by snappy little people with porridge in their brains.' He paused. 'Scottish porridge with salt, no sugar.'

Jenny laughed aloud.

The vet looked up from his work. 'Hey, I've got a hairy little terrier.'

'Exactly,' replied Henry. 'The point is proven.'

Jenny covered her open mouth and suppressed a fit of giggles.

Henry looked at her, a twinkle in his eye. 'The man is half Scottish,' he explained in a loud stage whisper. 'So he hangs on to his money, counts the pennies. The other half of him is Yorkshire, giving us yet again a man strangled by his own purse strings. The dog is very like him. Lots of hair on its face and a tendency to hang on. By the teeth. It's a nasty, ill-humoured little animal, owned by a nasty, ill-humoured little man.'

The vet wandered over, a needle threaded with suture in his hand. He waved this weapon as he spoke. 'Take no notice of him. When he's sick, he sends for me, won't have a doctor. I've cured him of tonsillitis, heartburn and distemper.'

Jenny stared. 'Isn't distemper a dog's thing?'

Stuart Cross nodded. 'The man is a dog, a miserable dog. And it's probably bad temper I cured him of. Bad temper is distemper gone too far.'

It was plain that Henry Skipton did have a friend, then. A friend who was close enough to be discourteous, even rude. She looked from one to the other, saw comradeship in the pretended reluctance of shared smiles. Well, that was a good thing. She had started to worry about Mr Skipton almost as much as she worried about his sick wife.

When the vet had finished, he told them to let the animal sleep and to try him with food in the morning. 'I'll forward my account in the post,' he said.

Henry looked at him with mock-disdain. 'I'm sure you will, old thing. Yes, that's one of the certainties in life.'

Stuart Cross snapped shut the clasp of his brown leather case. 'And another certainty is that you'll pay it when I get nasty.' He held out a hand to Jenny. 'Good night, miss. If he gets out of control, call me. No, not the dog, Henry here.' After shaking Jenny's hand, he waved his own at the master of Skipton Hall as if to dismiss him. 'Come and work for me, young lady. You'd make a fine receptionist.'

While they went to the front door, Jenny looked at the sleeping puppy. He was stretched out on the floor next to the table, Jenny's old cardigan tucked around him. In spite of unconsciousness, the animal looked peaceful, almost happy.

'What will you call him?'

Jenny jumped. She hadn't heard any footsteps, must have been too engrossed in the patient's welfare. 'You should choose his name, sir.'

'All right.' He squatted down beside her. 'He's a bit bald now, isn't he? Very enthusiastic with a razor, is old Stuart. I sometimes wonder if he shaves his head just to be different.'

She studied him closely. It was hard to tell when he was joking. 'He doesn't shave much of his face, though, does he?' she asked.

Henry Skipton tried not to laugh. 'No, without the

beard, he would be ordinary. And extraordinariness is Stuart's goal. Some people just like to be noticed. We'll call him Charlie, because he is a proper Charlie.' His eyes gleamed, seeming to send out sparks of light from the striped and multi-coloured irises.

'It's no use,' she said. 'I know you're talking about the dog.'

'Oh. So I can't fool you?' They rose simultaneously from their knees.

Jenny smoothed her filthy dressing gown. 'Not all the time, sir. Just now and again. The dog's a Charlie for running into your car. Right?'

He sighed with faked sadness. 'Right. Now, get off to your bed, young lady. I'll look after Charlie. And buy yourself some . . . something to replace the nightdress and the dressing gown.'

She looked down once more at her ruined garments. 'Mrs Skipton says I can have some of hers.'

He fixed his gaze on the dog. 'Will you accept them?'

Jenny shrugged. 'It'll save money,' she said.

He watched as she walked from the room. Yes, she would accept Eloise's bribes without knowing that bribery existed. And it was a case of not biting the hand that provided, he supposed. Also, she should perhaps be dressed in silks, not in plain cotton.

With the pup in his arms, he walked to his room. Plain cotton, he told himself firmly, had kept this house going for many years. His forefathers had built the mills, and it hadn't been a particularly easy life. Money ploughed back, no change for pleasures, the food on the table always plain. From the spinning and weaving of cotton, this house had risen. And anyway, she would look good in anything. Why did his mind keep straying back to her? Because she didn't need silks and powders and perfumes?

He leaned on his bedroom door, as if trying to shut out the world. The dog slept, Jenny would be asleep soon, sensible girl. And the lady dressed by the silkworm was probably oblivious to everything. A hurt dog, a sad maid, a worried husband – none of these trivialities would be allowed to encroach on her beauty rest.

'Charlie,' he said quietly, not really wanting to disturb the animal. 'Give me plain cotton any day of the week.'

Maria Hesketh felt that she ought to have grown by several inches. She was being pulled so many ways by so many people, that she went a bit stupid at times, had to start writing things on bits of paper. And if folk were going to carry on being so demanding of her time, she would end up like a long streak of grease, just a mark on the wall.

The money had gone on a gas oven, and the main thing was to save up that thirteen pounds odd and give it back to Jenny for the stone. So Maria worked all the hours God sent, every night on the printing, every day on alterations, linen-mending and even dressmaking. There had been no need to take in washing, so Anthony had never got stuck in the back yard with a posser and knickers. He sold headscarves when there were sufficient to make it a worthwhile exercise, and he worked the evening shift in the pub.

Josie had settled well. That was one thing to be grateful for. At first, the other children had laughed at her accent, but Josie's ways had won them all over, because she knew different games, pastimes that were new to the playground of Sts Peter and Paul Junior School. She had stopped being a mixed infant, and was pleased about that. Being mixed meant, both in Liverpool and in Bolton, sharing a playground with boys. Now, Josie was the queen of the girls' yard, and she carried her office with great pride and dignity. At least, she hoped it was dignity, because she tried not to abuse her position of power. This child was very like Maria, who had recognized the similarities during recent months. They would both get out; neither of them was content to sit, as their mother sat, in total chaos. They were both doers, and doers had to get out and do.

When the knock at the door came that summer afternoon, Maria expected nobody. As she was in the middle of cutting out a bridesmaid's dress, she was not best pleased by the interruption. With pins stuck between her teeth, she opened the front door, thinking that perhaps Denis had

called round again. He worked crazy hours, so the court-
ship had to fit in with the fire service, needlework and
household chores. Since Josie had taken up residence, the
two would-be lovers had spent exactly one hour and eight
minutes in privacy. Well, this might be the beginning of
their ninth minute, thought Maria as she swung back the
door.

Her jaw dropped. There was no need to remove the
pins, because they scattered on the step at her feet, making
small tinny noises as they bounced against the stone slab.
'Er . . . yes?' she managed at last.

The nearest one was big and fat, the stiff, white anchor
for the wimple seeming ready to jump from its moorings,
so tightly did it press against a round, rosy-bright face.
The other nun was tall and thin, with a face that looked as
if it had just eaten an extremely sour lemon.

Maria pulled at her work pinafore. She was sweaty and
tired and the oven was on a low light, crammed full with
printing. There'd be the tea to do in a minute as well, what
with Anthony eating enough for ten and Josie always
fetching somebody in for a bite. 'Come in, sisters,' she
said, her voice sounding far away.

They entered the front room and stood like ebony
statues next to Mavis's round table. From the back, they
looked carved and lifeless, completely without normal
things like blood and desires and bodily functions . . .
Maria stilled her wilful brain and stepped round them so
that she could see their faces. The fat one was smiling,
so she smiled back. 'Sit down, sisters. Will you have a cup
of tea?'

The thin one was the headmistress. She had interviewed
Maria and Josie before allowing the child into Standard
One, and Maria felt terrible because she had forgotten the
woman's chosen name. 'I'm sorry,' she said 'I'm hopeless
with names.'

Thin lips parted to allow life into a few measured words.
'Sister Beatrice,' she said. 'And this is Sister Vincentia. We
shall not take tea, thank you.'

Oh God, thought Maria. Somebody's rattled the convent
gates here, and it's likely our Josie. She tried to mould her

features into a shape that was expressionless, but the sweat continued to pour, while she could feel the tense worry-lines gathering like clouds between her eyebrows. 'All right,' she said finally. 'What's she done now?' It was no use beating about the bush, might as well get right down to it. If their Josie was planning on being a second Maria, then the school could well be razed to the ground by now.

Sister Beatrice didn't budge. Maria revised her view about sucking lemons. This face didn't need lemons – it probably always looked like a smacked bum.

'Are you meaning Josephine?' asked the fat nun. 'She's done nothing, nothing that we know of.'

'Thank God for that.' Maria fanned fevered cheeks with a newspaper. 'See, me dad's not what you might call straight. I don't mean he's an out and out sinner, but he's . . . he drinks and that,' she finished lamely. After a few moments of excruciating silence, she begain again. 'And our Josie's quick to pick things up.' Like threepenny bits and ornaments, she said silently. And anything else that doesn't move fast enough. 'She might be a bit unsettled with the move and all that.' Why couldn't she shut up? Why the hell did she always chatter like a stupid monkey whenever she was nervous? She shouldn't say why the hell, shouldn't even think it in front of nuns.

'Miss Hesketh,' said Sister Vincentia. 'Your sister is a brilliant child who should eventually go on to the convent at Deane. Mount St Joseph's. But we're not here about that. It's the First Communion. Did she make it ever? She seemed confused when we asked her about it.'

Maria blushed. There were so many comings and goings at home, nobody knew who was where or when or why. 'I'm not sure. Too many of us in the house, and I don't live there now. I live here.' She felt about three years old. Yes, they'd turned her into a child again, a kid who hadn't put her hand in the air quickly enough, an infant with wet pants and a bright red face. 'There'd be no frock for it at ours, so the kids usually lend one off somebody else's mam.' She lifted her chin defiantly. 'Josie's proud. She might not want to talk about how poor her family is and about having to lend a frock.'

'Borrow,' corrected Sister Beatrice in the immediate and automatic mode of one who has spent a lifetime in teaching.

'Borrow,' repeated Maria, wishing she could bite off her tongue as soon as the word had slipped out. She wasn't at school any more. They couldn't tell her what to do. She knew her times tables and her Catechism. And her pants were completely dry. Except for the sweat.

Sister Beatrice suddenly reached out a hand and touched Maria's hot arm. 'You look worn out, child. We just came to tell you that Josephine ought to make her firsts if she hasn't already done so. Find out from your mammy, then come to me. The sisters will make her a beautiful dress.' Her face didn't look mean any more. It was still thin, but a light had come on behind the eyes. In Sister Beatrice's rather idealistic book, the poor were Christ's nobility.

Maria's own eyes pricked. 'That's lovely of you, really it is.' She'd been with nuns before – Liverpool crawled with them – and they'd never been nice. Everybody called them penguins, but they were just ordinary women in queer clothes. 'I can make it,' she said. 'If I can get the stuff, I can sew nearly anything. In the top class at our school, we even done – I mean did – embroidery on vestments.'

'Isn't that wonderful, Beatrice?' beamed the fat nun.

Maria frowned. They called each other 'sister' where she'd come from. 'Anyway, I'll ask me mam.' Would she know, though? Would she notice who came and went in a white frock, in jodhpurs, in a hearse? There were days when she never lifted her head or a hand, days when she'd borrowed a good book or magazine.

Anthony came in, his hand resting for a frozen second on the latch as he noticed the room's occupants. The nuns rose as one woman, muttered their goodbyes and God blesses, then scuttled out of the house. Anthony grinned. 'I have that effect on women,' he said. 'As soon as I show me face, they bugger off.'

'Where've you been? You took no scarves and has our Josie made her First Communion?'

'Slow down, George—'

'What's George got to do with it?'

'Nothing, it's just a saying, and anyway—'

'Has she?'

'Eh?'

Maria ground her teeth silently and fought for composure. He was bloody daft, their Anthony, as soft as they came. 'Listen, you. Watch my lips. One, where've you been till now? Two, has our Josie made her firsts?'

'Firsts?'

'Confession and communion.'

'No. She'd no frock and wouldn't lend one.'

'Borrow.' She dug her nails into her palms. She'd be turning out like the blinking teaching nuns if she didn't watch it. Though one of the things she wanted was to talk nice and posh. 'Where've you been?' This was getting a bit repetitive for Maria and her printing would be set by now.

'Liverpool. I went to see Mam. And somebody else, somebody important.'

'And are you sure about our Josie?'

He nodded. 'I remember her crying. She wouldn't let me go and ask for a frock either.'

'And what did me mam do?'

He shifted about uncomfortably. 'We never told her.'

'Why? Why didn't you tell her one of her daughters needed a bit of attention? She's getting worse. It won't be long before she stops feeding them altogether.'

'Maria—'

'Now listen. I'm not saying anything behind her back that I wouldn't say to her face. If you want to know, I have said it to her, I've told her that she carries on wrong. I can see her point of view, like. I mean, it's not much of a life with me dad and all that. But they're her children, Anthony. You don't have babies then stick your head in a book for ten years. She could read as well, read when she's seen to the family.' She bit down on her lip with frustration. It was no use talking to Anthony. If Mam had committed cold-blooded murder, he would still have stood by her. 'All right. Who did you see that was so important?'

He shrugged. 'I might tell you. And then again, I might not.'

'Please yourself, I've printing to save.' She turned as if to make for the kitchen, but he grabbed her arm. 'It's Jenny's mother,' he said. 'Me mam found this old woman what knew her ages ago. So don't say Mam's no use. She got the bit between her teeth for Jenny when I asked.'

'All right, keep your shirt on. Well?'

He placed both thumbs in the waistband of his trousers, began rocking to and fro with the air of an alderman who is about to save the city from perdition. 'The old girl . . . well . . . she ran one called Oonagh.'

'Eh?'

'With a spot on her face too.'

Maria thumped her brother none too gently on the shoulder. 'What do you mean, "ran her"? Ran her where? To the bloody tram stop?'

'I wish you'd stop hitting me. I bruise easy, you know.'

'Shut up. Now, tell me.'

He grinned cheekily. 'How can I shut up and—' He rubbed the shoulder. That was twice in a few seconds, and on the same spot too. She didn't hit hard, but she did it carefully, working away in the same location until her victim suffered. She was like sandpaper, their Maria. Rubbed and scraped till she got through, till she got her own way . . .

'Anthony!'

'Oonagh worked the docks for a couple of months. The old girl looked after her, put a man on her tail, took half her earnings.'

Maria swallowed audibly. 'Christ Almighty. I'm not telling Jenny that, Ant.'

'Another thing. This Oonagh's daughter is supposed to have died. And Oonagh only had the one daughter – according to the old biddy, like – so that must have been Jenny.'

Maria blinked rapidly. 'But Jenny's alive.'

He nodded, keen to continue his interesting tale. 'See, Oonagh got a good job, left the old girl's place, went working legit in a big house. She wasn't a whore at heart, this Oonagh, only walked the streets for a few weeks, when she was desperate. But she used to come back and visit this

Mrs Moore, even after starting a proper job. It was all very pleasant, there was no bother about Oonagh going straight. Anyway, Oonagh would never tell Mrs Moore where she worked, or who her new boss was. She seemed to be some sort of housekeeper – judging by the bit she did say to the old dear.'

'Why did Jenny's mother go back to the brothel?'

'It wasn't a brothel. It's a two up two down, an ordinary house. Oonagh used it as an address for letters. So that was how it came out about the kiddy dying – it was all in some letter. Then somebody else died too, only the old woman didn't know who. Could have been anybody, one of the brothers or the mother of these Murphys. There was two letters in a couple of weeks. Oonagh did nothing but cry, then she went back to work, wherever that was.'

Maria eased herself into a chair. It was still hot from the fat nun. 'I can't tell Jenny any of that. What happened to Oonagh?'

He shook his head pensively. 'Just disappeared. The old girl got no more visits after these two notes about deaths. It was as if Oonagh expected no more messages. Anyway, nobody's heard from Oonagh since. But the letters were from Bolton. She noticed that, did Mrs Moore. And the envelopes was both in the same handwriting.'

Maria glanced towards the ceiling, suddenly realizing that the answers, or some of the answers, might be in the package upstairs. 'So somebody sent a letter saying Jenny was dead.'

'If it's the same Oonagh.'

'And then the person what wrote the first letter sent another. And that was the second person dying.'

He scratched his head. 'Something like that.'

'What do we do, Anthony?'

He was still scratching his head. 'We don't hurt her. She doesn't need to be told any of this.'

Maria wiped the sweat from her brow. There was only one thing for it. She would have to open those parcels. Not yet, she'd have to build up to it, give it some more thought. But with Jenny's mother turning into such a mystery, it might be as well if the worst was filtered out before Jenny got to it. 'Anthony?'

'What now?'

'Don't tell anybody at all. Me mam won't talk when she comes over, will she?'

He smiled sadly. 'She'll have forgotten it all by now, Maria. She's working her way through a pile of magazines what me dad came by.' He sighed. 'You're right. She does read too much.'

She went out to rescue her work. Jenny's story would probably turn out to be more riveting than anything in a woman's picture paper. And the last person to know the full history would be Jenny herself.

Chapter Nine

SHE LINGERED ON THE CORNER OUTSIDE ST PATRICK'S, A large handkerchief pressed against her swollen mouth. Most of the bleeding had stopped, much of her lifeblood was in a bucket at Mr Williams's surgery down Deansgate. Imelda, some minutes earlier, had crossed over to a large shop, intending to buy some new lamps with fringed shades, leaving Carla to 'rest' against the church wall. Fringed lampshades. Another symptom of a woman without taste. Plain braid edging was better, neater, didn't collect dust or end up knotted.

It was a real town church, no yard, no cemetery, its large, arched and very solid oak doors leading straight on to the pavement. This was where Imelda had brought her last week, where they had sat through a service that had sounded thoroughly foreign, all Latin and bells and Gregorian plainchant. She slipped into the porch to look for a chair, but there was no seating, just a rack full of pamphlets, a trusting money box by its side. There were other money boxes too, for missions, for the Knights of St Columba, for contributions to the support of resident pastors. None of them was fastened down or locked; obviously, there was no need to protect the contents.

She pushed hesitantly at the inner door, peeped inside, managed to assess that the comparatively dark interior was occupied by just a handful of women who were taking a break from shopping. In one of the back pews, she rested her shocked bones.

It had been dreadful, the worst experience of her whole life. She had fought the gas, choked and gagged for lack of oxygen. On waking, she had vomited, still too dizzy to aim properly for the proffered bowl. He had been kind, had nursed her in his arms like a baby. It had felt strange, being cuddled by a man. Strange and not unpleasant. Her new teeth had grinned at her continuously from a glass beaker on the counter. They had seemed to mock the whole procedure, sitting there frozen in an eternally complacent porcelain grin.

She leaned back against the small comfort of rigid wood. In a couple of hours, she would return and that smug smile would be pressed into flesh that was red-hot and raw. She could not imagine pain worse than this, but soon the suffering must intensify. The idea of a palate pushing against bloody sockets was terrifying. He had tried so hard to be comforting, telling her that this was the worst part, that the dentures would not hurt, that they would bed in and stop the bleeding completely. She struggled to believe this, to believe that the pain would ever stop.

'Excuse me.'

She turned slowly, handkerchief still pressed against a mouth that had travelled beyond mere soreness. The man was dressed in black, and the white collar of priesthood announced itself starkly against a healthy, tanned neck. She shook her head mutely, could not remove the cover from her mouth.

'Is it teeth?' he asked, noting bloodstains on white linen.

Her head seemed to jerk agreement of its own accord.

'Just you stay there quiet now.' The voice was educated Lancashire. 'I'm Father Entwistle — Jimmy Entwistle-as-was, the parishioners call me sometimes. As if I used to be normal, but then I stopped and turned into a priest overnight. Have you had a drink?'

Again, she nodded, her face aching anew from the dentist's assault. After half an hour of agony, she had sipped from a glass of water which had diluted the blood, and she had shivered against the taste of her own life-fluid.

'I'll be back in a minute,' whispered the priest. 'And try not to swallow. Spit the stuff into the handkerchief.' He turned away, turned again and offered, in the form of a genuflection towards the altar, a hasty afterthought to his Maker.

Carla gazed round the church, trying to force her attention to dwell outside of herself, away from a mouth in which her heart drummed loudly, as if it were forcing the blood to continue its slow but merciless dripping. There were tableaux on the walls, groups of sepia-coloured figures that seemed to be telling a story. This was the first time she had noticed these arrangements, and she studied the nearest ones, realizing that they depicted Christ's sufferings. They were rather beautiful things, almost matching the fabric of the church, blending in as part and parcel of the building.

She dropped her head pensively. They were the basis of this rather showy faith, so it was right that such scenes should fit in so well. Their very understatement spoke of importance, shouted that they were welded not only to the walls, but also to the soul of every good Catholic servant who entered the church of St Patrick.

Imelda came here because she imagined the church to be Irish. It was named after the good Patrick himself, therefore it deserved Imelda's patronage. Strangely, Carla liked it, enjoyed the coolness of the building, its silence, its absolute separateness from the bustle of Great Moor Street. The figures were nice too. They gave her the odd and very new concept that Christ had died for her, that on this particular day, He knew about the teeth and the pain. She had never experienced such feelings before, and did not trust them. She was currently vulnerable, therefore her thinking was not straight. Catholicism was here for the masses, for those who received little or nothing in this life. Because of the paucity of their existence, they trusted in perfection later on, in a wonderful afterlife.

The priest returned, a table napkin in his hand. It was of woven linen, the sort that she had seen at Skipton Hall many times. 'A fine napkin,' he said, a twinkle in his eye. 'From a fine parishioner with contacts abroad. Here, there's ice in it. Press it against your face, and suck at it sometimes. It will take some of the discomfort away.' He passed the bundle to her. 'Did you get the full lot out?'

She inclined her head.

'My dad did that when he was about fifty, gave us all merry hell for about three days. My mother was thinking of sending him back to the dentist to see if he could get them put back in. But he's been thankful since, because his new teeth don't rot. Imagine that. Never having to go to the dentist for a hole filling. Makes you wonder what sort of people want to be dentists, doesn't it? Perhaps they enjoy hearing us scream.'

Throughout the speech, Carla sat and listened with one ear, the rest of her faculties seeming to devote themselves to gratitude. The ice was lovely, really cooling and comforting. She looked at Jesus and His third fall beneath the weight of a cross, half-listened to the pleasant young man who sat by her side trying to help her through the agony. He had been ordinary, or so he had said. Then he had gone away into years of college in order to stop being run-of-the-mill, yet he remained an essentially normal person. Which was what Carla herself would like to be. Unremarkable, not different, something that didn't get stared at, pointed at, called names.

'Most people don't talk in church,' he was saying now. 'Except for communal prayers. But I look at it this way. We're visitors, aren't we? Visitors in God's house, the one we built for Him. And when you go visiting a friend, you don't sit there with your face in your boots. You talk. Everybody talks. Speech is a gift from God and we are in His house. So, like any caller, we can talk and offer it up as prayer. As long as we're not gossiping about the state of a neighbour's curtains.'

She glanced at him sideways. He was a nice-looking young chap with dark hair and bright eyes. And he talked a kind of sense, too, the sort of language she understood. Catholicism was supposed to be weird, wonderful and totally inaccessible to someone born outside its confines.

But he made of it an everyday thing, something that could embrace all circumstances, even the loss of teeth.

'You'll feel better when you get the others in,' he was saying now. 'There's something dehumanizing about having no teeth. Even snakes have four or six – I can't remember how many. But once you get the dentures, you'll be smiling again.'

I never smile, she thought, but I could smile now if I didn't have the pain. He's such a nice man. This religion must have made him generous, made him look for the good things in life. And yet he remained perfectly approachable. She wondered if she were getting silly in her old age, but fifty was not old enough for senile dementia. He was taking away her pain. The sculptures too were helping, but she didn't know how. Perhaps it was something about Christ's face looking so . . . so accepting beneath its crown of thorns. He had experienced pain in the head, pain from those biting spikes of wood. And there hadn't even been Aspros in Christ's day . . .

'I'm lending you my dad's beads,' he said, pushing a black rosary into her hands. 'If you're not a Catholic, just use them as worry-beads, count them while the dentist puts your teeth in. Or say a nursery rhyme in your head, something thoroughly foolish and inappropriate. That'll keep you from concentrating on what's being done. When you're better, bring the rosary back to the presbytery and we'll have a nice cuppa with a splash of whisky to celebrate your improvement.' He squeezed her hand, made the sign of the cross, then left her with beads and ice.

After he had gone from the church, a woman came down the centre aisle, headscarf tied tightly under her chin to comply with church rules. He must have known I wasn't a Catholic, thought Carla. A Catholic woman would have covered her head. Yet he hadn't minded, hadn't questioned . . .

'Are you all right, love?' asked the woman.

Carla nodded.

'There's nowt like teeth for cheering you up, eh?' She rummaged in her shopping bag. 'Here.' A coloured picture was shoved under Carla's nose. 'That's St Anthony of Padua. Have a word with him, I always do. He's done wonders for me bleeding piles.' She shuffled off towards the door.

Carla wanted to laugh, but she managed not to. This was all very strange, she thought. The priest going on about his father, then a parishioner talking in church about haemorrhoids. It was as if this place might be their home, or perhaps a second home, somewhere to come when they were bruised or broken. No, it wasn't funny, not at all. It was a sort of strength given to them by the church, by the building, the pomp and circumstance of its ritual, the normality of its everyday function. Her shoulders relaxed and the stiffness began to ease itself out of her spine. This was a place where she could come, where she would be treated as normal, ordinary, just another woman. Whether or not she was a Catholic did not matter. Whether or not she was ugly did not count. There was humanity here. Humanity and a charity that stopped short of, or perhaps went beyond, the merely charitable.

Imelda bustled in importantly, a lace mantilla thrown over her short hair. 'Ah, so you came in. It's a good place to be in times of stress. I got the lamps, pink ones with lovely long fringes. We shall be very London with all this finery. Hang on now till I say a prayer or two.' She dumped the large parcel in the aisle where everybody could fall over it.

Carla almost grinned behind the handkerchief. Imelda and Franklyn could never be 'London', not in a million years. But they were good, honest folk. She checked herself inwardly. What was she doing, sitting here in a Catholic church with no teeth and a head full of thoughts about people's goodness? She was going mad, that would be it. The traumas of the past month or so had caught up with her, softened her brain. She wasn't as tough as she used to be, didn't bounce back like a rubber ball every time she got kicked. The madness would be temporary, of course. Given another week or two, she'd be back to her old self.

She fixed her eyes on a figure she did not recognize as St Simon. All she saw was a bloke trying to help Jesus with the cross. It was nice to think that somebody had offered a hand in spite of Roman whips. It was a bit like Father Entwistle giving that bit of comfort today even though the recipient was not a Catholic.

The bleeding had stopped now. She slipped a sliver of ice into her mouth, thanking yet again the man who had given it to her. The ice burned, but at least this was an acceptable and explicable pain. Surely the rest of it would be easier? And there'd be no more 'Stonehenge', no more horrible teeth that entered a room before the rest of her did. They had imagined her to be ignorant of this latest nickname, but she had been adept at hiding behind doors. Even a large woman could be invisible when she chose.

Her old self. Who was that? And did she want to go back to it, did she really want to remain untouchable, unlovable? Something stirred in her stomach and she knew that this wasn't wind from lack of breakfast. Was this guilt, then? Was she giving birth to a new feeling, a lot of sentimental rubbish? It was the church. It was being in here that was making her uncomfortable. She glanced at Imelda, but her silly little employer was just about halfway round her pearl-finished white beads.

'Did ye want to go, Carla? We can go, you just say when.' She thought for a second. 'Ah yes, you can't say when, for you're not talking at all. If the bleeding's stopped, we can bring ourselves back to the dentist. I'm sure he'll fit you right away. Will we do that?'

Carla nodded her slow agreement. She had one hand to her face, while the other fingered the rosary in her coat pocket. This was a silly bargain she had just made inside her own head, because Anthony of Padua or wherever would not help such a terrible sinner. She had told the man in the picture, the picture that nestled now between purse and Uncle Joes, that she would come back and see the father if the new teeth didn't hurt.

As she followed Imelda from the church and into sunlight, she knew that it had all been a nonsense. A nonsense of her own stupid making. With her head down, she walked towards inevitable torture. There was no God, so there was no help.

Sara Browne continued to come in every day, sometimes staying for hours. Eloise's condition had not deteriorated visibly; the therapist was lingering simply to take Dan's place, to do the job he would have been expected to do. Each afternoon, when massage and exercises had been completed, the heavy-muscled woman carried Eloise downstairs and placed her in the strong new wheelchair. This item had found a different home, was currently housed in what Mrs Hardman called a 'glory hole' just inside the front door. Upstairs, the frailer chair had been retained just for the short journey between bed and bathroom.

Eloise was extremely well behaved these days. The job was so easy that Jenny found plenty of time for the growing pup, took him for long walks, began to discover the many joys of country living. The town girl had never thought about open spaces, had never imagined trees and acres of grass. These were things that had been unavailable and outside her usual experience; she had therefore been unable to long for them, had not been envious of people who enjoyed this way of life on a day-to-day basis.

The countryside did something to Jenny. As soon as she was out of reach, beyond listening ears and watchful eyes, she would throw off her shoes and leap about in the grass, the smiling, playful dog chasing her heels. She often wondered why she did this daft thing. It was connected somehow to the sky, that great open dome of blue, or white, or blue-and-white that topped the world. It was a feeling of space, a sensation of floating, as if she could take off like the birds and soar ever upwards into the future or the past, just go wherever she wanted to go, be whatever she chose to become. Her postponed childhood was at last on the loose, was taking her off the leash, or at least, giving her a good length of rein.

There were patterns all around her, the jewelled tracery of a rain-washed spider's web, a dense umbrella provided by lush, mobile leaves that kept time with the wind's breath, a random scattering of blue petals in a copse and, in the distance, the sectioned quilt made of many greens, its seams stitched out of dry walls and slim ribbons of cart track. At last, Maria's fascination with form was understandable. Jenny could now identify with her friend, could see the reasoning behind the translation of shape, the potential joy in sitting down to print, copy, reproduce the patterns of life itself.

She could not believe her own happiness, could never fully explain the joy that nature gave to her. And it was all free. She didn't have to pay at the door, wasn't forced to sit still in this wonderful private yet shared theatre. It was better than the Grand, better by far than the Theatre Royal. This was an all-the-year-round pantomime, a play that ran fifty-two weeks a year, no rest days for the actors.

She discovered the players by accident and decided to come dogless on her next visit. If she sneaked out the front way, Charlie would never miss her. The wood was a small one and the special place was near the middle. At least, she thought it was the middle. When she had asked about the foxes, Mr Skipton had made a joke about woods, had asked her how far one could walk into a forest. And she had known the answer this time. 'Halfway,' she had said. 'After that, you're walking out of it.'

She knelt beside the item she had christened 'Frozen Stump'. It was the age-silvered base of a severed, long-dead tree. Creatures lived under and around it, beautiful bugs that were almost too small to see. She had meant to ask for a loan of the magnifying glass, and she cursed her own forgetfulness. The tree-trunk was riddled with holes, tiny homes for tiny beings with tiny, busy lives. Next time, she told herself firmly. Next time, she would examine their determined domesticity.

The foxes were in a hole not far from Frozen Stump. There was a small clearing, a fussy arrangement of bushes on the far edge, then a slight dip in the land into which she could not see properly. She lay, her chin resting on one arm, the arm resting on the dead tree. She hoped that the tree-creatures would not mind the dark for a while. Her arm probably took the windows out of a hundred houses, and she apologized mutely for the intrusion. She could not speak. Mr Skipton had told her to be quiet and to find a day when the breeze blew towards her so that her scent would not be detected.

They were here! Jenny's heart seemed to lurch in her chest when the babies came out, three ecstatic cubs whose baby-fluff was made untidy by the arrival of stronger hair. They were growing. Mother came out and warned them, a low growl emerging from her throat. She was unbelievably beautiful, almost red and with a wonderful tail that followed her like an extravagant bridal train.

Jenny fought the sigh, but it made its wilful way out of her throat. How could they hunt these creatures? How could they sit astride such glorious horses, run such clever hounds in order to commit a crime so vile and bloody? Gentlemen made little sense, she thought. All dressed up in red, horses shining from the ministrations of a groom, a gleaming horn held to lips that had just swallowed the contents of a silver cup. And thus they went forth to murder an animal they would not eat, a small creature that accounted for the deaths of very few chickens.

The mother looked straight at her, just stood and stared in a terrible stillness that matched the frozen stump. Jenny met her eyes, tried to arrange her face in a shape that would look friendly and non-threatening, yet she knew that the wild one would refuse to accept the so-called manners of a species that could never be trusted. 'I'll go if you want,' she whispered. 'And I won't tell them where you are.' Even now, the fox did not move; nor did she reprove her gambolling offspring. Slowly, the nervous girl rose from her inadequate hide. When Jenny stood full height, the vixen lifted her nose and sniffed the air. Again, the animal chose not to run, did not dive towards her young.

'Hello.' Jenny kept her voice low.

The fox made a small sound, like one of Charlie's barks, but shrill and fractured in the middle, cut off before completion. The hind quarters lowered themselves to sit, and a lazy foot made a half-hearted stab at scratching, missing the mark completely, probably drugged by the day's merciless heat.

Jenny walked slowly round Frozen Stump until she and

the foxes shared the same patch, although they were separated by several yards. Completely vulnerable now, with the fragile barrier removed, the vixen showed no sign of bolting. The lovely animal stretched herself out, the black nose pointing towards her children. Jenny, almost overcome by the so-called shy creature's total lack of shyness, swallowed a huge lump in her throat. This was how it should be with all the beasts, including mankind. Though some of them did get eaten, she admitted to herself guiltily. Yes, even she enjoyed a lamb chop, never associated such luxuries with the leaping baby sheep in the fields. Perhaps from now on she would eat only vegetables?

She stayed until the misty beginnings of summer's dusk dulled the sky. With deliberation, she drew a curtain across thoughts of duty, denied her conscience, ignored its guilty pinpricks. Mrs Skipton needed her, but Jenny remained a sinner until the light was almost gone. This was a chance in a lifetime, something that would never leave her until the day she died. Would anyone believe that she had spent a whole afternoon with foxes? Did it matter? Anyway, Mr Skipton would listen. He said she had a way with animals, especially after she had sat up with Barney the chestnut. She had, according to Howie, saved the horse from 'mortal colic'. Yes, they would listen, Howie and the master.

She took her leave carefully, mindful of the drying twigs underfoot. There must be no noise, no shock that would scatter Mother Fox's cubs. As she walked in shadow towards the little pond, a small bark reached her ears. It was the vixen, and Jenny decided that a goodbye was being spoken.

The others were round the pond, little green fellows that had recently been tadpoles. The miniature frogs were agile and clever, taking leaps that seemed impossible for their size, cavorting in near-darkness over stones and clumps of grass. When she managed to catch one, he bounded happily from her hand, arching through the air like a winged creature. On other days, she had seen rabbits, even a bigger one, possibly a hare. There were badgers too, or so Mr Skipton had said. Black and white creatures who loved the night and hated people. A bite from one of those, she had been told, was a terribly painful thing. They were right, she thought, to stay away from mankind. Mankind killed what he did not understand, even when it didn't get in the way.

She walked the mile or so back to Skipton Hall. It was gone supper time, and Miss would be waiting for her food. Sara Browne always carried the mistress back upstairs at five o'clock, after tea had been taken on the lawn or in the dining room. Sara Browne would be long gone by this time.

When Jenny walked into the kitchen, Briony almost fell on her, arms reaching out as if to greet a prodigal. 'Jenny! Her's out of her little mind up yonder. Do you know what time it is? She's thinking on getting the blinking bobbies to look for you.'

Jenny had no watch, no way of assessing the time, except by the sun. The days were long now, longer than she had thought. 'I didn't realize.' Her face turned itself towards the clock. 'Oh heck. I never knew it was going on eight. Has she had her supper?'

The other girl nodded swiftly. 'Aye, and it was me took it to her. I thought she'd chuck it at me, but she never. Just went all weepy, asked me what had happened to you.'

'I've been . . . busy. She always lets me have time off when Miss Browne's here, and I just forgot to come back.'

Briony's nut-brown face was a picture of amazement. 'How long's she been behaving herself?' she asked quietly. 'I've never seen her so quiet and good, not when she wasn't getting her own road.'

'She's dying,' said Jenny baldly. 'Well, she's getting herself ready to die, trying to be fit for heaven. I'd best go to her.'

She dashed up the library stairs three at a time, mouthing a muted 'Good evening, sir,' as she fled past Mr Skipton.

Eloise was definitely overwrought. The good hand was clutching at the edge of her sheet, while the grey eyes were wide with something that looked like panic. 'Jenny!' she screamed. 'I thought you were dead or hurt or lost.' The words came out quickly, almost jumbled. 'Don't . . . ever . . . do . . .' These syllables were staccato, while the breathing behind them seemed laboured. 'I do tend to worry so,' she finally managed.

'I'm sorry, miss, but I didn't know what time it was.'

Eloise took a series of deep, calming breaths. 'Find one of my watches. Keep it. I don't need to know the time.'

'No.' Jenny's tone was firm. 'You've already given me enough nighties and negli— whatever they're called to clothe a houseful of folk. When I've got money for Auntie's stone, I shall likely save for a watch.'

'Jenny, you offend me.' The nose was tilted upwards, as if to demonstrate that its owner was indeed offended. 'You must learn to accept gifts gracefully. That's all part of being a lady.'

It was no use telling her about not being a lady and not wanting to be one. That particular conversation had worn itself out due to excessive use, and Eloise had emerged the victor. Jenny looked at the mistress. I could have won if I'd really wanted to, she thought. If you hadn't been so ill, I'd have told you where to put the elly-queue-shon. She almost smiled as she thought about Maria, Maria who wanted to get on, who would pay, if necessary, to be properly elly-cuted. 'Where is it, miss?' The tone was resigned, just as it usually was in the face of Mrs Skipton's kindness.

'Top drawer of the dressing table. There are four of them. Take the one with the square black face.'

Jenny opened the drawer. Watches, in Eloise's book, were utilitarian and they did not belong with real jewellery. But the square black one had a gold case, and the bracelet too gleamed suspiciously yellow. 'It's gold,' she breathed softly.

'Yes, of course it's gold.'

There was not much wrong with the hearing, then, thought Jenny. Oh well, she would have to accept the watch, just as she'd taken all those amazing clothes. There were day dresses, nightdresses, robes, underslips. Not to mention some very daring knickers, all lacy bits and elastic so thin that it would never take the strain of a working day. Yes, that lot were certainly on the list of unmentionables. Unwearable too, some of them.

She circled her slender wrist with the lovely watch, glimpsing a sight of herself in the mirror. She was tousled from rolling about in grass, and there were greenish stains on the white blouse. A solemn face gazed back at her. Well, it would have been serious enough without the streaks of dirt across chin and nose.

'What on earth have you been doing, Jenny?' She forced her teeth not to grind with anger. If young madam here had found herself a suitor, then all plans would go awry.

'I've been watching foxes and playing with frogs.'

Eloise expressed a shudder. Horrid little things, frogs. Nasty green and slimy skins. 'Were you alone?'

Jenny turned. 'Oh aye.'

'Yes, Jenny. Please say yes.' The girl must say yes in more ways than one . . .

'Yes. I was by meself. Myself. You can't take anybody with you to watch wildlife. If there's more than one of you, you'll talk and giggle. Animals don't like that.'

'I see. You seem fascinated by the subject of animals. Do you spend all your free time searching the countryside?'

Jenny shook her untidy head. 'No. I have a lot of baths. I like having baths.'

'You need one now.'

'Yes,' continued Jenny, impervious and happy. 'But I do go out and about, look at nature and all that. It's all new to me, miss. We used to walk in the park sometimes, before Auntie Mavis went all funny with her nerves. But I'd never seen countryside. All the green in Bolton is surrounded by works and other buildings, same as houses and that.' She paused. 'I mean buildings like houses, not same as.'

'Good girl. I can see that you are learning.'

'Yes, miss.'

'Now, go and have that bath.'

'Yes, miss.' She made for the door.

'Jenny?'

'Yes, miss?' This was getting a bit monotonous.

Eloise stroked the creased sheet that she had recently

mangled. 'Try not to be late in future.' A saintly smile sat on her face. She had taken care to learn this expression, had practised for hours with a hand mirror. 'Do you see much of my husband these days?'

Jenny shrugged. 'Now and again, I see him. He'll be reading at the moment in the library.' She paused. 'Do you want me to fetch him or tell him something?'

The beautiful, frail face crumpled. 'Not just now, Jenny. But I do need to talk to you soon. About my husband. When I am . . . gone,' she swallowed, 'he will be so alone.'

Jenny fumbled with the doorknob. He was alone now. They both were, both of them more alone than if they'd stayed single. Each knew that the other was there, yet each tried to deny the other's existence. That must surely be the loneliest way of life. And the saddest, especially if there had been love between them.

'There are reasons, my dear girl. Reasons that will explain the situation here.'

Jenny dropped her chin. 'Them reasons are private. You shouldn't tell them to me.'

'But I must.' The voice was thick with something that sounded like grief. 'Jenny, I cannot leave this life without telling someone about my deep trouble. And about Henry's agony too. I have chosen you because you are so good, so kind.'

Jenny braced herself against the door, a shoulder wedged under a strip of moulding. 'Can't you tell a friend, somebody you've known a long while?'

Eloise continued to wear the aura of sainthood, the face pale, eyes gleaming with faith, hope, even charity. Her real faith lay in herself, was invested in the abilities she felt so sure of. Hope was not really necessary. It was like luck, and she would make her own chances. Charity was what she used to get her own way; she gave so that she might receive. 'Friends do not stay, Jenny. Not when the blows of fate are so devastating. They see a cripple, a wounded woman where there used to be a vibrant, living person. No-one of my acquaintance visits me now. They are tired of me, bored because I take so long to die.'

Jenny coughed. Her eyes were wet, and it would be

better to pretend a slight chill. This particular mistress did not want sympathy, would not thank her for weeping openly. 'Then they're not real friends, miss. A proper friend stops with you no matter what, sticks by your side through thick and thin.' She took a step into the room. 'I know what it's like, though. I never had friends, because everybody knew Auntie Mavis and how strange she was. I've only one friend, and I didn't meet her till I came here.'

'Maria.' This was not a question.

'That's right.'

Blue-veined eyelids drooped, while thick lashes fluttered like soft, dark-winged moths against an alabaster surface. 'Am I not your friend, Jenny?'

'Well . . .' Jenny hesitated, unsure of how to cope with the question. 'You're my boss, miss. You and Mr Skipton – you pay my wages. It's hard to have a friend who's your boss. And I bet you've never had a maid who was your mate.'

'You're different.'

'Oh.'

'You're special, Jenny. As soon as I saw you, from the very first day, I knew that you were going to become my one and only confidante, someone in whom I might trust. I have fears. They don't show, because I was educated to hide my feelings. But I want to tidy up before I die.'

'Yes, miss.' Again, it was easier to simply agree. The woman was too ill for argument.

'Dying is rather like leaving a room in the evening, the place where you have sat since supper time. There are cushions to plump, ashtrays to empty, there's the fire to be settled safely. We all tidy these things. Death is like that, but bigger, because you will never enter that room again. Others will use it, so it must be left in a good state. Jenny, will you help me to tidy my life?'

Jenny nodded mutely.

'Yes, I knew that you were the one. It will have to be soon. Very soon.'

'All right, miss.'

'Very well is better than all right, Jenny.'

'Very well, miss.' She shifted her weight to the other foot. 'Shall I get my bath now?'

'Yes, dear. Come and see me later, before you go to bed.' She managed a wan smile. 'Don't worry, child. We shall not begin the spring cleaning this evening. Another day will do.'

'Right. I mean yes.'

When she was alone, Eloise Skipton's smile broadened. It was all coming together admirably. The girl had taken the garments, the things a siren might wear, items ordered by telephone, collected by Sara Browne who remained in blissful ignorance of the parcels' contents. There was nothing second-hand about Jenny's clothes, though the maid believed that they had all been worn before. It was vital that the garments should be unrecognizable.

Another splendid event had been the arrival of that cur, the mongrel whose barks she sometimes heard. He liked dogs. Jenny loved all animals, so that might draw them together. A shared interest, however innocent, could easily be misinterpreted. Especially if the spy could be someone rather biased. Someone like Sara. There'd been no Sara last time, and Eloise's approach had not been subtle. Yes, she must go slowly, softly, gently this time.

Sara was already on the alert, had been made aware of 'poor Mrs Skipton's' fears. Yes, she was watching, waiting for the terrible thing to happen, the thing that would finally break Eloise's fragile heart.

Poor Mrs Skipton took another orange cream from the box, cramming it greedily into a mouth that always seemed to crave sugar these days. Sara Browne had recently become the proud owner of a solid gold locket and chain, a charitable gift from a grateful employer. It was costing a lot, she mused as she swallowed yet another chocolate. But it would cost him more. A lot more.

Throwing caution to the winds, she celebrated her progress by polishing off the pieces of rich confection. This would finish him. And no phoenix would rise from ashes so thoroughly burnt. Tomorrow, she would order some more chocolate creams.

*

250

'She was as near to me as I am to you now, sir. I couldn't believe it. She never moved, never batted an eye.'

'It seems that you are trustworthy, then. I've never known a fox to allow close inspection.'

Jenny thought for a moment. 'Do you think she was ill or something? Happen she'd no strength to run.'

'No. From your description, she sounds quite fit to me.' And Jenny looked fit too, her face lightly tanned, hair gleaming with health, eyes sparkling and clear. But she was as black as a sweep, smudges all over her face, the blouse stained and crumpled. Like a child, she had run to report on her day, to tell an adult where she had been, what she had seen and done.

'Then there was frogs. Hundreds and hundreds of frogs. They are so lively – you don't know where they'll jump next.'

He grinned. 'Did you kiss one?'

'No. What for?'

'To see if it would turn into a handsome prince, of course.'

She giggled. 'That's daft, that is. It only happens in books, like stories they read at school in the infants. Anyway, I don't want a handsome prince, ta very much.'

'Really?' The eyebrows shot up again. 'I thought every girl wanted Prince Charming.'

She looked at him, then passed a hand through hair that had escaped the confines of pins and clips. 'Not me. If I ever get wed, I'll want somebody ordinary. Maria's found a fireman. Well, I think he found her. They go for walks and to the pictures, just the usual things. But you can see that they're happy. Better than a prince, Denis is. A prince has all that bother of being king when his dad dies.'

She would make a lovely life-companion for some lucky chap, he thought. Jenny was honest, faithful, essentially good and caring. His eyes narrowed suddenly. 'I see that you have acquired a watch?'

She glanced at it, hesitated briefly. 'Yes, I got given it to stop me being late.'

He inhaled, cleared his angry throat, then leaned back

in the chair. 'I remember buying that,' he said, his voice almost inaudible.

But she had heard. 'You can have it back if you want, sir.'

'I've no use for it.'

'Well, I don't want to be taking things of yours.'

'It isn't mine,' he said carefully. 'I made a gift of it. And the person to whom I gave it has passed it on to you.'

A bubble rose in Jenny's chest, depositing its red-hot contents on her tongue. 'It's your wife, sir. Why can't you say her name? Why? She's a very sick woman, nearly ready for dying and—'

'She has been preparing for death for ages. It's a ploy she uses when she gets bored. And she is often bored, Jenny.'

Her breathing had become fast and shallow, while all kinds of questions and answers chased around in her head. How could he say that Mrs Skipton was pretending? How did he know when he never went near, never asked about her condition? Could he not forgive her for being ill, could he not try to overcome his aversion towards sickness? And why had this marriage gone so wrong? Mrs Skipton was different now, calm and pleasant, reaching out for death, for release . . .

'Don't get sucked in. I told you, I warned you.'

'Yes, sir.' The bubble had burst, its contents were evaporating like steam from a kettle.

'Just do the job.'

'Yes, sir.'

He half-smiled. 'Jenny, are you being insolent?'

'No.' The blue eyes stared at him steadily, seriously. 'I am never insolent. Look at my school reports. I am a quiet, sensible and hard-working girl.'

Not for the first time, he got the impression that she was speaking on behalf of many people, those compelled to touch forelock and doff cap to the ruling classes, the bosses towards whom the most positive feeling was almost always contempt. He had heard them. 'Yon feller needs a bigger size in boots' and 'Has tha seen t' cut of 'is 'at? Sat theer like a bloody pea on a drum, swell-'eaded bugger, 'e

252

is.' Yes, he had been condemned many times, the criticisms often pertaining to one extreme of his body, either a big head or large, insensitive feet.

'I'm sorry, Mr Skipton. I'll get me bath now.' She moved away, her movements sad and slow.

He studied her, watched the drooping shoulders, the dragging feet. 'Jenny?'

She turned quickly, as if she wanted more than anything in the world to be his friend, to be forgiven for a sin she had not even committed. 'Yes?'

'Congratulations. The foxes – getting so close.'

She beamed at him, warming the room with a smile of a sweetness that was next to unbearable. 'Yes, it was good, that.' She approached him again. 'Do you want me to take you at the weekend? Only we can't talk.'

'Yes. I'll come with you.' Oh, how he wished he could bite back those words!

'Good.' She ran off towards the hall, feet skipping happily once more.

He swung round abruptly, forcing his unseeing gaze to the window. 'Jenny,' said the dangerous voice in his head. She was beautiful, so uncomfortably lovely. He wanted . . . he wanted what any normal man would want. That body, that smile, those eyes. But no, this was no item to turn into treasure, into a prize, a victory that was merely physical.

His stomach lurched. He loved her. She was under-educated, unsuitable, unreachable. She was far too young. But she was real, honest, alive, strong, healthy. And . . . and she would give someone children.

Pol took a step backwards, her handiwork completed. 'There ye go, Carla. Haven't we made a new woman of you?' Her sparkling eyes met her companion's expressionless gaze in the still flatness of a tall, oval mirror. 'What do you think?' Pol could not contain herself. It had been many years since she had experienced such a strong sensation of excitement, such a wonderful feeling of triumph.

Carla stared at the stranger who was herself. Of course, nothing could be done about the overhanging brows, the tiny, piggy eyes, the misshapen nose. Yet Pol had somehow managed to minimize the various distortions, had worked with coloured face-creams and powders to make the face look . . . acceptable was the word. 'I look quite nice,' she ventured at last. 'Ordinary. And that's all I want to be.' Never before had she opened up to anyone about her looks and the way they had affected – even infected – her life. 'No-one will stare at me now.' There was satisfaction in her tone. And something akin to gratitude.

Pol placed her hands on Carla's shoulders. 'I've got you a suit,' she said, her thumbs massaging the tense shoulders. 'And it's new, not something off me cart.'

Carla inhaled deeply. Not once in her life had she received such a gift. There had been scarves and handkerchiefs at Christmas, the statue of the Virgin, some books during childhood. But a suit? 'I don't know what to say to you.' This was, at least, the truth.

'Ah, away with your bother, woman. It's time somebody took you in hand, gave you a bit of joy, some pleasure. When I picked you up outside the tramsheds a few weeks ago, you looked as if a smile would crack your face in two. But since you've been with me and Imelda – Christ, have you seen that haircut? It looks like a basin job, silly cow she is – you've come on a treat. Take off that awful frock, now. I've a notion to see you dressed proper for once.'

While Pol went to fetch the suit, Carla examined herself in the glass. The teeth were marvellous. Her lips seemed to have thickened slightly too; perhaps the stretching they had endured for all those years had turned them inward over the dreadful teeth. And it hadn't hurt, not much. Mr Williams's mother had been a herbalist, and he had used some magical potion to numb Carla's mouth slightly. Even now, with the sockets beginning to heal, she sprinkled the palate with the yellowish powder before inserting the dentures.

This meant that she would have to go back to the church. Well, to the presbytery. Even leaving the dreams aside, she should return those beads. They had belonged to the young priest's father, they were merely out on loan. Though that wouldn't have worried her a few weeks ago.

She might have sent them back in her own good time, and then again, she might have kept them. Something was happening to her and she feared a loss of control.

The dreams were clear now. At first, they had been a jumbled mess of pews, stations of the cross and Jenny Crawley floating down the aisle with her hair flowing behind, a finger pointing in front. The digit pointed, of course, towards Carla.

But Jenny's voice screaming 'liar' had stopped at last. Now, it was the kindly priest holding a platter of solid gold beneath Carla's chin. There were some strange words too, something like '*in vitam aeternam*'. No, not something like – it definitely was that, with '*Jesu Christi*' just before it. Perhaps she'd remembered this from mass, because she had sat perfectly still, watching them all going up for that circle of bread, and Imelda had insisted on sitting right in front, almost on the altar steps.

She stood up and removed the dark grey dress. It was on the large side now, probably because Imelda Finnegan kept her on the go, always found yet another task to be fulfilled. At Skipton Hall, she had been able to delegate, and many of her hours had been spent sitting, taking snuff, pretending to do accounts and read menus. Yes, at the big house, she had lived off the fat of the land, and the fat had settled. Mostly on her hips.

Pol came in with the suit on a hanger. It was blue, but not a run-of-the-mill identifiable blue. It was not royal, not navy, but something in between. There was a sheen to the cloth, as if it had been dipped in some kind of transparent gloss. 'Isn't it just lovely?' crowed Pol. 'Sure, I was getting fed up of seeing you in these desperate greys. They only emphasize the grey in your hair, make you look like a moulting sparrow. I shall colour your hair tomorrow. And it's not a case of vanity, madam. It's a case of survival.'

Pol's good taste was evident in the suit's cut. It must have been expensive. 'How much?' asked Carla, sounding like her old grim self.

'Never mind that, don't be worrying. Did you think I'd get you something murderous, something like me own dressing-up clothes? I've two jobs, Carla, and they each

255

demand a certain mode of dress, like a uniform. In the dirndl and blouse, I look like a colourful poor tinker with a bit of character. And the evening clothes are worn to . . . well, for another purpose altogether. But I've good clothes too. When I wear them, I'm not Pol the rag-and-bone, nor Pol the good-time girl. When I wear my best, I'm a lady.'

It fitted perfectly. The jacket draped itself across the front, was caught with a single button on the left side. The calf-length skirt owed little to the fashions of the day and much to its designer. It carefully hid the bulges, making her straighter, taller and certainly slimmer.

Pol held up a brown paper bag. 'Three blouses,' she announced. 'A white, a rose and a green. The green's near emerald, and it looks very good with that blue.'

Carla's hands fell to her sides. 'Why have you done this?'

'Because you never would,' Pol said, almost snappily. 'You'd stagger round the rest of your life looking like the remains of Sunday's dinner, just a hotch-potch of ingredients. Speaking of staggering, there's shoes in the bag too. They're black and will go with anything at all. And they've a low heel for comfort.' She turned and looked out of the window, not wanting thanks. She had enjoyed herself, just as she enjoyed dressing stray children, even if the little ones tended to pick out odd and unsuitable things.

'How did you know my size?'

'I've eyes and brains, haven't I? And there's no lock on the bedroom door. I looked in your cupboards.'

'Oh.' The mirror told Carla that the right things had been done, that the teeth should have been relegated to the scrap bucket years ago. And in the suit, she looked marvellous, appeared to be a well-dressed matron with a few bob in the bank. At last, she was like other people. Not beautiful, not ugly, merely conformist. 'Thank you, Pol.' When had she last thanked another person?

'That's all right. Your pleasure in your new self is all the thanks I need. Come on, out of that suit. We'll go downstairs and drink a toast to Franklyn Finnegan, who allows himself to be browbeaten into paying for people's teeth.'

'You're right,' said Carla.

'Of course I am. The poor man used to be six foot four, but she's worn him down to a leprechaun.'

Carla folded the new skirt. 'I didn't mean that. I meant about her hair. She looks bloody awful.'

They laughed in that special way known only to women who share jokes with other women about other women, screaming and rolling about on the edge of hysteria. Even this was new to Carla, who had seldom given herself up to any extremes, who could not remember such head-spinning giddiness and elemental joy.

They wiped their eyes, but it was still unfinished. 'She made him kiss the blarney once,' gasped Pol. 'And when he got himself back in the normal position, he slipped and . . . oh God, I can't say it,' she howled.

'Go on,' begged Carla.

'Broke his ankle. So much for the luck of the blarney, eh?'

When they were slightly nearer to composure, Carla straightened her face and said, almost sadly, 'She told him off for having a hard head. I was in the kitchen making meat puddings and I nearly left out the suet. It was the best teapot, one from Dublin, I think. She threw it and his head got in the way. "You've a head on you thicker than that wall," she shouted. He had a black eye for two days.'

'She's a desperate dangerous woman when she's roused,' moaned Pol, her stomach aching from laughter. 'Wait till she throws him out.'

'What? She throws him out? She's only the size of a child—'

'She locks the doors and bolts them. He sleeps in the coal shed and the neighbours pass him butties and cups of tea. The bobby on the beat nips in and has a word with him, usually on the subject of woman's evil. Sometimes, poor old Franklyn books into a hotel for a bath.'

'I'm not looking forward to all this,' said Carla, pensive now. 'It's not the easiest job, but at least she's never thrown him out into the shed. I shan't know what to do. Whose side am I on when it happens?'

'Who pays you?'

'He does.'

Pol thought for a moment. 'Ah well, he's just the accountant. There's only one managing director to that company.'

They looked at one another, nodded their heads in unison, then chorused, 'Imelda Finnegan,' before going down to polish off the whisky.

Chapter Ten

'ANTHONY, WILL YOU GO OUT? JUST LOSE YOURSELF DOWN the market or somewhere. You were always good at that, getting lost. I remember our Bernard used to cover for you when you were earning and you didn't want me dad to find out.' She fixed her eyes on him, tried to wear a severe expression, but it didn't fit her face, hung too loosely to be a real frown.

'Stop trying to boss me about. I'm going nowhere.' As if to underline this statement, he propped his feet on the fireguard. 'After all, we've company coming. And I'm the man of the house.'

Her manufactured laughter was thin. 'You, a man? Well, if that's what you are, God help us if there's another war. With men like you, we'd have to wave the white flag after ten minutes.'

He nodded, obviously thinking about something else altogether. These days, his mind was frequently on Jenny, and he was trying to make light of the infatuation. For one thing, Maria was already aware that he had noticed the pretty girl, and he didn't want to furnish this quick-tongued sister of his with any more ammunition. The house was becoming a battle zone, inhabited by a pair versed in the art of verbal parrying. Number seventeen Claughton Street was too much like the old home, with every deep hurt, every joy plastered over, covered by a skin of loud and meaningless banter.

'What's up with you?' she asked.

He shrugged, coughed, chewed at a sharp edge on a thumbnail. 'It was always like this at our house in Liverpool,' he grumbled. 'Joking, nobody ever saying what they really thought. Life's been one bloody great joke up to now, even when there was nothing to laugh about.'

She put her head on one side and looked at him critically. 'Are you ill?'

'No. I'm just thinking, that's all. Thinking serious thoughts like what am I doing stuck in the middle of a cotton town where it's always raining. Wondering why I'm living with you when you've a tongue that could slice three-day-old bread.'

She bit her lower lip. He was falling for Jenny, tumbling into a trap that hadn't even been set for him, a cage he had built for himself. Jenny wasn't ready for him, wasn't ready for anyone. Anthony's head, usually held high, was drooping just slightly and, having given up the nail-biting, he was now plucking repeatedly at a cover on the chair arm. 'Just slow down,' she said softly.

'I'm fed up.' His tone was subdued, almost sad.

She wanted to run to him, put her arms round his shoulders, reassure him. Because it was plain that he sensed failure. Some part of his mind must be telling him that Jenny was unprepared or unsuitable for him. 'Don't let the buggers grind you down, Ant,' was all she managed.

'Maria . . .' He wanted to pour it all out, but that would only make it real for both of them. And, one way or another, Maria would finish up knee-deep in his outpourings. She'd either wade about in his emotions and burst out laughing at him, or she'd start feeling awkward with Jenny. 'Leave it,' he said. 'I'll be all right in a day or two.' He scratched his chin, felt the new growth of beard. Was there time, could he shave . . . ? No, he need not shave. And no, Maria would not laugh, not if she knew how much he was hurting.

She tried a lighter tack, realizing too late that she was reverting to banter. 'Take them bloody feet off that fireguard, will you? I only polished it this morning—'

His feet dropped to the floor with an exaggerated

clatter. The silence that followed was loud and uneasy.

Maria polished the dresser for the umpteenth time, simply seeking a task that would cut out the sight of her brother's confusion. Her own heart thrummed noisily, and she had to swallow very hard. He must not be damaged. She loved him, had always loved him. But sisterly affection could not shut out the world, could not protect Anthony from whatever awaited him. The dresser gleamed like red-brown glass. In the oval mirror, an ugly ginger-haired female watched a sad man in a fireside chair. There was no escape. Had she been blind, she would still have felt his loneliness.

'Anthony?'

'What?'

She made a great fuss of Auntie Mavis's candelabra, twisting it back and forth until it pleased her critical eye. 'Make sure you say nothing about her mam. If she finds out what the woman did for a living, she'll go bald.'

'As if I would. As if I'd harm one hair on her head. I've always fancied a blonde, Maria.' With deliberation, he lifted his tone, pushed a smile on to his lips. 'There's something about blonde women, they don't seem to age like redheads.' The bravado was back. He grinned widely, threw back his head, then mee-mawed noiselessly at her reflection.

Maria tapped a foot against the floor. The game must continue, then. If he was not prepared to talk, then the Hesketh comedy would raise its curtain again. Or perhaps it was lowering the curtain, putting up the customary barrier? 'You'll not rile me, Anthony Hesketh. But if you start messing and acting soft, you can find somewhere else to live. Don't bother saying anything.' She waved the bodkin in the direction of his open mouth. 'Don't you dare say one word about that bloody dock road and prostitutes.'

'Oonagh Murphy only worked the docks for about six or seven weeks—'

'It's not how long you do it for, it's the fact that you did it for money at all. She's very ladylike, is Jenny—'

'Yes, just like me mam.'

'I wasn't talking about me mam.'

'You were a few days ago. You said she should have been a lady, reading books and embroidering silk flowers on her winter vests. Jenny's no more a lady than you are. She's quiet, needs bringing out of herself, that's all.'

Maria placed the bodkin on the mantelpiece, her movements deliberately slow. 'Anthony, do you want to talk to me?'

'I am talking to you.'

She smiled tightly. 'Didn't you just complain about us never being serious? If there's something on your mind, spit it out.'

He studied her for a moment or two. She'd found her chap, or so it seemed. Maria hadn't mooned about, hadn't fretted and wondered about what she wanted. But Maria wasn't a man. She didn't need to think about rejection and money and finding a decent life, a good job, security for a family. Women just said yes or no – it was the men who did the proposing, all red necks and sweaty palms. 'It's not the right time,' he said clearly. 'And I have to admit that a joke helps, so we'll carry on as normal.'

'If you ever want help, I'm here, Ant.'

He nodded. 'And the same goes for me.'

She swallowed again, then pointed to the mantelpiece. 'Just remember I know where me bodkin is. If you start telling Jenny about her mam being a . . . one of them women, that bodkin'll be somewhere else altogether. In fact, they'll need a magnet to get it out.'

She walked past him and looked through the window. 'It's getting late. And I've saved her money – well – some of it. If it wasn't for Jenny, I'd never have had the nerve to set up on me own. She's letting me live here, lending me money.' She stared at him for a moment, then took a deep breath. It was probably too late, but she must try to warn him off. 'Please don't go after her, Anthony. If you start making up to her, I could lose a very good friend.' And you could be hurt, she said inwardly. Jenny was a bird recently released from a lifetime behind bars, and the wings had not yet been tested to their fullest span.

A look of innocence came over his pleasant features. 'Me? I've never been one for the girls, you know that.'

'Huh.' She walked to the table and began to fuss with the tea-tray, sorting out cups, saucers, milk jug. 'They was like fleas round a dog, all stood on the street corner waiting for you. They only had one box of rouge between seven, and they wore it out in a week getting ready for you. Oh, I saw them, don't you worry. It was "chests out, bellies in, he's here", all of them trying to look like Mae flaming West. That's why nobody in our street never had no socks. All the socks was stuffed down blouses.' Anthony was a good-looking lad. Perhaps Jenny might settle for him in time, but time was what she needed.

He smiled amiably. 'I never noticed them or their socks. And now, I've only got eyes for Jenny and six or seven others.'

She was about to frame yet another riposte when Jenny stepped into the house. Immediately, Anthony picked up yesterday's *Sketch* and pretended to read. Maria, peering over Jenny's shoulder during their hug of greeting, quickly realized that Anthony was indeed thoroughly smitten. Her feelings were mixed. She was angry with him, annoyed by his transparent attempt at nonchalance. Yet she harboured pity for his embarrassment, for the blush of youth that had crept up his cheeks. Abruptly, Maria turned away and left the two of them together while she went to brew the tea.

'Hello, Anthony.'

Feigning surprise, he looked up. He knew he was being stupid, knew that no-one could accuse him of failing to notice her arrival. Unless he had been deaf, blind or daft. Or all three at once. 'How's it going?' he asked, his voice higher than usual.

'I've been shopping.' She spread her acquisitions on the tablecloth. 'I've got some Dr Cassell's tablets for a start.'

He roared with forced laughter. 'Maria,' he yelled. 'We can open a chemist's, forget the printing.'

In the kitchen, Maria paused, a hand on the tea caddy. The Hesketh School of Acting had produced some good performers. He was at it again. He was doing all the things he had criticized, was hiding the mask of tragedy behind the smile of comedy. Anthony had graduated with honours, was ready now to face his public. She had no need to walk through the doorway. From her hide, Maria could picture the scene in the other room, could predict some of her brother's lines.

Jenny smiled benignly, enjoying her companion's clowning. He was a funny, cheerful boy, and she was glad that Maria shared the house with such a pleasant brother.

He bounced up and grabbed the container of Dr Cassell's pills. 'It says here they're for pale skins, people what's too thin, headache, wind and palpitation.' He looked her up and down, one eyebrow raised quizzically. 'What are you doing with gastritis, indigestion and nerves?'

She giggled. 'They're not for me. They're for Mrs Skipton, I'm trying to build her up.'

'Made in Manchester,' he read aloud. 'Fancy them finding a miracle cure in Manchester.'

Jenny nodded. 'Yes, you expect things like that to come from somewhere exciting, don't you?'

He shrugged. 'Never mind, it might improve their football, God knows they need it. And what the hell's this? DeWitt's kidney and bladder pills? What's up with her?'

'Everything.'

'Yes, it looks like it. Never mind, you've enough phosferine here to cure the Lancashire Fusiliers' neuralgia and debility. If you give her all that lot, she'll come first at the flaming dog track. Mind you, she might be running backwards if she puts herself outside that bottle of tonic wine. There's plenty there to give her the DTs.'

Jenny shook her head slowly. 'No, she won't. She's going to die. I think it's called multiple sclerosis, and she's very weak all the time, can hardly breathe some days.'

He replaced packets and bottle, his face colouring to the roots of his hair. 'I'm sorry. I was only messing about. Now I come to think, our Maria said something about Mrs Skipton being ill. I never thought . . .'

'It's all right. You weren't to know.' She sat at the table and put the medicines in her bag. 'Only nobody seems to bother about her. Mr Skipton's really nice, but . . . well, they don't get on, you see. So she depends on me and this nurse called Mrs Browne. Well, she's a sort of nurse, does massage and manipulation, I think she calls it. I got some money off Mrs Hardman, bought these bits and pieces. They might not help, but I'd like to be able to say I tried. They can't make her worse, any road.'

To hide his nervousness, he tried a stab at casual indifference, shins welded to the fireguard, hands in pockets, a careless half-smile making his mouth crooked. 'Do you like all that nursing?' he asked.

'No. No, I don't. It's awful, watching somebody die. And you feel so useless and stupid, as if you should be doing summat more.' She bit her lip. 'Something more,' she said beneath her breath, feeling really useless and stupid after this correction. She wasn't at Skipton Hall now; she could do as she pleased, talk the way she had always talked. 'She's going thinner all the while, same as a picture that fades away through standing in the light. Yes, she's . . . like gradually disappearing. Even breathing's looking hard work for her at times.'

He folded himself into the chair. At least he didn't have to stare at her constantly if he sat sideways on. He could look at Maria's daisies on the wall, or pretend to be enjoying the bunch of real marigolds in the grate. He cleared his throat. 'I made a wooden stamp for them.' One of his hands waved towards the daisies. 'She drew a flower for me, then I copied it in hard wood and cut into it. She'd tried bits of wood before, but she could never get a piece big enough. And,' he pushed out his chest in an exaggerated show of male pride, 'it takes a man to cut wood right. Course, she's not satisfied, she wants roses now.'

Maria ran in with the daisy print, excitement staining her cheeks and brightening her eyes. 'Look, he's put a nice big handle on it. I feel like a bloody government official stamping papers. But it's brilliant, Jenny. If we could make a really big one, and something mechanical to move it, we could print loads at once. And there'd have to be a machine for moving the cloth along too, like rollers – like big cotton bobbins, but even bigger. Then we'd want more rollers with the stamps on, and they could roll in the dye, then over the cloth.'

'She's off,' said Anthony good-humouredly. 'She's planning another industrial revolution, even talking about pulling a wall down upstairs and getting me to build her flaming machines.'

Maria took in Jenny's expression. 'It was only a thought, Jen. I can't do much in that back kitchen – it's like working in a cupboard. But I'll not do anything to the house. It was just an idea, and a soft one at that, 'cos if we made a big room, the stairway would be in the middle of it. He'd break his leg for a start,' she jerked a thumb towards her brother, 'and we'd all have to sleep downstairs.'

Jenny folded her arms and leaned back in the chair. 'I bet Mr Skipton could find room for you, help you to get somewhere, happen a bit of a mill or a shed built in one of his yards. It'd be better than trying to alter a rented house.'

Maria shrugged. 'I don't think so. There's big printers round and about, folk that can line his pockets. I can't. He'd have to wait till I'd stopped just breaking even. I'm not talking about real mass production, either. I want me own patterns, loads of them, then sewing machines and people to cut patterns and . . . Oh, I want too much. For a start, what could we use for rent and to pay for the electric? I mean, we'd need a power house with a steam generator in it, then the steam could make electricity. Anthony knows all about that stuff.'

'Not all,' he muttered defensively. 'Just some. She'll have me doing a flaming engineering course any minute.'

Jenny felt so sad for her friend. Here was somebody with real talent, fierce ambition, and a level of energy that seemed to have no limit. The cloth of daisies pinned to the wall was beautiful, simple straight-petalled blooms with yellow centres and pink tips. It must have taken ages to get those colours right, especially the pink blush on the edge of each petal. 'So you want to start with plain cloth and finish up with whole clothes?'

'Not just clothes. Things for the house, curtains, cushion covers, mats, tablecloths.' She took a sharp breath, as if the list might be endless, too long for her excitement and limited patience.

'She wants to do everything, Jenny.' There was admiration

in his face as he looked at his sister. 'And she'll do it. It might not happen tomorrow, or even next week, but she'll get there.'

'Even if I am only a girl.'

'That's right.' He grinned hugely. 'You'll have me behind you, anyway.'

'The man of the house,' chirped Maria. But she made no quips this time. Anthony was deeply vulnerable at the moment, just because Jenny was in the house. Although one of Maria's hobbies was the plaguing of her brother, she had never sought his final humiliation. To put him down in front of Jenny would not comply with her code, a code that forced her to defend her family against all outsiders. In her books, even her forgetful mother was perfect to the rest of the world. She stood, aware of the awkward silence. Jenny was no outsider – this was her house. Was Anthony turning Jenny into a stranger, then? Was his infatuation going to come between the two friends?

'Where's the tea, then?' he asked. It was almost as if he were pleading, begging Maria not to show him up in front of present company.

'It won't be long.' She smiled at Jenny. 'And I've got nine pounds eight bob towards your money – you know – for Auntie's stone.'

'I don't need it,' answered Jenny. 'I've been saving up, because we get big wages now. In a fortnight, I'll be able to go to the stonemason's and get it ordered. Keep the money, Maria. You likely need it more than me.'

'But that's not right.' Maria looked totally indignant. 'It's a lot of money, is that. You could have a fortnight in the best hotel in Blackpool for thirteen pounds, Jen.' The red head shook itself fiercely, causing the fringe to jump into an upright position. 'I'm not having it.'

'Neither am I.' There was an edge to Jenny's tone, a quiet strength. 'Leave it where it is, Maria, or buy some cloth with it. I'll not take it.' She looked through the doorway into the kitchen. 'Where's Josie?'

'Still at school, they've got choir practice. And you'll take that money if I have to cram it up your knicker leg.'

'Really?' Jenny was grinning broadly now. 'You and whose army? I'll tell you when I need it.'

'And that'll be never,' said Maria. 'You'll starve before you'll take that off me. There's a stubborn streak in you, Jennifer Crawley.'

Jenny laughed. 'I'll not starve. I like me dinners too much.'

Maria tapped her fingers on the edge of the table, her face occupied now by a thoughtful expression. 'Right,' she said finally. 'I'll keep the money, but you'll have to be another director of Maria Hesketh.'

Anthony whistled under his breath. 'Christ,' he whispered. 'No factory, no orders, no tea made, and we've got three directors. Three chiefs and no Indians? Still, never mind. Welcome to the company, Jenny.' He bowed like a courtier, hand sweeping low as if dusting the floor with a Cavalier's feathered hat. 'Ma'am,' he gushed. 'Permit me to introduce myself. I am the managing director. That means I manage without pay and without tea.' He pretended to glare at Maria. 'She's the artistic director, she mixes the paint and forgets to brew up. And what will you be, Miss Crawley?'

'Sales director,' answered Maria immediately. 'If a face like hers can't sell, then I'm a monkey's uncle. I mean auntie.'

They burst into loud laughter, each of them finding fun in the silly situation. Young, working-class, two of them female – the dream seemed completely unattainable. But Maria's laughter was restrained, because some small seed of faith still fought for life in the fertile soil of her imagination. No, this was more than imagination, she thought as the other two continued to giggle. This was sheer bloody-minded determination, the sort that bordered on mania. Somehow, she would get her factory. Even if everything had to be handmade, even if she had to sew the frocks and cushions herself. It would happen . . .

The tea eventually arrived, accompanied by fresh-baked potato cakes and some custard slices from Jenkins's bakery. 'I've not had time to cook proper,' explained Maria. 'I've been up nights with me daisies and making frocks for some wedding. And Anthony's been in and out, going to Liverpool, never saying what time he'll be back home.' She swallowed a piece of hot, buttered potato cake, wishing she could bite out her tongue. As she expected, Jenny picked up on the Liverpool theme.

'Did you find anything about my mother?'

His mouthful of tea went down the wrong way, and Maria jumped up, beating his back with more enthusiasm than was really necessary. 'He always eats too fast,' she commented to nobody in particular. 'Mind, you had to be quick in our house. If you left stuff on your plate, it got pinched before you could say chip butty.'

Anthony regained his composure, though his watering eyes owed much to Maria's 'help', little to the stray drops of tea. 'No,' he lied as smoothly as he could manage. 'Nobody's heard of her, nobody remembers any woman like her.'

'Shame, that,' said Maria, the resolve to protect Jenny making her voice smooth and convincing. 'It's not easy finding a person what's been lost for years.'

Jenny stared into her cup. 'I wish we could find her before me dad comes back from Blackpool. That would be a lovely surprise for him. But he searched for years, used all his holidays up travelling about and asking questions.'

She looked so sad, so beautiful, thought Anthony. She must have been getting out and about a bit, because there was a golden bloom to her skin, while her hair had lightened in places, had been sun-bleached into strands of pure platinum. 'I'll not give up, Jenny,' he said. 'Trouble is, I've been through all the people what have lived at our end for a long time. They'd be the most likely. And they've heard of no Oonagh Murphy.'

Jenny lifted her face. 'She could have changed her name.'

'I showed them your photo.'

The startling blue eyes seemed to be begging for help. 'Me dad says I look like her, but he might just think that. You know what it's like – "Ooh, you've got your mother's eyes" – them things are said all the time. She might be nothing like me.'

269

Anthony bit back the small piece of comfort he might have offered, the consolation that would have failed completely to console. Her eyes were huge and liquid, looked as if the tears were stored up and just waiting to break their sweet, lash-bordered banks. 'I'll keep asking.' His tone was hoarse and gruff all of a sudden. 'Maria said your auntie mentioned the docks, but she might have got it wrong. Oonagh would have gone to the docks if she'd been waiting for the ferry at the landing stage, but if she decided to stop in this country, she could have left Liverpool. And it's a city, you know. Yes, Liverpool's a big place, even if she did stop there. She wouldn't need to be as small as a needle to hide in that haystack.'

Jenny nodded. 'I wonder where she went to have me?'

Maria placed a thin hand on Jenny's wrist. 'Anywhere, it could have been anywhere. But after you were born, she must have been round here, 'cos she brought you back.'

'I know,' said Jenny. 'But Auntie Mavis, the last time I saw her, was talking as if my mother had been . . . one of those streetwomen after I was born.' When these terrible words had been released, she took a deep and painful breath. It might only have been Auntie's opinion, but it still hurt. And if Oonagh really had been working the streets, then Anthony should be informed of that, because it might tell him where to look. Jenny went on, 'I'm sure she meant after I was born. Anyway, she wouldn't walk the streets while she was expecting, would she?' Surely Oonagh would have kept herself clean during pregnancy? The alternative made Jenny's blood crawl, and she shivered for a moment. 'Auntie Mavis said some sailors knew her, and that would have to be after I'd been born.' The eyebrows seemed to reach for one another as her face crumpled into sadness. 'I hope she wasn't one of those women.'

Maria tapped her friend's hand gently. 'What if she was, Jen? What if she'd no other way of making money?'

'No.' Jenny's face was set, the jaw jutting determinedly forward.

'Well.' Maria licked her lips, giving herself time to think. 'It's not easy in a new town. And if she had no references, the big houses wouldn't have wanted her. Maybe she'd no option. If she had to choose between that and death, well, I know which I'd have picked.'

'So do I.' Jenny pulled back her hand and placed it with its twin beneath the table.

'You'd have died.' Anthony delivered this as statement rather than question.

Jenny made no reply, though her mind continued to work. No, she would not have sold her body just to stay alive. Yes, she would have starved before selling favours like . . . like something to be consumed, something everyday, commonplace, unimportant.

Maria ploughed ahead blindly. 'She'd want to earn money so she could come back for you. I bet she was saving up and—'

'She never came.' These words were delivered sharply and rather loudly for Jenny. Quieter now, she added, 'If she saved to get to me, then she didn't save enough.'

'These things happen.' Anthony sounded glum, almost depressed. 'People try to save up, but it goes in rent and food and bits of clothing. And she'd be handing money over to—' Maria's foot kicked him sharply on the ankle. 'Money for a minder.' His face was brightening towards crimson. 'I mean if she was . . . and I'm sure she wasn't . . . but if . . .'

Jenny fixed him with a steely gaze. 'Why would she do that? Why would she pay a minder?'

He gulped a large supply of air. Her eyes were so bright one minute, so cold the next. 'Them women what walk the streets – they have to pay protection money.'

'Oh?' The upward lift at the end of this syllable made plain the fact that she expected a more thorough explanation.

'Well,' he floundered, pulling at his collar. 'Them that work the streets – they sometimes get hurt. See, they don't always get picked up by the right type, the kind of man who just wants . . . just wants . . . you know.' He coughed, feeling as if this conversation would choke him at any moment. 'So she'd have a minder. If she was on the streets and we don't know—'

'Then she may be dead.' Jenny's hands strayed to the

table where they found employment in the twisting and turning of her cup. 'That's what must have happened. She went somewhere to have me, then moved to Liverpool and either died or got murdered.'

'Jenny?' Maria was almost pleading. 'Don't think about it, not yet. Let our Anthony make a few more enquiries.'

They sat then in absolute silence, the very air seeming to be heavy with the weight of Jenny's missing mother. Anthony, knowing that Oonagh's exit from the docks had been deliberate, wanted to comfort the girl, wanted to tell her that there was a chance that Oonagh had survived. But what would that accomplish? It would be no better than keeping quiet, because his knowledge would serve only to broaden the search, would send Jenny's hopes and fears soaring the length and breadth of England.

Maria continued to sit very still, feeling as if she too should talk. About those packages, the secrets she herself had approached time after time, scissors in hand, breath bated, knees shaking. The opening of Mavis's so-called legacy had not yet occurred, because Maria actually feared the contents of those parcels. Even so, not once had she considered passing them on intact to Jenny. Deceit, she had decided, would be preferable, some kind of made-up story. Yes, she might just hand them over opened, insist that they had been found like that, untied and spilling out. Or she could wrap them again, could leave out anything that might cause pain. But first, she had to find the courage to break those wax seals.

A soft but persistent tapping at the door served to break the spell. Each of them moved, keen to fracture the sombre quiet, but Maria was the one who actually responded to the knock. 'Oh, come in. How nice to see you,' she said, her English suddenly improved.

The two nuns entered the room. 'You've company,' said Sister Beatrice, waving a pale, thin hand that looked like a fluttering white moth against the severity of her dark sleeve. 'So we shall take up little of your time. Josie is on her way down the street. She said if she walked with us, she would be called a favourite by the other children. Didn't she say that, Vincentia?'

272

The fat nun stood rigidly still, a hand to her mouth as she stared at Jenny.

Sister Beatrice, probably accustomed to the other's daydreaming, continued, 'We've a lovely communion frock here for Josie.' She placed a brown paper bag on the table. 'But you'll have to work on it, Maria. Do as you like with it, but this is a beautiful white silk. We'll take it back afterwards, for we may get another child the shape of Josie next year.' While Maria thanked her profusely for the kind loan, Sister Beatrice studied her companion. 'What is it, sister?' she asked.

'I've seen you before,' said Sister Vincentia to Jenny.

'Well, I've been round here a while,' answered the victim of close scrutiny.

'Catholic?' asked the headmistress.

Jenny shook her head.

'But I've seen you,' said Vincentia slowly. 'And you seemed older.'

Beatrice smiled. 'She sees all sorts of things, this sister of mine. She had ten of us running round the chapel just last week, for she'd spotted a spider the size of which was unbelievable. We found it. It was a black tassel off Father Sheahan's summer cloak.'

Jenny smiled politely and somewhat uncomfortably.

'And the hair was different,' said the large nun. 'Yes, there's something about the hair that's different. But the face . . .'

'Sure, everybody has a double,' said Beatrice. 'Even meself, and may God have mercy on whoever she may be, poor soul.'

Maria's responding laughter was false, because the fat nun looked so sure, sounded so certain.

'Anyway, wherever I saw someone like you, it was not round here,' said Vincentia. 'It was somewhere else altogether, and I can't just place my thoughts on it.'

'She'll have mislaid it,' said the headmistress cheerfully. 'If her head wasn't joined by the neck to the rest of her, sure she'd be leaving that behind her some mornings. The good Lord knows we've few enough possessions, but some of us still manage to lose our stockings and shoes. We're just back from retreat in Warrington, and she mislaid two prayer books and a mass card, had to send for them by post.' She sniffed meaningfully. 'Come along now, Vincentia, or the child will stay outside till morning.'

The two nuns made for the door.

'Sister?' called Jenny.

They both turned.

'If you remember, please tell me.'

'Oh, I'll be sure to do that, though it's probably of no great importance. It was just for a moment you jogged my memory. God bless you all.'

They were gone. Maria, anxious to be busy, felt the teapot, judged it to be cool and carried it out for a refill.

'They were nice,' said Jenny.

Anthony shrugged. He needed to talk, to talk hard and fast before Jenny got the chance to broach a certain subject again. 'They were all right for nuns, and they were a damned sight better than our priest.' He was gabbling a load of nonsense and he knew it. Had Jenny taken notice of that nun's ravings? And was there any substance to Sister Whatsername's tale? He continued hurriedly with his off-the-cuff piece of distraction. 'Our priest reckons he owns all the houses, never knocks, just walks in. You could be doing anything at all, and he'd still walk in. Me dad was in the tin bath once, and they had this long talk about the Good Samaritan. Me dad never remembered it, like, 'cos he was drunk at the time and frozen to death in cold water, but I was on the stairs, so I heard it too. It's the only flaming parable I can remember.'

Jenny tapped her fingers gently on the edge of the table. 'I wonder what she meant?'

'Who?'

'That nice fat nun. I wonder who she saw?'

He grabbed at the nearest passing response. 'Aw, Jenny, she's getting on, you know. There's neither of them will see sixty again, and they age young in convents. See, your normal woman of sixty, sixty-five – she's still all there. Not nuns, though. Her mind's gone.'

'No.' Jenny's voice matched for stubbornness the tilt of her resolute chin. 'She might have seen my mother.'

274

'Where?' asked Anthony, his arms spread wide. 'They never go nowhere. They're locked up all the time, only come out to plague the daylights out of schoolkids. Where do you think she saw your mam? Blackpool beach? No, her brain'll be wandering, Jenny. They never leave Bolton, do they?'

Maria entered with Josie who had sneaked down the back street in order to avoid being named a 'teacher's pet'. 'They go on retreats,' said Maria. 'But that's no use either, 'cos they lock the doors and pray for about a month, can't even talk to each other. They have to write messages on the backs of holy pictures and get washed in freezing water.'

'Me dad knows all about cold water,' said Anthony, though nobody seemed to heed this attempt to claim attention and lighten the mood.

Josie grabbed a cold potato cake and stuffed it into her mouth.

'Josie!' chided Maria. 'I wish you'd drop that habit. You're not at home now, there's nobody going to pinch your dinner.'

'Sorry.' Josie's voice was indistinct. 'Anyway, they go shopping and that.' She swallowed loudly. 'In twos. They're always in twos. They go to Manchester sometimes. Sister Marie-Thérèse can even drive a car, but the priest won't lend it her any more 'cos she goes in a crooked line all the way to Manchester.'

'See?' said Jenny triumphantly. 'She could have seen somebody like me only older in Manchester.'

Anthony sank with deliberate drama into the rocking chair. 'Don't send me searching there,' he pleaded. 'It's bad enough here, people talking in foreign words. They might be even worse in Manchester.'

Jenny's tight lips managed to form a slight smile. 'Don't worry,' she said. 'The nun might remember soon.' She turned to Josie. 'Ask her sometimes. Ask Sister Vincentia if she remembers where she saw a woman who looks like me.'

'Right.' Josie, hungry, bored with the conversation, flashed a winning, if somewhat gappy smile at her sister.

'Can I have chips for me tea? And an egg and two sausages?'

Maria laughed. 'Course you can.' But on her way to the kitchen, the grin faded. She had saved one of them. But the rest, still in Liverpool, would be fighting over crumbs. One day, she told herself grimly. Yes, one day . . .

She stood above him on the bank of the stream, arms akimbo, mouth wide with laughter. Her breasts seemed to push against restraints provided by a blouse of white lawn and, underneath the blouse, some sort of underwear, possibly a camisole. Whatever, it had a pattern across its top, and this pressed itself against the outer garment. Perhaps, he thought irrelevantly, it was broderie anglaise. Yes, it would be just like Eloise to use pretty lingerie to bribe a young girl into submission. The blouse, too, was probably a gift, second-hand from the mistress of Skipton Hall. Eloise still needed to buy her friends, that was plain enough. These days, she used money. In the long-dead past, she had bartered her charms, had flirted outrageously . . .

He steadied himself on the next stone, wondering who the hell had placed the things here so unevenly, and why on earth they should be called stepping-stones. Slipping-and-breaking-your-neck-stones would have been slightly nearer the mark.

'Mr Skipton?'

'What now?'

She stifled a giggle. 'Don't concentrate on your feet so much. It's like when folk climb a mountain – they're told not to keep looking down.'

He almost growled. She had crossed the stream with the unthinking agility of a doe, and now she was mocking his clumsiness. He might have performed better had she not been watching, possibly criticizing his every move. Again, he cursed beneath his breath. He was an expert skier, ice-skater, horseman, golfer. But he couldn't cross this bit of water without falling in. The dog wasn't helping, of course. He stood next to Jenny, black fur dripping, mouth wide with canine glee, tail waving like a flag of victory.

'Don't fall in again, Mr Skipton. You're already wet through.'

'Jenny.' He gritted his teeth, so his words came out thin. 'I am quite well acquainted with my state of wetness.' After all, it was his own skin that was soaked.

'Woof,' said Charlie, anxious to be in on the conversation.

Jenny patted the soggy head. 'You're not supposed to be here. You were shut in so that I could show Mr Skipton the foxes.' She had put the dog in his kennel, but it was plain that he had found a loophole in the system.

Charlie, who didn't seem to mind being in the wrong place at the wrong time, woofed again.

Henry Skipton heaved himself up the bank. 'There's a last time for everything,' he said.

'Shall we come back by Ricketty Bridge, then?'

He frowned. 'Have you named that too?' She had a tendency, a rather touching and romantic need to christen bits of the countryside that had become important to her. 'Careful,' he said. 'That's my bridge. If you give it a name that makes it sound unsafe, the next drunken farm labourer who falls off it will have my hide in court.'

They walked along with the growing pup, whose one aim in life seemed to be to get underfoot as often as possible. When he wasn't chasing butterflies or barking at some unattainable bird, he was running round Jenny and Henry, causing them to stand still until the dog had got his bearings.

'Not very bright, is he?' Henry sounded glum. 'No wonder I knocked him over – the dog has no sense.'

'He's only a puppy, sir.'

Henry sighed deeply. 'In my very considerable experience, an animal shows signs of intelligence right from the start. Or, as in this case, signs of stupidity. The dog's an amiable fool.'

As if to illustrate the point, Charlie stuck his head down a rabbit hole, leaving his hind quarters wriggling uselessly and rather comically above the burrow.

They dug a little, pulled a little and finally the grinning

black face rewarded them with some sharp barking and much excited licking.

'Sloppy thing.' Jenny wiped her cheeks on a handker-chief. 'He's not daft,' she insisted. 'He just wants training, sir.'

'I'll try very hard to believe you.'

Jenny rummaged in the pocket of her skirt. 'Sit,' she said. The pup sat, hind legs quivering against this unwanted restriction.

'Don't you dare move,' said Jenny. Charlie did not dare.

She approached him, crooning something Henry failed to catch. Slowly, Jenny placed a piece of toffee on the dog's nose. 'No,' she whispered. 'Not yet.' She walked a few paces, leaving the dog shaking with suppressed energy. Charlie's eyes remained fixed on Jenny until she called, 'Now', whereupon he tossed the sweet into the air, caught it in his mouth and swallowed it in one huge gulp of loud relief.

'I told you he wasn't stupid, sir. A dog can only be clever if it's told what to do.'

Charlie, reverting to type, was trying to run up a tree after a crow. The bird tilted its head sideways at the howling pup, then seemed to shrug its dark wings before flying off. Jenny started to laugh. 'He's a nuisance with birds.'

'So I've noticed. Though you seem to have some influence on him. You may make something of him after all.'

'If I stay.' She raced off with Charlie, jumping nimbly over a gate while the pup squeezed through its bars.

Henry stopped in his tracks, staring at girl and animal as they frolicked along a footpath. She might not stay. And he was a damned fool of a man to allow that to make some difference. What did he want? What the dickens did he need, expect, deserve, desire? He turned away from the happy pair, fixing his eyes on a dipping orange sun. The sky was beautiful towards the horizon, a brilliant aqua-marine that was shot with golds and reds, streaked here and there by mackerel clouds that promised a fair tomorrow. Light sliced across the distant moors, lending

278

them tones that were almost autumnal, punctuating the many greens with amber and copper shades. Yes, it would be fine in the morning.

Tomorrow. Another day of the usual grind, cloth for the bleachworks, cloth back from the bleachworks, bleached cloth for the printer. Not that he had much contact with the actual work, but he could feel it, hear it going on day after relentless bloody day. Then, with figures checked and orders filled, he would return home. Just like today. Tomorrow would be another today.

He lit a small cigar, breathing so deeply that the acrid smoke scalded his lungs. Another today. A wheelchair parked at the front of his house, its thin occupant's face hidden beneath the wide brim of a straw hat. The nurse who was always there would bend her head in silent greeting as the master drove his car round the back. He had started to park round the back because of the wheelchair. She was watching him. They were both watching, she and the big nurse. What did they expect to witness? A reconciliation?

As always, the cigar tasted vile in the open air. True vices needed to be kept indoors – drinking, smoking, fornication. Yes, they were all indoor sports, not one of them could thrive in wind, rain or sun. He spun round on his heel in response to her voice. She was waving and jumping like a two-year-old, most of her hair cascading now to the slender shoulders. He grinned in spite of his sombre thoughts. The battle between Jenny and her hair was an unequal one, because the mane of yellow silk invariably found its own wilful way. He could identify the day on which it was newly washed, because they were the truly difficult times. It was so smooth that a pin could find no purchase, and she often left a trail of ironmongery in her wake. And she could be heard cursing in corridors and on stairs, threatening to cut it off. She must not do that. No, she must not lose that glorious hair.

He climbed over the stile and joined her. She was quiet now, one side of her face completely swamped by tumbling locks. The dog, clutched tightly in her arms, had buried his face in the fallen hair, and Henry envied

Charlie for his current station in life. Her free hand was pressed against her mouth, and he heard her make a low shushing sound.

The small fox posed like a statue, one foot raised as if ready to make off as soon as danger threatened. A wet, black nose sniffed the air suspiciously, while triangular ears pointed straight up to show that his position was guarded.

'It's one of her babies,' whispered Jenny. 'That's Max – he's whiter in front than the others.'

Henry, who had never seen a fox except in passing, froze and wondered what this girl had that was so . . . attractive. It wasn't her looks, though they were pleasing to the eye of any human animal. It was something much bigger, more important and elemental than mere appearances. As the vixen came out of the bushes to reclaim her offspring, Henry realized what it was, this gift of Jenny's. The older animal stood for a moment and looked directly at Jenny. Then she nosed her naughty youngster, pushing him sideways into the undergrowth. Just before leaving, the vixen raised her head and made a low sound that might easily have been a greeting. Or perhaps a farewell, thought Henry as the red fur flashed its way towards home. Jenny had love, and that was her gift. Love, compassion, sympathy, empathy. Most especially, she had love for animals.

He glanced at her as she placed Charlie on the ground. When she lifted her tousled head, he glimpsed the moist joy that had gathered in her eyes. The girl loved carthorses, dogs and foxes. The girl was therefore lovable. This pain in his chest owed little to mutton for dinner, nothing to heart trouble. At least, not the usual heart trouble.

'Isn't she beautiful, Mr Skipton?'

'Yes, Jenny. She is lovely.'

'She talks to me.'

'Yes.'

'And she looks after her babies.' She bent to pat Charlie's neck. 'She comes to the house sometimes. It isn't Charlie getting in the swill bin, you know.'

'I see.'

'Does it matter, sir? Does it matter if we feed wild animals as well as farm ones?'

He wished that he had hung on to that dreadful cigar. It might have tasted nasty, but it would have given him something to do, some reason to lift a hand to his face, to pause before speaking. 'No, it doesn't matter.'

She wiped the wetness from the corners of her eyes. 'Nature is a wonderful thing, sir. I'd seen books – you know – pictures of animals and trees and all that at school. But nature's . . . more real than that. Like the smell of a wet tree. Nobody can draw a picture of a smell. Or the noise a bird makes when it's taking off or flying fast, all them joined-up feathers hitting the air. And they can't make a drawing about the feel of spring water either, how smooth it is on your fingers. Books can explain a lot of stuff, but they can't make you live things. Books are just pretend.'

With this one fell swoop, Jenny condemned the whole of science and literature to the rag cart. The countryside was clearly important to her, and he found himself hoping that the magnetic pull of open land would keep her here until . . . until what? Until the wheelchair had gone?

She ran ahead towards the house, leaving him behind. He felt old, weary, neglected. All Jenny wanted was here. Sky, woods, fields, animals. The things she needed were free. Even the present government could not put tax on this girl's dreams. A cottage, a log fire, some chickens and a kitchen garden – these were probably Jenny Crawley's idea of heaven. She would perhaps marry a farmer, or somebody connected to the land, a plougher of crop fields, a keeper of cows or sheep. Or she might suddenly disappear into the bowels of that blasted town, back to her friends, the mills, those tall and belching chimney stacks. In which case, the countryside would become a place to visit at weekends. Money would not attract her, and all he had was money and the feeble chattels that went with it.

He found himself grinning ruefully as he walked the last mile. He was thinking stupid thoughts again, allowing his mind to wander into a paradise that was not for him. She was unsuitable. He had a wife, a wife who hung round his neck like an albatross, an invisible burden whose appetite still managed to diminish him. Even when she died – and surely the disease would kill her soon? – even then, Jenny would not be the one for him.

She had stopped to wait for him. A blur of black fur cavorted at her feet, while her hands were raised yet again to fight the troublesome hair. His steps were slow as he approached her. Perhaps he wanted to keep the picture, hold the vision, prolong his own sweet agony. His divided mind cursed and praised her simultaneously, swinging violently from one emotion to the next, leaving him dizzy and sick from the see-saw of his own confusion. It might be better if she did leave the house, if she went away and left him some kind of barren peace. There was no comfort for him just now, because he had become incapable of approaching the sort of woman who had soothed his flesh in the past. Jenny had altered the course of his life, yet she remained totally oblivious of her own indisputable power. Was it just her *naïveté* that had captured him so completely? The girl was as natural as the elements she had recently described. Whoever took her into womanhood would indeed be privileged.

The last few steps were painfully slow, exquisitely agonizing. Something in the rear of his head seemed to snap – he could almost hear the twang of severed nerve. His hands were on her, smoothing their way across her shoulders, down her arms. He heard someone speaking, a man saying that he needed her, wanted her to be kind, to help his pain. The dog was barking as fingers closed around the supple waist. Jenny had been right – true beauty could not be written on paper, because true loveliness was ill-served by mere words.

'Are you all right, sir?'

He blinked rapidly, his thoughts fighting to catch up with the movements of his eyelids. He coughed. 'Just a slight turn of the ankle, Jenny.'

'You said you wanted me to help. Shall I go and fetch Briony so you can lean on both of us?'

'No. The pain's going now.' A lie, but a decent one. He

was a decent man, after all, an honourable man who refused to allow his baser nature to take advantage of this precious girl. 'I can walk now.' His hands removed themselves reluctantly from her body. The smell of her was heady, a flower-scent that managed not to be cloying. And he had touched a lock, a strand that had found complete freedom halfway down her body. It was satin. She must not cut that hair.

'Charlie's hungry,' she said. 'A run always makes him hungry.'

'Yes.' He was famished too, but not for want of food.

'We'd best get home, sir.'

'That's a good idea, Jenny. I'm sorry if I startled you just now, but I do have a weak ankle. Something I acquired in my misspent youth.'

They walked. 'How did you misspend it?' she asked.

'Tennis, mostly.'

'Oh. I've never played that. I played rounders at school, but we mostly did exercises. The teacher used to stand there blowing a whistle while we did daft things like touching our toes. But we never played tennis.'

'No.' They were almost there. He began to breathe freely again, feeling as if he had barely missed having a dreadful accident. He glanced towards the house. She was still sitting there, although the air had started to cool. The huge nurse was by her side, head bent to listen to the orders of her mistress. Nothing had changed. Today was just yesterday's tomorrow. And tomorrow would be exactly the same.

'I see what you mean.' Sara Browne patted Eloise's shoulder. 'She looks as if she's been dragged through the bushes.'

Eloise sighed sadly. 'The poor child doesn't know the difference, of course. Between right and wrong, I mean. I brought her straight from the slums, tried to show her a decent life ...' A pale, thin hand raised itself then dropped heavily into her lap. With this gesture, Eloise demonstrated the depth of her grief, the measure of her uselessness.

'She must be told,' said the nurse sharply. 'Making off into the woods with your husband is hardly honourable. Surely she must realize that she is encouraging him?'

'It's all his doing.' Eloise sniffed delicately in order to illustrate the proximity of her tears. 'Jenny isn't the first and she is hardly likely to be the last of his victims.'

She watched them as they approached. The dog had been a bonus, of course, had dragged the two of them together in some form of bond. And this expedition to search for foxes had been ideal too, especially with the evening remaining warm enough for a cripple to sit outside and watch the sunset. 'It was good of you to stay, Sara. I did so long to see the sun go down again. Summer dusk was always my favourite time.' She waved as Jenny disappeared round the side of the house. 'See how she's following his every move? Poor innocent little soul.'

Sara made a clucking sound to show her heartfelt sympathy for Mrs Skipton. This was a brave and wonderful lady whose tolerance should be thoroughly admired. Even so . . . She turned the chair and looked at the fragile face. 'You are so kind,' she said. 'Really, you ought to teach him a lesson.'

Eloise nodded. 'He has been silly,' she said, hoping to sound reluctant in this weak condemnation of her husband's activities. 'And I have been advised to divorce him. But I could not bear to go through all that alone. I would need evidence, witnesses, someone strong to lean on—'

'There's me.' The large woman dropped to her knees. 'I'll be witness, if you like. And I'm strong. Please allow me to help you, Mrs Skipton. Your husband should not be allowed to treat you so shabbily.'

'I'll . . . I'll give it some thought.' Eloise, who had thought about nothing else for some years, grinned to herself as the nurse lifted her out of the chair. Sara Browne was strong in more ways than one. Eloise felt like a feather in the woman's arms, was confident of support from this particular quarter. Like many unattractive women, the nurse was devoted to her pretty patient, looked upon her as something of a goddess, a special creature who had been visited with the gift of beauty, only to be cursed in relative youth by the terrible blow of terminal illness. Yes, some ugly women were strangely romantic, thought Eloise. And enamoured of nice jewellery too.

'We must talk,' said the nurse before leaving Eloise to Jenny's tender evening mercies. 'We need a plan.'

Eloise fluttered prettily. 'Oh my dear, I need to be sure before asking for a divorce.'

Sara almost spat, 'Sure? How sure do you want to be? Jenny didn't get in that state from walking, you know. They've been . . . doing things.'

'Perhaps. I'll let you know my decision soon.'

'But Mrs Skipton—'

'Please, Sara. I've asked you before to call me Eloise.' She pretended to think deeply for a moment. 'Divorce is such an awful thing. It could ruin him. Think of the mills, think of all the people who depend on Skipton's for a living. I should not like to be responsible for starving children. No, I should hate to feel that I had thrown fathers and mothers out of work.'

Sara Browne rubbed her flat nose. It was really touching, the way this lovely lady cared about common folk. Well, she would do whatever Mrs Skipton wanted. Whatever Eloise wanted, she corrected herself firmly.

'Please don't say anything to Jenny.' The voice from the bed was weak and thin. 'Let me deal with it.'

'I wouldn't dream of interfering. You know I—'

'Sara, you are so good. Don't forget to take that little bracelet, dear. It will be so lovely as a present for your niece.'

Sara Browne made her farewell, picked up the latest donated item and left the room. Her eyes stung all the way down the stairs. Never in her life had she met anyone as good and selfless as Eloise Skipton. She must divorce that dreadful man.

The girl was putting the wheelchair into the large hall cupboard. She was cleaner now, and her hair was brushed into a fat, gleaming bun on the nape of her neck. Sara paused, a hand to her mouth.

'Can I help you?' asked Jenny.

With her blood threatening to boil, Sara studied this wayward person. She was either very innocent, or completely corrupt, probably the latter. Mrs Skipton – Eloise – always saw the best in people, always looked for the saving graces.

'Nurse? Did you want something?'

'No,' growled the seething woman. 'Nothing is required of you. Except that you take care of that lovely lady.'

'I do look after her,' answered Jenny. But she was addressing thin air, because the nurse had galloped off down the steps with a speed that was astonishing in a woman of her size.

Jenny stood for a moment, then shrugged away her slight unease. Perhaps the nurse had had a difficult day and had taken out her frustration on the nearest maid. Oh well, not to worry. Cocoa, a chat with Briony, then it would be time to settle the mistress. She yawned, tired out by fresh air and exercise.

For the first time in her life, Jenny Crawley was completely happy.

Chapter Eleven

SHE WAS TWO WOMEN. THERE WAS THE ONE WITH THE teeth, those huge protruding slabs that had seemed to enter a room several seconds before the rest of her. Then there was this new person, acceptable, ordinary, unremarkable. But the removal of the teeth had not taken away the uglier shadow; it still pursued her, haunted her at night, made her wake in the early mornings with a sick, leaden weight in her chest, a terrible fear that the dentistry itself had been the dream, while the reality remained and was unremovable. At such times, she would snatch at the light-pull that hung over her head, a facility made necessary by Pol's affection for thick curtains. The evidence was always there, of course. Sitting by the bed in their jar, twin rows of gleaming ivory-white dentures set in gums that were rather pinker than necessary.

Day after day, Carla fought to be rid of her former self. In her much-revised book, the old Carla Sloane was hideous inside and out, and she had no doubt that some of the inner ugliness remained. It was time for change, time for the new Carla to find a sensible goal in life, something attainable and decent. The word 'decent' was in her mind often these days. She wanted, needed to be a good woman, was desperate in her desire for a niche, a place where she might truly belong. Sometimes, she worried that she might have a split personality, because the two sides of her nature seemed to pull one against the other. Yet there was a core, a solid centre of self that sat in the middle and weathered, somehow, these fierce tugs-of-war. The good side, the decent side would win, because she, in the middle, had thrown her weight behind its cause.

On this summer evening, she sat in front of her mirror and studied the answering face. It was like looking at somebody else. Now that the pain had eased its slow way out of her face, she was more relaxed, had fewer lines criss-crossing about at the corners of her mouth. The skin was smoother, younger than it had been at thirty, there was a slight blush on her cheeks, and even her eyes looked brighter, bigger. She should have done this earlier, should have realized that the teeth had crippled her whole face. Of course, the brows still jutted out like a cliff overhanging her eyes, and the nose was far from straight, but she was no longer an object to be ridiculed. Things could have been so much easier if she'd only had the sense to . . .

She turned from the mirror, chiding herself inwardly for thinking backwards again. It had been a terrible life, but that was nobody's fault. The bitterness, the overwhelming anger, the gut-twisting agony that had accompanied her for so many years – all such bad feelings must be left behind. She was a new woman. Not a beautiful woman, she could never be that. In fact, even beauty would have meant being noticed. Blending in, becoming part and parcel of the colourless crowd – these were the ingredients of Carla's recipe for heaven on earth.

The cat had started coming to her, padding its silent, soft-pawed way up to her bedroom and stretching out on bed or ottoman, greeting her with a gentle purring growl whenever she came in. Carla had never liked cats. So sure of themselves they were, so arrogant and self-contained. It was their certainty that she had hated, that tendency to rub uninvited against a leg, to jump up expecting a welcome in just about anybody's lap. Sammy was winning her affection, was twisting her right round the little finger he didn't have. 'You're a monster,' she said almost cheerfully. He was indeed a monster, the size of a small dog, while the lush Persian coat of purplish grey made him fatter than he really was.

She put on her new suit while Sammy watched, his head cocked to one side as if he were assessing her appearance. He seemed satisfied enough, because he was fast asleep before she had fastened the last button. Looking nice was a new thing, so she lingered for a few moments in front of the glass, making sure that her shoes shone, that the skirt hung right, that her stockings were not twisted or wrinkled.

Pol put her head round the door. 'He's thrown another bloody shoe,' she said. 'And hurt himself into the bargain. I'll have to stable him for a week or two.'

Carla didn't need to ask. The pony was the love of Pol's life, though the relationship between woman and beast was interesting. Rather like the Finnegans' romance, thought Carla. Loving words one minute, expletives the next.

'Are you going out, then?' Pol threw herself on to the woven quilt. 'Courting, is it?'

'Don't be silly. I'm going to see Father Entwistle.'

'Ah well, you'll not get far with him, though there's one or two priests I could name who'd give their right arms to fall from grace in the celibacy department. Aren't you spending a lot of time hanging round these churches, now? Did Imelda fill your ears with tales of salvation?'

Carla lowered herself gingerly into a chair, anxious not to seat the best skirt. 'I'm thinking of being a Catholic,' she said. That was the way, the right path for her, and she had worked it out for herself. A fine, strong religion would give her the framework, the security she needed. And which faith was stronger, more powerful than the lavish, buoyant Christianity of Rome?

'Oh God Almighty!' Pol clapped a hand to her forehead. 'Now, there's some of us have got to be Catholic, for it's the way we were born and no questions asked, no quarter given. A Catholic is a trying thing to be. For a start, they stamp the word "guilty" across your soul and you can never be rid of it.' She fixed a serious stare on her companion's much improved face. 'Anyway, you might as well say you want to be Jewish. Born, not made – that's what we Catholics are.'

289

'No.' Carla thought for a moment. 'Jews are members of a race as well as a creed. Anybody can become a Catholic.'

Pol pretended to mop her fevered brow. 'Well, may the Lord save me from all converts. Ah, it's one thing to enter the world with a handicap, another matter altogether to bring it on yourself. And it's the same as somebody who's signed the pledge against drink – they want everybody else to stay dry too. You'll be novena-ing all over the house and going to confession twice a month, trying to drag me along at the back of you.'

'I won't do that.'

'Aye, but you'll look at me and call me a whore in your heart.'

Carla smiled faintly. 'Whatever you've done and whatever you are, I have done and been worse. I don't know what's happening to me, Pol. When I went to St Patrick's it felt . . . like home, like I was in the right place.' It would have sounded silly if she'd told the truth – that half of her had been in the right place, while the rest—

'Did you see a light?'

'Just a few candles.'

Pol dragged herself up the bed and leaned on the headboard. 'Well, at least it's not a miracle, then. I could never give house room to a saint. But honestly, I never did notice such a change in a person. Not just the way you look, but how you act. It was fun before, because I knew we were both after getting even with himself—'

'That's over.' It was, had to be. In fact, she would probably need to . . . no. She must not think about that. Not now, not yet.

'Is it?'

'Yes.' She peered through the window to see if the up-tram was on its way. When that went past, she would have a few minutes before the down-tram left the terminus to carry her to town. 'I've no feelings at all about him. Except some regrets. There are things I must put right, horrible things.' She bit into her lower lip. That was a new experience too, because she hadn't been able to bite her lip with her old teeth . . . Yes, there were wrongs to right, people to face, explanations to rehearse.

'But the way you were treated, Carla!'

She breathed deeply against the old and familiar indignation. The indignation belonged to another time, another place, a different woman. She would not let it in. 'I may have deserved it.' Even now, standing on the doorstep of redemption, she found difficulty in admitting to her sins. 'Look, I know the changes in me are hard to take. I don't understand this need for . . . God, because I never needed Him before. But I want to be part of a congregation, part of a faith. There's nothing else that matters to me.'

'Doesn't my friendship count?'

'Yes, of course it does. I never had a friend before. It's because of you that I've found what I needed – you sent me to Imelda.'

'May I be forgiven for that. Stop taking this so seriously. You can go to church without hanging round the priests once a week. You'll get talked about.'

'Being talked about is nothing new to either of us. And I am taking instructions. There are questions I need to ask before I get baptized. It's not a step I can take lightly. And I don't know whether I'm good enough.' She had been bad, really wicked, and the misery of past misdeeds hung heavily about her shoulders. Perhaps she would never be forgiven. In which case, she would be denied entry into the body of the church.

'I'm a Catholic,' said Pol. 'But you don't see me in church except at Easter for my duties.'

Carla turned slowly from the window. 'And why do you make your Easter duties?'

'Because if I didn't, I'd be excommunicated. Confession and communion at least once a year, and that at Easter or thereabouts,' she quoted from the list of church commandments.

'Exactly. That's how important it is.'

Pol chuckled. 'Politics and religion. Those are subjects that should never see the light of day between friends. Let's just agree that we differ.'

'Right. I'd better go for the tram.'

Pol followed Carla down to the hallway. 'Listen. Do you

think Jenny Crawley is his daughter? Skipton's, I mean?'

Carla straightened her spine, swallowing hard, pushing against the memory of her own part in this fairy tale. 'No. I don't believe that he's her father.'

'You never said that before.'

'I never said anything. I just let you say what you wanted to say. That was wrong, because I'm sure he isn't her father.'

'Well, I'm not so certain. And if his uncle's behaviour is anything to judge by . . .'

'What?'

Pol took a step backwards. 'Oh, nothing. Just a conversation I overheard once.'

Carla opened the door. Almost wearily, she said, 'Pol, leave it alone. There's been enough damage in that house.'

Pol watched as her friend crossed the road for the down-tram. There had been damage, all right. Damage to Pol's mother, to her grandmother, to Pol herself. He sat there in his castle, Henry bloody Skipton, with his servants and his fancy meals, a nice fat cigar, a read of the paper, a soft bed and no worries. Though he had looked worried that day in the street, but then he was possibly a good actor as well as a supposedly fair mill boss.

She slammed the door vigorously. What was fair about it? Christ, she was his cousin, she was a Skipton, though the very name made her shiver. There was land, there were antiques, there was a life that had been denied to the Skipton-Irish bastard whose name was Pol O'Gorman.

The cat wound his silken way around her legs, and she picked him up, hugging him so fiercely that he yowled. 'Sorry, Sammy,' she whispered. 'But I'll have my day with the man. Yes, I'll see himself out if it's the last bloody thing I do.'

Maria flounced into the house, threw her bag and scarf on to the table, then collapsed in a chair, her expression grim and disappointed.

'Where've you been?' He folded the sports section and placed it in the grate with the rest of the paper. 'I had to get a Jenkins's pie for me dinner again.'

'Anthony,' she sighed, forcing the air from deep inside her body. 'My piles bleed for you, they really do.'

'You haven't got piles.'

'If I had, they'd bleed.' She paused, teeth chewing at her lower lip. 'We can't do it,' she said eventually. 'We'll never, ever do it.'

He thought of a clever remark, then swallowed it when he saw the darkness in her eyes. Something or somebody had upset his sister and, like a true Hesketh, he was immediately on his guard. 'Is it that lad? Has he been talking out of turn?'

'Eh?' The cloud on her face dispersed for a second. 'No, it's not Denis.' She sniffed in that way of hers, the way that told her family that she was not best pleased. 'It'd cost a bloody fortune. I've been up to Mallinsons'. They've got me beat into a cocked hat before I've even run on the field. It was . . . terrifying. Wonderful, like, but frightening.'

'Maria.' He leaned forward in his chair. 'Pretend I'm about five, then tell me proper. I can't keep up with you. It's like a riddle, or one of me father's jokes – no beginning, no end, but a middle that lasts past bedtime.'

'I went for a job.'

'You don't need a job. I thought we were setting up—'

'I pretended I wanted a job. Shut up and listen. They needed cleaners, so I went up and they showed me round a couple of rooms. It was like looking at heaven – except the patterns were a load of no good, dead-looking, most of them, all greys and bottle greens. The noise, the smell . . .' A dreamy look occupied her face now. 'Etched copper, I think they were, the cylinders what they use for printing. And colours left to one side, lovely colours they could have used. But no, they stick to the safe stuff, stuff that doesn't cause any arguments because it's not worth talking about.'

'You've been to the printworks.'

At last he had her full attention. 'Ten out of ten,' she said smartly. 'Give out the writing slates and one sum book between two.'

'But you don't want to work on that scale, do you?'

She blinked a few times, plainly concentrating once

more on her life's ambition. 'The size of our operation would be dictated by public demand.'

He laughed. 'What did you have for breakfast? A dictionary?'

'Library,' she answered. 'And not for breakfast, either. I go in sometimes and read the papers, posh London ones that business people have. If we could get going, we'd have to do something that bit different, then we'd have to make folk want it. So at first, we'd have like a scarcity value. We'd be expensive and exclusive. Then a bit later on, we'd lower our prices so that ordinary people could buy our lines. The posh end of the market would say, "Ooh, we'll have to get something different, 'cos even the fishmonger's wife's got Maria Hesketh daisy table linen." That's when we'd put out another expensive line. When the rich folk had taken their money's worth, we'd drop the price and—'

'And start all over again.'

'Yes. Except it won't happen. It costs thousands, Ant.'

'Not if a few of us do it by hand with the blocks. I can find a way of pressing them down, weight the blocks in some way. And if we're going to be all exclusive and posh, we don't need brass cylinders and all that.'

'Copper.' Absently, she chewed at a fingernail, then pulled her hand away, examining the damage done by her sharp teeth. 'I'm chewing again. I always do that when I'm bothered. I chew me lips and me nails—'

'And you sniff.'

'Yes, I know.' She sniffed. 'It's like this. Blocks are all right for big patterns. Like curtains. If you have a nice huge room with nice huge windows, a big pattern can look smart. But say you want something small, delicate, like. You can't do it with wood, Ant. See, the wood pattern sticks up, and it splits if you cut the relief too fine. I read about that down the library. These copper ones are cut into the cylinder, so your dyes swill into them. It's the opposite way altogether.'

He decided to try a positive and hopeful tack. 'If we save, we can get some second-hand stuff.'

'There is none. And it costs an arm, a leg and all your flaming underwear, never mind your shirt. If we started saving every penny – no food, no new clothes – we'd still be sixty before we could afford the machinery. So, I'll have to forget about anything on a large scale. It'll have to carry on here, in the back kitchen, with blocks. No workshed, no machines, no finished product except for a few head-scarves and pinnies.'

He leaned back now, fingertips joined and touching his lower lip. 'I've been thinking.'

'What with?'

'Me big toe. Listen, you know all these women that work in these mills?'

'Not by name, no, but I've noticed they're there.'

He tapped his teeth for a little while longer, then jumped up and began to stride about the room, as if his body had begun to work as fast as his brain. 'Right. We think small, Maria.'

'We can't get any smaller—'

'Hold your horses, queen. Have you seen them going to the mill? All dowdy and grey, scarves on their heads backwards. You know what I mean, they make a triangle with the scarf, then wrap it round their heads into a sort of turban thing.'

'Yes, them that don't wear shawls.'

He paced about for a few moments, head bent forward, brow furrowed as his idea fought for life. 'Clogs and shawls and mucky old scarves – not a bit of colour in their lives. And all day, they stand at their mules and looms, nothing to see except other women in miserable clothes.'

'What are you getting at?'

He stared hard at her. 'How fine can you cut it, Maria?'

'As fine as it needs to be. No profit's all right with me as long as I can see a light at the end of the tunnel. And as long as there's a bit of scouse in the pan for our dinner.'

He turned to the dresser, rummaged in a drawer, came up with a scarf. 'This is their basic equipment – the younger ones who don't wear the shawl. Now, it's a good safety measure, is a scarf. There's been women scalped in mills, I've read about them in papers. If we made a turban, something with a bit of elastic in, something that didn't need tying and fiddling with every morning . . .' He folded

295

the scarf. 'It wouldn't take a lot of cloth. And they could hide their pipe cleaners under it, or their steel curlers – they'd still look smart. Four or five different colours so they can pick and choose . . .' He studied her again. 'It'd be a grand safety measure too, so the bosses would approve. What do you say, Maria?'

Her skin had whitened except for two spots of colour high on the fine cheekbones. 'Pinnies,' she shouted triumphantly. 'Wrap-overs to match. Then on top, or instead of a wrap-over, a plain-coloured apron made of two large pockets – like a pillowcase sewn down the middle and with ties on. It would match one of the colours in the turban, so they'd be smart and cheerful. They could keep their tubes in the apron, the tubes what the cotton gets spun on to. Plenty of room, 'cos they'd be all pocket, these aprons. And that would save them bending for a handful every two minutes.' She nodded excitedly. 'We'll call it the doffer's companion. They can go to work all colour co-ordinated. We can sell them from here, can't we?'

'Naw. We'll get a Saturday stall on the market. Week-days would be no good – they can't buy aprons and turbans while they're at work. I'll look into it. Don't be worrying about copper cylinders, girl. It was the tortoise won the race at the finish.'

She ran to him, flinging her arms around his neck. 'By the way, I'm getting married in a couple of weeks.'

He pushed her away, though not fiercely. 'Why didn't you tell me before?'

She laughed. 'There was nothing to tell. I only proposed last night.'

'You didn't!'

'Of course I did. When I see a good thing, I go for it.'

'You're a bloody tearaway, and that's a fact. So you saw a good thing—'

'And I went for it.'

He hugged her tightly. 'Can I still live here?'

'We'll not throw you out, lad.'

'And is my idea a good thing? About the turbans and aprons?'

'Brilliant. So I'm going for that, too.'

It was another beautiful day. Jenny stepped out of the bath and on to the thick towelling mat, rubbing at a steam-clouded mirror over the handbasin. Once she was dressed, she might go out, have a word with the horses, walk up and down the lanes for a while. Sara Browne was in charge today, giving the missus all that massage before taking the wheelchair out into the sun.

She smiled at herself, noticing how white her teeth looked in the sun-kissed face. 'You're becoming a real country urchin, Jenny Crawley,' she told herself. 'Whatever would Auntie Mavis say if she could see you running about barefoot in cow-muck?' For a moment or two, she thought about poor Mavis. Would she have been afraid of going out up here on the moors? Or would she have loved it just as much as Jenny did? There was no answer, because Auntie had never got the opportunity.

For a reason that was completely unclear, Jenny found herself thinking about Maria's brothers and sisters. This was a wonderful place for city children, young souls who had never seen past chimneys and brick walls and broken pavements. If only she could bring them up here, give them that special feeling of freedom that was born of endless sky and boundless green. A week or two of this every year would set them up, keep them strong for the winter. No chance, though. If Jenny stayed on here for-ever, she would retire to a cottage, but all the little Heskeths would be grown up by then.

She scuttled along the corridor to her own room, fearful of being seen in her robe. Once inside, she threw on her clothes, bundled the weighty hair into a hasty bun, then thrust her feet into a pair of flat shoes. 'I wish I could wear trousers,' she said aloud. 'It'd be easier to climb in trousers.'

Out on the landing once more, she watched the large nurse carrying Mrs Skipton down the stairs. She called herself a nurse, did Sara Browne, but really she was a manipulator, someone who specialized in getting atrophied muscle to work again. Jenny had looked up 'atrophy' in the dictionary downstairs. It meant wasting away, getting smaller. Well, the mistress was certainly doing that. Jenny sometimes wondered if Mrs Skipton would just disappear one windy day. If the poor woman wasn't strapped in that chair, she probably would get blown away, carried off into the distance like an autumn leaf. It was so sad. The lady wouldn't see another autumn, Jenny felt fairly certain of that. She was becoming transparent. Yet although her body had grown weak, her brain showed few signs of degeneration. In fact, the smoky eyes had become quicker, more alert, as if the fire behind them had been rekindled.

Jenny ran across the lawn and sat under an old apple tree with Charlie. The growing pup seemed to have some mining ancestry, because his various diggings of borders were deep and serious, serious enough for the gardener to be quite displeased. 'Why do you do it?' she asked, looking into the dark brown eyes. He skittered about, posing at the end of each darting movement with head on front paws, backside in the air, tail waving madly. 'You're not funny,' she said, trying not to giggle. 'Why do you bury the bones and dig them up when they're a nasty green? And why can't you ever remember where you buried them?'

Charlie lay down beside her. He had been in the world for several weeks now, and he still believed that the place was his, that it had been provided specially and exclusively for his entertainment. They were strange, these two-legged ones. They kept sitting down and resting when they could have had fun. But he didn't mind, not much. The food was good, the garden was large, and if he could just remember where, there was a nicely mouldered bone somewhere nearby.

The car came up the drive, and Jenny glanced at the sky for a rough assessment of time. It was early. Mr Skipton should not be home just yet, so he must have come to collect something. The sun filtered through the gently shivering leaves, lending Jenny some of its terrible laziness. With her back against the tree, she dozed, her sleep shallow enough for dreams populated by Maria and potatoes dipped in dye. Then everything changed, and she was back in Claughton Street. The bucket was at her feet, burning a hole in the floorboards. Auntie Mavis shouted 'Come to me', but Jenny's feet were stuck to the floor. And anyway, she didn't want to do the smoke – the smoke was wrong . . . wrong . . .

A finger touched her face. 'Jenny?'

She woke startled, her own hand against her pounding heart. 'Oh, I'm sorry, sir. Am I late?'

He replaced the handkerchief in his pocket. There had been just one tear on her face, and he had captured it on the corner of the cotton square, just beneath the intertwined H and S that formed his initials. 'Bad dream?'

'Can't remember.' She couldn't remember. It was strange how a dream could be so clear, how she could wake knowing that it had been clear, yet it still eluded her.

'You were crying.'

She shrugged. 'Probably sweat, Mr Skipton. Am I late?' she asked again.

'No. I came home specially to see you. I've been thinking about the household, you see, and I thought it might be best if you left . . . things to Nurse Browne. Things upstairs, I mean. There's plenty of work. Briony could use another pair of hands, and Mrs Hardman isn't as young as she was.'

Jenny thought about it. 'But I'm needed. She needs me – Mrs Skipton, I mean. That nurse lady is very good, but she doesn't live here.'

'Perhaps she can be persuaded to move in. I want you to do the work for which you were hired in the first place.'

She stared at him. 'Why?'

Unable to look at her, he studied his shoes. The dog sat between them, eyes moving from one to the other, as if he were refereeing a tennis match. She had asked for a reason. And he couldn't tell her the real truth. That something was brewing upstairs, that the famous scribe who had documented the life of Macbeth might have found a use for Eloise Skipton. Yes, the beloved wife of Henry Skipton would have been aptly placed on the wild, windswept marshes of Scotland, and in the company of two more hags – plus a cauldron of seething mischief. He had no proof that there was anything afoot, but Eloise had changed her habits so dramatically of late, while the watchful gaze of Sara Browne was often upon Henry. Being in the house was a bit like living in a bomb factory. He knew that the explosives were in the building, but he had no chance of pinpointing them. The fuse would be lit eventually, and he didn't want Jenny caught in the blast. 'A qualified nurse is needed upstairs.' His tone carried little conviction.

She dusted dry grass and weed from her skirt, then stood with Charlie between herself and the master. The man was at it again, trying to keep her away from the sickroom. The vet had said that Mr Skipton hated illness. She wasn't too keen on it herself, but he really should stop lending his fears to other people. 'I am old enough, you know. It doesn't bother me now, being with her, I mean. What will she say if you take me away from her?'

He cleared his throat. 'It is what . . . what she wants. She has asked the nurse to take your place full time. You may keep the room. Nurse Browne will take one of the front bedrooms.'

'I'm not bothered about the room,' she said, hoping that this wasn't a lie. After all, she'd grown used to the opulence, almost took it for granted these days. And that wonderful bathroom, how she loved that bathroom. She would be forced to share it now with Sara Browne. Inwardly, she chided herself. How easy it was to become selfish and demanding. There was more to life than having a bathtub, a lot less to life for people such as poor Mrs Skipton. 'If that's what the mistress wants,' she said lamely, feeling rather hurt and rejected. Just a short time ago, the lady of the house had thrown tantrums and china simply because Jenny had been removed from her side.

'It's for the best, Jenny.' His voice was quiet and gentle.

She looked him straight in the face. 'Because she's dying? Because you don't want a young girl like me finding her dead?'

He turned away from the searching stare, his hands thrust deep into the pockets of the suit. This hadn't been his sole reason for coming home. There had been papers to collect, items of post that he had forgotten this morning.

But, having seen Jenny under the tree, he had decided there and then to inform her of Eloise's latest dictum, the order that had been delivered, via the nurse, on the previous evening. Eloise, it seemed, wanted Jenny in the house but out of her room. Naturally, the message had contained words of concern. Jenny was too young to sit at a deathbed, Jenny was too frail to carry her mistress down the stairs, Jenny should not be weighted down by the cares of a dying woman. Cry wolf again, he thought. Eloise had been dying so many times that it was becoming something of a habit, an entertainment for a bored woman. She was bored, so she made trouble. She was bored, so she had decided to die. Again.

'Sir? Is that the reason – because I'm too young?' A few short weeks ago, she would have given almost anything to be out of that sickroom. Now, she felt inferior, as if she had been judged incapable – even useless.

'Something like that. There have been . . . other occasions when a nurse has been needed. It will pass.' What was Eloise concocting this time? And was Sara Browne an accomplice? 'Just do as I ask. Go up and see . . . Go upstairs, and you will be told what to do. I must get back to work.'

He walked away, feeling like a messenger from olden times. Centuries ago, they used to kill the bringer of discouraging news. Perhaps such deaths had been merciful after all, because he was now so low in spirit that he was almost depressed. She had looked terribly hurt, the poor girl. Clearly, her mistress's 'better behaviour' had fooled her, had led her to believe that she was valued by her female employer. Well, that female employer was up to no good, and a girl of Jenny's tender years would be better out of earshot. What could it be this time? Was Eloise in the process of attempting to turn the world against her husband? Some of the glares from beneath the straw hat had been hot enough to start a forest blaze. Was she finally gunning for him? Oh, let her try, let her get on with it. The final card, the ace of trumps, was up his sleeve and had remained there unused for many years. If push came to shove, he would threaten to dig up little Sophie. But that would be a last resort. Sophie should be left to rest in peace.

Eloise could not touch him, he thought determinedly as he walked to the car. In body, soul and mind, he was as far removed as possible. And if she wanted to play games with the staff, then he would indulge her. Jenny could only benefit from the proposed changes, while Sara Browne seemed tough enough to withstand her mistress's swings of mood.

But although he tried to comfort himself, his nerves were alert, keen to the point of rawness. Eloise was cooking again, stirring up the cauldron, throwing in her ingredients, mixing malevolence with her special recipe of madness and cold sanity. His spine tingled, while beads of sweat collected on his face. He was, he told himself firmly, a fanciful man.

All the way back to town, he wondered about Eloise's intentions. Perhaps she was looking for a showdown, a separation, even a divorce? Yes, she might well be confident that he would never mention Sophie to the authorities. After all this time, her guilt would be difficult to prove, especially without the co-operation of Carla Sloane. He shivered involuntarily at the thought of that ugly, twisted woman. She would never testify. He knew in his bones that Sloane's resentment would preclude any chance of help. And the fact that he and the housekeeper had kept quiet provided another difficulty. At best, they would be judged as accessories; at worst, Eloise's easily summoned 'grief' might bend a jury's mind, while her poor physical condition would endear her to the whole court. Whatever, she must have worked out that Henry's ace was useless, that the trumps had changed suit many moons ago.

What was she doing? The thought pursued him right into the mill yard. He parked the car and let himself into a weaving shed where the sound of flying shuttles filled his mind. It was too noisy to think. This was not the right place for decisions. Decisions he was precluded from making anyway. She was in bed, off her feet, confined to the same territory every day. But it was a territory she understood well, because she had the opportunity to study little else. Something was simmering, and he couldn't even trace the fire. She was boilermaker, engineer and driver. He shrugged away such imaginative notions. If she wanted to travel in a ghost train, what did it matter? A ghost train would never touch him, so let her do her relatively powerless worst.

'Jenny, I do so hope that you will understand. I am becoming a great deal weaker every day. Soon, I shall need everything doing for me.'

Jenny, who had, for some weeks, been doing everything for her mistress, kept quiet.

'You see, Sara understands my needs, she has a level of medical knowledge, some insight into my condition. While you would be better employed in the general running of this household. And there will be other tasks for you, my dear girl. Tasks that will prove so valuable to me. I need a friend, someone who will look after my interests. You will be my representative downstairs and you will see that the house is well run.'

Jenny still found no answer. Mrs Skipton had taken little notice of whatever went on outside her own room. Even weeks earlier, when she'd always been in bad moods, she had mentioned the rest of the house merely to complain about the cooking or the poor ironing of her bed linen. This sudden concern for the efficient running of Skipton Hall was indeed strange. Commendable in such a sick woman, but odd all the same. Jenny, feeling ridiculously unnerved, plucked at her skirt. Mrs Skipton was so difficult to fathom.

'Please.' The right hand waved weakly towards a chair that stood next to the vast bed. 'Sit down. We need to have a talk, woman to woman.' She dropped her voice conspiratorially. 'There are things I can trust to you and only to you.'

Jenny, fascinated in spite of herself, came to sit beside Eloise. Her hand was taken and held by five bone-white, thin and almost useless digits. Everything seemed worn out now, even the bits that had been fairly strong just weeks earlier. There was a damp and unhealthy coolness in the touch too, as if the fingers were made of something akin to wax. While most of the skin on Eloise's body had sagged and wrinkled, her hands remained unnaturally smooth, with the dermis stretched taut over knuckles. These, thought Jenny, were the hands of an old person. She had seen hands like this before, and they had almost invariably been attached to a woman well into her seventies. The last weeks of the mistress's life were galloping by, making her thoroughly aged. It seemed that Death needed an excuse, wanted to make this body prematurely old so that his proposed visit would seem more acceptable. Jenny blinked and shivered against the idea of a living death, a spectral figure with bright orange eyes and cloak made of sin, mankind's collective misdeeds woven into a hooded garment. He would not be on a horse, though. No horse would carry such a passenger . . .

'You shivered just then, Jenny.'

She made a light, shrugging movement. 'I've been sitting outside. Happen the grass was a bit wet.'

'Not "happen". You must say "perhaps".'

'Yes. I'll try to remember. Perhaps the grass was wet.'

Eloise sighed. Even this seemed an effort, because her face crumpled as air pushed itself out of her mouth. 'Jenny, I am so pleased that you will be staying here. As a maid, of course. But, as I said before, Sara is more suitable for my personal needs at present. You must appreciate that.'

'Yes, miss.'

'You sound like a schoolchild. But there again, I do tend to forget how young you really are. It is plain that you have spent your life in the company of adults. Well, just one adult, I suppose. You are such a comfort, such a clever girl.'

Jenny swallowed her embarrassment. 'Thank you, miss.'

Eloise licked her drying lips as she approached the real reason for this conversation. 'Henry likes you,' she said. 'And I want you to look after him for me.'

Jenny's jaw dropped, and she closed it with a determined snap. These were words from what was nearly a deathbed, so she had best sit still and listen, no matter what.

'I loved him so, Jenny.'

'Yes.' What else, what more could she say? 'Yes' was the most appropriate, the least contentious.

'And he adores me.'

Jenny's hand stiffened in the mistress's frail grip, but she managed to maintain her silence.

'When Sophie died, we were both grief-stricken, too wounded to even discuss the subject of our dear little daughter. Then, when things became a little easier, I was struck down by the first attack of this terrible disease. As time went by, it became plain that Henry could not bear to look at me. He would cry, Jenny. He would look at me and cry.'

'That must have been awful.'

Pale lids threaded with a network of fine, purple veins came down to cover the smoky eyes, as if making an effort to obliterate painful memories. 'You remember I told you that I was a wife in name only, and that I did not want the name used? That you must call me "miss" rather than by my proper title?'

Jenny, speechless with pity, nodded once.

'That was because I have failed him. I told you that I wished I had never set eyes on him – and that is the truth. If he had never met me, he might have had a healthy wife and some fine children. I have completely ruined the life of a very fine man, possibly the finest man in the whole of England. When I screamed that he hated me, that I hated him, I was really saying how much we both hated this illness. We cannot look at one another any more, Jenny. Our love is and always was wonderful, a beautiful and rare thing. This body of mine – this hideous wreckage – is the death of our love, Jenny. My body was once a temple, but now it is a sepulchre. It is so hard to watch love dying day after day.'

Jenny thought that this talk of temples and tombs was a bit on the dramatic side, but Mrs Skipton had been showing a tendency towards the fanciful for some time. It would be the approaching end that was making her speech so colourful and decorative. Oh, this was awful. She leaned a little closer. 'Please don't upset yourself—'

'Don't stop me!' The eyes flew open. 'This must be done, Jenny, things need to be clear in your mind as well as in mine. I am letting you go because he needs you, he needs a friend in this house. I charge you with the care of my husband.'

In the ensuing silence, Jenny pondered carefully. 'Mr Skipton usually has a good friend in this house. My dad. Yes, we could bring my dad back from Blackpool. In his letters, he says he's quite well enough for work. I think he wants to come back and get on with his job—'

'No!' Something like panic showed in the sickly-white face, but it was wiped out within a split second. 'The man needs to recuperate. Getting over pneumonia is a long and tedious process. I should know, because that has been one of my own complications over the past few years. Jenny, Dan has done very well for the Skiptons. When it comes to business, he takes some of the burden from Henry's shoulders. However, this is a different matter altogether. We are talking now of something that is best handled by a woman. The subject is grief, my husband's grief. You see, my poor man lost me years ago. When I actually die, he will—'

'Mr Skipton reckons you're not dying. He says you've been as ill as this before.' These words were supposed to be encouraging, but they came out as a flat, plain statement.

Eloise's eyes narrowed. 'That's because he can't face it. The thought of my death is so abhorrent that he fools himself with such talk.' She was almost screaming again, and she had intended to remain so cool, so tired and pitiable. She must summon up all her cleverness, all her wiles. She squeezed her eyes until two drops of moisture drifted down her cheeks. That was better. Silent weeping had always been a good, reliable tack.

It was strange, thought Jenny, how strong emotion could make a person forget the physical discomforts. Then she saw the tears, and she knew that the fragile woman still suffered.

'This time, my good friend, I shall die.'

Jenny blinked rapidly. There was something odd here, something that didn't quite ring true, yet she could not pinpoint what was missing, what was extra or out of place. She covered the waxy fingers with her other hand. It was all in her imagination. Mrs Skipton had nothing to gain, so Jenny must hang on, must find strength, must learn to stop questioning and wondering about simple, everyday things. Everybody died. Some people knew when they were going to die, and this was one of those people.

'I am about to leave this life behind, Jenny. Believe me, it is imminent. You must believe, you really must.'

It seemed as if she had made her mind up, then, as if she wanted to die and had ordered it to happen. 'Yes,' she said softly. 'I do believe you.'

'You can help me, Jenny.'

'How? How can I help if things are as bad as that? And why don't you send for him, ask him to come and see you?'

Eloise frowned. 'Because he could not bear to see me like this. He pretends not to care – that is his way of coping with my illness. I think he even pretends sometimes that I am already dead, so that when it does happen, he will not feel so much pain.' She sucked in the cheeks that were already sunken, knowing that this ploy made her look iller than ever. But she was strong, strong inside. Yes, she had little intention of shuffling off, was determined to hang on till this last charade had played its course. Her body might be weak, but her will was fierce enough to see her through another Christmas, a lucrative and extremely destructive divorce . . .

'Do you want me to talk to Mr Skipton, miss?'

'No!' The deafening shriek seemed inappropriate, so Eloise changed it to a loud howl of pain. 'My fingers, dear. Recently, they have become so sensitive.'

'Sorry.' Jenny removed her hands, noticing how huge and clumsy they looked when compared to Mrs Skipton's diseased fingers. It was all so unbearably sad and confusing. She blinked, because she would not cry.

'You must mention none of this to him, not to anyone. I want you to . . . keep him company, try to make him cheerful. My end will be so much happier if you will do that. But if you mention me to him, he will be on his guard. Oh my dear friend, you already have so much in common with Henry.'

'Really?' Jenny's eyes were rounded by surprise.

'Yes. You love animals. Didn't you stay up all night, both of you, when he found that dog?'

'Yes.'

Eloise smiled, carefully restricting the expression to her mouth. From now on, her eyes must remain sad and full of pain. Well, at least until her solicitor advised her that smiling would be safe. 'His nights are dreadful, Jenny. He paces up and down, up and down until the early hours. Sometimes, he roams about downstairs until dawn. You must watch for him. Watch, listen and keep him company. He must not be allowed to slide into depression.'

'Right, miss.'

Eloise inhaled deeply before taking the biggest plunge. This was make or break time. The girl was beautiful, inexperienced, yet cleverer than had been presumed. There was strong instinct here, instinct and a genuine in-born morality. But she liked a bit of luxury, did Jenny Crawley. That bathroom along the landing had never been used as frequently, as happily as it had been used in recent weeks. 'Jenny, I am just an ordinary person. You know my beginnings. Henry is not drawn to women of high social status.'

'Oh, I see.' What was coming now?

'He likes you. I know that he really likes you.'

Jenny studied her broken nails. She would never want them long, but she wished that they could be tidier. 'He seems a nice man,' she said lightly.

'He will need another wife.' There, the seed was planted. 'And you must make sure that he chooses the right person.'

Jenny straightened. 'It's nowt to do with me—'

'Nothing, dear.'

'Right, well it's still nothing to do with me.'

Eloise took another gasp of air, breathing as deeply as nerve-starved muscles would allow. 'He will listen to Dan. Dan is your father, so Dan will listen to you. Above all, stay close to Henry during the next few weeks. That's all I have, just a month or so. Support and comfort him, Jenny.' Yes, this was an astute girl. Under the veneer of simplicity there lurked a woman. And all true women were, by nature, acquisitive. Would she take this broad hint? Would she go now and push herself towards Henry, tempt him with her undeniable charms? Unless she was a complete idiot, nature would surely take its age-old course. And Jenny Crawley, for all her *naïveté*, was nobody's fool.

'Right. I'll do my best.' It was daft, all this. She'd no intention of staying up all night just to wander about looking for somebody who was wandering about. Not while there'd be fireplaces to clean and furniture to polish at the crack of every dawn.

'You must take this very seriously, Jenny. Do not talk about me, do not say that I have sent you to comfort him. If you mention my name, he will become extremely angry. Just sit with him, talk to him. Talk about your walks and the animals you see in the woods. Anything at all that will keep his mind occupied during the dark hours.'

'I'll try.'

Eloise forced a sad, weary smile to her lips before firing the final dart. 'From now on, you must stay away from me, forget that I exist.'

'Eh? What for?'

The colloquialisms were forgotten this time. Eloise had done what she could to improve the girl's speech, and it was too late for any further refinements. 'Because Henry will talk to you more openly if he knows that you are not spending time with me. He will be happier to take comfort from someone who has no contact with me, someone who won't be a constant reminder of this terrible disease.'

'Then why don't you tell Briony to take over? She doesn't come in here, so she can keep an eye out for Mr Skipton.'

'Briony has no sensitivity. With that girl, things are black or white. You are clever enough to see the shades of grey, kind enough to accept this dreadful situation. You understand Henry. Briony understands nothing.'

'Right.' Jenny rose to her feet. There was plainly no point in arguing. 'Shall I go now?'

Eloise wiped an imaginary tear from her cheek. 'Yes. Farewell, my dear friend. Thank you. Thank you so much for . . . for everything. If you wish to communicate with me, do it through Briony Mulholland. She shall be our messenger.'

When Jenny had closed the door, Eloise pushed her right hand into the bed and brought out a box of slightly melted mint creams. It was time to celebrate. All she needed now was a spy, a spy who had already been prepared to look for the worst. Yes, there was the opal ring. Eloise had never been keen on opals, but her nurse had expressed a liking for them. The opal ring would buy the evidence. And the evidence would buy the divorce which, in turn, would guarantee his final ruin and her own triumphal curtain call.

She licked the stickiness from her fingers, then lay back to dream of triumphs to come. Revenge and mint creams were both sweet, both better served cold. In future, she would keep the sweets in her bedside cabinet. Next to the telephone.

Chapter Twelve

IT WAS THE MOST HAUNTING MUSIC SHE HAD EVER HEARD. There were no words, but none were needed, because the composer had somehow managed to touch the soul of even the most inexperienced of listeners. Jenny was inexperienced. Music was something they had done at school, a few simple rhymes, a tambourine, some bells on loops of thick wire, and Miss Eccles playing on the out-of-tune piano, the shoulders of her perennial black cardigan spotted with dandruff, the air filled by the scents of chalk and unclean children. If music could really be described as food for the spirit, then Jenny's inner core was severely malnourished. Nevertheless, she chose now to listen, drinking in the sad cadences, enjoying the comfortably predictable bars.

He often played this tune at night, but she had never lingered before. Sometimes, the music got spoilt because the gramophone had slowed, or had been overwound. But tonight, it seemed to be just right, perfect and extremely beautiful.

Her face was wet. The tears surprised her, because she had not expected to be moved so easily, so thoroughly, by a mere tune. It was tiredness, she supposed. Housework was hard, tedious, repetitive, and it wearied her body while leaving her mind agile. During polishing and sweeping, she could worry about Maria with her terrible need for success, could remember Auntie Mavis's lonely death, often wondered about Amber and the other brewery dray horses. Looking after Mrs Skipton had involved mental strain, a stress Jenny missed now.

She sat just outside the library, her head leaning sleepily against the door jamb. The piece was a pavan – she had read that strange word on the record sleeve. Some fellow called Ravel had written it, and it seemed to be dedicated to a dead child. The words had been in French or Spanish – some foreign language, but she had guessed that 'infanta' meant child, and the other word had been something like defunct, which meant dead. So for Mr Skipton, this tune would be about Sophie. When it came to Sophie, Jenny truly pitied both her employers. Nothing on earth could possibly be as bad, as horrible as the death of a son or daughter.

She hadn't done as the mistress had asked, hadn't followed him about at night. For a start, the work was hard, a great deal harder than she remembered. Looking after just one room had softened her, and she often grew angry with her body for tiring so easily. And she was forced to wear a uniform again, that awful grey dress with the silly cap and apron. Never mind. Perhaps she would leave soon, as soon as Mrs Skipton was past suffering.

The other reason for not complying with her mistress's instructions lay in the fact that it all seemed a bit daft when she thought about it. What would a grown man want with a girl following him round while he was grieving and worrying? He would likely tell her to get off to bed and leave him alone. Sometimes, folk needed solitude, like when they were thoughtful or distressed. If he wanted to talk, he could find somebody his own age, somebody educated, like a doctor or that vet. Mrs Skipton had, more than likely, been raving again when she had asked Jenny to look after her husband. She might just have come to her senses by now, was perhaps realizing that Jenny was not suited to that particular task.

It was odd that the music did not make her think about the mistress. For some strange reason, she could not be truly sad about Mrs Skipton. Oh, she had felt sadness in that bedroom, had felt sympathy for the woman's appalling condition. But now, in her solitude, she was forced by Ravel to think yet again about horses, about Amber and Flora with their beautiful chestnut coats and rippling shoulder muscles. About the strain as they pulled the ale-laden cart up the hill, about those great feet feathered by wisps of curled hair. There was something unbearably touching about a carthorse's feet. All that strength, all that obedience. One blow from an iron-clad foot, and most bosses would make a bee-line for kingdom come. The miracle was that the enormous horses chose not to use their terrible power. And the tragedy was the same as the miracle.

'What are you thinking about, young lady?'

'Horses,' she answered before she could stop herself. She jumped up, smoothed her ugly grey skirt, and allowed the master a tight smile. 'I was listening to the music.'

'"Clair de Lune" on the other side,' he said.

'I know, I've tidied it away a few times.'

'Strange how they always put Debussy with Ravel. There are no similarities except that they were both born French. Do you like the pavan? And why should it make you think of horses?'

Jenny nodded. 'I think I like it, but it's very, very sad. And horses make me worry, especially the ones at the brewery near our house. So the music reminds me of the big dray horses, sir.'

He leaned against the wall at the other side of the doorway. 'A pavan is a dance, a Spanish dance. But I could not imagine anyone dancing to that.' He jerked a thumb towards the library as the music faded. There was a scratching sound from the needle while it circled sense-lessly in a groove of silence. 'Actually, I can't imagine a horse dancing to anything, though some people get them to do silly things in the name of sportsmanship. Dancing could be the next silly thing.' He waved a hand at the gramophone. 'It's dedicated to a dead Spanish princess.' He shifted, placed himself in a position that was more upright. 'Do you like Bach?' he asked now.

'What is it?' She knew she was stupid, could have bitten her tongue out there and then. Yet he seemed to

313

understand, because he gave her the time and space in which she might redeem herself. 'It's church music, isn't it?' she asked, hoping that she was right.

'Organ stuff, most of it. Most of mine, at least. Would you like to hear some?'

'Well . . .' She was tired, and she had to get up at six in the morning. Still, if she went into the library with him, if she listened to some of this Bach stuff, then she could know in her heart that she had, at least once, complied with Mrs Skipton's crazy spoken wishes. 'Yes, please,' she said.

The library fire was not lit, as the evening had been cloyingly warm, but the book-lined room was made cheerful by electric lamps dotted about on low tables. His desk was littered with papers and pens, and the daily and evening newspapers were strewn in the tiled hearth. Automatically, she bent to clear this mess, but his hand was on her shoulder. 'No, Jenny. You're off duty now. If a man can't pick up after himself, then he should be ashamed. I always take the papers to the kitchen before going to bed. Mrs Hardman either stores them for winter fires, or she uses them for Charlie's bedding. While he's tearing up the *Evening News*, he's not chewing through the table legs.'

She faced him. 'He's halfway through one corner. We shall have to be getting a new kitchen table, sir.'

He shrugged. 'It could make life a lot easier if he chews through another leg. You could put the food on one end and let it slide along. All you'd need to do would be to catch your plate before it hit the other side. It could add a whole new dimension to mealtimes, rather like travelling on a yacht in stormy weather.'

'And if we missed, Charlie could have it.'

'That, Jenny, is life. The dog gets your dinner and you get to clean up.' He was amazed to find this so easy. He could talk to her as if she were older, as if she were not a servant. Had she noticed this too? he wondered. And what had happened to make it so simple for him? After all, just a couple of weeks ago, he had scarcely been able to look at her. The infatuation had been stronger before, was changing into something else, something far more danger-ous. Yet in this small moment, he felt no fear, just a sense of comfort, a sense of having arrived home in the right company.

She sat on the brown leather chesterfield while he searched for Bach. Bach could not have been played for a long time, because he was at the bottom of the pile. Mr Skipton looked just like an ordinary man tonight, not a bit of the mill boss about him. The sleeves of his shirt were rolled to elbow level, and the dark blue waistcoat and jacket had been relegated to the back row of the stalls, on a chair under the window. Twin gold cufflinks rested on the hide-bound blotter, while his necktie hung with the detached shirt collar round the chin of a white plaster bust, probably some dead writer of words or music. She was surprised to see that Mr Skipton wore everyday braces, plain black ones like she'd seen on men in Claughton Street. The shaved parts of his face were dark with new beard-shadow, and the hair looked as if it hadn't seen a comb for a while. She thought about the well-dressed man who left this house at eight-thirty each morning. This might have been his brother, but only just.

'There's a crack in it,' he said mournfully.

'A crack in Bach,' answered Jenny without thinking.

His knees hit the floor and he laughed as he sat back on his heels. 'Very witty. If I were a poet, I would make something of that. And some music critics might even agree with you, my dear. He can be a bit sombre, old Bach, a bit on the dictatorial side. But that's what you get with pure genius.' He put the record on the velvet turntable and began to wind the handle. He looked like any working bloke doing a repetitive manual job, all sighs and wry smiles.

'What about the crack?' she asked.

He shrugged lightly. 'Johann will just have to miss out on his big opening. It's more of a chip than a crack, so we'll just have to pretend that he started writing his toccata in the middle. Or I could sing you the first bit.' He coughed, then hummed a few bars that seemed to have little rhythm and no tune at all. 'I forgot,' he said. 'I should have warned you that my pitch is less than perfect. In fact, as a singer, I make a jolly good cotton merchant.'

She could contain herself no longer. His singing was completely and utterly dreadful. He sounded like a member of a pipe band tuning up, with the emphasis very much on the drone. Her quiet giggle erupted into a laugh, and she hastily put a hand to her mouth.

'Let it out,' he chided gently. 'J. S. Bach can't sue you – he's long dead. Though he might be just about sufficiently alive to deal me a savage blow for murdering his life work.'

'I bet you were never in a choir,' she said.

He pretended to be hurt. 'I'll have you know that I was an exceptionally brilliant boy soprano. When I went carolling at Christmas time, the cottagers used to give me cakes and sweets and—'

'And anything else that would fill your mouth and stop you singing.' She looked hard at him. 'Sir,' she added.

He ignored the spinning turntable and met her gaze. 'I never thought of that,' he said seriously. 'So all that kindness, all that praise – it was a sham, Jenny. My life is built on sand, and I am all undone.' In the mode of a hammish actor, he placed a hand on his furrowed brow. 'Fate deals the ungentlest blows, fair maiden. Sometimes, it even dealt treacle toffee. Have you ever tried singing – even speaking – with a mouthful of that? Thus they cut off my voice, and thus they have cut out my soul.'

He was daft. She stared at him, giggled at him, laughed with him. This was a man who could mock himself; he was therefore a man who feared no other. He was extremely likeable, though. In a way, he reminded her of one of those comedians who jumped about on the screen at the pictures. Mr Skipton, like the filmstars, was a deliberate fool. He actually enjoyed being laughed at, didn't care how silly he looked, because he knew that people would still love and respect him. It was such a pity that his wife couldn't see him like this.

He jumped up, crossed the rug and sat next to her. She smelled of flower-perfumed soap and clean hair. He was making an idiot of himself just to please her, just to gain her attention. And her affection, was he after that, too? Good God, he was acting like a callow youth—

'Mr Skipton?'

He made his face serious. 'Yes, Jenny?'

She bit her lip. This couldn't be a secret any more, not while he was so nice, so completely approachable. The man was experienced in these things, might be a valuable ally too. And she must not ignore the possibilities, not while there was a chance of Jenny Crawley actually helping somebody at last. 'Do you know anything about printing?' she ventured.

'Books, newspapers?'

She bit her lip nervously. 'Cloth.'

He nodded. 'What sort of printing? Block, screen, roller?'

'I don't know. She does it with potatoes and wooden stamps, but she's interested in all kinds, I think.'

'Expensive business, printing, not a thing to be taken lightly. It usually gets left to the specialists and they, like cotton manufacturers, have a long history. Printing was going on before Jesus died – and long before He was born too, according to my bit of reading. Nobody knows who started it, Jenny. Like a lot of good ideas, it probably began in several different countries at about the same time. That's about as much as I have needed to know, and I've passed that on to you so that you will understand the jealous world of the fabric printer. Why, he'd cut off his own right arm before allowing you the chemical formula for a particular blue.'

'Sounds a bit nasty, then.'

'Cut-throat,' he said ominously. 'Anyway, take no notice of me – I just spin and weave the stuff, don't even do my own bleaching any more, not since I decided on more mules and better space for my workers. The bleaching took up too much room and time, and I farmed it out to those who do it best. Printing? Let me see . . .' He stroked his chin. 'I'd say Mallinson's the man for fabric design.'

'Mallinsons' in town? At the bottom of Daubhill?'

'That's your man if you want to poke around among the whys and wherefores, though I doubt he'd greet competition in a civil manner. Why? And who's printing with potatoes?'

Her confidence began to waver slightly. 'Just a friend, somebody I know. She does it in the house, and she's really clever. There's all these patterns in her head and she wants to make nice, bright things to cheer people up a bit. Everything seems to be brown or bottle green these days.'

'Perhaps brown and bottle green are what people want to buy.'

She shook her head. 'It doesn't work like that, sir. See, folk buy what's there. It's like a vicious circle according to Anthony.'

'Anthony?' Was this a follower, a suitor? And why was his heart pounding like the big hammer at the steelworks? He no longer felt certain and comfortable. He was acutely and painfully aware of her. She was a beautiful woman and he was just inches away from her. And a man's name had just fallen from her lips.

'Another friend. He says that printers think the housewives want dull colours because that's what they buy. So printers make a load more dull things. But really, it's the other way round. If you make something, then tell everybody that this is the latest fashion, they'll start buying it.'

'So the manufacturer can dictate the trend?'

'Yes.'

He concentrated on his hands. His fingers were shaking, so he fixed his eyes on them, as if his hard stare might make them behave suitably. 'When did you study marketing, Jenny? Your ideas are . . . invigorating.'

'It's not my idea, it's theirs. But it sounds sensible enough to me.'

He nodded. 'Might be risky, though. If a small man starts something up – let's use your friends as an example. Say they set up in printing, brought out unusual lines. How would they persuade the ordinary woman in the street that this was the 'in' thing? Bear in mind that your purchaser of fabric is almost invariably female. Now, women are natural conformists. If Mrs Jones next door has fawn antimacassars, then it's very difficult to go out and buy pink ones. It all sounds very daring to me.'

She knew that she was blushing, yet she still blundered on. 'I don't agree, sir.'

'Oh?' The eyebrows were up again, looked like a pair of small animals fleeing into the forest of his hair.

'Women are trend-setters. That's what M – my friend says. She says that if things got left to men, we'd all be in togas throwing Christians to the lions. Mind you, she's always on about Christians and lions, it seems to be one of her favourite stories. What she means is that women have courage about small things, and sometimes about things a bit bigger too. Like fashions, clothes and stuff – they decide where hemlines will be and how to cut their hair. And women teach their families how to behave – that means women make the next generation. So my friend reckons she'd be hitting the market that makes the real decisions. That's what she says, anyway. She says a woman rocks the cradle and feeds the world, so it's a woman that's in charge.' She smiled slightly. 'And this friend of mine believes that men can't even decide what they want for their breakfast. Oh, and if we left it all to men, they'd have tablecloths made out of last night's *Evening News*.'

A corner of his mouth quivered, though he maintained an air of near-sobriety. After all, this was beginning to look like fairly serious business. 'She may have something there. If I were asked what I wanted for breakfast, it might be supper time before I decided on a menu. Mrs Hardman removes my choices.'

'And Mrs Hardman is a woman, sir.'

He was deep in thought by this time. This girl and her friend had obviously done a bit of research. Perhaps they would go out and conquer the world? 'Change has to be gradual, Jenny.'

'She knows that. Start slowly, she says. Give them a brown edge and a pale orange flower, pull them slowly into the twentieth century. She's got the idea that this will be what she calls the era of colour. By 1950, everything will be bold and bright. She wants to make a daisy range of table stuff – cloths and napkins and all that – and the daisies will be so delicate that you'll hardly see them. She uses the word "discreet" a lot. The main thing is not to frighten people off. Oh, and she's keen on advertising.'

'Wise woman. Will you tell me her name?'

Jenny floundered. 'No. I mean it's all very hush-hush.' This sounded rude. 'I'll have to ask her.'

The turntable creaked to a miserable halt. 'We've had no Bach,' he said.

She glanced at the clock, eager to pursue the conversation until she got an answer. Either he would help, or he wouldn't, and she wanted to know tonight. The idea of finding courage to broach the subject again did not appeal. 'There's still time, Mr Skipton. You can't have me going through life thinking that Bach sounds like bagpipes.'

'Women – these deciders of everyone's fate – are also cruel,' he said as he went to rewind the gramophone. 'They ferret out a man's weaknesses, then they play on them to undermine his confidence.'

'I never asked you to sing, sir.'

'Point taken. May the Lord help us if you and your kind ever get the vote.' He dropped the needle into the groove. 'You'll place somebody very odd in Downing Street, and the power will go to your heads.'

She stared hard at him as the music started. It was quite loud, so she had to shout. 'We'll get the vote. It's inevitable.'

'Who told you that?'

Her face was warm with embarrassment. Sometimes, it was difficult to remember that this man was her boss. 'Anthony. He says we're all created equal, so every one of us should have a say in running the country. He calls women not voting a boil on the face of democracy. I think he heard it at some meeting. About the boil, I mean.'

'Well, I hope they gave him ointment and a bandage for the problem.' He dropped into a chair by the fireplace. Sitting next to her was not exactly uncomfortable, but nor was it necessarily wise. 'He's right. There will be a petticoat vote in ten or twenty years. And it will be no bad thing. After all, woman counts the pennies and runs the home. She should have a say about the world she lives in.'

Jenny listened to the music for a while. It was grand,

impressive stuff, but it wasn't her cup of tea. This would probably sound better in a church with all the notes echoing off stone walls and arches. It was too . . . big for the small room. She waited for a quiet bit. 'Mr Skipton? Do you think two women – and one man that never went to school – could run a business?'

He put his head on one side. 'Why not? My grandfather didn't have what you would call a decent education. According to legend, he spent most of his time mucking about in fields. He was interested in agricultural machinery. An uncle of mine followed him into the business of invention, and it killed him in the end. You'll find that many people with good ideas took their education from the streets or from elders in a profession that fascinated them.'

She shrugged lightly. 'But what about money? You know, to buy machines and rent a building? Who'd give money to two girls and a lad who spent his schooldays humping fruit and vegetables?'

'Well.' He measured his words carefully. 'You start small and you find a backer – someone who's already established, though not in the same line.' He glanced at her. 'Are you involved in the venture?'

She hesitated just fractionally. She had gone too far, so she might as well hang for a sheep. 'I'm one of the two women.'

'I see.' The music faded, and he rose to rescue the needle from its scratchy groove. 'And the end product is to be printed cloth?'

She inhaled deeply. Maria might kill her for telling him. The thought of a truly angry Maria was disconcerting, but Jenny had to do her bit, and this was the only bit she could do. 'No. The end product would be finished articles. We would print them, get patterns cut out, have them sewn into all sort of things. Then I'd sell them in a café.'

His eyebrows were wandering again, pushing the healthy skin of his forehead into a series of deep furrows. 'In a café?'

'I think so. See, the idea is that folk come in for a cuppa, then they notice the stuff on another counter. You don't push, according to Anthony. No pushing, just suggestion.'

'So they buy it?'

'Yes.'

He returned to the chair. 'That is what I might call an unusual venture, Jenny. Almost unusual enough to be attractive. But who will cut and sew your cloth?'

'Women. Women at home. They'll do the hemming and make frocks and pinnies. The printing needs a shed with a power house, like a generator for electric. I think that's to run rollers or something – I don't really understand it all yet. When the cloth's printed, Anthony will carry it to the women in houses for them to finish.'

Henry took a cigar from a box on a nearby table. He wanted to meet this Anthony who kept cropping up. 'Right. When can I speak to Maria?'

Jenny's mouth hung open for a split second. 'How did you know . . . ?'

'I remember Maria. Once seen, never forgotten. And I know what she did with those sheet lengths I gave her for the family.' He grinned. 'I am a good spy. And the kitchen door does not always creak. So I saw, I watched.'

Jenny put a hand to her suddenly constricted throat. He had known all along! She felt like a fool, was angry with him for trying to squeeze from her a name he had already known. Determinedly, she sat on her temper. For one thing, this man could have her on the street by morning, and although Mrs Skipton didn't need her any more, Jenny had promised to hang on till the end. And another reason for behaving herself lay in the fact that she desperately wanted Maria to succeed. It was important. Important for all ordinary working folk, and particularly vital to those who usually got called the gentler sex. She formed a reasoned reply. 'That way, she could make more for her family in the long run. If she'd given them the cotton, they would have had sheets for the beds. With her ideas, they could get a lot more than bed linen.'

He lit the cigar. 'Jenny, I am not criticizing your friend. If no-one takes a chance, nothing gets done. If nothing gets done, the country makes poor progress. Your friend Maria took a chance with a bit of cloth. Jenny, I come from

322

a long line of chancers. We won in the end, pulled the workers into the sheds. We made it, after a long fight.' His voice was soft, almost cajoling. 'Against all conceivable odds – and there were many – we did it. Maria and you can do the same.'

'So you want to see Maria and Anthony?' She would get something out of him, even if it was just a promised meeting. After all, he had treated her like a fish on a hook, letting her carry on like that about a secret that was general knowledge.

He nodded. 'In a week or two, yes. For the moment, I'm tied up at the mills. We're busy sorting out the rest areas.' He smiled in answer to her questioning eyes. 'It's not just the Barrow Bridge and Eagley mills that provide facilities for their workers, Jenny. I know that Prince Albert was impressed by those glorious communities in his time, but we all try, not just a chosen few. My mill is going to have a social club, a sports field and some night classes.' He turned to look at the clock. 'Have you forgiven me now?'

'What for? For giving nice things to your workers?' She had heard some of the old ones talking about their early working lives, about being fined a shilling for opening a window to escape the murderous heat, about bosses refusing them water. Some had even got the sack for smuggling in a jar of rain.

'For pulling your leg, pretending I didn't know about Maria.'

'It's all right. I'm not bothered, sir.'

'I'm not a cruel man.'

'No, sir.'

'I've put money into research for chest diseases and mill cancers, into investigation of eye diseases . . .' He decided to put a rein on his tongue, angry at himself for needing to impress her, angry with her for making him feel so damned vulnerable. She was just a child, far too young for him, too untutored for dalliance. 'It's time you were in bed, young woman.'

'Yes.' She looked at the bust with its inappropriate decoration of collar and tie. 'Who's that?'

'Mozart. Strange how he's always just a head and shoulders job. Perhaps his wife carried him round in her shopping basket.'

She gazed levelly at Henry Skipton, some words of Maria's echoing in her mind. Before she could stop herself, they had leapt to her tongue. 'There'd be nothing unusual about that, Mr Skipton. Most women carry their husbands. Even if it's only up the stairs when they stagger back from the pub.'

He laughed loudly. 'Are you going to campaign for your cause, Jenny?'

'What cause?'

'The liberation of the female, of course.'

Jenny thought for a moment. 'No,' she said. 'They can all look after themselves. Anybody with a bit of sense can find freedom, Mr Skipton. It's just a matter of doing what you want some of the time, and getting other people to do what you want some of the time.'

'And the rest of the time?' he asked.

'Well, you just do as you're told and get on with it, sir.' She rose and made for the door, turning when she reached it. 'I'll tell Maria what you've said. And thanks for the music.'

He listened as her footsteps died away, then he threw the cigar into the fireplace. He did not notice the figure deep in shadow, the figure that had remained there throughout his discussion with the maid.

Sara Browne stepped out of the corner and made for the stairs. She would have something to report now, something to tell at last. In fact, she might even apply a slight amount of decoration to the tale. After all, she would have to earn that opal ring.

Josie dragged the old man into the house. Billy Openshaw was extremely thin, looked as if the slightest puff of wind might send him up the chimney with the rest of the smoke. He was the colour of smoke, thought Maria. Grey clothes, thick, iron-grey hair, off-white face. One of his eyes looked strange, was fixed in the corner next to his nose, but the other light blue and age-ringed orb was alert enough, moving about in its socket to take in the room and its occupants.

Maria sighed. Josie had started bringing people home, people she'd taken a fancy to. Like the chap without legs who sold newspapers from a trolley, and an extremely smelly old lady with clothes pegs and a gap-toothed smile. If you didn't buy her pegs, the aged tinker was handy with a gypsy curse or two. And Maria, who was getting married in two days, didn't want any more litter bringing into the house. She chided herself inwardly. People were not litter; they were souls imprisoned in bodies that always let them down at the end.

'It's Billy Openshaw's grandad,' announced Josie, not without a degree of pride. 'He's called Billy as well – aren't you, Mr Openshaw?'

'Aye.' He removed his cap and placed it on the dresser.

'And,' Josie's thin chest was inflated with self-congratulation, 'he knows all about printing. Don't you, Mr Openshaw?'

'Aye.'

Anthony, who had been transferring one of Maria's designs on to a block of wood, jumped up and helped the old man into a straight-backed chair. He looked as if he needed the straight back; he might have folded himself up like an ancient piece of parchment if offered the questionable support of a padded chair. 'You all right there, Mr Openshaw?'

'Aye.'

Anthony looked at Maria; Maria looked at Anthony. So far, there'd been a few sniffs and three 'ayes'. What the heck was their Josie up to this time?

The child placed herself next to the ancient man. Anthony thought that the pair of them looked like ventriloquist and dummy. 'Cup of tea, Mr Openshaw?' he asked.

Maria's mouth opened, and she nodded in time to the fourth 'aye'. This was all getting a bit monotonous and she'd her wedding frock to finish. There was worry enough about the rest of her family, whether they would arrive at all, whether her father would be drunk, what state the children's clothes would be in, whether her mother would remember the significance of the date in the first place . . .

Josie placed a hand on the back of Mr Openshaw's chair, thereby reinforcing Anthony's unspoken belief that his little sister was pulling the tiny mannikin's strings. Struggling to cover a mixture of amusement and pity, he fled to the kitchen for the tea.

Josie fixed a look of steel on her face, her teeth almost gritted as she forced out her next words. 'I know he looks old, but he's not that old. Billy-in-my-class says Mallinson has a lot to answer for. There's Grandad's eye for a start.' She bent over the old man. 'Your eye for a start, eh, Grandad?'

'Aye,' he breathed. Maria bit her lip. Had he said 'aye' or 'eye'? And Anthony had nipped out, of course. He hadn't stood here to face this bloody farce. It was like something you might see at the pictures or at the Theatre Royal. Those were the places she and Denis visited when she was being his Tuppenny Girl.

'Tell her, Mr Openshaw.'

'Aye.' Everybody's breath was held. Maria could even 'hear' Anthony's stunned silence from the other room. There followed a long and very pregnant pause while Mr Openshaw arranged in his head what might be, after all, just another series of Lancashire yeses.

'Sithee, I cum on down yonder when I were nobbut a lad, like about sevenish you might say. An' they telt me what to do an' I did what I were telt.' He paused for breath and looked at Josie.

'He knows we're foreigners,' she said. 'So I have to tell you what he says. He worked from seven years old at Mallinsons' and he did what he was telt. I mean told.'

'I cum on up t' ranks as you might say, till I fettled reet, then they took me on proper an' I got me papers. Be gone twenty, I ran t' shop, nowt I couldn't tackle. I were thrutchin' one day like, same as mendin' a bit on t' lathe, an' I gets a metal spile in th' eye, an' t' doctor took it out wi' a magnet but th' eye 'ad gone turned. I were nobbut fifty, but they telt me I were done. Up'ards o' nigh on forty-odd year they 'ad out o' me. I can tell thee I were nowty ovver it.'

'He was angry,' said Josie. 'When he lost the eye. He can see all right with the other one, but they sacked him and he was a foreman.'

The old man's face broadened into a wrinkled smile. 'I didn't cum out wi' th' empty 'and, though. No brass, so I grabbed more nor brass.' He took from his pocket a note-book and a handkerchief, spat on the latter, then used it to wipe the cover of the former. 'Bin after me for this, the boogers 'ave, but I ne'er parted wi' it. I carried on same as I knew nowt about it.' He finished his bit of cleaning with a flourish, then placed the book in the centre of the table. It was, to him, a holy thing, and Maria found herself wonder-ing for a moment about Auntie Mavis placing sacred objects on the selfsame table. It was becoming something of an altar, this round piece of wood. 'What is it?' she asked Josie.

'It's a recipe book.' Josie, eminently pleased with herself, placed a grubby hand on the revered and age-marked notes. 'All the dyes, all the things you need for colours. And about the machinery, mending it and all that. He says,' she jerked a thumb at Billy Openshaw, 'he could start his own works up if he had the brass. I mean money.'

The old man's single rheumy eye fixed itself on Maria. 'Tha mun tek it, lass. Tha mun get me revenge, for I've no chance missen. Tek it an' use it reet. If tha can't fettle, I'll tek it back an' find sum other way. But I leave thee free to copy owt as tha chooses. Meks no diffs to me.'

Gingerly Maria picked up the thin notebook. The writing inside was small but clear, all in capitals, none of it joined up. It must have taken him years to collect this information. She dropped into the rocking chair while her greedy eyes digested the first few pages. How blind she had been, so much blinder than this one-eyed man. Without these notes, she would have known next to nothing about fixing and washing and a million other necessary processes. 'Mr Openshaw,' she began.

'Tha mu'n't thank me. Tha could find out all yon,' he waved a gnarled hand at the book, 'but it might tek a year or more. I've nobbut 'elped thee out.'

Maria stared at him, her vision slightly misted by an emotion she could not identify. She'd been a bit on the soft side lately, what with the wedding and everything. 'If we can get a place, will you work for us, Mr Openshaw?'

He blinked and sat up straight. His face was stretched once more into that wide grin, while the years seemed to be falling away from him, each beat of time taking him back, making him younger, more vigorous. 'Dost tha mean it, lass?'

Maria tried to smile. 'Aye,' she said.

'There's others an' all, folk wi' plenty o' nouse.'

'Let's start at the beginning,' said Maria gently. 'You can kick off here in my back kitchen, just a few block prints, get your hand back in and show me these mixes. Only meals and a couple of bob at first, 'cos we need to save.'

He was studying his hands, forcing them to become straighter, stronger. 'Lass, owt's better nor sittin' in th' 'ouse gerrin' under t' daughter's clogs. But tha'll be needin' thousands if tha wants a shed.'

'I know that, Mr Openshaw. Sooner or later, we'll have to borrow. That's why we need to do some beautiful work. We can show it round, get a bank to come in with us.'

Mr Openshaw looked at the determined tilt of the sharp chin. There was true life here, so there was true hope. 'I ne'er 'ad a woman fer me boss afore,' he said.

Maria chuckled. 'Then it's time you fettled,' she declared impishly. 'Because women are terrible perfectionists.'

'I know,' he answered gloomily. 'Tek me daughter – I wish somebody would tek 'er. No feet on t' fender, she says, no drinkin' tay out o' t' saucer. 'Ow can a man tek 'is ease wi'out 'is feet on top o' t' fire an' wi'out coolin' 'is tay in t' saucer afore scaldin' 'is gob wi' it?'

Anthony came in with a pint pot of 'tay'. 'Sorry, Mr Openshaw,' he said, maintaining the pretended atmosphere of misery. 'It's the same here. Feet on the floor, sit up straight, don't make the place untidy.'

The old man took a noisy slurp of tea. 'Then we mun mek a union,' he said. 'Me and thee agin yon lass.' He

328

pointed to Maria. 'An' we can kick off wi' you fetchin' me a saucer for this tay.'

'No chance,' she laughed. 'No chance of beating me, boys.'

'She's right.' Anthony sat down opposite the visitor.

'I know.' Billy Openshaw's speech cleared up miraculously as he said, 'There's folk and there's women, lad. And me and thee is only folk.'

'How close?' Eloise Skipton's eyebrows shot upward. She had half-expected this woman simply to lie, to make up some sort of evidence against Henry. 'How close were they?' she asked again.

'On the sofa together.'

Eloise sucked in her cheeks. She had planted the idea of a liaison between Henry and the pretty maid, had expected Sara Browne to latch on to the concept of perjury, but here the nurse was, standing at the side of the bed and telling Eloise that she had actually seen the two of them . . . making love? Was that it? Her heart fluttered crazily. She was in luck, because the plan seemed to be working!

'They appear to have some sort of understanding, Mrs Skipton. Jenny is plainly ambitious, and your husband seems prepared to back this printing business.'

Eloise immediately summoned up a frown of deep hurt. She had told Jenny to keep an eye on him, had hoped that Sara, having seen them together, might be persuaded to misinterpret the relationship between master and maid. But the evidence sounded real and solid after all. Was it happening, then? Was he really and truly being unfaithful at last? She'd been too clumsy before, with that Lucy girl and with one or two others. But this time, having promised Sara some jewellery, having begged Jenny to care for him, she had expected the business to be . . . well . . . more discreet. It would have been enough for Sara to pretend, to give evidence about seeing them together in a situation of intimacy, but for the nurse to actually insist that there was something going on . . . 'I don't believe it, Sara,' she said. 'He would never lower himself . . .'

'But he did with other servants. You told me that he had made love to other young maids.'

Eloise tried hard not to scream her triumph. If she screamed, all her efforts to appear quiet, docile and damaged would be ruined. She hung on grimly to the desire to sue him for adultery, and here was the evidence she needed. 'Are you absolutely definite about this? Or are you simply being supportive, trying to help me?'

Sara bridled. 'You sacked her from the nursemaid job because you thought she was too close to your husband. Well, your thoughts were right. He looks at her as if she's the most important thing in all the world. As if he adores her.'

Eloise's stomach seemed to be threatening to erupt at any moment. Her thoughts were running all over the place, skittering about like rats in a dark corner. 'All I wanted, Sara, was for you to be prepared to testify. The details are not important to me.' Her voice emerged thinner, weaker than ever. This was awful. She was reaching her finest hour, but the illness was overcoming her. 'I feel terrible,' she breathed softly.

'I'm not surprised,' said her companion. 'It's just one shock after another, isn't it? You'll feel better after some cocoa and a bit of extra massage.'

'Sara?' The grey eyes glowed with something like rage. 'Will I live to see this through?'

'Yes.' The fat face was crumpling with concern. 'You're not my first patient with multiple sclerosis. Your chest is strong, so you'll survive to bring a case against him.'

'Are you sure?' Panic overtook anger. 'I must live, I must.'

'You will. Just believe me.'

Eloise forced herself to relax. If only this had all happened earlier, when she had been stronger. If Lucy and others like her had managed to seduce him, then Eloise would have been younger, quicker, more alert. In spite of her spoken decision to require no details, she asked, 'Were they . . . kissing?'

Sara shrugged. 'They went into another part of the room for a while. I couldn't see them all the time, just when they were sitting together on the sofa. They laughed a lot.'

Eloise swallowed the vile taste that had risen into her mouth. Laughter was a big thing for Henry. He had often said that people who laughed together stayed together. The plan was working beautifully, so why did she feel so ill, so defeated? And surely this dolt of a nurse realized that the evidence need not be true? Was she lying, then, was she manufacturing this scene between Henry and Jenny? 'Sara, there is no need for embroidery, not until we get to court. At that point, you will have to say that you saw them . . . together. Very close together. But there's no need to convince me. There have been other occasions, times when I had no witness . . .' The lie faded on her lips when she saw the expression on Sara Browne's moonlike face. 'So. He has truly fallen at last.'

'Yes. He is in love, miss. He might not even know it yet, but he loves that girl. I don't blame you for sending her away, really I don't. You should have sent her right back where she came from.'

Eloise, suddenly feeling cold, used her good hand to pull the bed jacket close about her thin shoulders. Nothing had changed, she told herself. In fact, if she thought about it, this might be even better. If he really loved Jenny, then he stood to lose so much more than just money. Because if Jenny were a fortune-hunter, there would be nothing left for either of them. So he would lose everything – money and love. She settled back against the mound of pillows. 'Sara?'

'Yes, miss?'

'Well done. Keep it up. Watch them, both of them. I've a rather nice pink diamond somewhere. We shall seek it out tomorrow. It's very valuable, platinum set.'

'Oh. Right, miss.'

'Listen to the noises they make, Sara. You will not see them actually making love, but you might hear them. The judge will want your evidence.'

'Don't worry.' Sara lifted the cocoa cup from the bedside table. 'I'll make you another drink. And don't be sad. Come the day, I'll know what to say, miss . . . Eloise. And you are quite right. The relationship between master and maid is inappropriate, to say the least. Masters and maids do not listen to music together. And she was stating her price, telling him that she wanted him to back this printing business. You were right all along. I'll be back shortly.'

Once she was alone, Eloise cried many tears that were unusually real. She was getting what she wanted, she told herself repeatedly. Henry was being unfaithful here, in the house, right under his sick wife's nose. Once all this had been voiced in court, he would be completely routed.

She lifted her head and stared at the closed door. He had shut her away, had shut her out of his life. And the biggest shock of all was that it still hurt. Furiously, she sniffed back the tears. Pain was useful. Pain could be translated into anger and hatred. But the deepest anger was directed at herself. Because she still cared, still wanted his love. He must therefore be destroyed completely. No, this was not the illness overtaking her. What she was experiencing was just another example of his cold cruelty. And yes, she would live long enough to see him thoroughly punished.

Eloise Skipton was not the only sleepless one that night. Miles down the road, Carla Sloane sweated her way through restlessness. Decision time had arrived, and the thing she was being asked to do was unpalatable, to say the least.

The priest had questioned her closely about the biggest of her sins, the subject that she had been unable to broach during all her sessions of instruction. And finally, she had been forced to lay her cards on the table face up, with all her wickedness on show. He had gone away to pray for her, also for himself. He needed guidance, he had said, because her sin had been far-reaching. Some mortal sins, it appeared, were not forgivable. If you were to commit a murder, for example, a priest would not absolve you until society had been advised of your crime. Stealing was the same; absolution would arrive once the debt had been repaid, perhaps anonymously. If such repayment seemed impossible, then a donation to a suitable charity would be required.

She turned on to her side. A faint glimmer of light touched the glass on her table, the glass that contained her teeth. Everything had changed with the teeth. She had become a new woman, and this new woman seemed to want peace with God and with the world. To achieve peace with the latter, she would have to bare her soul and leave herself open to all kinds of ill-treatment. Why, she might even go to prison . . .

The door opened a crack. 'Can't you sleep, love?'

'No. It's too warm.'

Pol slid into the room and dumped herself on the edge of the bed. 'It's this conversion thing, isn't it?'

'I don't know.' That was a lie, fifth commandment broken.

'You were better off as you were before. I sometimes wonder if getting them teeth out was the right thing. Since you had the job done, you've spent every minute thinking. Thinking's not good for you. It wears out your brain.'

'Pol, I need to think. It's been very difficult for me, this religion business. How could I have known that within a matter of weeks of leaving the Hall, I'd be a Catholic with a new face? And don't believe for one minute that I didn't fight it. I did fight. It was like being two people, one good and one bad.'

Pol reached out and touched her friend's shoulder. 'You weren't bad. Hurt would be nearer. Hurt because of the way you looked and because of how you'd been treated.'

'All right, you've told me that often enough. So I was hurt. Well, I made sure everybody else was hurt too. It seemed that the only way I could be satisfied was by making other people feel even worse than I felt. So I lashed out, Pol. And it must all be put straight.'

'What must?'

Carla sighed. 'The thing I must do can't be spoken of, not till I've seen the people whose lives I affected.'

There was a short pause. 'Skipton?'

Carla made no reply.

'Let him stew, why don't you? He employs his own

daughter as a maid, a daughter he put out after poor Oonagh left her on the doorstep. It's time I spoke up—'

'You're wrong, Pol.'

Pol jumped up and made for the door. 'I'm no holy Josephine, if that's what you mean by wrong. I've me own score to settle.' She closed the door with a bang.

Carla turned over and faced the wall. Once she had worked out what to say, how to say it, she would go and deliver her piece. After that, if there was anything left of her, she would become a baptized Catholic. And therein lay the only hope for her ultimate salvation.

Chapter Thirteen

MARIA HESKETH FELT THAT SHE HAD LEARNED MORE IN THE past couple of days than she'd learned in nine years at St Andrew's school back in Liverpool. Mind, she told herself, nobody got much education there. Apart from times tables – which had remained a mystery for most of the parrots who had recited them, the emphasis had been mainly on religion. Religion meant getting the cane if you'd missed mass, getting it again if you didn't go to confession once a month, and if you hadn't managed to chant the allocated portion of the catechism, you got the cane once more. Or six times more, depending on who was standing at the holding end of the weapon.

Their Anthony had never been able to sit down at school, because his backside was always striped and red-raw from punishment, so he'd stopped going. According to him, the only good thing about school was being able to sit down without half a dozen baby brothers and sisters crawling all over him. So, when his bottom showed signs of always being too sore, he decided to get paid for standing up. If he couldn't get a decent rest in class, at least he would get paid for being disturbed during daylight hours.

Maria was different from Anthony. She had a hunger for learning, a terrible need to know things and to be doing something useful. It was also important to be the best at whatever she chose to do. Billy Openshaw's book was very useful, even if it only told her to be careful before dipping her toe in the water, or rather in the dye. It all looked too much, too complicated and a damned sight too expensive. Still, she could dream, she supposed. Dreams, even those carrying all the colours of the rainbow, were free.

There hadn't been much time, not with the wedding and everything, but she'd devoured some essential paragraphs of the valuable little book. After she'd managed to get rid of her family, members of which had looked as if they might hang on in Claughton Street until Christmas. She grinned. Her dad had been drunk, Mam had been even vaguer than usual, the bride had spent most of the 'reception' – beer and butties at number seventeen – with her head full of formulae for dyestuffs. Oh, and earlier on, they had all enjoyed one of the milder *pièces de résistance* for which the Heskeths were famous on their own patch. A five-year-old tearaway had got stuck on the church railings with a big spike through his jumper. People passing by had gone white, but Mrs Hesketh had simply lifted the child from his moorings, clouted him gently across the back of his ginger head, then carried on reading her missal for want of something more interesting. So, everything had gone according to a plan that had never been constructed in the first place. In other words, all continued well with the world.

She raised her left hand and smiled at the shiny gold band that decorated her ring finger. She was married and she liked being married. Denis was a good lad, very kind, gentle and easy-going. Nothing had frightened her so far. There'd been that bit of embarrassment when Anthony had gone off on their first night so that they could have the house to themselves. But once they'd got through that bit of giggling, and started on the serious bit of being married, it had been quite nice, really.

Maria Hesketh-as-was, now Maria Dandy, ambled slowly along Bradshawgate, wondering how she, a poor and supposedly underprivileged Lancastrian female, was going to leave some sort of mark on the world. Marriage appeared to have increased her need for success, had certainly not diminished her liveliness. All energy should be harnessed, she told herself as she stared into a window filled with dun-coloured clothes. A power house was no use unless its resources were translated into electricity.

Near Trinity Street, she came upon a large corner café with two windows, each overlooking a different road. For five minutes or more, she watched. Hardly anybody went in, and she could see that most of the tables were unoccupied. It was a grand big place too, plenty of room for other things as well as food. There would be a kitchen in the back, she thought, and a couple of rooms upstairs. She raised her gaze to the upper floor. Whatever went on up there needed no light, because the windows had been painted over in green.

It was near the train station and next to the tram stops, yet it was so ugly and uninviting that few people seemed to notice its existence. She wouldn't have noticed herself except for the fact that she was on the lookout. She grinned at her own foolishness. On the lookout for what? For a great big café with a great big rent that she'd never be able to pay in a month of Sundays? It should be painted yellow, she thought. A shade somewhere between primrose and buttercup, with a big sign at the front, MARIA HESKETH LTD PRINTED FABRICS.

Casually, she wandered across the road. There were just two people in the café, and one of them was a waitress and general dogsbody, sweating fit to burst in the heat of the day, made hotter, no doubt, by the tea urn and oven. A small woman sat in a corner nursing a thick white cup. She had probably been there all day, because she looked like one of the homeless, tattered bags spilling out on to surrounding chairs, a coat buttoned up to the wrinkled neck of a poor soul who was, more than likely, still thawing out thin, aged blood after another night spent on the streets.

Maria pushed the door wide and kicked a wedge of wood under it. 'Do you want it left open?' she asked the raven-haired waitress.

'I do.' She beckoned until Maria was within whispering distance. 'I keep wedging it open, then she gets up and shuts it, says she's cold.'

They both watched as the shabby woman staggered to

the door, this time bearing all her goods and chattels. 'Thank God for that,' said the waitress. 'I know it's a shame for the old biddy, but it must be about a hundred and ten in here, bad as the bloody mill. Do you want a lemonade, love?'

'That'll be nice.' She gazed round the room. 'Are you always this busy? It looks like a funeral after they've all gone home.'

The girl chuckled. 'It's better in winter. Or worse, depending on which way you look at it. In the cold months, I get all the tramps. For about tuppence each, they stop here till they're warm. That's why everybody calls it the dossers' café. I reckon he'll shut it down soon.'

'Who?'

'The boss. Big fat man, he is, what me mam calls a fly bugger. I've only seen him once, 'cos he comes from Manchester, has a proper restaurant there, all menus and wine.' She looked round the room as if it were full, then bent to Maria's ear. 'The real business is upstairs. I stop down here, take the money to the bank and keep me wages. Sometimes, there's hardly enough cash for me to pay meself. Not what you might call a thriving concern. Except for whatever goes on up yonder.' She jerked a thumb towards the ceiling. 'I get the feeling I'm just here as cover, but say nowt, eh? I call upstairs the prohibition den.'

'There's no law against booze in England, is there?'

A casual cloth waved itself about an inch above the counter, supposedly sweeping up crumbs. 'Aye, but I reckon there's a law against thievery.' She dropped the cloth, then poured a cold drink for herself. 'Still, least said soonest mended.'

Maria took a ladylike sip of her lemonade. 'What goes on upstairs?' she mouthed in the manner she had learned from the Lancashire mill women.

'I don't know. Sometimes, a gang of men comes, but not the fat one. He's called Burrows or Barrows – summat like that. They bring parcels in a van, big heavy-looking things. They use the back door, but I've seen them a few times. I reckon they do most of it at night when I'm shut.'

'Do you live here?'

The dark head shook. 'No, I live with me mother down Hatfield Road, and I'm right fed up. She's got a tongue as sharp as a barber's razor, my mam. I've had a job with a room, but it didn't work out, so our Hilda got me this. She's another fly piece, lives over Manchester way with her fancy man. Me mam doesn't know, like. She thinks our Hilda's in a nice flat in Wythenshawe with two nurses and a supervisor from Woolies'. But I'm sure she's Mr Barrows's – or Burrows's – bit on the side. Do you want a butty?'

'No, thanks. It's too hot to eat.' Maria leaned on the counter. The openness of the Bolton people seldom failed to amaze her. If they 'took to you', you could have their life story with chapter, verse and two cups of tea within ten minutes. If they didn't 'take', you could be out on your bum in a couple of seconds, no explanation, no chance to leave your calling card.

'Are you working, then?' asked the waitress.

Maria shrugged. 'Bit of sewing and mending for the big houses. I've a little sister living with me, so I have to stay in the house a lot. And I just got married on Saturday.'

'Ooh.' The coarse but pretty face blossomed into a full-blown smile. 'Isn't that lovely? Where are you from?'

'Liverpool.'

'Oh. Is your husband from there too?'

'No, he's a Bolton fireman.'

'Well, aren't you lucky? I think that's a real romantic job, saving folks' lives. Is he big and strong?'

'Yes. And he's nice. You know, considerate.'

The girl shook the wet curls from her forehead. 'I wish I could get wed. That's the only thing that would get Mam off me back. Or if I could get another live-in job – I'd like that. I wouldn't have to stand here like a spud in the oven if I could just find a man or a place in somebody's house, like a maid's job. The sweat's pouring down my back, rivers of it. Come on, we'll sit on the doorstep. If we both sit there, there'll be no room for any bloody customers carrying their paper bags and fleas into the shop.'

With a lemonade each, they sat on the stone step while Maria told her life story. She reached the bit about the cart bringing her to Bolton, then she faltered as she felt her companion stiffen beside her. 'Are you all right?'

The mouth snapped itself back into a less stunned position. 'Skipton? Skipton Hall, you mean?'

'Yes. Flaming Stonehenge – her real name's Sloane – was the housekeeper, a rotten, big ugly woman with some queer ways, then there was a great soft ha'p'orth upstairs chucking prunes. Anyway, I got sacked,' said Maria after another mouthful of lemonade. 'Well, if I'm going to be honest, I suppose I resigned. But I didn't give fair notice, so I sacked meself. See, me friend got chucked out, so I came out in sympathy. She's gone back, daft bat, she won't listen.'

The waitress nodded slowly. 'I didn't wait for the sack either,' she said softly. 'I slung me bloody hook when she started on me.' Her lips clamped themselves tight after this statement, as if the girl knew that she was in danger of going too far.

Maria turned so that she could see her companion's profile. 'Did you work up there too?'

A small cough was created to cover some hesitation. 'I did.'

'And you cleared off because of Stonehenge?'

'No.'

Maria stood up and walked to the middle of the shallow pavement. 'What happened?' She stared at the girl's face. Pretty, very pretty, in a thinnish, street-urchin way. Was this the famous pretty dark-haired one? 'Come on. What's your name?'

'Lucy. Lucy Turnbull. Don't let on you've seen me. Me mam had to go up for me stuff, clothes and that. Knowing her, she'll have already created fit to burn. I couldn't go up meself – there was no getting me within a mile of the place. I wouldn't tell me mam anything, except that I was homesick. I was sick, all right, but it were nowt to do with home. I didn't want to go home, but there were nowt else for it.' She paused, placed her thick glass of lemonade against the wall and folded her arms in a gesture of defence. 'It was her,' she declared at last. 'I don't want to say her name, I don't want her to find me. It was bad enough trying to get this rotten job without a reference. I'm working for a criminal, I know I am, but I'd sooner this than let her find me.'

Maria stooped forward and placed a hand on a rigid shoulder. 'Look, love, you've nothing to fear from me. Was it the missus?'

For answer, there was just a small nod.

'What did she do to you?'

Lucy jumped to her feet and ran into the café. 'I can't say,' she wailed. 'She'll get me if I tell. I know she will. She'll say it was all me, all in me mind. I'm just ordinary and she's rich. They can do owt they want, rich folk.' Maria, who had managed to keep up with Lucy's swift move across the café, stopped and placed her bag on a table. 'I'll say nothing. I promise you that I'll keep my trap shut. Only my best friend's up there nursing that Mrs Skipton. If there's anything she should know—'

'But it can't come from me!' shrieked Lucy, hysteria closing in now. 'If you mention my name—'

'Don't talk so soft. Do I look as if I was born yesterday? Do I?'

'No.' Lucy swallowed a sob. 'Is she pretty, your friend?'

'Yes.'

A groan forced itself out of the dark girl's mouth. 'It'll be her turn now.'

'What for? What the hell's going on at all? Look, that Stonehenge used to go on about Mrs S and pretty girls. What does she do? Lucy, tell me or I'll go up there this minute and—'

'It might not be happening this time.' The hot cheeks had faded to an uncomely greenish-white with bright patches of scarlet dotted about. 'She never managed it with me, so she might have left it all alone this time.'

'Left what alone?' Maria's voice was far from quiet. Lucy cast an anxious eye on the street, worried that someone might overhear the commotion. With fear-quickened steps, she ran to the door, slammed it, shot home the bolts and pulled down the blind. Slowly, with her breathing labouring under the weight of nerves and exercise, she turned to face Maria.

'Well?' A foot tapped on the scarred and poorly cleaned floor.

Lucy placed a hand beneath her heaving bosom. 'She offered me three hundred pounds if I'd ... I didn't. I didn't. I didn't do it and I didn't take her money.'

Maria kept quiet. The girl would tell her now, because there seemed to be no alternative.

'Cross your heart and hope to die, Maria?'

Maria crossed her heart.

'Oh God, it was horrible, it was sick. I had to wear this nightie, you could see right through it. And I hadn't to wear no underclothes. She made me grind a pill up and put it in his cocoa at supper time. It was to make him sleep. Then, I was supposed to ...' She straightened her shoulders, as if adjusting the cloak that was her own shredded dignity. 'I was supposed to get in bed with him.'

Maria heard her own gasp of horror. 'Sweet Jesus,' she muttered.

'That's not all,' said Lucy, much calmer now. 'She made special arrangements for a friend to stay the night. Everybody downstairs thought it was funny, 'cos Mrs Skipton never bothered with folk. It was somebody she'd been at school with, I think.'

'And?'

'Well, she had this friend in with her, talking till quite late about the old days. She was going to have one of her turns, then she was going to send this woman to get Mr Skipton. She said I'd be kept out of it, I'd just have to get dressed and go home to me mam. But I knew they'd use my name.'

'But what if the friend had seen you in bed with the master and hadn't told Mrs Skipton?'

Lucy grimaced. 'She'd catered for that and all. She could walk a bit with that metal frame, and she was going to follow the other woman into his bedroom.'

'So you scarpered.'

Lucy nodded vigorously. 'I did. I've often wondered what happened. They must have gone into Mr Skipton's room and found him fast asleep.'

'And on his own.'

'Yes. I've never told that to anybody.'

Maria frowned and studied her new ring. She was grown up now, a married woman, so she should be sensible. 'I know I promised, Lucy. I know I crossed me heart, but you can't keep this under your hat forever. You should tell him. Mr Skipton, I mean.'

Lucy folded her arms very tightly, as if she were literally holding herself together, and an expression of anger damaged her rather crude and shallow prettiness. 'Listen, it would have been all the same if I'd done what she asked. I'd have gone to court and told them about the three hundred pounds and the bribery – but she would have denied it, Maria. She made sure she told everybody that I knew the combination to her safe. She kept a small fortune in there, you know. It's hid behind that picture of a lad with yellow curls and daft clothes and men with buckets on their heads—'

'"When Did You Last See Your Father",' said Maria.

Lucy's face was further clouded by confusion. 'When I was about four. He went out for some baccy and an *Evening News*, hasn't been heard of since. So don't bring him into it, he's nowt to do with us any more. If he sets foot in Bolton, me mam'll have his guts for garters.'

Maria would have smiled, but she was too concerned about Jenny. 'That's the name of the picture,' she said. 'Roundheads and Cavaliers, something to do with Cromwell.' She paced back and forth, a hand to her mouth. 'Listen, we've got to go up there, me and you.'

Lucy let out a shattering scream, so loud that the clumsy cups rattled in their chipped saucers on the counter. 'I'm not going.' In contrast to the shriek, the words were whispered, as if the girl had run out of steam.

'Oh yes you are.' Maria put on her fiercest face, the one she had found useful when her younger brothers had needed frightening. Like every day. 'She's sick, Lucy. Mrs Skipton is a very ill woman—'

'I know that. I've seen it for meself, she were getting worse all the while.'

'Sick in the head,' said Maria. 'And he's got the right to

be told about it, he's her bloody husband when all's said and done.'

'He never bothers with her, never—'

'I have worked there, Lucy, so I know what's what. We've got to do it.' She paused for a moment. 'And I know a woman up Chorley New Road that's looking for a nice, clean maid. I can put a word in.'

Lucy stared suspiciously at her companion. 'What about me references?' she asked.

Maria fixed another steely stare on her unfortunate victim. Patterns were not her only forte, and she had no objection to breaking a few rules in a good cause. She could forge a convincing hand, and Anthony would find a 'safe' address in case the letter should be followed up. 'I'll see to all that. We're talented, us Liverpool people. If you want a job, I'll get you one, no problem.'

Lucy gazed round the café. It was all flaking plaster and damp-marks on the ceiling. The room was cold in winter, boiling hot in summer. And she wanted to get away from her mam. Sometimes, she understood about her dad and the baccy . . . 'Will I live in?'

'Yes. Nice room, lemon and white, I sewed the curtains. She's got a car, and she'll take you shopping in Southport. She likes Southport, says it's genteel. Her husband's a doctor, somebody important down the hospital.'

Lucy was still shaking. She pressed her trembling hands to her sides, but she could still feel them twitching. 'I don't know.'

'You'll get fleas here. Fleas and impetigo and all sorts. It's rotten, impetigo, and all the tramps have it. Takes months to clear up, leaves your skin all scarred and covered in white bits where the scabs were.'

A hand flew up and touched the terrified face. 'Right, all right, don't go on, you're worse than me flaming mother, and that's saying summat.' She paused, her eyes flicking from side to side as if they were seeking shelter from something diabolical. 'I don't want to be catching fleas and impy— what you said, but me mam'd flay me if I lost this job without another to go to. You don't know her, Maria. You'd stand a better chance against the flaming

Kaiser, I can tell you that for no money. And her up there, her with the silk sheets – she'll not do owt to me, will she? She might be in bed, but she's took all the chairs up with her, not much missing round her table. Aye, happen she is mad, but it's a very clever madness.'

Maria took pity on the poor girl. 'Listen, if push comes to shove, you can stop at ours, share our Josie's room. Our Josie wouldn't mind being squashed for a bit, it's what she's used to. We're already overcrowded – me brother sleeps downstairs since I got wed, so one more won't matter. There's nobody will hurt you while I'm about. But it won't come to that. I've told you, I'll get you a job. And there's no way that Lois Skipton will hurt you. They've too much to lose, that lot. But we've got to do it. I'll come in a day or two, when I've sorted Mr Openshaw out.' Yes, she'd have to get him going. He was a smashing bloke, he'd done wonders with the blocks and pin marks to make sure the pattern repeated evenly. And surely the situation at the big house could not get any worse within forty-eight hours? Oh, but she wished she'd known all this earlier. Jenny had called in at the wedding, just a whistle-stop visit, long enough to drink a toast and to hand over some nice new towels.

'What will I do with this place?' asked Lucy.

'Eh?' Maria dragged her reluctant mind away from the subject of Jenny. 'Shut it, nobody'll notice. The tramps can manage for half a day, poor devils.'

'I'm scared. You don't know what she's like, I—'

'Oh, but I do. She's gone all nice, Lucy. Butter wouldn't melt, and she's praying and treating everybody fair and square. She eats her food, never chucks it about, sends her bloody compliments to the cook, or her apologies if her plate's not licked clean. Hatching an egg or two, if I'm not sadly mistaken.'

Lucy's eyes were round. 'You're right, that's not her. She must be up to summat.'

Maria nodded. 'And my friend's in the middle of it, too soft to see what's staring her in the face. She's like that, tries to think the best of everybody.'

'What's her name?'

'Jenny. Jenny Crawley.' She paused for a second, remembering that Dan's paternity was now out in the open. 'She's Dan Crawley's daughter.'

Lucy smiled, the relief almost spilling out of her large blue eyes. 'He'll look after her, then. Just have a word with Mr Crawley, put him in the picture, like. There's no need to—'

'Oh, but there is. On Lois's recommendation, Dan's having a nice long holiday by the sea.' Maria was so cross with herself that she just about managed to refrain from stamping her foot like a five-year-old. She should have noticed before, should have realized that Jenny was at the mercy of . . . No. She was being irrational, unfair to herself. Until today, there had been no reason to suspect Mrs Skipton's motives.

Lucy's smile faded gradually, leaving the generous mouth downturned and sulky. 'Then there's nowt standing between Jenny and the missus.'

'Exactly.' Maria leaned on the table and watched while this girl matured. There was anger in the face now, a temper that might just overcome fear. Many people were forced to grow up all of a sudden, thought Maria. Something happened, often to somebody else, and bystanders were simply forced to put on years in order to cope. 'Are you all right, Lucy?'

'Aye.' She pushed yet another damp, black curl from her forehead. 'We'll go up when you're ready, Maria. Somebody's got to stop that bad bitch.'

Maria nodded thoughtfully. 'I know one thing, Lucy. Jenny'll get in no bed for money.' Yes, poor Jenny couldn't stand the thought of streetwomen and their likes, even though her own mother might have been . . . Maria shook herself inwardly to stop her wandering thoughts. 'I'm not criticizing you, girl. But she picks them, does chip shop Lois. I bet she knew your mother wasn't your favourite person, so she'd have been sure you'd keep your gob shut at home. Jenny's got no family except for Dan, and he's been shoved out of the way.'

Lucy hung her head. 'I could have bought me own house with that money, Maria. I was scared, like, and I

346

knew it were wrong, but that three hundred pounds could have changed me life.'

Maria placed her hands on the girl's shoulders. 'Listen, queen. For three hundred pounds, I'd have done it. As long as he'd stayed asleep and as long as I'd been guaranteed no trouble. But there would have been trouble. You saw that in time, and I'd have seen it too. Yes, a nice little house is very tempting. I understand, girl. You're no sinner, so don't be dragging yourself down all the while. She's the one, that Mrs S. Tempting you with property.'

'Yes. All I want, me own place.'

Maria stroked the girl's damp, dark hair into some semblance of order. 'She'll have taken a cleverer tack with Jenny. She'll have learned from her mistake with you. I'll call for you the day after tomorrow. Be ready. Don't let me down. Don't let Jenny down. Most of all, this is for you.'

'Yes, I know.'

'You'll be able to look yourself in the mirror and say you did the right thing.' She picked up her bag and made for the door. 'Ta-ra, love.'

Lucy raised her head, and the look in her eyes spoke of newborn pride and determination. 'Three o'clock, and don't be late,' she said.

'Keep me lemonade cold.'

Maria stepped out on to the pavement, glancing left into Manchester Road, then right into Bradshawgate before negotiating the busy stretch. She walked up Trinity Street, cutting towards the town centre by crossing the railway bridge. A huge engine coughed beneath her feet, its massive lungs sending up steam and smoke that smelled of tar and singed coal. The engineer waved, and she waved back just before becoming enveloped in the train's emissions.

Alone in her personal fog, she smiled. This reminded her of Maggie Pratt's repeated attempts at fumigation. The daft woman used to fill her house with some supposedly magic smoke, and the bugs loved it, often coming out to enjoy a drunken dance even before the safety of darkness had arrived to conceal their antisocial behaviour.

She leaned against the iron bridge, her eyes fixed on the disappearing monster. Why was she thinking about fleas? Oh yes, the tramps in the café. And thinking about fleas stopped her worrying about Jenny.

All the way down to St Patrick's, she determinedly fixed her mind on infestation and the various forms of treatment. The town man used to come with paint that stank, and he filled in all the bug cracks. So the bugs would move next door, then next door would get the town man in. All along the terrace the bugs would move, the lugubrious and very ancient town man staggering along in their wake. Until at the finish, the parasites started back at square one. No-one had ever worked out how the various species managed to travel from one end of the block to the other. But they did. They were alert, clever and one step ahead all the time.

Lois Skipton was a parasite. She bled folk dry, hopping from one to another and sucking their blood. She shouldn't be all pale and thin; she should be like a leech, all swollen by other folks' miseries. Oh, Jenny! Please don't let her get pulled in, prayed Maria silently. Don't let my friend be sucked dry . . .

She stopped outside the church. It was still warm, and she needed a rest. Lois, alias Eloise, didn't swell up. No, she stayed all weak and pitiable and fragile. How the hell could she pay somebody, actually pay them, to get in bed with Mr Skipton? Was she completely weird, or was she just clever? Yes, she was well clever enough to know how to go about divorce. Lucy's name would have been mud, and now poor Jenny . . . God, even thinking about fleas and bugs didn't help, she always came back to the same subject, the same worry.

She leaned against the rough-hewn stone wall of St Patrick's. A woman came out, a woman who looked vaguely familiar. But Maria couldn't place her, couldn't quite give a name to this ordinary-looking person. She was about 50, dressed in a good blue suit, and she kept staring at Maria, as if wondering whether to approach her. Maria, in no mood for approaches of any kind, crossed the road and made her way towards home. Her head was too full, too busy for sensible conversation. Halfway up Great Moor Street, she came to a sudden halt. No, it couldn't have been. That woman had looked nothing like Stonehenge. For a start, the body had been a lot thinner, and there had been no teeth sticking a mile out of her mouth.

Maria pulled herself together. There was a lot to be done in the next forty-eight hours. For a start, she'd better peel some spuds, the steak would be well stewed by now. Then there were the patterns to prepare for Mr Openshaw — he knew somebody who knew somebody with a drying cabinet. And Josie would have to call at the cobblers to get her school clogs mended, new rubbers on the soles. And . . . She turned, hoping to catch a glimpse of the woman in blue. But there was no sign of her. No sign at all.

Pol O'Gorman rested her aching bones in the doorway of the Prince William. A handcart was all well and good — a handcart was all well and necessary while Amos was mending his sore foot. But it was a desperate weight, and no mistake. If she carried on like this for much longer, she'd be getting fallen arches, housemaid's knee, and muscles on her arms like a prizefighter's.

She sighed meaningfully, turned on her heel and pushed open the door to the saloon bar, which would no doubt be occupied exclusively by the male of the species. Still, she was ready for all that. Just let them start when she was mortally thirsty and with a paddy on her that might have terrified Old Nick himself. Cart-pushing in hot weather was dry work and hard going. She nodded to herself as the double door swung shut in her wake. She was a bigger man than the lot of them put together.

The greetings were mixed, consisting of a solid fog of blue tobacco smoke, some singing that failed to keep time with a piano that failed to keep tune, and a red-feathered dart that whistled with near-mortal accuracy past her left ear. Another inch, and she would have been dead. Outwardly calm, she rescued the arrow from a wooden bust that stood on a plinth to the left of the door, probably a replica of Prince William himself. The royal personage bore many similar scars, particularly around a pitted hollow where the nose had been, and Pol wondered vaguely why the landlord didn't shift poor Will to somewhere out of the firing line.

A row of men had turned away, and she was presented with a series of carefully nonchalant rear views. There was some giggling, probably about the latest near miss, while the guilty party was no doubt being shielded by this solid rampart of male, beer-swilling defence. Pol sauntered to the counter, her ankle-length dirndl swinging even more widely than usual. 'Landlord!' she yelled. 'Get yourself away up here this minute!'

A small man with a complexion like withered cabbage came forward. Finding uncertain anchorage on his wet lower lip, a loose, handmade cigarette spilled tobacco and fire down a collarless shirt. The resulting incendiary missiles sat in the graveyards of their antecedents, a definite lacework of tiny brown-ringed holes on ale-spattered greyish-white cotton.

'I was just now nearly killed,' she announced. 'Did they never learn how to throw an arrow, these English peasants?' With a careless flourish, she tossed the dart in the general direction of the board. In that split second, the piano stopped, while the room grew sufficiently silent for the small twang of dart on wire to be adequately audible. 'A pint of mild, my good man,' she said, not bothering to assess the accuracy of her aim. 'And get yourself a fireproof vest, or ye'll have all the hair on your body singed.'

The landlord, who was totally bald, began to fill her glass. Pol turned to the nearest drinker. 'He must have hair on his chest. Surely he's not shiny-bare all over?'

No answer came. To a man, they were staring at the dart as it quivered inside the wire circle that surrounded the bulls-eye. After a while, they shifted along to give her space, and she leaned and talked and drank with the best (and the worst of them, she thought) until the session neared its end. Pol was not a good holder of drink – which is not to say that she was bad company when inebriated.

But her control had a tendency to slip after several pints and, as five or six were thrust upon her before the calling of time, she was in full flood when chucking-out time came.

There was a newsagent next to the pub, and the men gathered on the pavement to await the arrival of evening papers. Most were old, past retirement age, but the young and indolent were also represented, those who sought no work, those who drank the pennies earned by wives and mothers.

It was to such a mixed congregation that Pol preached. 'I am highborn,' she pronounced to no-one in particular. 'But he sits on it, on my father's money. He's a desperate bad bugger, may the good God pardon my swearing, but a saint would curse if a fortune got whipped from under his nose and no please or thank you or kiss my behind.' She belched unprettily, took a deep breath, and almost fell over when the oxygen hit her blood.

A shrivelled man in a flat cap approached her. 'Go home, sparrow,' he said. 'Tha'll regret this in t' mornin'.'

'Ah well.' She shook a limp finger. 'He's taken his own love-child back in, has he not? Jenny Crawley, left on his kitchen step eighteen years since. Reared not far from here, in Claughton Street. Oh aye, she's back in, the blue-eyed daughter. Not that I've anything against . . .' Against whom? What was she talking about, she must find her place in the script. Ah yes.

'But what about me? What about his father's . . . his father's brother's . . . ?' It was getting a bit complicated for a mind that wouldn't fix on anything, for a mouth too slack to form proper words. She was his father's brother's daughter. Her head moved in time with the three words. After a moment or two, 'father' and 'brother' and 'daughter' were quite firmly welded to the front of her brain. She dragged her blouse up on to her shoulder, wiped her nose on the sleeve and began again. 'I am Henry Skipton's father's brother's daughter.' The words rolled round in her mind again for a few seconds while she checked them for errors. 'That's right. I'm his cousin,' she declared triumphantly.

Flat Cap moved closer. 'Don't be slandering 'im. 'E's too big for us, too big for thee.'

'I'm bigger than everybody,' she yelled, spinning in a graceless arc with her arms stretched wide. Unfortunately, the delicate balance of her inner ears had already been disturbed by ale, so Pol ended up in the gutter with her underwear on show. Someone shouted, 'Nay lass, save that for Saturday neet.' Pol shook her head, making the dizziness even worse. 'I'm a Skipton without the name,' she screamed again and again.

Eventually, several of them managed to lean the hand-cart against the pub wall, then they placed Pol, none too carefully, in a half-lying half-standing attitude among the cart's collected treasures. She sang tearfully for a while, her mammy's songs from the old country, then she slept.

The men grouped outside the paper shop. 'What do you think?' and 'Take no notice, she was drunk, wasn't she?' were two of the many muttered questions and remarks.

Pol slept fitfully. Even in her drunken state, she knew that she had been and gone and done it. All these years she'd kept quiet, and now she'd told all the Prince William her secret. Jenny's too. She should not drink during the day. She was always mortallious if she drank in the afternoon.

The rags, which became decorated by the fruits of Pol's unhappy stomach, were relegated to the tip later that day. Pol put herself away in her room, determined not to come out for a year or two. It might all die down. And, if she lived, her stomach would recover. Given time.

Every evening was the same. She had to stay with the mistress, listen to all the talk, all the plans, then she was forced to monitor the movements of that girl. That girl usually went to bed at about half past ten. During the maid's preparation for bed, Sara Browne was expected to glue her ear to the communicating door. If Jenny was singing, then that had to be reported. If she was quiet, then that too had some sort of significance for Mrs Skipton. After a few such boring evenings, Sara was beginning to reflect on the real value of an opal ring.

'Come here, my dear.' Eloise stretched out a thin hand. 'You must be so tired.'

'Yes. Yes, I am a bit sleepy.' She sat in the chair, wishing that it were more comfortable, wishing that someone would come along and massage her aching limbs.

'I was wise, I think, to let her keep that room. The affair is so much easier to follow while she's just next door. And with the electric bell running across the landing, I can summon you at any time.'

'Yes, miss.' It had been three o'clock this morning when the bell had first shrilled its way into Sara's shocked ear. The mistress had wanted turning, had needed water and someone to listen while she described, for the hundredth time, how her husband would be repaid for his philandering.

'Did you yawn just then, Sara dear?'

'No, not at all. Would you like me to fix your pillows?'

'Thank you, perhaps later. Tell me again about the music.' She needed to keep hearing the words, needed the chance to cope with her feelings. It had been quite good fun before, working out how to have him sued for a liaison that had never happened. Now, it was more serious. If he were really fond of Jenny, then he was going to suffer very soon. Of course, if the love affair did turn out to be a fact of life, then Sara's only function would be to tell the truth. Which was, in a way, much easier than getting her to lie. But Eloise hated the thought of Henry enjoying comfort, however temporary, from any source. And, even now, the idea of someone else receiving his love was distasteful.

'They played the Ravel and some Bach and they laughed a lot.' This was such old hat now that it was delivered in a monotone. 'They sat together on the sofa. When he looked at her, there was desire in his eyes. When she looked at him, it was with admiration.'

'So,' said Eloise. 'When I die, he will bring that little trollop into my house.'

'Yes, miss,' sighed the long-suffering nurse.

'And she will benefit from all the comforts, all my wonderful ornaments and Louis Quinze furniture.'

'Yes, miss.'

'Oh, Sara, you must find some more evidence for me. You will be my friend, my voice in that terrible court. When the bond between myself and Henry is broken, you will wield the sword that severs the cord.'

'Yes, miss.' This was all waxing a bit lyrical again. Swords? All she wanted was a feather pillow and eight hours sleep.

'Sara.' Long, bony fingers entwined themselves in the dulling auburn locks. 'This will be your place, yours to run when all his property reverts to me. In this house, you will start a refuge for women who suffer from this cursed disease. It will be the Eloise Robinson Retreat. And you will be its foundation.'

Sara sat bolt upright, tiredness completely vanished. 'Me?' she asked softly.

'Oh yes. You will choose doctors and therapists for the clinic. The whole organization will fall to you. The salary should be somewhere in the region of ... oh ... a thousand pounds a year? And all your food and accommodation will be free.'

'But I'm only a—'

'Only a wonderful woman who understands a cripple's needs.' She stared at the exhausted face. 'Bring my box, Sara.'

Sara brought the box. This place, hers to run? That would be absolutely marvellous. She could see herself, hear herself lording it over the true medics, people who looked down on her as unqualified dross. Oh, she would pick and choose all right. They'd have to crawl on their bellies to be consulted by a patient from this place. And she would get some smart clothes, some—

'Sara?'

'Oh, sorry. I was miles away.'

'This is Victorian, but pretty all the same.' She held up a delicate four-bar gate bracelet. 'There's a piece of quartz there next to the lock. That quartz used to hang from my grandfather's watch chain.'

'It's beautiful.'

'Eighteen-carat.' She dangled it gently beneath the

woman's nose, as if she were using it to hypnotize. 'Get me more, Sara. Follow them. Find them together.'

'Yes, miss.'

'The bracelet will be here when you bring me more news.'

'Yes. I'll . . . I'll go and make my cocoa.' She scurried from the room. If she didn't see them together tonight, she would make it up, invent something. Her hand strayed along the banister. This would make a fine nursing home . . .

'Snap!' Briony's brown hand covered the cards. She shovelled them towards herself, gathering them in like a miser collecting his precious store of coins.

'You cheated,' said Jenny. 'I snapped at the same time as you, only you slapped your hand down over the cards as usual. It's not fair.'

Briony sniffed, screwing up her face in a ridiculous grimace. 'You're only jealous, Jenny Crawley. Just because I've got a feller and you haven't.'

Jenny laughed. 'You're welcome. He always smells of manure.'

'It's a good, clean smell,' shouted Briony. 'And he's very high thought of, is Mick. We're to have a cottage with a garden and some hens.'

Jenny tilted her head to one side. 'You'd have done better with me dad. He's high thought of, but not high with manure smells.'

'You what?' The lower lip dropped for a moment. 'How did you know? I mean, it's not true. I mean, who told you?'

'Everybody.'

'No!'

'Yes. The fact is, it showed. You used to look at him the same way Charlie looks at a bone before he jumps on it. Hungry, like.'

Briony's face fell again. She was a girl with mercurial feelings, swift to love, quick to dislike. But she was a great believer in the achievable, and Mick fell well within that category. Why, she hadn't thought about Mr Crawley for ages. Mr Crawley wasn't there any more, and Mick was there. 'I wasn't that bad, was I?'

Jenny chuckled. 'No, I'm just pulling your leg. Anyway, it was your business.'

Briony, seeking a change of subject, glanced at the kitchen clock. 'I think I'll go up. It's me on grates tomorrow, you're on polishing. You don't need to be up as early as me. Mind you, I don't know why we bother lighting fires while it's so hot. Nobody ever uses half the bloody rooms in this place.'

Jenny shrugged. 'It's to keep them aired. And the fires are all out by noon.'

'Aye, and they need cleaning out every flipping morning. I'll see you tomorrow.' She pushed the cards into their box. 'Night-night, Jenny.'

'Good night.'

Sara Browne came in just as Briony went out. She paused and stared at the other girl, the one who was her unwitting prey. Was it true? Was there something between Mr Skipton and this beautiful young girl? Oh what did it matter . . . ? 'Hello, Jenny. Are you ready for some cocoa?'

Jenny looked without malice at the woman who had stolen her job. Judging by the state of the nurse, minding Mrs Skipton must be getting harder by the minute. 'I'll make me own, ta.'

Sara lifted sugar from a shelf. 'Go and ask Mr Skipton if he would like a warm drink. He's in the library, I think.'

Jenny rose and pushed the playing cards into one of the table drawers. 'He looks after himself, nurse. He says he often makes a drink in the night.'

'Well, asking him would do no harm, especially while the pan's already on.'

Charlie crept to Jenny's side. He was developing a good ear for the language, so had managed to interpret Jenny's intentions. If he kept tail and profile fairly low, he could sneak behind her to the library. Once there, he would have his two favourite people together.

Luck was on Charlie's side. He followed her down the corridor, through the dining room and into the library. The rugs were well placed, enabling him to manage the distance without too many scratchings of claws on wooden floor.

The library was empty, but a faint glimmer from beneath the far door told that the study was occupied. The dog waited, breath held against a tongue that fought to come out panting. One of his ears pricked; he could sense a presence in the other direction, someone in the large dining room. The smell of the someone was not unfamiliar, so there was no need for his special 'intruder' bark. And he should not be here; silence would be the wisest option.

Jenny knocked on the study door and pushed it open. It was at this point that Charlie's puppiness got the better of him. Being good and quiet was easy up to a point, but he often got overstretched, too excited to be a real, grown-up dog. He howled gleefully, leapt forward and crashed into Jenny's legs as she turned in answer to the dog's commotion.

To Charlie's grief and total humiliation, Jenny crashed to the floor, her head making sharp contact with the wall on its way down. For a second or two, Charlie stood, head bowed, tail trailing towards the strip of carpet, heart beating loud in his ears. With every ounce of joy now banished from his body, the dog backed into the library, curling himself into the smallest ball he could manage with a body as clumsy as this one. He shivered and pushed his black leather nose beneath a paw. The other presence was near, but he was too grief-stricken for action.

Henry lifted Jenny's slack body in his arms. Even now, he thought about the poor dog. 'It's all right, boy. Not your fault.' But these words of comfort flowed over the poor animal like a breath of winter. He had been bad; he had damaged one of the leaders of a pack that had adopted him and fed him.

She was heavier than he might have expected. Hers was a slenderness that belied the true strength beneath the surface, a vigour she had developed since arriving in the country. The limbs and head drooped limply, yet he could see the healthy cords of young muscle in the longish column of her neck. 'Jenny?' he whispered. 'Good God, don't take her from me. Surely a crack on the head can't . . . ?' He placed her on the library sofa, then knelt beside her, rubbing the nearest hand. 'Jenny? Can you hear me?' He touched her neck, seeking the pulse that would reassure him. Yes, it was there.

He jumped up, strode across the room and snatched at a vase of chrysanthemums. The flowers were quickly cast into the grate, then he used the water to wet his handkerchief. 'Jenny?' This was louder and trimmed with something akin to panic. 'For pity's sake, girl, wake up!' He wet her forehead, his eyes glued to a swelling above the right eye. 'My mother always said that a swelling on the head was a good thing. You have a swelling, so your brain's intact. Come on, princess. Are you waiting for a kiss?' He bit hard on his lower lip, wishing that his mother's words of comfort would work now.

He edged himself on to the sofa, terrified of touching her, perching precariously so that he could watch her without causing further pain. Perhaps he should not have moved her from the floor. If she did not revive in a couple of minutes, he would seek help. The tips of his fingers were shaking as he began to stroke the lovely face from eyebrow to chin. Over and over, he traced the path of delicate bone and firm flesh, his own eyes misting ominously. 'Jenny,' he said again. 'Oh, my sweet girl.'

Charlie lifted his head as the shadow in the next room slid away to nothing. He felt bad inside, and not just about what he had done. That shadow, although he knew its owner, had not been friendly. His shiny black nose sniffed the air, translated the various scents, then dropped again to the cushion of paws. He would stay, no matter how long the vigil.

Henry smiled. The long, dark-bronze lashes quivered for a moment, then the eyes blazed forth in all their glory. 'Mr Skipton,' she said apologetically. 'Do you want some cocoa? Oh, and what hit me?'

He laughed quietly. 'Charlie. I'm sure he's very sorry. Any bones broken?'

She touched her head. 'This is the only bit that hurts,' she said. 'Oh well, if I fell on my head, I'll catch no harm. It always was my least sensitive point.'

Chapter Fourteen

RAIN LASHED THE WINDOWS CEASELESSLY, PUNISHING THE glass, slicing in long, diagonal stripes like raw wounds that refused to heal. Forks of summer lightning pierced ugly, low-slung cloud, the timpano of thunder not quite keeping time, as if Thor's orchestra had lain unrehearsed of late.

Henry Skipton sat motionless at his desk, a single sheet of paper drooping from a hand. While the elements quarrelled, he heard nothing apart from the thrumming of his own heart. Divorce. It was here, but hardly on a plate. Skipton v. Skipton – that much was all right. But further down the page, beneath the matrimonial address which was wrongly listed as Skiffton Hall, there stood another name. Jennifer Crawley. Jennifer Crawley would be served with papers within the next seven days, because Jennifer Crawley was the co-respondent.

The poky room was darkening, but he sought no further illumination. It was the smallest office in the building, just a desk, two chairs, some drawers for files, a hatstand to the right of a heavy door. He had never wanted space; those in the clamour of machinery that he currently failed to hear were the ones who needed room to move. It was nine o'clock and he had just opened his personal mail. A begging letter from an orphanage, the accountant's assessment of Skipton Mills' current state of financial health, a hastily compiled note from the solicitor.

'We need to talk,' the lawyer's attached understatement declared.

He could not talk. No part of his body seemed to be working. He was just a statue sitting on an earth tremor, the quaking caused by uneven beats of a heart that had not quite petrified. The phone was on the desk. He should drop this tangible tissue of lies, let it fall to the floor, pick up the receiver, fight for Jenny's sake. But the letter adhered to his hand, stuck to the palm like a sucking leech.

The headache was back, proving that some of his physical functions remained intact. He could feel pain, but not the right sort. Worry would arrive shortly, once his body had ceased to produce the analgesia born of shock. A quarter past nine. He had been sitting here for fifteen minutes and half the room had disappeared in the peripheral blindness that comes with migraine. The station clock above the door jerked its long finger another notch downward. His right eye was fixed on the time, while his left pupil swam in coloured waves of nauseating distress. There should be a cure for migraine; this was, after all, the twentieth century.

A head poked itself around the door, dragged the upper part of its owner into space that was already limited. 'We've three shuttles bust, Mr Skipton.'

The response was automatic, born of long practice. 'Send for Donald Appleton. Tell him to go through the lot while he's here.' Vocal chords were intact, then, though this small fact was scarcely deserving of applause. Still, he allowed himself a small measure of relief. At least he had not been struck dumb.

'Every loom?'

'That's right.' Henry shook his head slowly, tried to clear his vision.

'Are you all right, boss?'

'No.'

The rest of the body entered the office. 'Will I get some help, like? A doctor, or a nurse?'

'I don't need anybody, Sam.' Perhaps an undertaker would have been nearer the mark? This could ruin Jenny's life, might kill off her youth with one single, well-aimed arrow, the tip slimed with poisonous untruths. It was nine-teen minutes past nine. There was noise outside, thunder, a yellow-blue dart of lightning. He was still clutching the damned letter. There'd been fisticuffs in a carding room yesterday, something connected with a woman from Blenkinsop's bleachworks. He really ought to go down and see if the dust had settled. Not that it ever did, in a carding shop. It stuck to their lungs like glue – Pol O'Gorman knew all about that. 'They should have masks,' he declared.

The half of Sam's face that was visible to Henry clouded over. 'You what, sir?'

'Carding rooms. Get them some masks.'

'Oh. Aye. Right.' With each staccato word, the foreman retreated, his arm seeking a door handle and sanity. There was something up with the boss, something Sam couldn't put a finger on.

'Did they sort it out?' asked Henry.

'Eh?' Sam licked his lips and prayed for tea-break.

'The fight down below.'

The man's face cleared miraculously. 'Oh aye. It were just over Ida Melling, who's no better than she ought to be, according to my missus. They'd both been walking her out, see and—'

'Who won?' It was suddenly important that somebody should win.

Sam shrugged. 'They agreed to differ, like. So Ida's the one who lost, Mr Skipton. Both lads have took up with a pair of sisters from t' winding shed, treated theirselves to a fish supper and four seats in t' back row of t' pictures last night. That were t' tale flying round when th' 'ooter sounded, any road.'

Henry breathed deeply, rhythmically, fought to control a heartbeat that almost rattled beneath buried anxieties. 'So Ida lost. From now on, saint or sinner, she will always be known as a bad lot. Life's a fish-kettle, Sam.'

An oil-stained hand crept up the wall towards a brown Bakelite switch. 'Do you want me fer t' put t' light on, Mr Skipton? It's like t' bottom of a pit shaft in your office.'

'No. I've another headache. It will pass if I sit in the dark.'

He had been in the dark for a long time, he thought, as Sam clattered his clog-shod way down the corridor. A perfectly innocent relationship with a girl young enough to be his daughter had been interpreted as . . . Innocent? Had he been truly innocent?

Thunder crashed immediately overhead, its ferocity appearing to rattle the mill's very foundation. Some of the women would be screaming now, those who worked in quieter areas. Strange how people feared thunder. Jenny loved it, found it dramatic, exciting. She was an innocent lamb, must not be slaughtered on Eloise's satanic altar. No matter what he had thought or desired, no matter which vile slug had crawled from beneath the boulders of Henry Skipton's imagination, no guilt could be attached to the girl.

Jenny. His left eyeball was pulsating, throbbing in the midst of his inner storm. Outside, the furies continued at war, obeying some unseen conductor of cacophony as thunder and lightning arrived simultaneously, no split second of division.

The roar from his lips was drowned by a deafening crash in the blackened firmament. His hands jerked themselves on to the desk, sweeping murderously along its top, scattering blotter, envelopes, ink and diary. The sole survivor was the telephone, sitting smug, black and silent in a pool of purplish ink.

He lifted the receiver, spoke a number, waited for the connection. The discussion was short and sharp. Yes, Henry must come into the solicitor's office; no, there should be no details spoken via the telephone.

He cut himself off, sat for a while, his eyes glued to this instrument of communication as if it were a culpable part of the whole sadistic plot. It probably was a guilty party, because he'd heard the clicks. Not on this particular gadget, but at home. Strange how the sounds had never bothered him, how they had scarcely registered until now. Eloise had been reading his mind, or as much of his mind as he ever revealed on the telephone. Which would not be a great deal, he told himself firmly. He was very much a 'yes' or 'no' man when it came to the phone, did not indulge in long, crackling conversations.

The hand had become a fist, and the fist contained the solicitor's letter. He tossed the resulting paper ball into the waste basket, as if he might get rid of the printed message. But no, it was carved into his brain, with Jenny's name floodlit and in capitals.

His eyes began to clear. Perhaps he should have regular temper tantrums, because the outburst seemed to have worked more efficiently than aspirin. He would go out later, have a drink or two, steel himself in preparation for the afternoon appointment. The mill did not need him. Nobody needed him. The clock crawled. Jenny was at the Hall, under the same roof as a black widow spider. The lawyer's voice had been almost accusatory, coldly angry with Henry for his supposed indiscretion. It was still just a quarter to ten. Ink was seeping through cracks in floorboards at the edge of a tattered rug. The meteorological symphony continued to pour its wrath out of clouds low enough to touch rooftops. This tempest was appropriate; it reflected his own anger.

He stood, walked round the desk, reached for coat, hat, umbrella. The last item had been re-covered three or four times. This had been his father's gamp, a shabby item with a polished handle that was almost worn away. There had been a duck's head on the handle, but it had eroded now to a shape that was just about birdlike, all the carved feathers gone, eyes plucked out by Henry's childish hands years ago. 'Gertie Gamp' had been one of Henry's toys. He stroked the duck's head absently. She would be polishing now. Jenny would be touching wood as smooth as this, rubbing in the beeswax, humming under her breath. The hair, if newly washed, would be tumbling . . .

Gertie Gamp accompanied her master to the car, sat quietly collapsed beside him as he drove mindlessly over moorland, through villages, along tracks fit only for carts. She slipped just once in a nasty pothole, had to be righted so that the gear stick could be reached. At the edge of a reservoir, she was opened to the elements once more, spreading her taut, silky panels over her owner's head.

He stared at the water, watched the rain bouncing from

one greyness into another. Like the sky, the depths were sullen, dark and heavy as lead. From Gertie's wire frame, rain poured in eight ceaseless streams. He counted them, turning the umbrella, starting to score from the point with a hole to its left. There were eight prongs to a gamp, eight gores to its skirt. Jenny had a gored skirt, long, grey, part of the uniform. The skirt was tight at the waist, flaring out at the back as her travelling heels kicked its hem.

His mouth moved, almost of its own accord. 'I am not a weak man,' he said, the tone quiet, conversational. 'But, by Christ, I am at my limit now.' Two further strides, and he would be in the water; a dozen or so more wading steps, and the gently sloping banks of this green-edged storage vat would fail to support him. Gertie would float, would fail to mark the spot where the captain had gone down. 'And who would look after Jenny, then?' he asked a drowned dandelion. 'Her father? Could he help her out of this mess?'

He pushed back his shoulders, straightened his spine. If he were to die, then there would be no case for Jenny to answer, no mess for her to clear. And if he were to die, his death would be Eloise's victory. He gazed upward at the umbrella's dome where the eight points met. 'My weakness, then, is that I cannot let Eloise win. And, Gertie, I am not ready yet for a watery grave.'

Back in the car, he followed the road to Bolton. There were cobbles now, great stones that had been hammered into the earth a hundred years ago. It was a straight road, a way created by Romans, who had never let anything block the geometrical directness of their paths. He was skirting his own land, acres his family had worked to secure, fields that might be taken from him any day now in a court of so-called law.

The car juddered for want of fuel as Henry's toes came off the accelerator. He paused, swallowed, applied the brake. Slowly, his hand reached beneath the passenger seat, dragged out binoculars on a broken strap. He opened the door, stepped out, caught a dozen frail drops of rain on his face. The weather had exhausted itself, and a few beams of sun were penetrating diminished cloud.

Through the field glasses, he watched her. She was sitting on a wall of dry stone, a rusty-red stole about her slender shoulders. The hair, tucked up at the back, was beginning to break free, some skittish tendrils dancing in a light breeze. Her legs were crossed beneath a garment that seemed, from this distance, to match the wall for colour. Her left hand rested on the nearest stacked boulder.

Henry turned away, wiped the binoculars on a spotless handkerchief. He would look again in a moment. Yes, he would look again. After walking a short distance from the car, he raised the glasses once more. She had not moved an inch. From his new vantage point, he caught the sun as it finally divided the lower stratum of cloud, providing a backcloth that fell just short of haloed. This was how Jenny should be painted. With the light shining around her, with that wonderful hair unrestricted. To pose for a portrait, she should sit where she was now, not in a room, not in a gown of brocade or lace.

He lowered the binoculars. There was no point in cleaning them again, because that would improve nothing. This time, his vision was restricted not by migraine, but by unshed tears. 'I love you, Jenny,' he mumbled indistinctly.

Gears ground noisily as the car leapt along the road. Behind the wheel sat a man whose face seemed set against life itself, so grimly determined was the tilt of his jaw. He would survive. With God's help, and with a drop or two of scotch, Henry Skipton would endure.

The King's Arms on Deansgate was the first pub he noticed, so he literally fell in at the door, as he did not have the regulars' advantage of knowing about the two stone steps. Some elderly drinkers picked him up, dusted him down and placed him on a stool at the far end of the bar counter. 'Yer christened, now,' one of them said. 'Every new bugger has to get baptized over yon steps. Sometimes, we have bets, but mostly on a winter night when folk can't see th' end o' their noses. What's your excuse?'

'I just tripped,' answered Henry. 'Thanks for your help.' He ordered a double, nursed it for a while, had his hip flask filled by the plump and smiling landlord. Words ran about in the empty space where Henry's brain had used to lodge, lawyers' language, stilted and sombre, all whereto-fores and aforementioneds. He was in a pit, had neither wit nor wisdom to help himself out of it.

His eyes strayed to a nearby table, latched on to a session of dominoes. A player asked him to join, but he heard his own voice refusing the invitation. The game seemed serious, its participants' faces wearing deadpan expressions, while a cap full of coins squatted in a circle of pint glasses. In his current condition, he would not have managed to count the spots.

The landlord hovered. 'Anything to eat, sir? Me wife's took to laying on a supper, hotpot with red cabbage.'

'No. No, thank you.' He had not eaten since breakfast, though his stomach had complained for some hours. Where had he been all day? Ah yes, he had driven round for a while, had visited the solicitor, had driven round again. Round and round and round again. He lifted a hand to order some food, but the landlord had turned away, allowing Henry the view of a broad, red neck, a shiny waistcoat back and some hitched-up sleeves secured by metal rings around large upper arms. When the glass was drained, Henry picked up his flask and walked out into the quickened air that so often follows a storm.

The first rush of breeze sent him reeling into a shop doorway. Through the glazed panels, he saw some hanging flitches of bacon, then a pig's head sitting on the marble counter, an apple in its mouth. Everything was monumentally significant today, even a dead boar segmented for human consumption. He stared at the beast's half-open eyes. It might be a sow, he mused. Sometimes, the sow got slaughtered while the male pig continued alive.

Whisky and fresh air were not good companions for an empty stomach. He turned back towards the pub, thought about stew and red cabbage, rejected the concept immediately. Potato, carrot and meat floating in thin gravy, globules of fat swimming to the surface ... He gulped hard. A walk would do him good.

On Trinity Street bridge, he stopped, stared through the lattice of heavy metalwork that framed the sides.

Below him, iron rails criss-crossed over massive sleepers, and toffee papers played between the tracks, lifted by the wind into a game of run-and-catch. It was a long way down, perhaps not long enough. The jump had been tried, had been survived more than once when trains had shunted away on altered points. 'There are documents, dates and times, descriptions of your behaviour,' said a disembodied voice, the remembered tone deep, efficient, damning. Henry was not suicidal. He was, he told himself, not weak enough to kill himself, not strong enough to take that final leap.

Henry's hands came up, rested on rust-coloured metal-work. 'She killed my baby. She killed Sophie, smothered her with a cushion.' There had been a brief silence then, followed by a full analysis of Henry's accusation. Nought would come of this tardy notion of infanticide, not after all these years, not without other witnesses. A court would need to know why the crime had not been reported earlier – did Henry really want to dig his own grave? There had been no comfort, no help from the lawyer. And Carla Sloane, the solicitor had decided, would not be a reliable source should Henry care to air the business of Sophie's death.

Henry's knuckles were white, and the iron joist's edge was cutting into his palms. 'I have not been unfaithful with Jenny Crawley,' he heard himself saying. It had been so tidy, that lawyer's office, so righteous and cold. 'I have never made love to that young woman.' The solicitor had remained religiously unmoved.

A lecture had been duly delivered, a sermon on sympathy, quiet and emotionless words about a broken wife being wheeled in to state her case. Eloise would win, because the nurse, one Sara Browne, was so definite about what she had seen. Eloise would win, because the state of her health would break the iciest heart.

Henry groaned, rested his head against the bridge's frame.

'Is it jumping you're thinking of?'

He did not look up. 'Go away, damn you.' The four words were growled rather than spoken.

Pol came to stand next to him. Had he heard about her drunken behaviour? she wondered briefly. Did he know that she had, in her cups, claimed kinship with the Skiptons? They had been more than cups, she reflected soberly. More like buckets ... 'What's the matter with you?'

'Nothing that you can cure.'

She pondered. There was business on Bradshawgate tonight, enough to keep all the working girls occupied. So why was she standing here with a terrible man when she could be making a pound or five? 'I'm a mother confessor,' she declared. 'Half the businesses in this town would close if I spilled the odd bean. I should have become a head-doctor, for I'm remarkable at listening to the world's cares. And why are you drunk?'

'I'm not.' At last, he looked at her. This time, the suit was blue and the blouse seemed whiter than usual, possibly new. And she wasn't spitting.

Pol attempted a smile. 'Come along with me now till I talk to you.'

He blinked slowly, just once. 'Why don't you leave me alone?'

'Because you're near death. Come away to my place above the butcher's. You're in need of food. And how many times have those clothes been wet? Sure they've dried on you, and you must be chilled to the marrow.'

'The pork butcher's on Deansgate?' he asked. 'The one with a pig on the counter?'

'Aye. Me room's at the back and upstairs. It's not my home,' she said, jerking her chin with defiant pride. 'I've me own good house, but I keep this little room for entertaining.'

He nodded. 'So they sell flesh down below while you sell flesh up above?'

She ignored the question, judged it to be rhetorical. 'Henry Skipton,' she muttered, concealing the words from a courting couple who had just passed by. 'From a face as grey as yours, I would guess that you have taken spirits into an empty stomach. Either you eat, or you heave the lining of your gut down some bloody street grid with the world and his wife looking on. Such a tale would go down well with tomorrow morning's porridge and fried eggs.' She grabbed his arm, pulled him along like a child who was late home from school. 'You will come with me, and no nonsense, for I can manage a man twice your size with one hand tied behind me skirts.' She breathed more easily now. He had obviously not heard about her own recent indiscretion, the performance which had supposedly sent her to bed for the foreseeable future. The foreseeable future was a bit much for Pol, so she'd lasted just twelve hours.

She heaved him into Deansgate, content to believe that nothing would come of the Prince William episode. Anyway, whoever was going to be fool enough to believe that she was related to this man? Though he did look fairly ordinary at the moment, clothes wrinkled, shoes splashed with mud, whiskers matted from lack of grooming.

But Pol was feeling rather perplexed as they approached her *pied-à-terre*. Here was a man she disliked, from a family she disliked. And she liked him. Even when she cursed him, she liked him. It was impossible to like somebody if you also disliked him. It was unheard of to dislike somebody if really, deep down, you – oh, the hell with it. She would have to take him inside, dust him down, warm some soup on a gas ring. But what about the other thing she had screamed outside the Prince Will? What if he'd heard that she was calling him Jenny's father? Once he became stronger, he'd likely go for her, whether or not he was whoever's daddy. 'Pol,' she said aloud. 'You may as well hang for the whole sheep.'

'What sheep is that?' His sad eyes stared at her.

'The one next to the pig on a plate,' she answered tersely, nodding towards the butcher's window.

'But there was no—' He was cut off, manhandled up a fire escape to a door at first floor level.

The room was red, shining with oil-based paint that failed to conceal the cracks of ages running down walls. On a scarlet-covered bed, black silk undergarments lay in a tumbled heap. A single bare lamp hung from twisted flex, its roots embedded in a circular mirror on the ceiling. He was in a whorehouse. No, he was in the den of just one whore.

She bent down, and he heard the pop of igniting gas. 'We'll warm you up,' she said. He was not cold. The fire struggled in its casing of honeycombed refractories, the flames blue and weak. She had moved to a gas ring in the corner, was warming soup, cutting bread on a tiny table covered with thin oilcloth of blue-and-white check. .

There was no seating except for a low stool, its cushion of maroon plush stained by spillages Henry would not have cared to identify. Slowly, he bent and picked up the lingerie, placed it on the stool. His mind had stopped again, had gone on strike. The bed was comfortable, as soft as a mother's breast. He stretched out, amazed to discover how near to sleep he was. His last thoughts were not of Jenny, but of Pol. He was safe, she would look after him. Like the bed, she was as soft as a mother's . . .

Pol sat on the stool by the bed, listening first to Henry's steady breathing, then to his ramblings. At the start, he made little sense, just a few disjointed words and names. Carla Sloane got a mention, as did Jenny and somebody called Sam who was looking for masks.

She kept a long vigil, sometimes nodding, almost falling from her unsupportive seat, but she would not lie down with him. The man who was her cousin, the man she admired in spite of grim resolve, was too dignified to wake beside a lady of the night. He was troubled. She held the nearest twitching hand.

He was not drunk; this assessment was achieved quite quickly, as Pol was used to dealing with every stage of inebriation, from the pleasantly jolly to the totally paralysed. Henry had been drinking, but his trouble was exhaustion and lack of fuel. He had literally run out of steam. And he was talking in his sleep again, stringing phrases together, baring his soul in a room that had heard many a sad tale. And this, thought Pol, was the saddest of them all.

When he turned away and entered a peaceful phase, Pol walked to the tiny slit of window and glared out on an unkind world. He was not Jenny's father; those who communicated during sleep made poor liars. He loved little Jenny Crawley. Pol's eyes pricked. 'Forgive me, Mammy,' she whispered. 'But I must do my best now for the House of Skipton. This fellow is in a sore and desperate mess.'

She swivelled. His face had twisted again, looked crushed beneath a terrible weight of anxiety. With a feeling of great pity that was trimmed with a strange anger, she shook him to wakefulness. 'Let the cow divorce you,' she snarled. 'Come on, man, we shall drink some soup together. Don't worry about Jenny, for it will all come out in the laundry.'

He sat up, a hand to his brow, his faculties returning swiftly. 'Did I talk?'

'Yes.'

'Nonsense? I tend to talk nonsense in my sleep when the business is in difficulty—'

'Away with your bother.' She brandished a wooden spoon in the air. A second wooden spoon, inverted, waved in the mirror above the bed. 'That was the truth you spoke just now.'

He dropped his head, studied the mud on his shoes. 'What did I say?'

'Enough.' She poured the soup into thick, cracked mugs, pushed one of the steaming beakers under his nose. 'Drink,' she commanded.

He obeyed. After four swallows of the comforting liquid, he ventured, 'I'm in a pickle, and I'd be grateful if you'd—'

'Keep quiet?' She pointed to the door. 'Out there, I'll keep me gob shut. In here, in a place where I pay the rent, I'll say my piece. Jenny is named?'

He nodded.

'Unfairly, of course.' Her hand was in its customary place now, on an ample hip. 'You will ride this tide, Henry. Be it spring or neap, you will not drown. Will you take some soda bread?'

He nodded, sank his teeth into the proffered shive. He had never tasted better bread, was shocked by his hunger. How could he eat while the world rocked and shook, while

Jenny slept in sweet and blissful ignorance? He swallowed, drew a hand across his mouth. 'You're a good woman,' he said gruffly.

She sashayed up and down in the narrow space beside the bed. 'And you're in trouble, sunshine,' she said calmly. 'Different trouble from the sort I tried to bring for you, but a nasty mess all the same. I thought . . . I thought that Jenny Crawley was your love-child. I even wanted her to be yours, so that she would fight for her rights.' Kathleen O'Gorman had never fought. Kathleen O'Gorman's daughter should go into battle, yet she didn't want to . . . 'But you love her. Not as a daughter, as a woman. When a man's as tired as you are, he speaks no lie.'

Henry's flesh began to crawl. Drinking had never been the answer, certainly not for him. And now, it seemed, he had spilled enough beans to make a feast, and into such an inappropriate ear. Metaphors were silly things. Here he lay, shabby and miserable, thinking about ears and beans. 'Dan's her father,' he managed at last. 'Whatever else I have said while I've been here – please forget it.'

'No, I will not.'

He moved his aching head until he could see her. 'For pity's sake—'

'It isn't pity you're wanting, Henry Skipton. It's a bit of brainpower and some backbone, for God's sake. Are ye just going to lie there like a sack of praties waiting to be peeled for the pot? Dear God in heaven and all the saints, is it a coward we have here?'

His head swam. The picture rail was crooked; the building had subsided at some time. He was noticing irrelevancies, pinning thoughts on the edge of the map, never daring to home in on poor Jenny.

'I'm no coward,' he said eventually. 'And I'm no hero either.'

She sauntered over and sat on the edge of the bed. 'Are you afraid of gossip?'

'No.'

'Would a divorce damage your business?'

He wished with all his heart that she would keep still. Or

go away altogether. 'Initially it might. Long-term, not likely.' She was clicking her tongue, shaking her head.

'In future, don't drink on an empty stomach, for such behaviour addles the brain. Yes, you talked in your stupor and yes, I heard how you feel about Jenny and I know her name's on that paper. Well, you are going to walk tall, Henry Skipton, and I'll walk alongside. Where's Jenny's daddy?'

'Blackpool. Pneumonia. Keep still.'

'I've never moved in ages, it's your balance that's affected, not mine. Now, Jenny's father asked you to look after her during his absence. And you took a paternal interest while her father was away. Doesn't that sound good to you?'

'They won't listen. Nobody'll listen.'

Pol smiled. 'They will if your real mistress turns up. And if your real mistress has the sort of reputation that could curdle milk. Name me. I've nothing to lose. But perhaps your wife might be upset. After all, if you turned from her and chose someone as common as me—'

'Miss O'Gorman—'

'Pol,' she snapped. 'You call me Pol. And I've a notion brewing here in me brain . . .'

Henry swallowed painfully. He didn't want to hear anything about brewing or distilling ever again in his whole life.

'We'll all come in it. That's the job, that's the way to play it. We'll go along to your lawyer fellow, the whole bloody gang of us.'

'To my solicitor? But—?'

'Aye, we'll get all the girls' names on your list. You tell that wife of yours that you slept with every one of us.'

He blinked. The surface of his eyes felt like coarse sandpaper. 'Girls?'

She smiled. 'Working girls. Streetwomen. Sure, the whole town will see it for the tomfoolery it really is. Not that it'll ever get that far.'

'How many . . . working girls?'

Pol shrugged. 'Twenty or so.'

He clutched at the edge of the bed as if it were a life raft.

The sea was becoming stormier. What would he want with twenty women on paper? Or anywhere else, come to that?

'And each and every one of us will sign to say that you committed adultery with us all on the same day.'

A few beats of time crashed through his aching mind. 'But that's preposterous.'

'Exactly. Isn't it wonderful? If you ever do get to court, you'll be laughed out. The whole thing will be desperate and hilarious, sure you'll even get in the Sunday papers.'

'And you'll be done for prostitution – or perjury.'

'Away with your bother, for you never paid one of us. Perhaps we paid you?' She was doubled over now, laughing at the tragic fun of it.

Henry groaned. 'Well, I've heard of a *ménage à trois*, but a *ménage à vingt*'s a bit of a tall order.'

Pol stopped laughing. 'Listen, isn't it stupid to say that you committed adultery with that child? So why shouldn't we repay like with like? Your wife will drop the charge when she gets your confession. No way would she weather the mortal shame of a husband who acts like a stallion.'

'I don't know. I can't think, I need to be awake.'

She placed a card in his hand. 'When your brain stops being papier mâché, take a look at that, why don't you? There ye are, Miss Pol O'Gorman, dealer in fine antiques. The address is on there too. I'll wait to hear from you.'

'Right.' He rolled over towards the wall and away from the light. 'Thanks,' he muttered. Within seconds, he was fast asleep.

She gathered up her bag and stood in the doorway staring at him. So here was a situation that demonstrated why folk called the Irish daft, she thought. This man's uncle was her father. This man's uncle had ruined Pol's mother's life. But Henry was kin, even though he wasn't aware of it. So, like a true Western Irelander, she guarded her own. Duty didn't come into it, reason was not a part of it.

No. She was simply looking after her cousin. But all the same, she was daft.

Jenny shook the kitchen tablecloth outside the back door.

It was four o'clock, time to be shaping for the evening meals. She walked inside, spread the cloth on the table, picked up Mrs Skipton's afternoon tea tray. Since being expelled from the sickroom, she had carried the trays up daily, but had left them on the half-moon table for Sara Browne to collect.

She didn't like Sara Browne, didn't trust her. But, as she told herself often, that might have come about because the nurse had taken the job. However, there was something about the woman's eyes, as if she were greedy and out for herself. 'I'll take the tea up now, Mrs Hardman.'

'Good lass.' Minnie Hardman glanced at the clock. 'I wonder if he'll come home today? I've never known the master to stop out all night like that, not without some sort of message. I telephoned to the mill, and they said he came in late this morning. He must have gone to work without a clean shirt. Men. All the same, all children. I bet he was playing cards or something.' She looked at Jenny. Jenny was plainly worried by Mr Skipton's absence. 'Get yourself out for one of them walks. No use getting all wore out at your age—'

'But there's the vegetables.'

The cook grimaced. 'Aye, and let Briony help the daily with them. She's been doing her courting behind the stables, thought I hadn't noticed. She's supposed to be steeping sheets in the wash house, but she'd rather play with fire in the yard than with cold water in the shed. Time I rapped yon lady's knuckles for her.'

Jenny hummed to herself as she carried the tray upstairs. Briony's Mick was haunting the place, hanging about like a bad smell, according to Mrs Hardman. Well, good luck to Briony, thought Jenny. Marriage was all the girl wanted, and it looked as if her wish would be granted any day now.

On the landing, the humming stopped. Where was Mr Skipton and was he all right? When the tray was in its proper place, Jenny turned to walk downstairs. There was a bit of what Auntie Mavis used to call a kerfuffle going on, the main ingredient of which was Howie Bennett's raised voice. Again, Jenny smiled, pushed back the worry about the master. Howie, during Dan's absence, was working *in loco*, and this sudden though temporary elevation in status had gone to his head, so he shouted a lot.

'Yer can't go up there,' he was yelling. 'My guts'll be holding somebody's socks up by bedtime if you go marching through th' house like an 'erd of elephants.'

'I'll have you know I'm no elephant.' Was that Maria's voice? 'And take your hand off my arm, Howie Bennett. I'm a married woman now and entitled to some respect. If you want a holiday, I'll book you one. In traction down the infirmary.'

Jenny ran to the banisters. 'Maria!' she shouted. 'What are you doing here?'

'Being assaulted by laughing boy.' She turned to the offending stable lad. 'Go and muck something out. The mistress wants me to visit her – Jenny told me. And this is Lucy what worked here before, so she's a visitor too.'

Howie shrank away nursing his arm, a recipient of one of Maria's famous pinches.

'She'll not see you,' said Jenny, her eyes fixed to the white-faced girl who accompanied Maria. She looked terrified. Her large and vitreous blue eyes were fixed like a doll's, and even from this distance, Jenny could make out drops of sweat on the upper lip. 'It's not a good idea.' Jenny was determined to save her friend from embarrassment. 'She doesn't let anybody in any more, only doctors and the like.'

Maria patted her fringe to make sure that it was flat. 'We're going in,' she said. 'We're going in as company, like proper ladies paying a call. And don't try and stop me, Jenny Crawley, and don't ask me no questions.' She dragged Lucy along the landing, knocked on the mistress's door, then flung it wide. After stepping inside, she emerged again, pushed Lucy into the room, followed her through and slammed the door.

Jenny closed her mouth. Was the world going completely insane, and was she the daftest of the lot? Had she imagined the scene, was Mrs Skipton in her room alone, or with Sara Browne? As if Jenny's thoughts had resulted in some kind of manifestation, Sara Browne materialized and drifted across to her own room. Jenny, totally routed, sat on the top stair. And to crown it all, the tea was going cold on the half-moon table. Again, as if obeying Jenny's magic, the door opened and Maria came out. 'Just getting the tray,' she announced, managing to sound like a full-time maid again.

Jenny shook her head to clear it. Well, she would sit on the stairs till Christmas if necessary. There was something going on, and she would get to the bottom of it.

In Eloise Skipton's room, Maria watched, fascinated, while the face in the bed changed colour. This was a sick woman, so things should really proceed at a decent pace. But Maria, being Maria, simply waded in. She jerked a double-jointed thumb in Lucy's direction. 'You told her to get in bed with the master,' she stated without preamble. 'For three hundred pounds, you said. Well, I'm worried in case you're lining up the same game for Jenny.'

Eloise shivered in spite of the heat. 'I don't know what you're talking about,' she whispered.

'Tell her.' Maria prodded Lucy on the arm. 'And let her know we've a pretty good idea where Lizzie is too.'

'Lizzie?' The voice from the pillow was very unsteady.

'That's right, missus. Lizzie Calder, brownish-red hair, green eyes, worked here before Lucy did. We've heard that she buggered off in a blinking fit too, just disappeared back to town. Well, she works at the ropewalk, so we can easy find her, unless she's tied up, of course.' Maria pulled a wry face. Even now, with her temper up, she couldn't resist a feeble joke.

Eloise tried to smile. 'This must be some sort of mistake. So kind of you to visit me, but I'm no longer well enough for company You'll have to go, it's almost time for my massage.'

Maria sauntered round the room. 'We'll go when we're ready, queen. See, we've got you where we want you. The more you struggle, the more I'll find out.' She picked up a valuable figurine, blew on it to remove some imaginary dust, then replaced it. 'I'll search all Lancashire if needs be. Everybody you tried to bribe will come and visit you.

Isn't that a lovely idea? I bet we could fill the house with folk you've used.'

Eloise took in as much oxygen as her failing chest would accept. 'How can you do this to a sick woman? How can you make me suffer when I am so near to death? The shock could kill me. This room is supposed to be my refuge . . .'

Maria grabbed Lucy by the arm. 'Tell her. Let it come from the horse's mouth.'

Lucy blanched even further. 'I don't need to tell her, do I? She did it, so there's no point me telling her what she did.' Eloise was plainly frightened, and her fear emboldened the timid girl. 'You even gave me the nightie,' she said, her voice strengthening with every syllable. 'And you said my name wouldn't be used. Only I'm not as daft as you thought, eh? So I scarpered. Anyway.' She swallowed audibly. 'We'll go to the police if you do it to anybody else. Won't we, Maria?'

Maria's responding laugh was hollow. 'Police? No, we'll go to me dad. You've never met me dad, have you, Mrs Skipton?'

The lips tightened. 'No, I have not had that pleasure.'

'Pleasure? It's no pleasure. He's as sound as a pound till something gets on his nerves. Like people taking advantage of young girls what haven't a penny to their names. Times like that, he goes a bit wild, has a drink, then starts rampaging. It'd take a bit more than Howie Bennett to keep our owld feller away from your throat, Mrs S. Ooh, no. You don't want to be having me dad up here. Makes the police look like a boy scouts' picnic, me dad.'

Eloise forced herself to look into the girl's pale eyes. 'Are you threatening me?'

'Yes. I'm sorry – did I not make meself plain? Course I'm threatening – why else would I be here in me Sunday frock and second best stockings? Listen, first off, we've to see Mr Skipton, 'cos we're going to tell him anyway. It's time he knew your tricks, lady. Shall I pour your tea? Milk or lemon?'

Eloise, who looked as if she might just have a seizure at any minute, gripped the satin border on her sheet. 'Look, girls, this is a terrible misunderstanding.' She stared at their grim and immobile faces and knew that the game was up, that she had lost. This Maria person was so vigorous. Was she also needy? Needy and greedy? 'We can perhaps come to some arrangement about it. Would you like a little house, a place of your own?' She waited for a suitable length of time to elapse, time for them to calculate. 'Or a hundred pounds each, then another hundred at Christmas? There's no need to be silly. And no, I do not wish to take tea.'

Maria strode to the bed, dragging Lucy Turnbull with her. 'Listen, Lady Muck And Treacle, you can't bribe me. I know I'm not what you might call well bred, but I'm decent. So is she.' Maria prodded her companion with a none too gentle finger. 'Watch my lips, Lois. You hurt Jenny and you'll wish you'd never been born.'

Eloise gulped in a fashion that fell a long way short of ladylike. Panic swelled within the confines of a chest that was nearing paralysis. 'Don't tell my husband. Please don't—'

'Shurrup!' yelled Maria. 'He's our insurance policy.' She turned to Lucy. 'Right, I think that concludes our business for today. After you, old thing.' She followed Lucy to the door, then turned, a brilliant smile widening the thin face. 'Thank you for your hospitality, Mrs Skipton. We shall return the favour, of course. Feel free to call at any time. My card is in the receiving salver in the hall. Good day to you.'

Out on the landing, both girls collapsed against the wall. 'Jesus,' breathed Lucy. 'Did you see the sparks coming out of her eyes? If looks could kill, we'd be six feet under.'

'Well, they can't kill,' said Maria, the words emerging from a corner of her mouth. 'Stand up, shut up and leave this one to me, it'll need fancy footwork.'

Jenny arrived from the stairway. 'What did she say? How did you go on and why did you do it?'

Maria grinned in that disarming way she had developed during childhood. She had been a very small, thin girl in a very big, wide world, so her survival skills were well developed. 'We dared one another,' she said. 'I met Lucy in a café, and she told me she'd worked here too. So I said, "I'm game if you are", and here we stand, alive but only just.'

'Is she well? Is the mistress all right?'

Maria's face clouded just for a moment. 'She'll never be all right, Jen.'

Lucy, who had caught the double meaning, nodded. 'She's not getting any better.'

Maria took Jenny's arm. 'Come on, love. Let's see if there's a kettle on.' They walked through the house and into the kitchen, all talking and laughing, interrupting, tripping over each other's words. If Jenny had looked and listened closely, she might have noticed that Maria's gaiety was hollow, but she was too excited to pay close attention. Visitors were a rarity, and she intended to enjoy them to the full.

At the kitchen table, Maria buried her face in the pint mug of tea. The worst was yet to come. The worst would be telling the master.

The clock ticked. It was a large, loud clock, one Jenny had grown used to, because it provided a metronome for her dusting whenever she cleaned the library. The timepiece was usually her only audible company, but now she had no tin of polish in her hand, no feathered stick for reaching high shelves. This time, she was not alone and she was not working. Still, the worst was over. He'd said what he'd needed to say, while she, strangely, had remained almost untouched by any of it. Perhaps she was growing old; perhaps nothing would surprise her again.

'I am very sorry, Jenny. This has been a humiliating experience for both of us, but you are the completely innocent victim.'

She continued to stare through the window. 'It's not your fault.'

'I'm the one she's trying to hurt.'

A blackbird sat on the sundial, rubbing its yellow beak against curved metal. He was probably sharpening it, she thought. Did they fight, blackbirds? Was he arming himself against an aggressor? 'Do you want me to leave,

Mr Skipton?' After all, if she stayed, she would be, for him, a constant reminder of a grim time, a time that had been bad enough to make him stay away for a whole night.

He paused for a moment. 'No. I want you to do as you please. And . . . I like having you here.'

The bird flew off towards the woods, towards the foxes. If she left this house, she would see little countryside. 'I've never done what I've wanted to do.' She swung round slowly and looked at him. 'I've never known what I've wanted.'

'That sounds very sad. Surely, all young people have dreams? There must have been something?'

She thought about it. There had never been any choices, not with Auntie Mavis, school, mill, do as you're told and ask no questions, expect no favours. 'A father and a mother would have been nice.'

He coughed, drew a handkerchief from his pocket. Looking at her caused him pain. Pain and not a little guilt. He should have found out years ago what Eloise had been up to. He should have protected Jenny. 'You have a father.'

'You need a father when you're little. He was there all along, but he was Uncle Dan. I never told Uncle Dan how strange Auntie Mavis was becoming. She'd always been a bit odd, but she definitely got worse. I might have told a father.' She was sounding sorry for herself, and she hadn't intended that. 'Who's going to look after the missus now?' He had dismissed Sara Browne at lunchtime. 'She'll have to have somebody, sir. It's getting so bad, she can hardly get out of bed.'

'Mrs Hardman's been keeping an eye upstairs.'

'Mrs Hardman is the cook.' She spoke slowly, as if addressing a child. 'I'll do it.'

He jumped to his feet. 'You can't! That's preposterous.'

Jenny folded her arms. 'Sir, I don't intend any rudeness, but there's no use getting all excited about it. You'd be better with somebody who knows her, somebody who can keep one step ahead. I'm not frightened of her, and I'm not angry. She can't help half the things she does, and she'll get no second chance with me, will she? I'll be keeping me head well away from the block.'

'No.' He spread his hands on the table, dropping his head so low that he could see himself in the glassy, polished surface. 'Jenny, I can't send you back into that hell hole. What else will she try? I don't want you hurt again.'

'I'm not hurt. And she can only offer me three hundred pounds, like she did with Lucy. And why didn't Maria tell me the proper reason for coming up yesterday? Why did she lie to me?'

He lifted his head. 'It was my place to inform you, Jenny. Maria's a sensible girl and she didn't want to frighten you.'

Jenny dropped on to the window seat. 'The missus begged me to look after you, said she loved you. Then she must have put some ideas in Sara Browne's head. Huh. You and me? Whoever would believe that, sir? I don't know how she expected to get away with it. Just shows how ill she must be.'

He looked at her long and hard, wishing with all his heart that it could be possible. He found a part of himself that would have been happier if Eloise's vile plan had worked. This girl was worth more than mills, more than cash in the bank. 'You're a very beautiful young woman, Jenny.'

Her cheeks were glowing, she could feel the heat radiating out of her face. Could he see it too? She moved her head so that she presented him with her profile. Well, he could only see half of her blush now. 'You've been good to me, Mr Skipton. I . . . I trust you. I like you. It's not been master and servant, not since we found Charlie.'

'We've been friends,' he whispered.

'Yes, that's right.'

'Jenny, I . . .' No, he must not say it, must never tell her of his love. Was it love? Or only lust trimmed with loneliness? 'Let me do something for you, Jenny. There must be something you would like. New clothes, shoes – anything.'

She studied the window. There was a smear at one edge where the wash leather had missed its mark. She would

382

give it the once over later on. He was asking her what she wanted. He was telling her that she was beautiful. Perhaps she could make something happen, then. Not for herself, though. All she needed was here, or just outside in the fields, in the woods. 'I want a shop,' she heard herself say. 'It's on the corner of Bridgeman Place and Manchester Road.'

'I see,' he answered.

With her face cooling, she turned towards him. 'It's not for me, not really, but I want to make it happen. For Maria. A café with tables and chairs and a counter for her printing. I've no idea of what she'll do with it – Maria will have the answers.'

'Jenny, what about yourself?'

'I don't need anything. Anyway, I'm a company director, except there's no company yet. One day, Maria will make me rich.' She grinned hugely. 'She's decided. And when Maria makes her mind up, it's no use digging your heels in.'

He leaned against the edge of the table. 'Lucy – the one who came here with Maria the other day . . .' If only he'd been a fly on the wall during Maria's gladitorial display . . . 'Lucy works for Georgie Burrows – I used to be at school with him. If I'm not mistaken, he holds a lease on that corner premises.'

Jenny suddenly remembered something Lucy had said in the kitchen. 'Is he a criminal?' she asked.

'What? Georgie Burrows? No, he owns restaurants.'

'Mr Skipton, you can own restaurants and still be a criminal.'

Yes, it was love. Yes, he did love this sweet girl. 'He's going to be the sauce king of England,' he said.

Jenny scratched her chin. 'Why does he hide stuff upstairs, then?'

'Secret recipes and secret brewings. His name will be on every table in the land soon. I'll talk to him, see if I can get the shop. Is that all you want?'

'Yes.'

He stared at her for a second or two, then went out to the phone in his study. She followed and stood at the door that joined the two rooms. 'She's got a phone. Mrs Skipton, I mean. She listens to you and she phones shops, I think.'

'Thank you, Jenny.'

While he made the call, she wandered back to the window seat. He looked at her in a certain way, did Mr Skipton. The expression on his face was one she'd seen before. On Anthony's face. It was the sort of thing that made her uncomfortable sometimes, though she was learning to ignore it. At least, she ignored Anthony. But she couldn't ignore her boss, couldn't tell him not to be so soft.

'I've spoken to my solicitor, Jenny. He'll contact Georgie Burrows.'

'Thank you.' Briefly, she wondered what else she might have demanded from this man. Then she remembered, thought back to her first encounter with Eloise Skipton. 'Find a man and get out,' the woman had said. So this was the power, this was what she was supposed to use. Her prettiness, her acceptability, her body.

'You have taken this very well, Jenny,' he said. 'Your cool-headedness is remarkable.'

She wanted to tell him that she hadn't felt calm, that her original urge had been to run upstairs and scream at the mistress. But she kept quiet. In the future, Henry Skipton's good opinion of her might be valuable. So she simply smiled and left the room.

Upstairs, in the room next to Mrs Skipton's, she studied herself in the mirror, looking at the face as if it belonged to somebody else. As faces went, it was all right, she supposed. Everything was about the correct size and more or less the right shape. And it had to be her fortune, because she owned nothing else.

She released the cascade of hair that had been trying, for several hours, to escape from the knot into which it had been unwillingly forced. It fell about her shoulders, lent a frame to her features. Somewhat begrudgingly, she admitted that she was beautiful. This situation might last for another ten, fifteen years. By then, she would have used her appearance to . . . to what end? To get a man, to be rich, to have clothes and jewels?

'No,' she said aloud to the serious picture in the glass. 'Use it to be happy. And to help Maria.' Mr Skipton and Anthony each looked at her in that special way. She therefore had purchasing power. The worst part of it all was that Eloise Skipton had been right. All along, the woman had been right.

No, that wasn't true. This was nothing to do with trade, was not about swapping favours for a man's money, for security. A sob caught in her throat. She loved him. Jenny Crawley loved Henry Skipton.

Chapter Fifteen

IT WAS BECOMING DIFFICULT TO IMAGINE WINTER. THIS time last year, Jenny had never seen this place, had not imagined that a setting could be so idyllic. She simply loved country life and could not bear the thought of parting from any of it. Every hour of the day was special to her, because each phase brought its own very individual beauty, its own points of interest. So, when she had spare moments, she wondered about winter and autumn, and about larger changes to her world.

And it was her world, all of it. It belonged to everybody, but most especially to those who cared to notice and enjoy. Jenny was one of them, one of the watchers. In the mornings, she would stare at the moors still sleeping beneath their misty blankets, would watch them wakening, each square of green seeming to open its lustrous eyes as low cloud drifted away into the maw of a hungry sun.

The afternoons were bright and hot, filled by the lazy drone of fat bees and, occasionally, by the anxious buzz of a dragonfly searching for still water. Birds were slower, less worried now with nests emptied, young flown into their own hiding places. The Skipton horses swished tails and fed unenthusiastically, large teeth skimming over sweet green shoots. The grass would be here tomorrow, so there was no hurry.

Evensong was a moveable feast, prompted by the sun's behaviour, but it always happened. The choristers would preen in a tree, preen and call, preen and call. When mates were gathered in, one lone blackbird would sing the final anthem, his pure tone carried through a flawless sky as if to thank the Maker of the day. Thus it ended, only to begin again with the owls. She had heard them, but had never seen one. At some stage, she would stay up all night just to see an owl.

She stood at the window of her room, her eyes fixed on the horizon where a last rim of sun peeped shyly over the earth's edge. The sky was stained blood-red at its lowest, then washed with paler hues overhead, pinks, oranges, blues, even some greens. Tomorrow would be fine again. Dreadful, but fine. It was the dreadful bit that she sought to eliminate, and she knew that her efforts might well alter her life completely. Probably not for the better.

She went into the next room and lifted the cup from a withered hand. It was a special cup now, of thick, ugly, plain white pottery with a spout sticking out of its belly. Eloise Skipton could no longer take advantage of the fine china she had collected. The expensive new wheelchair sat permanently in the hall cupboard, its owner too weak and weary to remain upright on the padded seat. The doctor had visited several times, had pronounced to Jenny that the remission was over. This, it seemed, was an attack of the disease, and the end result was not a calculable equation. The patient might come out of it completely paralysed, or as well as she had been before. It was in the lap of the gods, and the gods did not seem to be on Mrs Skipton's side.

'Have you had enough, miss?'

'Yes.' Her voice, quiet, low, devoid of breath, still seemed to contain strong emotion – even hatred at times.

Jenny gazed down at the face of this woman. It was like a skull, just bone with no flesh or muscle beneath the skin. Her eyes were huge now, twin smouldering orbs of ashy grey set in wide, circular craters. It was a death's head, and Jenny was condemned to spend a part of each day in its company. Fiercely, she fought against her own revulsion and fear. This was a woman, and she would be treated as such for as long as she remained conscious. 'Do you need the bedpan?'

The eyes closed. Jenny knew how much it hurt, this terrible dependence, the close contact that was necessitated by such dire and needful weakness. She had done her best to be discreet, covering the bedpan with a cloth as soon as it had been used, carrying on a one-sided conversation about the wonders of the countryside while cleaning the poor woman's most private body parts. 'I am so sorry, miss. You'll get better. I'm sure you'll get well enough for the bathroom soon.'

'Jenny?'

'Yes?'

'Even . . . after what I did . . . to you . . . you still . . .'

'Save your breath. Yes, I still care about you. Whatever's wrong between you and the master must have got you down. It was nowt – I mean nothing – to do with me. I was just in the wrong place at the wrong time. Nobody holds anything against you.'

'He does.' A tear made its way along a cheek that was grey and haggard, the cheek of an eighty-year-old.

'No, he's not like that.' That was a real tear, Jenny thought. It was all the more touching because it was isolated, not accompanied and swallowed up by a manu-factured flood.

'He is. You don't know. All . . . all these years. Against me.'

'Please don't cry. You're not strong enough to cry.'

'Jenny, don't leave me. Don't . . . ever.'

'Stop your worrying, miss, 'cos I'm going nowhere. There's nobody else'll have me, because I'm a Jill of all trades. I can light fires, polish a bit, nurse a bit and cook a bit. But I can't do anything proper.'

'Properly.'

'Right. Now, I'm going for a bite of supper. If you want me, pull your cord and the bell will ring in the kitchen. All right? Or do you want a yellow pill?' The yellow pills were for when she panicked. With her breathing already impaired, a panic attack was becoming an unpleasant business.

'No. I want to be awake.'

Jenny straightened the bed covers and walked out to the landing. But instead of going towards the stairs, she walked past the master bathroom and stood outside Mr Skipton's room. She put her ear to the door, heard him moving about. Tentatively, she tapped.

'Who is it?'

'Jenny, sir.'

There was a short pause. 'Come in,' he called.

She opened the door. This room was new territory for her, and her natural inquisitiveness guided her eyes around the large area. It was very masculine, with big, dark wardrobes and an old-fashioned washstand with a marble top. There were three pictures, all of horses, and some brasses on straps over the mantelpiece. The bed was huge, a four-poster with tall corners but no curtains.

'What is it, Jenny?' he asked.

She leaned against the door after closing it firmly. 'I didn't want anybody except you to hear what I've got to say. Downstairs, you never know when Briony's going to appear, or one of the dailies. Nobody comes in here. Well, Briony cleans it, but not at this time of day.'

He sat on a stool, leaning one elbow on the washstand. 'Would you like to sit down?'

'No.'

He tapped a finger on the grey-streaked marble surface. 'Out with it, Jenny.'

She inhaled deeply. 'Look, I know it's none of my business, and you can throw me out if you like, but something's got to be done.'

A few seconds ticked by. 'About my wife.' This was not a question.

'Yes. I think you should send to London for an expert, somebody that knows about this multiple sclerosis. She's going down and down, and your doctor hasn't a clue about it.'

'Jenny, nobody knows about multiple sclerosis.'

'And nobody cares, either. She's shut in there — I bet there's loads of them, hundreds of them shut in places. What folk can't see, folk can't worry over. Well, I see it, Mr

Skipton. I see it, listen to it and clean up after it. She needs help, she's hardly any feeling left in her whole body.'

'Not much in her heart, either.' He muttered this under his breath, alarmed when he realized that she had heard it.

Jenny, who had always been even-tempered, tried to control her anger, but this time, her trick of breathing deeply had little effect. 'How would you like it, sir? How would you like to lie flat on your back all day with sores on your skin, sores you can't feel some of the time because your body's dying by inches? She's staring at the bloody ceiling, just staring. Even the horses in their stables have more to look at. And she's not an animal, she's not!' Her head bobbed furiously. She had never sworn in the past, but the 'bloody' that had slipped out served to make her even more heated.

He reached out a hand. 'Jenny—'

'No! Don't "Jenny" me, don't come over all nice and friendly. I know I'm only a servant, but I've got feelings the same as anybody else and she's suffering.'

'If it's too much for you, I'll find someone else.' His tone was cool, very controlled.

'It's not about me!' she yelled. 'It's not about me managing or not managing. It's about your wife, Eloise Skipton.' She lifted her chin defiantly. 'I know she's done some funny things in her time, but nobody deserves to be left like this. When I think how you cared about Charlie, how you sat with him, nursed him and saved that dog's life, I can't believe that the same person is . . . is fiddling about here waiting for supper time as if everything's all right in this house.'

He dropped his head in an attitude of deep thought. 'Very well,' he said at last. 'I shall seek yet another medical opinion.'

Jenny bit her lip. She'd already gone too far, so she might as well go for the full sheep. 'So you'll see to her body and to hell with her spirit?'

He raised his face, and the eyes seemed to darken, as if the marked spokes of colour had started to cling together. 'There is nothing I can do for her. You don't understand.'

She strode towards him. 'We did Bible at school, stories from the Testaments. And there was one about a whited sepulchre, Mr Skipton. That's a grave, all polished and clean on the outside, full of rotted flesh underneath. There's folk like that. The story is to warn us not to be like that, all nice on the top, evil in our hearts.'

He stared at her. Anger made her even more lovely. 'Jenny,' he whispered. 'My wife is the whited sepulchre in this house.'

'Is she?' A toe tapped against the rug. 'All right, she tried to make out that I was . . . that you and I were together. That might be part of the illness, something she can't help. I mean, look what it's done to her body. The brain's just another part of the body, so happen it's diseased. Or she may have been angry because you don't see her, won't talk to her, so she was paying you back. She has no power any more. She was a pretty woman, a rich woman too with a lovely house and nice things. Well, she's pretty no more, because this attack has made her old inside a couple of weeks. As for nice things, she's got a bed. That bed is her world.'

He stood up and looked steadily into the furious eyes. 'She tried to ruin you, tried to drag you into a divorce court.'

She tossed her head, as if throwing away such an unimportant detail. 'I would have lived, sir. The divorce court wouldn't have killed me. This is a big country and I'm young and healthy. Compared to your wife, I would still have been in clover.' She backed away from him slowly. 'They say you're a good boss, kind, reasonable, even sympathetic. That's the outside they're seeing. A real man would not treat his wife like this. No matter what she'd said or done.'

'Jenny, are you trying to force me to fire you?'

'No. I'm sticking up for what's right. And I can't leave her. When your bedroom is your whole life, you need somebody who cares whether you live or die. She needs me. She's got no family.' After a slight pause, she added, 'And most of all, she's got no husband.'

He dropped back on to the stool, elbows on the

washstand, hands running through his hair. 'This is hopeless,' he muttered.

'You loved her once.' She remembered her place now that she was calmer, but she did not add a 'sir'. 'How can you turn your back on someone you loved?'

'There is a reason.' His fingers were gripping his hair, holding on tight like a climber on a steep slope.

'There's no reason good enough for this kind of behaviour. A stranger would get better treatment—'

'THERE IS A REASON!' He jumped up and pounded a fist against the back of a nearby chair, sending it crashing to the floor with its spindly legs pointing towards the door. 'A very good reason.'

'So much for coming in here and keeping everything private. You don't need to shout so loud. If you want to advertise, paint it on the front wall.' She turned to walk out.

'Jenny?'

'What?' She did not look at him.

'One day, I'll tell you. After . . . After—'

'After she's dead?' She swivelled now and glared at him. 'It'll be a bit late then, Mr Skipton. And I won't be here. She's my reason for staying.' Her throat contracted involuntarily after this lie. 'When she dies, I leave.' She groped for the door handle.

'I love you,' he whispered.

'I know,' she replied immediately. 'And it doesn't mean anything. You must have loved her once, but it's done her no good. Did you tell her that you loved her? Or did you tell her the truth – that you'd love her as long as she did what you wanted her to do? Love like that's cheap, Mr Skipton. Any beggar can afford your price.' She wrenched the knob, flung the door so wide that it bounced against something in the room, she then fled through the house, a fist clenched against her mouth.

In the kitchen, she sobbed wildly, flinging herself into Briony's shocked arms. It was awful, terrible, she could not stay here. 'I love you,' he had said. 'I know,' she had replied. And the affection she felt for him was deep enough for the wound of disappointment to sear her soul.

He could not admit his mistakes. He could not face that poor, spurned woman.

'Come on, chuck,' said Briony. 'Has she died? Is that it?'

Jenny, still sobbing, shook her head.

'Eeh well, young girls like us shouldn't have to look after people as ill as that one. Jenny, you'd be best off going home. Shall I ask the master to send for Dan? Do you want your dad?'

The head shook again.

'You'll have to toughen up, Jenny. We care about you, me and Mrs Hardman. You can always run to us with your problems. See.' She pushed Jenny into the fireside rocker. 'Shall I run down the lane for Mrs Hardman? She's nobbut a stride away.'

'No,' managed Jenny.

Briony dropped to her hunkers. 'Don't cry. I'll just take Mr Skipton's tray into the study, then I won't be long. Will you be all right on your own for a few minutes? Only I might nip out and see if Mick's come down from the farm. Don't worry, I'll not stop with him long.' With her handkerchief, she mopped Jenny's tears.

'Yes. I'll be fine, stay as long as you like with Mick.' She wanted to be alone, needed to think. She was a bad girl. She loved a married man whose neglected wife was dying of a disease that was too evil to describe. He was good and kind, he was getting the shop for Maria, looking for a cheap printing place too. He was the devil in a good suit. He was a coward and a thief of hearts. He was a man who loved dogs and horses. All these words rattled round her head like marbles in a biscuit tin.

Briony went out with the tray. Jenny heard her own empty stomach complaining of starvation, but she had no need for food. She just wanted things right. Things between him and Eloise. Whatever the woman had done, she should not enter the next life in a loveless state.

Charlie whined at the door. She let him in, noticed feathers in his mouth. He placed the offering in the grate, then sniffed at the blue-black plumage. Jenny bent to the bird. There was not a mark on him, he must have been dead before Charlie found him. The yellow beak was slightly open and a beady, sightless eye stared up at her.

The tears returned. Was this the soloist, the one who saved his best till last every evening? So fragile, so small, all voice and no substance. And now, not even a voice.

Charlie whimpered, touched the bird with a tentative paw.

'You can't bring him back, lad,' she said. 'And you can stop in while I bury him.'

Henry Skipton watched from a window while his wife's nursemaid buried a cigar box. Later, when all was quiet, he came out and looked at the cross, two sticks of firewood bound with sewing cotton. On the wood, she had written, 'Sleep well little singer.' But it was a while before he read it, because his eyes were full of water.

'I don't want to finish up like me mother, that's all. She's like the old woman who lived in a shoe, so many children that she can't be bothered, has to escape in daft books. And other women in Liverpool – here, too – all weighed down with loads of children.'

Anthony smiled. 'Have you told Denis?'

'Course I have, you daft bat. I wouldn't be telling you first, would I?'

'Is he pleased?'

She shrugged sulkily. 'Like a dog with three tails and a beef bone. Oh Ant, I didn't want this, not now, not yet.'

'Anybody would think you were going to hatch thousands. It's only a baby, Maria. Just one small baby.'

She dropped into a chair. 'Things are starting to take off. We're to have that café, me and Lucy. And I've loads of stuff to do, like more printing and sewing. Mr Skipton thought the cheap mill clothes were a good idea, he's starting me off with a pile of free fents.'

Anthony studied his sister. She was pale and seemed to be losing the bit of weight she had gained since marriage. 'You're not frightened, are you?' he asked.

She nodded and sniffed her annoyed sniff. 'Not of giving birth, not that. It's afterwards that bothers me. Babies might be small, but they're big thieves of time. I can't feed a baby and print at the same time, can't sew with one hand and change a nappy with the other. I know it's awful, but I don't want this baby.'

'But you can't—'

'I know, I went to school, thou shalt not kill. Anyway, they always make a mess of you, abortionists. I'm having no bugger prodding me with a knitting needle and I'm not taking to the gin, either. But I feel so . . . like lonely. Lonely and disappointed.'

Anthony crossed the room and sat on the rug at her feet. 'We're already overcrowded,' he said. 'Me sleeping downstairs isn't doing you any good. It'll be worse when the baby comes. I'll move out and make space.'

She stroked his hair. 'I couldn't say any of this to Denis. He'd never understand, 'cos he loves kids. When there's a fire and he pulls a child out safe, he grins so much he nearly swallows his ears. Anthony, all I want is a business, something that's going to keep me out of the gutter where me mam lives. I've never thought about babies, never wanted one. I had a sickener at home with that lot. Never once did I play with a doll. I hated dolls. I was glad that there was no money to buy me one of my own.'

He dropped his head into her lap. 'We'll manage, queen,' he whispered. 'I'm here some of the day, and Denis works staggered hours.'

'Staggered's right,' she answered. 'He's tired right through to the bone when he comes in. The fact is, he's more exhausted when there's been no fires. Playing darts at the depot with his mates makes him fed up. He'll not be much use.'

'Maria, stop worrying.'

She rubbed fiercely at the end of her nose. She usually did that when near to tears. 'The fight's going out of me,' she muttered. 'I'm different, I feel strange, out of step with meself. Anyway, I can't see me working in a café with a hundredweight of coal under me skirt. It's already bloody difficult. Hand block-printing means we can only do a bit, and there'll be even less when I'm floating round like a boat with all its sails on show. See, we've got to make money to get into proper printing. And I feel as if somebody's stopped my clock.'

Anthony stood up and walked to the window. 'Have you seen a doctor?'

'Don't need to, there's signs. Remember, I watched Mam breeding like a rabbit year after year. At first, I thought she was fat sometimes, then thin. Every time she got fat, a baby arrived. Later on, I watched her, saw how weary she was. I know she seems calm, but there's a kind of panic behind her eyes when she's pregnant. You'd have to be female to notice it.'

He decided to have a stab at lightening the situation. 'Remember when the midwife came?'

'I do.' She sighed audibly.

'And we all used to sit on the stairs? We knew there was a baby in that black bag, so we tried to trip her up one time, tied a piece of string just inside the door. That way, she would have dropped her black bag and we would have been the first to see the new baby. Only she noticed the string straight away and we never got the bag.'

'And we all went to bed with sore bums. Oh, Anthony.'

'What, love?'

She was crying now. 'What's going to happen to my marriage? I'll not want him near me again, even though I love him. I do love him, Ant. And I want him, I want him close by me all the time. But if we can't . . . you know . . . he'll find some woman that will.'

He ran to her, plucked her from the chair and gathered the thin body to his chest. 'I'll do something, Maria, I'll find something for you. There's sponges and lotions. There's a thing for flushing yourself out afterwards. And never do it halfway through a month, you know what I mean.'

Her crying stopped abruptly. 'How do you know all that, Anthony Hesketh?'

He grinned. 'Man of the world, my dear. I'm a man of the world.'

Pol was throwing a dinner party to celebrate Carla's imminent reception into the one true faith. Pol had reservations about the whole matter. For a start, she was a once-a-year or troubled Catholic, in that apart from making her Easter duties, she saw a priest only when she was worried or in difficulties. She didn't fancy living with a convert, somebody who would drive her to church with a whip, if necessary. They were altogether too keen, those who arrived late at the gates of Rome.

Then again, she wasn't so sure about this single path to God. Everybody who was not Catholic supposedly went to hell, purgatory or limbo. Limbo was on offer as a temporary residence to the souls of the just who had died before Christ (they should all be well gone to glory everlasting by this time) or to good Christian people who had made something called a baptism of desire, which all sounded a bit vague and rather carnal to Pol. Purgatory was where those with little sins went to get their consciences cleansed, a kind of temporary hell. And hell itself didn't bear thinking about, especially if it was anything like the place Father Ryan used to rant about when he'd been at the unconsecrated communion wine. It was an altogether miserable business, religion. It was best left alone or taken in small doses after meals.

Nevertheless, she would go along with Carla, who had been down in the dumps for a while. Apparently, she had to get something simply enormous off her mind and soul before allowing herself to be properly plugged into the faith, and she'd been walking round like a bellyache on two legs.

Imelda and Franklyn were invited. This was a pleasure Pol anticipated with mixed feelings. By ten o'clock, they'd either be killing one another or making love in company, and Pol was prudish when it came to public demonstrations of affection between the sexes. It was a business for the bedroom, all that billing and cooing, not an item to be served up with the gravy and peas. Still, perhaps billing and cooing would be preferable to the throwing around of gravy and peas. Ah, she'd just have to wait and see. That was life, waiting and seeing.

She arranged the good silver, looking over her shoulder before breathing on the odd fork and polishing it on her pinny. Carla would go on about germs, like as not. Well, no germ would dare to encroach on an eighty-piece

Georgian canteen with fancy handles and only one teaspoon missing. The table looked lovely. They were to have melon to start, followed by lamb with just about everything, including the mint she'd grown herself, and she had baked a wonderful chocolate cake for pudding. It would be a culinary triumph. She hoped Carla would smile.

And what about the Jews? she thought suddenly. Did they not get considered for heaven, or were they, after all, the right ones? There'd be one hell of a fracas when their Messiah arrived. The world was big, but there was not the space for too many of these saviours. They were mostly good people, the Jews. Then there were all these Hindus and Muslims and Buddhists – were they all precluded from having a look at God in the end? It was all very silly. There were good and bad members in every religion.

And she knew some bad Catholics who waltzed into church every Sunday, communicated at the altar, genuflected and bobbed about as if they were on elastic. Oh yes, they'd be beating their breasts when the Blessed Sacrament was held aloft. Then they'd spend the rest of the week drowned in booze or battering their wives or stealing. Sometimes all three. But it was quite all right, because they could get their mucky souls laundered, dolly-blued and starched as a job lot come Wednesday evening, just throw the sins through the grille and let the priest drop a bit of Latin on to them. If the one true faith meant that you could do as you liked as long as you told a priest about it, then the one true faith was flawed.

Pol shook herself inwardly. She was becoming morbid about religion just lately – it was probably rubbing off Carla and contaminating the very air they breathed, the two of them. But it was beginning to bother her. Every year, she went to confession and promised to give up her evening trade. Every year she meant it, and every year she went back to the job within a week. She liked it, just as she liked collecting antiques and talking to children. Men were one of her hobbies and all her hobbies paid well. Was she going zealous all of a sudden? Would she finish up with a black missal, a good dark suit and a hump on her back from bending over each day at mass? 'God Almighty save me from such glories,' she muttered aloud.

She hadn't told Carla about her encounter with Henry Skipton. She was embarrassed about the whole thing, felt like a stupid turncoat. The man had been bad-mouthed in this house for so long that it was going to sound ridiculous when she finally said, 'He was ill and I helped him, he's family.' She still didn't understand why she'd done it, so explaining to somebody else was a near impossibility. But he was a good man. She had to admit that the nephew of the Skipton who had fathered her was a nice fellow.

'Pol?'

She placed the candles on the table before turning to look at her friend. 'Ah, so here you are. That print suits you a treat. Didn't I say it would?' Carla looked smart in a cotton dress of green and gold. 'You're a different woman outside and in. It's lovely to see you all dressed up and taking an interest in yourself.'

Carla looked at the table. 'That's splendid,' she said. 'I'm not sure that I deserve it. There's still the old Carla in here.' She touched her breast. 'Converting to Catholicism isn't the full answer, Pol. I still have anger.'

'Don't we all?'

Carla stared blankly at the wall for a moment. 'Yes, I suppose we do. But it rather depends on what you do with your rage. Mine got out of hand more than once. I hated the world and God because of the way I looked. And that ruined other lives.'

Pol sighed heavily. This was supposedly a joyous occasion, and here Carla was, all done up and wonderful, still worrying about something that had happened years ago. 'Will you not tell me about it?'

'No. I have to tell the people I destroyed first.'

Pol straightened a folded napkin, though it had been straight enough in the first place. It just gave her something to do, something to cover her own irritation. If this went on for much longer, she would have to ask Carla to leave. And she didn't want to do that. A bit of company in the house was suiting her so well that she dreaded the thought of living alone again. 'When will you get this thing sorted, Carla? Only it's gone on for so long, I'm sure we're all desperately tired of it. I don't mean to be rude, but it's getting me down. You've a face on you like a month of wet Sundays. Aren't you supposed to be happy now that you're entering the faith?'

'I'm sorry, Pol. It'll all be over in a few days. I've needed to build up my courage, you see. And this is not about happiness, though I'm sure I'll get some comfort from attending church. It's really about strength, you see. I need strength to do what has to be done, and I'm a very weak woman, used to giving in to myself. I need a world of prayer to back me up.'

Pol folded her arms and nodded thoughtfully. 'It's something to do with the Skiptons, isn't it? Look, I've been as bad as yourself, calling them for everything. My mother wasn't the first person to die young because of overwork, and I dare say she won't be the last. But I have learned to forgive myself for my shortcomings. You must do the same. Was your crime so big that you cannot ask for absolution? Did you murder someone, for goodness sake?'

Carla came across the room and put her arms round Pol. 'You are my dearest friend, my only true friend,' she said. 'What I did was just as bad as murder. In some ways, it was worse, because the suffering goes on this very day, has gone on for years. Hold me, Pol. Nobody has held me since I was a child. Even then, I got very short shrift because of my looks. Maude was the favourite, Maude was normal. And here I am, sounding sorry for myself again.'

Pol held on to the stiff body of this suffering woman. 'I'll look after you,' she whispered. 'You've had a raw deal up to now. But please, for my sake, try to enjoy the dinner.'

Carla sniffed back the tears. She hadn't realized how much she had missed physical contact with other humans. 'Oh, I'll enjoy it. After all, we shall be entertained by our visitors. I know it should be the other way round, but the Finnegans are a travelling circus.' She stepped back and dabbed at her eyes with a handkerchief. 'I'll be all right, Pol. Just be here next weekend if you can. That'll be the time when I'll need a shoulder.'

Pol jerked her head in assent. 'I'll go and baste the lamb,' she said. 'Get yourself a sherry and answer the door when they come. And stop worrying.'

Alone in the room, Carla poured a moderate drink for herself and stood at the window. It was another beautiful evening, though little of it showed here, because the sky was punctuated by buildings. She swallowed the sherry in one gulp, straightened her shoulders and waited for the knock at the door. Soon, she would be free of her burden, but the climax was yet to come. Would she have the backbone to go through with it? Would she?

The cat wound itself round her ankles, and she bent to pick him up. He was purring enormously and he smelled rather fishy. Carla had brushed him earlier in the day, and the beautiful coat gleamed with health. 'Had your dinner? I can smell it. No, don't pluck the dress, it's Pol's favourite.' She stroked his head. 'Will I have the courage, Sammy? Will I?'

He mewed, wriggled free and landed with a soft plop on the floor. The eyes were on her, those marvellous all-seeing cat's eyes. He mewed again, twitched his tail, then walked from the room. There was no help, no easy answer. Well, she would get through this day. That was how she was coping, a day at a time. And soon, *the* day would arrive. It would be faced, and squarely, because now there was no hiding place.

Jenny came in smiling. 'The papers are getting done,' she said once the greetings were complete. 'This Burrows is quite happy for you to have the lease, though I suppose Mr Skipton's name will be on it too. Mr Skipton's found a night watchman for the goings on upstairs, some old man from the mill. Mr Burrows is pleased that the building will be safe. He makes sauces, invents them.'

Maria smiled. 'That'll please Lucy. She thought they were storing bombs or poison gas.'

'Why, do the sauces smell so bad?'

'I don't know. She thought they were criminals, but she's a bit on the imaginative side, is Lucy.'

Jenny pondered for a moment. 'She didn't make that up, though. About Mrs Skipton bribing her. It happened to me too, only in a different way. The missus told me to look after him, then she got Sara Browne to follow us and find evidence for a divorce.'

Maria stepped back and placed a hand on the table. 'Bloody hell, is there no end to her? I knew she'd be up to something, I said to Lucy . . . And what the heck are you doing still looking after her? Can't you get away? Mrs Burke says Josie and Anthony can lodge with her – Josie's always there anyway. You could come back here, live with me and Denis.'

Jenny sat down. 'I'll stay till she dies.'

'But—'

'You heard me the first time, love. She's got nobody and she's in a terrible state, half an inch from death's door. I've tackled him, oh yes, I have.' Her head bobbed in time with the words. 'There was nothing to lose, so I barged in head down and . . .' Her voice faded. 'Anyway, it doesn't matter.'

'Jenny?' There was a warning uplift in the second syllable. 'What's on your mind?'

'Nothing.'

'Oh yes?' The thin arms folded themselves across a bosom that scarcely existed. 'And I'm a monkey's auntie. There's something on your mind, Jenny Crawley.'

Jenny shrugged. He was always in her thoughts, that lovely man who was kind to animals, who treated his wife like mud. 'I don't want to talk about it.'

Maria waited for a moment. Jenny's face was set, so it was no use asking any more questions. 'Oh, well talk about this. You're going to be needed. I'm expecting. I can't run everything with a baby on the way, and things'll get worse once she's born. It's got to be a girl. There's girls and there's creatures, and I know which I want. If I'm forced to have one.'

Jenny studied her friend through narrowed eyes, sensing somehow that congratulations were not in order. 'You're not happy, Maria.'

'No. I've never particularly wanted children, but don't tell Denis. He's already worried 'cos I'm a bit quiet. Anyway, the fact is that I can print and sew for a few months, but you and Lucy will have to front the shop. So you've got to leave the queen of the chip shop.'

'I can't.'

'You've left her now. Who's minding her while you're here?'

'Mrs Hardman. It's my half day. And I'm sorry, you'll have to take my name off the directors' list, because I can't pull my weight.'

'You're an investor.' The tone was becoming sharp. 'And if I get a chance, I'll make us rich. You'll be cleaning no bedrooms, Jenny. There'll be maids doing all that for you. Believe me, Maria Hesketh is going to be a big name.'

Jenny looked round the colourful room. It was full of bright cushions and chair covers. A pot of flowers stood in the grate and the curtains were covered in Maria's daisies. Very little of Auntie Mavis remained. Only the dresser looked familiar, and even that was decorated with a daisy runner. 'I don't want to be rich,' she said softly. 'I've never wanted that.' No, all she needed was a country cottage, some animals for company and enough money to feed them and herself. 'It's your dream, not mine.'

Maria placed herself in the opposite chair. 'What is your dream, then? Come on, you must want something.'

Jenny smiled. 'You've asked me that before. There's still my mother. I would like to find her. Apart from that, I just want countryside.'

'Countryside costs.' Maria spread her hands on the table and tapped the long, slender fingers against polished wood. 'There's a house for a start, at least two hundred pounds with a decent garden. Then you'll want your blessed animals, I suppose. We can get you all that. Just come and work with me and Anthony.'

'No.' She smoothed her hair calmly. 'I'm doing what I want, what I think is right. Nobody but me understands her.'

'Huh.' Maria wore a scornful look. 'Why should you understand a bitch like her, a woman who tries to drag everybody down? How can you sympathize with—'

'She's lonely. I know all about loneliness. Look, I'm glad about your baby and sad that you don't want it. That's something else I remember, not being wanted. But I can choose now, Maria. Nobody can tell me what I must do, not any more. You're a very strong person with some wonderful ideas, and I'm sure you will do well. But that's your thing, your dream. If you can't manage the child, I'll look after it up yonder if the master will allow it.'

'I don't want that woman near my daughter!'

'I thought you didn't care about your daughter.'

'Jenny, I wouldn't let a mad dog near the Skipton freak. Not after what she did to you and Lucy.'

They stared at one another for a few moments, Maria realizing that Jenny was, at last, making her own decisions. They might be the wrong ones, but they were her own.

Jenny had her reasons for being quiet, because her thoughts were elsewhere. She was nursing a dying woman whose husband had professed love. And she had not pushed him away hard enough. Perhaps she should leave the house, leave now while her heart was reasonably intact, but Mrs Skipton needed her, allowed Jenny to look after her properly. If another nurse arrived, there would be all that embarrassment again.

The door crashed open and Ena Burke leapt into the room, arms flailing, words sticking in her throat. 'They're inside . . . three of them . . . the empty house . . . can't get out . . .'

Jenny jumped to her feet and put an arm about the large woman's shoulder. 'Mrs Burke, please try to calm down.'

Maria, white-faced, had noted the knell of warning in the neighbour's tone. 'Is it our Josie?' she asked.

'Yes. Hurry up, come on, it's on fire.'

They all ran outside, but Maria was the fastest. A plume of smoke climbed up the sky, thick and purplish-grey. Fire bells clanged along the main road and a crowd had gathered on the pavement opposite the empty house. This place had been strictly out of bounds for all children. Every mother in Daubhill had warned her offspring not to play here. The floors were crumbling, some windows were boarded up, while others still pretended to be windows, though they housed just a few jagged pieces of glass.

Maria ran to the nearest fireman. 'My sister's in there. My little sister . . .'

He pulled her away from the building. 'Look, it's going to collapse any minute. Get across that road with the others.'

She threw back her head and screamed at the top of her not inconsiderable voice, 'Josie! Josie! It's Maria.' With the flat of her hand, she hit the fireman on the cheek as he fought to restrain her. 'I'll tell Denis about you. He's a fireman, my husband. I'll tell him you kept me away from saving my sister.' The words bubbled from her, powered by hysteria and single-minded panic. There was only one thing to do, and that was to save Josie. 'She'll come to me. Take your hands off me, you bugger. I'll kick you, I will.' And she did.

Jenny and Ena Burke arrived on the scene. With the help of two firemen, they managed to drag Maria across the road, though she kicked and spat like an alley cat every inch of the way. A group of women received them, relieving the fireman of their difficult burden. It took six to hold her down, but they managed, though some would be bruised tomorrow.

Suddenly, all was still. A man appeared in a gap that was once an upstairs window. Across his black-sleeved forearms, a limp child was draped. He dropped what looked like a large rag doll into a waiting blanket held by other members of the force, then he straightened and stared across the road. 'Don't worry, Tuppenny Girl,' he shouted. 'She's all right and I'm out next.'

'Denis,' she whispered. She saw that grin on his face, the ridiculous smile he always wore when a little one survived a fire. Again, she tried to break free as Josie was carried away, but the women held her back.

Denis climbed on to the sill and waited for the order to jump. Thick smoke pumped out from behind him, and some stray flames were beginning to lick upwards from the front door. When the blanket was ready to catch him, he steaded himself against the edging of brickwork that had surrounded the window. His knees were bent ready to launch him out when the house exploded. The noise was terrible, like a hundred huge guns all firing at once. Brick, glass and wood flew through the air, some of the debris injuring the crowd across the road. There was little oxygen, because the whole area was filled by choking dust. Within seconds, those with the ability to escape had run away, leaving the bleeding to manage as best they could.

Jenny had a huge shard of glass sticking out of her head, and she removed it with shaking fingers. Her hair had saved her life, though she was not aware of it then. She grabbed Maria, felt the stickiness of blood dripping from somewhere on Maria's face. Ena was just a heap on the floor, something that was not really visible yet. 'Maria? Are you badly hurt?'

No answer came.

'Maria! Talk to me. Are you hurt? Where's this blood coming from? We've got to get away, that was the gas main blowing and the whole road might go up.' The dust was clearing slightly, but Jenny didn't want to see what it had been hiding. Maria allowed herself to be led like an infant out of the mess. Not once did she speak or cry; not once did she struggle.

Jenny handed her dumbstruck friend to a group outside the Post Office. 'Look after her,' she whispered. 'Her husband's just been killed in that fire. See if you can clean her head, there's a cut over her eyebrow.' She steadied herself, then went back into the hell that was Derby Street. Ena was moaning, so at least she was alive. The charred bodies could be seen now, and not all of them were whole. There was a smell in the air, a nasty, greasy aroma. Jenny knew that this was the stink of burning human flesh. She cupped her mouth with both hands and screamed into the thinning greyness, 'Anyone who can walk, get out of here now. If you can't walk, crawl. Help one another.' She was a strong girl, so Ena Burke's weight was not too big a problem. Determinedly, she dragged the woman a yard at a time until she reached the Post Office, which had been turned into a temporary and very amateur first-aid centre.

An aged man tapped her on the shoulder. His face was black except where the tears had cleaned it. 'Don't go back in, lass.'

'I've got to.' She looked down at Ena. There was no damage on the surface, but she was unconscious. 'Get this lady inside, please.' Figures were emerging now from the smoke, some hobbling along, one or two looking dazed, a few crawling. Jenny steeled herself to help, not looking at charred faces or gushing wounds.

The police arrived and took over, ushering Jenny with the rest into the crowded Post Office. Maria was on the floor in a corner, her eyes blank, the clever hands totally still in her lap. She looked at nobody, spoke to nobody. It occurred to Jenny that her friend might have been deafened by the explosion, though she feared that Maria's injuries were far worse than that. The girl was in deep shock. Shock, Jenny had heard, could kill. And Denis, poor Denis . . . She leaned on the counter and broke her heart. She was lucky because she could cry. When would Maria cry? When?

A hand gripped her shoulder, the touch firm and certain. 'Jenny?'

She turned and saw him through a mist of tears. 'Denis is dead,' she managed. 'Denis, Maria's Denis.'

He pulled her into the safety of his arms. 'Oh, thank God you're alive. I ran all the way from the mill, didn't even think to bring the car.' It occurred to him that he might have been useful, might have taken some of the minor casualties down to the infirmary. 'Jenny, my love, are you hurt?'

She shook her head. 'Maria's gone funny.'

He attempted to dry the flood of tears, but his handkerchief was soaked in seconds. She looked like a child, a dirty lost child in a torn frock, but she felt like a woman. 'Stay there while I get Maria,' he said. He struggled through the crowded room until he found her in a corner. A man was bending over her with a cup of water, but she seemed to be staring straight through him. Gently, Henry eased the girl to her feet. Jenny had looked like a child; this one was a worn-out old woman, her face empty and unquestioning, dust and dirt sinking into premature lines on the poor little face. It was the emptiness that cut him like a knife, and he gathered her up in his arms as if to protect her. She was so light that a breeze might have blown her away. His throat was thick with emotion, so he simply nodded at Jenny to indicate that he was leaving.

With Jenny following behind, he carried Maria all the way home. They put her on the kitchen sofa, then Henry went to make tea. He was a Lancastrian, and right through the ages, Lancastrians had always made tea in times of stress, though he did wonder why. Maria was a nineteen-year-old widow. What would tea do to mend that?

'Mr Skipton?' Jenny's voice was hoarse with smoke. 'Will you get a doctor for me? I think she's losing her baby.'

This was too much for him. Just one sob came out of his mouth before he reached the door, then he raced towards the mill for his car, not seeing the reaching hands, not hearing the cries of amazement. Henry Skipton was crying like a baby in the street. Henry Skipton was crying about a baby. About two, really. As he drove for the best doctor money could buy, he mourned Maria's unborn child. And once again, he wept for Sophie.

Chapter Sixteen

THERE WAS SOMETHING APPROACHING A FULL HOUSE AT
Skipton Hall. After she had spent a few days in a nursing
home, Maria was brought to the house for a rest. Henry
insisted that her brother should come too, as the young
man was plainly in an agitated state about Maria's
condition. Each evening, Henry collected Ena Burke from
Claughton Street so that she could be on call during the
nights should Maria need help or company. The good
woman had recovered completely from concussion,
though she too had spent a night at the infirmary. Josie
was still in hospital, but the prognosis was encouraging,
and a third bedroom had been prepared for her, a pretty,
airy room, all yellow and cream.

So two of the front bedrooms were occupied, one by
Anthony, the other by Maria and Ena. During the days,
after Ena had been taken home, Briony looked after Maria
while Jenny continued in her usual job. Eloise seemed to
be decaying before Jenny's eyes, while poor Maria, whom
she visited each hour, continued withdrawn. Nobody had
dared to raise the subject of Denis's funeral, because she
was obviously unfit to attend.

After three days of almost total silence, Maria spoke to
Jenny. 'I've been thinking,' she said, her tone normal
though sad. 'I want a heart-shaped wreath with roses in it.
He liked roses, them very dark red ones.'

Jenny dropped a cup, didn't notice as it rolled across the

floor. 'Maria?' she whispered. 'Where've you been, love?'

The ginger head moved jerkily, like something in a film which was a bit stuck on the reel. 'In hell,' she answered. 'In my own brain, that's where hell is.'

Jenny bit her lip, forced back the emotion. 'I love you, Maria. Anthony loves you, so does Josie and all the rest of your family. We feel for you, every one of us. Even Mr Skipton's going out of his way, paying for you to go to that posh little hospital. Don't be in hell, or you'll take us there with you. 'Cos we're sticking to you. Wherever you go, there'll be the tribes of Israel after you, making sure you're all right.'

Tense and almost transparent hands plucked at the coverlet. Those pale, colourless eyes fixed themselves on a point above Jenny's head. 'One or two more seconds, and he might have had a chance. That's what I've been thinking, Jen, how long a second is. At that moment, a second was a lifetime for my man, because that's all his life was. A second. I wonder if he knew he was just a spit away from death at that moment?'

Jenny edged herself on to the bed in a sitting position, her hands meeting Maria's, holding them, stroking, soothing, patting gently. 'The firemen on the pavement died too. He'd have needed more than a second. A lot more. Everything blew up, Maria. We were lucky ourselves, even though we were on the other side.'

The eyes narrowed suddenly, while the grip on Jenny's hand tightened. 'Our Josie. He died saving our Josie. How many times did we warn her, how many—'

'Maria!' Jenny took hold of the sharp little chin and moved the head so that the tormented girl was forced to look at her. 'It wasn't Josie. Josie never went playing in what the kiddies call the haunted house. She's too full of stories, she'd soon have been getting nightmares. I've spoken to her in the infirmary, she was dead scared of the place, wouldn't set foot in it for a gold clock.'

A little of the old Maria was beginning to show. 'Then what the bloody hell was she doing in there? You can't go in a place and stop out at the same time, Jen. That's what you might call a physical impossibility.'

For answer, Jenny stood up and took a piece of folded and much-handled newsprint from her apron pocket. 'Just listen,' she said. 'It's all in the *Evening News*.'

She straightened the page, and began to read. 'The headline's called "A Day of Bravery".' Was Maria ready for this? she wondered. But she ploughed ahead, not knowing what was for the best or worst. '"Five firemen gave up their lives yesterday afternoon while rescuing a child from a blaze on Derby Street."' She looked up. 'Then there's a list of their names.'

'Is he . . . is Denis . . . ?'

'Yes, he's the first. They're in alphabetical order. Shall I go on?'

The head jerked just once.

'Little Josie Hesketh, a Liverpool girl who lives with her sister and attends the school of Sts Peter and Paul, has saved the lives of two Bolton four-year-olds. They had lit a fire in the empty house on Derby Street, and Josie did not consider her own safety when she entered the premises after the flames had taken hold. She dragged the unconscious infants to an outside door where a passer-by, Mr John Higgins, found them. Mr Higgins alerted the police and the fire service, who were quickly at the scene.

'"Unfortunately, Josie believed that more children were playing upstairs. She fought her way through dense smoke which eventually overcame her. Josie's life was saved by her own brother-in-law, fireman Denis Dandy, who threw her into a blanket. Ladders were not in place, because the building was judged to be unsafe.

'"Sadly, Mr Dandy's name is listed above. He and four other men lost their lives, while several bystanders were injured. We understand that Josie's sister, Mrs Maria Dandy, was among those taken to hospital after being restrained from entering the burning building to help bring Josie out."' Jenny paused.

Maria's face was grim. 'Read the rest of it,' she said.

'No, it's about other people, not you and Josie and Denis.'

'I want the full story. It's a day that will be with me forever, Jen, but please let me try and make a bit of sense out of it.'

411

Jenny folded the paper to reveal the final paragraphs. 'Is it making sense so far? Is it helping?'

'Yes.'

Jenny cleared her throat, which was still sticky from the fire. '"When the house exploded, probably due to a fractured main, Miss Jenny Crawley organized the evacuation of the injured in spite of thick dust and smoke. With no thought for herself, she dragged a neighbour away from danger and ordered other casualties to get out of the area.

'"Mr Henry Skipton, owner of the Skipton Mills, helped Maria and Jenny to their home in Claughton Street. We understand that the two sisters and Jenny Crawley will be staying at Skipton Hall when Josie is released from hospital. She is suffering from shock, also from the effects of smoke inhalation, but she received no burns."'

'Thank goodness,' said Maria, though her voice was devoid of any real emotion.

Jenny finished the piece. '"We pay tribute to those five firemen, also to Josie Hesketh, Jenny Crawley and Henry Skipton. In times of stress, the strong and the brave of all ages seem to rise to the surface. We offer our sincere condolences to the widows of the firemen, and to their children, ten in total. This was a day of great sadness, but also a time of courage. The people of Bolton and Liverpool can be proud of their fellows."' She pushed the page into Maria's stiff hand. 'You keep it, love.'

'It was nearly eleven,' said Maria.

'Eh?'

'Children. There were ten and a bit, and mine was the bit. It's gone now.'

Jenny, who remembered Maria's attitude to the pregnancy, said nothing. She didn't know whether to offer comfort for the loss, or support for Maria's desire to be childless. After all, that problem was solved now. A brutal solution, but . . .

'I was getting used to it, you know. I feel . . . empty.' She thought for a moment, her gaze fixed on Jenny now. 'When we were at school, we had this daft teacher called Miss Purcell. We used to sing, "Mary Purcell rang the bell, sent the children straight to hell", 'cos she had a little bell on her desk. She rang it when she was angry, so it rang all bloody day.' Her eyes seemed to glaze over, as if she were peering back through the mists of her own brief history. 'I've been hearing that rotten bell for days, the hell-bell.' She nodded slowly, pensively.

'She had a bug in her bonnet about nature study, old Purcell. She said we didn't have a proper life 'cos we never saw no flowers and stuff growing. So she gave us all some seeds and a pot, and we took them home to make them into flowers. One of the kids ate me seeds. We knew which one, it was the one with the green face and bellyache. I cried because I couldn't grow flowers.'

She paused and looked down at the newspaper cutting. 'This is the same, only a lot worse. It was Denis who planted this one. He's dead. I would have had something of his, a little bit of him. His little flower. I was going to call her Daisy, Daisy like my pattern. She would have been beautiful. I wonder if she would ever have forgiven me, though? For giving her a name like Daisy Dandy? But anyway, God punished me, Jen. He knew I shouldn't have a baby, that I wasn't good enough. God knew how I felt and He paid me back, took everything away from me, just wiped it all out like polishing a bit of dust off a window.'

Jenny walked slowly to the window, trying hard not to cry. If she looked outside, she would not cry. 'God's not like that,' she said. 'He didn't give you the shock that . . . ended your baby. God didn't kill Denis. Denis was too good to be a part of any revenge. He didn't deserve to die and you didn't deserve to lose him. And you did nothing to make yourself stop being pregnant. You were getting used to it.'

'I was going to take her to work with me in a nice pram. I had me eye on one belonging to a woman down Deane Road. Her baby had nearly grown out of it, so I put me name down for buying it. Daisy would have been all right, you know. Ena would have helped. Oh, Denis, Denis, what's wrong with me? Why can't I shed tears like normal women do?'

'Anyway . . .' Jenny rubbed her nose which seemed to

itch with her own desire to weep. 'Anyway, it wasn't your Josie's fault. That was the main thing I wanted you to understand. She's a little heroine. There's presents piling up for her in Claughton Street – Ena says her house is full to bursting with dolls and things. Somebody sent two hundred pounds in fivers, no name on the letter.' That particular money had been donated by Henry Skipton – she knew that deep in her bones. 'Altogether, there's going on five hundred pounds for Josie now.'

Maria made a choking sound. 'Oh yes, I heard what you said this time, Jenny. My ears always prick up at the sound of money. But it doesn't matter, does it? Money, I mean. I've been so greedy, planning how I'd do this and do that, never a thought for my own family.'

'Rubbish. You took Josie in—'

'Only 'cos she's a reflection of me. It's like looking in a mirror, seeing myself more than ten years ago. She's a piece of me. I was still thinking only of myself. Josie's bright, and she could have come in with us later on, after she'd been to the Catholic Grammar for a proper education. She'd be my other half, the educated half. Me, me, it's always bloody me, first, last, always and forever. I am a rotten, selfish bitch.' At last, there was life in the tone. She was angry, depressed, hitting herself. But she was feeling something. And all this talking was tiring her, because she'd scarcely opened her mouth for days.

'Maria,' scolded Jenny. 'Will you put a stop to all this daft stuff? What did you expect after a life of poverty? Did you think you'd want that to carry on, no decent clothes, too little to eat, afraid of the rentman? Is it wrong to try for a better way to live?' Maria was even blaming herself for her husband's death, and Jenny could see that only too clearly. Denis had been taken, the baby had been taken because of Maria's supposed selfishness. 'You're tough, Maria, but you're not hard, not selfish.'

Maria sat bolt upright in the bed, her upper body rocking to and fro. 'Jenny?'

'What?'

'He wouldn't . . .' She swallowed painfully. 'He wouldn't have suffered, would he?'

Jenny shook her head. 'Instantaneous. That's what the fire chief said when he came to the house.'

Maria put a hand to her mouth, then removed it to ask, 'Is he . . . in one piece? Is there something to bury?'

Jenny returned to the bed and stood beside it. 'They've put him in a closed coffin.' When she felt her hand being gripped tightly, she added, 'He's all there, Maria.' In truth, Jenny had no knowledge about the matter, but if her memory served her correctly, putting the bodies in order would have been no mean feat. And Denis, who had been right over the blast, had probably taken the full force.

'When's the funeral?'

'Tomorrow.'

Maria paused for thought. 'Can you lend me something black?'

'Yes, of course I can.'

'Then I must get up, get ready.' She threw back the covers and swung her legs over the edge of the bed, crumpling into a heap as soon as her feet touched the floor. 'I feel drunk,' she whispered.

Jenny dragged her back on to the bed. 'You've lost a lot of blood,' she said. 'If you're like this tomorrow, we'll have to take one of the wheelchairs.'

Maria, still panting from her recent small effort, found breath enough to say, 'No thanks. I want nothing of hers.'

This was not the time to argue, so Jenny simply set about the business of tidying the bed.

'And I'll walk to my husband's grave. There's no easy way to say goodbye to a good man, and I don't want it easy. I'll go under me own steam.' At last, the dam burst as she thought about tomorrow. Sorrow, guilt and happy memories flooded into her head and out of her mouth in a long, wordless scream. She could not imagine a future without him. The marriage had been short, but wonderful, because Denis had been not just her lover. Maria had also lost her best friend.

Briony ran in, her brown eyes wide and questioning. 'What's happened?'

As if a tap had been turned, Maria stopped crying. 'Just another fireman, Briony. Not the first, not the last. Just another one gone.' After this short statement, she cried again, but the screaming had stopped. She lay down and turned away from the other girls, drawing her legs up to her chest and sobbing until the pillow was soaked right through.

Briony crept away, leaving Jenny on a chair by the door. Jenny just needed to be there, just needed to sit through this first demonstration of raw grief. There would be more. And Jenny intended to be available to dry the tears.

'How was it?' Eloise had cheered up slightly, was trying to sit properly in the bed, though she was encased in a huge nest of pillows.

'Horrible.' Jenny took the feeding cup and laid it on the bedside table. 'I suppose all funerals are nasty. But with him being so young and so brave—'

'I'm young and I'm dying. Will you feel the same about me? Will you go to my funeral, even after I tried to blacken your name?' The upper lip curled into a slight but challenging sneer.

Jenny smoothed the bedcover. It was beautiful, made of eau-de-Nil satin lightly padded with down and stitched into fancy patterns. 'You've a way to go yet, miss. You've rallied again, so there's no reason why you shouldn't be here for a few years yet. You know what the doctor from Liverpool said the other day. You could live for ages.'

Eloise sniffed. 'This isn't living. Life's about enjoying yourself, dancing and eating and flirting with men. I'm just a shell, just a hollow husk waiting to be blown away in the wind.'

Jenny counted out the tablets. 'Well, swallow these before we get a storm. It's no use being blown away before you've taken your medicine.'

The woman in the bed studied her nursemaid covertly as the girl handed over the various medicaments that were supposed to keep a cabbage alive for as long as possible. Jenny Crawley was becoming rather flippant, rather quick with her answers. It was probably rubbing off the other one, that ugly girl with the haystack hair. 'Is she still here?'

she asked when her gullet finally overcame the last pill. 'The widow – is she staying here?'

'Yes.' She wasn't going to say anything about Mr Skipton's plan. He was intending to keep Maria and Anthony here until what he had christened 'the day of unveiling'. There was something going on, something that might please Maria and take her out of herself. According to Mr Skipton, only Lucy was in on the secret, so Jenny couldn't have said much anyway. 'The master says she needs a rest.'

A yellowing hand reached out and touched Jenny's arm. 'How near the mark was I?'

'I beg your pardon, miss?' There had been something in the tone, a sort of amused annoyance – if such a thing could be possible.

'You . . . like my husband?'

There was a pill on the floor, one of the white ones. She bent to retrieve it. 'Did you take two of these? You're supposed to have two. Have you had just one?'

Eloise almost giggled. 'I don't know, you're in charge of that sort of thing. Stick it back in the bottle. And why are you blushing?'

'I'm not. It's hot and I feel the heat.'

The auburn head nodded. 'I'm sure you do. Does he?'

Jenny made herself meet the cool grey gaze. 'I don't know. I'll ask him when I see him. It'll be hot in the spinning rooms, of course, but it's sweltering there even in the middle of winter.'

'You know what I mean, Jenny. Are you in love with my husband? Is he in love with you?'

Jenny banged the pills down on a tray which held dozens of similar jars and bottles. 'If you've nothing sensible to say, I'll go and have my walk now.'

Eloise had begun to laugh, though her breath was short and laboured. 'Methinks I have hit a nerve,' she cackled.

Jenny smiled grimly. 'Well, me can thinks whatever me likes, miss, it takes no skin off my rice pudding. And don't be getting yourself all worked up, or it'll be yellow pill time.' She wasn't afraid any more, wasn't even respectful. Mrs Skipton was ill, seriously ill, but she obviously wasn't too sick to make bother if she chose. As for the subject currently under scrutiny, Jenny didn't really want to think about him. He was a confusing man, appreciative and generous on the one hand, cold and calculating on the other. Anyway, he was just like an uncle, an older man who showed kindness to a young girl. An uncle, that's what he was. Well, almost . . .

'Oh, go and have your walk. You are becoming a bore, Jenny. You haven't told me one thing about the funeral. Such fun, funerals. But I always looked so good in black, you see.'

Jenny went out and banged the door. It hadn't been fun at all. Hundreds of people had been at the cemetery where Denis and two of the others had been buried. Hundreds of people, all silent except for the occasional sob. And Maria, white-faced and thinner than ever in the sombre clothes, had needed to lean on her strong brother. Denis's mother, eyes puffy from days and nights of weeping, had clung wordlessly to her husband, a shambling old man who only last week had been upright, a wizard at the dartboard, a trainer of the local schools' football teams. The firemen had carried their mates, and the strain on their faces had borne no relation to the weight of coffins. It was their spirits that had been heavy, that would continue so until time had stitched up the inner wounds.

At the top of the stairs, Jenny paused. Charlie was sitting in the hallway, a place that was strictly out of bounds. He was grinning expectantly, the pink tongue all aquiver as it hung from his silly mouth. Someone was speaking to him softly, and Jenny had to strain to hear the words, because the speaker was out of sight. 'She's a good girl,' said the invisible voice. 'She didn't deserve that, did she?'

Jenny sat on the stairs and listened to Anthony's unmistakeable Liverpool voice. 'Asleep now. They've given her a pill to knock her out. I liked Denis, he was all right. Josie's coming soon, you'll get on great with her. Well, I promised you a walk, so come on.'

Maintaining a discreet distance, she followed man and dog through the front door. If Anthony was anything like herself, he'd be saying things to Charlie, secret things that he might prefer to keep away from human ears. But Charlie, who always displayed few symptoms of discretion, saw her and leapt back to round her up like a wandering sheep.

'I'm sorry,' she said as she reached Anthony's side. 'Did you want to be by yourself?'

'No.' He patted the dog's head. 'I could do with company. Maria's flat on her back in dreamland, though I dare say she'll be having more nightmares than dreams, unless there's something funny about that pill we gave her. I don't know what to do for her, Jenny. I don't know what to say.'

She nodded and touched his arm. 'Just be there for her. They were made for one another, her and Denis. It would have lasted forever, because it was so right. They were friends as well as husband and wife. All you can do is watch, wait and be her friend as well as her brother.'

His eyes were wet, and he blinked to clear his vision. 'We never had anything, you know. She felt it more than most, no clean underwear, bug bites on her arms, nits behind her ears. She used to cut them out, the nits. Her hair was all over the place, little bald bits, tufts sticking up where the new lot was growing. She used to steal pennies for the slipper baths and she'd wash her clothes in the bath water. All she wanted was to get away from that, have a decent life with a good man and all the bills paid.'

She squeezed his arm. 'Don't. She'll get better in time. It's no use living in the past.'

He stared at her. 'The past is all we've got to learn from. It's like a house with bad foundations. You've still got to build, but you're hoping all the while that it won't sink into the sand. She'd got herself . . .' He gulped and tried again. 'She'd got herself some concrete and she'd shored herself up. And somebody's gone and dropped a ten ton bomb on all her buildings.'

'Anthony, please stop punishing yourself.'

'It should have been me. If I'd been there, I could have gone in and—'

'And got yourself blown up? Come on, let's walk this dog.' Charlie was jumping up and down in an effort to get things moving. Jenny stepped away from Anthony, her hand beckoning him to follow.

'Jenny?'

'What?'

He moved slowly towards her. 'It's a bad time, but I must tell you. When it's all over, when things are a bit easier, I'll be asking you . . . I'll be wanting to marry you.'

'Oh.' Her voice was squeaky, as high as a child's. 'You're right, this is not the best time,' she managed after a second or two of silence. He was gazing at her with such naked adoration that she had to avert her eyes. 'I'm not getting married yet, Anthony,' she announced quietly to her feet. 'I feel as if I'm only just growing up, as if I need some time to think about . . . well, just to think.'

'I can wait.'

She continued to look at her shoes. He was a lovely boy, he was an open book. With Anthony Hesketh, you got what you saw and saw what you would get. And she didn't want it. There were things she had to do, things she had to make happen. Her heart was . . . elsewhere. Or nowhere, perhaps it was nowhere. She searched for words, kind words that might tell the lad the truth in a way that would not hurt, but she found none. He was grieving for his sister's grief, and she dared not compound the problem. 'It will be a long time,' she said finally. 'I may not get married at all.'

'You will.' His voice was roughened by a plethora of conflicting emotions. 'You are the most beautiful thing that ever walked this earth, Jenny. If I have to wait fifty years, you will be my wife.'

She glanced quickly at the house, her pulse pounding in her ears. 'I'd best go in, I might be in trouble,' she lied. 'I think I forgot one of Mrs Skipton's pills.'

'I love you,' he said.

She had heard that before, and she didn't want to think, didn't need to hear it again. He was an echo, a repeat of another time. She kept pretending that the first time hadn't happened. So did he. Mr Skipton was very businesslike these days, almost abrupt with her. 'I love you,' he had said. 'I know,' she had answered. How could she know? Because that was where her heart lay? She forced herself to look at Anthony. 'I'm not ready. There's things I have to work out. I mean, I've only just found my father and God knows where my mother is. You said the past is important, and it is. I'm too young.' She tapped her forehead. 'In here, I'm still a child.'

His eyes were wise. 'Everybody's a child,' he said. 'People of seventy are still learning, still growing.'

'Please—'

'It doesn't matter.' He looked her up and down. 'One day, Jenny. One day.' He turned on his heel and dashed off with the frantic dog.

Jenny stood alone watching them getting smaller in the distance. After a while, Anthony and Charlie began to look like some strange six-legged creature, a mythical animal from a child's fairy tale. That was how it should be for man and dog, she thought. If a person could absorb a dog's innate goodness, then he would be whole and perfect. It was knowing where dog ended and man began that brought the differences, the inadequacies.

She stopped mid-stride. A figure was making its slow way up the wide drive, a well-dressed woman with a familiar walk. When Jenny saw the face, she shrugged away her thoughts. She did not know this person, could not possibly have recognized her. With her head down, Jenny went through the doorway. The stroll in the country must be forgotten for today. Anthony might double back, might find any of the various paths that criss-crossed the land hereabouts.

Back in her own room, she lay flat on her bed, the anxieties and questions she had avoided for so long arriving now to pound at the front of her brain, like visitors left too long on a doorstep. Anthony Hesketh loved her. Henry Skipton loved her. She hardly knew who she was, yet two men had professed their love. Could she love someone in return? Did she already . . . ? Oh, God. Was she sitting here waiting for Eloise's head to roll? Was she a Parisienne in disguise, off with their heads so that I can enjoy their riches?

Anthony was the right sort for her, the type she might

have expected to marry some day. But she didn't want him, didn't want a callow youth. She wanted ... she wanted to stop thinking. It would be easier just to exist, just to simply be. That way, everything could happen without any decision on her part. In which case, she would be less than poor Charlie, less than Flora and Amber who pulled the drays. It was no use, she had to face it head-on. She was waiting for Eloise to die so that she, Jenny Crawley, could become mistress of this house.

It was almost funny, she decided. How arrogant she was, lying here like a princess and assuming that Henry Skipton would marry her. She had doffed his tubes, guided his thread through the rings, swept his floors. She had sweated in his mill, perspired in his house, because Eloise did not allow for sweat. And now, like some street woman with a certain commodity to sell, Jenny Crawley was planning on auctioning her virtue to a very high bidder. But would he bid? Was this particular lot attractive enough for him to register even the mildest interest?

She turned on to her side and gazed through the window, her eyes fixed to a swaying treetop. Here was where she wanted to be. And if he did love her, he would marry her once Eloise was dead. She shivered at her own selfishness. To stand as witness to a woman's death was one thing; to have designs on her husband was another bowl of soup altogether. But this was her chance, this would be her one opportunity to make things happen. For Maria, for Anthony, for all the Heskeths. If she were to become Jenny Skipton, she would ease the way for many people.

The tree swayed again. She sang softly, 'Spinning Jenny, spinning round, turning up and turning down ...' Perhaps this was her forte, then. Perhaps she would be a planner, a spinner of webs, one of life's smaller architects. She was not an important person. Her mother had abandoned her, her father had only recently admitted parentage. The one thing she seemed to have was beauty, and this was a tool she could employ in order to find a use for herself at last. When Eloise died, Spinning Jenny could begin her task. Just before she drifted into sleep, she comforted herself with one small thought. She loved him. She loved Henry Skipton. She would make him want to marry her.

Behind the gaping front door, the hallway was empty. She placed her bag and gloves on a side table, noticing how badly her hands were trembling. He had advised her not to ring the bell, had promised that he would be here waiting for her. The grandfather clock said twenty minutes to four. In her anxiety, she had arrived far too early.

There were scratches on the parquet, marks that would have been punished to eradication in her day. The heavy curtains wanted a good shake too, would benefit from an hour or two in the fresh air. An unpolished bloom decorated the silver card bowl, the dish where visitors were supposed to leave messages and addresses. In the mornings, with the sun on it, this hall probably looked thoroughly filthy. She tried to visualize it with the sun slicing through, dust-motes dancing in the bright, piercing shafts. It did not matter. Her hand closed in her pocket, imprisoning the mock-pearl rosary on which she counted her prayers. Today, she would use the holy abacus to mark the number of her greatest sins.

Briony Mulholland came in, hesitated, stepped forward, ground to a confused halt. 'Can I help you?' The thick brown hair dangled to her shoulders, making her young and almost beautiful. The rule had been that hair must be encased, tied back, pinned off the face.

'I'm waiting for Mr Skipton.' Was the change so radical, then? Did the new teeth alter her so greatly? The unspoken question answered itself. She was completely different. Her hair was softer, gentler, the skin was smoother, the body finer. But the biggest change was to her mouth, because her jaw lined up at last, sat straight like everyone else's. 'Yes, it's me,' she said. 'Stonehenge.'

Briony dropped a duster and a tin of Beresford's Better Beeswax. It landed on its edge and rolled across the floor, stopping when it hit Carla's foot.

'Mrs Sloane?'

'The same.' She picked up the tin, crossed the small

space and handed the polish over. 'You look puzzled.'

'Well, you don't look the same. I mean, even your voice is different. I'd never have known you. You look . . .'

'Human?'

Briony pushed the tin into her pocket. 'Well, we all knew you were human, Mrs Sloane.'

'I was a gargoyle. I was also unfair at times.'

'Oh.' Briony found herself squeaking like a mouse. 'I've got to, I mean . . .' She cleared her throat and repitched the voice. 'It's the day for polishing the dining room.' She fled, her brown face aflame with embarrassment.

He came in then, seemed not to notice the woman standing in the hall. He was plainly waiting for somebody else, perhaps imagined that this particular Carla was an outsider, one of the nameless and faceless tradespersons who kept this place ticking. The house must have gone right to the dogs, then, because trade always used the back door. She stepped forward. 'Mr Skipton?'

He stared at her, seemed to be peering through her. 'My God,' he said. 'You have changed.'

'Yes. Yes, I have.'

His eyes seemed to be riveted to the new yet familiar face. Whatever she had done, whatever anybody had done, this was a vast improvement. But it wasn't just the shell that had altered. The face was younger, almost vulnerable. There was no malice in the tiny eyes, and the forehead was smooth and peaceful. He pulled at his tie, loosened a collar stud. 'Shall we go into the study, Miss Sloane?'

She noticed that he did not call her Mrs Sloane. The 'Mrs' had been a courtesy title, an award that had demonstrated her position as housekeeper. Now, she was 'Miss', and that made her glad. Mrs Sloane was dead and buried; today, the ghost would serve its time in purgatory. 'We need to go upstairs, sir.'

He assumed a puzzled look. 'Upstairs?'

'To your wife's room.'

'Oh.' He turned away from her, stood at the window, hands in pockets, weight swaying back and forth on his heels. 'That would not be convenient.'

She picked up the bag and gloves and walked towards him. 'It is extremely important that I talk to both of you.'

'No.' He stilled himself as he spoke the single word of refusal.

She inhaled sharply. It was so difficult, because she was fighting him as well as herself. The old Carla was still there, still inside the new casing. The old Carla was furious about the dusty hall, the wide open door, the feckless serving girl. Most of all, the old Carla did not want to be brought down by the new. Her hand gripped so tightly on the bag that it almost slipped from hot, clammy fingers. For a brief moment, she closed her eyes and prayed to St Jude. 'Then I must talk to both of you separately. That means that I shall suffer twice over.'

He detected the pain in her tone, caught a brief glimpse of tightly closed eyelids. She was asking him to step into a room he had not visited for . . . He did not care to remember the last time he had seen his wife's bedroom. There was an urgency about this woman, a terrible passion that bordered on desperation – even insanity. He had wondered in the past about her stability of mind. 'Very well.' He sounded terse, even unkind. He tried to remedy the fault. 'She is extremely ill.'

'Yes, I know that.'

'So the visit will be brief?'

'Yes.' It would be just long enough to cleanse her soul forever. Beyond that, she would not, dared not think.

He followed her up the staircase, keeping time with the funereal pace she had chosen. At his wife's door, they stopped while she patted her hair and straightened shoulders that had begun to droop beneath the weight of whatever was on her mind. As she turned the brass handle, a terrible pre-knowledge flooded his brain, almost causing him to stagger. He suddenly understood why she was here. The panic rose in his gorge, but he had no time to indulge it. They were in the room. He had stepped beyond what he had begun to call the gateway to hell.

Eloise looked dreadful. He stared at the ravaged face for what seemed a lifetime, then the housekeeper began to speak.

'You may not recognize me, Mrs Skipton. I am Carla Sloane.'

'Get out.' This pair of words was spat from between yellowing teeth that sat in the maw of a death's head.

'I shall not stay for long.' Hot beads of sweat coursed down her cheeks, and she mopped at them with a white glove. 'I lied. You know that I lied, Mrs Skipton. We both know that you did not kill that child,' she said.

Henry's legs threatened to buckle, so he slumped into a gilt chair opposite the end of the bed. Eloise was laughing. At least, he thought it was laughter, but her breath was so short that it might have been some sort of attack. There was a weaver at one of the mills with asthma. Yes, she sounded like the asthmatic weaver. Jimmy Clegg, that was his name. He took pills and drank a lot of water, needed to go out of the shed sometimes. What the hell was he doing sitting in a Louis Quinze chair thinking about Jimmy Clegg when words of moment were being spoken at a woman's deathbed?

'I hated you,' the visitor was saying. 'You called me ugly, made sure I heard you laughing at my misfortune. Never once did you allow me to touch Sophie. I used to come up and sing to her when you were out or downstairs. She liked me. I am not fond of children, but she was the exception to my rule.'

He was going to be sick. Any second now, his stomach would come up into his mouth. The room was turning gently; he could almost hear the cheap, metallic chime of a fairground organ as the world became a merry-go-round.

'That day, the day of Sophie's death, a friend had been to see you. I was out on the landing and I heard you saying that I was the ugliest thing ever created, that my mother should have drowned me at birth.'

Eloise's eyes were on him. She was boring right through to his soul. He could not look at her. The man in charge must have overwound the mechanism, because the round-about was jerking all over the place and the music was too fast.

'I cried that day, Mrs Skipton. I went out into the back yard and wept about my hideous face. After that, I seemed

426

harder, stronger.' She turned to look at Mr Skipton. He was doubled over like a man in pain, his head bent almost to the knees. 'Sophie probably choked on regurgitated milk as she lay alone in her cot,' she said softly. 'Mrs Skipton was leaning over the baby, pushing her fingers into the child's throat, trying to clear it. Then she took the cushion and placed it on Sophie's chest. Mrs Skipton was hitting the cushion. I think she was trying to jog the heart into starting again. When she realized that there was no hope, she covered Sophie's face with the cushion. She did not suffocate her. I saw everything that happened in those few seconds. Because of my hatred for your wife and my grief about Sophie, I made Mrs Skipton pay a price that was terrible. I ruined both your lives.'

Carla wiped her face again and turned to the woman on the bed. 'It was me you killed that day. I loathed you because you voiced the opinion that I should have been destroyed in infancy. So I simply transferred your guilt, swore that you had murdered another child. Your own daughter. You were a poor mother. Just as you judged me unfit to be seen, I judged you to be an appalling parent. I am here to apologize.'

'You destroyed me!' Strength had been found somewhere, had been dredged from any part of the body that remained alive. 'You evil bitch. My husband has not spoken to me for years.' Vainly, she tried to resurrect herself, tried to find a way to leap from the bed, but the miracle would not happen. Her eyes bulged in their hollow sockets, while the hands curled themselves into claws. 'Henry!' she shouted. 'There, I told you that this creature was lying.'

He stumbled into the bathroom he had shared with his wife for years. When the vomiting finished, he leaned against the handbasin, his raging head pressed against the cool mirror. Sophie. Sophie had died alone in her cot, had not been murdered by her mother. This happened to children sometimes, he told himself. They died in their cots, no illness, no explanation. Even the best mothers lost their little ones. And she had not been the best mother.

When he returned, Eloise was alone. They stared at one another for a time that seemed endless to him.

'Why didn't you believe me?' The quivering lip that had once been so attractive was horrible on the haggard face.

He breathed deeply through his mouth, fought another threat from his stomach. 'You were selfish and uncaring. Sophie was often left alone to cry. I know now that you didn't kill her. I also know that you didn't love her either. You are too selfish to love anyone.'

'I loved you,' she whispered.

He nodded slowly. 'You loved the fact that I loved you. I was a mere looking glass, something that reflected your beauty. But I am sorry that I accused you of murder. That was unfair.' He staggered to the landing door.

'Henry?'

'Yes?'

'Did you love me? Did you really love me?'

He did not look at her. 'Yes, I did.' Swiftly, he let himself out of the room. The woman was waiting on the landing. Her breathing was fast and shallow, almost as noisy as Eloise's had been. 'Are you all right?' he asked.

'Mr Skipton,' she gasped. 'What can I say to you? I have found God, or rather He has found me at last. What can you find now? No comfort from me, I think, no solace from what I have just said.' She stumbled against the wall. 'Do as you will. Prosecute me, I shall not fight the decision.'

Two doors opened simultaneously. A tousled Maria emerged from one room, Jenny poked her head out of the other. 'Oh,' she said. 'Sorry, sir. We didn't realize you had company.'

Maria, under the influence of sedative drugs, staggered forward a few paces. 'Is that you?' she asked stupidly, her brain still out of gear. 'I saw you in town and thought it might be you. Is it?'

'Yes.'

Jenny, who was receiving a rear view of Carla, asked, 'Who? Who is it?'

The large head turned slowly. 'Jenny?'

428

Jenny gripped the door handle tightly. 'Mrs Sloane? Is that really Mrs Sloane?'

'Yes. I've had some improvements done.' She talked as if she were a house that had been redecorated. With her breathing easier, she offloaded another sin. 'Please forgive me for the way in which you were treated – both of you.' She fixed her attention on Maria. 'I am so sorry,' she said. 'I saw it in the newspaper.'

Maria, thinking that she was in another strange dream, backed away and closed her door firmly. Some things, whether real or imagined, were best left alone.

Henry coughed against the dreadful taste in his mouth. 'There will be no repercussions, Miss Sloane. Please go now. What you have done today is a brave thing.'

'A pity I didn't do it earlier.'

He shrugged, but the movement was slight, as if he expected to shift little of the weight from his shoulders. 'Go and live your life,' he whispered. 'And leave me to exist as best I can.'

Jenny glanced quickly at the master, judged that he was in slightly better order than the visitor. 'Mrs Sloane?' she ventured. 'Would you like some refreshment, a cup of tea or coffee?'

Carla fixed her gaze on Jenny. 'You are a good girl and an extremely pretty one. Be careful how you use your appearance.' A sob managed to escape, was quickly covered by a glove. 'I used mine badly. Ugliness and beauty carry similar curses, because each makes its wearer noticeable. I shall not take tea. This is not a place where I can expect a welcome.' She walked to the stairhead.

Jenny followed her right through the hallway to the front door. At one time, she would not have dared to ask the question she now framed. 'What happened, Mrs Sloane?'

They stood side by side on the highest step at the front of the house. Stonehenge's sight was still working; she marked the fact that the forecourt needed a scrub. 'This is a happier place without me, isn't it? It must have been dreadful.'

'It wasn't easy. But why are you here?'

A huge sigh escaped from lips that were still thin,

though no longer disfigured. 'I told a lie, Jenny. Years ago, I spoiled their marriage. Beyond that, I can tell you nothing because they own the truth.' She waved a hand at the house. 'Look after them. I shall not come again.'

Jenny swallowed. 'Do you love this place, Mrs Sloane?'

The head dropped slightly. 'Yes. Before I went away, I had no feeling for Skipton Hall. Now, I miss it as if it had been my own home. The trouble was that I noticed little while I was here.' She pulled on her gloves with an air of finality. 'Goodbye, Jenny.'

Jenny watched as the woman strode away with all the determination she could muster. Her back looked sad. It was strange that someone's back could actually look sad. Perhaps Mrs Sloane would come back one day if things changed. It seemed impossible just now, because Mr Skipton had been so angry and upset. But it was a shame for Mrs Sloane, it really was. She had nothing and nobody, no reasons to be happy.

She went in and closed the door. Already, her mind was working, adding another name to the list of people she might help one day. Her mouth shaped itself into a sad smile. How had she managed to imagine all this power? Did she have what Auntie Mavis had called 'the sight', was she the real teller of fortunes and disasters?

The silver bowl wanted polishing. She picked it up and carried it into the kitchen. On the table, a feast of cold salmon and salad had been prepared by Mrs Hardman who had gone home now. Briony was singing somewhere in the house, a tuneless drone that murdered the 'London-derry Air'. Jenny sat on the doorstep with silver polish and rags, rubbed at the old bowl till it shone like a big harvest moon. Flora and Amber, she would help them too. Like an old cottager at the wheel, she spun the threads of her imagination. Even if none of it ever came true, she would have enjoyed the planning.

She rose and watched the birds for a moment, two large magpies riding on the air of early evening. Two magpies foretold joy, they too were sighted. Perhaps the children of Claughton Street had been right after all. She was Spinning Jenny.

Chapter Seventeen

IT WAS PAINTED IN THE CORRECT SHADE OF YELLOW, SOME-where between buttercup and primrose, a happy colour with the signwriter's fancy work picked out in black, all curly letters and bits of scroll. In the main window there was an old spinning wheel with cotton wound round its bobbin. The smaller window was occupied by a glass case enclosing mill documents from days gone by and some drawings of ancient machinery.

'It's great,' declared Anthony, trying to elicit some response from his quiet sister. 'You can see it for miles, everybody will come for a cuppa and to buy your scarves and work clothes.'

Maria said nothing. It was a lovely place, but she couldn't quite manage to summon up any real enthusiasm these days. It was easy enough to tell herself that things were simply back to normal, that all she needed was to pretend that Denis had never existed. Before meeting him, she had been ambitious, so what was the matter with her? It was the baby too, she was fairly sure of that. Her body had changed somehow during those brief days of pregnancy. After the initial shock had worn off, once she had accepted the idea of becoming a mother, she had felt really well, truly alive. Now she was empty and lonely and the cutting edge had almost disappeared from her conversation, from her thoughts.

Jenny stared at the sign. Mr Skipton had called the café

the Spinning Jenny. Why? She glanced at him. He was smiling somewhat shyly, avoiding everybody's eyes. 'There are some photographs on the walls inside,' he said. 'Pictures of spinners and weavers. And a couple of paintings done by mill staff. Perhaps you can sell them as a sideline – we've several gifted artists in Bolton. The counter for your work, Maria, is on the far side, away from cooking smells. I've had another little sign done. "Tuppenny Girl Prints", we called it. Jenny told me . . . your nickname.'

Maria stared at him. 'Denis called me that.'

'I know.'

'It was private.' Her eyes moved to Jenny. 'But it's nice. Yes, that was a good thing to do. Tuppenny Girl will one day be Maria Hesketh Fabrics.' If she could retrieve some energy, that was.

'Keep both,' said Henry. 'Heskeths' for the expensive stuff, Tuppenny for the more accessible end of the market.' He would find a printworks, somewhere, somehow.

'I'll see.' There was still a marked absence of feeling in her voice. 'You're a kind man,' she said to Henry. 'Jenny always knew it, she's a fair judge of character. Ages ago, at the start of summer, she told me to ask you for help. She was right.'

Henry studied the small, thin, damaged girl. 'Maria, I'm a businessman. I never back a loser. Once you get back into stride, you'll leave us all standing. Go on, now. You've got the key and Lucy will be along in a minute looking for instructions. Go and strut about, be the boss.' He was trying not to worry. The money didn't matter. It had cost just six months' advance rent, some paint and a few shillings for labour. But she looked as if the spirit had been whipped out of her. In fact, she seemed smaller than her little sister who, having made a noisy escape from hospital, was running about the moors and beginning to outgrow all her clothes. But Maria was gifted, and gifts always came back. At least, that was what he believed and hoped. He intended to watch and wait for the moment when Maria would be ready for a factory. Just now, the girl was ready for not much at all.

Anthony was leaning on a wall, one foot up behind him against the brickwork. He pretended to study the café across the road, but he was taking in more than buildings. Skipton was glancing at Jenny from time to time, looking while appearing not to look. And Jenny, probably without realizing it, stayed close to her master. If he moved, she moved. Only inches, but definitely in the same direction every time. Towards him. Towards a married man who was old enough to be her father. His heart lurched then sank like a chunk of stone. She had plans, then. The hard-faced little trollop was waiting for wife the first to die, hanging on till Skipton could shout, 'Come in number two, your time is up.' But no, surely not. Jenny was no schemer, Jenny would never take things for herself. His stomach churned and life began to beat once more in his throat. Dear God, was she doing all this for Maria, then? Was she . . . selling her body and soul for a café, then, later on, for a printworks?

Anthony grabbed Maria's arm. 'Come on, queen, there'll be work to do.' He glanced at Jenny, the girl who had said that she would never sell herself, not for any price. 'Are you going back up there?' he asked.

'Yes. Mr Skipton's taking me.'

Anthony stamped away with Maria trailing behind him. They crossed the road, opened the door and walked into the shop. Jenny shivered. She didn't like getting dirty looks, and the one she had just received from Anthony had felt as if everybody had scraped their boots on it – muddy boots, too.

'Shall we go?' He was touching her elbow. A small flame seemed to sit in his hand, spreading its warmth up her arm, through her shoulder and into her cheeks where, no doubt, it would shine like a beacon. Being in love with a married man was not easy. He probably knew all the signs and symptoms, was likely smiling inside himself, congratulating his manhood for this small victory over female flesh that was weak and frail. 'Yes,' she said quietly.

She sat in the passenger seat while he wound furiously at the starter handle. His own face was red with exertion and anger by the time the car showed signs of life. He threw himself into the seat beside hers. 'I shall write this thing's death certificate one of these days,' he grumbled. 'It acts as if rigor mortis is its next port of call. New car? It should have BC on its papers.'

They were alone and speeding through Bolton when she asked carefully, 'Why did Mrs Sloane come the other day?'

'Something she had to do.' He spoke with difficulty through teeth that were almost gritted. 'Just a small item she had forgotten.' He steered round a sharp corner and added, 'It had slipped her mind for about fifteen years.'

'Oh.' She hadn't called him 'sir' lately, and she couldn't quite work out why. 'She brought you and Mrs Skipton together, anyway. It's important that you talk to each other now. Mrs Skipton's going to die any day.' It was the next thing she had to engineer, this bringing of peace between man and dying wife.

He took in a deep breath, exhaling slowly through his mouth. 'My wife has been blamed for something she didn't do. The fact that she didn't do it does not alter my opinion of her. She is self-centered, ill-tempered, shallow and opinionated. The illness has made her neither better nor worse. It is easy to pretend that the disease is accountable, but I have a long memory.'

She flinched as if she had been struck. 'There is no forgiveness in you,' she whispered. 'I can't understand how a man who is good to his workers and kind to animals can treat a dying woman like dirt. And whatever you think of her, you shouldn't say it to just anybody.'

'I don't.' Impatient fingers clenched tightly on the steering wheel. 'You are not just anybody. But perhaps some thoughts should be kept to ourselves, Jenny.' He bit his lip. He hadn't meant to sound like a master addressing a servant, but nor did he wish to discuss Eloise. It seemed out of place and totally wrong, yet he longed to open up his heart to somebody, needed to express himself. 'I'm sorry,' he mumbled.

'It's all right. There's no need to apologize. I should know my place by now, Mr Skipton.'

'It isn't that. It's not a case of places. There are things I can't explain, things from years ago. I'm not completely sure that I understand them myself. Even people as old as I am get confused, you know.'

'Yes.'

He stared at the road ahead. 'I am . . . very fond of you.'

She swallowed, covered her mouth with a curled fist. 'You were fond of her once.'

'That's true. I try to remember when things went wrong, why they went wrong. She didn't kill Sophie—' He closed his mouth with a snap that echoed through his brain like a pistol shot. But he could not bite back the words, could never un-say what had just been spoken. 'Just ignore me,' he muttered. 'I'm not myself today.'

Jenny dropped her head. 'I thought it must be something like that, something big. Mrs Sloane must have been a very unhappy woman to let you believe that your Sophie had been murdered by her own mother. She came up to tell you the truth, I suppose.'

He stopped the car with an abruptness that shunted both of them forward. 'How the devil did you get to be so quick, Jenny? And why is it that you always see the best in people? So-and-so must have been so sad, so distressed to do this or that. You even like . . . my wife. Nobody has ever managed that, not completely.'

'You loved her.'

'Infatuation and lust are not the same as liking or loving. They're like gold plating – they always wear off in the end. And you're left with base metal. There's nothing wrong with iron and steel, Jenny, but there's a big sin called dressing up.'

'Pretending to be what you're not.'

'Yes, wearing a front of fools' gold.'

She sighed heavily. 'That, Mr Skipton, is a small sin, a very small one. We all do it, we all play parts.' She remembered Maria, 'You never know a man till you've seen him naked' – something like that. 'None of us is exactly what shows on the outside.'

He cleared his throat. 'You are. You are real.'

There was wisdom in her eyes as she looked straight at

him. 'I am just beginning, Mr Skipton. We don't know who I'll be, what I'll be like. Mrs Skipton is a naughty, spoilt child who wants her own way. Her parents made her like that, and you did nothing to mend it. We're all responsible for one another.' She smoothed a fold in her grey skirt. 'But I'll tell you this much for nothing. If you don't go in that bedroom and try to put things right with a woman who is living in mortal fear and danger, then I shan't speak to you again.'

He wiped a non-existent mark from the windscreen. 'Where did you come by all this power? How are we managing to sit here with you telling me what to do?'

She shrugged. 'Yes, I suppose you pay my wages. So, if you pay my wages, you buy my mind and my opinion. Failing that, you are paying for my silence.' It didn't matter any more. Once Mrs Skipton was dead, Jenny would leave. What she felt for him would go away in time, while he could soon find somebody to be his wife, somebody the right age and with the right background.

'Jenny . . .' He didn't know what to say. He loved her, she was becoming manipulative, even aggressive in her attitude. So honest, she was. This foundling was his wife's nursemaid, so the marital problems were plain to her. And she was demanding that he made an effort, she was telling him how to run his affairs. Anyone else would have been sacked on the spot. Yes, this was a spinning jenny. She was a quiet girl, a good girl, yet she could bend life to her own shape simply by being there. Hargreaves's mill jenny had been built to make strides in the fast production of yarn. This one had been born to torment him, and he should cast her out before his perverse affection grew any more.

'I know what it is not to be wanted, Mr Skipton. Speak to her.'

He drove off at top speed, tyres and brakes squealing their displeasure. There was no further conversation. When they reached Skipton Hall, she climbed out of the car, nodded her thanks, then stamped into the house. She had a sick woman to care for.

Her head was turned towards the door and held stiffly, as

if restrained by an invisible vice, though in truth, it was supported by a mountain of pillows. He was coming; she could feel him coming. Dan was back from Blackpool. It was September and his summer sabbatical was over. She had heard the girl laughing on the landing, had listened to Jenny Crawley celebrating the return of a father who had only recently admitted his part in her creation.

The item in Eloise's hand was no longer cold. In fact, it seemed to burn through her silk pyjamas, felt as if it might leave a scald mark on diminished flesh. She was cold, so cold. This thing in her bed had borrowed the final heat from her body, had drained the last life out of her soul. Only her eyes remained feverish as she carefully rationed the blinks of the eyelids. She would miss not one second of it. By now, he would have thought it through. By now, his lame apology would be prepared.

The door opened with excruciating slowness. While lying in her bed these past years, Eloise had become a part of the house, another piece of the various fabrics out of which it had been constructed. As an immobile watcher and listener, she imagined that she could read the minds of those who moved. Thus she had known that he would come today. She was brick, she was plaster, she was the silent witness.

He was not a large man, and she had always preferred the well-built male. He was ageing, his shoulders were rounded and the laughter had gone from his eyes and mouth. She remembered the laughter, treasured his pain. There was a stillness about him, a quiet sureness that might have made her squirm with anger had her nervous system remained totally alert. Now, she owned just a right hand, a right leg and the ability to take in sufficient oxygen to prevent choking. Soon, she would cease to swallow, and air alone would not keep her alive.

She stared at him, kept her face blank. The room smelled of death. Shakespeare had written something about all the perfumes of Arabia being incapable of drowning the stench of guilt. It was the same here. All the perfumes of Paris and London failed to mask the earthy odour of encroaching death. Death was the guilty party, while Eloise's determined opinion insisted that she had been an innocent victim for what seemed a lifetime. In the midst of life, we are in death, she thought irrelevantly. She watched his hand as it travelled to his face. He was cutting out the smell.

'Eloise, I am sorry,' he muttered. The voice was uncertain, failed to match his outward demeanour. She realized that he was nervous and that he had deliberately donned a cloak of calm before coming in to say four words. And the four words of supposed kindness consisted of her name, then four extra syllables stuck on after the Eloise. I and am and sorry.

Oh well, that made everything right, didn't it? He had chosen, in the past, to believe that she had committed a vile murder, an infanticide. He had chosen to believe the words of a female servant whose inside had been as distorted as the exterior. He was sorry. Bells should ring, flags should be draped across the lawn, perhaps a string quartet might play downstairs. 'I hate you,' she said, the tone conversational. 'I had nothing left, but even then you reduced me to less than nothing. The child died naturally.'

'I thought you didn't love her. After the birth, you became . . .' He searched for words that would not hurt. Petulant, demanding and quarrelsome were not suitable terms for the ears of a terminally ill woman. She would answer soon to her Maker, would be required to explain all her devious machinations. 'You became less than happy. She cried and you did not touch her.' He bit back the rest, the words she had used to describe the ugliness, the selfishness of a tiny, helpless human.

The right shoulder lifted itself in a small shrugging movement. 'She was a part of me, a part of us. I would have come to love her. Babies are not my forte.'

His hand was on the doorknob. He had kept the door open, was hanging on to the possibility of retreat. 'I was wrong,' he said lamely. The truth was terrible. The truth was that his already ailing love for Eloise had died with Sophie. Eloise's guilt or innocence had played no real part, because his heart had cooled even before the tiny, white coffin had been put below ground.

438

She continued to stare at him and his flesh was beginning to crawl under the cold, penetrating gaze. 'There is nothing else I can say to you.' He was useless, weak and stupid.

She filled what was left of her lungs. 'Then I shall do the talking.' A tremendous burst of energy flooded though her chest, a last crescendo of glorious anger. 'You are a bastard, Henry. You are a silly and insignificant man. The Crawley girl will twist you round her little finger.' She nodded quickly, warming to the subject. 'I know your intentions, Skipton. The girl is cleverer than I was, sweeter, purer. But she is a woman, and you are no match for any of us.'

He took a step towards her. 'Stop this. I am sorry for you, sorry about this awful bloody disease, for my neglect of you, my hatred . . .'

She cackled deep in her throat. 'If I had both legs, I would walk out of here and sue both of you, you and the new, slightly improved gargoyle. Amazing what a set of cheap porcelain teeth can do, isn't it? Well, I can't walk, and I failed in my attempts to ruin you. But this is my day. You will give me this one day.' It was too late now to summon a lawyer. She would not live to enjoy the scandalous outcome of any litigation.

'All right.' He folded his arms and backed away again. 'Have your say.' He owed her that and so much more. There was no way of apologizing properly, and he could not pretend an affection he did not feel. It had been a bad marriage. It would have been a bad marriage even if Sophie had lived. Once his young and hungry eyes had cleared, after that first flush of sensuality and indulgence, he would have seen past the shallow beauty who had inflamed his desire so expertly.

She smiled, but her eyes remained as fierce as twin glowing coals in a bed of ash. 'A telephone is such a valuable piece of equipment. With a telephone, one can do most things. I found a man who knew a man who knew another man. Second-hand dealers, you see. It's amazing what people sell in the wake of a war, valuables and so on. Some very interesting objects came to light.'

His pulse seemed to miss a beat. She was clearly working herself up to something. Even from this distance, he could see small flecks of foam gathering at the corners of her mouth.

Her lips parted as she took another deepish breath. 'I bought my peace, my freedom,' she screamed, surprised by her own returning energy. Perhaps she was going into remission, a period of improvement that would be, at this juncture, completely surplus to requirements. Insane laughter spilled from her, filled the room and poured out through the open door. 'I spit on you,' she howled. 'On you, your household, your business, I lay the curse of a dying woman. From this day, the Skipton mills will not thrive and Skipton Hall is finished.' She was hot now, so hot that her body was slick with rivulets of salt water. The stink of heated and decaying flesh rose up and drew itself into nostrils that were widened by temper. A guttural howling flooded the whole house as she forced her hand to do her bidding.

The bullet ripped easily through sheet and padded coverlet, its report slightly muffled by these soft barriers. A man stood behind Henry, a taller, brown man with a face refreshed by summer seaside air. The lead missile felled the nearest one, the prime target, then embedded itself in the newly-arrived butler. She was confused. She had meant to kill one man, not two. They made little sound as they hit the floor. It was as if they had been rendered boneless, had become twin, almost inseparable heaps of humanity in small, red pools of ebbing fluid.

A tiredness overcame her now, a sad and wearying weakness. There was no regret, no feeling of guilt. Silly words ran through her mind, phrases about killing two birds with one stone, about a bird in the hand and others in a bush. Jenny Crawley was standing over the corpses. She would suffer twice over, the girl with the sun-bleached hair and the saintly smile.

Finally, Eloise Skipton dragged together the last scraps of her dwindling power. She would save her face – or what was left of her face. With the hard nozzle wedged beneath a protruding rib on the left side of her body, she quickly

440

dismissed the soul whose flame flickered uncertainly within her withered frame. She died instantly and with a wide smile frozen on her shrunken features.

When Briony Mulholland rushed in, she found four bodies in the bedroom. Jenny, covered in her father's blood, cradled Dan's head in her own unconscious embrace. Eloise was slumped in the bed, and Mr Skipton lay still as a stone, his left arm oozing and twisted into a position that defied nature.

Instinctively, Briony ran out and halted Josie Hesketh's progress up the stairs. The girl was here for the good of her health, and the vision in the bedroom might have sent her straight back to hospital. Controlling her own hysteria with difficulty, Briony instructed the child to go to Mrs Hardman. When the coast was clear, the shaken servant made her first ever telephone call from the study.

The operator listened, sucked a sweet, alerted the usual forces then returned to her knitting. Tonight, she would have a good story for her husband. She could tell him that the lady of Skipton Hall had finally moved on, had needed company on her last journey. A dropped stitch, even in twenty-row cable, was a small price to pay for such a gem.

'I am your only living relative, stupid man, you are.' Pol nodded her head fiercely, causing untidy dark locks to tumble forward on to her face. 'And I want nothing from you, Henry Skipton. This is not about money, it's about me giving a bit of support to yourself.'

He glanced at her. 'Go away, Pol. I'm sorry for your mother and I'm sorry for you. What else is there?' He had thinking to do, and it needed doing now, today. Under different circumstances, the woman's company might have been appreciated, even enjoyed. Though she had changed the tune on her pseudo-Irish fiddle considerably since that meeting in the street, he mused briefly.

Pol paced about the small hospital room. 'Dear God in heaven,' she said to the ugly green curtains. 'Did you hear that? Himself is flat out here trying his best to get ruinated, while the other damn fool is in my house on hunger strike. She thinks she did it,' she announced to a small trolley. 'She thinks she held the gun that fired the bullet. I am surrounded by what Mammy would have called English eejits. And was ever a woman so right about this breed of stubborn people?' She tossed the curls from her face and stood, feet apart and arms akimbo, glowering at him with mock ferocity from the foot of the bed.

He groaned under his breath. He was denied even the small ability to turn over and face the wall. The shattered arm lay mummified in stiff bandages, strapped so tightly to his chest that breathing was becoming a luxury, something to be rationed. Pol had wittered on endlessly about her mother's search for Uncle Donald, about the poor woman working in the Skipton mills because the trade name had matched that of her erstwhile lover. 'She was mortificated to hear that he was dead,' Pol had said. 'And she could not even grieve over the bones of another English eejit who had got himself mangled in his corn thresher, for she was too ashamed to tell the tale of her own weakness.' Thus she had gone on. And on. At any other time, Pol's version of the tragedy would have been amusing, just as her home-made and wonderfully express-ive vocabulary might easily have raised smiles, spirits and eyebrows. But now he was too self-engrossed to heed her properly.

'I'm away just now for a cuppa and a smoke,' she announced. 'But I'll be back directly to knock some sense into that piece of concrete that sits on your shoulders pretending to be a head with a few specks of grey matter in it.' She stamped out noisily. Everything about her was loud – voice, clothing, footfalls.

Henry closed his eyes. If Eloise could only know what she had perpetrated, if she could but realize how well she had fared in the evil game she once played. Dan was dead and buried, wiped out by a bullet in his big, kind heart. Jenny, like Maria, had entered into a terrible grief, could scarcely speak to anyone without weeping. And Henry Skipton had lost the use of his left arm. It would never come back, the medical people had said. The nerves were torn to shreds and he would have to tuck the numbed hand into a pocket once the bandages were removed. Poor

Dan had been taller, had taken into his chest a bullet that had found an easy route through Henry's slighter frame.

He ran the fingers of his right hand over the stiff cast. This was how it had been for Eloise, then. Her body had stopped responding to messages from the brain. Inch by slow inch, the woman's life had been stolen from her. How magnificent her exit seemed now, though she was not visibly here to applaud herself. It was almost as if her ghost were sitting in this room, smiling as he fought to breathe, laughing at his redundant arm. She had failed to kill him, had killed a better man instead and by mistake. But she had taught him how precious life was, how to treasure each fought-for gasp of oxygen. This was her curtain call, a last gleeful message from beyond the grave. She was saying, 'Now you know, now you understand how I felt, though this is just an arm. Imagine your spine, Skipton. Imagine that central rope of nerve diminished, unfed, dying. This is how it begins, with an arm, a foot, a weakening joint . . .'

Acutely aware of his own selfishness, he dashed a tear from his cheek. He could be like her. Unless he took care, he might finish up just as selfish and ungrateful as she had been. Oh, how easy it would be to be bitter about his affliction. If he chose, he could stay at home, run the mills from a distance. It was a pleasant house, all the pleasanter now for her absence. There were walks, books, gramophone records. There were surely a million hobbies that might entertain a one-armed man. He could grow old now, could turn into a crabby bachelor with an uncertain temper, might even be nominated a character, something to be pointed out in the village like a landmark. Yes, it might even be fun to be listed with the early Victorian horse-trough and the medieval stocks.

No. There was a lesson to be learned here. It was probably something to do with forgiveness – damn that lovely girl for always being right. Was she suffering? If only he could comfort her. He searched among the tangled threads of his mind, found a point of reference, took up where he had left off. Jenny Crawley kept doing that, coming into his dreams and . . . It was about forgiveness. The forgiving of Eloise was almost academic now, an act of will that he would force himself to perform. The absolving of himself was not so easy, but that too would achieve itself in time. And he would work, work as he had never worked before. They would whisper about the wife who shot him, who killed the butler, took her own life. And their whispers would be covered eventually by the same layer of soot that enveloped most other things in a cotton town. It would, as they said, die down over the years.

Pol O'Gorman was his cousin. That was the first thing he had smiled about in days. He did not question her story, because there was something elementally honest about the fey woman. He would see her right, find a way of compensating for Uncle Donald's apparent heartlessness. He had been something of a black sheep, this uncle of his. Henry's father had seldom referred to the dead man, save to say that he'd been an inventor of sorts, a man with no love for cotton. But Henry remembered him well. Yes, he would do something for Pol. Eventually.

But first, he needed to get out of this sepulchral place. It was all grey and green, all miserable faces, charts about bodily functions, and it was populated by bow-legged nurses without humour. And, of course, there was the gaggle of self-important physicians who constantly congratulated themselves on finding a jolly good reason why every human being must perish. They acted as if they had invented death, as if they dished out life to the chosen few who must, of course, be grateful to the white-clad gods with double-barrelled names and pinched nostrils. They had all learned the trick of not breathing too deeply, it seemed. They did not allow the smell of the wards to enter their sacred noses. Bloody quacks, the lot of them. He stiffened, remembering his own reaction to the stench of decay at home. Yes, as the locals would say, he needed to sweep his own back yard before criticizing the housekeeping of others.

When Pol returned, he was on his feet beside the bed. 'Dress me, cousin,' he commanded. 'The stuff's in a green cupboard behind that green curtain next to the green wall.

Another hour, and I shall become as bilious as the paint.'

She dropped her bag, a capacious blue thing drawn together at the top by a red ribbon. She was glad that she hadn't worn her green frock. 'Are you out of here, then? Did you wear them out till they gave you the sack?'

'I'm sacking myself. They've had enough money out of me. I never realized until this week how much I dislike doctors. Our family man's a grand chap, but this lot here are just a cage of monkeys with a superiority complex. They imagine they're human.'

She stood for a moment as if considering things of deep importance, hands on hips as usual. 'Listen. Don't you be telling everybody I'm your cousin, for I could not bear the shame of it.'

He started to chuckle, then the laughter grew deeper and more painful, seemed to come right from the pit of his stomach. She was a grand woman, this Pol O'Gorman, with a good heart and more sense than ten men.

She heard the hysteria behind the glee. 'Watch it, son,' she said softly. 'There's tears in your heart, and the laughter will boil them up till they bubble out of the pot. Be calm. You've a mile of life to walk when you're out of here, and not every man will cheer your progress.'

He gulped, then swallowed carefully. Laughing with a squashed chest had taken some doing. 'He was a good and reliable chap, Pol. He had a gentleness about him, yet he was very much a man.' He glanced through the window, blinked the mist from his eyes. 'Dan Crawley was my best friend.'

'And he was Jenny's daddy,' she ventured. 'Had he lived, he might have been . . .'

He looked at her. 'What, Pol?'

'Your father-in-law.'

Their eyes met. It seemed that he had known her forever. She was one of those all-or-nothing people, was either with you or against you. The result of both situations was similar, though. She yelled a lot, but it was easier and infinitely more amusing to have her as an ally. 'I'm not ashamed of you, Pol,' he said.

She threw back her head and chuckled. 'It's easier from

445

where you stand. You can deign to notice a working girl, but I might be accused of kissing your arse for gain.' She threw open the ghastly cupboard and took out his clothes. 'Mind, from the looks of these garments, you'd be a pauper, for it's the suit you were shot in. Will you not have me bring something decent from the house?'

He shook his head. 'A prisoner has to grab a chance of escape. If you go away, so will my nerve.'

She understood. He had known that she would see his point. It seemed that he had lost one friend and gained another, though no-one would ever fill Dan's large shoes. She dressed him quickly, and with the efficiency of one who has dealt with the details of men's attire many times. At least he was sober. Most of the others had probably been magnificently inebriated as she had pushed them homeward, wifeward.

'You're a good girl, Pol. Thanks.'

She grinned. 'Well, you look like you're listing to starboard and the sails wanting wind, what with the sleeves all flapping.' She pushed the empty cuff into the pocket of his jacket. 'Let us sally forth, your honour.'

'Is the corridor empty?'

'Does it matter?'

'No.' He stood as straight as the strapping would allow. 'They can go to hell.'

Pol retrieved her large dolly-bag and opened the door. 'Now, that's the right attitude,' she said. 'Damnation on the lot of them.'

Briony held the door wide to admit Jenny, Maria, Josie and Anthony. All four of them were currently living in Claughton Street, the two grown girls at number seventeen, Anthony and his younger sister at twenty-nine with Ena Burke. They stood, a clutch of silent, unwilling and black-clad visitors, waiting to be put wherever they must go. Even Josie was subdued, but then she hadn't really been invited, had fought to come. It hadn't even been a real fight. Maria was so quiet and compliant these days that there was no fun in taunting her.

Maria looked with fondness on her sister, thankful for

the child's obvious powers of recovery. She was like a small wave in the Dead Sea, the only ripple of movement in an environment of leaden stillness. But she would not send the child home to Liverpool. Even this was better than home.

Jenny shivered, though the day was warm enough. Since the afternoon of her father's death, she had not set foot over this threshold. Even when Dan had been carried out to the hearse, she had waited on the drive. Maria had been right all along. Mrs Skipton must have been crazy. Only a demented woman would buy a gun and secrete it in the bed, use it to kill herself as well as others.

He sent for Jenny first. She walked slowly into the study, her eyes fixing themselves on his empty sleeve and on the bunched shirt that pretended to conceal what remained of his left arm.

'Jenny?'

She sat down opposite him. 'Is your arm really no use?' It had been in the paper, the stuff about his injury. And about the balance of Eloise's mind having been questionable, though there had been some trouble about that coming out before the inquest. The doctor had spoken out of turn to a reporter, had informed the press that Mrs Skipton had been suffering from a defective personality. So she'd had the lot on one plate, poor woman. Crazy and paralysed, locked in two prisons, one of the mind, the other of her numbed and unresponsive body. Mrs Skipton's had been a very special kind of lunacy too, because she had seemed so sane at times.

'I lost just one limb, Jenny. I am so sorry about Dan.'

'So am I.' She stared at him steadily, little expression in her eyes. 'It's been a bad time. Auntie Mavis, Denis, Maria's baby, my dad and the missus.' There was a slight pause. 'She couldn't help it, you know.'

He picked up a pencil and tapped it against the desk's edge. 'She was sane enough to know right from wrong. And the planning must have taken some intelligent thought.'

'People who are ill in their minds don't always sit screaming at the moon, Mr Skipton. It takes them all different ways.'

He leaned back against the chair's solid support. Even talking about Eloise made him ill. 'Where did you find all your excuses for everybody's bad behaviour? Are you a saint, or are you simply naïve?'

'Does it matter?' She sounded weary. 'I think folk are good, but things happen to them and make them act badly. Wickedness is something we learn. It's like a kitten taken too soon from its mother. It spits and scratches because no love was shown to it.'

He coughed. 'Eloise was shown love.'

She lowered her eyes. 'Then the love was not strong enough, or it was the wrong kind.'

'So I am to blame? Her parents too – were they guilty?'

Jenny drew a hand across her tired forehead. 'Their lives might have been difficult, yours too. It all goes back, a long way back. It goes as far back as God, Mr Skipton.'

So here sat a budding philosopher, he thought grimly. Her thinking was so transparently uncomplicated, so idealistic and hopeful. According to Jenny, goodness would breed goodness, would reproduce itself forever. He did not care to illustrate his unspoken argument, would not tell her of the numbers of solid parents who had spawned monsters. Were he to try, she would find some answers about poor schooling, naughty friends, deprivation on some or all levels. 'You had no mother's love, Jenny.'

'Perhaps that's why I'm so aware of what's needed.' She sighed tiredly. 'Why are we here?'

'Business,' he replied as briskly as he could manage. 'I'm buying another mill, a small one on Blackburn Road. There's a building nearby that will convert for printing. I shall talk to Maria and her brother about that in a moment.'

Seconds that seemed as long as hours ticked by, and she did not take her searching gaze from his face. She was numbed, unattached to everything and everyone. Though she could think and speak with a facsimile of normality, her isolation was total. He was just a man, another person who had been good to her in another time. 'What's it got to do with me?' she asked.

He was not reaching her. The body sitting on this chair in his study was almost unoccupied. Thought processes remained, the primitive philosophy was intact, but Jenny Crawley had ceased to be a part of the real world. She would return to normal, no doubt, once nature had formed a protective scab over her deep and invisible wound. 'You and Lucy might like to run the shop, the café in the centre of town.' He threw the pencil down and fiddled with his watch-chain. 'The mill will belong to me. Maria, Anthony and whoever they choose as workforce can use the printing shed. I shall sell the cotton to them at a decent price.'

Jenny nodded. 'Right.'

'This is to prevent the business going under. You see, Jenny, a small business needs help. Maria might get flooded with orders – that's what happens when small people start up. A competitor, or his friend, will fill your order books in ten seconds flat, but the small printed word will ruin you. When you fail to meet demands, they will buy you out. But with Skipton's behind you, there'll be a prop.'

At last she turned her head and gazed through the window. 'Then you should be talking to Maria, not to me.'

'I shall see her in a moment. Really, you are here so that I can let you go – officially – from Skipton Hall.'

'Yes.'

'Jenny?'

Her attention, severely limited by trauma, returned to him. 'What?'

He held the stopped watch to his ear. He could no longer wind the spring, and Dan was not here to do it for him, would never be here again to wind a watch or to comfort his poor lonely daughter. 'This is not the right place for you.'

There was no right place. She had never in all her life found the right place. 'Will you look after the dog?'

'Yes.'

'And get him a cat. That's all lies about dogs and cats. Let him have company. He'll learn there's more to life than dogs and people.'

'Very well.' He watched as she walked from the room. There was a small hole in the back of her stocking and the shoes wanted polish. Two years. He was going to make a long space for both of them, a time for recovery and a time to find new, as yet uncharted, directions. She might marry someone, so might he. It was all in the lap of some superior being who gave no clues, no guidelines. Henry Skipton was just a man with one arm and no aptitude for drawing maps. Even with ten fingers, he could never have ordained the future.

He rang the bell that would prompt Briony to send in the Heskeths. Any moment now, he would do business with a man who might draw the first line on blank paper. If Anthony married Jenny, that would remove one glorious possibility. Henry took a deep breath and gave himself up to the unpredictability of providence. And the watch remained unwound.

PART TWO
1922

Chapter Eighteen

LUCY TURNBULL STRAIGHTENED HER CAP, WHICH HAD slipped forward during this latest altercation with old Battersby. 'That is definitely an Eccles cake, Mr Battersby.' She hid crossed fingers behind her back, hoping that luck and a small measure of self-discipline might combine to prevent her losing temper and job. 'And it's got best butter on it, spread nice and thick too.'

He peered upward at her from beneath the peak of his greasy cap. 'I'm saying nowt about butter. Did you hear me say owt about butter? It's these currants. Half of them's raisins and there's too many, they stick under me top plate.' To demonstrate, he lowered the mouth furniture on to his greyish tongue, then flicked the teeth back into place with a level of expertise that might have been laudable in different circumstances.

Lucy's panicking eyes scanned the full-to-bursting café. She leaned across the counter and spoke from a corner of her tight mouth. 'Listen, sunshine. One more peep out of you, and I'll ram that bloody daft cap so hard on your head, it'll finish up as a garter. Which leg do you want it on?' She flashed her best 'customer' smile, which served only to confuse the old man even further.

'I fought for this country—'

'Never mind the Boers and the flaming Crimea, Bert. Just get sat down over there near the door and forget everything—'

'But me Eccles cake—'

'For this once, and only for this once, it's free, old son. Take it and the cheese on toast with my compliments.' She managed not to express the insane hope that he would choke on the feast. 'We don't make our own cakes no more, not since Miss Crawley took over upstairs in the gallery. We buy them in from Jenkins, so go and tell him about his dried fruit and your teeth. I'll have you know that Mr Jenkins's individual Eccles cakes are a byword in this town, very well thought of and—'

'They'll not be a byword in Eccles, where they got invented in the first place. Fruit should be added sparsely.' He preened himself after finding such a nice, uppity sort of word. 'Sparsely,' he repeated proudly.

'There's no parsley in them.' Bewilderment occupied Lucy's face for a split second, but then she often finished up puzzled when Bert was on the premises. He knew everything and was always right, especially when he was wrong.

He muttered a few choice phrases about education not being what it used to be, picked up his lunch and walked away.

Lucy mopped her fevered brow with the back of her hand. This place was a madhouse, even with two full-time and three part-time staff under her managerial eye. Yes, it was a bloody war zone. The more the staff captured and fed, the more the invaders carried on coming over the top like a constant wave of Lancashire flaming fusiliers. They needed telling that the war was over, that this was a place of tranquil relaxation. These days, everybody was too busy, too preoccupied and too damned selfish for words. Still, she got a good packet at the end of each week, and she'd finally escaped her mother's fierce clutches.

Except for odd bods like Bert Battersby, the Spinning Jenny boasted a rather up-market clientele at lunchtime. Mill owners, factory managers and office staff tended to patronize the café on weekdays, and it was quite a common thing for papers to be spread on a table so that business might mingle with the pleasure of eating. There were also the posh women who placed orders upstairs, then came in with their friends for *café au lait* or China tea with small dainties, bite-sized affairs constructed from iced marzipan or cream-filled and chocolate-drowned choux pastries.

Bert Battersby chewed morosely under Lucy's gimlet stare. One word to another customer, one attempt to polish his dentures on the tablecloth, and his cap wouldn't fit any more. Not on his head, at least. He knew it, she knew it, and they both knew that he'd be back tomorrow with another lively complaint.

The door opened and Maria stepped in. She was wearing a loose, dye-daubed smock, rather like something a Somerset yokel might have favoured. Her hair was long now, scraped back harshly from the narrow face and arranged in a plaited red bun just above her collar. Small circular spectacles in metal frames perched on the end of her nose, while the pierced ears boasted some unusual dangly earrings which were oddly reminiscent of items an angler might use on the end of a fishing line.

Lucy waved. 'Hiya, Maria.' This was her usual form of greeting to her unlikely boss, who had taken to pronouncing her own name as Mar-eye-a, so the two words of greeting rhymed. 'There'll be a table in a sec.' She glared at Bert Battersby who was taking his time over the small free meal.

Maria removed her smock and hung it on the hatstand. As ever, she was dressed in a suit of impeccable cut and quality, while the blouse was one of the Maria Hesketh range. She kicked off her canvas work slippers, dug in her bag and produced a pair of fashionable kid shoes. When the spectacles were in their case, she was a new woman, ready to face the world. No-one looked at her for more than a second or two. Bolton had grown used to the strange Liverpool lady who bounced around in a car and made all her own jewellery from odds and ends. She was just another character; the town was full of them.

At the counter, Maria spoke to Lucy in a stage whisper. 'Right, now I've got myself sorted, we'll get down to business. Where is he?'

'Who?'

'That stupid brother of mine. He's like a bad smell,

always hanging around. You know it's hiding somewhere, but you can never quite put your disinfectant on it.'

'He's not here.'

'I can see he's not here. Even with the glasses off, I can see he's not here.' She glanced from side to side, making sure that nobody was listening. 'Has he been?'

'Where?'

Maria ground her teeth impatiently. 'To China, you soft mare. Listen, has he been in for a drink of tea, or have you seen him going upstairs through the other door? Or coming down the stairs?'

'No.' Lucy cupped her mouth with a hand. 'Why are we whispering? Has he done something wrong?'

Maria rubbed at an indigo spot on her left wrist. 'Lucy, has he ever done anything right? Oh, he's brilliant with the machines, learned everything in five minutes flat, but . . . well, you know what I mean. It's getting past funny now.'

Lucy paused until two waitresses with trays had passed by. 'Is he still at it, then? Jenny's fed up. Last time he asked her, she promised to crown him with her cash register. I think she's got a temper, you know. One of these days, she'll give him a bloody good clouting. Why can't he take no for an answer?'

Maria almost growled, 'Because he's a man, because he thinks he's in love, and because he never had a brain in the first place. I'll have a ham salad and a pot of tea. Don't worry, I'll sit with Bert, his teeth don't bother me. After sixteen years down the dock road, I can put up with most things.'

Lucy chuckled to herself. Maria always wore the air of someone in a dreadful hurry, so it was her custom to change subject in the middle of a sentence, then to return to the original topic without warning. She took a bit of keeping up with, but she was all right, a good boss who wasn't frightened of work herself. 'Do you want a bit of bread and butter?'

Maria sniffed. 'No, I'll take it neat, I feel like living dangerously.' She wandered to the window and stared outside, not noticing the people in the café. As single-minded as ever, she raked her eyes up and down the road in search of her brother. She would belt him when she got hold of him this time, sneaking off in the middle of a job, leaving Ivy Nelson and Joan Higginbottom with the wrong rollers, no colours and enough cloth to make a couple of handkerchieves.

Bert stood up, pulled his cap so far down that it almost served as blinkers, then stormed out of the shop. He did the same thing every day, and nobody was impressed. Maria watched the shabby figure ambling off towards Bradshawgate, then she claimed the table, keeping her gaze on the window. Their Anthony was up to something. Again. If he turned up here, she would serve him as horseradish with the roast beef, stupid pillock he was.

She picked at her meal, wondering when she had last enjoyed food. The fork hung for a second or two in mid-air, halfway between plate and mouth. Potato pie with Denis, brown earthenware dishes balanced on knees in front of the fireplace, marigolds in the grate instead of flames. Shortcrust pastry wafer-thin, so thin that it was almost impossible to keep in one piece. The smile on his face, a shiny spot where his hair had worn away, soft kind eyes and hands big enough to save lives, gentle enough to soothe away her cares. Tasting nothing, she chewed the salad and swallowed like an obedient child. Food was a necessary evil, it kept her alive.

It had been a long two years of nights, but a short time of daylight. There were lines on her face and she was only twenty-one, but she had earned every one of her worry marks. It had cost thousands to set up Hesketh Fabrics, thousands of Henry Skipton's money. He always said that the money wasn't his, though, always insisted that it was the proceeds from forty-seven chip shops up and down the country. She took a sip of tea. She was drinking, wearing, printing, eating Eloise Skipton's fortune. It had been worth cleaning up the prunes after all. Every time she paid him some back, the bloody man turned up with more machines, more dyes, more cloth. She owed him everything and so did Anthony who had gone missing without a word to anyone.

An interior door opened, and Jenny Crawley stepped

into the café. There was a momentary lull in the various conversations. Jenny never failed to turn heads. She'd turned Anthony's almost full circle, thought Maria. He'd be wearing his shirt collars back to front if he didn't shape. She waved. 'Over here, Jenny.'

The beautiful blonde girl made her slow way to Maria's table. Although she used very little make-up, her lips were red and her cheeks glowed with a pleasant creamy-rose tint that owed nothing to artifice. The only concession she allowed to modernity was to pepper her nose with an occasional dab of powder which made her sneeze, but saved her skin from shining. 'Pol's in,' she said. 'Two oil paintings and a small statuette with a chip on its shoulder. She's so excited, you'd think she'd found a pair of long lost Rembrandts and Venus de Milo's arms. I've sold eighteen yards of Tuppenny and eleven yards of Hesketh. The violet range is going out well, so you'd better print some more. Lilac seems to be in vogue at the moment. Lilac and the pale cream snowdrop print.'

'Aye-aye, cap'n.' Maria touched an invisible forelock. 'He's gone missing again. I've six London orders in and that Cornish landlady's on about her bedroom curtains with ships on, keeps sending letters full of drawings of masts and sails. That's a block job, a one-off, so me and the girls can do it. But we should be rolling on with the London work, the equipment's cost a flaming fortune. And he's buggered off. Do you want a cup of tea? Have you seen him? And what about our Josie getting her scholarship a year early?' She preened herself, sticking out the non-existent chest and smoothing the tight cap of hair. 'She's clever, is Josie. I'm thinking of getting her a typewriter, give her a start for when she's company secretary. I'll take an inch out of that frock tomorrow,' she muttered finally. 'You've lost weight on your hips again.'

Jenny grinned. If she really listened to Maria, she would probably go stark raving lunatic. 'I've not seen him, Josie's doing very well, I like a bit of room in my clothes, I don't want tea and when are you going to London about that posh shop contract?'

'Next week. He could be anywhere, our Anthony, like a

458

cat on hot bricks these days. Mr Skipton's coming with me to read the small print. He says he wouldn't put it past these southerners to pull a fast one, 'cos they don't know we've Skipton's behind us. I've told him to wear a vest after that bad cold. He's out in all weathers, no coat and no sense.'

Jenny knew that her friend had skipped from the mill owner to Anthony, and she didn't wish to discuss either of them. Mr Skipton had spoken few words to her these past months, while Anthony kept repeating the same four. 'Will you marry me' was his usual refrain, sometimes accompanied by flowers, once by an old man with finger-less gloves and a worn-out melodian. It was becoming a farce, yet it was tragic because Anthony seemed to be so smitten, poor lad. 'Stop worrying, Maria,' was all she said.

'It's my nature to worry. I watched my mother pretend-ing not to worry, and look where that got her. Isolation hospital, kids scattered to the four winds and my dad sat in the house on his own with a jug of stout and no dinner. Switzerland will put her right, you'll see.' At last, her mother was living a life that suited her, books, mountain air and no screaming infants. But to reach her goal, she had needed to acquire tuberculosis of the lungs and a fair proportion of her oldest daughter's personal income. 'You'll not marry him, will you?' The tone was flat and resigned.

'No, I'm not marrying anybody at the moment, I'm going to have some dinner.'

'He's right for you, Jenny. And you'd set him straight, make him into a man. He's looked at nobody else since he first met you. This'll carry on till you marry some bugger. He'll not let go till you're out of reach.'

Jenny drew the tip of a finger round a crocus on the Hesketh tablecloth. She liked her life, loved it, even. When the man upstairs had finally moved out with his patented brown sauce, they had taken the lease and opened the Spinning Jenny Gallery. Pol, who had converted in the twinkling of an eye from prostitution to total respect-ability, brought in the goods. Jenny haunted the library, started to learn about collectable items. The breadth of the topic was overwhelming, and she knew that she could never absorb enough of the fascinating subject. She sold Maria's fabrics, dress patterns and household linens which were finished by homeworkers, women who did piecework for pin money. She also dealt in art materials, and sold paintings produced by local artists. But her favourite things were the old pieces, some of which she grieved over once they were sold.

'You're quiet, Jenny.'

She raised her eyes. 'Don't blame me for not marrying Anthony. I can't marry him.'

Maria sniffed. 'The other fellow's out and about with all kinds of women. He's not letting the grass grow, I can tell you. He might have a dead arm, but he manages somehow. Why are you waiting for him? He's old, too old for you.'

'Maria, I am waiting for nobody.' There was an edge to her voice, probably because she was propping up the lie. 'And I don't know why we're talking about this in here when we can do it at home.'

The thin girl sniffed again while her butterfly mind sought its next port of call. 'I know where he is when we're at home. I know he's either in the pub or he's six doors down with Ena and our Josie. Today, he could be anywhere, might have thrown himself in the cut with a brick round his neck—'

'And no vest on.'

Maria clicked her tongue. This Jenny Crawley was getting a bit quick and a bit stubborn. She used words economically, so it wasn't always easy to know what she was thinking. It was almost as if she were hatching some grand plan, and there was no shifting her off the nest to see the nature of the beast. It would all come out in the end, Maria presumed. And before that happened, Mavis's parcels must be opened in case their contents had some bearing on the direction of Jenny's life. She choked on a crisp bit of lettuce, then abandoned her meal. Most days, she managed not to think about the secret she was keeping from Jenny, but it cropped up occasionally, occupied the front of her thinking. This was one of those times. She could almost feel the age-dried and brittle paper in her hand.

Jenny looked calmly at her coughing friend. She did everything too quickly, that was Maria's problem. And underneath the neat and precise exterior, there lurked a darker side, a part of Maria that dared not show itself to a world that purchased pretty cloth. The sorrow over Denis and the baby had cut Maria down, so she had simply used a remembered pattern to rebuild a facsimile of her previous self. She was amusing, talented, bright. But this outer garment of poise was worn only when necessary. At home, in the evenings, she often sat in her lonely room, still and soundless with her thoughts and memories. And in the night, Maria sometimes cried out when sleep deprived her of the ability to control herself. She really did know the names of her brothers and sisters, because she called for them in her nightmares. Denis had died a thousand times. Jenny, in the next room, frequently shared the widow's sleep-drugged lament.

'I suppose I'd better get back,' said Maria. 'We can manage without him at a pinch. But he's always been there when we've set up a new line. And it's no use docking his wages, 'cos he's a director and only the directors get poor pay. Mr Skipton says these are our breadline days when everything's ploughed back. And my mother's taking a few bob—'

'None of us minds, Maria. If it had been my dad, we would have done the same.'

Maria placed a hand over Jenny's. 'I'm sorry, girl. With my own loss, I sometimes forget there's others suffering. He was a lovely bloke, your dad.'

Jenny shrugged lightly. 'He was only lent to me. It's the same for everybody and everything on the earth, we just borrow one another. All books go back to the library at the finish.'

Maria nodded swiftly, sniffed yet again, then jumped up and grabbed her work smock from the coat stand. 'If you see a book called Liverpool Layabout, stamp its front page and tell it it's overdue. And if any of its pages are dog-eared from drink, send for me. I'll bend his bloody membership card for him.'

Jenny gazed round the café after Maria had left. Where the Tuppenny Prints counter had stood, there were now four rectangular tables in alcoves, intimate areas where business could be discussed over cheese and coffee without the world's ear listening in. The rest of the tables were circular with long, floor-sweeping Hesketh Crocus cloths and comfortable padded chairs. The wallpaper had been specially commissioned to blend, and the curtains too were made from the subtly-patterned cotton. Cutlery was cheap, but plated with silver, while the china was plain white with a silver edge to cups and plates. It was a good place, a place they had hung on to fiercely. They could have used this floor for fabrics, the upper storey for antiques, had even considered employing seamstresses, but the café more than served its purpose. Maria also believed that a concern which looked small seemed more 'exclusive'. She therefore produced pattern books so that the gallery would not be filled by bales of cloth. She was clever, Jenny thought, clever enough to court London, astute enough to stimulate some large and moneyed imaginations.

Pol would be dealing with the customers now. Jenny tried not to giggle. She was so wonderfully funny, so honest and direct, yet manipulative in her own light-hearted way. A customer would come in for a Georgian figurine, and might well leave with two yards of cloth, a dress pattern for his daughter, a recipe for apple dumplings and some advice for an aching knee. Halfway down Bradshawgate, he would remember the figurine, return, buy it plus whatever else Pol had designated to the Special Offers box, then go home all the richer in soul for having met such a woman, all the poorer in pocket for a reason that was much the same.

Lucy placed a glass of lemonade and a Hovis cheese sandwich in front of Jenny. It was Thursday, and Thursdays were always cheese followed by apple pie. Like Maria, Jenny wanted things orderly, though her real reason for handing in a weekly menu had been so that she could browse through auction leaflets without interrruption. The auctions were the biggest treat. Pol, who was an old hand at most things, was always aware of value, knew when to bid, when to refrain and when to wipe everybody else off the face of the earth by paying a price that seemed ridiculous for something with no apparent worth. On such items, the Spinning Jenny Gallery often made up to 400 per cent.

London had noticed these activities as well as the swelling popularity of Hesketh Fabrics. Pol, who toured the North West with her pony and cart, apparently had the ability to syphon off all the best stuff. The woman was like a giant suction machine, gathering everything up, then spitting out the dross for the rag yards. A Londoner with an accentless voice, a pin-striped suit, a weedy moustache and no sense of humour had left his card. Anything large or monumentally unshiftable would be taken by him, commission to the gallery.

Jenny chewed. They were up in the world, but not far enough. Not yet, not far enough for Maria. The love of Maria's life was dead. Even her little unborn baby had been taken. Jenny knew that this dear friend of hers wanted to be kept busy and successful. She, Jenny Crawley, needed to do the next thing, make it all happen. I am a spinning jenny, she thought. I have to take all the threads and wind them on the bobbins at the same time. But I'll have to snip poor Anthony's moorings, let him float away like one of those wisps of fluff in a hot and damp mill room. That was the bit she hated, being unable to make all of them happy.

Pol would take care of the gallery this afternoon. Jenny would be off and away, picking up her next piece of carded cotton. It was hers for the picking. This knowledge was not born out of pride or misplaced and overgrown confidence. It was just there, like the wind and the rain were just there. It was a part of life itself.

He tried to summon up some energy, some way of sounding angry and amazed. But it was hard work, because he understood only too well the younger man's dilemma. 'I don't know how you have the nerve, the effrontery to stand here questioning me. I've been helpful, I hope, during recent years. My main concern is to ensure that the business does well, which is why I bought the mill and the printing shop. On a personal level, you and I are completely separate.' He threw a sample on to the table, seeking a change of subject, some solid ground that already existed between the pair of them. 'That's the new blanket, well shrunk and felted. It only wants sewing into a continuous band. The machines will print better with this under the cotton – those other blankets went sticky after a while because they were too cheap. Cotton's a vicious mistress, responds only to the best of everything.'

Anthony glowered and stared at his shoes. He hated this man, hated their benefactor, a poor creature with a useless left arm, a rich creature with money to burn. Being grateful was not Anthony's idea of fun. 'She'll not look at me. There's no harm me asking if you're in the picture. She never mentions you. When we do, she goes quiet.' He had come up here on a whim, a sudden and undeniable urge to get to the bottom of things, find out where he stood with Jenny. Probably nowhere, he thought gloomily. He probably stood in a corner all on his own with a dunce cap on his head. Just as he'd done on the few occasions when he'd attended school to get out of the rain and snow.

'She's always quiet,' said Henry, his manufactured annoyance running out of steam. He still remembered what it was to be a callow youth in pursuit of a lovely girl. 'She never made a lot of noise,' he added. Except when running through a field, clambering over stiles, singing to the horses, laughing at the dog's antics.

Anthony shifted, hands dug deep in trouser pockets, feet unsure about what to do, where to go. 'She says she'll marry nobody. I've tried flowers, jokes, chocolates – everything short of standing on me head in the middle of the rails while a train's coming.' Now, it was himself he disliked, for being weak enough to say all that, for not being tough enough to keep it where it belonged, unspoken and tucked in his own consciousness.

'Well, lad, there's nothing I can say or do to make you happy. As far as I'm concerned, she's a free woman. It's her mind, so she'll have to make it up when she's ready. I

464

have not proposed to her. I gather that was to be the gist of your question?'

Anthony blushed, shrugged helplessly. She was driving him twice round the bend, and here he was, meeting himself on the way back from round the bend, in an office with a supposed rival. And, as Maria would have said, with no vest on. 'She'll kill me when I get back.' He didn't need to speak his sister's name. 'I'm supposed to be lining up some new rollers and colours for this London job.'

Henry smiled politely. 'You'll be a rich man one day. Put your hours in now, work hard, then in the end, you'll have the money to pay somebody else.'

'And I'll sit in an office like yours.' He cast an eye round the small room. 'Mind, I'll want it a sight more cheerful than this.'

'It's away from the noise, that's the main thing. Cotton grows silently, then screams when we try to twist it. The man who invents a quiet mule will get my vote in the Chamber of Commerce.' He looked at the clock. 'Time for lunch. Have you tried taking her out for a meal, a nice dinner at a hotel? Some wine, petits fours with the coffee?' He was, he told himself, a scrupulously fair man. All was fair in love and war, and this young chap didn't stand a chance with her anyway.

Anthony shrugged. 'We've had fish and chips outside the Tivoli, and I bought her a cup of black peas once on the fair. Oh, and some of that spun candy, strawberry flavour.' He stared miserably at Henry. 'Not the same, is it? Cod and two penn'orth wrapped in the sports page of the *Daily Sketch* won't impress her. Specially with me forgetting she doesn't like vinegar.'

'Quite.' Henry rose to his feet, giving what he hoped was a clear signal of dismissal.

'Ta-ra, then,' said Anthony, making for the door. He turned slowly. 'It's all them knives and forks, I wouldn't know which to use. And I drop things, spill things. Still, I'll think about it.' He nodded, then walked out jauntily, creating the Anthony he wanted the world to see.

Henry sank back into the chair, leaning his right elbow on the desk, resting his thrumming forehead against the clenched fist. He had kept the bargain, the bargain he had made with himself. For two years, he had done the right things. After seven and a half months of so-called mourning, he had started to go out, had accepted dinner invitations, had gone to the theatre, to evening meetings and small gambling parties.

When the full twelve months had been served, the vultures had moved in on the carcass. Nieces, sisters, cousins and friends of friends had been dug up, dusted, dressed for the kill, then pushed in his direction. His smile had become fixed, and he had learned how to dance with one arm, just as he had come to manage a poker hand with half of his original allocation of fingers. The women had simpered and sighed, and most of them were now at the age where simpering just made the face powder set in the creases of cheek and chin. Or chins. He had played fast and loose with no-one; a peck on the cheek was the marked limit of his familiarity with a group he had come to term the hopeful virgins. He was cruel and inaccurate, because many of them were widows, but their coy ways had sharpened his wit to razors.

Jenny. He looked at his watch, remembered learning how to wind it. Maids cut his food for him, and Sam Nuttall from the local foundry had invented an implement for Henry, a 'spooforknife' with a cutting edge, three tines and a small scoop for gravies and sauces. Necessity was indeed the mother of invention. Or, in Sam and Henry's case, the father.

He was avoiding thinking about her. He was avoiding remembering the nights when he had stood in shadow at the end of Claughton Street, watching, waiting, hoping to catch a glimpse, praying that she would arrive home with Maria or Anthony. She would not marry Anthony. If the poor lad had been in the running, they would have got the wedding over just to improve their domestic arrangements. It was strange that they had stayed in that little street. Yet it was not strange, because Maria would spare not one penny from the business.

It was time now to go for her, to court her, win her hand. But she carried the trump cards, she had youth and beauty on her side. All he could offer was money, and money meant little to a girl who saw gold in buttercups, diamonds in raindrops, whose dream was a perfect world where the lion and the lamb would lie down together. He loved her. With all his heart, soul, mind and body, he loved that young woman. He saw her now, bare feet skimming the grass, arms widened to embrace the whole earth, voice raised in joyous laughter. No, she was not always quiet, his Jenny. How she had giggled after dashing through that field of cows and he had pointed to her stained toes. Her irrefutable answer had been, 'It's only grass, Mr Skipton, grass processed by cows.' She was so alive, so happy in the right circumstances. If she would have him, he would sell the Hall, find a new place, anything she wanted.

He failed to hear the door as it swung to on its weighted, self-closing hinge. When he looked up, he knew that his mind had gone, that he was finally ready for the van and the men in white coats. Her hair was like spun platinum, gossamer-light, shining and healthy. She was biting her lip to hold back a smile that was no longer timid. The finger-nails were short and neat; he remembered that she hated talons on women. He had summoned up this vision, this picture of her.

'Henry?' she said.

He swallowed nervously, shook his head as if clearing it after too much sleep or whisky. There was a pulse at the base of her throat, a tiny beat that he would not have seen in his imagination. The dress was a little too loose, and she was wearing a slender bangle of etched silver, a thing he had never seen before. 'Jenny?'

'Shall we go to lunch?' she asked. There was Bolton in her vowels. This sweet child would never deny her origins, would never polish herself to false perfection. Yet she spoke now like a woman, a well-versed woman who was sure of her own identity.

He stumbled to his feet. 'Jenny, I've only one arm, but will you marry me?' That was probably the daftest thing he had ever said, he thought ruefully.

'We have three between us,' she answered. 'I think we

can just about manage, don't you?' She walked towards him slowly, but then her movements were usually slow when restricted by walls and furniture. There was a languor about her, a deep and solid certainty. It occurred to him suddenly that she had always been sure, and that he was the thing she had been sure about. 'I love you so much,' she said softly. 'Shall we get married soon?'

Now he really felt the loss of the limb, because he was holding her, breathing her, tasting the sweetness of her willing lips. She was strong and willowy; he could have counted the supple vertebrae if he had chosen to use the moment foolishly. He threaded his fingers through silken hair, covered her throat with a dozen small kisses. His face was wet with tears that belonged to both of them. It was like a dam bursting, a huge wall breaking down to let out something that had been stored, contained and hidden.

They stood slightly apart while she used a handkerchief to mop up all the joy. 'I'll never wash that,' she said breathily. 'Because we're in it, you and me.'

'Jenny, I'm old—'

'Forty's not old.'

'Forty and a bit is. A big bit.'

She laughed. 'Then I'll buy plenty of embrocation and tonics, old man. You'll have me to keep up with, remember.'

He held on to her hand, afraid to let go, terrified that this might, after all, be just a dream. 'A new house,' he stammered. 'A fresh start—'

'No. There are no ghosts for me, Henry. We shall live at Skipton Hall, but at the front in what used to be the best spare room.' She smiled, and he caught a trace of that old shyness in her eyes. 'Just one bedroom. That's all we'll need for a while.'

'And later?'

'A nursery, of course.'

His heart was beating wildly, thrashing about in his chest like a wild thing in a trap. He still found it difficult to believe that this was really happening, that a woman so young and inexperienced could have known exactly what to do, what to expect from this odd situation. His love must have followed her, clung to her during the separation. Perhaps love had a life of its own, then. Perhaps love needed no calendar, no timepiece to monitor its course, no vehicle to transport it to its destination.

'Even while Eloise was alive, I loved you,' she whispered.

Words would not come to him easily, and he found himself almost stammering, 'Well, people will talk, you know.' He concentrated on his pulse, willed it to slow. 'There's the age difference and the undeniable fact that my wife killed your father.'

'And I'm a bastard,' she said soberly. 'What chance do we have? We've both had very odd lives, though we should be used to gossip. I was jeered at for living with Auntie Mavis, and you've always been talked about because of who you are.'

He was calmer now. 'How did you know? What brought you here today of all days?'

Her voice was full of laughter as she said, 'I was bored, had to find something to do. And I should like to carry on at the gallery after I'm married.'

He marked her correct use of language. Eloise had been right, this was a clever girl. Nevertheless, he intended to enjoy being twisted round Jenny's little finger. 'Have I guessed your price?' he asked. 'Do I get my lawyer to make a deed of gift for Maria and Anthony?'

She measured her response carefully. 'Yes. Even if you refuse to hand over the printworks, I shall still marry you. It's not a price, Henry Skipton. That is compensation.'

Henry shook his head sadly as he thought of Anthony Hesketh. 'He wants to marry you. He was here a few minutes ago, complaining about your ill-treatment of him. Anthony is very much in love with you.'

She felt a cloud of pity passing over her, as if Anthony were here in the room, listening as they discussed his fate. These days, there was often something akin to anger in the young man's attitude. 'Yes,' she said finally. 'And Maria needs steadying. She's searching hungrily, still rooting about like she did as a child. You can give her this one thing. After all, it's only money and you've plenty of that.'

He raised her chin with the tip of his forefinger.

469

'Everything I own is yours. Even now, today, you are my sole beneficiary. There's no need for you to commit yourself to marriage with an aged uncle.' He paused, studied her eyes, looked for doubt and saw none. 'And I can't replace Dan,' he said. 'Despite my age, I can never be a father to you.'

She rubbed her itching nose with the heel of a hand. This silly nose of hers always irritated when she became emotional. 'You said you loved me. Years ago, you said that. It was a long time before I realized that it was the truth. And I could not love you back. You were married and I was still too young in here.' She tapped her brow with a forefinger. 'I'm ready now.'

'Then we shall go to lunch and start the tongues wagging. The sooner they begin, the sooner they will wear themselves out.' He checked his left arm, made sure that the hand was tucked into the pocket. With all his being, he wished that he could be whole for her. Whole, younger, livelier.

Jenny watched, knowing his thoughts. The arm, the house, even the moors would remind her of that dreadful day. She had run to her father, because he had been the important one then. When the doctor had revived her, she had woken in her own room, well away from the smell of blood and smoking gun. She had grieved for the dead man, had not thought about Henry very frequently. She knew now that she had been in shock and that the trauma had hung over her for months. Maria had been the nearest, the dearest friend, pushing food at her, drying the tears when they finally came, sitting with her in a grim, dark silence that spoke clearly of their joint yet separate griefs.

She smiled, dismissing yet again the ghosts she had earlier denied. Henry did not need to leave his home, would not want that. And the moors were still the same, still precious, because she had visited them several times. As for the house, it was stone and brick and mortar. A house could not frighten her. She was the old one, because she was the one who had travelled light years in just a few years. Her maturation was complete; she could cope now with anything that life chose to throw at her.

Jenny Crawley took the good arm of the man she loved, walked free from her childhood and into a future that would begin at the bottom of the mill stairs. It was a leap forward for Maria too, and Jenny felt satisfied with what she had achieved. And the bonus for herself was that she truly loved this gentle man.

After a lunch during which they had pledged and re-pledged their love, Jenny went back to the gallery. Pol was busy in a corner, laughing and joking with a middle-aged couple. On the counter, there was a bunch of red roses. They were slightly the worse for wear, needed water and a tender touch. An accompanying card bore a single word, 'Anthony'. She stared at them, inhaled their extravagant perfume. But she didn't see the petals or the dry and curling leaves. Her eyes were riveted to the thorns, which were unusually large and spiky. In them, she saw Anthony's pain.

Maria was perched, as ever, on a high stool that allowed her to keep an eye on the workings of the shed. Her office, no more than ten square feet in area, bore all the hall-marks of a meticulously tidy and organized occupant. Two windowless walls were covered in neat drawings of print designs, while a great cabinet beneath the single window housed letters, orders and details of customers.

In the middle of all this, she would sit, wire-framed glasses slipping down the slender bridge of her nose, unsupported spine ramrod-straight, a drawing pad on her crossed knees. This was one of the few places where she managed to lose herself, where she felt useful, needed, almost happy. As soon as she locked the door each night, the desolation would return, that hollow and sick feeling in the pit of her stomach, desolate thoughts running round her mind, footsteps dragging until she reached her car. Once the motor was started, she was at ease again, because the motion of the vehicle seemed to rock her, lull her into a sense of security that was completely sham. Then there would be the night, the endless darkness with no arms to hold her, no shoulders for her tears. She was not getting over Denis.

She plucked at a thread on the front of her smock, then chewed hard on a pencil. Cream on white, that would be the theme for the spring collection, something subtle and bridal, things a young woman might put on her list to be collected for a new home. She would invent a flower, perhaps the Hesketh rose, then some green-fingered chap might get to grips with the production of a real pale cream hybrid of the same name – fame, at last? Was that what she craved?

Roses. There had been a withering bunch here this morning, and they had disappeared. So had Anthony. He was the sort of lad who didn't like to be seen carrying flowers, so they'd be lost by now, left in a bin or a tram shelter. They would have been bought, of course, for Jenny. Maria sighed. Jenny would not marry him. He was too young for her; there was something . . . mature about Jenny, something that had only shown itself these past few months.

She fixed her eyes on the half-glazed door that led to the print room. 'Maria Hesketh,' said aloud. 'You should be grateful and content. Just look at that, you silly mare. From potatoes to a production line and a full order book in two years.'

The thin shoulders drooped for a second. Her man, her own lovely man, wasn't here. He wasn't here to be proud of her, to look at her drawings, discuss colours, read letters of praise from London shops. It didn't mean anything. Success was a thing to be shared with a special, chosen person. She would not cry. They called her Wiry-Woman behind her back, those people running the machines. It was because of her thinness, the metal-framed spectacles and her quickness of movement. They thought she didn't know about the nickname, but nothing happened within these walls without Maria being fully aware of it. She knew when they slipped out for a smoke, when they coughed or ached with overwork – even when their marriages were in trouble. She saw all, heard all and said nowt. And they liked her.

The place was, for Maria, a miracle of modern science. Huge wheels turned, etched copper cylinders picked up colour, pressed patterns on to endless yards of cloth. A massive steam cabinet puffed and complained occasionally, but never faltered, never failed. There were pieces of equipment here that had cost hundreds, even thousands of Henry Skipton's pounds, yet Maria had calculated that the man would be fully reimbursed within six or seven years. The child would have been eight, perhaps nine by then, and she wouldn't think, no, she must not think.

She glanced at the clock. It would soon be three, and her brother was still conspicuous by his absence. Fortunately, the machines' vagaries were understood by one or two of the men she had courted away from other printers, so the new line was running. But she needed Anthony's brilliance when starting a fresh pattern. He gave her confidence, made her laugh, understood her Liverpool wit. And she would belt him with her sample book when he came in.

Bored with sitting still, she jumped down from her ivory tower, threw open the door and walked to the back of the shed to her own special department. Although the continuous printing made the real money, block work remained her personal forte and her favourite. Sometimes she stayed behind, not working, just looking at the carved wood, feeling the grain, the cuts, touching the press Anthony had made for her. It was crude, it was amateurish, but it produced the best work that ever came out of Hesketh Fabrics. It was the wood, good, hard timber that had lived and breathed, that had fed shoots and leaves and blossom. She was getting all fanciful, she thought. If she carried on like this, she'd finish up all lyrical about nature. Just like Jenny.

She leaned against a wall, her eyes travelling the length of the shed. If this was Henry Skipton's idea of a little print works, then a big one might well merit Ordnance Survey maps and road signs, even a compass and telescope. It was vast. There were dyes being mixed in pans, mordants getting measured, then a soaping area, the washing machines, drying cabinets, steamers, mangles, dungers, boilers, coolers – Uncle Tom Cobley and all, she mused.

Two years ago, she hadn't known what these oddly named machines were. Printing had been simple then. She would put colour on cloth, dry it, sell it, pray that it wouldn't run in the wash or in the rain. She half-smiled. There must have been dozens of Liverpool women running round with purple and green faces. No mordant to set fast the dye, no recipes for a surer bond.

The interior walls were of painted brick, done in a darkish cream so as not to further tax the eyes of printers. Maria made sure that every man and woman who worked close to pattern got a fifteen-minute rest period in each two hours. After a while, the printing danced, especially if it contained a small and busy design.

He shuffled up the shed, eyes on his boots, hands dug deep in trouser pockets. When he reached Maria's side, he stood stock still, maintaining the same air of . . . was this defeat?

'Where the bloody hell do you think you've been, Ant? We had a spill just after dinner – there's half of this lot going home with a new brand of chicken pox, not so much pink as mauve. They could be in isolation by tonight.' She slowed her thoughts, sniffed, waited.

'I hate him,' he said. 'I left the flowers downstairs, didn't want the king of the castle laughing at me. He owns us, you know.' His head bobbed, then returned to its lowered station. 'And I saw her going in. They came out together, arm in arm. And there was me thinking he was armless.' Spoken in such dull tones, the small quip fell flat. 'He's took my girl.'

Maria's agile mind sorted the information, assessed it, filed it. 'Jenny's nobody's girl. She wants the fun she never had as a kid, only it's grown-up fun she's looking for.'

'He took her to the Pack Horse.'

'That sounds like adult fun to me. She's getting what she can out of life, that's all.'

'They were in there over an hour.' He sighed and looked up. 'I took the flowers to the gallery. The bloody roses were nearly dead, faint from lack of nourishment, so I thought they were just the right thing. I know how they feel.' He gulped, took a slow breath. 'I can't stop in Bolton,

Maria. The way I feel about her, I just can't take the loss.'

She stood her ground. 'I've no choice, Anthony. My man's gone for good. At least she's still alive, and where there's life, there's always—'

'No hope at all. She'll marry him. At least you don't have to look at Denis with another woman. I'm sorry, Maria, but there's dignity in widowhood, and there's none in being passed over for a richer man.'

She could not fail to agree with that. On the surface, she was a woman with a sad past and a well-oiled future. Similarly, Anthony was a brash young man whose wit never failed him. The acting he would need to do now was perhaps a little too professional for him. Even Chaplin and Keaton would have difficulty carrying on daft with broken hearts. 'I can't do this without you, lad. If you leave, I'll shut down.'

He stared at her. 'No, you won't. Maria, you don't need a power house to keep yourself going. You're your own generator—'

'And you're a bloody company director!' Her voice had raised itself, and she was glad of the machines' buzzings and hummings.

'Rubbish. That's all my eye and Betty Martin. Bloody Skipton is the company.' He pulled at his shirt. 'He's bought the clothes I stand up in, the food I eat, the air I breathe in this place.'

'No, he's lent us the machines and we'll pay him back with interest. He's made jobs for fifty people. It's our bank, is Skipton Mills. He's just the banker and—'

'And I've mortgaged my soul.' He ran a hand through his dark red hair. 'I'm off home.'

She sniffed a few times. 'There is no home. Mam's in Switzerland, the young ones are fostered. There's just me dad and our Jimmy and our Frankie. It'll be wall-to-wall empties and him snoring on the floor with his stomach full of whatever he's pinched from some bonded warehouse.'

'I'm sorry, our kid.' And he was sorry, didn't want to leave her. But he had no choice. He would be no good for this sister of his anyway, because he'd just reinforce her own sadness with his depression. He pulled her into his strong arms and kissed her on both cheeks. She was being treated like some continental prime minister, she thought, some French bloke with leanings towards a life of diplomacy and cabinet decision-making. They were cold kisses, the embrace of hopelessness.

He released her. 'Ta-ra, love.'

Maria watched her brother as he walked from the factory. He made no goodbyes, didn't stop once to look at the people who hailed him. For almost a minute, the rollers remained unwatched while half a workforce studied Wiry-Woman.

She turned away, faced a wall covered with small recipes, 100 g starch, 290 g water, logwood, acetic acid, Persian berry. She knew them off by heart, didn't need to see them swimming under a pool of tears. Maria Hesketh was alone and the world was as cold as poor Anthony's kisses.

They didn't know what to do. The tough little woman, the much-loved little woman was breaking her heart in a small corner of her empire. It was Ivy who eventually came forward and led the sobbing boss to the tiny office. The dye-mixer sat her employer on the stool, then pulled down the paper blind on the door. Ivy asked no questions. She simply held the girl, wiped the tears, patted a bony shoulder. 'Let it all out, luv. Yer dinner won't sit right till t' tears dry. Whatever's up, we're on your side, lass. Yer've done us proud, Mrs Dandy. That's better. See I'll go now, 'cos I'm wanting chalk from t' stores.'

Maria waited until the door closed, picked up her pencil, designed a pattern of cream lilies in thirty seconds flat. She felt lilyish, funereal. When the sketch was complete, she raised the blind and waved to them. There was still a lump in her throat, though. Because all who saw her waved back. They loved her.

Chapter Nineteen

THE PARCELS LAY ON THE TABLE, TWIN BUNDLES OF decrepit and discoloured paper. Maria prodded them with a finger, still uncertain about touching them. She had carried them downstairs on a tray, quickly transferring them from wardrobe to tray, then from tray to table. Jenny was not twenty-one, but Jenny was to be married in a few days. Maria wished with all her heart that Dan had lived to be here during the next difficult hours.

She stepped away from the evidence of her own disloyalty. Had she been a true friend, she would have ignored the scribbled instructions, would have passed the damned things on to the addressee on the day of discovery. But even Anthony had warned her, had told his sister of Oonagh Murphy's questionable past. If these papers – or whatever – were to prove that Jenny's mother had indeed been a whore, then Jenny, at eighteen, had been too young for such information. Now, the girl was older, certainly more mature in attitude. And the oracle currently residing in the Swiss Alps with nuns and a drawerful of romantic novels had shared Anthony's view. Maria's own mother might be a dilatory type, but she was a good judge of character and situation. She had advised Maria to keep the parcels until such time as Jenny's life took a turn, made a change. And what bigger change than this very hasty marriage to an older, moneyed man?

With her hands twisting nervously, Maria stared at the

front door, willed it to open. Jenny had gone to Ena Burke's to pick up the 'something borrowed', a frilly blue garter previously worn by Ena's daughter. She was taking ages – how long did she need just to collect a piece of lace on elastic? Maria positively ached for this to be over, kept comforting herself with the small and vain hope that the packages contained nothing of particular consequence. The pendulum in her mind swung again, telling her that nobody would wrap and seal a bundle of trivia, no-one would go to such trouble unless the contents were vital, even life-altering.

At last, the door swung inward. Josie Hesketh's cheeky face appeared in the gap, quickly followed by Josie Hesketh's bony leg sporting a blue satin garter, all ribbons and frills. 'Da-da-da-da-da-DA . . A . . A . . aah,' sang Josie, creating her own fanfare. She came into the room, followed by Jenny and Henry.

Maria swept the parcels on to a seat, pushed the chair into its correct position at the table. 'I was just . . . I was having a bit of a clean in me wardrobe. I thought we should all have a fresh start, see . . . We didn't know you were coming, Mr Skipton . . .' Her over-strident tone faded to nothing, then she picked up another thread, anxious to darn the hole in a conversation that was plainly refusing to start, let alone stay in one piece. 'Anyway, you shouldn't see anything that's going to be worn by your bride, Mr Skipton.'

He whistled, then let out a sigh of mock despair. 'Call me Henry, please,' he said, not for the first time. He took the garter from the laughing child. 'This will not be visible,' he announced soberly. 'At least, I hope it will be hidden . . . Jenny?'

There was something wrong. Jenny had felt it as soon as Josie's loudly heralded entrance had raised no smile from Maria. 'Go back to Ena's,' she told the child. 'Make sure you get the hem on your bridesmaid frock sewn, and stand still while Ena's using pins.'

When Josie had left, Jenny sat at the table, motioning her fiancé to join her. Maria, rendered completely unsure by Henry's unexpected presence, stayed near the fireplace.

'Out with it.' Jenny's voice was quiet and firm. 'Is it Anthony? Has he come back, emigrated, got into trouble?'

'It's not him.' Maria's weight shifted itself from foot to foot. 'It's . . . like private.'

'Would you like me to go?' asked Henry, wishing to be helpful, keen not to intrude on a friendship that was obviously close.

Maria sank gracelessly into a fireside chair, folding herself like a marionette with broken strings, all angles and no sense of direction. 'I don't know what to do,' she wailed. 'You'll know about it in time, I suppose.' She looked directly at Henry. 'But Jenny might want to sort it out on her own first. Perhaps you and I should . . . adjourn to the kitchen for a pot of tea.'

Maria couldn't go out of the house, couldn't take Henry and leave Jenny on her own. Also, her friend might well need Henry after the Great Unwrapping. She sniffed, leaned forward and placed the packages on the table. Perhaps the contents were just little bits of birthday cards and other small mementoes. They were more than that, she thought as she stalked grimly into the other room with Jenny's groom-to-be, who kept pausing, thinking, who had to be dragged away in the end.

When they were finally in the kitchen, Maria pulled him towards the window and whispered, 'They're family papers, I think. They're for Jenny, just for her, it says so on the outside of the wrappings. It won't be much, just a few bits and pieces,' she lied amicably, determined to make him stay put for now. Maria worried too, yet she felt that Jenny should do this alone. The worry existed because Maria fancied that she felt misery folded into every crease, every yellowing fold and tear. She chided herself for becoming too imaginative, filled the kettle, found the caddy.

Jenny, alone and suddenly lonely, picked at faded red ribbon. The wax fell away in crumbs, stiff and dried out after years of storage. Flakes of newsprint shivered their curly way towards the floor, as silent as a sepia-coloured fall of snow. There were more folded papers inside, not as decayed as the wrappings had been.

The top item in the first packet was a letter from Mavis. The writing was childish and spidery, blotted here and there with a small pool of ink that had escaped the hand of someone unversed in the art of penmanship.

My Dear Jenny,

You are four years old and we have just moved to this house. You are upstairs sleeping. You are so beautiful. I want to write down how lovely you are and why I keep you with me. It has all been done for the best and because I love you. I don't want to live without you, Jenny. Life without you would not be worth anything.

Your mother will not tell me your father's name, but it must be somebody who lives near Skipton Hall. She trusted my brother Dan to find you a good home, so that is why you are with me. I have done my best for you, Jenny, with clothes and food and we have always had a warm house.

I can't explain what I have done. I can't find the right words. Some of your mother's letters to me are in here. Mine to her are wherever she is and I took no copies.

She could have found you through Dan, so I had to tell two big lies. Remember my love for you when you read your mother's letters. Jenny, my Jenny, I am a difficult woman with no friends. You are all I have in this world and you are all I need. Please forgive me. When you read this, I will be dead and you will be grown, I hope. There was no other way of making sure I kept you.

God bless you. My own spirit and the spirit of my guide will be with you forever.

MAVIS CRAWLEY.

The name was printed in capitals, then 'Auntie Mavis' had been scrawled beneath it in a terrible blur of anxious blots. Jenny blinked, then read the letter again. There was guilt in it, guilt, fear and the hungry and awful selfishness that Auntie Mavis had believed to be love. Good parents and guardians did not smother their charges, did not dog their steps, demand attention and total commitment. Mavis had

had needs, just like anyone else, but she had squeezed Jenny dry of childhood long ago, had dominated her, used her, depended on her. And Jenny had forgiven Mavis already, so the twice-read missive was quickly placed on one side.

Like the letter from Mavis, none of Oonagh's bore a date. Jenny touched paper her mother had touched, ran her fingers over the writing, breathed in the musty smell that always clings to old paper. On each single-page communication, 'LIVERPOOL' was hand-printed above the greeting 'Dear Miss Crawley'. The first dozen or so contained questions about Jenny's progress, her teeth, her growth, her favourite foods and games. Sometimes, there was a sentence referring vaguely to Oonagh's life, words like, 'Soon, I might get a job, a proper one. There are hungry people here . . .'

On letters that looked very slightly newer, there were statements that bordered on apology, that courted forgiveness. 'I shall give this up soon. I am sorry you had to find out, but it's only for a few weeks, then when I get a real job, I'll save and be back for my baby and a fresh start . . .'

Jenny's eyes were misting. Her mother had been starving, had done something terrible to stay alive. She knew what it was, knew what her mother had been forced to do. Oonagh had probably been waiting for the fuss to die down in Lancashire, for her brothers and her mother to give up their search. In daylight hours, she had stayed in, no doubt, would have waited to ply her trade under a blanket of darkness. Her mother had walked the streets that flanked the Mersey, the streets that contained Maria's family and many more deprived souls. Inner Lancashire was poor, but the dock road alleys were destitute, or so Maria had said.

The girl's hand trembled as she opened the second, smaller parcel. This was wrapped many times in fractured layers of age-crisped covering, and contained a small black-ribboned package with a ticket tied to it. The ticket had a message scribbled in ink that had faded to a sad and unsavoury mauve: 'Jenny, open the other parcel first.'

Well, at least she had done the jobs in the right order, however unwittingly.

There were two further letters from Oonagh, the messages smudged, possibly drowned in the writer's tears. The paper was newer, must have been obtained from a source where good writing materials were to hand. Perhaps from a large house? Jenny was motionless as she read her mother's answer to the first of Mavis's lies. Oonagh was heartbroken to hear that Jenny had died of a lung disease after the measles. Oonagh had saved enough money to come for Jenny, to give the child a decent life. Oonagh was sorry that she had missed her daughter's funeral. She recalled visiting Mavis 'two years ago, just before I got the good job. Jenny looked so well then. It is hard to believe that she is dead. I suppose you will have told your brother, my good friend Dan, what has happened to my poor little Jenny. I pray that she did not suffer. Please send me Dan's address in London so that I can thank him too for finding Jenny such a good home.'

Jenny wiped the beads of sweat from her forehead. Dan had never been out of Bolton except for a day's shopping now and then, and for that last rest in Blackpool. Why? Why had Mavis told Oonagh that he had moved? Mavis hadn't know that Dan was Jenny's father . . . She nodded. Under normal circumstances, Oonagh would have written to Dan about the dead foundling, would have sent the letter to Skipton Hall. But had Oonagh really believed that Dan would desert the love of his life, move to London without making sure that the mother of his child had the address?

It was all very confusing, working out who had known what and so on. A cup of tea appeared at Jenny's elbow. She had not noticed Maria slipping in. The cup was empty before she opened the final letter and everything became clear. Dan had been killed by a bolting horse just after his arrival in London. Oonagh was sorry again, and the letter was badly executed, written by someone who was feeling more than she allowed to show in the restrained printed words. 'It is a pity that your brother had to leave the Hall.

But Mr Skipton was kind to let Dan get some experience in London for a few months. Dan would have had the chance to work for a lord and that always looks good on a reference.'

Jenny blinked again, cleared her vision. Oonagh expressed her best wishes, hoped that Miss Crawley would enjoy living in Yorkshire, asked her to write again some time 'to the same address as always, that's where I pick them up because it's safer'. There was no address. The address was buried with a totem, a fat Buddha, some tarot cards and Auntie Mavis. The address was rotted away, no longer available.

There was a burnt bit on the rug, a black corner where Jenny had dropped a coal while transferring fire from one place to another. Sometimes, the fire had been in here, sometimes it had been in the kitchen. And sometimes, it had been upstairs in a 'holey' bucket which had been used for an unholy purpose. She almost smiled as the pun filtered through her thoughts. She was dead. Jenny Crawley was dead, so was the man who had been her father and her Uncle Dan. Now, he really was dead, but she wasn't. There was a birth certificate, mother Oonagh Murphy, father unknown. Henry had it, was using it for the wedding, something to do with the marriage licence. There was another certificate, similar to the first, but with father Daniel Crawley on it. Henry had that, too. There were pieces of paper that said who she was, other pieces here that said she was no more.

Was her mother still alive? That was the burning question. Again her eyes were fixed on the rug, she was back to the subject of burning, going round in ceaseless circles that made no sense. Who she used to be did not matter. She would shortly be Jenny Skipton, and that would be her identity for the rest of her life. With this clear thought in her mind, she pushed the past away from herself until it sat in its own pile of mould at the other side of the table. She would not look at these letters again.

They came in and sat with her then, silent and still, like mourners after a burial. She studied both of them in turn, her lovely friend with the tied-back red hair and the spectacles dangling from a chain round her neck, her friend who had found these packages. And Henry, his face setting in worry lines, the eyebrows raised again, pushed upward by a thousand questions that he had deliberately squashed, internalized. 'I think my mother is still alive,' she said quietly. 'Auntie Mavis made her believe that I died when I was very young, and that my father died at about the same time.' Her throat was dry, so she drained the cold dregs from her cup. 'You didn't use the strainer, Maria.' She picked some leaves from her tongue.

'Sorry.'

'It's all right. Really, everything's all right.'

Henry touched Jenny's hand. 'But she didn't know that Dan was your father – nobody knew that. So why did she need to . . . kill him off like that?'

Jenny squeezed his fingers. 'Oonagh would have expected some communication from Dan, because to all intents and purposes, particularly as far as Mavis was concerned, he was a trusted friend of my mother's.' She gazed past both of them. 'This is why I never played in the street. We were in hiding. The visit from my mother must have happened in secret, or my father would have mentioned it to me.'

Henry nodded slowly. 'Dan used to visit his sister regularly, so Mavis would know his movements. She probably picked a day when we were out on some sort of business. A clever woman. A very devious woman, too.' Yes, he knew all about that type . . .

'Did my mother never write to the Hall?' asked Jenny.

Henry thought about that. 'No. Before Dan died, when he told me about being your father, he said that Oonagh was terrified of her family. She was particularly concerned that she should not be found and that Dan should be safe. If she had written to him, he would have combed Liverpool more regularly and more thoroughly. But as things were, he only had Mavis's word that Oonagh was in Liverpool. It seems that she lost her temper, made some remark about sailors.' He coughed, cleared his throat. 'Dan was not aware of any letters or any visits by your mother.'

Jenny stared down at her hands, at Henry's strong,

supple fingers. He was a fine and lovable man, an injured man. It had cost a fortune to get the car converted so that he could continue to drive, continue to lead a normal existence. And here she was, piling more trouble on his head. 'There's nothing we can do,' she said at last. 'Life's no different, not really. Everything's the same as it was yesterday and the day before that.'

'I'll hire somebody,' he protested.

Jenny tried to smile. 'She could be anywhere between the south coast and Scotland. She might even be at home in Ireland. What if she's married, with a new family, other children? How would it be if I turned up out of the blue, "Hello, I'm your illegitimate daughter"? No. It's best left alone, all of it.' She rose, picked up the letters and bundled them without ceremony into the bottom of the dresser. The bottom of the dresser was a mess, full of life's miscellanea, bits and pieces that fell into no particular category. 'I'll make some more tea.' She went out, leaving them to their renewed silence.

Maria looked at him. He was a good bloke, too good to let this go. 'Be careful,' she mouthed. 'I know things, but don't be telling her anything that will upset her.'

He jerked his head in agreement.

Maria continued to whisper. 'Old woman down the docks. Anthony knows her. Oonagh stayed with her early on, when Jenny was small. Mavis's letters must have gone there, even after Oonagh got the good job. The old girl saw the letters, knew somebody was dead. Twice. I'll get the address. Don't say a word about it.'

He took some papers from his inner pocket, stared at them for a second or two, then placed them in front of Maria. 'That's the printing works. It's yours.' This was spoken in a normal and audible tone.

Maria's mouth dropped open, allowing her a somewhat vacant appearance, but the untypical expression was allowed to reside on her face for no more than a second. She snapped her jaw shut before saying, 'I want no charity and I need none. I'll pay you back, like we said before, for all the things you've bought for the factory. But these are the deeds and I'll never afford them. Not unless I live in a tent for the rest of me life, wear clogs and shawl, drink rainwater and eat fresh air—'

'I want you to have the works, lock stock and buckets of dye. It's not my scenario, Maria. I don't want the responsibility, the maintenance, the rates bills. This isn't charity. I do pay taxes, you know, and the giving away of that building will make me slightly poorer on paper. Take it. If you won't have it, I'll sell it to the highest bidder.' He paused. 'And the highest bidder will be another printer of fabrics.' He paused for effect. 'Probably Mallinson. He can't wait to get his hands on some of your workforce, pay them for your ideas and methods.'

She grinned wryly. 'You're a smart beggar, aren't you? You think you can twist me in any direction, just flick a switch and I'll move like a mechanical doll. After all, I'm just a woman, eh?' She grabbed the deeds. 'Right, you're on. But keep your prices competitive, Henry Skipton, or I'll be getting my calico from Shuttleworths'. He's already been sniffing around, old Cuthbert Shuttleworth, trying to offer me the world on a cardboard roll, no extra cost for best bleaching. You think this town's famous for spinning little bits of fluff into yarn, do you? Well, I'll leave you all stood at the starting gate, you and the rest of the milk-horses. You want to see Lancashire on the map? Wait for me, old son. My patterns'll take the whole bloody planet by storm.' After this speech, which was long even for Maria, she leaned back and took a deep breath.

'If I had two hands, I'd applaud,' he said.

She laughed. 'I've got to say thank you. I mean, I know that was all rubbish about taxes and rates. You're giving me the building because that's what Jenny wants. And Jenny wants it because I lost Denis and the baby. She's a good kid, our Jen. See you look after her.' She rolled the deeds into a tube. 'Because if you don't, I'll stick this where the sun don't shine. Are you with me?'

He joined in the laughter. 'Remind me never to make an enemy of you,' he chortled. 'And whatever Shuttleworth offers, get it quoted in writing and I'll better it.' He dropped his voice. 'I've friends in the police force. They can get the Liverpool end started. I'll need the name and address quickly.'

She nodded, then jumped up and moved to the door. 'Are you growing that tea, Jenny Crawley?'

'I'm cutting some parkin,' came the reply. 'Are you pleased about the works, Maria? Does it make you feel all wealthy and important?'

Maria, between two rooms, winked knowingly at Henry. 'Jenny Crawley,' she shouted. 'I've always been important. Ask me again about the rich in ten years.' There was a long road to travel yet. As she stood on the crack that was no man's land, the tiny strip of nowhere at the bottom of the stairs, Maria Hesketh made a momentous decision. She would marry again. With no particular candidate in mind, she began to plan her own wedding. The victim didn't matter – that was the easy bit and she would sort out that small detail at a later date.

'Are you all right?' asked Jenny.

'Fine.' It wouldn't be white, but it would be expensive. All her sisters could be bridesmaids – if she could find them – and the whole thing would be a Hesketh fashion show. Pale pink was chased through her head, replaced by soft green, then cream etched on to pale ivory. A massive church, a huge party with the press courted along, persuaded by promises of champagne and caviare. This was the best advertising campaign she had ever thought up. It would pay for itself in the long run.

Stationery. There should be Hesketh envelopes, invitation cards, writing paper. Not just for the wedding, the wedding without a groom, but for always. Being frightened of debt, of borrowing, was foolish. Henry Skipton, a man who managed to keep the wheels of three mills turning, had shown her that she was a viable and credible businesswoman. There were other factors of goods, different firms, products, contacts to make, visits to enjoy . . .

The business was getting bigger by the second, growing, shooting up here at the bottom of the stairs. There would be sub-contracts, work for other industries, for individual artists and craftspeople. Pottery? What about plates and bowls and cups to match the linen? Co-ordination, she thought, rolling this professional-sounding word across the front of her agile brain, taking a mental photograph, letting the dream try its wings. Stoke-on-Trent for the china, Nottingham for proper handmade laces. Pictures. Paintings for the walls of these colour-conscious rooms. Lancashire artists, commissions, success for everyone.

And. above all, she would seek out a shoulder for the tears. But first, she would enjoy the tea and parkin while wondering who would make the carpets to complete the furnishing of her fantasy. But this was no mere dream. This was achievable.

They were grinning at her. Jenny's smile had a sad edge, and that was only natural. But Henry's eyes were bright with hope, with faith in the slender red-haired girl who had started her apprenticeship with King Edward potatoes stolen from his larder. Maria knew why they were looking so happy and relieved. The cloud had lifted at last. Maria could survive without Denis. She could survive and even win.

Pol dashed into the house, her feet barely touching the floor as she rushed up the hall. She felt young again, full of childlike excitement. The last time she had experienced such a sensation had been at the Bolton Fair with her mother years ago. There had been a barrel organ with a wizened old gypsy turning the handle, all squeaks and groans and very little discernible music. A monkey in a red coat had sat on Pol's shoulders, and the funny little man had gone off for a pint, leaving Pol and her mother in charge. This was the same thing, pure glee and pride in herself. Because she, Pol O'Gorman, had found the missing spoon.

She stood at the bottom of the stairs, her mouth already forming the first syllable of 'Carla', then she remembered. There was no-one to tell. Carla had gone, had packed up and left after that nasty business at Skipton Hall.

Pol sat on the stairs, a small paper bag in her hands. Slowly, she unwrapped it to reveal an unimpressive object, all tarnished and brown, bits of fluff and dust sticking to it. There was glue or toffee in the bowl of the spoon, and the fancy handle was filthy, with greasy black marks in the nooks and crannies. But it was the spoon, a thing she had hunted for years and years. Now, she would have the full set. Now, she would clean up the case and give the whole canteen to Jenny and Henry as a wedding gift.

Sammy stalked by, his tail fluffed up like a bottle brush. He missed Carla. Carla had groomed him, spoken to him, offered her face for him to rub against. It was amazing how most of these two-legged ones had no concept of a real greeting, a good old head-to-head with a bit of purring thrown in, perhaps the odd mew of contentment and pleasure. Carla had made the right noises. This one just fed him and used him as a foot-warmer on winter evenings. He scratched an ear and waited for her to get off the stairs and cook his cod.

'I've the spoon at last, Sammy,' she said.

He yawned and turned to face the umbrella stand. At least with furniture he expected nothing, got nothing, knew where he stood.

'Bloody superior creature, you are,' said Pol, unwilling to admit her fondness for this terrible animal. She loved him, just as she loved the sulking pony. 'I'll send you to Carla, that I will and no mistake about it. It's all prayers and silent thought where she is, everything offered up to some bloke on a holy picture.' She bit her lip, hoped that God wasn't listening. He had to knock off sometimes, and early evening was a lowish-ebb time of day. Perhaps He'd be reading His paper, putting up His lordly feet for an hour. All the same, she muttered the short act of contrition before carrying the spoon into the kitchen.

When the small piece of silver had been immersed in suds to soften the dirt, she took some cods' heads from the meatsafe and began to poach them in milk and butter for her lunatic feline companion. He was beginning to celebrate what Pol called his 'mad half-hour', a festive occasion that fell somewhere between six and seven each evening. It was a time that was markedly worse preceding a full moon, and the moon was in its third quarter. She sighed, caught a glimpse of startled and upright fur as its wearer bolted with unnerving speed past the door. 'Will all the saints on high kindly preserve me this day,' she muttered. 'And preserve me doors too, for he's stripped half the paint off the bottoms and them only freshly done a couple of years back.'

He was swinging from the landing curtains again. She could hear that feverish clawing, the anxious tear of talon against rare, high-grade and long-stapled cotton, the most expensive of Bolton's woven fibres. Sammy was a big cat, and the curtains would probably be reduced to a ragged and uneven lacework by Christmas. She stood at the foot of the stairs, a large metal fish slice swishing through the air from an angry hand.

He was firmly and passionately attached to the blue cloth, ears flattened against his head, tail swinging from side to side, fangs bared, every hair on his body standing to full attention. The wickedness came from nowhere, just started itself up without warning. She had a weapon again, was ready to clout him across the rump. Not understanding his own daily craziness, Sammy was probably more sinned against than sinning. He dropped to the floor, rearranged his ears into a more decorous and civilized shape, concentrated on containing his own demons.

'Are you done, or is this just half-time?' she asked. 'There's Lucifer himself in those eyes of yours. Leave the curtains alone.'

He washed himself, carefully smoothing each strand of his beautiful bluish coat. A pre-prandial wash was unusual for him, but it seemed to calm the one who provided the food. She would go in a minute, then he could carry on sharpening wit and claw on the landing ottoman.

The front door opened, causing a blur of activity that took Pol's breath away. Someone stepped into the hall, then the cat flashed past like a fluffy cannonball, launching himself at the newcomer with all the confidence of a trapeze artiste whose trust is firmly placed in a strong safety net. There was, of course, no such happy landing for Sammy, who missed his goal and made an extremely undignified finish which culminated in a slalom run along oilcloth, no purchase for his widespread claws.

Carla picked him up, made a few 'iddums diddums'

sounds, then spoke to Pol. 'I've the evening off, thought I'd call in to see you.'

'Is it me you want, or the blessed cat?' Pol's eyes travelled up and down the figure of her friend. 'Wasting away, you are. Do they not feed you, these priests? And how come you've been given permission to be out during Angelus?'

The visitor sighed. 'I'm hardly in a convent, Pol. My life's no different from anyone else's. Don't think for one minute that it's all prayer and no fun, because it's a lovely job.'

Pol shrugged. 'For peanuts. You're working for monkey wages, girl. Why could you not stay put here, carry on working for Imelda and Franklyn? We were great pals, you and me.'

Carla smiled, showing off two rows of perfect and unnaturally white teeth. 'I wanted to do it, wanted to work for the church. I'm having a good time. We played poker again last night. Father Hourigan owes Father Weir three thousand pounds now, and the same fellow owes me two hundred and fifty. We're thinking of selling his violin to pay the debts and to save our ears. When he practises, I go shopping or do a bit of gardening. Even the birds stop singing when he's in full flood.'

Pol said nothing, just turned on her heel and marched off to save the fish heads from total cremation. She was daft, this friend of hers, throwing away a good job just to go and be housekeeper to a couple of holy Joes in Westhoughton, all statues, scratched furniture and lectures on the value of prayer. Pol flaked the fish, extracted the bones, set the cat's meal to cool on the sill.

She found Carla and Sammy in the dining room. They were carrying on like a pair of long-separated lovers, all touches and little noises, both as pleased as Punch after the policeman's been clobbered by the puppet's baton. Pol placed a cup and saucer on a side table. 'There's ham for tea, with a bit of tinned pineapple. Will you join me?'

'Thank you.'

Pol coughed politely, though her mood of mild derision was audible throughout this unnecessary and rather overdone throat-clearing. 'You will say grace, of course. After all, you're nearer to heaven than I am.'

After a few ticks of the clock, Carla picked up her cup and took a sip of Horniman's best. 'Pol, I've a debt to pay. I can't pay it directly to those I injured—'

'Then sell the bloody violin—'

'But I can put things straight with God. By serving the priests, I am trying to make myself a better person. Money isn't important any more. If you only knew how wicked I was, how cold and unfeeling, jealous, restless, looking for compensation, revenge—'

'Because of how you looked. You were treated badly by the world, so you kicked back.'

Carla's head dropped. 'I ruined a young woman's life.'

Pol sat in a dining chair, placed her joined hands on the table. 'You should speak to Henry. Your lie just put the tin hat on a marriage that was already deteriorating. The woman is dead, and it doesn't pay to speak ill, but she was a selfish brat with no depth to her, no thought for anything but her own adornment. He's happy now with Jenny, even recognizes me as a cousin. Remember I told you just before you left about my mother and Donald Skipton? Well, I'm the antiques specialist for the gallery now. I still collect rags, still talk to the children, get about like before, but he's given me status. He's a man big enough to forgive you, if it's forgiveness you're seeking.' She stopped for a moment. 'But you won't forgive yourself, Carla Sloane.'

Carla stroked the cat. 'Like any prisoner of conscience, I shall simply serve my time. If I ever manage to feel absolved, then perhaps my life will change.' Her tone was determined, even stubborn. 'Until then, I shall continue working at the presbytery.'

It was a total waste of energy. Pol watched the cat-hater, the people-hater who had been so interesting, so angry and different. She had found God, she loved cats and people alike, and she was now about as intriguing as cold cabbage water. 'You've changed,' she complained. 'I thought you were a marvellous woman when I met you, a survivor of cruel fate.'

Carla nodded. 'Been reading Dickens again?'

The Irish woman rose and pulled herself to full height. 'I do not read those fancy books.' She did read them, but never admitted her weakness. English writers should carry no weight in the values of a displaced person who was simply saving up to get back to the old country. 'I have better things to do.' This was said haughtily and with the head held so high that it almost faced the ceiling.

Carla again seemed to read Pol's thoughts. 'You'll never go back, except for a visit. Your life is too comfortable and you've friends here.'

Now this was going too far. The blue eyes sparkled ominously, as if someone had lit an impossible icy fire in their attractive depths. With her elbows sharply angled, the hands resting on rounded hips, Pol threw away her temper and laid into Carla. 'Don't you be sitting there all Queen of Sheba or the other one who washed her hair in asses' milk. I can go where I want and do what I like and no problems about crazy women with guns in their beds. She was as cracked as an old cup anyway, she was as mad as a rabid bitch when he met her, but all he could see was her charm. And you're hitting yourself because you made her worse – aren't you the stupid one? So you've come over all holy, need to punish yourself. Well, I'm not like that. There's nothing keeping me in the one place with a scrubbing brush and a pan of Irish stew and two fellers with their collars back to front playing poker and violins.' She was losing her breath, so she allowed a slight pause.

'I might have been a whore, Carla Sloane, but I'll take no punishment and make no excuse for it. If I want to go to Ireland, then I'll go, no permission from you is needed. You're so stupid and calm and pious, I could just now bite the head off you and spit it in the pig bin. Of late, you have come over all . . .' Frustrated by the marked limits of her self-organized education, she searched for the word. 'All sanctifimonious,' she concluded triumphantly.

A terrible silence descended on the room. Carla looked at the furniture, much of it draped in old clothes and curtains and bits of tat. A statue of the Virgin struggled to see with one eye, the other obscured by a pair of tea-rose directoire knickers, a relic from one of Pol's rag-collecting missions. A silver snuff-box sat on the mantelpiece, carefully extracted, no doubt, from a pocket or a bag that had been thrown on to the cart in exchange for donkeystone, balloons, goldfish. Pol was an astute woman, a clever opportunist. Carla tried to concentrate on the cat, but the bubble was bursting. Sanctifimonious. The laughter escaped, spilled into the cluttered room.

Pol pondered, stared at the helpless figure in the chair. 'Are you as daft as the chip shop lady? Whatever are you laughing at?'

'Sanctifi—' Carla hiccupped, swallowed the rest of the word.

'Don't you be mocking my way of speech, now. I talk the way me mammy did, and her mammy before her.' But the infection had spread, and Pol too was overcome by senseless mirth.

Eventually, they dried their streaming eyes. Pol fixed her friend with a stare that was sharper than needles, except for when unbidden glee tripped out of her mouth in tiny giggles. 'Do you want this bloody ham or not?'

'Is it English?' Carla managed.

'Of course it is. I eat only English pigs, told you before. Well?' A toe tapped the floor in pretended impatience.

'Is it salty?'

'How the hell should I know? Wouldn't you have to taste it before you got the answer?'

'The colour.' Carla pushed the damp handkerchief into her pocket. 'What colour is it?'

Pol nodded, her eyes glistening with devilment. 'Green, of course. With a purple rind and yellow spots here and there.'

The cat mewed as Carla stood up. 'That sounds eminently suitable,' she said. 'I'll have plenty of custard with mine.'

They looked at one another for several seconds. This unlikely friendship would survive to the grave, it seemed. Because the awful silence had been so quickly replaced by something else, something that wanted no words. What held them together was understanding, tolerance for one another's vagaries.

A yowling Persian stood between them, hair on end again as he demanded his food. They glanced at Sammy, laughed again, then went to cook their own multi-coloured supper, differences aired, tempers cooled. And the ham was not too salty.

Charlie chewed his bone thoughtfully. It had been a long walk, but these two were so wrapped in each other that there had been few throws of the stick. He yawned and went to wash the cat. He always washed the cat when life got a bit boring. She was a soppy tortoiseshell who seemed to accept the washes as a piece of some plot against her, a vicious decision on the part of whoever had created cat-dom. Charlie's tongue was long, pink, wet and extremely enthusiastic. Sometimes, she scratched him, but it was only a gesture of obedience to that other law, the unwritten edict stating that cats and dogs must fight.

Jenny sat at the kitchen table, her eyes glued to this demonstration of peace and happiness. 'Aren't they lovely together?'

Henry was cleaning some mud from his boots, determined as ever to cope with one hand. He lived with the animals, saw more of them. 'She's tolerating him,' he said. 'One of these days, she'll take a lump out of one of his ears. The dog has no sense at all, and Purdy knows that. She needs to grow a bit, then she'll be the boss.' Without warning, he changed the subject. 'Do you still love me? And if so, why? And if not, why not?'

She was getting used to him. The one predictable thing about him was that he was always unpredictable. 'Yes, I love you. I don't know why, it's just something that has to happen. Like it's out of our hands, that sort of thing.'

'Ah.' He straightened, looked ruefully at the dirt on his palm. 'A fatalist, are you?' Careless as ever, he transferred the dirt from hand to old sweater. 'Never bargained on getting one of those.'

Jenny, who thought that she didn't belong to any particular school of thought, watched while one of the richest men in Bolton got himself as dirty as any street urchin. 'You are the most terrible mess,' she said. 'Why can't you have a rinse under the kitchen tap?' She brought a cloth and sponged his hand. 'It's plain to me that you weren't brung up proper,' she said gravely. 'Josie's cleaner than you are.'

He put out his tongue, and she flicked it with the washcloth. 'Any more cheek from you, my lad, and you'll go in the corner by yourself on your own with nobody.'

He buried his face in her blouse, spoiling the loving gesture by blowing a very loud raspberry into the fine cotton. She pushed him away and studied her clothing. He was a clown. This was a new blouse, and he should know, because he bought it. 'Just thank your lucky stars that you got no mud on me, Henry Skipton. There's more to me than meets the eye, so you might as well know it before it's too late. Never mind the dog and the cat – it'll be me biting bits out of somebody's ear.'

'Promises,' he said disdainfully.

She walked to the sink, looked down at her left hand, turned it so that the three diamonds would catch what remained of the daylight. Henry had no choice about a wedding ring. Many men did not wear them, but this man had not the ability to sport a gold band. Unless he put it on his right hand, which would render the intention meaningless anyway.

She was growing used to the house again, had chased out most of the memories. Eloise's room had been stripped completely, and all the sets of china and crystal were in boxes at the gallery. Soon, they would be scattered about Lancashire, would decorate at least ten living rooms. She wished joy upon the anonymous purchasers, hoped that they would gain pleasure from owning such beautiful things. Eloise had not enjoyed them, had not enjoyed anything. 'What happened?' she asked suddenly, her back towards him. 'Before Sophie, I mean. What did Eloise do to make you dislike her so much?'

He rubbed at his boot again with a ruined handkerchief, sat up and looked at his bride-to-be as she returned to her seat. 'A lot of small things,' he answered. 'Like layers of thin tissue piling up until they made cardboard. She spent a lot of money, money I needed for the mills. At first, I didn't worry, because she'd money of her own. But once she'd exhausted that supply, she made inroads into cash that was needed for the mills.'

'That's a big thing.'

His eyebrows lifted. 'Is it? I've never considered money to be big.'

She frowned slightly. 'You would if you'd never had any, if you'd lived in a back-to-back and nothing to pay the rent, no pennies for fun. The nearest we came to entertainment was the night-soil men coming to empty the closets. They wore big wellingtons right up to their knees and wallowed in filth, dug it out with spades and poured some awful stuff down to kill the germs. I used to watch them from my window.' She smiled, remembering the small and misguided excitements of childhood. 'Money is important if it means a bathroom and carpets on the stairs,' she concluded.

'Yes.' He inclined his head thoughtfully. 'I suppose I do rather take things for granted.' But not like she had, not like the woman who had shot him and killed poor Jenny's father. 'She whined a lot,' he said, almost to himself. 'Wheedled and cajoled, always about some darling dress or some sweet piece of Wedgwood, Doulton, Waterford. There was always something she just had to have, couldn't live without.' He waited for a moment before adding, 'I think she was always unbalanced.'

Jenny watched him, felt his misery, opened her heart to take it in, soak it up and relieve him of some of it. 'She couldn't help it, Henry. It was the way she had been brought up.'

'She had food fads,' he went on, as if he had not heard her speak. 'Small tantrums at first, a pout, a refusal to eat anything unattractive. Then it got worse. She started to miss meals, began to eat chocolates and biscuits in the bedroom, pretty boxes of expensive rubbish with ribbons and royal seals. We lost three cooks in a month because of the refusal to eat. I forced her to sit at the table, and she would spread the food round her plate and sulk like a child. Then she threw a dish at a maid. After that, she made her own arrangements and I ate alone.' He smiled gently at Jenny. 'Perhaps I should have sent the boy for fish and chips. That was a menu she would surely have understood.'

Jenny swallowed guiltily. He looked so sad, so broken. She should not ask these questions, should never refer to the past. But how could either of them dismiss half his life, treat it as if it had never happened? 'There's someone at the back door,' she said, grateful for the interruption. It would not be easy, this life with the man she loved so much. They each had things to forget, though Jenny could hardly forget a mother she had never known in the first place. Again, she squashed the need to dash off to Liverpool. She was here to make everything work, and she could hardly do that while haunting a large and overpopulated city. Finding her mother was not necessary, she told herself firmly for the umpteenth time.

He got up, walked to the door, opened it and stood in a silence that seemed to be stunned. 'What do you want?' he asked finally.

Jenny crept up behind him, peeped over his shoulder. It was Pol and some other woman. Jenny swallowed painfully. It was Stonehenge, improved but still herself, still the nasty woman who had driven Jenny out and caused pain to all the staff here.

Pol stared at him. 'We're here to see you, Mr Skipton.'

'About what?' He took the watch from his pocket. 'And how did you get here?'

'Amos,' answered Pol.

'It's late.' He pushed the hunter back into the pocket of his waistcoat. 'There'll be no light for you to get back.'

'We'll manage. You know my companion, I take it?'

'Indeed I do.'

Pol waited for more from him, but nothing was forthcoming. 'She's changed,' shouted Pol excitedly. 'She's a different person altogether, all church and praying these days. She's sorry, Mr Skipton.'

He sighed. 'My name is Henry and you should not be here.'

'I'll go,' muttered Carla Sloane.

'That you will not,' yelled Pol. 'She didn't know what she was doing at the time, Mr Skipton. Henry. She was all bitter and twisted up like barley sugar without the sugar, what with being so ugly she made the milk curdle and the rice pudding set like brick. With a face like hers, you'd be hard put to lead a normal life, and that's for certain sure. And she was all angry with God and with her own mother and Maude who was so pretty with the ribbons and the nice frocks and—'

'Pol,' he called loudly. 'Shut up.'

Jenny touched his shoulder. She was getting married, and all this should be put aside so that the time could be a happy one.

'Leave the pony and cart here,' he said. 'I've to take Jenny home, and there are two seats in the back of the car. But you should not be here, Pol O'Gorman.' He paused, rocked back on his heels. 'You may take my arm, cousin,' he said. 'But I've no other arm to offer you, Miss Sloane.'

Pol hesitated. 'I was going to drive Carla back to Westhoughton.'

'I'll do that.' He pushed them away from the door. 'Do not come here again,' he said. 'This is the tradesman's entrance. Family and visitors are received at the front of the house. You, Pol, are family.' He stared at Carla for what seemed like ages. 'And you are a visitor. Come along, we shall walk to the front and Jenny will let us in.'

Jenny bit her lip as they walked away along the side path. Charlie followed, with Purdy bringing up the rear, her tortoiseshell tail erect, as if she were on important government business, best foot forward, eyes front and no faltering. How much did cats know? Jenny wondered. She watched until the little procession disappeared round the corner. There had been tears in old Stonehenge's little grey eyes; the woman was human after all. But the most human among a million human beings was this man who would be Jenny's husband very soon. He had even managed to forgive Carla Sloane for a lie big enough to start a war.

Jenny patted her hair, straightened her collar, then walked through the house that would soon be her home. As she welcomed the visitors, pride and joy combined to make her easy. She would be a good hostess. And she would be the best wife in the world.

Chapter Twenty

SHE HAD NEVER BEEN GIVEN A BIRTHDAY PARTY BEFORE. THE room was filled with light, conversation and people. It was hard to believe that so many would gather to help her celebrate a day which had, until now, remained as unmarked as any other.

Her husband was right at the other end of the table, laughing and joking with the daft vet and the retired family doctor, a man of advanced years who coughed, smoked cigars and drank copious amounts of anything and everything that contained alcohol. Perhaps he knew the secret of everlasting life, then, because he looked aged enough to have been under the sod a couple of times already. Had he re-emerged, not quite dead, with a glass in one hand and a Havana in the other? Henry winked at her. He was thinking along similar lines, no doubt. It was amazing how often one of them would make a remark, and the other would say, 'I was thinking that.'

Maria sat next to Jenny, had swapped seats to be nearer a young accountant called Josh, a senior apprentice with Hadley & Co., the firm used by Skipton Mills. Maria and Josh had been engaged in lively conversation all evening, something to do with interest, compound and simple. Obviously, Maria found the subject . . . interesting? Jenny sipped at the Mouton Cadet, swallowed a giggle with the wine.

Josh was clearly smitten by the lively red-haired young

woman. She had qualities that didn't show on the surface, was a complex character whose agile soul lit up a face that might have been deemed plain by some poor creature without Josh Kennedy's vision. He had judged her to be unlovely on first contact. Now, he was becoming putty in her clever hands. This was a lady to be reckoned with, someone different, a woman of great financial vision. A lover of figures, he was halfway smitten already, fascinated by a female who understood and appreciated the logical beauty of calculation.

Jenny watched while he lolled casually on one hand, the elbow resting on damask and in a bit of spilled trifle, but Jenny did not want to break the mood of comradeship which had sprung up between these two people. If she had sent one of the new maids for a cloth, then Josh would have become all embarrassed and gauche. Better to leave the stain, let Maria notice it. That would be the first barrier down, the first physical contact. Jenny smiled inwardly. Here she was, a bride of two months' experience, turning herself into a matchmaker.

Further down the table, Briony Mulholland gazed adoringly into the eyes of her own brand new husband. The young farmhand, who had been awkward at first, was now delivering a soliloquy on drainage and rotation, subjects that seemed to fascinate Pol O'Gorman. Pol leaned forward, large and creamy breasts threatening to spill over the top of clinging red satin. The young farmer's boy flinched; no doubt Briony had kicked his ankle under the table, punishing him for staring at Pol's voluptuous and abundant fleshly charms.

Carla Sloane was, as usual, with Pol. They were constant friends, these two, separating only when the housekeeper needed to stay at the presbytery. Henry had been heard to remark that the pair were joined at the hip, but Jenny knew better. That part of life which dictated the future, which catalogued and categorized people, had put them together. Most people called that organization God, but Jenny wasn't so sure. There was the same thing in nature, at all levels of the animal kingdom. These women needed each other, needed the security of easy comradeship.

At present, the housekeeper was still and silent, working hard at chewing with the porcelain teeth, though everyone else had finished their meal. Even the geriatric doctor had done thorough justice to five courses, each of which had been a fine example of Mrs Hardman's ability to read, understand and obey a wedding gift that would have made a good doorstop. It had over a thousand pages and bore on its leather-bound cover the words *Continental Cookery for the English Country House*, the silliest title Jenny had ever read.

She looked down at her own plate, didn't want to be seen studying folk so closely and rudely. If anyone had advised her two years ago that they would all sit down in peace together, Maria, Jenny, Stonehenge and Briony, she might well have told the prophet not to talk so daft. But it was all a part of it, all a part of everything working out and coming right. Jenny might be a quiet person, but she could feel things happening, could even influence fate. Just by being alive, she could change the world. It wasn't pride that told her that. It was a simple knowledge deep within herself, the portion of her that was connected to flower and tree, to bird and beast. In spite of her attitude to Auntie Mavis's calling, she might just have inherited a touch of 'the sight' herself, a small amount of prescience. Animals had it, an awareness, a quiet sense of things to come, of inevitability.

Maria touched Jenny's arm. 'Are you happy?' she mouthed.

'Oh yes.' She blushed, glanced at Henry who was guffawing again, probably laughing at some joke unfit for female ears. She would get him to repeat it later. The only difficulty in being married to him was that 'later' didn't last all day and all night. She enjoyed him, lusted after him. Perhaps she would cool in time, though she hoped not. Physical pleasures were definitely wonderful, especially the latest addition to her list of indulgences.

'You're blushing.' Maria's tone was light and happy.

Jenny laughed, drank, accused the wine of bringing colour to her cheeks. Her senses had always been acute; since the marriage, everything had intensified. She looked with new eyes, found so much beauty in the countryside that she sometimes had to look away for fear of weeping. Her taste buds too had come alive, though she had already sported a reputation for loving food. Now, the smell of new bread seemed sultry, earthy, part of herself.

He raised his glass and she answered with her own, tasting their love in the wine. Even music was more beautiful these days, whether it was on the records in the library or spilling from the clever throat of a songbird. And she had heard her first cuckoo in the woods, had frozen against a sycamore, afraid of disturbing the mating birds. She would be looking for a nest now, Mrs Cuckoo. There would be an egg, a big foreigner in some thrush's home. Jenny had been a cuckoo, a foundling with no real place. It didn't matter now. She and the cuckoos could survive motherless guardianship, had been doing it for years.

In her belly, she thought she carried her own secret, but she would wait till she was absolutely sure, until a doctor had confirmed her suspicions. A baby was growing, his and hers. They would be a family, a real family with Christmas trees, swings in the garden, holidays by the sea.

Under the cover of general hubbub and movement away from the table, Carla Sloane was walking in Jenny's direction, the thinner face anxious and pink, healthier than it had ever been. She placed a box next to Jenny's plate. 'I saved to get you something special,' she whispered. 'I am so sorry—'

Jenny pressed the woman's hand. 'We all make mistakes, especially me. I suppose if we didn't muck things up sometimes, we'd learn nothing.' There was laughter in her voice, a comradely undertone of happy acceptance. A lecture was not required here. She opened the box to reveal a gold Madonna on a substantial chain. 'That is so beautiful, Miss Sloane,' she said carefully. It wasn't Mrs any more. Only resident cooks and housekeepers were called 'Mrs' whatever their marital status. 'Thank you.'

The woman stared, small eyes twinkling damply under the cap of grey hair. 'Eighteen-carat,' she mumbled softly. 'You are the most beautiful girl I ever saw in my whole life.' Her neck moved as she swallowed her own pain. 'And that is why I treated you so poorly.'

To end the difficult and stilted conversation, Jenny stood up and led the fretful woman out of the huge dining room. 'Wait here,' she said when they reached the library. 'Henry wants to talk to you. It's nothing serious, so don't start all that worrying you're so good at. He wouldn't tell me what it's about. He probably just ... wants to put things straight.'

Carla slumped in a chair. 'It will never be straight.'

Jenny stood back and studied her old enemy. 'It will be all right. Trust him. He's somebody who can be trusted.'

'I do know that, Jenny.'

The blonde head nodded. 'Trust yourself, Miss Sloane, be your own best friend. We all need other people, but most of all, we need to love ourselves. If we can't do that, then we can't love anyone at all.'

Carla dabbed at her eyes with a neat square of white cotton, a sensible handkerchief with no frills, no border of lace. 'You are so young. Where did you get the wisdom?'

Jenny grinned impishly. 'It's not wisdom. I make it up as I go along. Henry calls it my philosophy, says it's very simplistic. But I just feel that all things have a reason, like a part to play. My part is to be quiet, act as some kind of listener and watcher. It's probably because I was alone so much as a child.'

'Alone?' The handkerchief was twisting in work-reddened fingers. 'Why? Didn't you play with the other children?'

'No.'

The grey head drooped slightly. 'Neither did I. They were frightened of me, especially when the second lot of teeth came in so crooked.'

Jenny bit down on her lip. This was such a sad and sorry woman. 'I was locked away apart from school. Mavis didn't want my mother to find me. It's hard to grow up when you've had an odd childhood. I had no idea of the right things to say and do, so I watched and listened. When I first came here, I was like a ten-year-old, still a baby.'

'And I treated you like a dog.'

'It made me watch out for myself. You probably helped in a way.'

Carla looked directly into the incredibly blue eyes of this young person who was now mistress of Skipton Hall. 'And look at you now,' she said.

'And look at you too. I'd say we have both improved. Wouldn't you say the same?'

The door opened. Henry and Jenny smiled but did not speak as their paths crossed. He wanted to be alone with Carla, sought to clear out some more of the stale air that had filled these rooms for many a year. No, it had been more than stale, thought Jenny as she walked back to her party. Rank would be a nearer description. She did not wonder about what her husband was saying, didn't question his motive or his need.

Pol was flirting outrageously with the retired doctor. The vet's wife was having a quiet bout of hysteria in a corner, unable to suppress her glee at the sight of a nonagenarian being courted by a professional. Maria and Josh stood by a window, where the last rays of sun were finding brief residence in the slight girl's burnished hair. Even the gingerness seemed to have toned itself down, providing a more suitable backdrop for Maria's recent sobriety. She was laughing, and the laughter was no longer shrill, had ceased to be a product of crowded slum alleys where only the loud and belligerent were noticed.

Jenny glanced up at a chandelier, newly lit with warm, soft colour. Even her birthday had been useful, had caused this gathering to form. Carla Sloane would eventually settle and live peaceably with her past, Pol O'Gorman was a reformed – well, almost reformed character. Maria was probably looking for a husband, had become positive, constructive at last. Jenny was happy, so was Henry. And little Briony had a young man to boss around, a lad who needed a push, a bit of organizing. Briony had replaced his mother. That was often the secret of marriage, Jenny thought, a strong female who would say, 'Follow me, I'm right behind you.' She smiled. Only Pol would have understood a thought like that.

A hand slipped into each of hers, Lucy Turnbull from

the café on one side, little Josie Hesketh on the other. 'This is the best party what I've ever been to,' said Josie. 'And I think our Maria's got herself a feller.'

Ena Burke staggered over to them, resplendent in a violet suit with a difficult hobble skirt that caused the heavy body to lean forward, as if her head were hurrying while the rest of her person took its own time. She had not removed her hat throughout the meal, and her refusal to be parted from such an intricate structure had caused stifled giggles all round. Each time she had turned her head, the vet had crouched over his plate to avoid being assaulted by a deadly feather. Josie, who had sat on the other side of Ena, had enjoyed the fortune of a younger and therefore lower position in the scheme of things, so it had all gone over her head.

'Thank you for coming,' smiled Jenny, her eyes riveted to the garishly dyed plume which had snapped at some point, and was dangling aimlessly above her old neighbour's substantial shoulder.

'Eeh, I'm that proud of you,' said Ena breathlessly. 'You're a grand lass, our Jenny. It's like you're me own daughter, ooh, I could cry, I could that.' She pulled a hanky from her sleeve. This, of course, was also violet, but of a more moderate shade.

The love from these people surrounded Jenny like a warm blanket, especially as it was a two-way thing, because she loved them too, all of them. She retrieved her hands from Lucy and Josie, threw her arms round Ena's neck. Deep in her heart, in the one tiny place that remained cool, lonely and unoccupied, she tried to force her imagination to stretch to a point where Ena could be her mother. And although she made a good effort, the trick did not work.

'There's no need to stand up,' said Henry. 'There's never been a lot of ceremony here, we're not the landed gentry, you know.' Deftly, he placed a cigar on a tray, nipped off the end with some silver clippers, coaxed the lighter to work. 'You won't mind if I smoke?' he asked somewhat belatedly, wreathed in a thin blue fug.

'No.'

He brought a small enamelled box from a side table. 'This is your poison, I believe. Try it, it's a good brand.'

Carla had given up the snuff, but she took some just to show willing. The resulting bout of sneezing lasted several seconds, during which Henry settled himself into a leather chair. 'Now,' he said after another thoughtful puff, 'I understand that you have shut yourself away in West-houghton with some gambling priests and an out-of-tune violin. Getting a story out of Pol is not easy, you know. She tends to colour things with her tongue, uses it as a paintbrush. So, what's going on?'

Carla hesitated. 'They don't gamble, not for money. It's just recreation, a game they play when they're resting. And they're nice men, very easy to feed. I don't mind being there, I'm quite content with my lot.'

Ash dropped to the floor, and he noticed that her eyes did not follow its descent, that she no longer condemned the perpetrator of such a crime against good housekeeping. 'There is no need to punish yourself,' he said softly. 'I was as much to blame for believing your story, for thinking that Eloise could have stooped so low.'

She shook her greying head. 'No, the sin was mine.'

The woman was determined to make herself suffer. He leaned forward. 'What you did was terrible. I know it, you know it, but it's done, finished.' He rooted about in his memory, tried to dredge up a bit of scripture, something that might impress this new Christian. At last, he latched on to a legend that could just about prove appropriate. 'Take old Lucifer,' he suggested. 'If he'd apologized on his way to hell, even when he'd one foot in the flames, God would have forgiven him and brought him back to heaven as an archangel or a seraph or whatever he used to be before becoming power crazy. You are wrong in not accepting God's grace.' Further inspired, he added, 'In fact, it might be a sin if you don't stop doing this endless penance. It could well be a form of self-indulgence. And we all know that true despair is a crime against God.' Well satisfied with his speech, he settled back to smoke the cigar.

'I can only follow the dictates of my conscience,' she replied. 'And anyway, I'm not really suffering. People think working with priests is some sort of burden, but it's not. I just need to make my contribution, need to make up for the trouble I caused in this house. With the fathers, I am doing a worthy job, helping those who mediate on behalf of sinners like myself.'

He was not getting very far, he admitted silently. So he would have to use different tactics, a plan he had hoped would not be needed. He sat very still, the words forming in his mind, his tongue unwilling to give them audible shape. The cigar burned in his hand; he had lost the taste for it.

'Is that all you wanted to say to me?' she asked. 'Because we should get back to the others.'

He sighed, dropped his head, raising it again quickly, as if preparing for a big occasion. 'I know how you feel,' he said at last.

'How can you? I caused mayhem to your wife, gave you unbearable pain that lasted for years and—'

'I bore it. There has been no pain so far that I could not cope with.'

'But a child,' she cried, her hands wringing together. 'I accused a mother of murdering a baby. It looked like that at the end, the cushion, the little body, Mrs Skipton standing over and . . . But she didn't do it. She was trying to revive the—'

'Stop this! Just accept that I really do know how you feel.' There was authority, finality in the tone. He would clearly brook no nonsense at this point. After stubbing out his cigar, he rose and walked to the window, stood and rocked on his heels for at least half a minute.

Something of moment was about to happen. She stiffened in the chair, forced herself to relax, became rigid again. There were twenty-four panes in the bay where he stood, two dozen leaded lights looking out on to the garden. She counted them twice, trying to occupy her mind. The curtains were of a loose weave, moss-green in colour, matching the shades on twin lamps. It was a man's room, brown and green with a lot of polished

508

wood, leather chairs, the smell of expensive tobaccos.

He did not look at her. 'I had an uncle called Donald, my father's younger brother. He was something of a rake, a ladies' man with a liking for drink and riotous living.'

Carla nodded to herself. The subject of this monologue was the man who had fathered Pol.

'He hated cotton, loathed the stuff, never went in a mill, or so I was told. The great outdoors was the place for him. Well, that and the smoking room of a local inn. He refused to come into the business, said the only connection he wanted with cotton was a decent shirt to his back. He might have been interested in growing the plant if the climate had been different, and he even spent some time researching into mallows, hollyhocks and the like.' He glanced at her. 'Hollyhocks are cousins of cotton,' he offered helpfully. 'Donald thought he might breed a hardy strain. If hollyhocks grew in England, he said, then so should other mallows.' He averted his face once more. 'The venture failed. All Donald's experiments were slightly eccentric. So was he. An interesting chap, but rather off-beam.'

She waited for him to continue, realizing suddenly that he was skirting the central point, or building up to it in a way that might prove less painful for himself.

'He liked farming, particularly the mechanical aspect. Terribly keen on making a farmer's lot a better one, wanted to introduce more machinery. He made ploughs, automatic rakes and hoes, a potato sorter, even a machine for hulling strawberries of all things. Nothing quite worked. Everything he tried was a whisker short of viability, probably because he would lose patience and move on to the next experiment. The next invention was always going to be a winner, the maker of his fortune. But Uncle Donald was as happy as a playing child, no responsibilities, a bit of money from his share of the mills, a roof over his head.' He paused again, remembering a man who had brightened his childhood.

Carla shifted in her chair, feeling uncomfortable with this story. It was leading to a distasteful end, she could sense it coming. His shoulders were sloping and the voice had been low and sad. She opened her mouth to punctuate the silence, to ask him to stop, but he picked up the threads of his tale.

'What I am about to tell you has never been spoken of until today. All my life, since I was nine years old, I have lived with the consequences. Don't repeat it. No-one needs to know, because it would improve no lives. Jenny must never hear of it.' He sighed, breathed deeply, dragged the words from the soles of his feet. 'I killed my Uncle Donald.'

Even had she known the right words, she could not have spoken them at that moment. Her throat was stiff, as if the normal secretions in her mouth had dried up or turned to concrete. She swallowed noisily and painfully, wrapped her fingers round the arms of the chair.

'We were messing about on old Sugden's farm, trying out Donald's thresher. It was another hit-and-miss contraption, seldom worked, looked as if it had been cobbled together from a bicycle and a set of saucepans. Typical. He was adjusting a blade at the front and he called to me, "Don't touch anything, Harry." He always called me Harry or Henry the Ninth.' He rested, saw the fine young Donald in his mind's eye. 'I was the sort of child who tended to investigate. Forbidding me to do something was the same as offering me an open invitation. In fact, if he'd asked me to fiddle with the damned thing, I should probably have walked away. I touched a lever, pressed a knob and . . .' He stopped, gulped, began again. 'It was a bloody mess in the literal sense.'

'Mr Skipton,' she managed. 'There's no need for you to—'

'Oh, but there is.' He swung round and looked at her, anger in the hazel eyes. 'It was a while before I remembered what had happened. Shock and so on. But I did remember. And I never told anyone until today. I made a mistake that cost a man his life. And I do not punish myself for it.'

She met his gaze, knew that the fury was directed inward, at himself. 'But you were a child, just a boy.'

'I had reached the age of reason, Carla. May I call you that?'

510

She jerked her head in agreement.

'Not only that, I stuck to the lie, even when I became a man. Just as you refused to tell the truth, so did I. Sometimes, an unbroken silence breaks the rules, makes a sin against man.' He walked, stopped and turned, walked again, finally settling once again near the window.

'I knew the risks,' he went on. 'At the time of the accident, I had seen the thing actually working for a few seconds occasionally. Some devil in me wanted to take a chance at playing with fire. But I excuse myself, just as you must. We are human, weak, stupid at times. A mistake is a mistake no matter what its size. It's just that you and I had the bad luck to be tempted when the odds were against us.'

She bowed her head, stopped listening. He had picked Pol up, dusted her off and turned her into a true dealer in antiques. Maria Hesketh, really Maria Dandy, was on the way to success, making a name for her prints. Even Briony was happy and settled. Now here he was trying to comfort a woman who had blackmailed him for years. Jenny was behind this. It was her goodness, her quiet gentleness that had made this man so bountiful. 'You're a bountiful man and a great comfort,' she said. 'I shall think about this over the next few weeks. Perhaps I shall come back to Pol, live in her house again. I miss her, you know. I really do miss that woman.'

He relaxed, the fingers of his good hand uncurling slowly. 'There will be work for you. There's the café, the gallery, the printworks, this house, three mills. We shall fit you in.' He managed a boyish grin. 'Welcome home,' he said.

She shook his hand, flashed a wide smile that advertised well the expertise of some dental technician, then went back to Pol. The party was over and people were drifting through the house and spilling out on to the lawns. Jenny was being chased by a black dog while a cat sat by and washed itself, one critical eye on its canine companion and adversary.

Maria touched Carla's arm. 'How are you?'

This was when control almost snapped, when the older woman had to slow down, think, relax. Maria had hated her, and there was nothing but warmth now in the pale eyes. 'Fine. And you?'

Maria shrugged. 'Up and down, pulling myself together, I think.'

'Good.' She tried to smile. 'I'm sorry about . . . that business. Jenny and you leaving so suddenly, the lies and the humiliation.'

Maria pulled back her slim shoulders. 'Don't worry about it. Come and meet Josh, he knows all about money. That medal you gave Jenny is lovely, did you get it in Westhoughton? And you look great now, with the weight off and your teeth straight. Have you had a drink?'

At last, old Stonehenge relaxed, almost feeling her nickname melting away into history. She was ordinary, she was free. And the man in the library had renewed her confidence, given her some hope. 'You're a fine girl, Maria.'

Maria stopped, looked through the open french windows. 'Jenny's the great one,' she replied. 'There's more to her than meets the eye. A lot more.'

'Who's put all this bloody wheat starch in here?' Maria, who always acted in a supervisory capacity when dyes were being mixed, tossed a small empty sack to one side. 'No wonder it looks like blue treacle. You were supposed to thicken it, not set it like flaming putty round a window.' Her head whipped round. 'John,' she yelled to a passing young man. 'Get up that line, find whatever's squeaking and put it out of its misery immediately if not sooner. It wants oil or a quick death, I'll leave you to decide.' She was not in the best of moods. There was a letter from Anthony, who was also in a fit of couldn't-care-less-if-I-live-or-not. Men. They thought the world revolved around them and their problems.

The spectacles tumbled from her nose, dangled on their silver chain. Even her earrings clanked, loops of bevelled metal, twin figures of eight that hung down the long neck until they almost reached the shoulders.

Well, she wasn't going to contact him, that was for sure. He could take a running jump into the cut with a brick round his neck, Mr Personality 1922, nice to meet you and all that. She was seething, and it wasn't Anthony who occupied her thoughts. Anthony had acted soft, would come round in time. But Josh Kennedy wasn't interested, hadn't bothered to contact her. It had all been a joke, just a laugh on Jenny's birthday. After all, what would a good-looking lad want with a sparrow-legged scarecrow with ginger hair, freckles and colourless eyes that only worked half the time?

She blinked, crammed the glasses on to her nose, waited till the ability to focus returned. It was close work that did it, made her eyes tired, and she'd been up half the night with a set square, working on an abstract pattern which got smaller and smaller until it disappeared up its own right-angled turns.

'Mr Skipton's in the office,' said the returned John, oil can in one hand, screwdriver in the other. 'He's waiting for you, and the squeak was from one of the washing machines.' In truth, the place was full of noise, so he had simply nominated the nearest item. 'I've cured it.'

'Go to the top of the class and give out the pencils,' she replied smartly. Her shoulders drooped. 'Sorry, lad. It's just one of them days. Go and have a cuppa if there's a brew on, and take no notice of me. I'll sort myself out in a minute.'

She walked into the office, face pink, fringe darkened by sweat, plastered so flat on her forehead that it looked as if it had been etched there. But once she was seated on her stool, an item that had been christened by the workers her 'high horse', she breathed a sigh of relief. No longer uncomfortable in Henry's company, she forced a smile and complained about the heat.

'Get fans in,' he said. 'It's not like the mill, you'll lose no stock because of fresh air. There's enough power from the generator to carry a couple of fans.'

She dug in a pocket of her farmer's smock, removed some fluff and a small sample of Diazo Brilliant Scarlet cloth, finally found the folded note. 'Read it if you want,' she said. 'But there's nothing in it. The old woman died a couple of months ago, so the trail's gone cold.'

He scanned the letter, noting that its brief message spoke loudly of Anthony's sadness. 'He's sickening for Jenny,' he remarked.

'He's sickening full stop. She never encouraged him, she told him he was just a good friend. They went on the rides at the fair and saw Buster Keaton a couple of times at the fleapit, but there was no romance. He's just mad because he didn't get his own way. Living with me dad won't make him any happier. He should come back and help me before the devil finds work for his idle hands.'

Henry paced about the floor, his expression thoughtful. 'No news from the police either. Oonagh Murphy simply disappeared, it seems. The good job, the one she spoke of in the letters, must have been in a house, possibly a merchant's or some other professional's place. It's too long ago, Maria. But I understand Jenny so well, almost as if I've always known her. She needs, above all else, to find her mother.'

Maria shrugged helplessly. 'She says not. She says if her mother's settled with a new life, a husband and children, then Jenny turning up might be troublesome.'

He considered this once again. 'If that were to happen, Jenny would not introduce herself. She only needs a place, an address, some sort of basis for her own existence. It's a very small requirement, a perfectly natural wish just to know who her mother is, just to catch a glimpse now and then.'

Maria rubbed at a spot of yellow on her wrist. They were more than fast, these dyes, they were, for the most part, totally unshiftable. 'She's clever, is Jenny, cleverer than we give her credit for.' She nodded three times, picked up a pencil, chewed on it, pushed it into her plaited bun where it sat like a geisha ornament. 'It's all sorted out in Jenny's mind, life and the meaning of things. She makes everybody happy just by being there, does Jen. When I first met her, she was as soft as muck, scared of her own shadow. But she grew up so fast, I hardly noticed. Till one day, there she was with a mind of her own and a sort of quiet stubbornness, like she'd suddenly found out who she was.'

'An amazing girl,' he said softly. 'Very close to nature,

which is strange when you consider her upbringing, four walls and a back yard, no toys, no friends.'

Maria was still fiddling, this time with pinking shears. 'She'll be all right without her mother. Jenny accepts these things—'

'She wouldn't if the roles were reversed. If you or I were seeking a relative, she'd turn every stone for us.'

Maria made sure the door was closed, though a person's ears would have needed to be specially talented to hear anything above the din of the workshop. 'Listen to me. What if Oonagh's a rotten cow? Or if she's turned out like Pol, all smiles and favours for gentlemen? Have you thought about that side of it?'

He cocked his head on one side. 'That's why we need to find her first.'

'Oh no, I'm not having that,' said Maria firmly. 'If I'm in it, then Jenny gets to see her mother and make her own mind up.'

His eyebrows stood to attention, stiff and puzzled. 'But you said she mustn't get hurt by hearing—'

'I've changed me mind.' As ever, she reverted to Liverpool tones when roused. 'She needs telling, good or bad. Jenny's what me mam would call a seeker of truth. So I'm warning you now, it might be better to stop looking – for fear of what we might find.' It might be better still if Oonagh had died in the intervening years, Maria thought. Some mothers were best kept in a closet behind the coal buckets. Her own was nothing to write home about, though Maria clung to the fierce hope that Switzerland would do its magic . . . 'Anyway, you can't hide anything from Jenny. You two read one another like a couple of open books.'

His brain was dashing all over the place, birth registers, baptismal records, the size of Ireland and how long it would take to visit every church. 'We could try Oonagh's family,' he said. 'Her mother and her brothers.' Dan would have done that if it had been feasible. But perhaps Dan had recognized the futility of such a plan. Oonagh had been disgraced and had compounded her felony by not returning to Ireland to serve a lifelong penance, probably under the disapproving roof of some aunt or grand-mother. And the Murphys had not been interested in Jenny, who was merely the fruit of her mother's sin.

Maria's response was simple and direct. 'Don't bother,' she said, her lips tightening with distaste. 'Leave the Murphys wherever they are. Pol says they were no good, and Pol's usually right.'

He moved to the door. 'Oh, by the way, Josh Kennedy was asking after you this morning. He's been away, had to step in at the Manchester branch. He intends to call on you today.'

Maria was off the stool before Henry had completed his statement. Josh was interested after all! He'd been away working, and she needed to shampoo her hair, get some lipstick on. Well, the lipstick would be available, but she couldn't go home and wash her hair, not with so many new patterns on the go. And he might come while she was in Claughton Street completing her beautification . . .

She tore off the stained smock, smoothed her hair, kicked her canvas slippers into a corner, searched for shoes. 'They're here somewhere,' she muttered to herself. 'I'll swear they can walk on their own, always bloody disappearing.'

Henry's eyes followed her, found difficulty in keeping up with the movements. She was like quicksilver, every-where at once, completely uncontainable. Josh Kennedy would have his work cut out here, he mused. There again, Josh might be a match for Maria, because he wasn't slow to come forward. He tried to visualize the two of them, sparks flying, ideas pouring out of her, financial advan-tages and pitfalls being weighed in the young accountant's quick mind. He nodded to himself. It might be best to keep all the sharp knives in one drawer. The match might even work.

It had been confirmed. Jenny told him after supper, watched the different emotions chasing across his face. He was a transparent man, could never quite hide his feelings. There was joy first, then concern for her, some worry about her youth, perhaps about the state of her health. He kissed her hands, her face, her neck, burying confusion just above her shoulder. Because after a few moments, he began to remember Sophie. Jenny felt the tension in his rigid spine, knew that he was seeing again the sweet face of that pretty child.

'I'll not be able to sleep,' he muttered unclearly, his face still hidden. 'They die in their cots, just slip away in sleep, no warning, no symptom of illness. That's what happened, though for years I thought . . . even worse than that. She was a good baby—' He cut himself off, stood back, looked at his young wife. He should not voice these things, was wrong to frighten her, to impose his past. 'I'm sorry. It won't happen again, lightning seldom strikes twice.'

'Henry, stop worrying. I'm perfectly well except for the mornings. There's no reason why everything won't be fine.'

'She won't die,' he said solemnly.

'It could be a he, and he won't die either.'

He hadn't thought of that. 'Of course, this might be a son. Henry the Tenth.' He thought about Donald, saw the clear eyes, the furrowed forehead of a dear man who had sought to change the world with his box of unworkable tricks. 'My uncle used to call me Henry the Ninth, said I'd be a riot on the throne of England.'

She laughed. 'The last Henry was bad enough, cutting folks' heads off.'

He tried to echo the sound of her merriment, but all he could see was a mutilated body, cuts, pieces . . . He shuddered. This should be a happy time, and Uncle Donald would not wish to intrude and spoil it. Since Henry had told Carla the truth, it had become real, like something that had happened yesterday. Sometimes, it was better not to verbalize a nightmare, because the spoken word served only to make it more terrifying. 'When is the baby due?' he asked.

'End of November.' She touched his face. 'What is the matter?'

He knew then that he would have to tell her. Not today, not next week, probably not during the pregnancy. But at some stage, he must try to rip it out of himself. She didn't deserve the burden, yet she was the other half of him, the part that had been missing for years. And he could keep no secret from himself. 'There's an illness going about at the mills, it seems to breed in the heat. Like a cold, but with stomach and head pains. I may have picked it up.'

He looked a bit headachy, she thought. She'd known about his migraines, even before they were married. Of late, they had become less frequent, and she hoped that the current epidemic would not trigger his long-term problem.

They lay in bed like a pair of spoons, he with his face in her hair, she doing calculations on her fingers, trying to remember whether to add ten months minus one week or nine months plus two weeks or . . . Her eyes closed and she dreamed of frilled cribs and infant cries, a yellow room with the sun streaming through pretty curtains, then a smart baby carriage containing a bundle of new life, birds celebrating the day . . .

When she woke, there was a stillness in the room, a terrible feeling that she could not explain or even identify. He was on his back, and she reached out, touched his weak left arm. For an endless moment, she thought he was dead, then she moved her hand to his chest, felt the rhythm of his breathing.

After her bath, she returned to take morning tea with him, sat at the dressing table, combed her hair, waited for Mary to arrive with the tray. He was sleeping late today, but he needed the rest. After all, she was not the only one who expected a baby. He would want to adjust, to encompass the concept of fatherhood again. If Sophie had lived, he might have been a grandad in a few years.

Mary tapped on the door, came in, placed the tray at Jenny's side of the bed. 'Madam?' she asked quietly.

Jenny was almost used to this title. 'What is it, Mary?'

The maid tiptoed to Jenny's side. 'He looks funny,' she whispered. 'His face has gone all to one side.' She placed a hand on her mistress's arm. 'I've seen this before. Don't touch him, I'll phone for the doctor.' She turned and ran out of the room.

Jenny was frozen to the stool for several seconds. She

didn't want to move, didn't want to look at him. If she waited, it would all go right again and he'd wake up grinning and with his hair on end. Yes, it would all be normal if she sat very still. Every morning, she smiled at his hair, thought it looked like a bird's nest . . . He was so still. Henry was not one to wake calmly; he usually thrashed about for half an hour before coming round, often made a real mess of the bed, all twists and turns and creases.

There was an ache in her belly, not quite a pain, more like a pulse, a rhythmic beat that was situated just about where the baby must be. It was as if that small cluster of cells could read her thoughts and was reacting to her fears. It was ten minutes to eight. By this time, he would have bathed, shaved, grabbed the morning paper.

Slowly, she rose and walked to the bed. His mouth was twisted and the right side of his face seemed waxy and stiff. Apart from the breathing, there was no movement at all. She pulled back the covers. The useless left arm lay straight against his side, but the good hand was closed so tightly that the knuckles showed white beneath tanned flesh. Dumbfounded, she sat with him, caressed his hair until Mary returned.

'I think he's had a stroke, madam.'

'Oh.' She couldn't think what to say. 'Will he get better?' she asked after a long pause.

'Me grandma did. We had to learn her how to talk, and one side of her was always a bit stiff, but she lived another ten years, drove us all mad. It's just that . . . well . . . it's happened on the wrong side for Mr Skipton, hasn't it?'

Jenny lifted her head. 'What do you mean?'

The maid licked her lips nervously. 'If it'd been the other side, it wouldn't have mattered, not for his arm, 'cos it's already out of order. But, I mean . . .' Her voice tailed away, refused to underline the point.

Eloise had had only one arm, the arm she had used when throwing food, when handling a gun, when taking Henry's arm away from him, when killing Dan. She breathed against the panic. Was this the pound of flesh, then? Was Eloise reaching from beyond, teaching this lovely man another of her misguided lessons? Oh God, were both arms going to be still? How could he hold a baby, how would he live and work? No! screamed Jenny's inner voice. There were no demons, no ghosts. Henry had always suffered from headaches, this was not punishment, could not be that. It was a condition he had lived with for years and he would recover, must get better . . .

The doctor came in, examined his patient while Mary consoled the young wife. 'Too ill to move,' he pronounced finally. 'Try to get some fluid into him. I'll be back in an hour with a colleague.' He put a hand on Jenny's shoulder. 'Bear up, now,' he said. 'I've seen worse than this walking out of hospital within four weeks. As long as he doesn't have another attack, he's in with a good chance. Strong constitution should see him through.'

Henry Skipton died at five minutes past two that same afternoon. He did not regain consciousness, was blessedly relieved of the sight of Jenny's long period of suffering. Except for journeys to the bathroom for water and towels, she did not leave his side during that time. When she knew that he had gone, she pulled the sheet over his face and rang the bell for Mary.

At half past three, Jenny Skipton ran across the Ricketty Bridge and into the wood. She lay spread-eagled under a canopy of trees, poured her grief into the earth. She didn't notice when the birds sang, when the long grass, disturbed by small animals, shivered and shook in the dappled light. Charlie found her, sat quietly by her side while she screamed out in sorrow and anger.

Finally exhausted, she heaved herself up and placed her spine against the rigid support of an ancient birch. The pattern had gone wrong. She must tell Maria that the pattern didn't work. She, Jenny Skipton, had been placed in this world with a map in her hand, and she had followed the route carefully since reaching the age where she understood the directions. Marrying Henry had been right, so why had he been taken? Was she here simply to provide an heir, to continue the line? Surely not. The love had been good, too good to die. Loneliness crushed her, made her so weak that her head dropped heavily.

Charlie chose his moment, pushed the snout of wet black leather into her hand. She lifted her face and looked into the solemn brown eyes. He knew. A paw came up, touched her arm, then the black face pointed itself skyward. His howling was primeval and loud, like the roar of an untamed beast. She buried her nose in the thick fur of his neck. It was right to grieve, it was normal.

They trudged homeward and stood together on the front path. A carriage waited outside the door, an old-fashioned vehicle with a black horse in the shafts. The undertaker was here. Jenny sat on the steps with Charlie, watched the sun as it sank low in the sky. Henry would not see a new day, would never again watch the birth of morning. Large black birds argued in a tree. Henry had used to call them a quarrel of crows, had said that 'quarrel' was an apt collective noun for such a wilful set of characters.

The stone beneath her was warm, retained the heat that had served Henry's last day. She would not meet his like again, nor would she seek it. With Charlie at her heels, she walked through the house and into the library, not seeing, not feeling the hands that reached out to comfort her. As the strains of Ravel's lament for a dead princess filled the room, she fell asleep in her husband's favourite chair. Charlie kept watch, whimpering from time to time. Some of the life had gone out of Skipton Hall, but he would guard his mistress for as long as he was needed. The music ended and the great house slept.

Chapter Twenty-One

JOSIE HESKETH HAD EXCELLED HERSELF AS QUEEN OF THE Rainbow. Dressed in every colour under the sun, she had been the star turn of the Sts Peter and Paul Junior Players, six songs, a bit of tap-dancing and only one forgotten line. She curtseyed at the edge of the makeshift stage, wiped her nose on a floating sleeve, beamed magnificently upon the front row where Maria and Jenny sat, then took a final vigorous bow that almost propelled her into the body of the school hall. This was the first outing for Jenny since her husband's death, and Josie was pleased to have been the architect behind the expedition.

Jenny, her hands sore from clapping, wriggled in a chair which had been designed for a ten-year-old bottom. The manufacturer of this furniture had certainly given no quarter to a woman in mid-pregnancy, but then he could hardly have been aware that such an occupant of a junior chair would ever exist.

'Are you uncomfortable?' asked Maria, knowing the answer before it came. She skewered the spectacles on to her nose, peered closely at her companion. 'What's up with you?' Jenny was wearing a smile that contained wonderment and sadness, an expression that might have sat well on the Mona Lisa if Leonardo had tried a bit harder. It was a stupid painting, Maria thought, just a vacuous face, completely devoid of any expression.

Jenny took Maria's hand and placed it on her belly.

'Josie's woken him,' she whispered. 'That's the first time he's ever moved. Can you feel it? Can you?'

Maria sat perfectly still. 'Good God,' she said at last. 'You want to put his name down for the heavyweight championship of 1940. I think he's already got boots and gloves on. What have you been eating?'

Jenny thought for a moment. 'Spinach.'

'You what? There's iron in that, queen. You'll have him fighting his way out with a full set of weights and muscles like a docker. In my experience – which is vast – they're better on orange peel. Me mam went through a cartload of that with our Jimmy and he never said a word till he was four. Peace, perfect peace. Mind, he was a funny colour when he was born. It was supposed to be jaundice, but we knew it was all wind and pith. From the oranges, like.'

Jenny found herself laughing, actually laughing aloud. And there was no hysteria in the scene this time, no backdrop of guilt and misery. She was allowed to be happy, would occasionally grant herself this small permission. 'Maria, you should be on the stage, some variety act.'

Maria pretended to give serious consideration to the suggestion. 'Naw,' she said. 'I couldn't be doing with the fame, all them stage-door johnnies lining up with bunches of flowers. We've only got one vase, so I'd never cope.'

Ena Burke staggered up the hall, swathed in a green frock with lots of pintucks and a square neckline, out of which her squat pink neck poked itself forward, busy as usual. The face was pinker still, rosy with delight because 'her' Josie had done them all proud. 'Yon lass is a little marvel,' she said triumphantly. 'Specially when you think back. I mean, she couldn't even talk proper two years since, it was all "gizzago" and "fair" coats.'

Maria hooted loudly. The Bolton accent made her hair stand on end, so slow and flat, so blinking dull. At least you got a bit of pace with the Scouse, a bit of life in it. 'It's you lot what doesn't talk right,' she said, deliberately laying on the Liverpool.

'Hmmph,' muttered Ena. 'I'm telling you now, we can be

understood, not like a load of foreigners.' She raised her chins, wobbled them about a bit in an imitation of anger. 'And how's our Jenny? Are you bearing up, love?'

Maria dug a gentle, if somewhat pointed elbow into her companion's upper arm. 'She's not bearing down, that's for sure. If she was, all these nuns would be even flappier than usual.'

'I'm fine,' answered Jenny. 'I'm sleeping at Maria's tonight.' She had not left the Hall since Henry's death. The gallery was in Maria's keeping for the time being, so the busy girl had organized regular hours for Pol and some part-time work for a retired teacher of history, a quiet little man who was proving to be a mine of information, some of it useless, much of it apt. He was good with the customers, that was the main thing.

Maria jumped up, held out her hands to Jenny, heaved Jenny out of the low chair. Josie arrived at a gallop, hair ribbons falling down her face, the diaphanous panels of the rainbow costume floating behind her. 'We've got new nuns,' she announced. 'Just to help with the show and our fair next Saturday. They're over there.' She pointed to a pair of Cross and Passion sisters who were talking animatedly to some parents. 'We've all got to come to the fair on Saturday, because it's the school fund, money for books and stuff.'

The place was dotted with nuns of every shape and size, all different, yet all made the same by heavy uniforms, mostly black but with white wimples. Each sister had a huge rosary strung from the waist and, pinned to the chest, a heart-shaped badge with a cross above the heart. 'We've swapped some,' said Josie. 'Our nuns have gone to Warrington for a few days and some of theirs have come here. It's called an exchange.'

Maria didn't have much time for the good sisters, though the pair who visited her in Claughton Street had managed to become acceptable. But those two weren't here, were probably a part of the exchange arrangements. 'I hope it stays fine for them,' she muttered caustically. 'Come on, let's get out before we're cornered by a penguin with a begging bowl.'

They all moved to the door with Maria bringing up the rear. As the rest of the party went out into the playground, something made Maria turn and glance over her shoulder. It was a face, someone familiar who seemed to have been caught in her none too perfect peripheral vision. But as she scanned the room, noting the faces of parents and neighbours, she saw nothing unusual, no reason to linger. She would need to get the glasses changed, she thought.

Anthony was waiting for them at number seventeen. He jumped up when they entered the house, his face colouring as he noticed Jenny stepping into the room. He pushed agitated fingers through his hair, planted his feet wide apart and said, 'I'm back.'

Maria glared at him. 'I'd never have known if you hadn't said, Anthony. No, we wouldn't have noticed you standing there with your hair on end. Would we, Josie?'

But Josie had hurled herself at her brother, was swinging from his neck. 'You never saw me in the concert. Why didn't you come? Billy Burke was sick all over Tommy Dewhurst. Tommy Dewhurst was crying, 'cos he was supposed to be a tree and he stank rotten and Sister Margaret had to pull most of his leaves off. Where were you?' She sniffed the air, then made her judgement. 'In the pub. You pong nearly as bad as Tommy Dewhurst.'

Anthony relieved himself of the loud burden. 'Shut up, Josie,' he said, not unkindly. 'I went for some dutch courage in case our Maria took off at me.'

Maria threw her bag on the table, motioned Jenny to sit in a dining chair. 'Dutch courage? Where were you when me drive belt went and we could get nothing dry? You never even stopped long enough to put the new blankets on me rollers. Some use you are as a partner.'

He shuffled his feet, grabbed Josie's hand for comfort and tangible support. 'Me dad's gone off,' he muttered.

Maria laughed, though there was no humour in the sound. 'Gone off? He went off years ago, lad. If you threw a handful of grass and peelings on him, he could be taken for a compost heap, 'cos he's never had a proper bath since 1914.' She looked at Jenny. 'The soldiers hosed him down before they rejected him for the army. They needed to find out what they were dealing with when me dad tried to be a hero.' Her head swung round again towards Anthony. 'And where's me brothers and sisters?'

He pulled a sheet of paper from his top pocket. 'I've got them written on here, the addresses. They're all right, but the owld feller's done a bunk, disappeared off the face of the earth.'

'So?' Maria's bravado was cracking slightly.

'There's no house. The landlord's got the bum bailey in, rentman says we can't go back. So me dad won't know where to lay his weary head when he finds himself.'

Maria stared at the floor. This was bloody awful. Her mam was in Switzerland trying to get better, her dad had disappeared, and her siblings were farmed out with strangers. Once again, she thanked God that she had saved Josie. 'What about them that's working?' she asked without lifting her head.

'Lodgings,' he replied.

'Me family's falling apart.' She sank into the chair next to Jenny's. A thought rattled about in Maria's brain, a loud item that sounded like a small stone in an empty tin. The face. Had it been her father? She rooted round in her suddenly depleted memory. No. Surely she would have recognized her own dad, even after just half a glimpse? Anyway, it had been female. She knew no more than that, but it had definitely not been a man. 'I can't think why I bother,' she said lamely. 'They're hopeless. The Hopeless Heskeths, star turn of the dock road. We even do a bloody disappearing act.'

Josie wept quietly, her face pressed into Anthony's jacket.

'It'll be all right,' said Maria. 'I'll find them all, Josie. Me and our Anthony will see to everything. When Mam comes home, I'll try to get them all to move here. Joe Soap'll get you a house, he knows me and Jenny are good payers. Go on, love. Go to Ena's and stop there tonight.' Of late, Josie had enjoyed two homes, had taken meals in either or both, had begun to feel secure, wanted, cared for. The little girl hugged her brother, her sister, Jenny, then went off to pour the sorry tale into Ena's ever-receptive ear.

'Well,' mused Maria. 'There's one good thing to all this. Me mam won't have any more babies when she gets home. If he can't find her, he can't put her in the club again.' She straightened her spine. 'But I'm not telling her he's done a runner. No, she can stay ignorant. No good warning her that there'll be no home for her when she gets back, it'll only make her lungs heal slower. He'll be in the flaming Mersey with the rest of the trash.' She sighed. 'I love the rotten bugger, you know.'

Anthony nodded, joined the two girls at the table. 'We used to have some funny stuff in our house – she'd never credit it, would she, Maria? Best smuggler for miles, me dad.'

Maria smiled wistfully. 'Fifteen parrots upstairs, we had. All squawking and spitting sunflower seeds at each other, like the battle of Waterloo. Me dad used to send the lot of us outside to make a noise so that nobody would hear these bloody birds he'd pinched.'

'Thirty-five boots, all for left feet,' said Anthony, sober in spite of three pints. 'Then Dad tried to sell them to Smelly Watson from the pawnshop, said there was a demand for odd shoes with all the cripples after the war. Smelly was that drunk, he nearly bought them too. Till he worked out that some folk must have lost their left foot. It took all night, that argument.' It was good, sitting here with Maria and Jenny. This was how it should have been, the three of them, perhaps four if Maria found another bloke. He knew about Henry. Ena Burke's next door neighbour had told him earlier on when he'd been looking for his sisters. He hated himself for the relief, the hope that had been born from this terrible news.

'Are you coming back to work?' Maria asked.

He shrugged. 'Might as well.'

'I want you committed, Ant.'

'To a lunatic asylum?'

She punched his arm. 'To the printing. It's going to take every ounce of our energy to make a go of it. He . . . er . . . left it to me,' she added. Her eyes swept Jenny's face for a split second as the lie was spoken. 'Henry left me the print factory.' It sounded better that way, more acceptable from

527

the dead than from the living. Surely he would not call it charity if it came from a dead donor?

'Oh.' He lifted his face, gazed at Jenny. 'I'm sorry, girl. He was a fine man.'

Jenny's face remained serene while she took a business-like stance. 'The mills will continue to offer calico for printing at the same reduced rate. The lawyer's looking after everything, drawing up some papers. And he's appointed managers and auditors to watch the business for me.' She touched Maria's hand. 'I made sure Josh was given a chance and some responsibility. He'll get a fee and learn the business.'

He noticed Maria's blush, guessed that one of these young widows had made a new friend. Anthony began to think properly now about Jenny. He was not being cold and heartless about the dead man, because both he and Henry Skipton had loved her. One was dead, the other alive, while Jenny herself would, at some time, become available. He felt warmer, calmer. Perhaps he was now assuming that he would get her in time, would be so good to her, become so indispensable that Jenny's need for him would grow.

'Jenny's pregnant,' announced Maria baldly. 'So we're having to run the gallery and the café as well as the works. She wants to make sure she hangs on to this baby, don't you, queen?'

'I do.' She looked straight at Anthony. 'The baby will be all that's left of Henry. As the lawyer says, this is the legitimate heir to the mills.'

He didn't mind, didn't care. She'd be depending on him all the more once the child was born. It was right that a man like Skipton should have someone to carry on the line. 'He went quick, Jenny,' he said softly. 'Her next door to Ena told me it all happened in one day.'

Jenny thought about that for a moment. 'He had a lot of headaches. For years he suffered with his head, thought it was migraine. Perhaps we should have taken notice and—'

'Shush.' Maria's voice was comforting. 'There's people with no headaches that die with a stroke, Jen. By the time they've got the pain in their head, it's too late. It must have been migraine if it lasted years. Look at me, I've got to wear these stupid specs because I get pain in my head.' She paused, lifted the spectacles, polished them on her handkerchief. 'Anyway, there's nothing will bring our men back, love. Henry and Denis have gone, so we start again.'

Jenny stared down at the tablecloth, one of the Tuppenny Girl cheaper items, still prettily flowered, perfectly acceptable. 'I hope things work out between you and Josh, but I shan't remarry.' She could not have him waiting. The idea of Anthony hanging around hopefully was not appealing. She wanted fewer burdens, not more and heavier loads to carry on her shoulders. The pattern was coming together again, but slowly. Each day, she got nearer to knowing the next step and, although the outline was still vague, warp and weft were beginning to weave a picture. Anthony was not a part of the unfinished design.

He moved to the door, his face turned away from both of them. 'I'll sleep at Ena's,' he said. 'Good night.' The door closed quietly behind him.

'Well,' said Maria. 'That's his feathers ruffled for the next ten days.'

Jenny lifted head and voice, 'But I can't—'

'Shut up. He'll have one of his lugholes pinned to the letterbox.' She jumped up, lifted the flap, looked outside. 'I think he's gone,' she whispered, turning then to her friend. 'I know you can't. Not now, not yet. You're carrying Henry's baby, and that child might be ten years old before you want another marriage.' She jerked her thumb in the direction of Ena's house. 'He'll wait till the day one of you dies. I know him, he's as stubborn as me dad.' She paused. 'Me father what's missing.'

Jenny realized the depth of Maria's worry. The young woman had started to 'talk proper' much of the time, only reverted to Scouse when she was upset or fooling. 'There's me with a dad I found too late,' said Jenny. 'And a mother I can't find at all. And here you are with two parents, both of them removed.'

Maria pondered, a hand sliding along the dresser. 'He's not removed. Me dad'll be wandering about with the rest of the dock tramps, drinking biddy and seeing what he can pinch to sell. And if they've found him, the cops, he could be in the bridewell breaking his heart.' She raised her shoulders until they almost touched her ears. 'Me dad's a total idiot,' she concluded.

'Do you want to go and look for him?'

'I can't. There's the works to run and I wouldn't know what to do with him if I did clap eyes on the daft beggar.'

Jenny thought, waited for the idea to form. 'Send him to me. He can help in the garden, live in my dad's rooms.'

Maria's eyes were so round that they seemed ready to pop out of their sockets. 'You what? Let him loose with pounds' worth of flori-bloody-bunda? You'd have a desert in a fortnight.' She nodded quickly. 'Or a swamp.'

'He can do the paths, work with Howie Bennett. Then he could help old George with the weeding. George comes three times a week, so he could keep an eye on Mr Hesketh.'

Maria staggered to the table, fell into a chair. 'Eh? Keep an eye? You'd have to use restraints, never mind an eye. There's silver in them cupboards, Jenny. He'd strip you bare overnight, turn it all over in Liverpool for a few bottles of whisky.'

Jenny maintained her calm pose. 'Your father will take nothing from me, Maria. When did he last rob a friend?'

'He's got no blinking friends. And them he drinks with haven't two pennies between them, so they're not worth the bother.'

Jenny stood up. 'I'm off to bed. Tell Anthony to find your dad. I'll sort him out.' Mr Hesketh was probably a piece of the jig-saw anyway. 'Maria, I'll fix it. Just get him to the Hall and I'll do the rest.'

'What if he's in prison?'

'Then I'll pay the fine or the bail or whatever.' She felt better, happier than she'd felt in weeks. The last time, Henry had been with her and they'd searched for foxes. This little silver-edged cloud of memory passed quickly. 'Do as you're told, Maria,' she said firmly. 'For once, let someone else make a decision.' She stalked out and went up to bed.

Maria gazed at the tablecloth, wondered obliquely

whether to introduce a bit more green into the pattern. Or aqua, she liked that shade. He'd never cleared a path in his life. And the pale yellow was a touch sickly, perhaps needed more definition. Wouldn't know his rake from his hoe, wasn't used to work. Most of his life, he'd been propping up a wall or a bar counter.

And Jenny Skipton was taking too much on, thinking she could manage to sort out everybody's life. Maria's dad considered work to be nothing but a dirty word, something to be tossed about with the rest of his colourful language when he was in drink. Oh well, let Jenny try. It had all been done before, boots from the welfare sold the same day for ale, coats and trousers swapped for scotch. She decided on the aqua, then went to bed.

Pol slammed the door. 'I'm going there no more,' she said loudly. 'They cheat. I'm just after being deprived of me dignity, getting beaten into the ground by a child of twenty-five and an old bugger with six aces up his sleeve. Invited to play cards with them, was I? Huh. I stepped into a den of thieves, so I did, a den of bloody robbers.'

Carla picked up the cat, which was winding round and round her ankles like a furry spinning top. 'Sorry, Pol. But they say all's fair in love and cards. And I did promise that we would visit them after you persuaded me to come back here.'

'It's war, all's fair in love and war. And it was a battle too. Call themselves Catholic priests? They'd the divil himself on their side, changing the rules all the while. I'd a full house! How come he beat me with that little pair of sevens? And him Irish-trained in Dublin with a daddy who's big in politics. God help us, that was just the young one. The old feller's teaching him bad ways, the boy will be a desperate criminal in five years.'

Carla laughed. 'They let me leave on one condition – I have to play poker with them from time to time. When they play cards, they're not priests, they're just men having a bit of fun.'

Pol wrinkled her nose. 'I could show them better fun, but it's not in their contract. Anyway, himself and the infant priest could work a casino between them, make a fortune for Rome.' She had never had so much enjoyment in her whole life. She would go back – after a bit of schooling from a certain gentleman in Bolton. He owed her. After all, during her sinful days, she'd shown the so-called gentleman a trick or two. Tit for tat, trick for trick. And she'd have the trousers beaten off the clergy in Westhoughton.

Carla fed Sammy, put the kettle to boil. They had a cup of tea, settled down in the sitting room which, at last, looked like a parlour. Pol's good bits and pieces were in the gallery; some had already gone for excellent prices. Carla read, Pol sorted through lists of antiques, referred occasionally to a manual.

'Well now, isn't this just typical?' asked Pol rhetorically when someone knocked on the front door. 'You get nicely settled, cup of tea, something to read, and the world comes to stand on the doorstep with his dog and a full pipe band.' She marched out, returned seconds later in a cooler state, Jenny Skipton following behind.

Jenny and Carla looked at one another. 'Shall I go out?' asked Carla. In a sense, these two were related, so they might be wanting to talk family business.

Jenny's expression remained the same, not smiling, not frowning, simply neutral. 'Please stay. I want to talk to both of you.'

They settled themselves, Carla and Pol in fireside chairs, Jenny on an uncomfortable but firm sofa with lots of ill-matched arm covers and antimacassars, almost every piece edged with its own singular border of handmade lace.

She declined the offer of tea, placed her bag on a cushion, crossed her ankles, leaned against a backrest that must have been invented for a very odd-shaped person. 'It's the house,' she said finally. 'I'm forming a trust which will last my lifetime, and I shall be the chairman or whatever they call the man in charge. Except it'll be a woman this time. I want you two as members.'

Pol scratched her head. 'Why me?' she asked, her face a picture of bewilderment.

'Because you love children.' Jenny turned to the once-loathed housekeeper. 'And you can run that house with your eyes closed, Miss Sloane.'

'But I . . .' The words tailed away to nothing.

'She'd not feel comfortable in that place,' declared Pol, prepared, as always, to speak up for her friend. 'She'd be remembering things that are best under the carpet. After all, haven't we all sinned in our time? But a constant reminder is not a good thing. I was ages getting her to leave her penance behind at that presbytery with the marked cards and the fancy violins and two buggers who should be in jail the state of them.' This last long sentence was said in one breath.

Jenny was determined not to be confused by Pol's wandering speech. She spoke directly to Carla Sloane. 'I was in that house when my father was murdered. I saw it, made statements to the police, went to court as a witness, yet I still married Henry. A home is not what happened before, it's what's happening now and what's planned for the future. Come and look at the house, Miss Sloane. Look at it with new eyes.'

Carla dropped her head and said nothing.

Pol was suddenly concerned with the practicalities. 'A trust for what?' she asked.

Jenny paused for a moment, shifted slightly as the infant in her womb quickened yet again. 'For city children, those who have never seen a field or a tree. They will come for a holiday, get some good, fresh air and food. The schools and churches will select the most needy. We will take them from Bolton, Manchester and Liverpool.'

'And will you live there?' Pol asked.

'No. I shall have two farm cottages knocked into one. There's a pair at the other side of Sniggery Wood.'

Carla studied her shoes. She knew those cottages. Even joined together, they would not make much of a house. 'You intend to give up the Hall?'

Jenny spread her hands wide. 'What would I want with a place that size? My child will inherit it, so he or she can decide whether or not to extend the trust. I shall look after the horses with Howie, get someone in to teach the children how to ride, how to care for a creature. Skipton

Hall needs filling, wants noise and laughter and children scraping those perfect floors with their clogs.' She took a paper from her bag. 'Here is a list of young ones whose mother is ill in Switzerland. Until she comes back, they can live permanently at the Hall. When their mother is recovered, she'll be able to rent another place.'

'Where are they now?' Pol's expression was full of concern.

'All over Liverpool,' answered Jenny. 'Spread out and separated from each other.'

'Jesus, Mary and Joseph, the poor little mites.' Pol took the paper, read the list. 'We'll do it,' she said. 'And when the mammy is better, they can live here – unless they prefer Liverpool, because this will be empty if Carla and meself are elsewhere.' She nodded excitedly. 'We can bring Sammy and Amos, give them a whole new life.' In accordance with her mercurial character, she now chose to give no thought to her lodger's difficulties. Children were children, and they came first, with animals a close second.

At last, Carla looked up. 'Just a moment, Pol,' her voice was low, bore no resemblance to the sergeant-major type of tone she had used a few years ago. 'Let's talk about it first, it's no use making these quick decisions. You've a nice home and a good job—'

'And you've no work at all since Imelda took in those young Irish girls.' She glanced at Jenny. 'Ugly colleens, the both of them – and they're hard to come by, because the Irish are a notoriously beautiful race. But Imelda can't let her stud of a husband live with danger. Franklyn is a man above all men, he's so attractive, so gracious—' She cut herself off. 'And why would you be laughing, Carla? I'm only after telling the truth.'

Carla wiped her eyes. 'I should be the last to mock the physically unfortunate,' she mumbled. Her hands were twisting together as she spoke to Jenny. 'If you don't mind me asking, where will the money come from?'

'I'll have an income from the mills, and my needs are few. There'll also be some backing from various bodies in towns and cities.'

Pol stared at the young woman. 'You could have the life

of Riley, Jenny. You could sit on a cushion and sew a fine seam—'

'Strawberries with sugar and cream give me a rash.' Jenny smiled after this remark. She had started the ball rolling, was beginning to follow her instincts and her conscience. 'I love the countryside, but I'm not particular about a grand house. Anyway, think about it, talk about it. My mind's made up, but you two must not be influenced by me. I just thought you should be given a chance. It will be a good life and a fulfilling one, looking after city children, watching them play and grow.'

Carla gazed through the window, though her sights were fixed on nothing in particular. Jenny Skipton's sights were definitely fixed, fastened to a dream of a happier world. How could a person like Carla fit into such a plan? She was still short-tempered, continued to keep a rein on her old self. What if the old Carla were to suddenly come out from behind the new, pleasanter mask?

'You'll be all right.' Yet again, Pol was reading thoughts. 'You'll have me behind you – and the house won't be the same at all. There'll be others there, teachers and mothers and folk from churches.' She flashed a glance in Jenny's direction. 'Isn't that so?' She failed to wait for a reply. 'And you can finally bury the ghost of whoever you used to be, Carla.'

After the usual words of farewell, Jenny left the house and climbed into Henry's car. Howie, who had promoted himself to part-time chauffeur, had turned out to be an exceptionally able driver. They turned round, travelled through the town.

Jenny settled back, a faint smile of something approaching triumph playing on her mouth. Pol would be a wonderful addition to the project. Life was strange, she thought. One of the best people she had ever met had once been a prostitute. Well, a lot more than once, she mused ruefully. Pol was a giver, Carla was an organizer. And I, said Jenny to herself as they passed the gallery, am a catalyst. She had found the word in Henry's large dictionary. A catalyst made things happen, altered life quietly, then lost its importance. She would be there, on

Henry's land, on her own land, but she would be no more than an agent. She was Spinning Jenny, and the yarn was almost spun, almost ready to complete the tapestry.

She remembered Henry, allowed his dear face to enter the eye of her mind. He had told her that she was important, had built up her confidence, made her feel loved, needed, useful. For him, she had been a new, if somewhat short, lease of being. But a catalyst was a necessity too, because it brought life together, melded elements, changed the picture, supported many threads. That had been Hargreaves's idea when the first jenny had been made. It took a lot of machinery to carry several strands, a large powerhouse to feed it too.

She was glad she had the energy, the drive to see this through. Jenny would touch and educate many lives, simply because she existed. And the unborn baby was kicking again.

There were nuns everywhere again. Maria, who nursed memories of chanted Catechism and six strokes of the cane for missing mass, patronized the stalls run by lay people. Jenny had drifted off with Josie, was probably ruining the girl with gifts and sweets. She spoiled everybody, did Jenny, was too soft by a long chalk. Even the newly-discovered Ernest Hesketh was up at the Hall, had been dragged there on train, tram and coal wagon by Anthony, whose temper had not been improved by the exercise, so both were absent from the Sts Peter and Paul fair.

She sighed heavily. Her father was probably sleeping off a drinking marathon, while Anthony nursed a head made sore by the man's ravings. Her family tree was moulting again. She sympathized with the boy in the concert, the lad who had been stripped of his leaves. Life, at the moment, was what Ena Burke might call 'a right rum do'.

Maria bought a cup of lemonade, leaned against railings, sipped the frothy drink. Mam was nearly better. She'd had an all-clear on the latest sputum test, would probably be home in a few months if the improvement continued. Maria, her face ablaze, had given her father a rollicking about self-control and birth control. Teaching upwards, to an older generation, was never pleasant. He had sat there in Mr Skipton's study, eyes wandering over valuables, tongue wandering over his lips when the decanters had come into view. And he'd told her to mind her own so-and-so business, the so-and-so having consisted of several new and unfamiliar swear words.

Oh well, not to worry, it would all come out in the bleach tub. She emptied the cup, gazed round the playground. The decanters had been moved to the cellar and daft Jenny had been moved by Ernie's condition, had given him bed and board. She'd regret it, the silly mare. Her eyes raked back and forth across the cobbled area, trying to pick out Jenny's blue blouse, Josie's pink frock.

When a weakness in her legs threatened to render her prone, Maria placed the cup on a nearby white elephant stall and grasped one of the iron railings. Something had disturbed her, and she couldn't manage to think or stand properly. With the other trembling hand, she dragged the spectacles to her nose, forced them into position, scanned the area again. It was a remembered feeling, one she had experienced last Monday after the concert. Perhaps she ought to stay away from Catholic schools. After all, she'd been in every conceivable kind of trouble during her own brief years of education in one of these prisons.

She swallowed, unusually thirsty so soon after a drink. Pol's favourite cry of 'Jesus, Mary and Joseph' chased itself through her brain. No wonder the hair had been different. There was no hair, none that showed. She forced herself upright, staggered across the yard to where she had last seen Jenny. Josie skipped out of a side entrance, Jenny following close behind. 'I showed Jenny my pictures,' yelled the child. 'She said they are the best in the whole school.'

Maria stared blankly at her young sister. Yes, Josie would be good for the printing business in a few years. Like Maria, she had designs etched on her soul. 'Here.' Maria thrust a sixpence at Josie. 'Go and buy something for Ena.'

When the child had disappeared, Maria pulled her friend to one side. 'Jenny,' she mumbled.

'What?' The clear blue eyes studied Maria. 'What's up? Has Josh proposed?'

'Eh?' The mouth hung for a second, was completely untypical of the quick-thinking girl. 'No. I mean yes, he has, but it's not that. It's . . . something else.'

'Congratulations.'

'You what? Oh, oh . . . yes. Thanks. Shall we go home?'

'Why?'

Maria searched her store of ideas, found it as cluttered as a Victorian drawing room. 'I'm tired,' she managed. 'It's me eyes. I've forgot me specs.'

'They're on your nose.' Jenny made a note of the revived Liverpool accent, the obvious confusion which had created this lie about the glasses. 'Spit it out.'

'See?' Maria gulped, swallowed again. 'They're no good. I mean, I didn't even know I was wearing them. Let's go and get me eyes tested, shall we? I'm no good as a designer while I've no proper sight.'

Jenny, who had been persuaded to stay with Maria all week, and who knew by heart the diary of forthcoming events, reminded Maria of the facts. 'This is Saturday. At two o'clock on Monday, you are going for an eye test.'

'Oh. I forgot.' The tone was crippled. 'I'm getting a bit that way, forgetful. I just want to go home.'

Jenny turned away, looked for Josie. Across the yard, next to six stone steps, there was a woollens stall. New and good second-hand knitted garments were being sold by a nun, a tall, slim woman with a happy face. With Jenny's face. She gripped Maria's arm. 'Oh, my God.' The voice was muted almost to the point of non-existence. 'You saw her first, didn't you?' She did not look at Maria, because her gaze was fastened on the nun's familiar features.

Maria sighed, shifted her feet. 'I didn't know what to do, Jen. I thought the best of a bad job would be to take you home and tell you there.' Pulling together the jagged threads of mislaid composure, she dragged Jenny through the door and into a seemingly endless dark green corridor. 'Jenny? They saw her, the nuns who came to our house.

538

They'd been on retreat, said they'd caught sight of someone like you, but they couldn't remember the blonde hair. It's no wonder . . . Jenny?' Maria became frantic as the fair head rested itself against a poster about lice and house-bugs. 'Are you all right, queen? Why are you holding on to your stomach? Does it hurt, is it the baby?' No, no, not Jenny too, cried her inner voice.

'No pain.' She straightened, turned, placed her spine against the wall. 'She's beautiful, so much nicer than me. She's nearly a granny and so young . . .'

Maria stood back, peered through the open door. She summoned all her strength, denied the quaking of her knees. 'Listen, it might just be somebody who looks like her – like you, I mean. I wish they wouldn't wear these stupid wimples and that white bit round their faces. Stop there till I come back. Don't move, else I'll flatten you. I'll buy a jersey for me dad.' She ran outside again.

Jenny waited, almost counting the beats of her heart. She knew that the nun was her mother. She did not need to look again, did not want to ask unnecessary questions. The nun was Oonagh Murphy. The woman's child was dead, her man was dead, so she had given her life to God's work. And she had put herself where her own mother and her brothers would not search for her.

How must she feel, then, about being part of the exchange? Bolton was bound to hold memories for her, would not be a place for her to visit voluntarily. There was an open inner door just opposite the poster. Three canes hung from a hook, three instruments with which children were regularly tortured. Was Oonagh one of these heartless people who punished babies?

Jenny put a hand to her mouth. Oonagh would have no teaching certificate, would probably be a domestic, one of those nuns who normally worked behind the scenes. Beating infants into submission would not be her task. And no mother of Jenny's could ever use a cane, Jenny felt sure of that. Her heart slowed down to its normal pace. Her mother was a few yards away, but her baby was nearer, needed peace and calm, a regulated place in which to grow strong and healthy.

Maria fell in at the door, arms and legs everywhere, looking about the same age as Josie. 'It's there. The mark on her head, the birthmark. Nearly covered, but—'

'We'll go home now.' Jenny looked perfectly composed by this time.

'Aren't you going to . . . ? Oh, I see. Not in front of all these people, eh? Will you come back and go to the convent? They'll be stopping up Deane Road, I think, with the High School sisters. Her name's Sister Mary Magdalene.'

Jenny blinked against the wetness in her eyes. Mary Magdalene had been a sinner, had loved Jesus enough to give up her bad ways. Oonagh had given up too, long before entering the convent. And she had chosen the name of a lovely saint. Jenny whispered the words, tasted them, listened to the separated syllables.

Pol was another such person, someone who was full of love. Promiscuity was not such a bad thing, then, thought Jenny. Those who had indulged in it seemed warm and giving, had probably learned generosity of spirit after so much contact with unhappy men. She raised her chin. 'Home, Maria.'

After Josie had been found, Jenny emerged from the school, her head covered by a scarf, face averted from the knitwear stall. She walked swiftly through the yard, not pausing until she had reached the pavement on Pilkington Street. Josie caught up with her. 'Have you got sunstroke?' she asked.

'Something like that,' answered Jenny as Maria reached her side. 'Yes, it's something like sunstroke.'

Howie was coming to collect her tonight. He had been once this week to take her to Pol's house, and Jenny had asked him then to pick her up on Saturday evening. This was Saturday evening. Anthony and Josie were at Ena's preparing to go to the Tivoli picture house. Jenny, in the kitchen of number seventeen, pushed away her empty plate, thanked Maria for the meal.

'Well?' The little red-haired girl, who was not renowned for her patience, could contain herself no longer. 'When are you going to see her?'

Jenny wiped her mouth with a Tuppenny Girl napkin, a reject with smudged leaves in the pattern. 'I'm not,' she said quietly.

Maria dropped a plate, bent slowly to retrieve the unbroken item. 'What the hell are you playing at, Jenny Crawley – I mean Skipton? You've been searching for years, your dad was searching for even longer. Anthony got up off his bum too and traced her to—' She closed her mouth tightly.

'To where she had been working as a prostitute?'

'Er . . . yeah.' Maria, temporarily deflated, bit her lip before continuing. 'The old lady's dead now, the one who looked after your mam.' She inhaled some courage. 'We've all been mithered with it and now, when you find her, you don't want to talk to her.' She slammed the plate down, her agile spirit happily revived.

'You'll break that in a minute.'

'Better this than your neck. Whatever are you thinking of, madam?'

'Nothing.' Jenny rose and walked into the front room placing herself in a chair at the best table.

Maria, determined not to be outdone or outrun, was fast on Jenny's heels. 'You can't just . . .' The voice faded as she saw that look on Jenny's face, the expression that spoke volumes about inner determination. 'Jenny, you can't.'

'You remember how I said that I wouldn't go to her if she had a husband and other children?'

'Yes, but—'

'Well, she has.'

Maria threw herself into the opposite chair. 'Has she hell as like! She's a bloody nun, in case you hadn't noticed, like.'

'I noticed. She's married to God and the order looks after children.' The face danced before her eyes, a face that would be her own property in a few short years. 'The woman is content.'

Maria fiddled with her glasses' chain. 'She's got a daughter, for God's sake. She'll have a grandchild in a few months. How can you keep all this from her?'

For the first time ever, Jenny rose completely to the bait.

'Maria, do not tell me what to do.' Anger coloured her skin, made the eyes brighter, larger. 'This is my life, a life I shall organize for myself. I'm grateful for what you have done for me, and I'm grateful to Anthony too. But you will not tell me what I must do. That is my mother, mine.' She beat a fist against her chest. 'One day, I may go to see her. But the date will be of my choosing. This is my design, not a Tuppenny or a Hesketh. This is a Skipton.'

Maria stared silently at the tablecloth. Yes, there was a mile more to Jenny than met the eye. 'I suppose she'd be shocked in a way,' she conceded.

Jenny had thought of that, had wondered about the possible reactions if she had turned up at the convent to see Sister Mary Magdalene. Oonagh had buried her 'dead', had done her suffering. And she had lost a baby, a four-year-old, not some great lump of a woman with a child of her own on the way. Jenny would have been forced to kill Dan again too, poor Dan who had been dead for years in Oonagh's mind. Yes, Jenny would have told the real story.

But Oonagh Murphy had found her peace, her joy and her own way of living. It would be wrong to intrude, just as it would have been wrong to disturb a complete family. In fact, the sisterhood was a family, so Mary Magdalene was not alone, not lonely and grieving.

'Jenny, you are as old as the hills,' said Maria. 'You're so . . . so wise.'

'No.' The blonde head shook and she repeated something she had said to another woman some time ago. 'I make it up as I go along.' And that, she mused, was the truth.

Ernest Hesketh walked in front, his back straighter than it had been in years. He was an odd-job man now, and it was a very odd job, a bit of this and that, no rhythm to it, three good meals a day. He paused outside the gallery where his rumbustious daughter was making one of her flying visits, waved his country walking stick at the red-haired woman in her dye-spattered smock. She was all right, their Maria. Plenty of go in her, plenty of the Hesketh blood. After all, hadn't he worked hard all his life to support the huge family?

Jenny followed, her belly rounded by eight months of pregnancy. She was well, more than capable of keeping up with this very unusual procession. The empty purse dangled from a hand. She had paid cash, something to do with income tax. It had cost a small fortune too, the sort of money that would have fed an army for weeks. But she didn't care, because her two friends were a part of the whole thing, a part of her past, and she was leading them into a tranquil future.

Amber and Flora swished their tails, puffed excitement through distended nostrils. Something was happening, and whatever it was, it was going to be good. They were proud, as proud as when they had been used for real parades and shows. Blue and red rosettes were pinned among brasses on their leather trappings. They had been winners many times, and now they sensed reward.

All along Deansgate, shoppers stopped to stare at the odd group. It was Jenny Skipton, the young widow of that mill chap, him who'd had a funny first wife. Whatever was she thinking of, messing about with horses on the tramlines and her ready to give birth at any second? Mind, she was a bit on the fey side, always dashing around in fields, by all accounts. The man at the front was a rum one as well, capering about with his daft stick, shouting 'Mindyerbacks' and ''ellomissus' to folk who weren't in the way and to others who didn't know him. Liverpool, he was. They were always on the familiar side, the lads from the pool.

Out of town and halfway up Tonge Moor, they stopped for a rest. Ernest fetched a bucket of water from the chemist's shop, gave it to the thirsty mares. He grinned at Jenny. 'Should 'ave bought the bloody cart too,' he said. 'Then you could of rode in style, like.'

Jenny sat on a garden wall. It was October and the sun was less cruel, more beautiful, lower in the sky. The whole world was bathed in a golden light, a sort of pale amber. That was a good omen, then. She had chosen the right time to release Amber and Flora from their life of toil.

She turned her head and gazed up the road. They would all be there, Pol and Carla, Mrs Hesketh and the children, Howie and Mary and the little one-eyed maid called Edith who was so grateful for the job. Anthony too would arrive later on, was supposed to be bringing a cart to transport his whole family to Pol's old house. All was well.

Jenny shifted her uneven weight into a more comfortable position. Auntie Mavis had 'seen' something that night, the night when Jenny had found her father. Mavis had seen cotton, money and late love in Jenny's tarot. It was all a nonsense, of course. The love had come early, had lasted for just a few sweet weeks.

Jenny watched the horses, saw their silent patience. She didn't mind any more. Anthony would wait, she could allow him to wait. The pattern was changing all the time . . .